The Mary Shelley Reader

FRANKENSTEIN'S CREATURE

*"By the glimmer of the half-extinguished light, I saw the dull, yellow eye
of the creature open; it breathed hard, and a convulsive motion
agitated its limbs,*** I rushed out of the room."*

T. Holst, del. · W. Chevalier, sculp.
(Frontispiece from 1831 *Frankenstein*.)

The
Mary Shelley
Reader

containing *Frankenstein, Mathilda,* Tales and Stories,
Essays and Reviews, and Letters

Edited by

BETTY T. BENNETT

CHARLES E. ROBINSON

New York   Oxford
OXFORD UNIVERSITY PRESS
1990

Oxford University Press

Oxford   New York   Toronto
Delhi   Bombay   Calcutta   Madras   Karachi
Petaling Jaya   Singapore   Hong Kong   Tokyo
Nairobi   Dar es Salaam   Cape Town
Melbourne   Auckland
and associated companies in
Berlin   Ibadan

Published by Oxford University Press, Inc.,
200 Madison Avenue, New York, New York 10016

Oxford is a registered trademark of Oxford University Press

Library of Congress Cataloging-in-Publication Data
Shelley, Mary Wollstonecraft, 1797–1851.
The Mary Shelley reader : containing *Frankenstein, Mathilda,*
tales and stories, essays and reviews, and letters
edited by Betty T. Bennett and Charles E. Robinson.
p. cm. Includes bibliographical references.
ISBN 0-19-506258-2
ISBN 0-19-506259-0 (pbk.)
I. Bennett, Betty T.   II. Robinson, Charles E.   III. Title.
PR5397.A4   1990   823'.7—dc20   89-26584

1 3 5 7 9 8 6 4 2
Printed in the United States of America
on acid-free paper

For

MATTHEW T. *and* PETER T. BENNETT

and

CLARE K. *and* JOHN C. ROBINSON

Preface

In Mary Shelley's *Frankenstein,* books define each of the narrators: the destinies of the explorer Robert Walton, the scientist Victor Franken-stein, and the unnamed creature are determined by their reading. Had they read more or different texts (for example, the poetry and romances that made up the studies of Elizabeth Lavenza and Henry Clerval), they might have been less tragic characters, less destructive in their relations with others. That is to say, the redemptive value of a broad and humanis-tic education is one of Mary Shelley's themes in *Frankenstein* as well as in her other works. This theme and many other ideas of the "Author of *Frankenstein*" go unrecognized, however, because most modern readers of Mary Shelley have not read enough of her works: they interpret the au-thor on limited evidence, frequently on the basis of *Frankenstein* alone. Hence this new *Mary Shelley Reader* by which we offer additional texts that can lead to a better understanding and, it is hoped, appreciation of a major nineteenth-century author.

This reader is in many ways a primer: it begins with *Frankenstein* in its original form, the text of the first edition of 1818, considerably differ-ent from that with which most readers are familiar, namely the revised 1831 edition. This 1818 novel has its own integrity and reflects to a greater extent the circumstances of Mary Shelley's initial inspiration, composition, and publication—all before she turned twenty-one. When she was thirty-four years old, she revised the novel and explained the ori-gin of her fantastic tale in a new Introduction that we reprint after the 1818 text. Then follows her complete novella *Mathilda* (written 1819, first published 1959, but since then out-of-print), in which the reader will encounter a complicated persona who, "in a strange state of mind," strug-gles as a self-conscious tragic actress in a drama about the taboo subject of incest. Mary Shelley frequently experimented with both theme and style in her narratives, and we offer seven of her shorter tales and stories to demonstrate further her fictional strategies. Three of these narratives ("Roger Dodsworth," "Transformation," and "The Mortal Immortal") reveal her continuing interest in the supernatural; two others ("The Bride of Modern Italy" and "The False Rhyme"), her abilities as a gentle satirist. These stories are followed by eight essays, reviews, and prefaces—grouping for the first time a series of texts by which Mary Shelley's aesthetic principles can be deduced and evaluated. Finally, the more personal voice of the author is represented by eleven of her more than twelve hundred extant letters.

Readers of this edition will discover that Mary Shelley's public voice, especially in her essays and reviews, speaks eloquently, precisely, and also personally about the issues of the English Romantic period. In her essay on "Giovanni Villani," for example, she explains how much she welcomes an author's "intrusion of self" into works of art. This does not mean for Mary Shelley (or for any other Romantic writer) that art must be autobiographical in a literal or limited sense. As she explained in her review of her father's novel *Cloudesley,* "merely copying from our own hearts will no more form a first-rate work of art, than will the most exquisite representation of mountains, water, wood, and glorious clouds, form a good painting, if none of the rules of grouping or colouring are followed." Adherence to these rules transforms and transmutes life into art, thereby producing what William Hazlitt and Mary Shelley call "keeping"; or what Samuel Taylor Coleridge calls the secondary imagination's struggle "to idealize and to unify"; or what Percy Bysshe Shelley calls "the creation of actions according to the unchangeable forms of human nature, as existing in the mind of the creator, which is itself the image of all other minds." In Mary Shelley's own words from "Modern Italy," "Works of art belong to the imagination, certain forms of which they realize."

Did Mary Shelley as artist realize these forms? The editors believe so. And so do most readers of *Frankenstein,* which subsumes and conflates the two central myths about knowledge in the Graeco-Roman and Judaeo-Christian traditions: those of Prometheus and of Adam, Eve, and Satan. *Frankenstein* itself has attained mythic status, and Victor's creature can be read as a symbol of humanity, of perfectibilitarian theory, of the French Revolution, of art—even, self-reflexively, of the very novel that Mary Shelley was writing: in her Introduction to the 1831 edition, she bade her famous novel as a "hideous progeny [to] go forth and prosper." So it has; and we hope it will flourish even more in this new *Reader,* where the other texts collectively reveal that Mary Shelley made many and substantial contributions to nineteenth-century literature.

Acknowledgments: The editors have many debts, especially for support from The American University and the University of Delaware. We are most grateful for the assistance of Meoghan M. Byrne, University of Delaware, who untiringly provided us information for the annotations. And we thank other colleagues who have assisted our labors: especially Ingeborg F. Dim, Edward L. Kessler, and Joan Rush at The American University; and James P. Crowley, Carl Dawson, James M. Dean, Gabriella Finizio, H. Anne Hatfield, Deborah S. Lyall, and George Miller at the University of Delaware. We also acknowledge the kindness of The Johns Hopkins University Press for permission to reprint selections of Mary Shelley's *Letters* and *Tales and Stories*. Finally, we thank The University of North Carolina Press for permission to reprint Mary Shelley's *Mathilda*.

Note on the Texts: We have reprinted verbatim from the modern editions of *Letters* and of *Tales and Stories*. The letters reproduce the spelling, punctuation, and other particulars of the original manuscripts; the tales and stories are not modernized but follow the text of the first printing, except for corrections of the original compositors' errors or inconsistencies. For further information, consult the editorial policies outlined in *Letters* and *Tales and Stories*. In the cases of *Frankenstein, Mathilda*, and the essays and reviews, we again reproduce the texts of the original publication, but we silently correct errors in spelling and punctuation. Nineteenth-century spellings and forms (e.g., "groupe," "desart," "to-day," "to-morrow") are retained if they are used consistently within a text; otherwise, we would silently emend to respect the more frequent or more modern spelling of a word within a text. No attempt, however, has been made to regularize spellings throughout this edition: hence the reader may encounter "shew" in one story and "show" in another. All other emendations (e.g., the addition or deletion or changing of a word) are indicated by brackets in or footnotes to the text.

Emendations to the text of *Mathilda* have been more numerous. Our copy-text was Elizabeth Nitchie's 1959 diplomatic edition, which reproduced Mary Shelley's fair-copy manuscript, with its occasionally incorrect or inconsistent spellings and punctuation. Nitchie's frequent brackets for such items are silently deleted here, as are inadvertently doubled words, but we have retained square brackets for interpolated words needed to complete a syntactical pattern. Again, substantive editorial alterations other than those specified above are identified with footnotes.

Washington, D.C.   B. T. B.
Newark, Del.   C. E. R.
May 1990

Contents

Illustrations

Short Titles

JOURNALS

The Journals of Mary Shelley 1814–1844.
Edited by Paula R. Feldman and Diana Scott-Kilvert.
2 vols.
Oxford: Clarendon Press,
1987.

LETTERS

The Letters of Mary Wollstonecraft Shelley.
Edited by Betty T. Bennett.
3 vols.
Baltimore: The Johns Hopkins University Press,
1980, 1983, 1988.

TALES AND STORIES

Mary Shelley:
Collected Tales and Stories,
with Original Engravings.
Edited by Charles E. Robinson.
Baltimore: The Johns Hopkins University Press,
1976.

Chronology

1814

30 March	Mary Godwin returns home from Scotland
13 May	Mary Godwin and Shelley meet again
28 July	Mary Godwin and Shelley accompanied by her stepsister Jane Clairmont elope to the Continent
July–August	Travel through France, Switzerland, Germany, and Holland
13 September	Return of Mary Godwin, Shelley, and Jane Clairmont to London
30 November	Birth of Charles Shelley, Shelley and Harriet Shelley's second child

1815

22 February	Birth of Mary Godwin and Shelley's premature daughter
6 March	Death of premature daughter

1816

24 January	Birth of William Shelley
3 May	Mary Godwin, Shelley, their son William, and Claire Clairmont leave England for Switzerland to meet Lord Byron
?16–23 June	Mary Godwin begins *Frankenstein*
29 August	Mary Godwin, with Shelley, William, and Claire leave Switzerland to return to England
9 October	Fanny Imlay commits suicide
November	Harriet Shelley commits suicide: body discovered 10 December; Shelley informed 15 December
30 December	Mary Godwin and Shelley marry at St. Mildred's, Bread Street, London

1817

12 January	Birth of Claire Clairmont and Byron's daughter Allegra
27 March	Shelley denied custody of his and Harriet Shelley's two children in Chancery Court proceedings
May	Mary Shelley completes *Frankenstein*
2 September	Birth of the Shelleys' daughter Clara Everina Shelley
November	Publication of *History of a Six Weeks' Tour*

1818

1 January	Publication of *Frankenstein*
12 March	The Shelleys, Claire Clairmont, and Allegra depart for Italy
17 August	Shelley and Claire Clairmont depart for Venice and Este
5 September	Mary Shelley and children join them at Este
24 September	Death of Clara Everina Shelley in Venice

1819

7 June	Death of William Shelley in Rome
August–February 1820	Mary Shelley writes *Mathilda*
12 November	Birth of Percy Florence Shelley at Florence

1820

April–May	Mary Shelley writes mythological dramas, *Proserpine* and *Midas*
November	The Shelleys meet Emilia Viviani

1821

January	The Shelleys meet Edward and Jane Williams in Pisa
November	Byron arrives in Pisa

1822

January	Edward John Trelawny arrives in Pisa
20 April	Death of Allegra Byron
16 June	Mary Shelley has miscarriage
8 July	Shelley and Edward Williams drown in the Gulf of Spezia
16 August	Shelley's body cremated at Viareggio

1823

21 January	Shelley's ashes interred in the Protestant Cemetery, Rome
February	Publication of Mary Shelley's *Valperga*
?July	Mary Shelley writes her poem, "The Choice"

25 July	Mary Shelley leaves Italy for England, arriving on 25 August
29 August	Mary Shelley sees *Presumption,* dramatic adaptation of *Frankenstein*
27 November	Mary Shelley receives repayable allowance of £100 per year for Percy Florence's support

1824

19 April	Death of Byron in Greece
June	Publication of Mary Shelley's edition of *Posthumous Poems of Percy Bysshe Shelley*
August	Allowance from Sir Timothy Shelley increased to £200 per year

1826

February	Publication of *The Last Man*
14 September	Death of Charles Bysshe Shelley, Shelley and Harriet Shelley's son; Percy Florence becomes heir to baronetcy

1827

May	Allowance from Sir Timothy Shelley increased to £250 per year
July–October	Mary Shelley with Isabella Robinson and Mary Diana Dods ("Mr. and Mrs. Walter Sholto Douglas") in south of England

1828

11 April	Mary Shelley's trip to Paris to see "Douglases." Ill with smallpox, she meets Prosper Mérimée and General Lafayette
26 May	Mary Shelley returns from Paris to England

1829

June–January 1830	Mary Shelley assists Cyrus Redding in publishing the Paris Galignani edition of Shelley's poems
1 June	Allowance from Sir Timothy Shelley increased to £300 per year

1830

May	Publication of Mary Shelley's *The Fortunes of Perkin Warbeck*

1831

November | Publication of revised edition of *Frankenstein* and of *Proserpine* (*Midas*, her other mythological drama, published in 1922)

1832

8 September | Death of William Godwin, Jr.

29 September | Percy Florence enters Harrow

1835

February | Publication of Mary Shelley's *Lives of the Most Eminent Literary and Scientific Men of Italy, Spain and Portugal,* Vol. I (Vol. II followed by October 1835; Vol. III, by November 1837)

March | Publication of Mary Shelley's *Lodore*

1836

7 April | Death of William Godwin

1837

February | Publication of Mary Shelley's *Falkner*

October | Percy Florence enters Trinity College, Cambridge

1838

c. August | Sir Timothy Shelley allows Mary Shelley to publish Shelley's works

August | Publication of Mary Shelley's *Lives of the Most Eminent Literary and Scientific Men of France,* Vol. I (Vol. II followed by August 1839)

1839

January | Periods of severe illness begin for Mary Shelley

January–May | Publication of Mary Shelley's edition of *Poetical Works of Percy Bysshe Shelley* (4 vols.)

November | Publication of Mary Shelley's edition of *Poetical Works of Percy Bysshe Shelley* (1 vol.)

December | Publication of Mary Shelley's edition of Shelley's *Essays, Letters from Abroad, Translations and Fragments*

1840

June–January 1841   Mary Shelley's tour of the Continent with Percy Florence and his friends

1841

January   Percy Florence graduates from Trinity College, Cambridge

January   Allowance from Sir Timothy Shelley increased to £400 per year

1842

June–August 1843   Second tour of the Continent with Percy Florence and his friends

1844

24 April   Death of Sir Timothy Shelley; Percy Florence inherits estate and title

July   Publication of Mary Shelley's *Rambles in Germany and Italy*

1845

September   Attempted blackmail of Mary Shelley by Gatteschi

October   Attempted blackmail of Mary Shelley by George "Byron"

1848

22 June   Marriage of Sir Percy Florence and Jane St. John

1851

1 February   Death of Mary Shelley, Chester Square, London; burial on 8 February in St. Peter's Churchyard, Bournemouth

The Mary Shelley Reader

Introduction

Mary Wollstonecraft Shelley's *Frankenstein* (1818), her first and most celebrated novel, contrasts a scientist of good family and seemingly lofty aspirations with his own malformed creature. The creature is a noble savage, loving and humanistic until driven to murder by human cruelty. The scientist, representing the values of his culture, emerges as egocentric and irresponsible—a failed "New Prometheus." His obsessive quest for power leads to his own and his creature's moral and physical destruction, symbolizing a central dilemma of the early nineteenth century: how will the dawning age establish moral values that keep pace with rapidly changing technological advances and political ideologies? In Mary Shelley's era, the question applied equally to formative research in air-flight and electricity as it did to government based on an increasingly expanded and enlightened electorate deciding the fate of the nation. Substitute nuclear energy and gene research, and we recognize the questions as the same we continue to struggle with today.

All of Mary Shelley's major works are infused with the basic themes she explored in her first, singular novel: the problem of creating a social order based on love, reciprocity with nature, and education rather than on power and domination. Her first adult publication, *A Six Weeks' Tour* (1817), melds the story of the Shelleys' unconventional elopement adventure with reflections about war-torn Europe and the abiding beauties of nature; her novella *Mathilda* (1819; pub. 1959) explores the devastating effects of incestuous love on a father and daughter; *Valperga* (1823), a historical novel, argues for democratic governance and individual valor (in this case, female) in opposition to unlimited power; *The Last Man* (1826), an apocalyptical novel, interweaves personal and political struggle; *Perkin Warbeck* (1830), another historical novel that opposes unlimited power, again underscores female wisdom and valor; *Lodore*

(1835) and *Falkner* (1837), both domestic novels, resolve familial conflicts through the actions of young women.

Between 1835 and 1839, Mary Shelley wrote five volumes of essays about the lives of eminent Italian, Spanish, Portuguese, and French literary and scientific figures set in their sociopolitical context for Lardner's *Cabinet Cyclopædia*. In 1844, seven years before her death, she closed her writing career with the personal and political *Rambles in Germany and Italy,* based on her 1840–43 travels with her son (see her letter of 20 July [1840] below). In addition to the longer works, she published the mythological drama *Proserpine,* at least two dozen short stories, as well as essays, translations, reviews, and poems. And as Shelley's editor, she brought out not only Shelley's *Posthumous Poems* (1824), but also his *Poetical Works* (1839) (see her letter of 14 July [1841] below) and his *Essays, Letters* (1839, dated 1840), these later editions containing her biographical notes, which remain an invaluable resource for Shelley scholarship. She was a highly regarded author, many of whose novels went into at least second printings and were pirated by foreign publishers in her lifetime. *Frankenstein* was not only revised, republished, and translated, it also began its long history of dramatizations. In 1823, Mary Shelley went to see the first stage production and afterwards wrote to a friend: "But lo & behold! I found myself famous" (see her letter of 9–11 September [1823] below).

The question of how Mary Shelley could have conceived so complex a work as *Frankenstein* has often been asked, both because she was nineteen and a female. In her own time, Sir Walter Scott and many others initially believed that the anonymously published work was written by a man (see her letter of 14 June 1818 below). When word spread that a woman wrote the quickly popular *Frankenstein,* contemporaries accepted it with the "compliment" then common for intellectual women: she was a woman of "masculine understanding."[1] In our time, some critics[2] have continued to have difficulty accepting her authorship, arguing that Shelley materially changed, or even co-authored, the novel despite manuscript evidence that his contributions were primarily editorial—no more, in fact, than Mary Shelley provided for Shelley's works when she posthumously published them. To understand Mary Shelley as the author of this remarkable book, as well as her other works, we need to examine how her particular genius was shaped by her family and her world.

Mary Wollstonecraft Godwin Shelley was born in London on 30 August

1. Leigh Hunt, *Examiner,* 5 October 1817, p. 626n.
2. See, e.g., P. D. Fleck, "Mary Shelley's Notes to Shelley's Poems and *Frankenstein,*" *Studies in Romanticism* 6 (1967): 226–54; and James Rieger, ed., "Introduction," *Frankenstein; or, The Modern Prometheus: The 1818 Text* (Chicago: The University of Chicago Press, 1982).

1797 to parents who played leading roles in trying to reshape late eighteenth-century Britain as it moved from an agrarian society to an age of
industry and technology. Her mother, Mary Wollstonecraft, was a radical
writer and sociopolitical reformer who rejected "proper" female passivity,
dependency, unintelligence. Instead, she became one of that rare breed of
eighteenth-century women who struggled to develop a writing career and
to support herself. She wrote novels, political tracts, educational primers,
travel works, and reviews, advocating a democratic society based on universal freedom. Her 1792 *Vindication of the Rights of Woman,* now recognized as the progenitor of the women's rights movement, argued that a
democratic, moral society could not exist unless women were given equal
education, career opportunities, and civil rights. Mary Wollstonecraft
traveled abroad unescorted in an era that frowned on "ladies" even walking in the street alone; she supported the French Revolution, sharing the
hope with other British radicals that democracy established in France
would influence British politics, and she expressed her political views in
an era that regarded politics as the exclusive realm of men. Her daring
extended to her personal life as well. Her first daughter, Fanny Imlay,
was born out of wedlock, fathered by a man she believed shared her
political ideals as well as her disapproval of legalized marriage. In 1796,
Wollstonecraft formed a liaison with William Godwin that led to their
marriage just five months before the birth of their daughter. Ten days
after her namesake was born, Mary Wollstonecraft died, leaving her
daughter an extraordinary legacy.

That legacy was severely tested during Mary Shelley's childhood, when
the reform movement in Britain, begun with such high expectations, was
all but eliminated in the wake of Britain's grueling war with France that
lasted, with only an eighteen-month interruption, from 1793 to Napoleon's final defeat at Waterloo in 1815. The British government brought
radical reformers to trial, accusing them of treason for their prorevolu-
tionary beliefs. In the conservatism that pervaded the end of the decade
and extended into the next century, Mary Wollstonecraft's name and
writings were vilified as much for her radical politics as for her illegiti-
mate child. But Mary Shelley met her mother through Godwin's loving
memories and through Wollstonecraft's own works. Despite the condem-
nations of Wollstonecraft, Mary Shelley revered her mother. She found solace and spiritual communication while sitting beside her mother's grave at
St. Pancras Churchyard; for most of her life she used the name Wollstonecraft in her signature; she took special pleasure in hearing her mother
praised and being told she resembled her.[3] And her mother's indepen-

3. *Letters,* I: 4, 376; II: 3-4.

dence and politics strongly influenced Mary Shelley's own politics and her conception of a world that accepted the unconventional in herself and others.

But Mary Shelley had a role model for unconventional behavior in her father as well. William Godwin was a professional man of letters who achieved wide prominence in 1793 with his radical *Enquiry Concerning Political Justice,* in which he advocated a society structured on reason, mass education, shared property, and minimal government. One year later, he published *Caleb Williams,* the first detective story in the English language and a fictionalization of the destructiveness of current systems of social structure and power. Both works achieved their initial fame in an era in which radical reform of British government seemed imminent. With the increasing government attack on reformers during the 1790s, Godwin and his works fell into the shadows.

With Mary Wollstonecraft's death, Godwin took the responsibility of raising Fanny Imlay and Mary Godwin. Four years later, he married Mary Jane Clairmont, who brought with her two children. And two years after this second marriage, the Godwins added a son to their entourage. In a period of six years, Godwin had gone from bachelorhood to head of a household with five children. And for the remainder of his life, he struggled to mesh his unswerving daily routine of reading and writing each morning with finding the means to overcome almost constant financial insolvency. For his daughter, the Godwin household provided immediate lessons in complex politics: a half-sister, step-brother and step-sister, baby brother; a step-mother, with whom she did not get on; a beloved learned father committed to maintaining ideals and his family life; and above the mantle, the ever present portrait of Mary Wollstonecraft reminding her of her own special heritage.

Godwin's life style and his writing substantially influenced his daughter, who acknowledged her own "excessive & romantic attachment" to him before she met Shelley.[4] Godwin early recognized her precocity; and she prospered under his tutelage that included access to his extensive library, attendance at public lectures, and exposure to conversations about politics, literature, and philosophy by such writers as Samuel Taylor Coleridge, William Hazlitt, Thomas Holcroft, and Charles Lamb. She also became familiar with the world of publishing through her father and step-mother's publishing firm of M. J. Godwin, founded to try to support their family. And Mary Shelley's first published work, *Mounseer Nongtongpaw; or, the Discoveries of John Bull in a Trip to Paris,* a poetic parody, was published in booklet form in 1808 by M. J. Godwin & Co., with sales sufficient to bring out a fourth edition in 1812.

4. *Letters,* II: 215.

Mary Shelley valued her father's opinions of her work and welcomed his suggestions of subjects to write about. Generally, he held her work in the highest regard. At times, however, he turned her away from some projects: for example, from writing dramas because he believed she lacked the craft for that medium and from publishing *Mathilda* because of its incest theme. A dedicated student of Godwin's works, she found in his fiction an important model for her own: both *Caleb Williams* and *Frankenstein* illustrate the darker side of corrupt social systems in warning of the need to develop new, egalitarian values. Mary Shelley also adopted her father's work habits: a lifelong pattern of reading and writing; and intensive historical research, which provided the foundation of her novels *Valperga* and *Perkin Warbeck* as well as the five volumes of biographical essays in Lardner's *Cabinet Cyclopædia*. After her return to England a year after Shelley's death in 1822, she took her place in Godwin's circle, frequently visiting her father and providing financial support for him from her own meager funds, until his death in 1836.

Mary Shelley's reaction to her parents was not rebellion but an eager and learned discipleship, one which eventually was shared with Percy Bysshe Shelley, who was also a student and follower of Godwin's and Wollstonecraft's egalitarian ideology. But it was a heritage she reshaped according to her own intellect and life experiences. The most important of those experiences began when Mary Shelley daringly eloped with Shelley on 28 July 1814 (see her letters of 25 October and 3 November 1814 below). Almost seventeen, she carried with her the belief from childhood that it was her "fate" to become a writer. In Shelley, she found the perfect mate to share her passions and her intellect. Shelley, almost twenty-two, was a political reformer and a poet: passionate, intense, brilliant, idealistic. He was also married, the father of one child, and expecting a second. But for Shelley, Godwin's and Wollstonecraft's blessed "child of light" was the embodiment of the ideals he shared with her parents. On their elopement, the couple took with them works by Godwin and Wollstonecraft as well as early "productions" of Mary Shelley. They began the joint journal of their tour that later became the basis of Mary Shelley's *Six Weeks' Tour*. And it is possible that Mary Shelley was already expecting their first child, born seven months later.

The Shelleys fashioned an independent, unconventional life that was almost a paradigm for today's world of movement and change. In their eight years together, because of finances, friendships, health, they lived in many places: London, Windsor, Lake Geneva, Bath, Leghorn, Pisa, Baths of Lucca, Rome, Naples, Florence, Spezia. Each locale inspired, and often became the settings for, their writings. Shelley was frequently ill; Mary Shelley, frequently pregnant. Of five conceptions, the last ending in a near fatal miscarriage just weeks before Shelley's own death, only Percy Florence, born 12 November 1819, survived his parents. Their elopement child, a daughter, lived only two weeks after her birth on 22 February 1815; William lived from January 1816 to June 1819; and Clara Everina, September 1817 to September 1818. Mary Shelley recorded her anguished experience of these losses in her letters, her journal, and her fiction.

Her childhood provided Mary Shelley with a far richer intellectual experience than women of that period ordinarily enjoyed. Shelley, himself a student of Enlightenment and Romantic thinkers who believed that the world would necessarily improve, continued that education. He opened to her the advantages of his elitist schooling, together with his own diverse and avid reading. With Shelley, Mary Shelley entered into the world of the younger Romantics that included Lord Byron (see her letter of [?14 December 1822] below), John Keats, Leigh Hunt. And Shelley added a critical concept to her parents' egalitarian ideals: the new society must be based on expansive, humanitarian love rather than on power. This concept, expressed through Mary Shelley's own vision, became fundamental to her life and writing.

From the beginning, Shelley encouraged his eager companion to write and develop her own ideas. Despite their hectic life, Mary Shelley learned Italian, French, Greek, and some Latin; expanded her reading in the great writers and thinkers of the past and present; discussed with Shelley the works each wrote and hoped to write. Unquestionably, Mary Shelley was profoundly influenced by Shelley's artistry, intellect, and sociopolitical philosophy. But their relationship, filled with creativity and excitement, also brought to the young artist, developing her own identity, unusual strains: Shelley's interest in other women; domestic responsibilities; financial worries; the deaths of their children; and a transient existence.

That life was abruptly ended when Shelley drowned in 1822 leaving Mary Shelley a widow at twenty-five (see her letter of 15 August 1822 below). Her newly published letters to Jane Williams show how completely she erased all blemish from her memory of Shelley and began her devoted task of gathering and publishing his writings. Accustomed to worshiping her dead mother and communing with her through her mother's works, she would now relate to Shelley through his poetry and prose. She committed herself to raising her son, to writing, to publishing and achieving for her lost Shelley the literary prominence she believed was his due.

Her hopes of financial aid from Shelley's family were quickly disappointed. Sir Timothy Shelley, after trying to wrest her one child from her, finally agreed to provide support for the boy with the provisos that they live in England and that the allowance be repaid against the estate she would inherit as Shelley's heir when Sir Timothy died. Refusing ever to meet her or to communicate directly with her, he employed an attorney as intermediary. When she published Shelley's *Posthumous Poems,* Sir Timothy stopped that allowance until she agreed to halt the further distribution of the *Poems* and to publish no more of Shelley's works. She did agree, thinking the injunction would not last long because of the elderly Sir Timothy's ill health; however, he died only seven years before she did. And not until 1838 did he relent and permit her to publish Shelley's works, which resulted in her great 1839 editions of his poetry and prose.

After Shelley's death, forced to live in England rather than her beloved Italy, the widowed Mary Shelley struggled to establish a new life for herself and her son. With income entirely dependent on her own writing and her father-in-law's whims, she met the challenge both socially and financially of making her own way in a society that increasingly demanded that a woman's place be within the home. She formed many new friendships that included prominent literary, political, and social figures. And among those, special ties to women, with a special affinity for those regarded as social outcasts. No doubt identifying her own blemished social position and constant financial insecurity with theirs, she assisted the writer Caroline Norton with her successful pamphlet arguing that divorce law should be revised to grant custody of young children to their mothers; and she arranged false passports so that two women could disguise themselves as man and wife and start a new life in France. Many of her letters, as well as Godwin's journal, record a busy social schedule, including tea visits, the occasional dinner party, passes to the theater and opera. But at the same time her letters, her journals, and her fiction express a deep loneliness, rooted not in the absence of friends and family but in the loss of the special intimacy she and Shelley had shared, in retrospect hallowed by her imagination, and never to be replaced.

For the first five years of widowhood, Mary Shelley remained deeply rooted in the world the Shelleys had shared. But by 1827 she was treading new paths on her own. From 1827 to 1844, her most prolific years as an author and editor, she successfully fulfilled the three major goals of her life: she provided a gentleman's education for her son; she continued to write and publish (see chronology); and she collected and published Shelley's works in the 1839 editions. And despite occasional feelings of ambivalence and frustrations about her career, she continued to write, earning a professional living and an international reputation.

Until the end of Mary Shelley's life, certain themes, both personal and literary, recurred in her writing. A sophisticated observer of the political scene, she reminded readers in the preface to Shelley's *Poetical Works* that the poet had been treated with extreme hostility by critics because of his support of political reform. And in the 1844 *Rambles,* she again publicly voiced her abiding opposition to despotic government and her support of sociopolitical reform. She also continued to express a self-consciousness as a writer, and a confidence in imagination—her own and others—as the means to define the world. And she believed love and nature were equally sublime and restorative.

The sociopolitical ardor, the passion, and the imagination that pervaded the life and works of this complex, extraordinary woman place her solidly in the mainstream of the English Romantic literary tradition. Unfortunately, for many years few of her works beyond *Frankenstein* were available to readers. Recently, however, her *Tales, Letters, Journals,* and a number of biographical studies have provided a new context for interpreting Mary Shelley. The object of this collection is to advance that contextual reading of Mary Shelley so that we may better understand her masterpiece, the author herself, and the multifaceted Romanticism that extends from her time to ours.

Frankenstein;

or,

The Modern Prometheus[1]

Did I request thee, Maker, from my clay
To mould me man? Did I solicit thee
From darkness to promote me?——
                              Paradise Lost.

---

1. Reprinted from *Frankenstein; or, The Modern Prometheus,* 3 vols. (London: Lackington, Hughes, Harding, Mavor, & Jones, 1818). The epigraph is from Milton's *Paradise Lost* X.743-45.

To

WILLIAM GODWIN,

Author of Political Justice, Caleb Williams, &c.

THESE VOLUMES

Are Respectfully Inscribed by the Author.

Preface[2]

The event on which this fiction is founded has been supposed, by Dr. Darwin,[3] and some of the physiological writers of Germany, as not of impossible occurrence. I shall not be supposed as according the remotest degree of serious faith to such an imagination; yet, in assuming it as the basis of a work of fancy, I have not considered myself as merely weaving a series of supernatural terrors. The event on which the interest of the story depends is exempt from the disadvantages of a mere tale of spectres or enchantment. It was recommended by the novelty of the situations which it developes; and, however impossible as a physical fact, affords a point of view to the imagination for the delineating of human passions more comprehensive and commanding than any which the ordinary relations of existing events can yield.

I have thus endeavoured to preserve the truth of the elementary principles of human nature, while I have not scrupled to innovate upon their combinations. The *Iliad,* the tragic poetry of Greece,—Shakespeare, in the *Tempest* and *Midsummer Night's Dream,*—and most especially Milton, in *Paradise Lost,* conform to this rule; and the most humble novelist, who seeks to confer or receive amusement from his labours, may, without presumption, apply to prose fiction a licence, or rather a rule, from the adoption of which so many exquisite combinations of human feeling have resulted in the highest specimens of poetry.

The circumstance on which my story rests was suggested in casual conversation. It was commenced, partly as a source of amusement, and partly as an expedient for exercising any untried resources of mind. Other motives were mingled with these, as the work proceeded. I am by no means

2. According to Mary Shelley's Introduction to the 1831 edition, this Preface was "entirely written by" Percy B. Shelley.
3. Erasmus Darwin (1731–1802), physician and poet-naturalist.

indifferent to the manner in which whatever moral tendencies exist in the sentiments or characters it contains shall affect the reader; yet my chief concern in this respect has been limited to the avoiding the enervating effects of the novels of the present day, and to the exhibition of the amiableness of domestic affection, and the excellence of universal virtue. The opinions which naturally spring from the character and situation of the hero are by no means to be conceived as existing always in my own conviction; nor is any inference justly to be drawn from the following pages as prejudicing any philosophical doctrine of whatever kind.

It is a subject also of additional interest to the author, that this story was begun in the majestic region where the scene is principally laid, and in society which cannot cease to be regretted. I passed the summer of 1816 in the environs of Geneva. The season was cold and rainy, and in the evenings we crowded around a blazing wood fire, and occasionally amused ourselves with some German stories of ghosts, which happened to fall into our hands. These tales excited in us a playful desire of imitation. Two other friends (a tale from the pen of one of whom would be far more acceptable to the public than any thing I can ever hope to produce) and myself agreed to write each a story, founded on some supernatural occurrence.[4]

The weather, however, suddenly became serene; and my two friends left me on a journey among the Alps, and lost, in the magnificent scenes which they present, all memory of their ghostly visions. The following tale is the only one which has been completed.[5]

4. See Mary Shelley's more elaborate description of these circumstances in her Introduction to the 1831 *Frankenstein*: the ghost stories were *Fantasmagoriana* (Paris, 1812), published anonymously by J. B. B. Eyriès (1767–1846); the two "other friends" were Lord Byron and Percy B. Shelley; Byron was the one whose tale "would be far more acceptable"; Byron's doctor, John William Polidori, was a fourth participant in the storytelling.

5. In the 1831 edition, Mary Shelley here dated this Preface "Marlow, September, 1817."

Volume I

To Mrs. Saville, England.

St. Petersburgh, Dec. 11th, 17—.
You will rejoice to hear that no disaster has accompanied the commencement of an enterprise which you have regarded with such evil forebodings. I arrived here yesterday; and my first task is to assure my dear sister of my welfare, and increasing confidence in the success of my undertaking.

I am already far north of London; and as I walk in the streets of Petersburgh, I feel a cold northern breeze play upon my cheeks, which braces my nerves, and fills me with delight. Do you understand this feeling? This breeze, which has travelled from the regions towards which I am advancing, gives me a foretaste of those icy climes. Inspirited by this wind of promise, my day dreams become more fervent and vivid. I try in vain to be persuaded that the pole is the seat of frost and desolation; it ever presents itself to my imagination as the region of beauty and delight. There, Margaret, the sun is for ever visible; its broad disk just skirting the horizon, and diffusing a perpetual splendour. There—for with your leave, my sister, I will put some trust in preceding navigators—there snow and frost are banished; and, sailing over a calm sea, we may be wafted to a land surpassing in wonders and in beauty every region hitherto discovered on the habitable globe. Its productions and features may be without example, as the phænomena of the heavenly bodies undoubtedly are in those undiscovered solitudes. What may not be expected in a country of eternal light? I may there discover the wondrous power which attracts the needle; and may regulate a thousand celestial observations, that require only this voyage to render their seeming eccentricities consistent for ever. I shall satiate my ardent curiosity with the sight of a part of the world never before visited, and may tread a land never before imprinted by the foot of man. These are my enticements, and they are sufficient to conquer all fear of danger or death, and to induce me to commence this laborious voyage with the joy a child feels when he embarks in a little boat, with his holiday mates, on an expedition of discovery up his native river. But, supposing all these conjectures to be false, you cannot contest the inestimable benefit which I shall confer on all mankind to the last generation, by discovering a passage near the pole to those countries, to reach which at present so many months are requisite; or by ascertaining the secret of the magnet, which, if at all possible, can only be effected by an undertaking such as mine.

These reflections have dispelled the agitation with which I began my letter, and I feel my heart glow with an enthusiasm which elevates me to heaven; for nothing contributes so much to tranquillize the mind as a steady purpose,—a point on which the soul may fix its intellectual eye. This expedition has been the favourite dream of my early years. I have read with ardour the accounts of the various voyages which have been made in the prospect of arriving at the North Pacific Ocean through the seas which surround the pole. You may remember, that a history of all the voyages made for purposes of discovery composed the whole of our good uncle Thomas's library. My education was neglected, yet I was passionately fond of reading. These volumes were my study day and night, and my familiarity with them increased that regret which I had felt, as a child, on learning that my father's dying injunction had forbidden my uncle to allow me to embark in a sea-faring life.

These visions faded when I perused, for the first time, those poets whose effusions entranced my soul, and lifted it to heaven. I also became a poet, and for one year lived in a Paradise of my own creation; I imagined that I also might obtain a niche in the temple where the names of Homer and Shakespeare are consecrated. You are well acquainted with my failure, and how heavily I bore the disappointment. But just at that time I inherited the fortune of my cousin, and my thoughts were turned into the channel of their earlier bent.

Six years have passed since I resolved on my present undertaking. I can, even now, remember the hour from which I dedicated myself to this great enterprise. I commenced by inuring my body to hardship. I accompanied the whale-fishers on several expeditions to the North Sea; I voluntarily endured cold, famine, thirst, and want of sleep; I often worked harder than the common sailors during the day, and devoted my nights to the study of mathematics, the theory of medicine, and those branches of physical science from which a naval adventurer might derive the greatest practical advantage. Twice I actually hired myself as an under-mate in a Greenland whaler, and acquitted myself to admiration. I must own I felt a little proud, when my captain offered me the second dignity in the vessel, and entreated me to remain with the greatest earnestness; so valuable did he consider my services.

And now, dear Margaret, do I not deserve to accomplish some great purpose. My life might have been passed in ease and luxury; but I preferred glory to every enticement that wealth placed in my path. Oh, that some encouraging voice would answer in the affirmative! My courage and my resolution is firm; but my hopes fluctuate, and my spirits are often depressed. I am about to proceed on a long and difficult voyage; the emergencies of which will demand all my fortitude: I am required not only to raise the spirits of others, but sometimes to sustain my own, when their's are failing.

This is the most favourable period for travelling in Russia. They fly quickly over the snow in their sledges; the motion is pleasant, and, in my opinion, far more agreeable than that of an English stage-coach. The cold is not excessive, if you are wrapt in furs, a dress which I have already adopted; for there is a great difference between walking the deck and remaining seated motionless for hours, when no exercise prevents the blood from actually freezing in your veins. I have no ambition to lose my life on the post-road between St. Petersburgh and Archangel.

I shall depart for the latter town in a fortnight or three weeks; and my intention is to hire a ship there, which can easily be done by paying the insurance for the owner, and to engage as many sailors as I think necessary among those who are accustomed to the whale-fishing. I do not intend to sail until the month of June: and when shall I return? Ah, dear sister, how can I answer this question? If I succeed, many, many months, perhaps years, will pass before you and I may meet. If I fail, you will see me again soon, or never.

Farewell, my dear, excellent, Margaret. Heaven shower down blessings on you, and save me, that I may again and again testify my gratitude for all your love and kindness.

Your affectionate brother,
R. Walton.

LETTER II

To Mrs. Saville, England.

Archangel, 28th March, 17—.

How slowly the time passes here, encompassed as I am by frost and snow;

yet a second step is taken towards my enterprise. I have hired a vessel, and am occupied in collecting my sailors; those whom I have already engaged appear to be men on whom I can depend, and are certainly possessed of dauntless courage.

But I have one want which I have never yet been able to satisfy; and the absence of the object of which I now feel as a most severe evil. I have no friend, Margaret: when I am glowing with the enthusiasm of success, there will be none to participate my joy; if I am assailed by disappointment, no one will endeavour to sustain me in dejection. I shall commit my thoughts to paper, it is true; but that is a poor medium for the communication of feeling. I desire the company of a man who could sympathize with me; whose eyes would reply to mine. You may deem me romantic, my dear sister, but I bitterly feel the want of a friend. I have no one near me, gentle yet courageous, possessed of a cultivated as well as of a capacious mind, whose tastes are like my own, to approve or amend my plans. How would such a friend repair the faults of your poor brother! I am too ardent in execution, and too impatient of difficulties. But it is a still greater evil to me that I am self-educated: for the first fourteen years of my life I ran wild on a common, and read nothing but our uncle Thomas's books of voyages. At that age I became acquainted with the celebrated poets of our own country; but it was only when it had ceased to be in my power to derive its most important benefits from such a conviction, that I perceived the necessity of becoming acquainted with more languages than that of my native country. Now I am twenty-eight, and am in reality more illiterate than many school-boys of fifteen. It is true that I have thought more, and that my day dreams are more extended and magnificent; but they want (as the painters call it) *keeping*; and I greatly need a friend who would have sense enough not to despise me as romantic, and affection enough for me to endeavour to regulate my mind.

Well, these are useless complaints; I shall certainly find no friend on the wide ocean, nor even here in Archangel, among merchants and seamen. Yet some feelings, unallied to the dross of human nature, beat even in these rugged bosoms. My lieutenant, for instance, is a man of wonderful courage and enterprise; he is madly desirous of glory. He is an Englishman, and in the midst of national and professional prejudices, unsoftened by cultivation, retains some of the noblest endowments of humanity. I first became acquainted with him on board a whale vessel: finding that he was unemployed in this city, I easily engaged him to assist in my enterprise.

The master is a person of an excellent disposition, and is remarkable in the ship for his gentleness, and the mildness of his discipline. He is, indeed, of so amiable a nature, that he will not hunt (a favourite, and almost the only amusement here), because he cannot endure to spill blood. He is, moreover, heroically generous. Some years ago he loved a young Russian lady, of moderate fortune; and having amassed a considerable sum in prize-money, the father of the girl consented to the match. He saw his mistress once before the destined ceremony; but she was bathed in tears, and, throwing herself at his feet, entreated him to spare her, confessing at the same time that she loved another, but that he was poor, and that her father would never consent to the union. My generous friend reassured the suppliant, and on being informed of the name of her lover instantly abandoned his pursuit. He had already bought a farm with his money, on which he had designed to pass the remainder of his life; but he bestowed the whole on his rival, together with the remains of his prize-money to purchase stock, and then himself solicited the young woman's father to consent to her marriage with her lover. But the old man decidedly refused, thinking himself bound in honour to my friend; who, when he found the father inexorable, quitted his country, nor returned until he heard that his former mistress was married according to her inclinations. "What a noble fellow!" you will exclaim. He is so; but then he has passed all his life on board a vessel, and has scarcely an idea beyond the rope and the shroud.

But do not suppose that, because I complain a little, or because I can conceive a consolation for my toils which I may never know, that I am wavering in my resolutions. Those are as fixed as fate; and my voyage is only now delayed until the weather shall permit my embarkation. The winter has been dreadfully severe; but the spring promises well, and it is considered as a remarkably early season; so that, perhaps, I may sail sooner than I expected. I shall do nothing rashly; you know me sufficiently to confide in my prudence and considerateness whenever the safety of others is committed to my care.

I cannot describe to you my sensations on the near prospect of my undertaking. It is impossible to communicate to you a conception of the trembling sensation, half pleasurable and half fearful, with which I am preparing to depart. I am going to unexplored regions, to "the land of mist and snow;"[6] but I shall kill no albatross, therefore do not be alarmed for my safety.

Shall I meet you again, after having traversed immense seas, and returned by the most southern cape of Africa or America? I dare not expect such success, yet I cannot bear to look on the reverse of the picture. Continue to write to me by every opportunity: I may receive your letters

---

6. S. T. Coleridge (1772–1834), "The Rime of the Ancient Mariner," first published in *Lyrical Ballads* (1798).

(though the chance is very doubtful) on some occasions when I need them most to support my spirits. I love you very tenderly. Remember me with affection, should you never hear from me again.

Your affectionate brother,
Robert Walton.

LETTER III

To Mrs. Saville, England.

July 7th, 17—.

My dear Sister,

I write a few lines in haste, to say that I am safe, and well advanced on my voyage. This letter will reach England by a merchant-man now on its homeward voyage from Archangel; more fortunate than I, who may not see my native land, perhaps, for many years. I am, however, in good spirits: my men are bold, and apparently firm of purpose; nor do the floating sheets of ice that continually pass us, indicating the dangers of the region towards which we are advancing, appear to dismay them. We have already reached a very high latitude; but it is the height of summer, and although not so warm as in England, the southern gales, which blow us speedily towards those shores which I so ardently desire to attain, breathe a degree of renovating warmth which I had not expected.

No incidents have hitherto befallen us, that would make a figure in a letter. One or two stiff gales, and the breaking of a mast, are accidents which experienced navigators scarcely remember to record; and I shall be well content, if nothing worse happen to us during our voyage.

Adieu, my dear Margaret. Be assured, that for my own sake, as well as your's, I will not rashly encounter danger. I will be cool, persevering, and prudent.

Remember me to all my English friends.

Most affectionately yours,
R. W.

LETTER IV

To Mrs. Saville, England.

August 5th, 17—.

So strange an accident has happened to us, that I cannot forbear recording it, although it is very probable that you will see me before these
papers can come into your possession.

Last Monday (July 31st), we were nearly surrounded by ice, which
closed in the ship on all sides, scarcely leaving her the sea room in which
she floated. Our situation was somewhat dangerous, especially as we were
compassed round by a very thick fog. We accordingly lay to, hoping that
some change would take place in the atmosphere and weather.

About two o'clock the mist cleared away, and we beheld, stretched out
in every direction, vast and irregular plains of ice, which seemed to have
no end. Some of my comrades groaned, and my own mind began to grow
watchful with anxious thoughts, when a strange sight suddenly attracted
our attention, and diverted our solicitude from our own situation. We
perceived a low carriage, fixed on a sledge and drawn by dogs, pass on
towards the north, at the distance of half a mile: a being which had the
shape of a man, but apparently of gigantic stature, sat in the sledge, and
guided the dogs. We watched the rapid progress of the traveller with our
telescopes, until he was lost among the distant inequalities of the ice.

This appearance excited our unqualified wonder. We were, as we believed, many hundred miles from any land; but this apparition seemed to
denote that it was not, in reality, so distant as we had supposed. Shut in,
however, by ice, it was impossible to follow his track, which we had observed with the greatest attention.

About two hours after this occurrence, we heard the ground sea; and
before night the ice broke, and freed our ship. We, however, lay to until
the morning, fearing to encounter in the dark those large loose masses
which float about after the breaking up of the ice. I profited of this time
to rest for a few hours.

In the morning, however, as soon as it was light, I went upon deck, and
found all the sailors busy on one side of the vessel, apparently talking to
some one in the sea. It was, in fact, a sledge, like that we had seen before,
which had drifted towards us in the night, on a large fragment of ice.
Only one dog remained alive; but there was a human being within it,
whom the sailors were persuading to enter the vessel. He was not, as the
other traveller seemed to be, a savage inhabitant of some undiscovered
island, but an European. When I appeared on deck, the master said,
"Here is our captain, and he will not allow you to perish on the open sea."

On perceiving me, the stranger addressed me in English, although with a foreign accent. "Before I come on board your vessel," said he, "will you have the kindness to inform me whither you are bound?"

You may conceive my astonishment on hearing such a question addressed to me from a man on the brink of destruction, and to whom I should have supposed that my vessel would have been a resource which he would not have exchanged for the most precious wealth the earth can afford. I replied, however, that we were on a voyage of discovery towards the northern pole.

Upon hearing this he appeared satisfied, and consented to come on board. Good God! Margaret, if you had seen the man who thus capitulated for his safety, your surprise would have been boundless. His limbs were nearly frozen, and his body dreadfully emaciated by fatigue and suffering. I never saw a man in so wretched a condition. We attempted to carry him into the cabin; but as soon as he had quitted the fresh air, he fainted. We accordingly brought him back to the deck, and restored him to animation by rubbing him with brandy, and forcing him to swallow a small quantity. As soon as he shewed signs of life, we wrapped him up in blankets, and placed him near the chimney of the kitchen-stove. By slow degrees he recovered, and ate a little soup, which restored him wonderfully.

Two days passed in this manner before he was able to speak; and I often feared that his sufferings had deprived him of understanding. When he had in some measure recovered, I removed him to my own cabin, and attended on him as much as my duty would permit. I never saw a more interesting creature: his eyes have generally an expression of wildness, and even madness; but there are moments when, if any one performs an act of kindness towards him, or does him any the most trifling service, his whole countenance is lighted up, as it were, with a beam of benevolence and sweetness that I never saw equalled. But he is generally melancholy and despairing; and sometimes he gnashes his teeth, as if impatient of the weight of woes that oppresses him.

When my guest was a little recovered, I had great trouble to keep off the men, who wished to ask him a thousand questions; but I would not allow him to be tormented by their idle curiosity, in a state of body and mind whose restoration evidently depended upon entire repose. Once, however, the lieutenant asked, Why he had come so far upon the ice in so strange a vehicle?

His countenance instantly assumed an aspect of the deepest gloom; and he replied, "To seek one who fled from me."

"And did the man whom you pursued travel in the same fashion?"

"Yes."

"Then I fancy we have seen him; for, the day before we picked you up, we saw some dogs drawing a sledge, with a man in it, across the ice."

This aroused the stranger's attention; and he asked a multitude of questions concerning the route which the dæmon, as he called him, had pursued. Soon after, when he was alone with me, he said, "I have, doubtless, excited your curiosity, as well as that of these good people; but you are too considerate to make inquiries."

"Certainly; it would indeed be very impertinent and inhuman in me to trouble you with any inquisitiveness of mine."

"And yet you rescued me from a strange and perilous situation; you have benevolently restored me to life."

Soon after this he inquired, if I thought that the breaking up of the ice had destroyed the other sledge? I replied, that I could not answer with any degree of certainty; for the ice had not broken until near midnight, and the traveller might have arrived at a place of safety before that time; but of this I could not judge.

From this time the stranger seemed very eager to be upon deck, to watch for the sledge which had before appeared; but I have persuaded him to remain in the cabin, for he is far too weak to sustain the rawness of the atmosphere. But I have promised that some one should watch for him, and give him instant notice if any new object should appear in sight.

Such is my journal of what relates to this strange occurrence up to the present day. The stranger has gradually improved in health, but is very silent, and appears uneasy when any one except myself enters his cabin. Yet his manners are so conciliating and gentle, that the sailors are all interested in him, although they have had very little communication with him. For my own part, I begin to love him as a brother; and his constant and deep grief fills me with sympathy and compassion. He must have been a noble creature in his better days, being even now in wreck so attractive and amiable.

I said in one of my letters, my dear Margaret, that I should find no friend on the wide ocean; yet I have found a man who, before his spirit had been broken by misery, I should have been happy to have possessed as the brother of my heart.

I shall continue my journal concerning the stranger at intervals, should I have any fresh incidents to record.

August 13th, 17—.

My affection for my guest increases every day. He excites at once my admiration and my pity to an astonishing degree. How can I see so noble a creature destroyed by misery without feeling the most poignant grief? He is so gentle, yet so wise; his mind is so cultivated; and when he speaks, although his words are culled with the choicest art, yet they flow with rapidity and unparalleled eloquence.

He is now much recovered from his illness, and is continually on the deck, apparently watching for the sledge that preceded his own. Yet, although unhappy, he is not so utterly occupied by his own misery, but that he interests himself deeply in the employments of others. He has asked me many questions concerning my design; and I have related my little history frankly to him. He appeared pleased with the confidence, and suggested several alterations in my plan, which I shall find exceedingly useful. There is no pedantry in his manner; but all he does appears to spring solely from the interest he instinctively takes in the welfare of those who surround him. He is often overcome by gloom, and then he sits by himself, and tries to overcome all that is sullen or unsocial in his humour. These paroxysms pass from him like a cloud from before the sun, though his dejection never leaves him. I have endeavoured to win his confidence; and I trust that I have succeeded. One day I mentioned to him the desire I had always felt of finding a friend who might sympathize with me, and direct me by his counsel. I said, I did not belong to that class of men who are offended by advice. "I am self-educated, and perhaps I hardly rely sufficiently upon my own powers. I wish therefore that my companion should be wiser and more experienced than myself, to confirm and support me; nor have I believed it impossible to find a true friend."

"I agree with you," replied the stranger, "in believing that friendship is not only a desirable, but a possible acquisition. I once had a friend, the most noble of human creatures, and am entitled, therefore, to judge respecting friendship. You have hope, and the world before you, and have no cause for despair. But I——I have lost everything, and cannot begin life anew."

As he said this, his countenance became expressive of a calm settled grief, that touched me to the heart. But he was silent, and presently retired to his cabin.

Even broken in spirit as he is, no one can feel more deeply than he does the beauties of nature. The starry sky, the sea, and every sight afforded by these wonderful regions, seems still to have the power of elevating his soul from earth. Such a man has a double existence: he may suffer misery, and be overwhelmed by disappointments; yet when he has retired into himself, he will be like a celestial spirit, that has a halo around him, within whose circle no grief or folly ventures.

Will you laugh at the enthusiasm I express concerning this divine wanderer? If you do, you must have certainly lost that simplicity which was once your characteristic charm. Yet, if you will, smile at the warmth of my expressions, while I find every day new causes for repeating them.

August 19th, 17—.

Yesterday the stranger said to me, "You may easily perceive, Captain Walton, that I have suffered great and unparalleled misfortunes. I had determined, once, that the memory of these evils should die with me; but you have won me to alter my determination. You seek for knowledge and wisdom, as I once did; and I ardently hope that the gratification of your wishes may not be a serpent to sting you, as mine has been. I do not know that the relation of my misfortunes will be useful to you, yet, if you are inclined, listen to my tale. I believe that the strange incidents connected with it will afford a view of nature, which may enlarge your faculties and understanding. You will hear of powers and occurrences, such as you have been accustomed to believe impossible: but I do not doubt that my tale conveys in its series internal evidence of the truth of the events of which it is composed."

You may easily conceive that I was much gratified by the offered communication; yet I could not endure that he should renew his grief by a recital of his misfortunes. I felt the greatest eagerness to hear the promised narrative, partly from curiosity, and partly from a strong desire to ameliorate his fate, if it were in my power. I expressed these feelings in my answer.

"I thank you," he replied, "for your sympathy, but it is useless; my fate is nearly fulfilled. I wait but for one event, and then I shall repose in peace. I understand your feeling," continued he, perceiving that I wished to interrupt him; "but you are mistaken, my friend, if thus you will allow me to name you; nothing can alter my destiny: listen to my history, and you will perceive how irrevocably it is determined."

He then told me, that he would commence his narrative the next day when I should be at leisure. This promise drew from me the warmest thanks. I have resolved every night, when I am not engaged, to record, as nearly as possible in his own words, what he has related during the day. If I should be engaged, I will at least make notes. This manuscript will doubtless afford you the greatest pleasure: but to me, who know him, and who hear it from his own lips, with what interest and sympathy shall I read it in some future day!

CHAPTER I

I am by birth a Genevese; and my family is one of the most distinguished of that republic. My ancestors had been for many years counsellors and syndics; and my father had filled several public situations with honour and reputation. He was respected by all who knew him for his integrity and indefatigable attention to public business. He passed his younger days perpetually occupied by the affairs of his country; and it was not until the decline of life that he thought of marrying, and bestowing on the state sons who might carry his virtues and his name down to posterity.

As the circumstances of his marriage illustrate his character, I cannot refrain from relating them. One of his most intimate friends was a merchant, who, from a flourishing state, fell, through numerous mischances, into poverty. This man, whose name was Beaufort, was of a proud and unbending disposition, and could not bear to live in poverty and oblivion in the same country where he had formerly been distinguished for his rank and magnificence. Having paid his debts, therefore, in the most honourable manner, he retreated with his daughter to the town of Lucerne, where he lived unknown and in wretchedness. My father loved Beaufort with the truest friendship, and was deeply grieved by his retreat in these unfortunate circumstances. He grieved also for the loss of his society, and resolved to seek him out and endeavour to persuade him to begin the world again through his credit and assistance.

Beaufort had taken effectual measures to conceal himself; and it was ten months before my father discovered his abode. Overjoyed at this discovery, he hastened to the house, which was situated in a mean street, near the Reuss. But when he entered, misery and despair alone welcomed him. Beaufort had saved but a very small sum of money from the wreck of his fortunes; but it was sufficient to provide him with sustenance for some months, and in the mean time he hoped to procure some respectable employment in a merchant's house. The interval was consequently spent in inaction; his grief only became more deep and rankling, when he had leisure for reflection; and at length it took so fast hold of his mind, that at the end of three months he lay on a bed of sickness, incapable of any exertion.

His daughter attended him with the greatest tenderness; but she saw with despair that their little fund was rapidly decreasing, and that there was no other prospect of support. But Caroline Beaufort possessed a mind of an uncommon mould; and her courage rose to support her in her adversity. She procured plain work; she plaited straw; and by various means contrived to earn a pittance scarcely sufficient to support life.

Several months passed in this manner. Her father grew worse; her time was more entirely occupied in attending him; her means of subsistence decreased; and in the tenth month her father died in her arms, leaving her an orphan and a beggar. This last blow overcame her; and she knelt by Beaufort's coffin, weeping bitterly, when my father entered the chamber. He came like a protecting spirit to the poor girl, who committed herself to his care, and after the interment of his friend he conducted her to Geneva, and placed her under the protection of a relation. Two years after this event Caroline became his wife.

When my father became a husband and a parent, he found his time so occupied by the duties of his new situation, that he relinquished many of his public employments, and devoted himself to the education of his children. Of these I was the eldest, and the destined successor to all his labours and utility. No creature could have more tender parents than mine. My improvement and health were their constant care, especially as I remained for several years their only child. But before I continue my narrative, I must record an incident which took place when I was four years of age.

My father had a sister, whom he tenderly loved, and who had married early in life an Italian gentleman. Soon after her marriage, she had accompanied her husband into his[7] native country, and for some years my father had very little communication with her. About the time I mentioned she died; and a few months afterwards he received a letter from her husband, acquainting him with his intention of marrying an Italian lady, and requesting my father to take charge of the infant Elizabeth, the only child of his deceased sister. "It is my wish," he said, "that you should consider her as your own daughter, and educate her thus. Her mother's fortune is secured to her, the documents of which I will commit to your keeping. Reflect upon this proposition; and decide whether you would prefer educating your niece yourself to her being brought up by a stepmother."

My father did not hesitate, and immediately went to Italy, that he might accompany the little Elizabeth to her future home. I have often heard my mother say, that she was at that time the most beautiful child she had ever seen, and shewed signs even then of a gentle and affectionate disposition. These indications, and a desire to bind as closely as possible the ties of domestic love, determined my mother to consider Elizabeth as my future wife; a design which she never found reason to repent.

From this time Elizabeth Lavenza became my playfellow, and, as we grew older, my friend. She was docile and good tempered, yet gay and

7. Incorrectly printed as "her" in the 1818 edition.

playful as a summer insect. Although she was lively and animated, her feelings were strong and deep, and her disposition uncommonly affectionate. No one could better enjoy liberty, yet no one could submit with more grace than she did to constraint and caprice. Her imagination was luxuriant, yet her capability of application was great. Her person was the image of her mind; her hazel eyes, although as lively as a bird's, possessed an attractive softness. Her figure was light and airy; and, though capable of enduring great fatigue, she appeared the most fragile creature in the world. While I admired her understanding and fancy, I loved to tend on her, as I should on a favourite animal; and I never saw so much grace both of person and mind united to so little pretension.

Every one adored Elizabeth. If the servants had any request to make, it was always through her intercession. We were strangers to any species of disunion and dispute; for although there was a great dissimilitude in our characters, there was an harmony in that very dissimilitude. I was more calm and philosophical than my companion; yet my temper was not so yielding. My application was of longer endurance; but it was not so severe whilst it endured. I delighted in investigating the facts relative to the actual world; she busied herself in following the aerial creations of the poets. The world was to me a secret, which I desired to discover; to her it was a vacancy, which she sought to people with imaginations of her own.

My brothers were considerably younger than myself; but I had a friend in one of my schoolfellows, who compensated for this deficiency. Henry Clerval was the son of a merchant of Geneva, an intimate friend of my father. He was a boy of singular talent and fancy. I remember, when he was nine years old, he wrote a fairy tale, which was the delight and amazement of all his companions. His favourite study consisted in books of chivalry and romance; and when very young, I can remember, that we used to act plays composed by him out of these favourite books, the principal characters of which were Orlando, Robin Hood, Amadis, and St. George.

No youth could have passed more happily than mine. My parents were indulgent, and my companions amiable. Our studies were never forced; and by some means we always had an end placed in view, which excited us to ardour in the prosecution of them. It was by this method, and not by emulation, that we were urged to application. Elizabeth was not incited to apply herself to drawing, that her companions might not outstrip her; but through the desire of pleasing her aunt, by the representation of some favourite scene done by her own hand. We learned Latin and English, that we might read the writings in those languages; and so far from study being made odious to us through punishment, we loved application, and our amusements would have been the labours of other children. Perhaps we did not read so many books, or learn languages so quickly, as those who are disciplined according to the ordinary methods; but what we learned was impressed the more deeply on our memories.

In this description of our domestic circle I include Henry Clerval; for he was constantly with us. He went to school with me, and generally passed the afternoon at our house; for being an only child, and destitute of companions at home, his father was well pleased that he should find associates at our house; and we were never completely happy when Clerval was absent.

I feel pleasure in dwelling on the recollections of childhood, before misfortune had tainted my mind, and changed its bright visions of extensive usefulness into gloomy and narrow reflections upon self. But, in drawing the picture of my early days, I must not omit to record those events which led, by insensible steps to my after tale of misery: for when I would account to myself for the birth of that passion, which afterwards ruled my destiny, I find it arise, like a mountain river, from ignoble and almost forgotten sources; but, swelling as it proceeded, it became the torrent which, in its course, has swept away all my hopes and joys.

Natural philosophy is the genius that has regulated my fate; I desire therefore, in this narration, to state those facts which led to my predilection for that science. When I was thirteen years of age, we all went on a party of pleasure to the baths near Thonon: the inclemency of the weather obliged us to remain a day confined to the inn. In this house I chanced to find a volume of the works of Cornelius Agrippa.[8] I opened it with apathy; the theory which he attempts to demonstrate, and the wonderful facts which he relates, soon changed this feeling into enthusiasm. A new light seemed to dawn upon my mind; and, bounding with joy, I communicated my discovery to my father. I cannot help remarking here the many opportunities instructors possess of directing the attention of their pupils to useful knowledge, which they utterly neglect. My father looked carelessly at the title-page of my book, and said, "Ah! Cornelius Agrippa! My dear Victor, do not waste your time upon this; it is sad trash."

If, instead of this remark, my father had taken the pains to explain to me, that the principles of Agrippa had been entirely exploded, and that a modern system of science had been introduced, which possessed much greater powers than the ancient, because the powers of the latter were chimerical, while those of the former were real and practical; under such circumstances, I should certainly have thrown Agrippa aside, and, with

8. Cornelius Agrippa (1486–1535), German writer on the occult.

my imagination warmed as it was, should probably have applied myself to the more rational theory of chemistry which has resulted from modern discoveries. It is even possible, that the train of my ideas would never have received the fatal impulse that led to my ruin. But the cursory glance my father had taken of my volume by no means assured me that he was acquainted with its contents; and I continued to read with the greatest avidity.

When I returned home, my first care was to procure the whole works of this author, and afterwards of Paracelsus and Albertus Magnus.[9] I read and studied the wild fancies of these writers with delight; they appeared to me treasures known to few beside myself; and although I often wished to communicate these secret stores of knowledge to my father, yet his indefinite censure of my favourite Agrippa always withheld me. I disclosed my discoveries to Elizabeth, therefore, under a promise of strict secrecy; but she did not interest herself in the subject, and I was left by her to pursue my studies alone.

It may appear very strange, that a disciple of Albertus Magnus should arise in the eighteenth century; but our family was not scientifical, and I had not attended any of the lectures given at the schools of Geneva. My dreams were therefore undisturbed by reality; and I entered with the greatest diligence into the search of the philosopher's stone and the elixir of life. But the latter obtained my most undivided attention: wealth was an inferior object; but what glory would attend the discovery, if I could banish disease from the human frame, and render man invulnerable to any but a violent death!

Nor were these my only visions. The raising of ghosts or devils was a promise liberally accorded by my favourite authors, the fulfilment of which I most eagerly sought; and if my incantations were always unsuccessful, I attributed the failure rather to my own inexperience and mistake, than to a want of skill or fidelity in my instructors.

The natural phænomena that take place every day before our eyes did not escape my examinations. Distillation, and the wonderful effects of steam, processes of which my favourite authors were utterly ignorant, excited my astonishment; but my utmost wonder was engaged by some experiments on an air-pump, which I saw employed by a gentleman whom we were in the habit of visiting.

The ignorance of the early philosophers on these and several other points served to decrease their credit with me: but I could not entirely throw them aside, before some other system should occupy their place in my mind.

9. The Swiss Paracelsus (1493–1541) and the German Albertus Magnus (c. 1193–1280) were men of letters also associated with occult knowledge.

When I was about fifteen years old, we had retired to our house near Belrive, when we witnessed a most violent and terrible thunder-storm. It advanced from behind the mountains of Jura; and the thunder burst at once with frightful loudness from various quarters of the heavens. I remained, while the storm lasted, watching its progress with curiosity and delight. As I stood at the door, on a sudden I beheld a stream of fire issue from an old and beautiful oak, which stood about twenty yards from our house; and so soon as the dazzling light vanished, the oak had disappeared, and nothing remained but a blasted stump. When we visited it the next morning, we found the tree shattered in a singular manner. It was not splintered by the shock, but entirely reduced to thin ribbands of wood. I never beheld any thing so utterly destroyed.

The catastrophe of this tree excited my extreme astonishment; and I eagerly inquired of my father the nature and origin of thunder and lightning. He replied, "Electricity;" describing at the same time the various effects of that power. He constructed a small electrical machine, and exhibited a few experiments; he made also a kite, with a wire and string, which drew down that fluid from the clouds.

This last stroke completed the overthrow of Cornelius Agrippa, Albertus Magnus, and Paracelsus, who had so long reigned the lords of my imagination. But by some fatality I did not feel inclined to commence the study of any modern system; and this disinclination was influenced by the following circumstance.

My father expressed a wish that I should attend a course of lectures upon natural philosophy, to which I cheerfully consented. Some accident prevented my attending these lectures until the course was nearly finished. The lecture, being therefore one of the last, was entirely incomprehensible to me. The professor discoursed with the greatest fluency of potassium and boron, of sulphates and oxyds, terms to which I could affix no idea; and I became disgusted with the science of natural philosophy, although I still read Pliny and Buffon[10] with delight, authors, in my estimation, of nearly equal interest and utility.

My occupations at this age were principally the mathematics, and most of the branches of study appertaining to that science. I was busily employed in learning languages; Latin was already familiar to me, and I began to read some of the easiest Greek authors without the help of a lexicon. I also perfectly understood English and German. This is the list of my accomplishments at the age of seventeen; and you may conceive that my hours were fully employed in acquiring and maintaining a knowledge of this various literature.

10. Pliny (23–79), Roman naturalist; Georges Louis Leclerc, comte de Buffon (1707–88), French naturalist.

Another task also devolved upon me, when I became the instructor of my brothers. Ernest was six years younger than myself, and was my principal pupil. He had been afflicted with ill health from his infancy, through which Elizabeth and I had been his constant nurses: his disposition was gentle, but he was incapable of any severe application. William, the youngest of our family, was yet an infant, and the most beautiful little fellow in the world; his lively blue eyes, dimpled cheeks, and endearing manners, inspired the tenderest affection.

Such was our domestic circle, from which care and pain seemed for ever banished. My father directed our studies, and my mother partook of our enjoyments. Neither of us possessed the slightest pre-eminence over the other; the voice of command was never heard amongst us; but mutual affection engaged us all to comply with and obey the slightest desire of each other.

CHAPTER II

When I had attained the age of seventeen, my parents resolved that I should become a student at the university of Ingolstadt.[11] I had hitherto attended the schools of Geneva; but my father thought it necessary, for the completion of my education, that I should be made acquainted with other customs than those of my native country. My departure was therefore fixed at an early date; but, before the day resolved upon could arrive, the first misfortune of my life occurred—an omen, as it were, of my future misery.

Elizabeth had caught the scarlet fever; but her illness was not severe, and she quickly recovered. During her confinement, many arguments had been urged to persuade my mother to refrain from attending upon her. She had, at first, yielded to our entreaties; but when she heard that her favourite was recovering, she could no longer debar herself from her society, and entered her chamber long before the danger of infection was past. The consequences of this imprudence were fatal. On the third day my mother sickened; her fever was very malignant, and the looks of her attendants prognosticated the worst event. On her death-bed the fortitude and benignity of this admirable woman did not desert her. She joined the hands of Elizabeth and myself: "My children," she said, "my firmest hopes of future happiness were placed on the prospect of your union.

11. The University of Ingolstadt (1472–1800), located on the Danube in Upper Bavaria, had a medical school. Because the society of Illuminati had been founded there in 1776, Ingolstadt also suggests progressive or revolutionary thought.

This expectation will now be the consolation of your father. Elizabeth, my love, you must supply my place to your younger cousins. Alas! I regret that I am taken from you; and, happy and beloved as I have been, is it not hard to quit you all? But these are not thoughts befitting me; I will endeavour to resign myself cheerfully to death, and will indulge a hope of meeting you in another world."

She died calmly; and her countenance expressed affection even in death. I need not describe the feelings of those whose dearest ties are rent by that most irreparable evil, the void that presents itself to the soul, and the despair that is exhibited on the countenance. It is so long before the mind can persuade itself that she, whom we saw every day, and whose very existence appeared a part of our own, can have departed for ever—that the brightness of a beloved eye can have been extinguished, and the sound of a voice so familiar, and dear to the ear, can be hushed, never more to be heard. These are the reflections of the first days; but when the lapse of time proves the reality of the evil, then the actual bitterness of grief commences. Yet from whom has not that rude hand rent away some dear connexion; and why should I describe a sorrow which all have felt, and must feel? The time at length arrives, when grief is rather an indulgence than a necessity; and the smile that plays upon the lips, although it may be deemed a sacrilege, is not banished. My mother was dead, but we had still duties which we ought to perform; we must continue our course with the rest, and learn to think ourselves fortunate, whilst one remains whom the spoiler has not seized.

My journey to Ingolstadt, which had been deferred by these events, was now again determined upon. I obtained from my father a respite of some weeks. This period was spent sadly; my mother's death, and my speedy departure, depressed our spirits; but Elizabeth endeavoured to renew the spirit of cheerfulness in our little society. Since the death of her aunt, her mind had acquired new firmness and vigour. She determined to fulfil her duties with the greatest exactness; and she felt that that most imperious duty, of rendering her uncle and cousins happy, had devolved upon her. She consoled me, amused her uncle, instructed my brothers; and I never beheld her so enchanting as at this time, when she was continually endeavouring to contribute to the happiness of others, entirely forgetful of herself.

The day of my departure at length arrived. I had taken leave of all my friends, excepting Clerval, who spent the last evening with us. He bitterly lamented that he was unable to accompany me: but his father could not be persuaded to part with him, intending that he should become a partner with him in business, in compliance with his favourite theory, that learning was superfluous in the commerce of ordinary life. Henry had a refined mind; he had no desire to be idle, and was well pleased to become his father's partner, but he believed that a man might be a very good trader, and yet possess a cultivated understanding.

We sat late, listening to his complaints, and making many little arrangements for the future. The next morning early I departed. Tears gushed from the eyes of Elizabeth; they proceeded partly from sorrow at my departure, and partly because she reflected that the same journey was to have taken place three months before, when a mother's blessing would have accompanied me.

I threw myself into the chaise that was to convey me away, and indulged in the most melancholy reflections. I, who had ever been surrounded by amiable companions, continually engaged in endeavouring to bestow mutual pleasure, I was now alone. In the university, whither I was going, I must form my own friends, and be my own protector. My life had hitherto been remarkably secluded and domestic; and this had given me invincible repugnance to new countenances. I loved my brothers, Elizabeth, and Clerval; these were "old familiar faces;"[12] but I believed myself totally unfitted for the company of strangers. Such were my reflections as I commenced my journey; but as I proceeded, my spirits and hopes rose. I ardently desired the acquisition of knowledge. I had often, when at home, thought it hard to remain during my youth cooped up in one place, and had longed to enter the world, and take my station among other human beings. Now my desires were complied with, and it would, indeed, have been folly to repent.

I had sufficient leisure for these and many other reflections during my journey to Ingolstadt, which was long and fatiguing. At length the high white steeple of the town met my eyes. I alighted, and was conducted to my solitary apartment, to spend the evening as I pleased.

The next morning I delivered my letters of introduction, and paid a visit to some of the principal professors, and among others to M. Krempe, professor of natural philosophy. He received me with politeness, and asked me several questions concerning my progress in the different branches of science appertaining to natural philosophy. I mentioned, it is true, with fear and trembling, the only authors I had ever read upon those subjects. The professor stared: "Have you," he said, "really spent your time in studying such nonsense?"

I replied in the affirmative. "Every minute," continued M. Krempe with warmth, "every instant that you have wasted on those books is utterly and entirely lost. You have burdened your memory with exploded systems, and

12. Charles Lamb (1775–1834), "The Old Familiar Faces" (poem) (1798).

useless names. Good God! in what desert land have you lived, where no one was kind enough to inform you that these fancies, which you have so greedily imbibed, are a thousand years old, and as musty as they are ancient? I little expected in this enlightened and scientific age to find a disciple of Albertus Magnus and Paracelsus. My dear Sir, you must begin your studies entirely anew."

So saying, he stept aside, and wrote down a list of several books treating of natural philosophy, which he desired me to procure, and dismissed me, after mentioning that in the beginning of the following week he intended to commence a course of lectures upon natural philosophy in its general relations, and that M. Waldman, a fellow-professor, would lecture upon chemistry the alternate days that he missed.

I returned home, not disappointed, for I had long considered those authors useless whom the professor had so strongly reprobated; but I did not feel much inclined to study the books which I procured at his recommendation. M. Krempe was a little squat man, with a gruff voice and repulsive countenance; the teacher, therefore, did not prepossess me in favour of his doctrine. Besides, I had a contempt for the uses of modern natural philosophy. It was very different, when the masters of the science sought immortality and power; such views, although futile, were grand: but now the scene was changed. The ambition of the inquirer seemed to limit itself to the annihilation of those visions on which my interest in science was chiefly founded. I was required to exchange chimeras of boundless grandeur for realities of little worth.

Such were my reflections during the first two or three days spent almost in solitude. But as the ensuing week commenced, I thought of the information which M. Krempe had given me concerning the lectures. And although I could not consent to go and hear that little conceited fellow deliver sentences out of a pulpit, I recollected what he had said of M. Waldman, whom I had never seen, as he had hitherto been out of town.

Partly from curiosity, and partly from idleness, I went into the lecturing room, which M. Waldman entered shortly after. This professor was very unlike his colleague. He appeared about fifty years of age, but with an aspect expressive of the greatest benevolence; a few gray hairs covered his temples, but those at the back of his head were nearly black. His person was short, but remarkably erect; and his voice the sweetest I had ever heard. He began his lecture by a recapitulation of the history of chemistry and the various improvements made by different men of learning, pronouncing with fervour the names of the most distinguished discoverers. He then took a cursory view of the present state of the science, and explained many of its elementary terms. After having made a few preparatory experiments, he concluded with a panegyric upon modern chemistry, the terms of which I shall never forget:—

"The ancient teachers of this science," said he, "promised impossibilities, and performed nothing. The modern masters promise very little; they know that metals cannot be transmuted, and that the elixir of life is a chimera. But these philosophers, whose hands seem only made to dabble in dirt, and their eyes to pour over the microscope or crucible, have indeed performed miracles. They penetrate into the recesses of nature, and shew how she works in her hiding places. They ascend into the heavens; they have discovered how the blood circulates, and the nature of the air we breathe. They have acquired new and almost unlimited powers; they can command the thunders of heaven, mimic the earthquake, and even mock the invisible world with its own shadows."

I departed highly pleased with the professor and his lecture, and paid him a visit the same evening. His manners in private were even more mild and attractive than in public; for there was a certain dignity in his mien during his lecture, which in his own house was replaced by the greatest affability and kindness. He heard with attention my little narration concerning my studies, and smiled at the names of Cornelius Agrippa, and Paracelsus, but without the contempt that M. Krempe had exhibited. He said, that "these were men to whose indefatigable zeal modern philosophers were indebted for most of the foundations of their knowledge. They had left to us, as an easier task, to give new names, and arrange in connected classifications, the facts which they in a great degree had been the instruments of bringing to light. The labours of men of genius, however erroneously directed, scarcely ever fail in ultimately turning to the solid advantage of mankind." I listened to his statement, which was delivered without any presumption or affectation; and then added, that his lecture had removed my prejudices against modern chemists; and I, at the same time, requested his advice concerning the books I ought to procure.

"I am happy," said M. Waldman, "to have gained a disciple; and if your application equals your ability, I have no doubt of your success. Chemistry is that branch of natural philosophy in which the greatest improvements have been and may be made; it is on that account that I have made it my peculiar study; but at the same time I have not neglected the other branches of science. A man would make but a very sorry chemist, if he attended to that department of human knowledge alone. If your wish is to become really a man of science, and not merely a petty experimentalist, I should advise you to apply to every branch of natural philosophy, including mathematics."

He then took me into his laboratory, and explained to me the uses of his various machines; instructing me as to what I ought to procure, and promising me the use of his own, when I should have advanced far enough in the science not to derange their mechanism. He also gave me the list of books which I had requested; and I took my leave.

Thus ended a day memorable to me; it decided my future destiny.

CHAPTER III

From this day natural philosophy, and particularly chemistry, in the most comprehensive sense of the term, became nearly my sole occupation. I read with ardour those works, so full of genius and discrimination, which modern inquirers have written on these subjects. I attended the lectures, and cultivated the acquaintance, of the men of science of the university; and I found even in M. Krempe a great deal of sound sense and real information, combined, it is true, with a repulsive physiognomy and manners, but not on that account the less valuable. In M. Waldman I found a true friend. His gentleness was never tinged by dogmatism; and his instructions were given with an air of frankness and good nature, that banished every idea of pedantry. It was, perhaps, the amiable character of this man that inclined me more to that branch of natural philosophy which he professed, than an intrinsic love for the science itself. But this state of mind had place only in the first steps towards knowledge: the more fully I entered into the science, the more exclusively I pursued it for its own sake. That application, which at first had been a matter of duty and resolution, now became so ardent and eager, that the stars often disappeared in the light of morning whilst I was yet engaged in my laboratory.

As I applied so closely, it may be easily conceived that I improved rapidly. My ardour was indeed the astonishment of the students; and my proficiency, that of the masters. Professor Krempe often asked me, with a sly smile, how Cornelius Agrippa went on? whilst M. Waldman expressed the most heartfelt exultation in my progress. Two years passed in this manner, during which I paid no visit to Geneva, but was engaged, heart and soul, in the pursuit of some discoveries, which I hoped to make. None but those who have experienced them can conceive of the enticements of science. In other studies you go as far as others have gone before you, and there is nothing more to know; but in a scientific pursuit there is continual food for discovery and wonder. A mind of moderate capacity, which closely pursues one study, must infallibly arrive at great proficiency in that study; and I, who continually sought the attainment of one object of pursuit, and was solely wrapt up in this, improved so rapidly, that, at the end of two years, I made some discoveries in the improvement of some chemical instruments, which procured me great esteem and admiration at the university. When I had arrived at this point, and had become as well acquainted with the theory and practice of natural philosophy as depended on the lessons of any of the professors at Ingolstadt, my residence there being no longer conducive to my improvements, I thought of returning to my friends and my native town, when an incident happened that protracted my stay.

One of the phænomena which had peculiarly attracted my attention was the structure of the human frame, and, indeed, any animal endued with life. Whence, I often asked myself, did the principle of life proceed? It was a bold question, and one which has ever been considered as a mystery; yet with how many things are we upon the brink of becoming acquainted, if cowardice or carelessness did not restrain our inquiries. I revolved these circumstances in my mind, and determined thenceforth to apply myself more particularly to those branches of natural philosophy which relate to physiology. Unless I had been animated by an almost supernatural enthusiasm, my application to this study would have been irksome, and almost intolerable. To examine the causes of life, we must first have recourse to death. I became acquainted with the science of anatomy: but this was not sufficient; I must also observe the natural decay and corruption of the human body. In my education my father had taken the greatest precautions that my mind should be impressed with no supernatural horrors. I do not ever remember to have trembled at a tale of superstition, or to have feared the apparition of a spirit. Darkness had no effect upon my fancy; and a church-yard was to me merely the receptacle of bodies deprived of life, which, from being the seat of beauty and strength, had become food for the worm. Now I was led to examine the cause and progress of this decay, and forced to spend days and nights in vaults and charnel houses. My attention was fixed upon every object the most insupportable to the delicacy of the human feelings. I saw how the fine form of man was degraded and wasted; I beheld the corruption of death succeed to the blooming cheek of life; I saw how the worm inherited the wonders of the eye and brain. I paused, examining and analysing all the minutiæ of causation, as exemplified in the change from life to death, and death to life, until from the midst of this darkness a sudden light broke in upon me—a light so brilliant and wondrous, yet so simple, that while I became dizzy with the immensity of the prospect which it illustrated, I was surprised that among so many men of genius, who had directed their inquiries towards the same science, that I alone should be reserved to discover so astonishing a secret.

Remember, I am not recording the vision of a madman. The sun does not more certainly shine in the heavens, than that which I now affirm is true. Some miracle might have produced it, yet the stages of the discovery were distinct and probable. After days and nights of incredible labour and fatigue, I succeeded in discovering the cause of generation and life; nay, more, I became myself capable of bestowing animation upon lifeless matter.

The astonishment which I had at first experienced on this discovery soon gave place to delight and rapture. After so much time spent in painful labour, to arrive at once at the summit of my desires, was the most gratifying consummation of my toils. But this discovery was so great and overwhelming, that all the steps by which I had been progressively led to it were obliterated, and I beheld only the result. What had been the study and desire of the wisest men since the creation of the world, was now within my grasp. Not that, like a magic scene, it all opened upon me at once: the information I had obtained was of a nature rather to direct my endeavours so soon as I should point them towards the object of my search, than to exhibit that object already accomplished. I was like the Arabian who had been buried with the dead, and found a passage to life aided only by one glimmering, and seemingly ineffectual light.

I see by your eagerness, and the wonder and hope which your eyes express, my friend, that you expect to be informed of the secret with which I am acquainted; that cannot be: listen patiently until the end of my story, and you will easily perceive why I am reserved upon that subject. I will not lead you on, unguarded and ardent as I then was, to your destruction and infallible misery. Learn from me, if not by my precepts, at least by my example, how dangerous is the acquirement of knowledge, and how much happier that man is who believes his native town to be the world, than he who aspires to become greater than his nature will allow.

When I found so astonishing a power placed within my hands, I hesitated a long time concerning the manner in which I should employ it. Although I possessed the capacity of bestowing animation, yet to prepare a frame for the reception of it, with all its intricacies of fibres, muscles, and veins, still remained a work of inconceivable difficulty and labour. I doubted at first whether I should attempt the creation of a being like myself or one of simpler organization; but my imagination was too much exalted by my first success to permit me to doubt of my ability to give life to an animal as complex and wonderful as man. The materials at present within my command hardly appeared adequate to so arduous an undertaking; but I doubted not that I should ultimately succeed. I prepared myself for a multitude of reverses; my operations might be incessantly baffled, and at last my work be imperfect: yet, when I considered the improvement which every day takes place in science and mechanics, I was encouraged to hope my present attempts would at least lay the foundations of future success. Nor could I consider the magnitude and complexity of my plan as any argument of its impracticability. It was with these feelings that I began the creation of a human being. As the minuteness of the parts formed a great hindrance to my speed, I resolved, contrary to my first intention, to make the being of a gigantic stature; that is to say, about eight feet in height, and proportionably large. After having formed this determination, and having spent some months in successfully collecting and arranging my materials, I began.

No one can conceive the variety of feelings which bore me onwards, like a hurricane, in the first enthusiasm of success. Life and death appeared to me ideal bounds, which I should first break through, and pour a torrent of light into our dark world. A new species would bless me as its creator and source; many happy and excellent natures would owe their being to me. No father could claim the gratitude of his child so completely as I should deserve their's. Pursuing these reflections, I thought, that if I could bestow animation upon lifeless matter, I might in process of time (although I now found it impossible) renew life where death had apparently devoted the body to corruption.

These thoughts supported my spirits, while I pursued my undertaking with unremitting ardour. My cheek had grown pale with study, and my person had become emaciated with confinement. Sometimes, on the very brink of certainty, I failed; yet still I clung to the hope which the next day or the next hour might realize. One secret which I alone possessed was the hope to which I had dedicated myself; and the moon gazed on my midnight labours, while, with unrelaxed and breathless eagerness, I pursued nature to her hiding places. Who shall conceive the horrors of my secret toil, as I dabbled among the unhallowed damps of the grave, or tortured the living animal to animate the lifeless clay? My limbs now tremble, and my eyes swim with the remembrance; but then a resistless, and almost frantic impulse, urged me forward; I seemed to have lost all soul or sensation but for this one pursuit. It was indeed but a passing trance, that only made me feel with renewed acuteness so soon as, the unnatural stimulus ceasing to operate, I had returned to my old habits. I collected bones from charnel houses; and disturbed, with profane fingers, the tremendous secrets of the human frame. In a solitary chamber, or rather cell, at the top of the house, and separated from all the other apartments by a gallery and staircase, I kept my workshop of filthy creation; my eyeballs were starting from their sockets in attending to the details of my employment. The dissecting room and the slaughter-house furnished many of my materials; and often did my human nature turn with loathing from my occupation, whilst, still urged on by an eagerness which perpetually increased, I brought my work near to a conclusion.

The summer months passed while I was thus engaged, heart and soul, in one pursuit. It was a most beautiful season; never did the fields bestow a more plentiful harvest, or the vines yield a more luxuriant vintage: but my eyes were insensible to the charms of nature. And the same feelings which made me neglect the scenes around me caused me also to forget those friends who were so many miles absent, and whom I had not seen for so long a time. I knew my silence disquieted them; and I well remembered the words of my father: "I know that while you are pleased with yourself, you will think of us with affection, and we shall hear regularly from you. You must pardon me, if I regard any interruption in your correspondence as a proof that your other duties are equally neglected."

I knew well therefore what would be my father's feelings; but I could not tear my thoughts from my employment, loathsome in itself, but which had taken an irresistible hold of my imagination. I wished, as it were, to procrastinate all that related to my feelings of affection until the great object, which swallowed up every habit of my nature, should be completed.

I then thought that my father would be unjust if he ascribed my neglect to vice, or faultiness on my part; but I am now convinced that he was justified in conceiving that I should not be altogether free from blame. A human being in perfection ought always to preserve a calm and peaceful mind, and never to allow passion or a transitory desire to disturb his tranquillity. I do not think that the pursuit of knowledge is an exception to this rule. If the study to which you apply yourself has a tendency to weaken your affections, and to destroy your taste for those simple pleasures in which no alloy can possibly mix, then that study is certainly unlawful, that is to say, not befitting the human mind. If this rule were always observed; if no man allowed any pursuit whatsoever to interfere with the tranquillity of his domestic affections, Greece had not been enslaved; Cæsar would have spared his country; America would have been discovered more gradually; and the empires of Mexico and Peru had not been destroyed.

But I forget that I am moralizing in the most interesting part of my tale; and your looks remind me to proceed.

My father made no reproach in his letters; and only took notice of my silence by inquiring into my occupations more particularly than before.

Winter, spring, and summer, passed away during my labours; but I did not watch the blossom or the expanding leaves—sights which before always yielded me supreme delight, so deeply was I engrossed in my occupation. The leaves of that year had withered before my work drew near to a close; and now every day shewed me more plainly how well I had succeeded. But my enthusiasm was checked by my anxiety, and I appeared rather like one doomed by slavery to toil in the mines, or any other unwholesome trade, than an artist occupied by his favourite employment. Every night I was oppressed by a slow fever, and I became nervous to a most painful degree; a disease that I regretted the more because I had hitherto enjoyed most excellent health, and had always boasted of the firmness of my nerves. But I believed that exercise and amusement would soon drive away such symptoms; and I promised myself both of these, when my creation should be complete.

CHAPTER IV

It was on a dreary night of November, that I beheld the accomplishment of my toils. With an anxiety that almost amounted to agony, I collected the instruments of life around me, that I might infuse a spark of being into the lifeless thing that lay at my feet. It was already one in the morning; the rain pattered dismally against the panes, and my candle was nearly burnt out, when, by the glimmer of the half-extinguished light, I saw the dull yellow eye of the creature open; it breathed hard, and a convulsive motion agitated its limbs.

How can I describe my emotions at this catastrophe, or how delineate the wretch whom with such infinite pains and care I had endeavoured to form? His limbs were in proportion, and I had selected his features as beautiful. Beautiful!—Great God! His yellow skin scarcely covered the work of muscles and arteries beneath; his hair was of a lustrous black, and flowing; his teeth of a pearly whiteness; but these luxuriances only formed a more horrid contrast with his watery eyes, that seemed almost of the same colour as the dun white sockets in which they were set, his shrivelled complexion, and straight black lips.

The different accidents of life are not so changeable as the feelings of human nature. I had worked hard for nearly two years, for the sole purpose of infusing life into an inanimate body. For this I had deprived myself of rest and health. I had desired it with an ardour that far exceeded moderation; but now that I had finished, the beauty of the dream vanished, and breathless horror and disgust filled my heart. Unable to endure the aspect of the being I had created, I rushed out of the room, and continued a long time traversing my bed-chamber, unable to compose my mind to sleep. At length lassitude succeeded to the tumult I had before endured; and I threw myself on the bed in my clothes, endeavouring to seek a few moments of forgetfulness. But it was in vain: I slept indeed, but I was disturbed by the wildest dreams. I thought I saw Elizabeth, in the bloom of health, walking in the streets of Ingolstadt. Delighted and surprised, I embraced her; but as I imprinted the first kiss on her lips, they became livid with the hue of death; her features appeared to change, and I thought that I held the corpse of my dead mother in my arms; a shroud enveloped her form, and I saw the grave-worms crawling in the folds of the flannel. I started from my sleep with horror; a cold dew covered my forehead, my teeth chattered, and every limb became convulsed; when, by the dim and yellow light of the moon, as it forced its way through the window-shutters, I beheld the wretch—the miserable monster whom I had created. He held up the curtain of the bed; and his eyes, if eyes they may be called, were fixed on me. His jaws opened, and he muttered some inarticulate sounds, while a grin wrinkled his cheeks. He might have spoken, but I did not hear; one hand was stretched out, seemingly to detain me, but I escaped, and rushed down stairs. I took refuge in the court-yard belonging to the house which I inhabited; where I remained during the rest of the night, walking up and down in the greatest agitation, listening attentively, catching and fearing each sound as if it were to announce the approach of the demoniacal corpse to which I had so miserably given life.

Oh! no mortal could support the horror of that countenance. A mummy again endued with animation could not be so hideous as that wretch. I had gazed on him while unfinished; he was ugly then; but when those muscles and joints were rendered capable of motion, it became a thing such as even Dante could not have conceived.

I passed the night wretchedly. Sometimes my pulse beat so quickly and hardly, that I felt the palpitation of every artery; at others, I nearly sank to the ground through languor and extreme weakness. Mingled with this horror, I felt the bitterness of disappointment: dreams that had been my food and pleasant rest for so long a space, were now become a hell to me; and the change was so rapid, the overthrow so complete!

Morning, dismal and wet, at length dawned, and discovered to my sleepless and aching eyes the church of Ingolstadt, its white steeple and clock, which indicated the sixth hour. The porter opened the gates of the court, which had that night been my asylum, and I issued into the streets, pacing them with quick steps, as if I sought to avoid the wretch whom I feared every turning of the street would present to my view. I did not dare return to the apartment which I inhabited, but felt impelled to hurry on, although wetted by the rain, which poured from a black and comfortless sky.

I continued walking in this manner for some time, endeavouring, by bodily exercise, to ease the load that weighed upon my mind. I traversed the streets, without any clear conception of where I was, or what I was doing. My heart palpitated in the sickness of fear; and I hurried on with irregular steps, not daring to look about me:

> Like one who, on a lonely road,
>   Doth walk in fear and dread,
> And, having once turn'd round, walks on,
>   And turns no more his head;
> Because he knows a frightful fiend
>   Doth close behind him tread.[13]

Continuing thus, I came at length opposite to the inn at which the various diligences and carriages usually stopped. Here I paused, I knew not why; but I remained some minutes with my eyes fixed on a coach that was coming towards me from the other end of the street. As it drew nearer, I observed that it was the Swiss diligence: it stopped just where I was standing; and, on the door being opened, I perceived Henry Clerval, who, on seeing me, instantly sprung out. "My dear Frankenstein," exclaimed he, "how glad I am to see you! how fortunate that you should be here at the very moment of my alighting!"

Nothing could equal my delight on seeing Clerval; his presence brought back to my thoughts my father, Elizabeth, and all those scenes of home so dear to my recollection. I grasped his hand, and in a moment forgot my horror and misfortune; I felt suddenly, and for the first time during many months, calm and serene joy. I welcomed my friend, therefore, in the most cordial manner, and we walked towards my college. Clerval continued talking for some time about our mutual friends, and his own good fortune in being permitted to come to Ingolstadt. "You may easily believe," said he, "how great was the difficulty to persuade my father that it was not absolutely necessary for a merchant not to understand any thing except book-keeping; and, indeed, I believe I left him incredulous to the last, for his constant answer to my unwearied entreaties was the same as that of the Dutch school-master in the Vicar of Wakefield: 'I have ten thousand florins a year without Greek, I eat heartily without Greek.'[14] But his affection for me at length overcame his dislike of learning, and

13. Coleridge's "Ancient Mariner." [Mary Shelley's note.]
14. From Chapter 20 of Oliver Goldsmith's *The Vicar of Wakefield* (1766).

he has permitted me to undertake a voyage of discovery to the land of knowledge."

"It gives me the greatest delight to see you; but tell me how you left my fathers, brothers, and Elizabeth."

"Very well, and very happy, only a little uneasy that they hear from you so seldom. By the bye, I mean to lecture you a little upon their account myself.—But, my dear Frankenstein," continued he, stopping short, and gazing full in my face, "I did not before remark how very ill you appear; so thin and pale; you look as if you had been watching for several nights."

"You have guessed right; I have lately been so deeply engaged in one occupation, that I have not allowed myself sufficient rest, as you see: but I hope, I sincerely hope, that all these employments are now at an end, and that I am at length free."

I trembled excessively; I could not endure to think of, and far less to allude to the occurrences of the preceding night. I walked with a quick pace, and we soon arrived at my college. I then reflected, and the thought made me shiver, that the creature whom I had left in my apartment might still be there, alive, and walking about. I dreaded to behold this monster; but I feared still more that Henry should see him. Entreating him therefore to remain a few minutes at the bottom of the stairs, I darted up towards my own room. My hand was already on the lock of the door before I recollected myself. I then paused; and a cold shivering came over me. I threw the door forcibly open, as children are accustomed to do when they expect a spectre to stand in waiting for them on the other side; but nothing appeared. I stepped fearfully in: the apartment was empty; and my bed-room was also freed from its hideous guest. I could hardly believe that so great a good-fortune could have befallen me; but when I became assured that my enemy had indeed fled, I clapped my hands for joy, and ran down to Clerval.

We ascended into my room, and the servant presently brought breakfast; but I was unable to contain myself. It was not joy only that possessed me; I felt my flesh tingle with excess of sensitiveness, and my pulse beat rapidly. I was unable to remain for a single instant in the same place; I jumped over the chairs, clapped my hands, and laughed aloud. Clerval at first attributed my unusual spirits to joy on his arrival; but when he observed me more attentively, he saw a wildness in my eyes for which he could not account; and my loud, unrestrained, heartless laughter, frightened and astonished him.

"My dear Victor," cried he, "what, for God's sake, is the matter? Do not laugh in that manner. How ill you are! What is the cause of all this?"

"Do not ask me," cried I, putting my hands before my eyes, for I thought I saw the dreaded spectre glide into the room; "*he* can tell.—Oh, save me! save me!" I imagined that the monster seized me; I struggled furiously, and fell down in a fit.

Poor Clerval! what must have been his feelings? A meeting, which he anticipated with such joy, so strangely turned to bitterness. But I was not the witness of his grief; for I was lifeless, and did not recover my senses for a long, long time.

This was the commencement of a nervous fever, which confined me for several months. During all that time Henry was my only nurse. I afterwards learned that, knowing my father's advanced age, and unfitness for so long a journey, and how wretched my sickness would make Elizabeth, he spared them this grief by concealing the extent of my disorder. He knew that I could not have a more kind and attentive nurse than himself; and, firm in the hope he felt of my recovery, he did not doubt that, instead of doing harm, he performed the kindest action that he could towards them.

But I was in reality very ill; and surely nothing but the unbounded and unremitting attentions of my friend could have restored me to life. The form of the monster on whom I had bestowed existence was for ever before my eyes, and I raved incessantly concerning him. Doubtless my words surprised Henry: he at first believed them to be the wanderings of my disturbed imagination; but the pertinacity with which I continually recurred to the same subject persuaded him that my disorder indeed owed its origin to some uncommon and terrible event.

By very slow degrees, and with frequent relapses, that alarmed and grieved my friend, I recovered. I remember the first time I became capable of observing outward objects with any kind of pleasure, I perceived that the fallen leaves had disappeared, and that the young buds were shooting forth from the trees that shaded my window. It was a divine spring; and the season contributed greatly to my convalescence. I felt also sentiments of joy and affection revive in my bosom; my gloom disappeared, and in a short time I became as cheerful as before I was attacked by the fatal passion.

"Dearest Clerval," exclaimed I, "how kind, how very good you are to me. This whole winter, instead of being spent in study, as you promised yourself, has been consumed in my sick room. How shall I ever repay you? I feel the greatest remorse for the disappointment of which I have been the occasion; but you will forgive me."

"You will repay me entirely, if you do not discompose yourself, but get well as fast as you can; and since you appear in such good spirits, I may speak to you on one subject, may I not?"

I trembled. One subject! what could it be? Could he allude to an object on whom I dared not even think?

"Compose yourself," said Clerval, who observed my change of colour, "I will not mention it, if it agitates you; but your father and cousin would be very happy if they received a letter from you in your own hand-writing. They hardly know how ill you have been, and are uneasy at your long silence."

"Is that all? my dear Henry. How could you suppose that my first thought would not fly towards those dear, dear friends whom I love, and who are so deserving of my love."

"If this is your present temper, my friend, you will perhaps be glad to see a letter that has been lying here some days for you: it is from your cousin, I believe."

CHAPTER V

Clerval then put the following letter into my hands.

"To V. Frankenstein.

"My dear Cousin,

"I cannot describe to you the uneasiness we have all felt concerning your health. We cannot help imagining that your friend Clerval conceals the extent of your disorder: for it is now several months since we have seen your hand-writing; and all this time you have been obliged to dictate your letters to Henry. Surely, Victor, you must have been exceedingly ill; and this makes us all very wretched, as much so nearly as after the death of your dear mother. My uncle was almost persuaded that you were indeed dangerously ill, and could hardly be restrained from undertaking a journey to Ingolstadt. Clerval always writes that you are getting better; I eagerly hope that you will confirm this intelligence soon in your own hand-writing; for indeed, indeed, Victor, we are all very miserable on this account. Relieve us from this fear, and we shall be the happiest creatures in the world. Your father's health is now so vigorous, that he appears ten years younger since last winter. Ernest also is so much improved, that you would hardly know him: he is now nearly sixteen, and has lost that sickly appearance which he had some years ago; he is grown quite robust and active.

"My uncle and I conversed a long time last night about what profession Ernest should follow. His constant illness when young has deprived him of the habits of application; and now that he enjoys good health, he is continually in the open air, climbing the hills, or rowing on the lake. I therefore proposed that he should be a farmer; which you know, Cousin, is a favourite scheme of mine. A farmer's is a very healthy happy life; and the least hurtful, or rather the most beneficial profession of any. My uncle had an idea of his being educated as an advocate, that through his interest he might become a judge. But, besides that he is not at all fitted for such an occupation, it is certainly more creditable to cultivate the earth for the sustenance of man, than to be the confidant, and sometimes the accomplice, of his vices; which is the profession of a lawyer. I said, that the employments of a prosperous farmer, if they were not a more honourable, they were at least a happier species of occupation than that of a judge, whose misfortune it was always to meddle with the dark side of human nature. My uncle smiled, and said, that I ought to be an advocate myself, which put an end to the conversation on that subject.

"And now I must tell you a little story that will please, and perhaps amuse you. Do you not remember Justine Moritz? Probably you do not; I will relate her history, therefore, in a few words. Madame Moritz, her mother, was a widow with four children, of whom Justine was the third. This girl had always been the favourite of her father; but, through a strange perversity, her mother could not endure her, and, after the death of M. Moritz, treated her very ill. My aunt observed this; and, when Justine was twelve years of age, prevailed on her mother to allow her to live at her house. The republican institutions of our country have produced simpler and happier manners than those which prevail in the great monarchies that surround it. Hence there is less distinction between the several classes of its inhabitants; and the lower orders being neither so poor nor so despised, their manners are more refined and moral. A servant in Geneva does not mean the same thing as a servant in France and England. Justine, thus received in our family, learned the duties of a servant; a condition which, in our fortunate country, does not include the idea of ignorance, and a sacrifice of the dignity of a human being.

"After what I have said, I dare say you well remember the heroine of my little tale: for Justine was a great favourite of your's; and I recollect you once remarked, that if you were in an ill humour, one glance from Justine could dissipate it, for the same reason that Ariosto gives concerning the beauty of Angelica—she looked so frank-hearted and happy.[15] My aunt conceived a great attachment for her, by which she was induced to give her an education superior to that which she had at first intended. This benefit was fully repaid; Justine was the most grateful little creature in the world: I do not mean that she made any professions, I never heard

15. The heroine of *Orlando Furioso* (1532) by Ludovico Ariosto (1474–1533).

one pass her lips; but you could see by her eyes that she almost adored her protectress. Although her disposition was gay, and in many respects inconsiderate, yet she paid the greatest attention to every gesture of my aunt. She thought her the model of all excellence, and endeavoured to imitate her phraseology and manners, so that even now she often reminds me of her.

"When my dearest aunt died, every one was too much occupied in their own grief to notice poor Justine, who had attended her during her illness with the most anxious affection. Poor Justine was very ill; but other trials were reserved for her.

"One by one, her brothers and sister died; and her mother, with the exception of her neglected daughter, was left childless. The conscience of the woman was troubled; she began to think that the deaths of her favourites was a judgment from heaven to chastise her partiality. She was a Roman Catholic; and I believe her confessor confirmed the idea which she had conceived. Accordingly, a few months after your departure for Ingolstadt, Justine was called home by her repentant mother. Poor girl! she wept when she quitted our house: she was much altered since the death of my aunt; grief had given softness and a winning mildness to her manners, which had before been remarkable for vivacity. Nor was her residence at her mother's house of a nature to restore her gaiety. The poor woman was very vacillating in her repentance. She sometimes begged Justine to forgive her unkindness, but much oftener accused her of having caused the deaths of her brothers and sister. Perpetual fretting at length threw Madame Moritz into a decline, which at first increased her irritability, but she is now at peace for ever. She died on the first approach of cold weather, at the beginning of this last winter. Justine has returned to us; and I assure you I love her tenderly. She is very clever and gentle, and extremely pretty; as I mentioned before, her mien and her expressions continually remind me of my dear aunt.

"I must say also a few words to you, my dear cousin, of little darling William. I wish you could see him; he is very tall of his age, with sweet laughing blue eyes, dark eye-lashes, and curling hair. When he smiles, two little dimples appear on each cheek, which are rosy with health. He has already had one or two little *wives*, but Louisa Biron is his favourite, a pretty little girl of five years of age.

"Now, dear Victor, I dare say you wish to be indulged in a little gossip concerning the good people of Geneva. The pretty Miss Mansfield has already received the congratulatory visits on her approaching marriage with a young Englishman, John Melbourne, Esq. Her ugly sister, Manon, married M. Duvillard, the rich banker, last autumn. Your favourite schoolfellow, Louis Manoir, has suffered several misfortunes since the departure of Clerval from Geneva. But he has already recovered his spirits, and is reported to be on the point of marrying a very lively pretty Frenchwoman, Madame Tavernier. She is a widow, and much older than Manoir; but she is very much admired, and a favourite with every body.

"I have written myself into good spirits, dear cousin; yet I cannot conclude without again anxiously inquiring concerning your health. Dear Victor, if you are not very ill, write yourself, and make your father and all of us happy; or——I cannot bear to think of the other side of the question; my tears already flow. Adieu, my dearest cousin.

"Elizabeth Lavenza.
"Geneva, March 18th, 17—."

"Dear, dear Elizabeth!" I exclaimed when I had read her letter, "I will write instantly, and relieve them from the anxiety they must feel." I wrote, and this exertion greatly fatigued me; but my convalescence had commenced, and proceeded regularly. In another fortnight I was able to leave my chamber.

One of my first duties on my recovery was to introduce Clerval to the several professors of the university. In doing this, I underwent a kind of rough usage, ill befitting the wounds that my mind had sustained. Ever since the fatal night, the end of my labours, and the beginning of my misfortunes, I had conceived a violent antipathy even to the name of natural philosophy. When I was otherwise quite restored to health, the sight of a chemical instrument would renew all the agony of my nervous symptoms. Henry saw this, and had removed all my apparatus from my view. He had also changed my apartment; for he perceived that I had acquired a dislike for the room which had previously been my laboratory. But these cares of Clerval were made of no avail when I visited the professors. M. Waldman inflicted torture when he praised, with kindness and warmth, the astonishing progress I had made in the sciences. He soon perceived that I disliked the subject; but, not guessing the real cause, he attributed my feelings to modesty, and changed the subject from my improvement to the science itself, with a desire, as I evidently saw, of drawing me out. What could I do? He meant to please, and he tormented me. I felt as if he had placed carefully, one by one, in my view those instruments which were to be afterwards used in putting me to a slow and cruel death. I writhed under his words, yet dared not exhibit the pain I felt. Clerval, whose eyes and feelings were always quick in discerning the sensations of others, declined the subject, alleging, in excuse, his total ignorance; and the conversation took a more general turn. I thanked my friend from my heart, but I did not speak. I saw plainly that he was surprised, but he never attempted to draw my secret from me; and although I loved him with a mixture of affection and reverence that knew no bounds, yet I could never persuade myself to confide to him that event which was so often present to my recollection, but which I feared the detail to another would only impress more deeply.

M. Krempe was not equally docile; and in my condition at that time, of almost insupportable sensitiveness, his harsh blunt encomiums gave me even more pain than the benevolent approbation of M. Waldman. "D—n the fellow!" cried he; "why, M. Clerval, I assure you he has outstript us all. Aye, stare if you please; but it is nevertheless true. A youngster who, but a few years ago, believed Cornelius Agrippa as firmly as the gospel, has now set himself at the head of the university; and if he is not soon pulled down, we shall all be out of countenance.—Aye, aye," continued he, observing my face expressive of suffering, "M. Frankenstein is modest; an excellent quality in a young man. Young men should be diffident of themselves, you know, M. Clerval; I was myself when young: but that wears out in a very short time."

M. Krempe had now commenced an eulogy on himself, which happily turned the conversation from a subject that was so annoying to me.

Clerval was no natural philosopher. His imagination was too vivid for the minutiæ of science. Languages were his principal study; and he sought, by acquiring their elements, to open a field for self-instruction on his return to Geneva. Persian, Arabic, and Hebrew, gained his attention, after he had made himself perfectly master of Greek and Latin. For my own part, idleness had ever been irksome to me; and now that I wished to fly from reflection, and hated my former studies, I felt great relief in being the fellow-pupil with my friend, and found not only instruction but consolation in the works of the orientalists. Their melancholy is soothing, and their joy elevating to a degree I never experienced in study-ing the authors of any other country. When you read their writings, life appears to consist in a warm sun and garden of roses,—in the smiles and frowns of a fair enemy, and the fire that consumes your own heart. How different from the manly and heroical poetry of Greece and Rome.

Summer passed away in these occupations, and my return to Geneva was fixed for the latter end of autumn; but being delayed by several accidents, winter and snow arrived, the roads were deemed impassable, and my journey was retarded until the ensuing spring. I felt this delay very bitterly; for I longed to see my native town, and my beloved friends. My return had only been delayed so long from an unwillingness to leave Clerval in a strange place, before he had become acquainted with any of its inhabitants. The winter, however, was spent cheerfully; and although the spring was uncommonly late, when it came, its beauty compensated for its dilatoriness.

The month of May had already commenced, and I expected the letter daily which was to fix the date of my departure, when Henry proposed a pedestrian tour in the environs of Ingolstadt that I might bid a personal farewell to the country I had so long inhabited. I acceded with pleasure to this proposition: I was fond of exercise, and Clerval had always been my favourite companion in the rambles of this nature that I had taken among the scenes of my native country.

We passed a fortnight in these perambulations; my health and spirits had long been restored, and they gained additional strength from the salubrious air I breathed, the natural incidents of our progress, and the conversation of my friend. Study had before secluded me from the intercourse of my fellow-creatures, and rendered me unsocial; but Clerval called forth the better feelings of my heart; he again taught me to love the aspect of nature, and the cheerful faces of children. Excellent friend! how sincerely did you love me, and endeavour to elevate my mind, until it was on a level with your own. A selfish pursuit had cramped and narrowed me, until your gentleness and affection warmed and opened my senses; I became the same happy creature who, a few years ago, loving and beloved by all, had no sorrow or care. When happy, inanimate nature had the power of bestowing on me the most delightful sensations. A serene sky and verdant fields filled me with ecstacy. The present season was indeed divine; the flowers of spring bloomed in the hedges, while those of summer were already in bud: I was undisturbed by thoughts which during the preceding year had pressed upon me, notwithstanding my endeavours to throw them off, with an invincible burden.

Henry rejoiced in my gaiety, and sincerely sympathized in my feelings: he exerted himself to amuse me, while he expressed the sensations that filled his soul. The resources of his mind on this occasion were truly astonishing: his conversation was full of imagination; and very often, in imitation of the Persian and Arabic writers, he invented tales of wonderful fancy and passion. At other times he repeated my favourite poems, or drew me out into arguments, which he supported with great ingenuity.

We returned to our college on a Sunday afternoon: the peasants were dancing, and every one we met appeared gay and happy. My own spirits were high, and I bounded along with feelings of unbridled joy and hilarity.

CHAPTER VI

On my return, I found the following letter from my father:—

"To V. Frankenstein.

"My dear Victor,

"You have probably waited impatiently for a letter to fix the date of your return to us; and I was at first tempted to write only a few lines, merely mentioning the day on which I should expect you. But that would be a cruel kindness, and I dare not do it. What would be your surprise, my son, when you expected a happy and gay welcome, to behold, on the contrary, tears and wretchedness? And how, Victor, can I relate our misfortune? Absence cannot have rendered you callous to our joys and griefs; and how shall I inflict pain on an absent child? I wish to prepare you for the woeful news, but I know it is impossible; even now your eye skims over the page, to seek the words which are to convey to you the horrible tidings.

"William is dead!—that sweet child, whose smiles delighted and warmed my heart, who was so gentle, yet so gay! Victor, he is murdered!

"I will not attempt to console you; but will simply relate the circumstances of the transaction.

"Last Thursday (May 7th) I, my niece, and your two brothers, went to walk in Plainpalais. The evening was warm and serene, and we prolonged our walk farther than usual. It was already dusk before we thought of returning; and then we discovered that William and Ernest, who had gone on before, were not to be found. We accordingly rested on a seat until they should return. Presently Ernest came, and inquired if we had seen his brother: he said, that they had been playing together, that William had run away to hide himself, and that he vainly sought for him, and afterwards waited for him a long time, but that he did not return.

"This account rather alarmed us, and we continued to search for him until night fell, when Elizabeth conjectured that he might have returned to the house. He was not there. We returned again, with torches; for I could not rest, when I thought that my sweet boy had lost himself, and was exposed to all the damps and dews of night: Elizabeth also suffered extreme anguish. About five in the morning I discovered my lovely boy, whom the night before I had seen blooming and active in health, stretched on the grass livid and motionless: the print of the murderer's finger was on his neck.

"He was conveyed home, and the anguish that was visible in my countenance betrayed the secret to Elizabeth. She was very earnest to see the corpse. At first I attempted to prevent her; but she persisted, and entering the room where it lay, hastily examined the neck of the victim, and clasping her hands exclaimed, 'O God! I have murdered my darling infant!'

"She fainted, and was restored with extreme difficulty. When she again lived, it was only to weep and sigh. She told me, that that same evening William had teazed her to let him wear a very valuable miniature that she possessed of your mother. This picture is gone, and was doubtless the temptation which urged the murderer to the deed. We have no trace of him at present, although our exertions to discover him are unremitted; but they will not restore my beloved William.

"Come, dearest Victor; you alone can console Elizabeth. She weeps continually, and accuses herself unjustly as the cause of his death; her words pierce my heart. We are all unhappy; but will not that be an additional motive for you, my son, to return and be our comforter? Your dear mother! Alas, Victor! I now say, Thank God she did not live to witness the cruel, miserable death of her youngest darling!

"Come, Victor; not brooding thoughts of vengeance against the assassin, but with feelings of peace and gentleness, that will heal, instead of festering the wounds of our minds. Enter the house of mourning, my friend, but with kindness and affection for those who love you, and not with hatred for your enemies.

"Your affectionate and afflicted father,

Alphonse Frankenstein.

"Geneva, May 12th, 17—."

Clerval, who had watched my countenance as I read this letter, was surprised to observe the despair that succeeded to the joy I at first expressed on receiving news from my friends. I threw the letter on the table, and covered my face with my hands.

"My dear Frankenstein," exclaimed Henry, when he perceived me weep with bitterness, "are you always to be unhappy? My dear friend, what has happened?"

I motioned to him to take up the letter, while I walked up and down the room in the extremest agitation. Tears also gushed from the eyes of Clerval, as he read the account of my misfortune.

"I can offer you no consolation, my friend," said he; "your disaster is irreparable. What do you intend to do."

"To go instantly to Geneva: come with me, Henry, to order the horses."

During our walk, Clerval endeavoured to raise my spirits. He did not do this by common topics of consolation, but by exhibiting the truest sympathy. "Poor William!" said he, "that dear child; he now sleeps with his angel mother. His friends mourn and weep, but he is at rest: he does not now feel the murderer's grasp; a sod covers his gentle form, and he knows no pain. He can no longer be a fit subject for pity; the survivors are the greatest sufferers, and for them time is the only consolation. Those maxims of the Stoics, that death was no evil, and that the mind of man ought to be superior to despair on the eternal absence of a beloved object, ought not to be urged. Even Cato wept over the dead body of his brother."

Clerval spoke thus as we hurried through the streets; the words impressed themselves on my mind, and I remembered them afterwards in solitude. But now, as soon as the horses arrived, I hurried into a cabriole,[16] and bade farewell to my friend.

My journey was very melancholy. At first I wished to hurry on, for I longed to console and sympathize with my loved and sorrowing friends; but when I drew near my native town, I slackened my progress. I could hardly sustain the multitude of feelings that crowded into my mind. I passed through scenes familiar to my youth, but which I had not seen for nearly six years. How altered every thing might be during that time? One sudden and desolating change had taken place; but a thousand little circumstances might have by degrees worked other alterations which, although they were done more tranquilly, might not be the less decisive. Fear overcame me; I dared not advance, dreading a thousand nameless evils that made me tremble, although I was unable to define them.

I remained two days at Lausanne, in this painful state of mind. I contemplated the lake: the waters were placid; all around was calm, and the snowy mountains, "the palaces of nature,"[17] were not changed. By degrees the calm and heavenly scene restored me, and I continued my journey towards Geneva.

The road ran by the side of the lake, which became narrower as I approached my native town. I discovered more distinctly the black sides of Jura, and the bright summit of Mont Blanc; I wept like a child: "Dear mountains! my own beautiful lake! how do you welcome your wanderer? Your summits are clear; the sky and lake are blue and placid. Is this to prognosticate peace, or to mock at my unhappiness?"

I fear, my friend, that I shall render myself tedious by dwelling on these preliminary circumstances; but they were days of comparative happiness, and I think of them with pleasure. My country, my beloved country! who but a native can tell the delight I took in again beholding thy streams, thy mountains, and, more than all, thy lovely lake.

Yet, as I drew nearer home, grief and fear again overcame me. Night also closed around; and when I could hardly see the dark mountains, I felt still more gloomily. The picture appeared a vast and dim scene of

16. Variant spelling of "cabriolet," a two-wheeled chaise drawn by one horse.
17. Lord Byron (1788–1824), *Childe Harold's Pilgrimage*, Canto III (1816), stanza 62.

evil, and I foresaw obscurely that I was destined to become the most wretched of human beings. Alas! I prophesied truly, and failed only in one single circumstance, that in all the misery I imagined and dreaded, I did not conceive the hundredth part of the anguish I was destined to endure.

It was completely dark when I arrived in the environs of Geneva; the gates of the town were already shut; and I was obliged to pass the night at Secheron, a village half a league to the east of the city. The sky was serene; and, as I was unable to rest, I resolved to visit the spot where my poor William had been murdered. As I could not pass through the town, I was obliged to cross the lake in a boat to arrive at Plainpalais. During this short voyage I saw the lightnings playing on the summit of Mont Blanc in the most beautiful figures. The storm appeared to approach rapidly; and, on landing, I ascended a low hill, that I might observe its progress. It advanced; the heavens were clouded, and I soon felt the rain coming slowly in large drops, but its violence quickly increased.

I quitted my seat, and walked on, although the darkness and storm increased every minute, and the thunder burst with a terrific crash over my head. It was echoed from Salêve, the Juras, and the Alps of Savoy; vivid flashes of lightning dazzled my eyes, illuminating the lake, making it appear like a vast sheet of fire; then for an instant every thing seemed of a pitchy darkness, until the eye recovered itself from the preceding flash. The storm, as is often the case in Switzerland, appeared at once in various parts of the heavens. The most violent storm hung exactly north of the town, over that part of the lake which lies between the promontory of Belrive and the village of Copêt. Another storm enlightened Jura with faint flashes; and another darkened and sometimes disclosed the Môle, a peaked mountain to the east of the lake.

While I watched the storm, so beautiful yet terrific, I wandered on with a hasty step. This noble war in the sky elevated my spirits; I clasped my hands, and exclaimed aloud, "William, dear angel! this is thy funeral, this thy dirge!" As I said these words, I perceived in the gloom a figure which stole from behind a clump of trees near me; I stood fixed, gazing intently: I could not be mistaken. A flash of lightning illuminated the object, and discovered its shape plainly to me; its gigantic stature, and the deformity of its aspect, more hideous than belongs to humanity, instantly informed me that it was the wretch, the filthy dæmon to whom I had given life. What did he there? Could he be (I shuddered at the conception) the murderer of my brother? No sooner did that idea cross my imagination, than I became convinced of its truth; my teeth chattered, and I was forced to lean against a tree for support. The figure passed me quickly, and I lost it in the gloom. Nothing in human shape could have destroyed that fair child. *He* was the murderer! I could not doubt it. The mere presence of the idea was an irresistible proof of the fact. I thought of pursuing the devil; but it would have been in vain, for another flash discovered him to me hanging among the rocks of the nearly perpendicular ascent of Mont Salêve, a hill that bounds Plainpalais on the south. He soon reached the summit, and disappeared.

I remained motionless. The thunder ceased; but the rain still continued, and the scene was enveloped in an impenetrable darkness. I revolved in my mind the events which I had until now sought to forget: the whole train of my progress towards the creation; the appearance of the work of my own hands alive at my bed side; its departure. Two years had now nearly elapsed since the night on which he first received life; and was this his first crime? Alas! I had turned loose into the world a depraved wretch, whose delight was in carnage and misery; had he not murdered my brother?

No one can conceive the anguish I suffered during the remainder of the night, which I spent, cold and wet, in the open air. But I did not feel the inconvenience of the weather; my imagination was busy in scenes of evil and despair. I considered the being whom I had cast among mankind, and endowed with the will and power to effect purposes of horror, such as the deed which he had now done, nearly in the light of my own vampire, my own spirit let loose from the grave, and forced to destroy all that was dear to me.

Day dawned; and I directed my steps toward the town. The gates were open; and I hastened to my father's house. My first thought was to discover what I knew of the murderer, and cause instant pursuit to be made. But I paused when I reflected on the story that I had to tell. A being whom I myself had formed, and endued with life, had met me at midnight among the precipices of an inaccessible mountain. I remembered also the nervous fever with which I had been seized just at the time that I dated my creation, and which would give an air of delirium to a tale otherwise so utterly improbable. I well knew that if any other had communicated such a relation to me, I should have looked upon it as the ravings of insanity. Besides, the strange nature of the animal would elude all pursuit, even if I were so far credited as to persuade my relatives to commence it. Besides, of what use would be pursuit? Who could arrest a creature capable of scaling the overhanging sides of Mont Salêve? These reflections determined me, and I resolved to remain silent.

It was about five in the morning when I entered my father's house. I told the servants not to disturb the family, and went into the library to attend their usual hour of rising.

Six years had elapsed, passed as a dream but for one indelible trace, and I stood in the same place where I had last embraced my father before my departure for Ingolstadt. Beloved and respectable parent! He still remained to me. I gazed on the picture of my mother, which stood over the mantlepiece. It was an historical subject, painted at my father's desire, and represented Caroline Beaufort in an agony of despair, kneeling by the coffin of her dead father. Her garb was rustic, and her cheek pale; but there was an air of dignity and beauty, that hardly permitted the sentiment of pity. Below this picture was a miniature of William; and my tears flowed when I looked upon it. While I was thus engaged, Ernest entered: he had heard me arrive, and hastened to welcome me. He expressed a sorrowful delight to see me: "Welcome, my dearest Victor," said he. "Ah! I wish you had come three months ago, and then you would have found us all joyous and delighted. But we are now unhappy; and, I am afraid, tears instead of smiles will be your welcome. Our father looks so sorrowful: this dreadful event seems to have revived in his mind his grief on the death of Mamma. Poor Elizabeth also is quite inconsolable." Ernest began to weep as he said these words.

"Do not," said I, "welcome me thus; try to be more calm, that I may not be absolutely miserable the moment I enter my father's house after so long an absence. But, tell me, how does my father support his misfortunes? and how is my poor Elizabeth?"

"She indeed requires consolation; she accused herself of having caused the death of my brother, and that made her very wretched. But since the murderer has been discovered——"

"The murderer discovered! Good God! how can that be? who could attempt to pursue him? It is impossible; one might as well try to overtake the winds, or confine a mountain-stream with a straw."

"I do not know what you mean; but we were all very unhappy when she was discovered. No one would believe it at first; and even now Elizabeth will not be convinced; notwithstanding all the evidence. Indeed, who would credit that Justine Moritz, who was so amiable, and fond of all the family, could all at once become so extremely wicked?"

"Justine Moritz! Poor, poor girl, is she the accused? But it is wrongfully; every one knows that; no one believes it, surely, Ernest?"

"No one did at first; but several circumstances came out, that have almost forced conviction upon us: and her own behaviour has been so confused, as to add to the evidence of facts a weight that, I fear, leaves no hope for doubt. But she will be tried to-day, and you will then hear all."

He related that, the morning on which the murder of poor William had been discovered, Justine had been taken ill, and confined to her bed; and, after several days, one of the servants, happening to examine the apparel she had worn on the night of the murder, had discovered in her pocket the picture of my mother, which had been judged to be the temptation of the murderer. The servant instantly shewed it to one of the others, who, without saying a word to any of the family, went to a magistrate; and, upon their deposition, Justine was apprehended. On being charged with the fact, the poor girl confirmed the suspicion in a great measure by her extreme confusion of manner.

This was a strange tale, but it did not shake my faith; and I replied earnestly, "You are all mistaken; I know the murderer. Justine, poor, good Justine, is innocent."

At that instant my father entered. I saw unhappiness deeply impressed on his countenance, but he endeavoured to welcome me cheerfully; and, after we had exchanged our mournful greeting, would have introduced some other topic than that of our disaster, had not Ernest exclaimed, "Good God, Papa! Victor says that he knows who was the murderer of poor William."

"We do also, unfortunately," replied my father; "for indeed I had rather have been for ever ignorant than have discovered so much depravity and ingratitude in one I valued so highly."

"My dear father, you are mistaken; Justine is innocent."

"If she is, God forbid that she should suffer as guilty. She is to be tried to-day, and I hope, I sincerely hope, that she will be acquitted."

This speech calmed me. I was firmly convinced in my own mind that Justine, and indeed every human being, was guiltless of this murder. I had no fear, therefore, that any circumstantial evidence could be brought forward strong enough to convict her; and, in this assurance, I calmed myself, expecting the trial with eagerness, but without prognosticating an evil result.

We were soon joined by Elizabeth. Time had made great alterations in her form since I had last beheld her. Six years before she had been a pretty, good-humoured girl, whom every one loved and caressed. She was now a woman in stature and expression of countenance, which was uncommonly lovely. An open and capacious forehead gave indications of a good understanding, joined to great frankness of disposition. Her eyes were hazel, and expressive of mildness, now through recent affliction allied to sadness. Her hair was of a rich dark auburn, her complexion fair, and her figure slight and graceful. She welcomed me with the greatest affection. "Your arrival, my dear cousin," said she, "fills me with hope. You perhaps will find some means to justify my poor guiltless Justine. Alas! who is safe, if she be convicted of crime? I rely on her innocence as certainly as I do upon my own. Our misfortune is doubly hard to us; we have not only lost that lovely darling boy, but this poor girl, whom

I sincerely love, is to be torn away by even a worse fate. If she is condemned, I never shall know joy more. But she will not, I am sure she will not; and then I shall be happy again, even after the sad death of my little William."

"She is innocent, my Elizabeth," said I, "and that shall be proved; fear nothing, but let your spirits be cheered by the assurance of her acquittal."

"How kind you are! every one else believes in her guilt, and that made me wretched; for I knew that it was impossible: and to see every one else prejudiced in so deadly a manner, rendered me hopeless and despairing." She wept.

"Sweet niece," said my father, "dry your tears. If she is, as you believe, innocent, rely on the justice of our judges, and the activity with which I shall prevent the slightest shadow of partiality."

CHAPTER VII

We passed a few sad hours, until eleven o'clock, when the trial was to commence. My father and the rest of the family being obliged to attend as witnesses, I accompanied them to the court. During the whole of this wretched mockery of justice, I suffered living torture. It was to be decided, whether the result of my curiosity and lawless devices would cause the death of two of my fellow-beings: one a smiling babe, full of innocence and joy; the other far more dreadfully murdered, with every aggravation of infamy that could make the murder memorable in horror. Justine also was a girl of merit, and possessed qualities which promised to render her life happy: now all was to be obliterated in an ignominious grave; and I the cause! A thousand times rather would I have confessed myself guilty of the crime ascribed to Justine; but I was absent when it was committed, and such a declaration would have been considered as the ravings of a madman, and would not have exculpated her who suffered through me.

The appearance of Justine was calm. She was dressed in mourning; and her countenance, always engaging, was rendered, by the solemnity of her feelings, exquisitely beautiful. Yet she appeared confident in innocence, and did not tremble, although gazed on and execrated by thousands; for all the kindness which her beauty might otherwise have excited, was obliterated in the minds of the spectators by the imagination of the enormity she was supposed to have committed. She was tranquil, yet her tranquillity was evidently constrained; and as her confusion had before been adduced as a proof of her guilt, she worked up her mind to an appearance of courage. When she entered the court, she threw her eyes round it, and quickly discovered where we were seated. A tear seemed to dim her eye when she saw us; but she quickly recovered herself, and a look of sorrowful affection seemed to attest her utter guiltlessness.

The trial began; and after the advocate against her had stated the charge, several witnesses were called. Several strange facts combined against her, which might have staggered any one who had not such proof of her innocence as I had. She had been out the whole of the night on which the murder had been committed, and towards morning had been perceived by a market-woman not far from the spot where the body of the murdered child had been afterwards found. The woman asked her what she did there; but she looked very strangely, and only returned a confused and unintelligible answer. She returned to the house about eight o'clock; and when one inquired where she had passed the night, she replied, that she had been looking for the child, and demanded earnestly, if any thing had been heard concerning him. When shewn the body, she fell into violent hysterics, and kept her bed for several days. The picture was then produced, which the servant had found in her pocket; and when Elizabeth, in a faltering voice, proved that it was the same which, an hour before the child had been missed, she had placed round his neck, a murmur of horror and indignation filled the court.

Justine was called on for her defence. As the trial had proceeded, her countenance had altered. Surprise, horror, and misery, were strongly expressed. Sometimes she struggled with her tears; but when she was desired to plead, she collected her powers, and spoke in an audible although variable voice:—

"God knows," she said, "how entirely I am innocent. But I do not pretend that my protestations should acquit me: I rest my innocence on a plain and simple explanation of the facts which have been adduced against me; and I hope the character I have always borne will incline my judges to a favourable interpretation, where any circumstance appears doubtful or suspicious."

She then related that, by the permission of Elizabeth, she had passed the evening of the night on which the murder had been committed, at the house of an aunt at Chêne, a village situated at about a league from Geneva. On her return, at about nine o'clock, she met a man, who asked her if she had seen any thing of the child who was lost. She was alarmed by this account, and passed several hours in looking for him, when the gates of Geneva were shut, and she was forced to remain several hours of the night in a barn belonging to a cottage, being unwilling to call up the inhabitants, to whom she was well known. Unable to rest or sleep, she quitted her asylum early, that she might again endeavour to find my brother. If she had gone near the spot where his body lay, it was without her knowledge. That she had been bewildered when questioned by the market-woman, was not surprising, since she had passed a sleepless night, and the fate of poor William was yet uncertain. Concerning the picture she could give no account.

"I know," continued the unhappy victim, "how heavily and fatally this one circumstance weighs against me, but I have no power of explaining it; and when I have expressed my utter ignorance, I am only left to conjecture concerning the probabilities by which it might have been placed in my pocket. But here also I am checked. I believe that I have no enemy on earth, and none surely would have been so wicked as to destroy me wantonly. Did the murderer place it there? I know of no opportunity afforded him for so doing; or if I had, why should he have stolen the jewel, to part with it again so soon?

"I commit my cause to the justice of my judges, yet I see no room for hope. I beg permission to have a few witnesses examined concerning my character; and if their testimony shall not overweigh my supposed guilt, I must be condemned, although I would pledge my salvation on my innocence."

Several witnesses were called, who had known her for many years, and they spoke well of her; but fear, and hatred of the crime of which they supposed her guilty, rendered them timorous, and unwilling to come forward. Elizabeth saw even this last resource, her excellent dispositions and irreproachable conduct, about to fail the accused, when, although violently agitated, she desired permission to address the court.

"I am," said she, "the cousin of the unhappy child who was murdered, or rather his sister, for I was educated by and have lived with his parents ever since and even long before his birth. It may therefore be judged indecent in me to come forward on this occasion; but when I see a fellow-creature about to perish through the cowardice of her pretended friends, I wish to be allowed to speak, that I may say what I know of her character. I am well acquainted with the accused. I have lived in the same house with her, at one time for five, and at another for nearly two years. During all that period she appeared to me the most amiable and benevolent of human creatures. She nursed Madame Frankenstein, my aunt, in her last illness with the greatest affection and care; and afterwards attended her own mother during a tedious illness, in a manner that excited the admiration of all who knew her. After which she again lived in my uncle's house, where she was beloved by all the family. She was warmly attached to the child who is now dead, and acted towards him like a most affectionate mother. For my own part, I do not hesitate to say, that, notwithstanding all the evidence produced against her, I believe and rely on her perfect innocence. She had no temptation for such an action: as to the bauble on which the chief proof rests, if she had earnestly desired it, I should have willingly given it to her; so much do I esteem and value her."

Excellent Elizabeth! A murmur of approbation was heard; but it was excited by her generous interference, and not in favour of poor Justine, on whom the public indignation was turned with renewed violence, charging her with the blackest ingratitude. She herself wept as Elizabeth spoke, but she did not answer. My own agitation and anguish was extreme during the whole trial. I believed in her innocence; I knew it. Could the dæmon, who had (I did not for a minute doubt) murdered my brother, also in his hellish sport have betrayed the innocent to death and ignominy. I could not sustain the horror of my situation; and when I perceived that the popular voice, and the countenances of the judges, had already condemned my unhappy victim, I rushed out of the court in agony. The tortures of the accused did not equal mine; she was sustained by innocence, but the fangs of remorse tore my bosom, and would not forego their hold.

I passed a night of unmingled wretchedness. In the morning I went to the court; my lips and throat were parched. I dared not ask the fatal question; but I was known, and the officer guessed the cause of my visit. The ballots had been thrown; they were all black, and Justine was condemned.

I cannot pretend to describe what I then felt. I had before experienced sensations of horror; and I have endeavoured to bestow upon them adequate expressions, but words cannot convey an idea of the heart-sickening despair that I then endured. The person to whom I addressed myself added, that Justine had already confessed her guilt. "That evidence," he observed, "was hardly required in so glaring a case, but I am glad of it; and, indeed, none of our judges like to condemn a criminal upon circumstantial evidence, be it ever so decisive."

When I returned home, Elizabeth eagerly demanded the result.

"My cousin," replied I, "it is decided as you may have expected; all judges had rather that ten innocent should suffer, than that one guilty should escape. But she has confessed."

This was a dire blow to poor Elizabeth, who had relied with firmness upon Justine's innocence. "Alas!" said she, "how shall I ever again believe in human benevolence? Justine, whom I loved and esteemed as my sister, how could she put on those smiles of innocence only to betray; her mild eyes seemed incapable of any severity or ill-humour, and yet she has committed a murder."

Soon after we heard that the poor victim had expressed a wish to see my cousin. My father wished her not to go; but said, that he left it to her own judgment and feelings to decide. "Yes," said Elizabeth, "I will go, although she is guilty; and you, Victor, shall accompany me: I cannot go alone." The idea of this visit was torture to me, yet I could not refuse.

We entered the gloomy prison-chamber, and beheld Justine sitting on some straw at the further end; her hands were manacled, and her head rested on her knees. She rose on seeing us enter; and when we were left alone with her, she threw herself at the feet of Elizabeth, weeping bitterly. My cousin wept also.

"Oh, Justine!" said she, "why did you rob me of my last consolation. I relied on your innocence; and although I was then very wretched, I was not so miserable as I am now."

"And do you also believe that I am so very, very wicked? Do you also join with my enemies to crush me?" Her voice was suffocated with sobs.

"Rise, my poor girl," said Elizabeth, "why do you kneel, if you are innocent? I am not one of your enemies; I believed you guiltless, notwithstanding every evidence, until I heard that you had yourself declared your guilt. That report, you say, is false; and be assured, dear Justine, that nothing can shake my confidence in you for a moment, but your own confession."

"I did confess; but I confessed a lie. I confessed, that I might obtain absolution; but now that falsehood lies heavier at my heart than all my other sins. The God of heaven forgive me! Ever since I was condemned, my confessor has besieged me; he threatened and menaced, until I almost began to think that I was the monster that he said I was. He threatened excommunication and hell fire in my last moments, if I continued obdurate. Dear lady, I had none to support me; all looked on me as a wretch doomed to ignominy and perdition. What could I do? In an evil hour I subscribed to a lie; and now only am I truly miserable."

She paused, weeping, and then continued—"I thought with horror, my sweet lady, that you should believe your Justine, whom your blessed aunt had so highly honoured, and whom you loved, was a creature capable of a crime which none but the devil himself could have perpetrated. Dear William! dearest blessed child! I soon shall see you again in heaven, where we shall all be happy; and that consoles me, going as I am to suffer ignominy and death."

"Oh, Justine! forgive me for having for one moment distrusted you. Why did you confess? But do not mourn, my dear girl; I will every where proclaim your innocence, and force belief. Yet you must die; you, my playfellow, my companion, my more than sister. I never can survive so horrible a misfortune."

"Dear, sweet Elizabeth, do not weep. You ought to raise me with thoughts of a better life, and elevate me from the petty cares of this world of injustice and strife. Do not you, excellent friend, drive me to despair."

"I will try to comfort you; but this, I fear, is an evil too deep and poignant to admit of consolation, for there is no hope. Yet heaven bless thee, my dearest Justine, with resignation, and a confidence elevated beyond this world. Oh! how I hate its shews and mockeries! when one creature is murdered, another is immediately deprived of life in a slow torturing manner; then the executioners, their hands yet reeking with the blood of innocence, believe that they have done a great deed. They call this *retribution*. Hateful name! When that word is pronounced, I know greater and more horrid punishments are going to be inflicted than the gloomiest tyrant has ever invented to satiate his utmost revenge. Yet this is not consolation for you, my Justine, unless indeed that you may glory in escaping from so miserable a den. Alas! I would I were in peace with my aunt and my lovely William, escaped from a world which is hateful to me, and the visages of men which I abhor."

Justine smiled languidly. "This, dear lady, is despair, and not resignation. I must not learn the lesson that you would teach me. Talk of something else, something that will bring peace, and not increase of misery."

During this conversation I had retired to a corner of the prison-room, where I could conceal the horrid anguish that possessed me. Despair! Who dared talk of that? The poor victim, who on the morrow was to pass the dreary boundary between life and death, felt not as I did, such deep and bitter agony. I gnashed my teeth, and ground them together, uttering a groan that came from my inmost soul. Justine started. When she saw who it was, she approached me, and said, "Dear Sir, you are very kind to visit me; you, I hope, do not believe that I am guilty."

I could not answer. "No, Justine," said Elizabeth; "he is more convinced of your innocence than I was; for even when he heard that you had confessed, he did not credit it."

"I truly thank him. In these last moments I feel the sincerest gratitude towards those who think of me with kindness. How sweet is the affection of others to such a wretch as I am! It removes more than half my misfortune; and I feel as if I could die in peace, now that my innocence is acknowledged by you, dear lady, and your cousin."

Thus the poor sufferer tried to comfort others and herself. She indeed gained the resignation she desired. But I, the true murderer, felt the never-dying worm alive in my bosom, which allowed of no hope or consolation. Elizabeth also wept, and was unhappy; but her's also was the misery of innocence, which, like a cloud that passes over the fair moon, for a while hides, but cannot tarnish its brightness. Anguish and despair had penetrated into the core of my heart; I bore a hell within me, which nothing could extinguish. We staid several hours with Justine; and it was with great difficulty that Elizabeth could tear herself away. "I wish," cried she, "that I were to die with you; I cannot live in this world of misery."

Justine assumed an air of cheerfulness, while she with difficulty repressed her bitter tears. She embraced Elizabeth, and said, in a voice of half-suppressed emotion, "Farewell, sweet lady, dearest Elizabeth, my beloved and only friend; may heaven in its bounty bless and preserve you; may this be the last misfortune that you will ever suffer. Live, and be happy, and make others so."

As we returned, Elizabeth said, "You know not, my dear Victor, how much I am relieved, now that I trust in the innocence of this unfortunate girl. I never could again have known peace, if I had been deceived in my reliance on her. For the moment that I did believe her guilty, I felt an anguish that I could not have long sustained. Now my heart is lightened. The innocent suffers; but she whom I thought amiable and good has not betrayed the trust I reposed in her, and I am consoled.

Amiable cousin! such were your thoughts, mild and gentle as your own dear eyes and voice. But I—I was a wretch, and none ever conceived of the misery that I then endured.

END OF VOL. I.

Volume II

CHAPTER I

Nothing is more painful to the human mind, than, after the feelings have been worked up by a quick succession of events, the dead calmness of inaction and certainty which follows, and deprives the soul both of hope and fear. Justine died; she rested; and I was alive. The blood flowed freely in my veins, but a weight of despair and remorse pressed on my heart, which nothing could remove. Sleep fled from my eyes; I wandered like an evil spirit, for I had committed deeds of mischief beyond description horrible, and more, much more, (I persuaded myself) was yet behind. Yet my heart overflowed with kindness, and the love of virtue. I had begun life with benevolent intentions, and thirsted for the moment when I should put them in practice, and make myself useful to my fellow-beings. Now all was blasted: instead of that serenity of conscience, which allowed me to look back upon the past with self-satisfaction, and from thence to gather promise of new hopes, I was seized by remorse and the sense of guilt, which hurried me away to a hell of intense tortures, such as no language can describe.

This state of mind preyed upon my health, which had entirely recovered from the first shock it had sustained. I shunned the face of man; all sound of joy or complacency was torture to me; solitude was my only consolation—deep, dark, death-like solitude.

My father observed with pain the alteration perceptible in my disposition and habits, and endeavoured to reason with me on the folly of giving way to immoderate grief. "Do you think, Victor," said he, "that I do not suffer also? No one could love a child more than I loved your brother;" (tears came into his eyes as he spoke); "but is it not a duty to the survivors, that we should refrain from augmenting their unhappiness by an appearance of immoderate grief? It is also a duty owed to yourself; for excessive sorrow prevents improvement or enjoyment, or even the discharge of daily usefulness, without which no man is fit for society."

This advice, although good, was totally inapplicable to my case; I should have been the first to hide my grief, and console my friends, if remorse had not mingled its bitterness with my other sensations. Now I could only answer my father with a look of despair, and endeavour to hide myself from his view.

About this time we retired to our house at Belrive. This change was particularly agreeable to me. The shutting of the gates regularly at ten o'clock, and the impossibility of remaining on the lake after that hour, had rendered our residence within the walls of Geneva very irksome to me. I was now free. Often, after the rest of the family had retired for the night, I took the boat, and passed many hours upon the water. Sometimes, with my sails set, I was carried by the wind; and sometimes, after rowing into the middle of the lake, I left the boat to pursue its own course, and gave way to my own miserable reflections. I was often tempted, when all was at peace around me, and I the only unquiet thing that wandered restless in a scene so beautiful and heavenly, if I except some bat, or the frogs, whose harsh and interrupted croaking was heard only when I approached the shore—often, I say, I was tempted to plunge into the silent lake, that the waters might close over me and my calamities for ever. But I was restrained, when I thought of the heroic and suffering Elizabeth, whom I tenderly loved, and whose existence was bound up in mine. I thought also of my father, and surviving brother: should I by my base desertion leave them exposed and unprotected to the malice of the fiend whom I had let loose among them?

At these moments I wept bitterly, and wished that peace would revisit my mind only that I might afford them consolation and happiness. But that could not be. Remorse extinguished every hope. I had been the author of unalterable evils; and I lived in daily fear, lest the monster whom I had created should perpetrate some new wickedness. I had an obscure feeling that all was not over, and that he would still commit some signal crime, which by its enormity should almost efface the recollection of the past. There was always scope for fear, so long as any thing I loved remained behind. My abhorrence of this fiend cannot be conceived. When I thought of him, I gnashed my teeth, my eyes became inflamed, and I ardently wished to extinguish that life which I had so thoughtlessly bestowed. When I reflected on his crimes and malice, my hatred and revenge burst all bounds of moderation. I would have made a pilgrimage to the highest peak of the Andes, could I, when there, have precipitated him to their base. I wished to see him again, that I might wreak the utmost extent of anger on his head, and avenge the deaths of William and Justine.

Our house was the house of mourning. My father's health was deeply shaken by the horror of the recent events. Elizabeth was sad and desponding; she no longer took delight in her ordinary occupations; all pleasure seemed to her sacrilege towards the dead; eternal woe and tears she then thought was the just tribute she should pay to innocence so blasted and destroyed. She was no longer that happy creature, who in earlier youth wandered with me on the banks of the lake, and talked with ecstacy of our future prospects. She had become grave, and often conversed of the inconstancy of fortune, and the instability of human life.

"When I reflect, my dear cousin," said she, "on the miserable death of Justine Moritz, I no longer see the world and its works as they before appeared to me. Before, I looked upon the accounts of vice and injustice, that I read in books or heard from others, as tales of ancient days, or imaginary evils; at least they were remote, and more familiar to reason than to the imagination; but now misery has come home, and men appear to me as monsters thirsting for each other's blood. Yet I am certainly unjust. Every body believed that poor girl to be guilty; and if she could have committed the crime for which she suffered, assuredly she would have been the most depraved of human creatures. For the sake of a few jewels, to have murdered the son of her benefactor and friend, a child whom she had nursed from its birth, and appeared to love as if it had been her own! I could not consent to the death of any human being; but certainly I should have thought such a creature unfit to remain in the society of men. Yet she was innocent. I know, I feel she was innocent; you are of the same opinion, and that confirms me. Alas! Victor, when falsehood can look so like the truth, who can assure themselves of certain happiness? I feel as if I were walking on the edge of a precipice, towards which thousands are crowding, and endeavouring to plunge me into the abyss. William and Justine were assassinated, and the murderer escapes; he walks about the world free, and perhaps respected. But even if I were condemned to suffer on the scaffold for the same crimes, I would not change places with such a wretch."

I listened to this discourse with the extremest agony. I, not in deed, but in effect, was the true murderer. Elizabeth read my anguish in my countenance, and kindly taking my hand said, "My dearest cousin, you must calm yourself. These events have affected me, God knows how deeply; but I am not so wretched as you are. There is an expression of despair, and sometimes of revenge, in your countenance, that makes me tremble. Be calm, my dear Victor; I would sacrifice my life to your peace. We surely shall be happy: quiet in our native country, and not mingling in the world, what can disturb our tranquillity?"

She shed tears as she said this, distrusting the very solace that she gave;

but at the same time she smiled, that she might chase away the fiend that lurked in my heart. My father, who saw in the unhappiness that was painted in my face only an exaggeration of that sorrow which I might naturally feel, thought that an amusement suited to my taste would be the best means of restoring to me my wonted serenity. It was from this cause that he had removed to the country; and, induced by the same motive, he now proposed that we should all make an excursion to the valley of Chamounix. I had been there before, but Elizabeth and Ernest never had; and both had often expressed an earnest desire to see the scenery of this place, which had been described to them as so wonderful and sublime. Accordingly we departed from Geneva on this tour about the middle of the month of August, nearly two months after the death of Justine.

The weather was uncommonly fine; and if mine had been a sorrow to be chased away by any fleeting circumstance, this excursion would certainly have had the effect intended by my father. As it was, I was somewhat interested in the scene; it sometimes lulled, although it could not extinguish my grief. During the first day we travelled in a carriage. In the morning we had seen the mountains at a distance, towards which we gradually advanced. We perceived that the valley through which we wound, and which was formed by the river Arve, whose course we followed, closed in upon us by degrees; and when the sun had set, we beheld immense mountains and precipices overhanging us on every side, and heard the sound of the river raging among rocks, and the dashing of waterfalls around.

The next day we pursued our journey upon mules; and as we ascended still higher, the valley assumed a more magnificent and astonishing character. Ruined castles hanging on the precipices of piny mountains; the impetuous Arve, and cottages every here and there peeping forth from among the trees, formed a scene of singular beauty. But it was augmented and rendered sublime by the mighty Alps, whose white and shining pyramids and domes towered above all, as belonging to another earth, the habitations of another race of beings.

We passed the bridge of Pelissier, where the ravine, which the river forms, opened before us, and we began to ascend the mountain that overhangs it. Soon after we entered the valley of Chamounix. This valley is more wonderful and sublime, but not so beautiful and picturesque as that of Servox, through which we had just passed. The high and snowy mountains were its immediate boundaries; but we saw no more ruined castles and fertile fields. Immense glaciers approached the road; we heard the rumbling thunder of the falling avalanche, and marked the smoke of its passage. Mont Blanc, the supreme and magnificent Mont Blanc, raised itself from the surrounding *aiguilles*,[18] and its tremendous *dome* overlooked the valley.

During this journey, I sometimes joined Elizabeth, and exerted myself to point out to her the various beauties of the scene. I often suffered my mule to lag behind, and indulged in the misery of reflection. At other times I spurred on the animal before my companions, that I might forget them, the world, and, more than all, myself. When at a distance, I alighted, and threw myself on the grass, weighed down by horror and despair. At eight in the evening I arrived at Chamounix. My father and Elizabeth were very much fatigued; Ernest, who accompanied us, was delighted, and in high spirits: the only circumstance that detracted from his pleasure was the south wind, and the rain it seemed to promise for the next day.

We retired early to our apartments, but not to sleep; at least I did not. I remained many hours at the window, watching the pallid lightning that played above Mont Blanc, and listening to the rushing of the Arve, which ran below my window.

CHAPTER II

The next day, contrary to the prognostications of our guides, was fine, although clouded. We visited the source of the Arveiron, and rode about the valley until evening. These sublime and magnificent scenes afforded me the greatest consolation that I was capable of receiving. They elevated me from all littleness of feeling; and although they did not remove my grief, they subdued and tranquillized it. In some degree, also, they diverted my mind from the thoughts over which it had brooded for the last month. I returned in the evening, fatigued, but less unhappy, and conversed with my family with more cheerfulness than had been my custom for some time. My father was pleased, and Elizabeth overjoyed. "My dear cousin," said she, "you see what happiness you diffuse when you are happy; do not relapse again!"

The following morning the rain poured down in torrents, and thick mists hid the summits of the mountains. I rose early, but felt unusually melancholy. The rain depressed me; my old feelings recurred, and I was miserable. I knew how disappointed my father would be at this sudden change, and I wished to avoid him until I had recovered myself so far

18. "Mountain peaks."

as to be enabled to conceal those feelings that overpowered me. I knew that they would remain that day at the inn; and as I had ever inured myself to rain, moisture, and cold, I resolved to go alone to the summit of Montanvert. I remembered the effect that the view of the tremendous and ever-moving glacier had produced upon my mind when I first saw it. It had then filled me with a sublime ecstacy that gave wings to the soul, and allowed it to soar from the obscure world to light and joy. The sight of the awful and majestic in nature had indeed always the effect of solemnizing my mind, and causing me to forget the passing cares of life. I determined to go alone, for I was well acquainted with the path, and the presence of another would destroy the solitary grandeur of the scene.

The ascent is precipitous, but the path is cut into continual and short windings, which enable you to surmount the perpendicularity of the mountain. It is a scene terrifically desolate. In a thousand spots the traces of the winter avalanche may be perceived, where trees lie broken and strewed on the ground; some entirely destroyed, others bent, leaning upon the jutting rocks of the mountain, or transversely upon other trees. The path, as you ascend higher, is intersected by ravines of snow, down which stones continually roll from above; one of them is particularly dangerous, as the slightest sound, such as even speaking in a loud voice, produces a concussion of air sufficient to draw destruction upon the head of the speaker. The pines are not tall or luxuriant, but they are sombre, and add an air of severity to the scene. I looked on the valley beneath; vast mists were rising from the rivers which ran through it, and curling in thick wreaths around the opposite mountains, whose summits were hid in the uniform clouds, while rain poured from the dark sky, and added to the melancholy impression I received from the objects around me. Alas! why does man boast of sensibilities superior to those apparent in the brute; it only renders them more necessary beings. If our impulses were confined to hunger, thirst, and desire, we might be nearly free; but now we are moved by every wind that blows, and a chance word or scene that that word may convey to us.

> We rest; a dream has power to poison sleep.
>   We rise; one wand'ring thought pollutes the day.
> We feel, conceive, or reason; laugh, or weep,
>   Embrace fond woe, or cast our cares away;
> It is the same: for, be it joy or sorrow,
>   The path of its departure still is free.
> Man's yesterday may ne'er be like his morrow;
>   Nought may endure but mutability![19]

19. Percy B. Shelley, "Mutability," published with his *Alastor; or, The Spirit of Solitude: and Other Poems* (1816).

It was nearly noon when I arrived at the top of the ascent. For some time I sat upon the rock that overlooks the sea of ice. A mist covered both that and the surrounding mountains. Presently a breeze dissipated the cloud, and I descended upon the glacier. The surface is very uneven, rising like the waves of a troubled sea, descending low, and interspersed by rifts that sink deep. The field of ice is almost a league in width, but I spent nearly two hours in crossing it. The opposite mountain is a bare perpendicular rock. From the side where I now stood Montanvert was exactly opposite, at the distance of a league; and above it rose Mont Blanc, in awful majesty. I remained in a recess of the rock, gazing on this wonderful and stupendous scene. The sea, or rather the vast river of ice, wound among its dependent mountains, whose aerial summits hung over its recesses. Their icy and glittering peaks shone in the sunlight over the clouds. My heart, which was before sorrowful, now swelled with something like joy; I exclaimed—"Wandering spirits, if indeed ye wander, and do not rest in your narrow beds, allow me this faint happiness, or take me, as your companion, away from the joys of life."

As I said this, I suddenly beheld the figure of a man, at some distance, advancing towards me with superhuman speed. He bounded over the crevices in the ice, among which I had walked with caution; his stature also, as he approached, seemed to exceed that of man. I was troubled: a mist came over my eyes, and I felt a faintness seize me; but I was quickly restored by the cold gale of the mountains. I perceived, as the shape came nearer, (sight tremendous and abhorred!) that it was the wretch whom I had created. I trembled with rage and horror, resolving to wait his approach, and then close with him in mortal combat. He approached; his countenance bespoke bitter anguish, combined with disdain and malignity, while its unearthly ugliness rendered it almost too horrible for human eyes. But I scarcely observed this; anger and hatred had at first deprived me of utterance, and I recovered only to overwhelm him with words expressive of furious detestation and contempt.

"Devil!" I exclaimed, "do you dare approach me? and do not you fear the fierce vengeance of my arm wreaked on your miserable head? Begone, vile insect! or rather stay, that I may trample you to dust! and, oh, that I could, with the extinction of your miserable existence, restore those victims whom you have so diabolically murdered!"

"I expected this reception," said the dæmon. "All men hate the wretched; how then must I be hated, who am miserable beyond all living things! Yet you, my creator, detest and spurn me, thy creature, to whom thou art bound by ties only dissoluble by the annihilation of one of us. You purpose to kill me. How dare you sport thus with life? Do your duty towards me, and I will do mine towards you and the rest of mankind. If you will comply with my conditions, I will leave them and you at peace; but if you refuse, I will glut the maw of death, until it be satiated with the blood of your remaining friends."

"Abhorred monster! fiend that thou art! the tortures of hell are too mild a vengeance for thy crimes. Wretched devil! you reproach me with your creation; come on then, that I may extinguish the spark which I so negligently bestowed."

My rage was without bounds; I sprang on him, impelled by all the feelings which can arm one being against the existence of another.

He easily eluded me, and said,

"Be calm! I entreat you to hear me, before you give vent to your hatred on my devoted head. Have I not suffered enough, that you seek to increase my misery? Life, although it may only be an accumulation of anguish, is dear to me, and I will defend it. Remember, thou hast made me more powerful than thyself; my height is superior to thine; my joints more supple. But I will not be tempted to set myself in opposition to thee. I am thy creature, and I will be even mild and docile to my natural lord and king, if thou wilt also perform thy part, the which thou owest me. Oh, Frankenstein, be not equitable to every other, and trample upon me alone, to whom thy justice, and even thy clemency and affection, is most due. Remember, that I am thy creature: I ought to be thy Adam; but I am rather the fallen angel, whom thou drivest from joy for no misdeed. Every where I see bliss, from which I alone am irrevocably excluded. I was benevolent and good; misery made me a fiend. Make me happy, and I shall again be virtuous."

"Begone! I will not hear you. There can be no community between you and me; we are enemies. Begone, or let us try our strength in a fight, in which one must fall."

"How can I move thee? Will no entreaties cause thee to turn a favourable eye upon thy creature, who implores thy goodness and compassion. Believe me, Frankenstein: I was benevolent; my soul glowed with love and humanity: but am I not alone, miserably alone? You, my creator, abhor me; what hope can I gather from your fellow-creatures, who owe me nothing? they spurn and hate me. The desert mountains and dreary glaciers are my refuge. I have wandered here many days; the caves of ice, which I only do not fear, are a dwelling to me, and the only one which man does not grudge. These bleak skies I hail, for they are kinder to me than your fellow-beings. If the multitude of mankind knew of my existence, they would do as you do, and arm themselves for my destruction. Shall I not then hate them who abhor me? I will keep no terms with my enemies. I am miserable, and they shall share my wretchedness. Yet it is in your power to recompense me, and deliver them from an evil which it only remains for you to make so great, that not only you and your family, but thousands of others, shall be swallowed up in the whirlwinds of its rage. Let your compassion be moved, and do not disdain me. Listen to my tale: when you have heard that, abandon or commiserate me, as you shall judge that I deserve. But hear me. The guilty are allowed, by human laws, bloody as they may be, to speak in their own defence before they are condemned. Listen to me, Frankenstein. You accuse me of murder; and yet you would, with a satisfied conscience, destroy your own creature. Oh, praise the eternal justice of man! Yet I ask you not to spare me: listen to me; and then, if you can, and if you will, destroy the work of your hands."

"Why do you call to my remembrance circumstances of which I shudder to reflect, that I have been the miserable origin and author? Cursed be the day, abhorred devil, in which you first saw light! Cursed (although I curse myself) be the hands that formed you! You have made me wretched beyond expression. You have left me no power to consider whether I am just to you, or not. Begone! relieve me from the sight of your detested form."

"Thus I relieve thee, my creator," he said, and placed his hated hands before my eyes, which I flung from me with violence; "thus I take from thee a sight which you abhor. Still thou canst listen to me, and grant me thy compassion. By the virtues that I once possessed, I demand this from you. Hear my tale; it is long and strange, and the temperature of this place is not fitting to your fine sensations; come to the hut upon the mountain. The sun is yet high in the heavens; before it descends to hide itself behind yon snowy precipices, and illuminate another world, you will have heard my story, and can decide. On you it rests, whether I quit for ever the neighbourhood of man, and lead a harmless life, or become the scourge of your fellow-creatures, and the author of your own speedy ruin."

As he said this, he led the way across the ice: I followed. My heart was full, and I did not answer him; but, as I proceeded, I weighed the various arguments that he had used, and determined at least to listen to his tale. I was partly urged by curiosity, and compassion confirmed my resolution. I had hitherto supposed him to be the murderer of my brother, and I eagerly sought a confirmation or denial of this opinion. For the first time, also, I felt what the duties of a creator towards his creature were, and that I ought to render him happy before I complained of his wickedness. These motives urged me to comply with his demand. We crossed the ice, therefore, and ascended the opposite rock. The air was cold, and the rain again began to descend: we entered the hut, the fiend with an air of exultation, I with a heavy heart, and depressed spirits. But I consented to listen; and, seating myself by the fire which my odious companion had lighted, he thus began his tale.

CHAPTER III

"It is with considerable difficulty that I remember the original æra of my being: all the events of that period appear confused and indistinct. A strange multiplicity of sensations seized me, and I saw, felt, heard, and smelt, at the same time; and it was, indeed, a long time before I learned to distinguish between the operations of my various senses. By degrees, I remember, a stronger light pressed upon my nerves, so that I was obliged to shut my eyes. Darkness then came over me, and troubled me; but hardly had I felt this, when, by opening my eyes, as I now suppose, the light poured in upon me again. I walked, and, I believe, descended; but I presently found a great alteration in my sensations. Before, dark and opaque bodies had surrounded me, impervious to my touch or sight; but I now found that I could wander on at liberty, with no obstacles which I could not either surmount or avoid. The light became more and more oppressive to me; and, the heat wearying me as I walked, I sought a place where I could receive shade. This was the forest near Ingolstadt; and here I lay by the side of a brook resting from my fatigue, until I felt tormented by hunger and thirst. This roused me from my nearly dormant state, and I ate some berries which I found hanging on the trees, or lying on the ground. I slaked my thirst at the brook; and then lying down, was overcome by sleep.

"It was dark when I awoke; I felt cold also, and half-frightened as it were instinctively, finding myself so desolate. Before I had quitted your apartment, on a sensation of cold, I had covered myself with some clothes; but these were insufficient to secure me from the dews of night. I was a poor, helpless, miserable wretch; I knew, and could distinguish, nothing; but, feeling pain invade me on all sides, I sat down and wept.

"Soon a gentle light stole over the heavens, and gave me a sensation of pleasure. I started up, and beheld a radiant form rise from among the trees. I gazed with a kind of wonder. It moved slowly, but it enlightened my path; and I again went out in search of berries. I was still cold, when under one of the trees I found a huge cloak, with which I covered myself, and sat down upon the ground. No distinct ideas occupied my mind; all was confused. I felt light, and hunger, and thirst, and darkness; innumerable sounds rung in my ears, and on all sides various scents saluted me: the only object that I could distinguish was the bright moon, and I fixed my eyes on that with pleasure.

"Several changes of day and night passed, and the orb of night had greatly lessened when I began to distinguish my sensations from each other. I gradually saw plainly the clear stream that supplied me with drink, and the trees that shaded me with their foliage. I was delighted when I first discovered that a pleasant sound, which often saluted my ears, proceeded from the throats of the little winged animals who had often intercepted the light from my eyes. I began also to observe, with greater accuracy, the forms that surrounded me, and to perceive the boundaries of the radiant roof of light which canopied me. Sometimes I tried to imitate the pleasant songs of the birds, but was unable. Sometimes I wished to express my sensations in my own mode, but the uncouth and inarticulate sounds which broke from me frightened me into silence again.

"The moon had disappeared from the night, and again, with a lessened form, shewed itself, while I still remained in the forest. My sensations had, by this time, become distinct, and my mind received every day additional ideas. My eyes became accustomed to the light, and to perceive objects in their right forms; I distinguished the insect from the herb, and, by degrees, one herb from another. I found that the sparrow uttered none but harsh notes, whilst those of the blackbird and thrush were sweet and enticing.

"One day, when I was oppressed by cold, I found a fire which had been left by some wandering beggars, and was overcome with delight at the warmth I experienced from it. In my joy I thrust my hand into the live embers, but quickly drew it out again with a cry of pain. How strange, I thought, that the same cause should produce such opposite effects! I examined the materials of the fire, and to my joy found it to be composed of wood. I quickly collected some branches; but they were wet, and would not burn. I was pained at this, and sat still watching the operation of the fire. The wet wood which I had placed near the heat dried, and itself became inflamed. I reflected on this; and, by touching the various branches, I discovered the cause, and busied myself in collecting a great quantity of wood, that I might dry it, and have a plentiful supply of fire. When night came on, and brought sleep with it, I was in the greatest fear lest my fire should be extinguished. I covered it carefully with dry wood and leaves, and placed wet branches upon it; and then, spreading my cloak, I lay on the ground, and sunk into sleep.

"It was morning when I awoke, and my first care was to visit the fire. I uncovered it, and a gentle breeze quickly fanned it into a flame. I observed this also, and contrived a fan of branches, which roused the embers when they were nearly extinguished. When night came again, I found, with pleasure, that the fire gave light as well as heat; and that the discovery of this element was useful to me in my food; for I found some of the offals that the travellers had left had been roasted, and tasted much more savoury than the berries I gathered from the trees. I tried, therefore, to dress my food in the same manner, placing it on the live embers. I found that the berries were spoiled by this operation, and the nuts and roots much improved.

"Food, however, became scarce; and I often spent the whole day searching in vain for a few acorns to assuage the pangs of hunger. When I found this, I resolved to quit the place that I had hitherto inhabited, to seek for one where the few wants I experienced would be more easily satisfied. In this emigration, I exceedingly lamented the loss of the fire which I had obtained through accident, and knew not how to re-produce it. I gave several hours to the serious consideration of this difficulty; but I was obliged to relinquish all attempts to supply it; and, wrapping myself up in my cloak, I struck across the wood towards the setting sun. I passed three days in these rambles, and at length discovered the open country. A great fall of snow had taken place the night before, and the fields were of one uniform white; the appearance was disconsolate, and I found my feet chilled by the cold damp substance that covered the ground.

"It was about seven in the morning, and I longed to obtain food and shelter; at length I perceived a small hut, on a rising ground, which had doubtless been built for the convenience of some shepherd. This was a new sight to me; and I examined the structure with great curiosity. Finding the door open, I entered. An old man sat in it, near a fire, over which he was preparing his breakfast. He turned on hearing a noise; and, perceiving me, shrieked loudly, and, quitting the hut, ran across the fields with a speed of which his debilitated form hardly appeared capable. His appearance, different from any I had ever before seen, and his flight, somewhat surprised me. But I was enchanted by the appearance of the hut: here the snow and rain could not penetrate; the ground was dry; and it presented to me then as exquisite and divine a retreat as Pandæmonium appeared to the dæmons of hell after their sufferings in the lake of fire. I greedily devoured the remnants of the shepherd's breakfast, which consisted of bread, cheese, milk, and wine; the latter, however, I did not like. Then overcome by fatigue, I lay down among some straw, and fell asleep.

"It was noon when I awoke; and, allured by the warmth of the sun, which shone brightly on the white ground, I determined to recommence my travels; and, depositing the remains of the peasant's breakfast in a wallet I found, I proceeded across the fields for several hours, until at sunset I arrived at a village. How miraculous did this appear! the huts, the neater cottages, and stately houses, engaged my admiration by turns. The vegetables in the gardens, the milk and cheese that I saw placed at the windows of some of the cottages, allured my appetite. One of the best of these I entered; but I had hardly placed my foot within the door, before the children shrieked, and one of the women fainted. The whole village was roused; some fled, some attacked me, until, grievously bruised by stones and many other kinds of missile weapons, I escaped to the open country, and fearfully took refuge in a low hovel, quite bare, and making a wretched appearance after the palaces I had beheld in the village. This hovel, however, joined a cottage of a neat and pleasant appearance; but, after my late dearly-bought experience, I dared not enter it. My place of refuge was constructed of wood, but so low, that I could with difficulty sit upright in it. No wood, however, was placed on the earth, which formed the floor, but it was dry; and although the wind entered it by innumerable chinks, I found it an agreeable asylum from the snow and rain.

"Here then I retreated, and lay down, happy to have found a shelter, however miserable, from the inclemency of the season, and still more from the barbarity of man.

"As soon as morning dawned, I crept from my kennel, that I might view the adjacent cottage, and discover if I could remain in the habitation I had found. It was situated against the back of the cottage, and surrounded on the sides which were exposed by a pig-stye and a clear pool of water. One part was open, and by that I had crept in; but now I covered every crevice by which I might be perceived with stones and wood, yet in such a manner that I might move them on occasion to pass out: all the light I enjoyed came through the stye, and that was sufficient for me.

"Having thus arranged my dwelling, and carpeted it with clean straw, I retired; for I saw the figure of a man at a distance, and I remembered too well my treatment the night before, to trust myself in his power. I had first, however, provided for my sustenance for that day, by a loaf of coarse bread, which I purloined, and a cup with which I could drink, more conveniently than from my hand, of the pure water which flowed by my retreat. The floor was a little raised, so that it was kept perfectly dry, and by its vicinity to the chimney of the cottage it was tolerably warm.

"Being thus provided, I resolved to reside in this hovel, until something should occur which might alter my determination. It was indeed a paradise, compared to the bleak forest, my former residence, the rain-dropping branches, and dank earth. I ate my breakfast with pleasure, and was about to remove a plank to procure myself a little water, when I heard a step, and, looking through a small chink, I beheld a young creature, with a pail on her head, passing before my hovel. The girl was young and of gentle demeanour, unlike what I have since found cottagers and farm-house servants to be. Yet she was meanly dressed, a coarse blue petticoat and a linen jacket being her only garb; her fair hair was plaited, but not adorned; she looked patient, yet sad. I lost sight of her; and in about a quarter of an hour she returned, bearing the pail, which was now partly filled with milk. As she walked along, seemingly incommoded by the burden, a young man met her, whose countenance expressed a deeper despondence. Uttering a few sounds with an air of melancholy, he took the pail from her head, and bore it to the cottage himself. She followed, and they disappeared. Presently I saw the young man again, with some tools in his hand, cross the field behind the cottage; and the girl was also busied, sometimes in the house, and sometimes in the yard.

"On examining my dwelling, I found that one of the windows of the cottage had formerly occupied a part of it, but the panes had been filled up with wood. In one of these was a small and almost imperceptible chink, through which the eye could just penetrate. Through this crevice, a small room was visible, white-washed and clean, but very bare of furniture. In one corner, near a small fire, sat an old man, leaning his head on his hands in a disconsolate attitude. The young girl was occupied in arranging the cottage; but presently she took something out of a drawer, which employed her hands, and she sat down beside the old man, who, taking up an instrument, began to play, and to produce sounds, sweeter than the voice of the thrush or the nightingale. It was a lovely sight, even to me, poor wretch! who had never beheld aught beautiful before. The silver hair and benevolent countenance of the aged cottager, won my reverence; while the gentle manners of the girl enticed my love. He played a sweet mournful air, which I perceived drew tears from the eyes of his amiable companion, of which the old man took no notice, until she sobbed audibly; he then pronounced a few sounds, and the fair creature, leaving her work, knelt at his feet. He raised her, and smiled with such kindness and affection, that I felt sensations of a peculiar and overpowering nature: they were a mixture of pain and pleasure, such as I had never before experienced, either from hunger or cold, warmth or food; and I withdrew from the window, unable to bear these emotions.

"Soon after this the young man returned, bearing on his shoulders a load of wood. The girl met him at the door, helped to relieve him of his burden, and, taking some of the fuel into the cottage, placed it on the fire; then she and the youth went apart into a nook of the cottage, and he shewed her a large loaf and a piece of cheese. She seemed pleased;

and went into the garden for some roots and plants, which she placed in water, and then upon the fire. She afterwards continued her work, whilst the young man went into the garden, and appeared busily employed in digging and pulling up roots. After he had been employed thus about an hour, the young woman joined him, and they entered the cottage together.

"The old man had, in the mean time, been pensive; but, on the appearance of his companions, he assumed a more cheerful air, and they sat down to eat. The meal was quickly dispatched. The young woman was again occupied in arranging the cottage; the old man walked before the cottage in the sun for a few minutes, leaning on the arm of the youth. Nothing could exceed in beauty the contrast between these two excellent creatures. One was old, with silver hairs and a countenance beaming with benevolence and love; the younger was slight and graceful in his figure, and his features were moulded with the finest symmetry; yet his eyes and attitude expressed the utmost sadness and despondency. The old man returned to the cottage; and the youth, with tools different from those he had used in the morning, directed his steps across the fields.

"Night quickly shut in; but, to my extreme wonder, I found that the cottagers had a means of prolonging light, by the use of tapers, and was delighted to find, that the setting of the sun did not put an end to the pleasure I experienced in watching my human neighbours. In the evening, the young girl and her companion were employed in various occupations which I did not understand; and the old man again took up the instrument, which produced the divine sounds that had enchanted me in the morning. So soon as he had finished, the youth began, not to play, but to utter sounds that were monotonous, and neither resembling the harmony of the old man's instrument or the songs of the birds; I since found that he read aloud, but at that time I knew nothing of the science of words or letters.

"The family, after having been thus occupied for a short time, extinguished their lights, and retired, as I conjectured, to rest.

CHAPTER IV

"I lay on my straw, but I could not sleep. I thought of the occurrences of the day. What chiefly struck me was the gentle manners of these people; and I longed to join them, but dared not. I remembered too well the treatment I had suffered the night before from the barbarous villagers, and resolved, whatever course of conduct I might hereafter think it right to pursue, that for the present I would remain quietly in my hovel, watching, and endeavouring to discover the motives which influenced their actions.

"The cottagers arose the next morning before the sun. The young woman arranged the cottage, and prepared the food; and the youth departed after the first meal.

"This day was passed in the same routine as that which preceded it. The young man was constantly employed out of doors, and the girl in various laborious occupations within. The old man, whom I soon perceived to be blind, employed his leisure hours on his instrument, or in contemplation. Nothing could exceed the love and respect which the younger cottagers exhibited towards their venerable companion. They performed towards him every little office of affection and duty with gentleness; and he rewarded them by his benevolent smiles.

"They were not entirely happy. The young man and his companion often went apart, and appeared to weep. I saw no cause for their unhappiness; but I was deeply affected by it. If such lovely creatures were miserable, it was less strange that I, an imperfect and solitary being, should be wretched. Yet why were these gentle beings unhappy? They possessed a delightful house (for such it was in my eyes), and every luxury; they had a fire to warm them when chill, and delicious viands when hungry; they were dressed in excellent clothes; and, still more, they enjoyed one another's company and speech, interchanging each day looks of affection and kindness. What did their tears imply? Did they really express pain? I was at first unable to solve these questions; but perpetual attention, and time, explained to me many appearances which were at first enigmatic.

"A considerable period elapsed before I discovered one of the causes of the uneasiness of this amiable family; it was poverty; and they suffered that evil in a very distressing degree. Their nourishment consisted entirely of the vegetables of their garden, and the milk of one cow, who gave very little during the winter, when its masters could scarcely procure food to support it. They often, I believe, suffered the pangs of hunger very poignantly, especially the two younger cottagers; for several times they placed food before the old man, when they reserved none for themselves.

"This trait of kindness moved me sensibly. I had been accustomed, during the night, to steal a part of their store for my own consumption; but when I found that in doing this I inflicted pain on the cottagers, I abstained, and satisfied myself with berries, nuts, and roots, which I gathered from a neighbouring wood.

"I discovered also another means through which I was enabled to assist their labours. I found that the youth spent a great part of each day in collecting wood for the family fire; and, during the night, I often took his tools, the use of which I quickly discovered, and brought home firing sufficient for the consumption of several days.

"I remember, the first time that I did this, the young woman, when she opened the door in the morning, appeared greatly astonished on seeing a great pile of wood on the outside. She uttered some words in a loud voice, and the youth joined her, who also expressed surprise. I observed, with pleasure, that he did not go to the forest that day, but spent it in repairing the cottage, and cultivating the garden.

"By degrees I made a discovery of still greater moment. I found that these people possessed a method of communicating their experience and feelings to one another by articulate sounds. I perceived that the words they spoke sometimes produced pleasure or pain, smiles or sadness, in the minds and countenances of the hearers. This was indeed a godlike science, and I ardently desired to become acquainted with it. But I was baffled in every attempt I made for this purpose. Their pronunciation was quick; and the words they uttered, not having any apparent con- nexion with visible objects, I was unable to discover any clue by which I could unravel the mystery of their reference. By great application, how- ever, and after having remained during the space of several revolutions of the moon in my hovel, I discovered the names that were given to some of the most familiar objects of discourse; I learned and applied the words *fire, milk, bread,* and *wood.* I learned also the names of the cottagers themselves. The youth and his companion had each of them several names, but the old man had only one, which was *father.* The girl was called *sister,* or *Agatha*; and the youth *Felix, brother,* or *son.* I cannot describe the delight I felt when I learned the ideas appropriated to each of these sounds, and was able to pronounce them. I distinguished several other words, without being able as yet to understand or apply them; such as *good, dearest, unhappy.*

"I spent the winter in this manner. The gentle manners and beauty of the cottagers greatly endeared them to me; when they were unhappy, I felt depressed; when they rejoiced, I sympathized in their joys. I saw few human beings beside them; and if any other happened to enter the cottage, their harsh manners and rude gait only enhanced to me the su- perior accomplishments of my friends. The old man, I could perceive, often endeavoured to encourage his children, as sometimes I found that he called them, to cast off their melancholy. He would talk in a cheerful accent, with an expression of goodness that bestowed pleasure even upon me. Agatha listened with respect, her eyes sometimes filled with tears, which she endeavoured to wipe away unperceived; but I generally found that her countenance and tone were more cheerful after having listened to the exhortations of her father. It was not thus with Felix. He was always the saddest of the groupe; and, even to my unpractised senses, he appeared to have suffered more deeply than his friends. But if his countenance was more sorrowful, his voice was more cheerful than that of his sister, especially when he addressed the old man.

"I could mention innumerable instances, which, although slight, marked the dispositions of these amiable cottagers. In the midst of poverty and want, Felix carried with pleasure to his sister the first little white flower that peeped out from beneath the snowy ground. Early in the morning before she had risen, he cleared away the snow that obstructed her path to the milk-house, drew water from the well, and brought the wood from the outhouse, where, to his perpetual astonishment, he found his store always replenished by an invisible hand. In the day, I believe, he worked sometimes for a neighbouring farmer, because he often went forth, and did not return until dinner, yet brought no wood with him. At other times he worked in the garden; but, as there was little to do in the frosty season, he read to the old man and Agatha.

"This reading had puzzled me extremely at first; but, by degrees, I discovered that he uttered many of the same sounds when he read as when he talked. I conjectured, therefore, that he found on the paper signs for speech which he understood, and I ardently longed to comprehend these also; but how was that possible, when I did not even understand the sounds for which they stood as signs? I improved, however, sensibly in this science, but not sufficiently to follow up any kind of conversation, atlhough I applied my whole mind to the endeavour: for I easily perceived that, although I eagerly longed to discover myself to the cottagers, I ought not to make the attempt until I had first become master of their language; which knowledge might enable me to make them overlook the deformity of my figure; for with this also the contrast perpetually presented to my eyes had made me acquainted.

"I had admired the perfect forms of my cottagers—their grace, beauty, and delicate complexions: but how was I terrified, when I viewed myself in a transparent pool! At first I started back, unable to believe that it was indeed I who was reflected in the mirror; and when I became fully convinced that I was in reality the monster that I am, I was filled with the bitterest sensations of despondence and mortification. Alas! I did not yet entirely know the fatal effects of this miserable deformity.

"As the sun became warmer, and the light of day longer, the snow vanished, and I beheld the bare trees and the black earth. From this time Felix was more employed; and the heart-moving indications of impending famine disappeared. Their food, as I afterwards found, was coarse, but it was wholesome; and they procured a sufficiency of it. Several new kinds of plants sprung up in the garden, which they dressed; and these signs of comfort increased daily as the season advanced.

"The old man, leaning on his son, walked each day at noon, when it did not rain, as I found it was called when the heavens poured forth its waters. This frequently took place; but a high wind quickly dried the earth, and the season became far more pleasant than it had been.

"My mode of life in my hovel was uniform. During the morning I attended the motions of the cottagers; and when they were dispersed in various occupations, I slept: the remainder of the day was spent in observing my friends. When they had retired to rest, if there was any moon, or the night was star-light, I went into the woods, and collected my own food and fuel for the cottage. When I returned, as often as it was necessary, I cleared their path from the snow, and performed those offices that I had seen done by Felix. I afterwards found that these labours, performed by an invisible hand, greatly astonished them; and once or twice I heard them, on these occasions, utter the words *good spirit, wonderful*; but I did not then understand the signification of these terms.

"My thoughts now became more active, and I longed to discover the motives and feelings of these lovely creatures; I was inquisitive to know why Felix appeared so miserable, and Agatha so sad. I thought (foolish wretch!) that it might be in my power to restore happiness to these deserving people. When I slept, or was absent, the forms of the venerable blind father, the gentle Agatha, and the excellent Felix, flitted before me. I looked upon them as superior beings, who would be the arbiters of my future destiny. I formed in my imagination a thousand pictures of presenting myself to them, and their reception of me. I imagined that they would be disgusted, until, by my gentle demeanour and conciliating words, I should first win their favour, and afterwards their love.

"These thoughts exhilarated me, and led me to apply with fresh ardour to the acquiring the art of language. My organs were indeed harsh, but supple; and although my voice was very unlike the soft music of their tones, yet I pronounced such words as I understood with tolerable ease. It was as the ass and the lap-dog; yet surely the gentle ass, whose intentions were affectionate, although his manners were rude, deserved better treatment than blows and execration.

"The pleasant showers and genial warmth of spring greatly altered the aspect of the earth. Men, who before this change seemed to have been hid in caves, dispersed themselves, and were employed in various arts of cultivation. The birds sang in more cheerful notes, and the leaves began to bud forth on the trees. Happy, happy earth! fit habitation for gods, which, so short a time before, was bleak, damp, and unwholesome. My spirits were elevated by the enchanting appearance of nature; the past was blotted from my memory, the present was tranquil, and the future gilded by bright rays of hope, and anticipations of joy.

CHAPTER V

"I now hasten to the more moving part of my story. I shall relate events that impressed me with feelings which, from what I was, have made me what I am.

"Spring advanced rapidly; the weather became fine, and the skies cloudless. It surprised me, that what before was desert and gloomy should now bloom with the most beautiful flowers and verdure. My senses were gratified and refreshed by a thousand scents of delight, and a thousand sights of beauty.

"It was on one of these days, when my cottagers periodically rested from labour—the old man played on his guitar, and the children listened to him—I observed that the countenance of Felix was melancholy beyond expression; he sighed frequently; and once his father paused in his music, and I conjectured by his manner that he inquired the cause of his son's sorrow. Felix replied in a cheerful accent, and the old man was recommencing his music, when some one tapped at the door.

"It was a lady on horseback, accompanied by a countryman as a guide. The lady was dressed in a dark suit, and covered with a thick black veil. Agatha asked a question; to which the stranger only replied by pronouncing, in a sweet accent, the name of Felix. Her voice was musical, but unlike that of either of my friends. On hearing this word, Felix came up hastily to the lady; who, when she saw him, threw up her veil, and I beheld a countenance of angelic beauty and expression. Her hair of a shining raven black, and curiously braided; her eyes were dark, but gentle, although animated; her features of a regular proportion, and her complexion wondrously fair, each cheek tinged with a lovely pink.

"Felix seemed ravished with delight when he saw her, every trait of sorrow vanished from his face, and it instantly expressed a degree of ecstatic joy, of which I could hardly have believed it capable; his eyes sparkled, as his cheek flushed with pleasure; and at that moment I thought him as beautiful as the stranger. She appeared affected by different feelings; wiping a few tears from her lovely eyes, she held out her hand to Felix, who kissed it rapturously, and called her, as well as I could distinguish, his sweet Arabian. She did not appear to understand him, but smiled. He assisted her to dismount, and, dismissing her guide, conducted her into the cottage. Some conversation took place between him and his father; and the young stranger knelt at the old man's feet, and would have kissed his hand, but he raised her, and embraced her affectionately.

"I soon perceived, that although the stranger uttered articulate sounds, and appeared to have a language of her own, she was neither understood by, or herself understood, the cottagers. They made many signs which I did not comprehend; but I saw that her presence diffused gladness through the cottage, dispelling their sorrow as the sun dissipates the morning mists. Felix seemed peculiarly happy, and with smiles of delight welcomed his Arabian. Agatha, the ever-gentle Agatha, kissed the hands of the lovely stranger; and, pointing to her brother, made signs which appeared to me to mean that he had been sorrowful until she came. Some hours passed thus, while they, by their countenances, expressed joy, the cause of which I did not comprehend. Presently I found, by the frequent recurrence of one sound which the stranger repeated after them, that she was endeavouring to learn their language; and the idea instantly occurred to me, that I should make use of the same instructions to the same end. The stranger learned about twenty words at the first lesson, most of them indeed were those which I had before understood, but I profited by the others.

"As night came on, Agatha and the Arabian retired early. When they separated, Felix kissed the hand of the stranger, and said, 'Good night, sweet Safie.' He sat up much longer, conversing with his father; and, by the frequent repetition of her name, I conjectured that their lovely guest was the subject of their conversation. I ardently desired to understand them, and bent every faculty towards that purpose, but found it utterly impossible.

"The next morning Felix went out to his work; and, after the usual occupations of Agatha were finished, the Arabian sat at the feet of the old man, and, taking his guitar, played some airs so entrancingly beautiful, that they at once drew tears of sorrow and delight from my eyes. She sang, and her voice flowed in a rich cadence, swelling or dying away, like a nightingale of the woods.

"When she had finished, she gave the guitar to Agatha, who at first declined it. She played a simple air, and her voice accompanied it in sweet accents, but unlike the wondrous strain of the stranger. The old man appeared enraptured, and said some words, which Agatha endeavoured to explain to Safie, and by which he appeared to wish to express that she bestowed on him the greatest delight by her music.

"The days now passed as peaceably as before, with the sole alteration, that joy had taken place of sadness in the countenances of my friends. Safie was always gay and happy; she and I improved rapidly in the knowledge of language, so that in two months I began to comprehend most of the words uttered by my protectors.

"In the meanwhile also the black ground was covered with herbage, and the green banks interspersed with innumerable flowers, sweet to the scent and the eyes, stars of pale radiance among the moonlight woods; the sun became warmer, the nights clear and balmy; and my nocturnal rambles were an extreme pleasure to me, although they were considerably shortened by the late setting and early rising of the sun; for I never ventured abroad during day-light, fearful of meeting with the same treatment as I had formerly endured in the first village which I entered.

"My days were spent in close attention, that I might more speedily master the language; and I may boast that I improved more rapidly than the Arabian, who understood very little, and conversed in broken accents, whilst I comprehended and could imitate almost every word that was spoken.

"While I improved in speech, I also learned the science of letters, as it was taught to the stranger; and this opened before me a wide field for wonder and delight.

"The book from which Felix instructed Safie was Volney's *Ruins of Empires*.[20] I should not have understood the purport of this book, had not Felix, in reading it, given very minute explanations. He had chosen this work, he said, because the declamatory style was framed in imitation of the eastern authors. Through this work I obtained a cursory knowledge of history, and a view of the several empires at present existing in the world; it gave me an insight into the manners, governments, and religions of the different nations of the earth. I heard of the slothful Asiatics; of the stupendous genius and mental activity of the Grecians; of the wars and wonderful virtue of the early Romans—of their subsequent degeneration—of the decline of that mighty empire; of chivalry, Christianity, and kings. I heard of the discovery of the American hemisphere, and wept with Safie over the hapless fate of its original inhabitants.

"These wonderful narrations inspired me with strange feelings. Was man, indeed, at once so powerful, so virtuous, and magnificent, yet so vicious and base? He appeared at one time a mere scion of the evil principle, and at another as all that can be conceived of noble and godlike. To be a great and virtuous man appeared the highest honour that can befall a sensitive being; to be base and vicious, as many on record have been, appeared the lowest degradation, a condition more abject than that of the blind mole or harmless worm. For a long time I could not conceive how one man could go forth to murder his fellow, or even why

---

20. Constantin François Chassebœuf, comte de Volney (1757–1820), *Les Ruines ou méditations sur les révolutions des empires* (1791).

there were laws and governments; but when I heard details of vice and bloodshed, my wonder ceased, and I turned away with disgust and loathing.

"Every conversation of the cottagers now opened new wonders to me. While I listened to the instructions which Felix bestowed upon the Arabian, the strange system of human society was explained to me. I heard of the division of property, of immense wealth and squalid poverty; of rank, descent, and noble blood.

"The words induced me to turn towards myself. I learned that the possessions most esteemed by your fellow-creatures were, high and unsullied descent united with riches. A man might be respected with only one of these acquisitions; but without either he was considered, except in very rare instances, as a vagabond and a slave, doomed to waste his powers for the profit of the chosen few. And what was I? Of my creation and creator I was absolutely ignorant; but I knew that I possessed no money, no friends, no kind of property. I was, besides, endowed with a figure hideously deformed and loathsome; I was not even of the same nature as man. I was more agile than they, and could subsist upon coarser diet; I bore the extremes of heat and cold with less injury to my frame; my stature far exceeded their's. When I looked around, I saw and heard of none like me. Was I then a monster, a blot upon the earth, from which all men fled, and whom all men disowned?

"I cannot describe to you the agony that these reflections inflicted upon me; I tried to dispel them, but sorrow only increased with knowledge. Oh, that I had for ever remained in my native wood, nor known or felt beyond the sensations of hunger, thirst, and heat!

"Of what a strange nature is knowledge! It clings to the mind, when it has once seized on it, like a lichen on the rock. I wished sometimes to shake off all thought and feeling; but I learned that there was but one means to overcome the sensation of pain, and that was death—a state which I feared yet did not understand. I admired virtue and good feelings, and loved the gentle manners and amiable qualities of my cottagers; but I was shut out from intercourse with them, except through means which I obtained by stealth, when I was unseen and unknown, and which rather increased than satisfied the desire I had of becoming one among my fellows. The gentle words of Agatha, and the animated smiles of the charming Arabian, were not for me. The mild exhortations of the old man, and the lively conversation of the loved Felix, were not for me. Miserable, unhappy wretch!

"Other lessons were impressed upon me even more deeply. I heard of the difference of sexes; of the birth and growth of children; how the father doated on the smiles of the infant, and the lively sallies of the older child; how all the life and cares of the mother were wrapt up in the precious charge; how the mind of youth expanded and gained knowledge; of brother, sister, and all the various relationships which bind one human being to another in mutual bonds.

"But where were my friends and relations? No father had watched my infant days, no mother had blessed me with smiles and caresses; or if they had, all my past life was now a blot, a blind vacancy in which I distinguished nothing. From my earliest remembrance I had been as I then was in height and proportion. I had never yet seen a being resembling me, or who claimed any intercourse with me. What was I? The question again recurred, to be answered only with groans.

"I will soon explain to what these feelings tended; but allow me now to return to the cottagers, whose story excited in me such various feelings of indignation, delight, and wonder, but which all terminated in additional love and reverence for my protectors (for so I loved, in an innocent, half painful self-deceit, to call them).

CHAPTER VI

"Some time elapsed before I learned the history of my friends. It was one which could not fail to impress itself deeply on my mind, unfolding as it did a number of circumstances each interesting and wonderful to one so utterly inexperienced as I was.

"The name of the old man was De Lacey. He was descended from a good family in France, where he had lived for many years in affluence, respected by his superiors, and beloved by his equals. His son was bred in the service of his country; and Agatha had ranked with ladies of the highest distinction. A few months before my arrival, they had lived in a large and luxurious city, called Paris, surrounded by friends, and possessed of every enjoyment which virtue, refinement of intellect, or taste, accompanied by a moderate fortune, could afford.

"The father of Safie had been the cause of their ruin. He was a Turkish merchant, and had inhabited Paris for many years, when, for some reason which I could not learn, he became obnoxious to the government. He was seized and cast into prison the very day that Safie arrived from Constantinople to join him. He was tried, and condemned to death. The injustice of his sentence was very flagrant; all Paris was indignant; and it was judged that his religion and wealth, rather than the crime alleged against him, had been the cause of his condemnation.

"Felix had been present at the trial; his horror and indignation were uncontrollable, when he heard the decision of the court. He made, at that moment, a solemn vow to deliver him, and then looked around for the means. After many fruitless attempts to gain admittance to the prison, he found a strongly grated window in an unguarded part of the building, which lighted the dungeon of the unfortunate Mahometan; who, loaded with chains, waited in despair the execution of the barbarous sentence. Felix visited the grate at night, and made known to the prisoner his intentions in his favour. The Turk, amazed and delighted, endeavoured to kindle the zeal of his deliverer by promises of reward and wealth. Felix rejected his offers with contempt; yet when he saw the lovely Safie, who was allowed to visit her father, and who, by her gestures, expressed her lively gratitude, the youth could not help owning to his own mind, that the captive possessed a treasure which would fully reward his toil and hazard.

"The Turk quickly perceived the impression that his daughter had made on the heart of Felix, and endeavoured to secure him more entirely in his interests by the promise of her hand in marriage, so soon as he should be conveyed to a place of safety. Felix was too delicate to accept this offer; yet he looked forward to the probability of that event as to the consummation of his happiness.

"During the ensuing days, while the preparations were going forward for the escape of the merchant, the zeal of Felix was warmed by several letters that he received from this lovely girl, who found means to express her thoughts in the language of her lover by the aid of an old man, a servant of her father's who understood French. She thanked him in the most ardent terms for his intended services towards her father; and at the same time she gently deplored her own fate.

"I have copies of these letters; for I found means, during my residence in the hovel, to procure the implements of writing; and the letters were often in the hands of Felix or Agatha. Before I depart, I will give them to you, they will prove the truth of my tale; but at present, as the sun is already far declined, I shall only have time to repeat the substance of them to you.

"Safie related, that her mother was a Christian Arab, seized and made a slave by the Turks; recommended by her beauty, she had won the heart of the father of Safie, who married her. The young girl spoke in high and enthusiastic terms of her mother, who, born in freedom spurned the bondage to which she was now reduced. She instructed her daughter in the tenets of her religion, and taught her to aspire to higher powers of intellect, and an independence of spirit, forbidden to the female followers of Mahomet. This lady died; but her lessons were indelibly impressed on the mind of Safie, who sickened at the prospect of again returning to Asia, and the being immured within the walls of a haram, allowed only to occupy herself with puerile amusements, ill suited to the temper of her soul, now accustomed to grand ideas and a noble emulation for virtue. The prospect of marrying a Christian, and remaining in a country where women were allowed to take a rank in society, was enchanting to her.

"The day for the execution of the Turk was fixed; but, on the night previous to it, he had quitted prison, and before morning was distant many leagues from Paris. Felix had procured passports in the name of his father, sister, and himself. He had previously communicated his plan to the former, who aided the deceit by quitting his house, under the pretence of a journey, and concealed himself, with his daughter, in an obscure part of Paris.

"Felix conducted the fugitives through France to Lyons, and across Mont Cenis to Leghorn, where the merchant had decided to wait a favourable opportunity of passing into some part of the Turkish dominions.

"Safie resolved to remain with her father until the moment of his departure, before which time the Turk renewed his promise that she should be united to his deliverer; and Felix remained with them in expectation of that event; and in the mean time he enjoyed the society of the Arabian, who exhibited towards him the simplest and tenderest affection. They conversed with one another through the means of an interpreter, and sometimes with the interpretation of looks; and Safie sang to him the divine airs of her native country.

"The Turk allowed this intimacy to take place, and encouraged the hopes of the youthful lovers, while in his heart he had formed far other plans. He loathed the idea that his daughter should be united to a Christian; but he feared the resentment of Felix if he should appear lukewarm; for he knew that he was still in the power of his deliverer, if he should choose to betray him to the Italian state which they inhabited. He revolved a thousand plans by which he should be enabled to prolong the deceit until it might be no longer necessary, and secretly to take his daughter with him when he departed. His plans were greatly facilitated by the news which arrived from Paris.

"The government of France were greatly enraged at the escape of their victim, and spared no pains to detect and punish his deliverer. The plot of Felix was quickly discovered, and De Lacey and Agatha were thrown into prison. The news reached Felix, and roused him from his dream of pleasure. His blind and aged father, and his gentle sister, lay in a noisome dungeon, while he enjoyed the free air, and the society of her whom he loved. This idea was torture to him. He quickly arranged with the Turk, that if the latter should find a favourable opportunity for escape before Felix could return to Italy, Safie should remain as a boarder at a convent at Leghorn; and then, quitting the lovely Arabian, he hastened to Paris, and delivered himself up to the vengeance of the law, hoping to free De Lacey and Agatha by this proceeding.

"He did not succeed. They remained confined for five months before the trial took place; the result of which deprived them of their fortune, and condemned them to a perpetual exile from their native country.

"They found a miserable asylum in the cottage in Germany, where I discovered them. Felix soon learned that the treacherous Turk, for whom he and his family endured such unheard-of oppression, on discovering that his deliverer was thus reduced to poverty and impotence, became a traitor to good feeling and honour, and had quitted Italy with his daughter, insultingly sending Felix a pittance of money to aid him, as he said, in some plan of future maintenance.

"Such were the events that preyed on the heart of Felix, and rendered him, when I first saw him, the most miserable of his family. He could have endured poverty, and when this distress had been the meed of his virtue, he would have gloried in it: but the ingratitude of the Turk, and the loss of his beloved Safie, were misfortunes more bitter and irreparable. The arrival of the Arabian now infused new life into his soul.

"When the news reached Leghorn, that Felix was deprived of his wealth and rank, the merchant commanded his daughter to think no more of her lover, but to prepare to return with him to her native country. The generous nature of Safie was outraged by this command; she attempted to expostulate with her father, but he left her angrily, reiterating his tyrannical mandate.

"A few days after, the Turk entered his daughter's apartment, and told her hastily, that he had reason to believe that his residence at Leghorn had been divulged, and that he should speedily be delivered up to the French government; he had, consequently, hired a vessel to convey him to Constantinople, for which city he should sail in a few hours. He intended to leave his daughter under the care of a confidential servant, to follow at her leisure with the greater part of his property, which had not yet arrived at Leghorn.

"When alone, Safie resolved in her own mind the plan of conduct that it would become her to pursue in this emergency. A residence in Turkey was abhorrent to her; her religion and feelings were alike adverse to it. By some papers of her father's, which fell into her hands, she heard of the exile of her lover, and learnt the name of the spot where he then resided. She hesitated some time, but at length she formed her determination. Taking with her some jewels that belonged to her, and a small sum of money, she quitted Italy, with an attendant, a native of Leghorn, but who understood the common language of Turkey, and departed for Germany.

"She arrived in safety at a town about twenty leagues from the cottage of De Lacey, when her attendant fell dangerously ill. Safie nursed her with the most devoted affection; but the poor girl died, and the Arabian was left alone, unacquainted with the language of the country, and utterly ignorant of the customs of the world. She fell, however, into good hands. The Italian had mentioned the name of the spot for which they were bound; and, after her death, the woman of the house in which they had lived took care that Safie should arrive in safety at the cottage of her lover.

CHAPTER VII

"Such was the history of my beloved cottagers. It impressed me deeply. I learned, from the views of social life which it developed, to admire their virtues, and to deprecate the vices of mankind.

"As yet I looked upon crime as a distant evil; benevolence and generosity were ever present before me, inciting within me a desire to become an actor in the busy scene where so many admirable qualities were called forth and displayed. But, in giving an account of the progress of my intellect, I must not omit a circumstance which occurred in the beginning of the month of August of the same year.

"One night, during my accustomed visit to the neighbouring wood, where I collected my own food, and brought home firing for my protectors, I found on the ground a leathern portmanteau, containing several articles of dress and some books. I eagerly seized the prize, and returned it to my hovel. Fortunately the books were written in the language the elements of which I had acquired at the cottage; they consisted of *Paradise Lost,* a volume of *Plutarch's Lives,* and the *Sorrows of Werter.*21 The possession of these treasures gave me extreme delight; I now continually studied and exercised my mind upon these histories, whilst my friends were employed in their ordinary occupations.

"I can hardly describe to you the effect of these books. They produced in me an infinity of new images and feelings, that sometimes raised me to ecstacy, but more frequently sunk me into the lowest dejection. In the *Sorrows of Werter,* besides the interest of its simple and affecting story, so many opinions are canvassed, and so many lights thrown upon what had hitherto been to me obscure subjects, that I found in it a never-ending source of speculation and astonishment. The gentle and domestic man-

21. Milton, *Paradise Lost*; Plutarch (?46–?120), *Parallel Lives*; J. W. von Goethe (1749–1832), *The Sorrows of Young Werther* (1774).

ners it described, combined with lofty sentiments and feelings, which had for their object something out of self, accorded well with my experience among my protectors, and with the wants which were for ever alive in my own bosom. But I thought Werter himself a more divine being than I had ever beheld or imagined; his character contained no pretension, but it sunk deep. The disquisitions upon death and suicide were calculated to fill me with wonder. I did not pretend to enter into the merits of the case, yet I inclined towards the opinions of the hero, whose extinction I wept, without precisely understanding it.

"As I read, however, I applied much personally to my own feelings and condition. I found myself similar, yet at the same time strangely unlike the beings concerning whom I read, and to whose conversation I was a listener. I sympathized with, and partly understood them, but I was un-formed in mind; I was dependent on none, and related to none. 'The path of my departure was free;'[22] and there was none to lament my anni-hilation. My person was hideous, and my stature gigantic: what did this mean? Who was I? What was I? Whence did I come? What was my des-tination? These questions continually recurred, but I was unable to solve them.

"The volume of *Plutarch's Lives* which I possessed, contained the his-tories of the first founders of the ancient republics. This book had a far different effect upon me from the *Sorrows of Werter*. I learned from Wer-ter's imaginations despondency and gloom: but Plutarch taught me high thoughts; he elevated me above the wretched sphere of my own reflec-tions, to admire and love the heroes of past ages. Many things I read surpassed my understanding and experience. I had a very confused knowl-edge of kingdoms, wide extents of country, mighty rivers, and boundless seas. But I was perfectly unacquainted with towns, and large assemblages of men. The cottage of my protectors had been the only school in which I had studied human nature; but this book developed new and mightier scenes of action. I read of men concerned in public affairs governing or massacring their species. I felt the greatest ardour for virtue rise within me, and abhorrence for vice, as far as I understood the signification of those terms, relative as they were, as I applied them, to pleasure and pain alone. Induced by these feelings, I was of course led to admire peaceable law-givers, Numa, Solon, and Lycurgus, in preference to Romulus and Theseus. The patriarchal lives of my protectors caused these impressions to take a firm hold on my mind; perhaps, if my first introduction to humanity had been made by a young soldier, burning for glory and slaughter, I should have been imbued with different sensations.

"But *Paradise Lost* excited different and far deeper emotions. I read it,

22. Paraphrased line from Percy B. Shelley's "Mutability" (1816).

as I had read the other volumes which had fallen into my hands, as a true history. It moved every feeling of wonder and awe, that the picture of an omnipotent God warring with his creatures was capable of exciting. I often referred the several situations, as their similarity struck me, to my own. Like Adam, I was created apparently united by no link to any other being in existence; but his state was far different from mine in every other respect. He had come forth from the hands of God a perfect creature, happy and prosperous, guarded by the especial care of his Creator; he was allowed to converse with, and acquire knowledge from beings of a superior nature: but I was wretched, helpless, and alone. Many times I considered Satan as the fitter emblem of my condition; for often, like him, when I viewed the bliss of my protectors, the bitter gall of envy rose within me.

"Another circumstance strengthened and confirmed these feelings. Soon after my arrival in the hovel, I discovered some papers in the pocket of the dress which I had taken from your laboratory. At first I had neglected them; but now that I was able to decypher the characters in which they were written, I began to study them with diligence. It was your journal of the four months that preceded my creation. You minutely described in these papers every step you took in the progress of your work; this history was mingled with accounts of domestic occurrences. You, doubtless, recollect these papers. Here they are. Every thing is related in them which bears reference to my accursed origin; the whole detail of that series of disgusting circumstances which produced it is set in view; the minutest description of my odious and loathsome person is given, in language which painted your own horrors, and rendered mine ineffaceable. I sickened as I read. 'Hateful day when I received life!' I exclaimed in agony. 'Cursed creator! Why did you form a monster so hideous that even you turned from me in disgust? God in pity made man beautiful and alluring, after his own image; but my form is a filthy type of your's, more horrid from its very resemblance. Satan had his companions, fellow-devils, to admire and encourage him; but I am solitary and detested.'

"These were the reflections of my hours of despondency and solitude; but when I contemplated the virtues of the cottagers, their amiable and benevolent dispositions, I persuaded myself that when they should become acquainted with my admiration of their virtues, they would compassionate me, and overlook my personal deformity. Could they turn from their door one, however monstrous, who solicited their compassion and friendship? I resolved, at least, not to despair, but in every way to fit myself for an interview with them which would decide my fate. I postponed this attempt for some months longer; for the importance attached to its success inspired me with a dread lest I should fail. Besides, I found that my understanding improved so much with every day's experience, that I was unwilling to commence this undertaking until a few more months should have added to my wisdom.

"Several changes, in the mean time, took place in the cottage. The presence of Safie diffused happiness among its inhabitants; and I also found that a greater degree of plenty reigned there. Felix and Agatha spent more time in amusement and conversation, and were assisted in their labours by servants. They did not appear rich, but they were contented and happy; their feelings were serene and peaceful, while mine became every day more tumultuous. Increase of knowledge only discovered to me more clearly what a wretched outcast I was. I cherished hope, it is true; but it vanished, when I beheld my person reflected in water, or my shadow in the moon-shine, even as that frail image and that inconstant shade.

"I endeavoured to crush these fears, and to fortify myself for the trial which in a few months I resolved to undergo; and sometimes I allowed my thoughts, unchecked by reason, to ramble in the fields of Paradise, and dared to fancy amiable and lovely creatures sympathizing with my feelings and cheering my gloom; their angelic countenances breathed smiles of consolation. But it was all a dream: no Eve soothed my sorrows, or shared my thoughts; I was alone. I remembered Adam's supplication to his Creator;[23] but where was mine? he had abandoned me, and, in the bitterness of my heart, I cursed him.

"Autumn passed thus. I saw, with surprise and grief, the leaves decay and fall, and nature again assume the barren and bleak appearance it had worn when I first beheld the woods and the lovely moon. Yet I did not heed the bleakness of the weather; I was better fitted by my conformation for the endurance of cold than heat. But my chief delights were the sight of the flowers, the birds, and all the gay apparel of summer; when those deserted me, I turned with more attention towards the cottagers. Their happiness was not decreased by the absence of summer. They loved, and sympathized with one another; and their joys, depending on each other, were not interrupted by the casualties that took place around them. The more I saw of them, the greater became my desire to claim their protection and kindness; my heart yearned to be known and loved by these amiable creatures: to see their sweet looks turned towards me with affection, was the utmost limit of my ambition. I dared not think that they would turn them from me with disdain and horror. The poor that stopped

23. Probably referring to *Paradise Lost* X.743–45, which Mary Shelley used as the epigraph to *Frankenstein*.

at their door were never driven away. I asked, it is true, for greater treasures than a little food or rest; I required kindness and sympathy; but I did not believe myself utterly unworthy of it.

"The winter advanced, and an entire revolution of the seasons had taken place since I awoke into life. My attention, at this time, was solely directed towards my plan of introducing myself into the cottage of my protectors. I revolved many projects; but that on which I finally fixed was, to enter the dwelling when the blind old man should be alone. I had sagacity enough to discover, that the unnatural hideousness of my person was the chief object of horror with those who had formerly beheld me. My voice, although harsh, had nothing terrible in it; I thought, therefore, that if, in the absence of his children, I could gain the good-will and mediation of the old De Lacey, I might, by his means, be tolerated by my younger protectors.

"One day, when the sun shone on the red leaves that strewed the ground, and diffused cheerfulness, although it denied warmth, Safie, Agatha, and Felix, departed on a long country walk, and the old man, at his own desire, was left alone in the cottage. When his children had departed, he took up his guitar, and played several mournful, but sweet airs, more sweet and mournful than I had ever heard him play before. At first his countenance was illuminated with pleasure, but, as he continued, thoughtfulness and sadness succeeded; at length, laying aside the instrument, he sat absorbed in reflection.

"My heart beat quick; this was the hour and moment of trial, which would decide my hopes, or realize my fears. The servants were gone to a neighbouring fair. All was silent in and around the cottage: it was an excellent opportunity; yet, when I proceeded to execute my plan, my limbs failed me, and I sunk to the ground. Again I rose; and, exerting all the firmness of which I was master, removed the planks which I had placed before my hovel to conceal my retreat. The fresh air revived me, and, with renewed determination, I approached the door of their cottage.

"I knocked. 'Who is there?' said the old man—'Come in.'

"I entered; 'Pardon this intrusion,' said I, 'I am a traveller in want of a little rest; you would greatly oblige me, if you would allow me to remain a few minutes before the fire.'

"'Enter,' said De Lacey; 'and I will try in what manner I can relieve your wants; but, unfortunately, my children are from home, and, as I am blind, I am afraid I shall find it difficult to procure food for you.'

"'Do not trouble yourself, my kind host, I have food; it is warmth and rest only that I need.'

"I sat down, and a silence ensued. I knew that every minute was precious to me, yet I remained irresolute in what manner to commence the interview; when the old man addressed me—

" 'By your language, stranger, I suppose you are my countryman;—are you French?'

" 'No; but I was educated by a French family, and understand that language only. I am now going to claim the protection of some friends, whom I sincerely love, and of whose favour I have some hopes.'

" 'Are these Germans?'

" 'No, they are French. But let us change the subject. I am an unfortunate and deserted creature; I look around, and I have no relation or friend upon earth. These amiable people to whom I go have never seen me, and know little of me. I am full of fears; for if I fail there, I am an outcast in the world for ever.'

" 'Do not despair. To be friendless is indeed to be unfortunate; but the hearts of men, when unprejudiced by any obvious self-interest, are full of brotherly love and charity. Rely, therefore, on your hopes; and if these friends are good and amiable, do not despair.'

" 'They are kind—they are the most excellent creatures in the world; but, unfortunately, they are prejudiced against me. I have good dispositions; my life has been hitherto harmless, and, in some degree, beneficial; but a fatal prejudice clouds their eyes, and where they ought to see a feeling and kind friend, they behold only a detestable monster.'

" 'That is indeed unfortunate; but if you are really blameless, cannot you undeceive them?'

" 'I am about to undertake that task; and it is on that account that I feel so many overwhelming terrors. I tenderly love these friends; I have, unknown to them, been for many months in the habits of daily kindness towards them; but they believe that I wish to injure them, and it is that prejudice which I wish to overcome.'

" 'Where do these friends reside?'

" 'Near this spot.'

"The old man paused, and then continued, 'If you will unreservedly confide to me the particulars of your tale, I perhaps may be of use in undeceiving them. I am blind, and cannot judge of your countenance, but there is something in your words which persuades me that you are sincere. I am poor, and an exile; but it will afford me true pleasure to be in any way serviceable to a human creature.'

" 'Excellent man! I thank you, and accept your generous offer. You raise me from the dust by this kindness; and I trust that, by your aid, I shall not be driven from the society and sympathy of your fellow-creatures.'

" 'Heaven forbid! even if you were really criminal; for that can only drive you to desperation, and not instigate you to virtue. I also am unfortunate; I and my family have been condemned, although innocent: judge, therefore, if I do not feel for your misfortunes.'

" 'How can I thank you, my best and only benefactor? from your lips first have I heard the voice of kindness directed towards me; I shall be for ever grateful; and your present humanity assures me of success with those friends whom I am on the point of meeting.'

" 'May I know the names and residence of those friends?'

"I paused. This, I thought, was the moment of decision, which was to rob me of, or bestow happiness on me for ever. I struggled vainly for firmness sufficient to answer him, but the effort destroyed all my remaining strength; I sank on the chair, and sobbed aloud. At that moment I heard the steps of my younger protectors. I had not a moment to lose; but, seizing the hand of the old man, I cried, 'Now is the time!—save and protect me! You and your family are the friends whom I seek. Do not you desert me in the hour of trial!'

" 'Great God!' exclaimed the old man, 'who are you?'

"At that instant the cottage door was opened, and Felix, Safie, and Agatha entered. Who can describe their horror and consternation on beholding me? Agatha fainted; and Safie, unable to attend to her friend, rushed out of the cottage. Felix darted forward, and with supernatural force tore me from his father, to whose knees I clung: in a transport of fury, he dashed me to the ground, and struck me violently with a stick. I could have torn him limb from limb, as the lion rends the antelope. But my heart sunk within me as with bitter sickness, and I refrained. I saw him on the point of repeating his blow, when, overcome by pain and anguish, I quitted the cottage, and in the general tumult escaped unperceived to my hovel.

CHAPTER VIII

"Cursed, cursed creator! Why did I live? Why, in that instant, did I not extinguish the spark of existence which you had so wantonly bestowed? I know not; despair had not yet taken possession of me; my feelings were those of rage and revenge. I could with pleasure have destroyed the cottage and its inhabitants, and have glutted myself with their shrieks and misery.

"When night came, I quitted my retreat, and wandered in the wood; and now, no longer restrained by the fear of discovery, I gave vent to my anguish in fearful howlings. I was like a wild beast that had broken the toils; destroying the objects that obstructed me, and ranging through the wood with a stag-like swiftness. Oh! what a miserable night I passed! the cold stars shone in mockery, and the bare trees waved their branches above me: now and then the sweet voice of a bird burst forth amidst the universal stillness. All, save I, were at rest or in enjoyment: I, like the arch fiend, bore a hell within me; and, finding myself unsympathized with, wished to tear up the trees, spread havoc and destruction around me, and then to have sat down and enjoyed the ruin.

"But this was a luxury of sensation that could not endure; I became fatigued with excess of bodily exertion, and sank on the damp grass in the sick impotence of despair. There was none among the myriads of men that existed who would pity or assist me; and should I feel kindness towards my enemies? No: from that moment I declared everlasting war against the species, and, more than all, against him who had formed me, and sent me forth to this insupportable misery.

"The sun rose; I heard the voices of men, and knew that it was impossible to return to my retreat during that day. Accordingly I hid myself in some thick underwood, determining to devote the ensuing hours to reflection on my situation.

"The pleasant sunshine, and the pure air of day, restored me to some degree of tranquillity; and when I considered what had passed at the cottage, I could not help believing that I had been too hasty in my conclusions. I had certainly acted imprudently. It was apparent that my conversation had interested the father in my behalf, and I was a fool in having exposed my person to the horror of his children. I ought to have familiarized the old De Lacey to me, and by degrees have discovered myself to the rest of his family, when they should have been prepared for my approach. But I did not believe my errors to be irretrievable; and, after much consideration, I resolved to return to the cottage, seek the old man, and by my representations win him to my party.

"These thoughts calmed me, and in the afternoon I sank into a profound sleep; but the fever of my blood did not allow me to be visited by peaceful dreams. The horrible scene of the preceding day was for ever acting before my eyes; the females were flying, and the enraged Felix tearing me from his father's feet. I awoke exhausted; and, finding that it was already night, I crept forth from my hiding-place, and went in search of food.

"When my hunger was appeased, I directed my steps towards the well-known path that conducted to the cottage. All there was at peace. I crept into my hovel, and remained in silent expectation of the accustomed hour when the family arose. That hour past, the sun mounted high in the heavens, but the cottagers did not appear. I trembled violently, apprehending some dreadful misfortune. The inside of the cottage was dark, and I heard no motion; I cannot describe the agony of this suspence.

"Presently two countrymen passed by; but, pausing near the cottage, they entered into conversation, using violent gesticulations; but I did not understand what they said, as they spoke the language of the country, which differed from that of my protectors. Soon after, however, Felix approached with another man: I was surprised, as I knew that he had not quitted the cottage that morning, and waited anxiously to discover, from his discourse, the meaning of these unusual appearances.

" 'Do you consider,' said his companion to him, 'that you will be obliged to pay three months' rent, and to lose the produce of your garden? I do not wish to take any unfair advantage, and I beg therefore that you will take some days to consider of your determination.'

" 'It is utterly useless,' replied Felix, 'we can never again inhabit your cottage. The life of my father is in the greatest danger, owing to the dreadful circumstance that I have related. My wife and my sister will never recover [from] their horror. I entreat you not to reason with me any more. Take possession of your tenement, and let me fly from this place.'

"Felix trembled violently as he said this. He and his companion entered the cottage, in which they remained for a few minutes, and then departed. I never saw any of the family of De Lacey more.

"I continued for the remainer of the day in my hovel in a state of utter and stupid despair. My protectors had departed, and had broken the only link that held me to the world. For the first time the feelings of revenge and hatred filled my bosom, and I did not strive to controul them; but, allowing myself to be borne away by the stream, I bent my mind towards injury and death. When I thought of my friends, of the mild voice of De Lacey, the gentle eyes of Agatha, and the exquisite beauty of the Arabian, these thoughts vanished, and a gush of tears somewhat soothed me. But again, when I reflected that they had spurned and deserted me, anger returned, a rage of anger; and, unable to injure any thing human, I turned my fury towards inanimate objects. As night advanced, I placed a variety of combustibles around the cottage; and, after having destroyed every vestige of cultivation in the garden, I waited with forced impatience until the moon had sunk to commence my operations.

"As the night advanced, a fierce wind arose from the woods, and quickly dispersed the clouds that had loitered in the heavens: the blast tore along like a mighty avalanche, and produced a kind of insanity in my spirits, that burst all bounds of reason and reflection. I lighted the dry branch of a tree, and danced with fury around the devoted cottage, my eyes still fixed on the western horizon, the edge of which the moon nearly touched. A part of its orb was at length hid, and I waved my brand; it sunk, and, with a loud scream, I fired the straw, and heath, and bushes, which I had collected. The wind fanned the fire, and the cottage was quickly enveloped by the flames, which clung to it, and licked it with their forked and destroying tongues.

"As soon as I was convinced that no assistance could save any part of the habitation, I quitted the scene, and sought for refuge in the woods.

"And now, with the world before me,[24] whither should I bend my steps? I resolved to fly far from the scene of my misfortunes; but to me, hated and despised, every country must be equally horrible. At length the thought of you crossed my mind. I learned from your papers that you were my father, my creator; and to whom could I apply with more fitness than to him who had given me life? Among the lessons that Felix had bestowed upon Safie geography had not been omitted: I had learned from these the relative situations of the different countries of the earth. You had mentioned Geneva as the name of your native town; and towards this place I resolved to proceed.

"But how was I to direct myself? I knew that I must travel in a southwesterly direction to reach my destination; but the sun was my only guide. I did not know the names of the towns that I was to pass through, nor could I ask information from a single human being; but I did not despair. From you only could I hope for succour, although towards you I felt no sentiment but that of hatred. Unfeeling, heartless creator! you had endowed me with perceptions and passions, and then cast me abroad an object for the scorn and horror of mankind. But on you only had I any claim for pity and redress, and from you I determined to seek that justice which I vainly attempted to gain from any other being that wore the human form.

"My travels were long, and the sufferings I endured intense. It was late in autumn when I quitted the district where I had so long resided. I travelled only at night, fearful of encountering the visage of a human being. Nature decayed around me, and the sun became heatless; rain and snow poured around me; mighty rivers were frozen; the surface of the earth was hard, and chill, and bare, and I found no shelter. Oh, earth! how often did I imprecate curses on the cause of my being! The mildness of my nature had fled, and all within me was turned to gall and bitterness. The nearer I approached to your habitation, the more deeply did I feel the spirit of revenge enkindled in my heart. Snow fell, and the waters were hardened, but I rested not. A few incidents now and then directed me, and I possessed a map of the country; but I often wandered wide from my path. The agony of my feelings allowed me no respite: no incident

24. Echo of "The World was all before them" from the conclusion of Milton's *Paradise Lost* XII.646.

occurred from which my rage and misery could not extract its food; but a circumstance that happened when I arrived on the confines of Switzerland, when the sun had recovered its warmth, and the earth again began to look green, confirmed in an especial manner the bitterness and horror of my feelings.

"I generally rested during the day, and travelled only when I was secured by night from the view of man. One morning, however, finding that my path lay through a deep wood, I ventured to continue my journey after the sun had risen; the day, which was one of the first of spring, cheered even me by the loveliness of its sunshine and the balminess of the air. I felt emotions of gentleness and pleasure, that had long appeared dead, revive within me. Half surprised by the novelty of these sensations, I allowed myself to be borne away by them; and, forgetting my solitude and deformity, dared to be happy. Soft tears again bedewed my cheeks, and I even raised my humid eyes with thankfulness towards the blessed sun which bestowed such joy upon me.

"I continued to wind among the paths of the wood, until I came to its boundary, which was skirted by a deep and rapid river, into which many of the trees bent their branches, now budding with the fresh spring. Here I paused, not exactly knowing what path to pursue, when I heard the sound of voices, that induced me to conceal myself under the shade of a cypress. I was scarcely hid, when a young girl came running towards the spot where I was concealed, laughing as if she ran from some one in sport. She continued her course along the precipitous sides of the river, when suddenly her foot slipt, and she fell into the rapid stream. I rushed from my hiding place, and, with extreme labour from the force of the current, saved her, and dragged her to shore. She was senseless; and I endeavoured, by every means in my power, to restore animation, when I was suddenly interrupted by the approach of a rustic, who was probably the person from whom she had playfully fled. On seeing me, he darted towards me, and, tearing the girl from my arms, hastened towards the deeper parts of the wood. I followed speedily, I hardly knew why; but when the man saw me draw near, he aimed a gun, which he carried, at my body, and fired. I sunk to the ground, and my injurer, with increased swiftness, escaped into the wood.

"This was then the reward of my benevolence! I had saved a human being from destruction, and, as a recompence, I now writhed under the miserable pain of a wound, which shattered the flesh and bone. The feelings of kindness and gentleness, which I had entertained but a few moments before, gave place to hellish rage and gnashing of teeth. Inflamed by pain, I vowed eternal hatred and vengeance to all mankind. But the agony of my wound overcame me; my pulses paused, and I fainted.

"For some weeks I led a miserable life in the woods, endeavouring to cure the wound which I had received. The ball had entered my shoulder, and I knew not whether it had remained there or passed through; at any rate I had no means of extracting it. My sufferings were augmented also by the oppressive sense of the injustice and ingratitude of their infliction. My daily vows rose for revenge—a deep and deadly revenge, such as would alone compensate for the outrages and anguish I had endured.

"After some weeks my wound healed, and I continued my journey. The labours I endured were no longer to be alleviated by the bright sun or gentle breezes of spring; all joy was but a mockery, which insulted my desolate state, and made me feel more painfully that I was not made for the enjoyment of pleasure.

"But my toils now drew near a close; and, two months from this time, I reached the environs of Geneva.

"It was evening when I arrived, and I retired to a hiding-place among the fields that surround it, to meditate in what manner I should apply to you. I was oppressed by fatigue and hunger, and far too unhappy to enjoy the gentle breezes of evening, or the prospect of the sun setting behind the stupendous mountains of Jura.

"At this time a slight sleep relieved me from the pain of reflection, which was disturbed by the approach of a beautiful child, who came running into the recess I had chosen with all the sportiveness of infancy. Suddenly, as I gazed on him, an idea seized me, that this little creature was unprejudiced, and had lived too short a time to have imbibed a horror of deformity. If, therefore, I could seize him, and educate him as my companion and friend, I should not be so desolate in this peopled earth.

"Urged by this impulse, I seized on the boy as he passed, and drew him towards me. As soon as he beheld my form, he placed his hands before his eyes, and uttered a shrill scream: I drew his hand forcibly from his face, and said, 'Child, what is the meaning of this? I do not intend to hurt you; listen to me.'

"He struggled violently; 'Let me go,' he cried; 'monster! ugly wretch! you wish to eat me, and tear me to pieces—You are an ogre—Let me go, or I will tell my papa.'

"'Boy, you will never see your father again; you must come with me.'

"'Hideous monster! let me go; My papa is a Syndic—he is M. Franken-stein—he would punish you. You dare not keep me.'

"'Frankenstein! you belong then to my enemy—to him towards whom I have sworn eternal revenge; you shall be my first victim.'

"The child still struggled, and loaded me with epithets which carried despair to my heart: I grasped his throat to silence him, and in a moment he lay dead at my feet.

"I gazed on my victim, and my heart swelled with exultation and hellish triumph: clapping my hands, I exclaimed, 'I, too, can create desolation; my enemy is not impregnable; this death will carry despair to him, and a thousand other miseries shall torment and destroy him.'

"As I fixed my eyes on the child, I saw something glittering on his breast. I took it; it was a portrait of a most lovely woman. In spite of my malignity, it softened and attracted me. For a few moments I gazed with delight on her dark eyes, fringed by deep lashes, and her lovely lips; but presently my rage returned: I remembered that I was for ever deprived of the delights that such beautiful creatures could bestow; and that she whose resemblance I contemplated would, in regarding me, have changed that air of divine benignity to one expressive of disgust and affright.

"Can you wonder that such thoughts transported me with rage? I only wonder that at that moment, instead of venting my sensations in exclamations and agony, I did not rush among mankind, and perish in the attempt to destroy them.

"While I was overcome by these feelings, I left the spot where I had committed the murder, and was seeking a more secluded hiding-place, when I perceived a woman passing near me. She was young, not indeed so beautiful as her whose portrait I held, but of an agreeable aspect, and blooming in the loveliness of youth and health. Here, I thought, is one of those whose smiles are bestowed on all but me; she shall not escape: thanks to the lessons of Felix, and the sanguinary laws of man, I have learned how to work mischief. I approached her unperceived, and placed the portrait securely in one of the folds of her dress.

"For some days I haunted the spot where these scenes had taken place; sometimes wishing to see you, sometimes resolved to quit the world and its miseries for ever. At length I wandered towards these mountains, and have ranged through their immense recesses, consumed by a burning passion which you alone can gratify. We may not part until you have promised to comply with my requisition. I am alone, and miserable; man will not associate with me; but one as deformed and horrible as myself would not deny herself to me. My companion must be of the same species, and have the same defects. This being you must create."

CHAPTER IX

The being finished speaking, and fixed his looks upon me in expectation of a reply. But I was bewildered, perplexed, and unable to arrange my ideas sufficiently to understand the full extent of his proposition. He continued—

"You must create a female for me, with whom I can live in the interchange of those sympathies necessary for my being. This you alone can do; and I demand it of you as a right which you must not refuse."

The latter part of his tale had kindled anew in me the anger that had died away while he narrated his peaceful life among the cottagers, and, as he said this, I could no longer suppress the rage that burned within me.

"I do refuse it," I replied; "and no torture shall ever extort a consent from me. You may render me the most miserable of men, but you shall never make me base in my own eyes. Shall I create another like yourself, whose joint wickedness might desolate the world. Begone! I have answered you; you may torture me, but I will never consent."

"You are in the wrong," replied the fiend; "and, instead of threatening, I am content to reason with you. I am malicious because I am miserable; am I not shunned and hated by all mankind? You, my creator, would tear me to pieces, and triumph; remember that, and tell me why I should pity man more than he pities me? You would not call it murder, if you could precipitate me into one of those ice-rifts, and destroy my frame, the work of your own hands. Shall I respect man, when he contemns me? Let him live with me in the interchange of kindness, and, instead of injury, I would bestow every benefit upon him with tears of gratitude at his acceptance. But that cannot be; the human senses are insurmountable barriers to our union. Yet mine shall not be the submission of abject slavery. I will revenge my injuries: if I cannot inspire love, I will cause fear; and chiefly towards you my arch-enemy, because my creator, do I swear inextinguishable hatred. Have a care: I will work at your destruction, nor finish until I desolate your heart, so that you curse the hour of your birth."

A fiendish rage animated him as he said this; his face was wrinkled into contortions too horrible for human eyes to behold; but presently he calmed himself, and proceeded—

"I intended to reason. This passion is detrimental to me; for you do not reflect that you are the cause of its excess. If any being felt emotions of benevolence towards me, I should return them an hundred and an hundred fold; for that one creature's sake, I would make peace with the whole kind! But I now indulge in dreams of bliss that cannot be realized. What I ask of you is reasonable and moderate; I demand a creature of another sex, but as hideous as myself: the gratification is small, but it is all that I can receive, and it shall content me. It is true, we shall be monsters, cut off from all the world; but on that account we shall be more attached to one another. Our lives will not be happy, but they will be harmless, and free from the misery I now feel. Oh! my creator, make me happy; let me feel gratitude towards you for one benefit! Let me see that I excite the sympathy of some existing thing; do not deny me my request!"

I was moved. I shuddered when I thought of the possible consequences of my consent; but I felt that there was some justice in his argument. His tale, and the feelings he now expressed, proved him to be a creature of fine sensations; and did I not, as his maker, owe him all the portion of happiness that it was in my power to bestow? He saw my change of feeling, and continued—

"If you consent, neither you nor any other human being shall ever see us again: I will go to the vast wilds of South America. My food is not that of man; I do not destroy the lamb and the kid, to glut my appetite; acorns and berries afford me sufficient nourishment. My companion will be of the same nature as myself, and will be content with the same fare. We shall make our bed of dried leaves; the sun will shine on us as on man, and will ripen our food. The picture I present to you is peaceful and human, and you must feel that you could deny it only in the wantonness of power and cruelty. Pitiless as you have been towards me, I now see compassion in your eyes; let me seize the favourable moment, and persuade you to promise what I so ardently desire."

"You propose," replied I, "to fly from the habitations of man, to dwell in those wilds where the beasts of the field will be your only companions. How can you, who long for the love and sympathy of man, persevere in this exile? You will return, and again seek their kindness, and you will meet with their detestation; your evil passions will be renewed, and you will then have a companion to aid you in the task of destruction. This may not be; cease to argue the point, for I cannot consent."

"How inconstant are your feelings! but a moment ago you were moved by my representations, and why do you again harden yourself to my complaints? I swear to you, by the earth which I inhabit, and by you that made me, that, with the companion you bestow, I will quit the neighbourhood of man, and dwell, as it may chance, in the most savage of places. My evil passions will have fled, for I shall meet with sympathy; my life will flow quietly away, and, in my dying moments, I shall not curse my maker."

His words had a strange effect upon me. I compassionated him, and sometimes felt a wish to console him; but when I looked upon him, when I saw the filthy mass that moved and talked, my heart sickened, and my feelings were altered to those of horror and hatred. I tried to stifle these sensations; I thought, that as I could not sympathize with him, I had no right to withhold from him the small portion of happiness which was yet in my power to bestow.

"You swear," I said, "to be harmless; but have you not already shewn a degree of malice that should reasonably make me distrust you? May not even this be a feint that will increase your triumph by affording a wider scope for your revenge?"

"How is this? I thought I had moved your compassion, and yet you still refuse to bestow on me the only benefit that can soften my heart, and render me harmless. If I have no ties and no affections, hatred and vice must be my portion; the love of another will destroy the cause of my crimes, and I shall become a thing, of whose existence every one will be ignorant. My vices are the children of a forced solitude that I abhor; and my virtues will necessarily arise when I live in communion with an equal. I shall feel the affections of a sensitive being, and become linked to the chain of existence and events, from which I am now excluded."

I paused some time to reflect on all he had related, and the various arguments which he had employed. I thought of the promise of virtues which he had displayed on the opening of his existence, and the subsequent blight of all kindly feeling by the loathing and scorn which his protectors had manifested towards him. His power and threats were not omitted in my calculations: a creature who could exist in the ice caves of the glaciers, and hide himself from pursuit among the ridges of inaccessible precipices, was a being possessing faculties it would be vain to cope with. After a long pause of reflection, I concluded, that the justice due both to him and my fellow-creatures demanded of me that I should comply with his request. Turning to him, therefore, I said—

"I consent to your demand, on your solemn oath to quit Europe for ever, and every other place in the neighbourhood of man, as soon as I shall deliver into your hands a female who will accompany you in your exile."

"I swear," he cried, "by the sun, and by the blue sky of heaven, that if you grant my prayer, while they exist you shall never behold me again. Depart to your home, and commence your labours: I shall watch their progress with unutterable anxiety; and fear not but that when you are ready I shall appear."

Saying this, he suddenly quitted me, fearful, perhaps, of any change in my sentiments. I saw him descend the mountain with greater speed than the flight of an eagle, and quickly lost him among the undulations of the sea of ice.

His tale had occupied the whole day; and the sun was upon the verge of the horizon when he departed. I knew that I ought to hasten my descent towards the valley, as I should soon be encompassed in darkness; but my heart was heavy, and my steps slow. The labour of winding among the little paths of the mountains, and fixing my feet firmly as I advanced, perplexed me, occupied as I was by the emotions which the occurrences of the day had produced. Night was far advanced, when I came to the half-way resting-place, and seated myself beside the fountain. The stars shone at intervals, as the clouds passed from over them; the dark pines rose before me, and every here and there a broken tree lay on the ground: it was a scene of wonderful solemnity, and stirred strange thoughts within me. I wept bitterly; and, clasping my hands in agony, I exclaimed, "Oh! stars, and clouds, and winds, ye are all about to mock me: if ye really pity me, crush sensation and memory; let me become as nought; but if not, depart, depart and leave me in darkness."

These were wild and miserable thoughts; but I cannot describe to you how the eternal twinkling of the stars weighed upon me, and how I listened to every blast of wind, as if it were a dull ugly siroc[25] on its way to consume me.

Morning dawned before I arrived at the village of Chamounix; but my presence, so haggard and strange, hardly calmed the fears of my family, who had waited the whole night in anxious expectation of my return.

The following day we returned to Geneva. The intention of my father in coming had been to divert my mind, and to restore me to my lost tranquillity; but the medicine had been fatal. And, unable to account for the excess of misery I appeared to suffer, he hastened to return home, hoping the quiet and monotony of a domestic life would by degrees alleviate my sufferings from whatsoever cause they might spring.

For myself, I was passive in all their arrangements; and the gentle affection of my beloved Elizabeth was inadequate to draw me from the depth of my despair. The promise I had made to the dæmon weighed upon my mind, like Dante's iron cowl on the heads of the hellish hypocrites. All pleasures of earth and sky passed before me like a dream, and that thought only had to me the reality of life. Can you wonder, that sometimes a kind of insanity possessed me, or that I saw continually about me a multitude of filthy animals inflicting on me incessant torture, that often extorted screams and bitter groans?

By degrees, however, these feelings became calmed. I entered again into the every-day scene of life, if not with interest, at least with some degree of tranquillity.

END OF VOL. II.

25. Variant spelling of "sirocco," an oppressively hot wind that blows from North Africa over the Mediterranean and Southern Europe.

Volume III

CHAPTER I

Day after day, week after week, passed away on my return to Geneva; and I could not collect the courage to recommence my work. I feared the vengeance of the disappointed fiend, yet I was unable to overcome my repugnance to the task which was enjoined me. I found that I could not compose a female without again devoting several months to profound study and laborious disquisition. I had heard of some discoveries having been made by an English philosopher, the knowledge of which was material to my success, and I sometimes thought of obtaining my father's consent to visit England for this purpose; but I clung to every pretence of delay, and could not resolve to interrupt my returning tranquillity. My health, which had hitherto declined, was now much restored; and my spirits, when unchecked by the memory of my unhappy promise, rose proportionably. My father saw this change with pleasure, and he turned his thoughts towards the best method of eradicating the remains of my melancholy, which every now and then would return by fits, and with a devouring blackness overcast the approaching sunshine. At these moments I took refuge in the most perfect solitude. I passed whole days on the lake alone in a little boat, watching the clouds, and listening to the rippling of the waves, silent and listless. But the fresh air and bright sun seldom failed to restore me to some degree of composure; and, on my return, I met the salutations of my friends with a readier smile and a more cheerful heart.

It was after my return from one of these rambles that my father, calling me aside, thus addressed me:—

"I am happy to remark, my dear son, that you have resumed your former pleasures, and seem to be returning to yourself. And yet you are still unhappy, and still avoid our society. For some time I was lost in conjecture as to the cause of this; but yesterday an idea struck me, and if it is well founded, I conjure you to avow it. Reserve on such a point would be not only useless, but draw down treble misery on us all."

I trembled violently at this exordium, and my father continued—

"I confess, my son, that I have always looked forward to your marriage with your cousin as the tie of our domestic comfort, and the stay of my declining years. You were attached to each other from your earliest infancy; you studied together, and appeared, in dispositions and tastes, entirely suited to one another. But so blind is the experience of man, that what I conceived to be the best assistants to my plan may have entirely destroyed it. You, perhaps, regard her as your sister, without any wish that she might become your wife. Nay, you may have met with another whom you may love; and, considering yourself as bound in honour to your cousin, this struggle may occasion the poignant misery which you appear to feel."

"My dear father, re-assure yourself. I love my cousin tenderly and sincerely. I never saw any woman who excited, as Elizabeth does, my warmest admiration and affection. My future hopes and prospects are entirely bound up in the expectation of our union."

"The expression of your sentiments on this subject, my dear Victor, gives me more pleasure than I have for some time experienced. If you feel thus, we shall assuredly be happy, however present events may cast a gloom over us. But it is this gloom, which appears to have taken so strong a hold of your mind, that I wish to dissipate. Tell me, therefore, whether you object to an immediate solemnization of the marriage. We have been unfortunate, and recent events have drawn us from that every-day tranquillity befitting my years and infirmities. You are younger; yet I do not suppose, possessed as you are of a competent fortune, that an early marriage would at all interfere with any future plans of honour and utility that you may have formed. Do not suppose, however, that I wish to dictate happiness to you, or that a delay on your part would cause me any serious uneasiness. Interpret my words with candour, and answer me, I conjure you, with confidence and sincerity."

I listened to my father in silence, and remained for some time incapable of offering any reply. I revolved rapidly in my mind a multitude of thoughts, and endeavoured to arrive at some conclusion. Alas! to me the idea of an immediate union with my cousin was one of horror and dismay. I was bound by a solemn promise, which I had not yet fulfilled, and dared not break; or, if I did, what manifold miseries might not impend over me and my devoted family! Could I enter into a festival with this deadly weight yet hanging round my neck, and bowing me to the ground. I must perform my engagement, and let the monster depart with his mate, before I allowed myself to enjoy the delight of an union from which I expected peace.

I remembered also the necessity imposed upon me of either journeying to England, or entering into a long correspondence with those philosophers of that country, whose knowledge and discoveries were of indispensable use to me in my present undertaking. The latter method of obtaining the desired intelligence was dilatory and unsatisfactory: besides, any variation was agreeable to me, and I was delighted with the idea of spending a year or two in change of scene and variety of occupation, in absence from my family; during which period some event might happen which would restore me to them in peace and happiness: my promise might be fulfilled, and the monster have departed; or some accident might occur to destroy him, and put an end to my slavery for ever.

These feelings dictated my answer to my father. I expressed a wish to visit England; but, concealing the true reasons of this request, I clothed my desires under the guise of wishing to travel and see the world before I sat down for life within the walls of my native town.

I urged my entreaty with earnestness, and my father was easily induced to comply; for a more indulgent and less dictatorial parent did not exist upon earth. Our plan was soon arranged. I should travel to Strasburgh, where Clerval would join me. Some short time would be spent in the towns of Holland, and our principal stay would be in England. We should return by France; and it was agreed that the tour should occupy the space of two years.

My father pleased himself with the reflection, that my union with Elizabeth should take place immediately on my return to Geneva. "These two years," said he, "will pass swiftly, and it will be the last delay that will oppose itself to your happiness. And, indeed, I earnestly desire that period to arrive, when we shall all be united, and neither hopes or fears arise to disturb our domestic calm."

"I am content," I replied, "with your arrangement. By that time we shall both have become wiser, and I hope happier, than we at present are." I sighed; but my father kindly forbore to question me further concerning the cause of my dejection. He hoped that new scenes, and the amusement of travelling, would restore my tranquillity.

I now made arrangements for my journey; but one feeling haunted me, which filled me with fear and agitation. During my absence I should leave my friends unconscious of the existence of their enemy, and unprotected from his attacks, exasperated as he might be by my departure. But he had promised to follow me wherever I might go; and would he not accompany me to England? This imagination was dreadful in itself, but soothing, inasmuch as it supposed the safety of my friends. I was agonized with the idea of the possibility that the reverse of this might happen. But through the whole period during which I was the slave of my creature, I allowed myself to be governed by the impulses of the moment; and my present sensations strongly intimated that the fiend would follow me, and exempt my family from the danger of his machinations.

It was in the latter end of August that I departed, to pass two years of exile. Elizabeth approved of the reasons of my departure, and only regretted that she had not the same opportunities of enlarging her experience, and cultivating her understanding. She wept, however, as she bade me farewell, and entreated me to return happy and tranquil. "We all," said she, "depend upon you; and if you are miserable, what must be our feelings?"

I threw myself into the carriage that was to convey me away, hardly knowing whither I was going, and careless of what was passing around. I remembered only, and it was with a bitter anguish that I reflected on it, to order that my chemical instruments should be packed to go with me: for I resolved to fulfil my promise while abroad, and return, if possible, a free man. Filled with dreary imaginations, I passed through many beautiful and majestic scenes; but my eyes were fixed and unobserving. I could only think of the bourne of my travels, and the work which was to occupy me whilst they endured.

After some days spent in listless indolence, during which I traversed many leagues, I arrived at Strasburgh, where I waited two days for Clerval. He came. Alas, how great was the contrast between us! He was alive to every new scene; joyful when he saw the beauties of the setting sun, and more happy when he beheld it rise, and recommence a new day. He pointed out to me the shifting colours of the landscape, and the appearances of the sky. "This is what it is to live;" he cried, "now I enjoy existence! But you, my dear Frankenstein, wherefore are you desponding and sorrowful?" In truth, I was occupied by gloomy thoughts, and neither saw the descent of the evening star, nor the golden sun-rise reflected in the Rhine.—And you, my friend, would be far more amused with the journal of Clerval, who observed the scenery with an eye of feeling and delight, than to listen to my reflections. I, a miserable wretch, haunted by a curse that shut up every avenue to enjoyment.

We had agreed to descend the Rhine in a boat from Strasburgh to Rotterdam, whence we might take shipping for London. During this voyage, we passed by many willowy islands, and saw several beautiful towns. We staid a day at Manheim, and, on the fifth from our departure from Strasburgh, arrived at Mayence. The course of the Rhine below Mayence becomes much more picturesque. The river descends rapidly, and winds between hills, not high, but steep, and of beautiful forms. We saw many ruined castles standing on the edges of precipices, surrounded by black woods, high and inaccesible. This part of the Rhine, indeed, presents a singularly variegated landscape. In one spot you view rugged hills, ruined castles overlooking tremendous precipices, with the dark Rhine rushing beneath; and, on the sudden turn of a promontory, flourishing vineyards, with green sloping banks, and a meandering river, and populous towns, occupy the scene.

We travelled at the time of the vintage, and heard the song of the labourers, as we glided down the stream. Even I, depressed in mind, and my spirits continually agitated by gloomy feelings, even I was pleased. I lay at the bottom of the boat, and, as I gazed on the cloudless blue sky, I seemed to drink in a tranquillity to which I had long been a stranger. And if these were my sensations, who can describe those of Henry? He felt as if he had been transported to Fairy-land, and enjoyed a happiness seldom tasted by man. "I have seen," he said, "the most beautiful scenes of my own country; I have visited the lakes of Lucerne and Uri, where the snowy mountains descend almost perpendicularly to the water, casting black and impenetrable shades, which would cause a gloomy and mournful appearance, were it not for the most verdant islands that relieve the eye by their gay appearance; I have seen this lake agitated by a tempest, when the wind tore up whirlwinds of water, and gave you an idea of what the water-spout must be on the great ocean, and the waves dash with fury the base of the mountain, where the priest and his mistress were overwhelmed by an avalanche, and where their dying voices are still said to be heard amid the pauses of the nightly wind; I have seen the mountains of La Valais, and the Pays de Vaud: but this country, Victor, pleases me more than all those wonders. The mountains of Switzerland are more majestic and strange; but there is a charm in the banks of this divine river, that I never before saw equalled. Look at that castle which overhangs yon precipice; and that also on the island, almost concealed amongst the foliage of those lovely trees; and now that group of labourers coming from among their vines; and that village half-hid in the recess of the mountain. Oh, surely, the spirit that inhabits and guards this place has a soul more in harmony with man, than those who pile the glacier, or retire to the inaccessible peaks of the mountains of our own country."

Clerval! beloved friend! even now it delights me to record your words, and to dwell on the praise of which you are so eminently deserving. He was a being formed in the "very poetry of nature."[26] His wild and enthusiastic imagination was chastened by the sensibility of his heart. His soul overflowed with ardent affections, and his friendship was of that devoted and wondrous nature that the worldly-minded teach us to look for only in the imagination. But even human sympathies were not sufficient

26. Leigh Hunt's "Rimini." [Mary Shelley's note referring to Leigh Hunt (1784–1859), *The Story of Rimini, A Poem* (1816) II.47.]

to satisfy his eager mind. The scenery of external nature, which others regard only with admiration, he loved with ardour:

> ———— The sounding cataract
> Haunted *him* like a passion: the tall rock,
> The mountain, and the deep and gloomy wood,
> Their colours and their forms, were then to him
> An appetite; a feeling, and a love,
> That had no need of a remoter charm,
> By thought supplied, or any interest
> Unborrowed from the eye.[27]

And where does he now exist? Is this gentle and lovely being lost for ever? Has this mind so replete with ideas, imaginations fanciful and magnificent, which formed a world, whose existence depended on the life of its creator; has this mind perished? Does it now only exist in my memory? No, it is not thus; your form so divinely wrought, and beaming with beauty, has decayed, but your spirit still visits and consoles your unhappy friend.

Pardon this gush of sorrow; these ineffectual words are but a slight tribute to the unexampled worth of Henry, but they soothe my heart, overflowing with the anguish which his remembrance creates. I will proceed with my tale.

Beyond Cologne we descended to the plains of Holland; and we resolved to post the remainder of our way; for the wind was contrary, and the stream of the river was too gentle to aid us.

Our journey here lost the interest arising from beautiful scenery; but we arrived in a few days at Rotterdam, whence we proceeded by sea to England. It was on a clear morning, in the latter days of December,[28] that I first saw the white cliffs of Britain. The banks of the Thames presented a new scene; they were flat, but fertile, and almost every town was marked by the remembrance of some story. We saw Tilbury Fort, and remembered the Spanish armada; Gravesend, Woolwich, and Greenwich, places which I had heard of even in my country.

At length we saw the numerous steeples of London, St. Paul's towering above all, and the Tower famed in English history.

27. Wordsworth's "Tintern Abbey." [Mary Shelley's note referring to William Wordsworth (1770–1850), "Lines Written a Few Miles Above Tintern Abbey," published in *Lyrical Ballads* (1798).]

28. But see the fifth paragraph of the next chapter, where Mary Shelley specifies "the beginning of October" for arriving in England.

CHAPTER II

London was our present point of rest; we determined to remain several months in this wonderful and celebrated city. Clerval desired the intercourse of the men of genius and talent who flourished at this time; but this was with me a secondary object; I was principally occupied with the means of obtaining the information necessary for the completion of my promise, and quickly availed myself of the letters of introduction that I had brought with me, addressed to the most distinguished natural philosophers.

If this journey had taken place during my days of study and happiness, it would have afforded me inexpressible pleasure. But a blight had come over my existence, and I only visited these people for the sake of the information they might give me on the subject in which my interest was so terribly profound. Company was irksome to me; when alone, I could fill my mind with the sights of heaven and earth; the voice of Henry soothed me, and I could thus cheat myself into a transitory peace. But busy uninteresting joyous faces brought back despair to my heart. I saw an insurmountable barrier placed between me and my fellow-men; this barrier was sealed with the blood of William and Justine; and to reflect on the events connected with those names filled my soul with anguish.

But in Clerval I saw the image of my former self; he was inquisitive, and anxious to gain experience and instruction. The difference of manners which he observed was to him an inexhaustible source of instruction and amusement. He was for ever busy; and the only check to his enjoyments was my sorrowful and dejected mien. I tried to conceal this as much as possible, that I might not debar him from the pleasures natural to one who was entering on a new scene of life, undisturbed by any care or bitter recollection. I often refused to accompany him, alleging another engagement, that I might remain alone. I now also began to collect the materials necessary for my new creation, and this was to me like the torture of single drops of water continually falling on the head. Every thought that was devoted to it was an extreme anguish, and every word that I spoke in allusion to it caused my lips to quiver, and my heart to palpitate.

After passing some months in London, we received a letter from a person in Scotland, who had formerly been our visitor at Geneva. He mentioned the beauties of his native country, and asked us if those were not sufficient allurements to induce us to prolong our journey as far north as Perth, where he resided. Clerval eagerly desired to accept this invitation; and I, although I abhorred society, wished to view again mountains and streams, and all the wondrous works with which Nature adorns her chosen dwelling-places.

We had arrived in England at the beginning of October, and it was now February. We accordingly determined to commence our journey towards the north at the expiration of another month. In this expedition we did not intend to follow the great road to Edinburgh, but to visit Windsor, Oxford, Matlock, and the Cumberland lakes, resolving to arrive at the completion of this tour about the end of July. I packed my chemical instruments, and the materials I had collected, resolving to finish my labours in some obscure nook in the northern highlands of Scotland.

We quitted London on the 27th of March, and remained a few days at Windsor, rambling in its beautiful forest. This was a new scene to us mountaineers; the majestic oaks, the quantity of game, and the herds of stately deer, were all novelties to us.

From thence we proceeded to Oxford. As we entered this city, our minds were filled with the remembrance of the events that had been transacted there more than a century and a half before. It was here that Charles I. had collected his forces. This city had remained faithful to him, after the whole nation had forsaken his cause to join the standard of parliament and liberty. The memory of that unfortunate king, and his companions, the amiable Falkland, the insolent Goring,[29] his queen, and son, gave a peculiar interest to every part of the city, which they might be supposed to have inhabited. The spirit of elder days found a dwelling here, and we delighted to trace its footsteps. If these feelings had not found an imaginary gratification, the appearance of the city had yet in itself sufficient beauty to obtain our admiration. The colleges are ancient and picturesque; the streets are almost magnificent; and the lovely Isis, which flows beside it through meadows of exquisite verdure, is spread forth into a placid expanse of waters, which reflects its majestic assemblage of towers, and spires, and domes, embosomed among aged trees.

I enjoyed this scene; and yet my enjoyment was embittered both by the memory of the past, and the anticipation of the future. I was formed for peaceful happiness. During my youthful days discontent never visited my mind; and if I was ever overcome by *ennui*, the sight of what is beautiful in nature, or the study of what is excellent and sublime in the productions of man, could always interest my heart, and communicate elasticity to my spirits. But I am a blasted tree; the bolt has entered my soul; and I felt then that I should survive to exhibit, what I shall soon cease to be—a

---

29. Incorrectly named as "Gower" in 1818; Mary Shelley corrected the error in 1831, naming instead George, Baron Goring (1608–57), a general who supported Charles I (1600–1649), whose amiable secretary of state was Lucius Cary, 2d Viscount Falkland (1610–43).

miserable spectacle of wrecked humanity, pitiable to others, and abhorrent to myself.

We passed a considerable period at Oxford, rambling among its environs, and endeavouring to identify every spot which might relate to the most animating epoch of English history. Our little voyages of discovery were often prolonged by the successive objects that presented themselves. We visited the tomb of the illustrious Hampden,[30] and the field on which that patriot fell. For a moment my soul was elevated from its debasing and miserable fears to contemplate the divine ideas of liberty and self-sacrifice, of which these sights were the monuments and the remembrancers. For an instant I dared to shake off my chains, and look around me with a free and lofty spirit; but the iron had eaten into my flesh, and I sank again, trembling and hopeless, into my miserable self.

We left Oxford with regret, and proceeded to Matlock, which was our next place of rest. The country in the neighbourhood of this village resembled, to a greater degree, the scenery of Switzerland; but every thing is on a lower scale, and the green hills want the crown of distant white Alps, which always attend on the piny mountains of my native country. We visited the wondrous cave, and the little cabinets of natural history, where the curiosities are disposed in the same manner as in the collections at Servox and Chamounix. The latter name made me tremble, when pronounced by Henry; and I hastened to quit Matlock, with which that terrible scene was thus associated.

From Derby still journeying northward, we passed two months in Cumberland and Westmoreland. I could now almost fancy myself among the Swiss mountains. The little patches of snow which yet lingered on the northern sides of the mountains, the lakes, and the dashing of the rocky streams, were all familiar and dear sights to me. Here also we made some acquaintances, who almost contrived to cheat me into happiness. The delight of Clerval was proportionably greater than mine; his mind expanded in the company of men of talent, and he found in his own nature greater capacities and resources than he could have imagined himself to have possessed while he associated with his inferiors. "I could pass my life here," said he to me; "and among these mountains I should scarcely regret Switzerland and the Rhine."

But he found that a traveller's life is one that includes much pain amidst its enjoyments. His feelings are for ever on the stretch; and when he begins to sink into repose, he finds himself obliged to quit that on which he rests in pleasure for something new, which again engages his attention, and which also he forsakes for other novelties.

---

30. John Hampden (1594–1643), cousin of Oliver Cromwell, who died near Oxford in the English Civil Wars.

We had scarcely visited the various lakes of Cumberland and West-moreland, and conceived an affection for some of the inhabitants, when the period of our appointment with our Scotch friend approached, and we left them to travel on. For my own part I was not sorry. I had now neglected my promise for some time, and I feared the effects of the dæmon's disappointment. He might remain in Switzerland, and wreak his vengeance on my relatives. This idea pursued me, and tormented me at every moment from which I might otherwise have snatched repose and peace. I waited for my letters with feverish impatience: if they were delayed, I was miserable, and overcome by a thousand fears; and when they arrived, and I saw the superscription of Elizabeth or my father, I hardly dared to read and ascertain my fate. Sometimes I thought that the fiend followed me, and might expedite my remissness by murdering my companion. When these thoughts possessed me, I would not quit Henry for a moment, but followed him as his shadow, to protect him from the fancied rage of his destroyer. I felt as if I had committed some great crime, the consciousness of which haunted me. I was guiltless, but I had indeed drawn down a horrible curse upon my head, as mortal as that of crime.

I visited Edinburgh with languid eyes and mind; and yet that city might have interested the most unfortunate being. Clerval did not like it so well as Oxford; for the antiquity of the latter city was more pleasing to him. But the beauty and regularity of the new town of Edinburgh, its romantic castle, and its environs, the most delightful in the world, Arthur's Seat, St. Bernard's Well, and the Pentland Hills, compensated him for the change, and filled him with cheerfulness and admiration. But I was impatient to arrive at the termination of my journey.

We left Edinburgh in a week, passing through Coupar, St. Andrews, and along the banks of the Tay, to Perth, where our friend expected us. But I was in no mood to laugh and talk with strangers, or enter into their feelings or plans with the good humour expected from a guest; and ac-cordingly I told Clerval that I wished to make the tour of Scotland alone. "Do you," said I, "enjoy yourself, and let this be our rendezvous. I may be absent a month or two; but do not interfere with my motions, I en-treat you: leave me to peace and solitude for a short time; and when I return, I hope it will be with a lighter heart, more congenial to your own temper."

Henry wished to dissuade me; but, seeing me bent on this plan, ceased to remonstrate. He entreated me to write often. "I had rather be with you," he said, "in your solitary rambles, than with these Scotch people, whom I do not know: hasten then, my dear friend, to return, that I may again feel myself somewhat at home, which I cannot do in your absence."

Having parted from my friend, I determined to visit some remote spot of Scotland, and finish my work in solitude. I did not doubt but that the monster followed me, and would discover himself to me when I should have finished, that he might receive his companion.

With this resolution I traversed the northern highlands, and fixed on one of the remotest of the Orkneys as the scene [of my] labours. It was a place fitted for such a work, being hardly more than a rock, whose high sides were continually beaten upon by the waves. The soil was barren, scarcely affording pasture for a few miserable cows, and oatmeal for its inhabitants, which consisted of five persons, whose gaunt and scraggy limbs gave tokens of their miserable fare. Vegetables and bread, when they indulged in such luxuries, and even fresh water, was to be procured from the main land, which was about five miles distant.

On the whole island there were but three miserable huts, and one of these was vacant when I arrived. This I hired. It contained but two rooms, and these exhibited all the squalidness of the most miserable penury. The thatch had fallen in, the walls were unplastered, and the door was off its hinges. I ordered it to be repaired, bought some furniture, and took possession; an incident which would, doubtless, have occasioned some surprise, had not all the senses of the cottagers been benumbed by want and squalid poverty. As it was, I lived ungazed at and unmolested, hardly thanked for the pittance of food and clothes which I gave; so much does suffering blunt even the coarsest sensations of men.

In this retreat I devoted the morning to labour; but in the evening, when the weather permitted, I walked on the stony beach of the sea, to listen to the waves as they roared, and dashed at my feet. It was a monotonous, yet ever-changing scene. I thought of Switzerland; it was far different from this desolate and appalling landscape. Its hills are covered with vines, and its cottages are scattered thickly in the plains. Its fair lakes reflect a blue and gentle sky; and, when troubled by the winds, their tumult is but as the play of a lively infant, when compared to the roarings of the giant ocean.

In this manner I distributed my occupations when I first arrived; but, as I proceeded in my labour, it became every day more horrible and irksome to me. Sometimes I could not prevail on myself to enter my laboratory for several days; and at other times I toiled day and night in order to complete my work. It was indeed a filthy process in which I was engaged. During my first experiment, a kind of enthusiastic frenzy had blinded me to the horror of my employment; my mind was intently fixed on the sequel of my labour, and my eyes were shut to the horror of my proceedings. But now I went to it in cold blood, and my heart often sickened at the work of my hands.

Thus situated, employed in the most detestable occupation, immersed in a solitude where nothing could for an instant call my attention from the actual scene in which I was engaged, my spirits became unequal; I grew restless and nervous. Every moment I feared to meet my persecutor. Sometimes I sat with my eyes fixed on the ground, fearing to raise them lest they should encounter the object which I so much dreaded to behold. I feared to wander from the sight of my fellow-creatures, lest when alone he should come to claim his companion.

In the mean time I worked on, and my labour was already considerably advanced. I looked towards its completion with a tremulous and eager hope, which I dared not trust myself to question, but which was intermixed with obscure forebodings of evil, that made my heart sicken in my bosom.

CHAPTER III

I sat one evening in my laboratory; the sun had set, and the moon was just rising from the sea; I had not sufficient light for my employment, and I remained idle, in a pause of consideration of whether I should leave my labour for the night, or hasten its conclusion by an unremitting attention to it. As I sat, a train of reflection occurred to me, which led me to consider the effects of what I was now doing. Three years before I was engaged in the same manner, and had created a fiend whose unparalleled barbarity had desolated my heart, and filled it for ever with the bitterest remorse. I was now about to form another being, of whose dispositions I was alike ignorant; she might become ten thousand times more malignant than her mate, and delight, for its own sake, in murder and wretchedness. He had sworn to quit the neighbourhood of man, and hide himself in deserts; but she had not; and she, who in all probability was to become a thinking and reasoning animal, might refuse to comply with a compact made before her creation. They might even hate each other; the creature who already lived loathed his own deformity, and might he not conceive a greater abhorrence for it when it came before his eyes in the female form? She also might turn with disgust from him to the superior beauty of man; she might quit him, and he be again alone, exasperated by the fresh provocation of being deserted by one of his own species.

Even if they were to leave Europe, and inhabit the deserts of the new world, yet one of the first results of those sympathies for which the dæmon thirsted would be children, and a race of devils would be propagated upon the earth, who might make the very existence of the species of man a condition precarious and full of terror. Had I a right, for my own benefit, to inflict this curse upon everlasting generations? I had before been moved by the sophisms of the being I had created; I had been struck senseless by his fiendish threats: but now, for the first time, the wickedness of my promise burst upon me; I shuddered to think that future ages might curse me as their pest, whose selfishness had not hesitated to buy its own peace at the price perhaps of the existence of the whole human race.

I trembled, and my heart failed within me; when, on looking up, I saw, by the light of the moon, the dæmon at the casement. A ghastly grin wrinkled his lips as he gazed on me, where I sat fulfilling the task which he had allotted to me. Yes, he had followed me in my travels; he had loitered in forests, hid himself in caves, or taken refuge in wide and desert heaths; and he now came to mark my progress, and claim the fulfilment of my promise.

As I looked on him, his countenance expressed the utmost extent of malice and treachery. I thought with a sensation of madness on my promise of creating another like to him, and, trembling with passion, tore to pieces the thing on which I was engaged. The wretch saw me destroy the creature on whose future existence he depended for happiness, and, with a howl of devilish despair and revenge, withdrew.

I left the room, and, locking the door, made a solemn vow in my own heart never to resume my labours; and then, with trembling steps, I sought my own apartment. I was alone; none were near me to dissipate the gloom, and relieve me from the sickening oppression of the most terrible reveries.

Several hours past, and I remained near my window gazing on the sea; it was almost motionless, for the winds were hushed, and all nature reposed under the eye of the quiet moon. A few fishing vessels alone specked the water, and now and then the gentle breeze wafted the sound of voices, as the fishermen called to one another. I felt the silence, although I was hardly conscious of its extreme profundity until my ear was suddenly arrested by the paddling of oars near the shore, and a person landed close to my house.

In a few minutes after, I heard the creaking of my door, as if some one endeavoured to open it softly. I trembled from head to foot; I felt a presentiment of who it was, and wished to rouse one of the peasants who dwelt in a cottage not far from mine; but I was overcome by the sensation of helplessness, so often felt in frightful dreams, when you in vain endeavour to fly from an impending danger, and was rooted to the spot.

Presently I heard the sound of footsteps along the passage; the door opened, and the wretch whom I dreaded appeared. Shutting the door, he approached me, and said, in a smothered voice—

"You have destroyed the work which you began; what is it that you intend? Do you dare to break your promise? I have endured toil and misery: I left Switzerland with you; I crept along the shores of the Rhine, among its willow islands, and over the summits of its hills. I have dwelt many months in the heaths of England, and among the deserts of Scotland. I have endured incalculable fatigue, and cold, and hunger; do you dare destroy my hopes?"

"Begone! I do break my promise; never will I create another like yourself, equal in deformity and wickedness."

"Slave, I before reasoned with you, but you have proved yourself unworthy of my condescension. Remember that I have power; you believe yourself miserable, but I can make you so wretched that the light of day will be hateful to you. You are my creator, but I am your master;—obey!"

"The hour of my weakness is past, and the period of your power is arrived. Your threats cannot move me to do an act of wickedness; but they confirm me in a resolution of not creating you a companion in vice. Shall I, in cool blood, set loose upon the earth a dæmon, whose delight is in death and wretchedness. Begone! I am firm, and your words will only exasperate my rage."

The monster saw my determination in my face, and gnashed his teeth in the impotence of anger. "Shall each man," cried he, "find a wife for his bosom, and each beast have his mate, and I be alone? I had feelings of affection, and they were requited by detestation and scorn. Man, you may hate; but beware! Your hours will pass in dread and misery, and soon the bolt will fall which must ravish from you your happiness for ever. Are you to be happy, while I grovel in the intensity of my wretchedness? You can blast my other passions; but revenge remains—revenge, henceforth dearer than light or food! I may die; but first you, my tyrant and tormentor, shall curse the sun that gazes on your misery. Beware; for I am fearless, and therefore powerful. I will watch with the wiliness of a snake, that I may sting with its venom. Man, you shall repent of the injuries you inflict."

"Devil, cease; and do not poison the air with these sounds of malice. I have declared my resolution to you, and I am no coward to bend beneath words. Leave me; I am inexorable."

"It is well. I go; but remember, I shall be with you on your wedding-night."

I started forward, and exclaimed, "Villain! before you sign my death-warrant, be sure that you are yourself safe."

I would have seized him; but he eluded me, and quitted the house with precipitation: in a few moments I saw him in his boat, which shot across the waters with an arrowy swiftness, and was soon lost amidst the waves.

All was again silent; but his words rung in my ears. I burned with rage to pursue the murderer of my peace, and precipitate him into the ocean. I walked up and down my room hastily and perturbed, while my imagination conjured up a thousand images to torment and sting me. Why had I not followed him, and closed with him in mortal strife? But I had suffered him to depart, and he had directed his course towards the main land. I shuddered to think who might be the next victim sacrificed to his insatiate revenge. And then I thought again of his words—"*I will be with you on your wedding-night.*" That then was the period fixed for the fulfilment of my destiny. In that hour I should die, and at once satisfy and extinguish his malice. The prospect did not move me to fear; yet when I thought of my beloved Elizabeth,—of her tears and endless sorrow, when she should find her lover so barbarously snatched from her,—tears, the first I had shed for many months, streamed from my eyes, and I resolved not to fall before my enemy without a bitter struggle.

The night passed away, and the sun rose from the ocean; my feelings became calmer, if it may be called calmness, when the violence of rage sinks into the depths of despair. I left the house, the horrid scene of the last night's contention, and walked on the beach of the sea, which I almost regarded as an insuperable barrier between me and my fellow-creatures; nay, a wish that such should prove the fact stole across me. I desired that I might pass my life on that barren rock, wearily it is true, but uninterrupted by any sudden shock of misery. If I returned, it was to be sacrificed, or to see those whom I most loved die under the grasp of a dæmon whom I had myself created.

I walked about the isle like a restless spectre, separated from all it loved, and miserable in the separation. When it became noon, and the sun rose higher, I lay down on the grass, and was overpowered by a deep sleep. I had been awake the whole of the preceding night, my nerves were agitated, and my eyes inflamed by watching and misery. The sleep into which I now sunk refreshed me; and when I awoke, I again felt as if I belonged to a race of human beings like myself, and I began to reflect upon what had passed with greater composure; yet still the words of the fiend rung in my ears like a death-knell, they appeared like a dream, yet distinct and oppressive as a reality.

The sun had far descended, and I still sat on the shore, satisfying my appetite, which had become ravenous, with an oaten cake, when I saw a fishing-boat land close to me, and one of the men brought me a packet; it contained letters from Geneva, and one from Clerval, entreating me to join him. He said that nearly a year had elapsed since we had quitted Switzerland, and France was yet unvisited. He entreated me, therefore, to leave my solitary isle, and meet him at Perth, in a week from that time, when we might arrange the plan of our future proceedings. This letter in a degree recalled me to life, and I determined to quit my island at the expiration of two days.

Yet, before I departed, there was a task to perform, on which I shuddered to reflect: I must pack my chemical instruments; and for that purpose I must enter the room which had been the scene of my odious work, and I must handle those utensils, the sight of which was sickening to me. The next morning, at day-break, I summoned sufficient courage, and unlocked the door of my laboratory. The remains of the half-finished creature, whom I had destroyed, lay scattered on the floor, and I almost felt as if I had mangled the living flesh of a human being. I paused to collect myself, and then entered the chamber. With trembling hand I conveyed the instruments out of the room; but I reflected that I ought not to leave the relics of my work to excite the horror and suspicion of the peasants, and I accordingly put them into a basket, with a great quantity of stones, and laying them up, determined to throw them into the sea that very night; and in the mean time I sat upon the beach, employed in cleaning and arranging my chemical apparatus.

Nothing could be more complete than the alteration that had taken place in my feelings since the night of the appearance of the dæmon. I had before regarded my promise with a gloomy despair, as a thing that, with whatever consequences, must be fulfilled; but I now felt as if a film had been taken from before my eyes, and that I, for the first time, saw clearly. The idea of renewing my labours did not for one instant occur to me; the threat I had heard weighed on my thoughts, but I did not reflect that a voluntary act of mine could avert it. I had resolved in my own mind, that to create another like the fiend I had first made would be an act of the basest and most atrocious selfishness; and I banished from my mind every thought that could lead to a different conclusion.

Between two and three in the morning the moon rose; and I then, putting my basket aboard a little skiff, sailed out about four miles from the shore. The scene was perfectly solitary: a few boats were returning towards land, but I sailed away from them. I felt as if I was about the commission of a dreadful crime, and avoided with shuddering anxiety any encounter with my fellow-creatures. At one time the moon, which had before been clear, was suddenly overspread by a thick cloud, and I took advantage of the moment of darkness, and cast my basket into the sea; I listened to the gurgling sound as it sunk, and then sailed away from the spot. The sky became clouded; but the air was pure, although chilled by the north-east breeze that was then rising. But it refreshed me, and filled me with such agreeable sensations, that I resolved to prolong my stay on the water, and fixing the rudder in a direct position, stretched myself at the bottom of the boat. Clouds hid the moon, every thing was obscure, and I heard only the sound of the boat, as its keel cut through the waves; the murmur lulled me, and in a short time I slept soundly.

I do not know how long I remained in this situation, but when I awoke I found that the sun had already mounted considerably. The wind was high, and the waves continually threatened the safety of my little skiff. I found that the wind was north-east, and must have driven me far from the coast from which I had embarked. I endeavoured to change my course, but quickly found that if I again made the attempt the boat would be instantly filled with water. Thus situated, my only resource was to drive before the wind. I confess that I felt a few sensations of terror. I had no compass with me, and was so little acquainted with the geography of this part of the world that the sun was of little benefit to me. I might be driven into the wide Atlantic, and feel all the tortures of starvation, or be swallowed up in the immeasurable waters that roared and buffeted around me. I had already been out many hours, and felt the torment of a burning thirst, a prelude to my other sufferings. I looked on the heavens, which were covered by clouds that flew before the wind only to be replaced by others: I looked upon the sea, it was to be my grave. "Fiend," I exclaimed, "your task is already fulfilled!" I thought of Elizabeth, of my father, and of Clerval; and sunk into a reverie, so despairing and frightful, that even now, when the scene is on the point of closing before me for ever, I shudder to reflect on it.

Some hours passed thus; but by degrees, as the sun declined towards the horizon, the wind died away into a gentle breeze, and the sea became free from breakers. But these gave place to a heavy swell; I felt sick, and hardly able to hold the rudder, when suddenly I saw a line of high land towards the south.

Almost spent, as I was, by fatigue, and the dreadful suspense I endured for several hours, this sudden certainty of life rushed like a flood of warm joy to my heart, and tears gushed from my eyes.

How mutable are our feelings, and how strange is that clinging love we have of life even in the excess of misery! I constructed another sail with a part of my dress, and eagerly steered my course towards the land. It had a wild and rocky appearance; but as I approached nearer, I easily perceived the traces of cultivation. I saw vessels near the shore, and found myself suddenly transported back to the neighbourhood of civilized man. I eagerly traced the windings of the land, and hailed a steeple which I at length saw issuing from behind a small promontory. As I was in a state of extreme debility, I resolved to sail directly towards the town as a place where I could most easily procure nourishment. Fortunately I had money with me. As I turned the promontory, I perceived a small neat town and a good harbour, which I entered, my heart bounding with joy at my unexpected escape.

As I was occupied in fixing the boat and arranging the sails, several people crowded towards the spot. They seemed very much surprised at my appearance; but, instead of offering me any assistance, whispered together with gestures that at any other time might have produced in me a slight sensation of alarm. As it was, I merely remarked that they spoke English; and I therefore addressed them in that language: "My good friends," said I, "will you be so kind as to tell me the name of this town, and inform me where I am?"

"You will know that soon enough," replied a man with a gruff voice. "May be you are come to a place that will not prove much to your taste; but you will not be consulted as to your quarters, I promise you."

I was exceedingly surprised on receiving so rude an answer from a stranger; and I was also disconcerted on perceiving the frowning and angry countenances of his companions. "Why do you answer me so roughly?" I replied: "surely it is not the custom of Englishmen to receive strangers so inhospitably."

"I do not know," said the man, "what the custom of the English may be; but it is the custom of the Irish to hate villains."

While this strange dialogue continued, I perceived the crowd rapidly increase. Their faces expressed a mixture of curiosity and anger, which annoyed, and in some degree alarmed me. I inquired the way to the inn; but no one replied. I then moved forward, and a murmuring sound arose from the crowd as they followed and surrounded me; when an ill-looking man approaching, tapped me on the shoulder, and said, "Come, Sir, you must follow me to Mr. Kirwin's, to give an account of yourself."

"Who is Mr. Kirwin? Why am I to give an account of myself? Is not this a free country?"

"Aye, Sir, free enough for honest folks. Mr. Kirwin is a magistrate; and you are to give an account of the death of a gentleman who was found murdered here last night."

This answer startled me; but I presently recovered myself. I was innocent; that could easily be proved: accordingly I followed my conductor in silence, and was led to one of the best houses in the town. I was ready to sink from fatigue and hunger; but, being surrounded by a crowd, I thought it politic to rouse all my strength, that no physical debility might be construed into apprehension or conscious guilt. Little did I then expect the calamity that was in a few moments to overwhelm me, and extinguish in horror and despair all fear of ignominy or death.

I must pause here; for it requires all my fortitude to recall the memory of the frightful events which I am about to relate, in proper detail, to my recollection.

CHAPTER IV

I was soon introduced into the presence of the magistrate, an old benevolent man, with calm and mild manners. He looked upon me, however, with some degree of severity; and then, turning towards my conductors, he asked who appeared as witnesses on this occasion.

About half a dozen men came forward; and one being selected by the magistrate, he deposed, that he had been out fishing the night before with his son and brother-in-law, Daniel Nugent, when, about ten o'clock, they observed a strong northerly blast rising, and they accordingly put in for port. It was a very dark night, as the moon had not yet risen; they did not land at the harbour, but, as they had been accustomed, at a creek about two miles below. He walked on first, carrying a part of the fishing tackle, and his companions followed him at some distance. As he was proceeding along the sands, he struck his foot against something, and fell all his length on the ground. His companions came up to assist him; and, by the light of their lantern, they found that he had fallen on the body of a man, who was to all appearance dead. Their first supposition was, that it was the corpse of some person who had been drowned, and was thrown on shore by the waves; but, upon examination, they found that the clothes were not wet, and even that the body was not then cold. They instantly carried it to the cottage of an old woman near the spot, and endeavoured, but in vain, to restore it to life. He appeared to be a handsome young man, about five and twenty years of age. He had apparently been strangled; for there was no sign of any violence, except the black mark of fingers on his neck.

The first part of this deposition did not in the least interest me; but when the mark of the fingers was mentioned, I remembered the murder of my brother, and felt myself extremely agitated; my limbs trembled, and a mist came over my eyes, which obliged me to lean on a chair for support. The magistrate observed me with a keen eye, and of course drew an unfavourable augury from my manner.

The son confirmed his father's account: but when Daniel Nugent was called, he swore positively that, just before the fall of his companion, he saw a boat, with a single man in it, at a short distance from the shore; and, as far as he could judge by the light of a few stars, it was the same boat in which I had just landed.

A woman deposed, that she lived near the beach, and was standing at the door of her cottage, waiting for the return of the fishermen, about an hour before she heard of the discovery of the body, when she saw a boat, with only one man in it, push off from that part of the shore where the corpse was afterwards found.

Another woman confirmed the account of the fishermen having brought the body into her house; it was not cold. They put it into a bed, and rubbed it; and Daniel went to the town for an apothecary, but life was quite gone.

Several other men were examined concerning my landing; and they agreed, that, with the strong north wind that had arisen during the night, it was very probable that I had beaten about for many hours, and had been obliged to return nearly to the same spot from which I had departed. Besides, they observed that it appeared that I had brought the body from another place, and it was likely, that as I did not appear to know the shore, I might have put into the harbour ignorant of the distance of the town of ——— from the place where I had deposited the corpse.

Mr. Kirwin, on hearing this evidence, desired that I should be taken into the room where the body lay for interment that it might be observed what effect the sight of it would produce upon me. This idea was probably suggested by the extreme agitation I had exhibited when the mode of the murder had been described. I was accordingly conducted, by the magistrate and several other persons, to the inn. I could not help being struck by the strange coincidences that had taken place during this eventful night; but, knowing that I had been conversing with several persons in the island I had inhabited about the time that the body had been found, I was perfectly tranquil as to the consequences of the affair.

I entered the room where the corpse lay, and was led up to the coffin. How can I describe my sensations on beholding it? I feel yet parched with horror, nor can I reflect on that terrible moment without shuddering and agony, that faintly reminds me of the anguish of the recognition. The trial, the presence of the magistrate and witnesses, passed like a dream from my memory, when I saw the lifeless form of Henry Clerval stretched before me. I gasped for breath; and, throwing myself on the body, I exclaimed, "Have my murderous machinations deprived you also, my dearest Henry, of life? Two I have already destroyed; other victims await their destiny: but you, Clerval, my friend, my benefactor"——

The human frame could no longer support the agonizing suffering that I endured, and I was carried out of the room in strong convulsions.

A fever succeeded to this. I lay for two months on the point of death: my ravings, as I afterwards heard, were frightful; I called myself the murderer of William, of Justine, and of Clerval. Sometimes I entreated my attendants to assist me in the destruction of the fiend by whom I was tormented; and, at others, I felt the fingers of the monster already grasping my neck, and screamed aloud with agony and terror. Fortunately, as I spoke my native language, Mr. Kirwin alone understood me; but my gestures and bitter cries were sufficient to affright the other witnesses.

Why did I not die? More miserable than man ever was before, why did I not sink into forgetfulness and rest? Death snatches away many blooming children, the only hopes of their doating parents: how many brides and youthful lovers have been one day in the bloom of health and hope, and the next a prey for worms and the decay of the tomb! Of what materials was I made, that I could thus resist so many shocks, which, like the turning of the wheel, continually renewed the torture.

But I was doomed to live; and, in two months, found myself as awaking from a dream, in a prison, stretched on a wretched bed, surrounded by gaolers, turnkeys, bolts, and all the miserable apparatus of a dungeon. It was morning, I remember, when I thus awoke to understanding: I had forgotten the particulars of what had happened, and only felt as if some great misfortune had suddenly overwhelmed me; but when I looked around, and saw the barred windows, and the squalidness of the room in which I was, all flashed across my memory, and I groaned bitterly.

This sound disturbed an old woman who was sleeping in a chair beside me. She was a hired nurse, the wife of one of the turnkeys, and her countenance expressed all those bad qualities which often characterize that class. The lines of her face were hard and rude, like that of persons accustomed to see without sympathizing in sights of misery. Her tone expressed her entire indifference; she addressed me in English, and the voice struck me as one that I had heard during my sufferings:

"Are you better now, Sir?" said she.

I replied in the same language, with a feeble voice, "I believe I am; but if it be all true, if indeed I did not dream, I am sorry that I am still alive to feel this misery and horror."

"For that matter," replied the old woman, "if you mean about the gentleman you murdered, I believe that it were better for you if you were dead, for I fancy it will go hard with you; but you will be hung when the next sessions come on. However, that's none of my business, I am sent to nurse you, and get you well; I do my duty with a safe conscience, it were well if every body did the same."

I turned with loathing from the woman who could utter so unfeeling a speech to a person just saved, on the very edge of death; but I felt languid, and unable to reflect on all that had passed. The whole series of my life appeared to me as a dream; I sometimes doubted if indeed it were all true, for it never presented itself to my mind with the force of reality.

As the images that floated before me became more distinct, I grew feverish; a darkness pressed around me; no one was near me who soothed me with the gentle voice of love; no dear hand supported me. The physician came and prescribed medicines, and the old woman prepared them for me; but utter carelessness was visible in the first, and the expression of brutality was strongly marked in the visage of the second. Who could be interested in the fate of a murderer, but the hangman who would gain his fee?

These were my first reflections; but I soon learned that Mr. Kirwin had shewn me extreme kindness. He had caused the best room in the prison to be prepared for me (wretched indeed was the best); and it was he who had provided a physician and a nurse. It is true, he seldom came to see me; for, although he ardently desired to relieve the sufferings of every human creature, he did not wish to be present at the agonies and miserable ravings of a murderer. He came, therefore, sometimes to see that I was not neglected; but his visits were short, and at long intervals.

One day, when I was gradually recovering, I was seated in a chair, my eyes half open, and my cheeks livid like those in death, I was overcome by gloom and misery, and often reflected I had better seek death than remain miserably pent up only to be let loose in a world replete with wretchedness. At one time I considered whether I should not declare myself guilty, and suffer the penalty of the law, less innocent than poor Justine had been. Such were my thoughts, when the door of my apartment was opened, and Mr. Kirwin entered. His countenance expressed sympathy and compassion; he drew a chair close to mine, and addressed me in French—

"I fear that this place is very shocking to you; can I do any thing to make you more comfortable?"

"I thank you; but all that you mention is nothing to me: on the whole earth there is no comfort which I am capable of receiving."

"I know that the sympathy of a stranger can be but of little relief to one borne down as you are by so strange a misfortune. But you will, I hope, soon quit this melancholy abode; for, doubtless, evidence can easily be brought to free you from the criminal charge."

"That is my least concern: I am, by a course of strange events, become the most miserable of mortals. Persecuted and tortured as I am and have been, can death be any evil to me?"

"Nothing indeed could be more unfortunate and agonizing than the strange chances that have lately occurred. You were thrown, by some surprising accident, on this shore, renowned for its hospitality: seized immediately, and charged with murder. The first sight that was presented to your eyes was the body of your friend, murdered in so unaccountable a manner, and placed, as it were, by some fiend across your path."

As Mr. Kirwin said this, notwithstanding the agitation I endured on this retrospect of my sufferings, I also felt considerable surprise at the knowledge he seemed to possess concerning me. I suppose some astonishment was exhibited in my countenance; for Mr. Kirwin hastened to say—

"It was not until a day or two after your illness that I thought of examining your dress, that I might discover some trace by which I could send to your relations an account of your misfortune and illness. I found several letters, and, among others, one which I discovered from its commencement to be from your father. I instantly wrote to Geneva: nearly two months have elapsed since the departure of my letter.—But you are ill; even now you tremble: you are unfit for agitation of any kind."

"This suspense is a thousand times worse than the most horrible event: tell me what new scene of death has been acted, and whose murder I am now to lament."

"Your family is perfectly well," said Mr. Kirwin, with gentleness; "and some one, a friend, is come to visit you."

I know not by what chain of thought the idea presented itself, but it instantly darted into my mind that the murderer had come to mock at my misery, and taunt me with the death of Clerval, as a new incitement for me to comply with his hellish desires. I put by hand before my eyes, and cried out in agony—

"Oh! take him away! I cannot see him; for God's sake, do not let him enter!"

Mr. Kirwin regarded me with a troubled countenance. He could not help regarding my exclamation as a presumption of my guilt, and said, in rather a severe tone—

"I should have thought, young man, that the presence of your father would have been welcome, instead of inspiring such violent repugnance."

"My father!" cried I, while every feature and every muscle was relaxed from anguish to pleasure. "Is my father, indeed, come? How kind, how very kind. But where is he, why does he not hasten to me?"

My change of manner surprised and pleased the magistrate; perhaps he thought that my former exclamation was a momentary return of delirium, and now he instantly resumed his former benevolence. He rose, and quitted the room with my nurse, and in a moment my father entered it.

Nothing, at this moment, could have given me greater pleasure than the arrival of my father. I stretched out my hand to him, and cried—

"Are you then safe—and Elizabeth—and Ernest?"

My father calmed me with assurances of their welfare, and endeavoured, by dwelling on these subjects so interesting to my heart, to raise my desponding spirits; but he soon felt that a prison cannot be the abode of cheerfulness. "What a place is this that you inhabit, my son!" said he, looking mournfully at the barred windows, and wretched appearance of the room. "You travelled to seek happiness, but a fatality seems to pursue you. And poor Clerval—"

The name of my unfortunate and murdered friend was an agitation too great to be endured in my weak state; I shed tears.

"Alas! yes, my father," replied I; "some destiny of the most horrible kind hangs over me, and I must live to fulfil it, or surely I should have died on the coffin of Henry."

We were not allowed to converse for any length of time, for the precarious state of my health rendered every precaution necessary that could insure tranquillity. Mr. Kirwin came in, and insisted that my strength should not be exhausted by too much exertion. But the appearance of my father was to me like that of my good angel, and I gradually recovered my health.

As my sickness quitted me, I was absorbed by a gloomy and black melancholy, that nothing could dissipate. The image of Clerval was for ever before me, ghastly and murdered. More than once the agitation into which these reflections threw me made my friends dread a dangerous relapse. Alas! why did they preserve so miserable and detested a life? It was surely that I might fulfil my destiny, which is now drawing to a close. Soon, oh, very soon, will death extinguish these throbbings, and relieve me from the mighty weight of anguish that bears me to the dust; and, in executing the award of justice, I shall also sink to rest. Then the appearance of death was distant, although the wish was ever present to my thoughts; and I often sat for hours motionless and speechless, wishing for some mighty revolution that might bury me and my destroyer in its ruins.

The season of the assizes approached. I had already been three months in prison; and although I was still weak, and in continual danger of a relapse, I was obliged to travel nearly a hundred miles to the county-town, where the court was held. Mr. Kirwin charged himself with every care of collecting witnesses, and arranging my defence. I was spared the disgrace of appearing publicly as a criminal, as the case was not brought before the court that decides on life and death. The grand jury rejected the bill, on its being proved that I was on the Orkney Islands at the hour the body of my friend was found, and a fortnight after my removal I was liberated from prison.

My father was enraptured on finding me freed from the vexations of a criminal charge, that I was again allowed to breathe the fresh atmosphere, and allowed to return to my native country. I did not participate in these feelings; for to me the walls of a dungeon or a palace were alike hateful. The cup of life was poisoned for ever; and although the sun shone upon me, as upon the happy and gay of heart, I saw around me nothing but a dense and frightful darkness, penetrated by no light but the glimmer of two eyes that glared upon me. Sometimes they were the expressive eyes of Henry, languishing in death, the dark orbs nearly covered by the lids, and the long black lashes that fringed them; sometimes it was the watery clouded eyes of the monster, as I first saw them in my chamber at Ingolstadt.

My father tried to awaken in me the feelings of affection. He talked of Geneva, which I should soon visit—of Elizabeth, and Ernest; but these words only drew deep groans from me. Sometimes, indeed, I felt a wish for happiness; and thought, with melancholy delight, of my beloved cousin; or longed, with a devouring *maladie du pays*,[31] to see once more the blue lake and rapid Rhone, that had been so dear to me in early childhood: but my general state of feeling was a torpor, in which a prison was as welcome a residence as the divinest scene in nature; and these fits were seldom interrupted, but by paroxysms of anguish and despair. At these moments I often endeavoured to put an end to the existence I loathed; and it required unceasing attendance and vigilance to restrain me from committing some dreadful act of violence.

I remember, as I quitted the prison, I heard one of the men say, "He may be innocent of the murder, but he has certainly a bad conscience." These words struck me. A bad conscience! yes, surely I had one. William, Justine, and Clerval, had died through my infernal machinations; "And whose death," cried I, "is to finish the tragedy? Ah! my father, do not remain in this wretched country; take me where I may forget myself, my existence, and all the world."

My father easily acceded to my desire; and, after having taken leave of Mr. Kirwin, we hastened to Dublin. I felt as if I was relieved from a heavy weight, when the packet sailed with a fair wind from Ireland, and I had quitted for ever the country which had been to me the scene of so much misery.

It was midnight. My father slept in the cabin; and I lay on the deck, looking at the stars, and listening to the dashing of the waves. I hailed

31. "Homesickness."

the darkness that shut Ireland from my sight, and my pulse beat with a feverish joy, when I reflected that I should soon see Geneva. The past appeared to me in the light of a frightful dream; yet the vessel in which I was, the wind that blew me from the detested shore of Ireland, and the sea which surrounded me, told me too forcibly that I was deceived by no vision, and that Clerval, my friend and dearest companion, had fallen a victim to me and the monster of my creation. I repassed, in my memory, my whole life; my quiet happiness while residing with my family in Geneva, the death of my mother, and my departure for Ingolstadt. I remembered shuddering at the mad enthusiasm that hurried me on to the creation of my hideous enemy, and I called to mind the night during which he first lived. I was unable to pursue the train of thought; a thousand feelings pressed upon me, and I wept bitterly.

Ever since my recovery from the fever I had been in the custom of taking every night a small quantity of laudanum; for it was by means of this drug only that I was enabled to gain the rest necessary for the preservation of life. Oppressed by the recollection of my various misfortunes, I now took a double dose, and soon slept profoundly. But sleep did not afford me respite from thought and misery; my dreams presented a thousand objects that scared me. Towards morning I was possessed by a kind of night-mare; I felt the fiend's grasp in my neck, and could not free myself from it; groans and cries rung in my ears. My father, who was watching over me, perceiving my restlessness, awoke me, and pointed to the port of Holyhead, which we were now entering.

CHAPTER V

We had resolved not to go to London, but to cross the country to Portsmouth, and thence to embark for Havre. I preferred this plan principally because I dreaded to see again those places in which I had enjoyed a few moments of tranquillity with my beloved Clerval. I thought with horror of seeing again those persons whom we had been accustomed to visit together, and who might make inquiries concerning an event, the very remembrance of which made me again feel the pang I endured when I gazed on his lifeless form in the inn at ———.

As for my father, his desires and exertions were bounded to the again seeing me restored to health and peace of mind. His tenderness and attentions were unremitting; my grief and gloom was obstinate, but he would not despair. Sometimes he thought that I felt deeply the degradation of being obliged to answer a charge of murder, and he endeavoured to prove to me the futility of pride.

"Alas! my father," said I, "how little do you know me. Human beings, their feelings and passions, would indeed be degraded, if such a wretch as I felt pride. Justine, poor unhappy Justine, was as innocent as I, and she suffered the same charge; she died for it; and I am the cause of this—I murdered her. William, Justine, and Henry—they all died by my hands."

My father had often, during my imprisonment, heard me make the same assertion; when I thus accused myself, he sometimes seemed to desire an explanation, and at others he appeared to consider it as caused by delirium, and that, during my illness, some idea of this kind had presented itself to my imagination, the remembrance of which I preserved in my convalescence. I avoided explanation, and maintained a continual silence concerning the wretch I had created. I had a feeling that I should be supposed mad, and this for ever chained my tongue, when I would have given the whole world to have confided the fatal secret.

Upon this occasion my father said, with an expression of unbounded wonder, "What do you mean, Victor? are you mad? My dear son, I entreat you never to make such an assertion again."

"I am not mad," I cried energetically; "the sun and the heavens, who have viewed my operations, can bear witness of my truth. I am the assassin of those most innocent victims; they died by my machinations. A thousand times would I have shed my own blood, drop by drop, to have saved their lives; but I could not, my father, indeed I could not sacrifice the whole human race."

The conclusion of this speech convinced my father that my ideas were deranged, and he instantly changed the subject of our conversation, and endeavoured to alter the course of my thoughts. He wished as much as possible to obliterate the memory of the scenes that had taken place in Ireland, and never alluded to them, or suffered me to speak of my misfortunes.

As time passed away I became more calm: misery had her dwelling in my heart, but I no longer talked in the same incoherent manner of my own crimes; sufficient for me was the consciousness of them. By the utmost self-violence, I curbed the imperious voice of wretchedness, which sometimes desired to declare itself to the whole world; and my manners were calmer and more composed than they had ever been since my journey to the sea of ice.

We arrived at Havre on the 8th of May, and instantly proceeded to Paris, where my father had some business which detained us a few weeks. In this city, I received the following letter from Elizabeth:—

"To Victor Frankenstein.

"My dearest Friend,

"It gave me the greatest pleasure to receive a letter from my uncle dated at Paris; you are no longer at a formidable distance, and I may hope to see you in less than a fortnight. My poor cousin, how much you must have suffered! I expect to see you looking even more ill than when you quitted Geneva. This winter has been passed most miserably, tortured as I have been by anxious suspense; yet I hope to see peace in your countenance, and to find that your heart is not totally devoid of comfort and tranquillity.

"Yet I fear that the same feelings now exist that made you so miserable a year ago, even perhaps augmented by time. I would not disturb you at this period, when so many misfortunes weigh upon you; but a conversation that I had with my uncle previous to his departure renders some explanation necessary before we meet.

"Explanation! you may possibly say; what can Elizabeth have to explain? If you really say this, my questions are answered, and I have no more to do than to sign myself your affectionate cousin. But you are distant from me, and it is possible that you may dread, and yet be pleased with this explanation; and, in a probability of this being the case, I dare not any longer postpone writing what, during your absence, I have often wished to express to you, but have never had the courage to begin.

"You well know, Victor, that our union had been the favourite plan of your parents ever since our infancy. We were told this when young, and taught to look forward to it as an event that would certainly take place. We were affectionate playfellows during childhood, and, I believe, dear and valued friends to one another as we grew older. But as brother and sister often entertain a lively affection towards each other, without desiring a more intimate union, may not such also be our case? Tell me, dearest Victor. Answer me, I conjure you, by our mutual happiness, with simple truth—Do you not love another?

"You have travelled; you have spent several years of your life at Ingolstadt; and I confess to you, my friend, that when I saw you last autumn so unhappy, flying to solitude, from the society of every creature, I could not help supposing that you might regret our connexion, and believe yourself bound in honour to fulfil the wishes of your parents, although they opposed themselves to your inclinations. But this is false reasoning. I confess to you, my cousin, that I love you, and that in my airy dreams of futurity you have been my constant friend and companion. But it is your happiness I desire as well as my own, when I declare to you, that our marriage would render me eternally miserable, unless it were the dictate of your own free choice. Even now I weep to think, that, borne down as you are by the cruelest misfortunes, you may stifle, by the word *honour,* all hope of that love and happiness which would alone restore you to yourself. I, who have so interested an affection for you, may increase your miseries ten-fold, by being an obstacle to your wishes. Ah, Victor, be assured that your cousin and playmate has too sincere a love for you not to be made miserable by this supposition. Be happy, my friend; and if you obey me in this one request, remain satisfied that nothing on earth will have the power to interrupt my tranquillity.

"Do not let this letter disturb you; do not answer it to-morrow, or the next day, or even until you come, if it will give you pain. My uncle will send me news of your health; and if I see but one smile on your lips when we meet, occasioned by this or any other exertion of mine, I shall need no other happiness.

"Elizabeth Lavenza.

"*Geneva, May 18th, 17—.*"

This letter revived in my memory what I had before forgotten, the threat of the fiend—"*I will be with you on your wedding-night!*" Such was my sentence, and on that night would the dæmon employ every art to destroy me, and tear me from the glimpse of happiness which promised partly to console my sufferings. On that night he had determined to consummate his crimes by my death. Well, be it so; a deadly struggle would then assuredly take place, in which if he was victorious, I should be at peace, and his power over me be at an end. If he were vanquished, I should be a free man. Alas! what freedom? such as the peasant enjoys when his family have been massacred before his eyes, his cottage burnt, his lands laid waste, and he is turned adrift, homeless, pennyless, and alone, but free. Such would be my liberty, except that in my Elizabeth I possessed a treasure; alas! balanced by those horrors of remorse and guilt, which would pursue me until death.

Sweet and beloved Elizabeth! I read and re-read her letter, and some softened feelings stole into my heart, and dared to whisper paradisaical dreams of love and joy; but the apple was already eaten, and the angel's arm bared to drive me from all hope. Yet I would die to make her happy. If the monster executed his threat, death was inevitable; yet, again, I considered whether my marriage would hasten my fate. My destruction might indeed arrive a few months sooner; but if my torturer should suspect that I postponed it, influenced by his menaces, he would surely find other, and perhaps more dreadful means of revenge. He had vowed *to be with me on my wedding-night,* yet he did not consider that threat as binding him to peace in the mean time; for, as if to shew me that he was not yet satiated with blood, he had murdered Clerval immediately after the enunciation of his threats. I resolved, therefore, that if my immediate union with my cousin would conduce either to her's or my father's happiness, my adversary's designs against my life should not retard it a single hour.

In this state of mind I wrote to Elizabeth. My letter was calm and affectionate. "I fear, my beloved girl," I said, "little happiness remains for us on earth; yet all that I may one day enjoy is concentered in you. Chase away your idle fears; to you alone do I consecrate my life, and my endeavours for contentment. I have one secret, Elizabeth, a dreadful one; when revealed to you, it will chill your frame with horror, and then, far from being surprised at my misery, you will only wonder that I survive what I have endured. I will confide this tale of misery and terror to you the day after our marriage shall take place; for, my sweet cousin, there must be perfect confidence between us. But until then, I conjure you, do not mention or allude to it. This I most earnestly entreat, and I know you will comply."

In about a week after the arrival of Elizabeth's letter, we returned to Geneva. My cousin welcomed me with warm affection; yet tears were in her eyes, as she beheld my emaciated frame and feverish cheeks. I saw a change in her also. She was thinner, and had lost much of that heavenly vivacity that had before charmed me; but her gentleness, and soft looks of compassion, made her a more fit companion for one blasted and miserable as I was.

The tranquillity which I now enjoyed did not endure. Memory brought madness with it; and when I thought on what had passed, a real insanity possessed me; sometimes I was furious, and burnt with rage, sometimes low and despondent. I neither spoke nor looked, but sat motionless, bewildered by the multitude of miseries that overcame me.

Elizabeth alone had the power to draw me from these fits; her gentle voice would soothe me when transported by passion, and inspire me with human feelings when sunk in torpor. She wept with me, and for me. When reason returned, she would remonstrate, and endeavour to inspire me with resignation. Ah! it is well for the unfortunate to be resigned, but for the guilty there is no peace. The agonies of remorse poison the luxury there is otherwise sometimes found in indulging the excess of grief.

Soon after my arrival my father spoke of my immediate marriage with my cousin. I remained silent.

"Have you, then, some other attachment?"

"None on earth. I love Elizabeth, and look forward to our union with delight. Let the day therefore be fixed; and on it I will consecrate myself, in life or death, to the happiness of my cousin."

"My dear Victor, do not speak thus. Heavy misfortunes have befallen us; but let us only cling closer to what remains, and transfer our love for those whom we have lost to those who yet live. Our circle will be small, but bound close by the ties of affection and mutual misfortune. And when time shall have softened your despair, new and dear objects of care will be born to replace those of whom we have been so cruelly deprived."

Such were the lessons of my father. But to me the remembrance of the threat returned: nor can you wonder, that, omnipotent as the fiend had yet been in his deeds of blood, I should almost regard him as invincible; and that when he had pronounced the words, *"I shall be with you on your wedding-night,"* I should regard the threatened fate as unavoidable. But death was no evil to me, if the loss of Elizabeth were balanced with it; and I therefore, with a contented and even cheerful countenance, agreed with my father, that if my cousin would consent, the ceremony should take place in ten days, and thus put, as I imagined, the seal to my fate.

Great God! if for one instant I had thought what might be the hellish intention of my fiendish adversary, I would rather have banished myself for ever from my native country, and wandered a friendless outcast over the earth, than have consented to this miserable marriage. But, as if possessed of magic powers, the monster had blinded me to his real intentions; and when I thought that I prepared only my own death, I hastened that of a far dearer victim.

As the period fixed for our marriage drew nearer, whether from cowardice or a prophetic feeling, I felt my heart sink within me. But I concealed my feelings by an appearance of hilarity, that brought smiles and joy to the countenance of my father, but hardly deceived the ever-watchful and nicer eye of Elizabeth. She looked forward to our union with placid contentment, not unmingled with a little fear, which past misfortunes had impressed, that what now appeared certain and tangible happiness, might soon dissipate into an airy dream, and leave no trace but deep and ever-lasting regret.

Preparations were made for the event; congratulatory visits were received; and all wore a smiling appearance. I shut up, as well as I could, in my own heart the anxiety that preyed there, and entered with seeming earnestness into the plans of my father, although they might only serve as the decorations of my tragedy. A house was purchased for us near Cologny, by which we should enjoy the pleasures of the country, and yet be so near Geneva as to see my father every day; who would still reside within the walls, for the benefit of Ernest, that he might follow his studies at the schools.

In the mean time I took every precaution to defend my person, in case the fiend should openly attack me. I carried pistols and a dagger constantly about me, and was ever on the watch to prevent artifice; and by these means gained a greater degree of tranquillity. Indeed, as the period approached, the threat appeared more as a delusion, not to be regarded as worthy to disturb my peace, while the happiness I hoped for in my marriage wore a greater appearance of certainty, as the day fixed for its solemnization drew nearer, and I heard it continually spoken of as an occurrence which no accident could possibly prevent.

Elizabeth seemed happy; my tranquil demeanour contributed greatly to calm her mind. But on the day that was to fulfil my wishes and my destiny, she was melancholy, and a presentiment of evil pervaded her; and perhaps also she thought of the dreadful secret, which I had promised to reveal to her the following day. My father was in the mean time over-joyed, and, in the bustle of preparation, only observed in the melancholy of his niece the diffidence of a bride.

After the ceremony was performed, a large party assembled at my father's; but it was agreed that Elizabeth and I should pass the afternoon and night at Evian, and return to Cologny the next morning. As the day was fair, and the wind favourable, we resolved to go by water.

Those were the last moments of my life during which I enjoyed the feeling of happiness. We passed rapidly along: the sun was hot, but we were sheltered from its rays by a kind of canopy, while we enjoyed the beauty of the scene, sometimes on one side of the lake, where we saw Mont Salêve, the pleasant banks of Montalêgre, and at a distance, sur-mounting all, the beautiful Mont Blanc, and the assemblage of snowy mountains that in vain endeavour to emulate her; sometimes coasting the opposite banks, we saw the mighty Jura opposing its dark side to the ambition that would quit its native country, and an almost insurmount-able barrier to the invader who should wish to enslave it.

I took the hand of Elizabeth: "You are sorrowful, my love. Ah! if you knew what I have suffered, and what I may yet endure, you would en-deavour to let me taste the quiet, and freedom from despair, that this one day at least permits me to enjoy."

"Be happy, my dear Victor," replied Elizabeth; "there is, I hope, noth-ing to distress you; and be assured that if a lively joy is not painted in my face, my heart is contented. Something whispers to me not to depend too much on the prospect that is opened before us; but I will not listen to such a sinister voice. Observe how fast we move along, and how the clouds which sometimes obscure, and sometimes rise above the dome of Mont Blanc, render this scene of beauty still more interesting. Look also at the innumerable fish that are swimming in the clear waters, where we can distinguish every pebble that lies at the bottom. What a divine day! how happy and serene all nature appears!"

Thus Elizabeth endeavoured to divert her thoughts and mine from all reflection upon melancholy subjects. But her temper was fluctuating; joy for a few instants shone in her eyes, but it continually gave place to distraction and reverie.

The sun sunk lower in the heavens; we passed the river Drance, and observed its path through the chasms of the higher, and the glens of the lower hills. The Alps here come closer to the lake, and we approached the amphitheatre of mountains which forms its eastern boundary. The spire of Evian shone under the woods that surrounded it, and the range of mountain above mountain by which it was overhung.

The wind, which had hitherto carried us along with amazing rapidity, sunk at sunset to a light breeze; the soft air just ruffled the water, and caused a pleasant motion among the trees as we approached the shore, from which it wafted the most delightful scent of flowers and hay. The sun sunk beneath the horizon as we landed; and as I touched the shore, I felt those cares and fears revive, which soon were to clasp me, and cling to me for ever.

CHAPTER VI

It was eight o'clock when we landed; we walked for a short time on the shore, enjoying the transitory light, and then retired to the inn, and contemplated the lovely scene of waters, woods, and mountains, obscured in darkness, yet still displaying their black outlines.

The wind, which had fallen in the south, now rose with great violence in the west. The moon had reached her summit in the heavens, and was beginning to descend; the clouds swept across it swifter than the flight of the vulture, and dimmed her rays, while the lake reflected the scene of the busy heavens, rendered still busier by the restless waves that were beginning to rise. Suddenly a heavy storm of rain descended.

I had been calm during the day; but so soon as night obscured the shapes of objects, a thousand fears arose in my mind. I was anxious and watchful, while my right hand grasped a pistol which was hidden in my bosom; every sound terrified me; but I resolved that I would sell my life dearly, and not relax the impending conflict until my own life, or that of my adversary, were extinguished.

Elizabeth observed my agitation for some time in timid and fearful silence; at length she said, "What is it that agitates you, my dear Victor? What is it you fear?"

"Oh! peace, peace, my love," replied I, "this night, and all will be safe: but this night is dreadful, very dreadful."

I passed an hour in this state of mind, when suddenly I reflected how dreadful the combat which I momentarily expected would be to my wife, and I earnestly entreated her to retire, resolving not to join her until I had obtained some knowledge as to the situation of my enemy.

She left me, and I continued some time walking up and down the passages of the house, and inspecting every corner that might afford a retreat to my adversary. But I discovered no trace of him, and was beginning to conjecture that some fortunate chance had intervened to prevent the execution of his menaces; when suddenly I heard a shrill and dreadful scream. It came from the room into which Elizabeth had retired. As I heard it, the whole truth rushed into my mind, my arms dropped, the motion of every muscle and fibre was suspended; I could feel the blood trickling in my veins, and tingling in the extremities of my limbs. This state lasted but for an instant; the scream was repeated, and I rushed into the room.

Great God! why did I not then expire! Why am I here to relate the destruction of the best hope, and the purest creature of earth? She was there, lifeless and inanimate, thrown across the bed, her head hanging down, and her pale and distorted features half covered by her hair. Every where I turn I see the same figure—her bloodless arms and relaxed form flung by the murderer on its bridal bier. Could I behold this, and live? Alas! life is obstinate, and clings closest where it is most hated. For a moment only did I lose recollection; I fainted.

When I recovered, I found myself surrounded by the people of the inn; their countenances expressed a breathless terror: but the horror of others appeared only as a mockery, a shadow of the feelings that oppressed me. I escaped from them to the room where lay the body of Elizabeth, my love, my wife, so lately living, so dear, so worthy. She had been moved from the posture in which I had first beheld her; and now, as she lay, her head upon her arm, and a handkerchief thrown across her face and neck, I might have supposed her asleep. I rushed towards her, and embraced her with ardour; but the deathly languor and coldness of the limbs told me, that what I now held in my arms had ceased to be the Elizabeth whom I had loved and cherished. The murderous mark of the fiend's grasp was on her neck, and the breath had ceased to issue from her lips.

While I still hung over her in the agony of despair, I happened to look up. The windows of the room had before been darkened; and I felt a kind of panic on seeing the pale yellow light of the moon illuminate the chamber. The shutters had been thrown back; and, with a sensation of horror not to be described, I saw at the open window a figure the most hideous and abhorred. A grin was on the face of the monster; he seemed to jeer, as with his fiendish finger he pointed towards the corpse of my wife. I rushed towards the window, and drawing a pistol from my bosom, shot; but he eluded me, leaped from his station, and, running with the swiftness of lightning, plunged into the lake.

The report of the pistol brought a crowd into the room. I pointed to the spot where he had disappeared, and we followed the track with boats; nets were cast, but in vain. After passing several hours, we returned hopeless, most of my companions believing it to have been a form conjured by my fancy. After having landed, they proceeded to search the country, parties going in different directions among the woods and vines.

I did not accompany them; I was exhausted: a film covered my eyes, and my skin was parched with the heat of fever. In this state I lay on a bed, hardly conscious of what had happened; my eyes wandered round the room, as if to seek something that I had lost.

At length I remembered that my father would anxiously expect the return of Elizabeth and myself, and that I must return alone. This reflection brought tears into my eyes, and I wept for a long time; but my thoughts rambled to various subjects, reflecting on my misfortunes, and their cause. I was bewildered in a cloud of wonder and horror. The death of William, the execution of Justine, the murder of Clerval, and lastly of my wife; even at that moment I knew not that my only remaining friends were safe from the malignity of the fiend; my father even now might be writhing under his grasp, and Ernest might be dead at his feet. This idea made me shudder, and recalled me to action. I started up, and resolved to return to Geneva with all possible speed.

There were no horses to be procured, and I must return by the lake; but the wind was unfavourable, and the rain fell in torrents. However, it was hardly morning, and I might reasonably hope to arrive by night. I hired men to row, and took an oar myself, for I had always experienced relief from mental torment in bodily exercise. But the overflowing misery I now felt, and the excess of agitation that I endured, rendered me incapable of any exertion. I threw down the oar; and, leaning my head upon my hands, gave way to every gloomy idea that arose. If I looked up, I saw the scenes which were familiar to me in my happier time, and which I had contemplated but the day before in the company of her who was now but a shadow and a recollection. Tears streamed from my eyes. The rain had ceased for a moment, and I saw the fish play in the waters as they had done a few hours before; they had then been observed by Elizabeth. Nothing is so painful to the human mind as a great and sudden change. The sun might shine, or the clouds might lour; but nothing could appear to me as it had done the day before. A .fiend had snatched from me every hope of future happiness: no creature had ever been so miserable as I was; so frightful an event is single in the history of man.

But why should I dwell upon the incidents that followed this last overwhelming event. Mine has been a tale of horrors; I have reached their *acme,* and what I must now relate can but be tedious to you. Know that, one by one, my friends were snatched away; I was left desolate. My own strength is exhausted; and I must tell, in a few words, what remains of my hideous narration.

I arrived at Geneva. My father and Ernest yet lived; but the former sunk under the tidings that I bore. I see him now, excellent and venerable old man! his eyes wandered in vacancy, for they had lost their charm and their delight—his niece, his more than daughter, whom he doated on with all that affection which a man feels, who, in the decline of life, having few affections, clings more earnestly to those that remain. Cursed, cursed be the fiend that brought misery on his grey hairs, and doomed him to waste in wretchedness! He could not live under the horrors that were accumulated around him; an apoplectic fit was brought on, and in a few days he died in my arms.

What then became of me? I know not; I lost sensation, and chains and darkness were the only objects that pressed upon me. Sometimes, indeed, I dreamt that I wandered in flowery meadows and pleasant vales with the friends of my youth; but awoke, and found myself in a dungeon. Melancholy followed, but by degrees I gained a clear conception of my miseries and situation, and was then released from my prison. For they had called me mad; and during many months, as I understood, a solitary cell had been my habitation.

But liberty had been a useless gift to me had I not, as I awakened to reason, at the same time awakened to revenge. As the memory of past misfortunes pressed upon me, I began to reflect on their cause—the monster whom I had created, the miserable dæmon whom I had sent abroad into the world for my destruction. I was possessed by a maddening rage when I thought of him, and desired and ardently prayed that I might have him within my grasp to wreak a great and signal revenge on his cursed head.

Nor did my hate long confine itself to useless wishes; I began to reflect on the best means of securing him; and for this purpose, about a month after my release, I repaired to a criminal judge in the town, and told him that I had an accusation to make; that I knew the destroyer of my family; and that I required him to exert his whole authority for the apprehension of the murderer.

The magistrate listened to me with attention and kindness: "Be assured, sir," said he, "no pains or exertions on my part shall be spared to discover the villain."

"I thank you," replied I; "listen, therefore, to the deposition that I have to make. It is indeed a tale so strange, that I should fear you would not credit it, were there not something in truth which, however wonderful, forces conviction. The story is too connected to be mistaken for a dream, and I have no motive for falsehood." My manner, as I thus addressed him, was impressive, but calm; I had formed in my own heart a resolution to pursue my destroyer to death; and this purpose quieted my agony, and provisionally reconciled me to life. I now related my history briefly, but with firmness and precision, marking the dates with accuracy, and never deviating into invective or exclamation.

The magistrate appeared at first perfectly incredulous, but as I continued he became more attentive and interested; I saw him sometimes shudder with horror, at others a lively surprise, unmingled with disbelief, was painted on his countenance.

When I had concluded my narration, I said, "This is the being whom I accuse, and for whose detection and punishment I call upon you to exert your whole power. It is your duty as a magistrate, and I believe and hope that your feelings as a man will not revolt from the execution of those functions on this occasion."

This address caused a considerable change in the physiognomy of my auditor. He had heard my story with that half kind of belief that is given to a tale of spirits and supernatural events; but when he was called upon to act officially in consequence, the whole tide of his incredulity returned. He, however, answered mildly, "I would willingly afford you every aid in your pursuit; but the creature of whom you speak appears to have powers which would put all my exertions to defiance. Who can follow an animal which can traverse the sea of ice, and inhabit caves and dens, where no man would venture to intrude? Besides, some months have elapsed since the commission of his crimes, and no one can conjecture to what place he has wandered, or what region he may now inhabit."

"I do not doubt that he hovers near the spot which I inhabit; and if he has indeed taken refuge in the Alps, he may be hunted like the chamois, and destroyed as a beast of prey. But I perceive your thoughts: you do not credit my narrative, and do not intend to pursue my enemy with the punishment which is his desert."

As I spoke, rage sparkled in my eyes; the magistrate was intimidated; "You are mistaken," said he, "I will exert myself; and if it is in my power to seize the monster, be assured that he shall suffer punishment proportionate to his crimes. But I fear, from what you have yourself described to be his properties, that this will prove impracticable, and that, while every proper measure is pursued, you should endeavour to make up your mind to disappointment."

"That cannot be; but all that I can say will be of little avail. My revenge is of no moment to you; yet, while I allow it to be a vice, I confess that it is the devouring and only passion of my soul. My rage is unspeakable, when I reflect that the murderer, whom I have turned loose upon society, still exists. You refuse my just demand: I have but one resource; and I devote myself, either in my life or death, to his destruction."

I trembled with excess of agitation as I said this; there was a phrenzy in my manner, and something, I doubt not, of that haughty fierceness, which the martyrs of old are said to have possessed. But to a Genevan magistrate, whose mind was occupied by far other ideas than those of devotion and heroism, this elevation of mind had much the appearance of madness. He endeavoured to soothe me as a nurse does a child, and reverted to my tale as the effects of delirium.

"Man," I cried, "how ignorant art thou in thy pride of wisdom! Cease; you know not what it is you say."

I broke from the house angry and disturbed, and retired to meditate on some other mode of action.

CHAPTER VII

My present situation was one in which all voluntary thought was swallowed up and lost. I was hurried away by fury; revenge alone endowed me with strength and composure; it modelled my feelings, and allowed me to be calculating and calm, at periods when otherwise delirium or death would have been my portion.

My first resolution was to quit Geneva for ever; my country, which, when I was happy and beloved, was dear to me, now, in my adversity, became hateful. I provided myself with a sum of money, together with a few jewels which had belonged to my mother, and departed.

And now my wanderings began, which are to cease but with life. I have traversed a vast portion of the earth, and have endured all the hardships which travellers, in deserts and barbarous countries, are wont to meet. How I have lived I hardly know; many times have I stretched my failing limbs upon the sandy plain, and prayed for death. But revenge kept me alive; I dared not die, and leave my adversary in being.

When I quitted Geneva, my first labour was to gain some clue by which I might trace the steps of my fiendish enemy. But my plan was unsettled;

and I wandered many hours around the confines of the town, uncertain what path I should pursue. As night approached, I found myself at the entrance of the cemetery where William, Elizabeth, and my father, reposed. I entered it, and approached the tomb which marked their graves. Every thing was silent, except the leaves of the trees, which were gently agitated by the wind; the night was nearly dark; and the scene would have been solemn and affecting even to an uninterested observer. The spirits of the departed seemed to flit around, and to cast a shadow, which was felt but seen not, around the head of the mourner.

The deep grief which this scene had at first excited quickly gave way to rage and despair. They were dead, and I lived; their murderer also lived, and to destroy him I must drag out my weary existence. I knelt on the grass, and kissed the earth, and with quivering lips exclaimed, "By the sacred earth on which I kneel, by the shades that wander near me, by the deep and eternal grief that I feel, I swear; and by thee, O Night, and by the spirits that preside over thee, I swear to pursue the dæmon, who caused this misery, until he or I shall perish in mortal conflict. For this purpose I will preserve my life: to execute this dear revenge, will I again behold the sun, and tread the green herbage of earth, which otherwise should vanish from my eyes for ever. And I call on you, spirits of the dead; and on you, wandering ministers of vengeance, to aid and conduct me in my work. Let the cursed and hellish monster drink deep of agony; let him feel the despair that now torments me."

I had begun my adjuration with solemnity, and an awe which almost assured me that the shades of my murdered friends heard and approved my devotion; but the furies possessed me as I concluded, and rage choaked my utterance.

I was answered through the stillness of night by a loud and fiendish laugh. It rung on my ears long and heavily; the mountains re-echoed it, and I felt as if all hell surrounded me with mockery and laughter. Surely in that moment I should have been possessed by phrenzy, and have destroyed my miserable existence, but that my vow was heard, and that I was reserved for vengeance. The laughter died away: when a well-known and abhorred voice, apparently close to my ear, addressed me in an audible whisper—"I am satisfied: miserable wretch! you have determined to live, and I am satisfied."

I darted towards the spot from which the sound proceeded; but the devil eluded my grasp. Suddenly the broad disk of the moon arose, and shone full upon his ghastly and distorted shape, as he fled with more than mortal speed.

I pursued him; and for many months this has been my task. Guided by a slight clue, I followed the windings of the Rhone, but vainly. The blue

Mediterranean appeared; and, by a strange chance, I saw the fiend enter by night, and hide himself in a vessel bound for the Black Sea. I took my passage in the same ship; but he escaped, I know not how.

Amidst the wilds of Tartary and Russia, although he still evaded me, I have ever followed in his track. Sometimes the peasants, scared by this horrid apparition, informed me of his path; sometimes he himself, who feared that if I lost all trace I should despair and die, often left some mark to guide me. The snows descended on my head, and I saw the print of his huge step on the white plain. To you first entering on life, to whom care is new, and agony unknown, how can you understand what I have felt, and still feel? Cold, want, and fatigue, were the least pains which I was destined to endure; I was cursed by some devil, and carried about with me my eternal hell; yet still a spirit of good followed and directed my steps, and, when I most murmured, would suddenly extricate me from seemingly insurmountable difficulties. Sometimes, when nature, overcome by hunger, sunk under the exhaustion, a repast was prepared for me in the desert, that restored and inspirited me. The fare was indeed coarse, such as the peasants of the country ate; but I may not doubt that it was set there by the spirits that I had invoked to aid me. Often, when all was dry, the heavens cloudless, and I was parched by thirst, a slight cloud would bedim the sky, shed the few drops that revived me, and vanish.

I followed, when I could, the courses of the rivers; but the dæmon generally avoided these, as it was here that the population of the country chiefly collected. In other places human beings were seldom seen; and I generally subsisted on the wild animals that crossed my path. I had money with me, and gained the friendship of the villagers by distributing it, or bringing with me some food that I had killed, which, after taking a small part, I always presented to those who had provided me with fire and utensils for cooking.

My life, as it passed thus, was indeed hateful to me, and it was during sleep alone that I could taste joy. O blessed sleep! often, when most miserable, I sank to repose, and my dreams lulled me even to rapture. The spirits that guarded me had provided these moments, or rather hours, of happiness, that I might retain strength to fulfil my pilgrimage. Deprived of this respite, I should have sunk under my hardships. During the day I was sustained and inspirited by the hope of night: for in sleep I saw my friends, my wife, and my beloved country; again I saw the benevolent countenance of my father, heard the silver tones of my Elizabeth's voice, and beheld Clerval enjoying health and youth. Often, when wearied by a toilsome march, I persuaded myself that I was dreaming until night should come, and that I should then enjoy reality in the arms of my dear-

est friends. What agonizing fondness did I feel for them! how did I cling
to their dear forms, as sometimes they haunted even my waking hours,
and persuade myself that they still lived! At such moments vengeance,
that burned within me, died in my heart, and I pursued my path towards
the destruction of the dæmon, more as a task enjoined by heaven, as the
mechanical impulse of some power of which I was unconscious, than as
the ardent desire of my soul.

What his feelings were whom I pursued, I cannot know. Sometimes, indeed, he left marks in writing on the barks of the trees, or cut in stone,
that guided me, and instigated my fury. "My reign is not yet over,"
(these words were legible in one of these inscriptions); "you live, and my
power is complete. Follow me; I seek the everlasting ices of the north,
where you will feel the misery of cold and frost, to which I am impassive.
You will find near this place, if you follow not too tardily, a dead hare;
eat, and be refreshed. Come on, my enemy; we have yet to wrestle for
our lives; but many hard and miserable hours must you endure, until
that period shall arrive."

Scoffing devil! Again do I vow vengeance; again do I devote thee, miserable fiend, to torture and death. Never will I omit my search, until he or
I perish; and then with what ecstacy shall I join my Elizabeth, and those
who even now prepare for me the reward of my tedious toil and horrible
pilgrimage.

As I still pursued my journey to the northward, the snows thickened,
and the cold increased in a degree almost too severe to support. The
peasants were shut up in their hovels, and only a few of the most hardy
ventured forth to seize the animals whom starvation had forced from
their hiding-places to seek for prey. The rivers were covered with ice, and
no fish could be procured; and thus I was cut off from my chief article
of maintenance.

The triumph of my enemy increased with the difficulty of my labours.
One inscription that he left was in these words: "Prepare! your toils only
begin: wrap yourself in furs, and provide food, for we shall soon enter
upon a journey where your sufferings will satisfy my everlasting hatred."

My courage and perseverance were invigorated by these scoffing words;
I resolved not to fail in my purpose; and, calling on heaven to support
me, I continued with unabated fervour to traverse immense deserts, until
the ocean appeared at a distance, and formed the utmost boundary of the
horizon. Oh! how unlike it was to the blue seas of the south! Covered
with ice, it was only to be distinguished from land by its superior wildness
and ruggedness. The Greeks wept for joy when they beheld the Mediterranean from the hills of Asia, and hailed with rapture the boundary of
their toils. I did not weep; but I knelt down, and, with a full heart,

thanked my guiding spirit for conducting me in safety to the place where I hoped, notwithstanding my adversary's gibe, to meet and grapple with him.

Some weeks before this period I had procured a sledge and dogs, and thus traversed the snows with inconceivable speed. I know not whether the fiend possessed the same advantages; but I found that, as before I had daily lost ground in the pursuit, I now gained on him; so much so, that when I first saw the ocean, he was but one day's journey in advance, and I hoped to intercept him before he should reach the beach. With new courage, therefore, I pressed on, and in two days arrived at a wretched hamlet on the sea-shore. I inquired of the inhabitants concerning the fiend, and gained accurate information. A gigantic monster, they said, had arrived the night before, armed with a gun and many pistols; putting to flight the inhabitants of a solitary cottage, through fear of his terrific appearance. He had carried off their store of winter food, and, placing it in a sledge, to draw which he had seized on a numerous drove of trained dogs, he had harnessed them, and the same night, to the joy of the horror-struck villagers, had pursued his journey across the sea in a direction that led to no land; and they conjectured that he must speedily be destroyed by the breaking of the ice, or frozen by the eternal frosts.

On hearing this information, I suffered a temporary access of despair. He had escaped me; and I must commence a destructive and almost endless journey across the mountainous ices of the ocean,—amidst cold that few of the inhabitants could long endure, and which I, the native of a genial and sunny climate, could not hope to survive. Yet at the idea that the fiend should live and be triumphant, my rage and vengeance returned, and, like a mighty tide, overwhelmed every other feeling. After a slight repose, during which the spirits of the dead hovered round, and instigated me to toil and revenge, I prepared for my journey.

I exchanged my land sledge for one fashioned for the inequalities of the frozen ocean; and, purchasing a plentiful stock of provisions, I departed from land.

I cannot guess how many days have passed since then; but I have endured misery, which nothing but the eternal sentiment of a just retribution burning within my heart could have enabled me to support. Immense and rugged mountains of ice often barred up my passage, and I often heard the thunder of the ground sea, which threatened my destruction. But again the frost came, and made the paths of the sea secure.

By the quantity of provision which I had consumed I should guess that I had passed three weeks in this journey; and the continual protraction of hope, returning back upon the heart, often wrung bitter drops of despondency and grief from my eyes. Despair had indeed almost secured her prey, and I should soon have sunk beneath this misery; when once, after the poor animals that carried me had with incredible toil gained the summit of a sloping ice mountain, and one sinking under his fatigue died, I viewed the expanse before me with anguish, when suddenly my eye caught a dark speck upon the dusky plain. I strained my sight to discover what it could be, and uttered a wild cry of ecstacy when I distinguished a sledge, and the distorted proportions of a well-known form within. Oh! with what a burning gush did hope revisit my heart! warm tears filled my eyes, which I hastily wiped away, that they might not intercept the view I had of the dæmon; but still my sight was dimmed by the burning drops, until, giving way to the emotions that oppressed me, I wept aloud.

But this was not the time for delay; I disencumbered the dogs of their dead companion, gave them a plentiful portion of food; and, after an hour's rest, which was absolutely necessary, and yet which was bitterly irksome to me, I continued my route. The sledge was still visible; nor did I again lose sight of it, except at the moments when for a short time some ice rock concealed it with its intervening crags. I indeed perceptibly gained on it; and when, after nearly two days' journey, I beheld my enemy at no more than a mile distant, my heart bounded within me.

But now, when I appeared almost within grasp of my enemy, my hopes were suddenly extinguished, and I lost all trace of him more utterly than I had ever done before. A ground sea was heard; the thunder of its progress, as the waters rolled and swelled beneath me, became every moment more ominous and terrific. I pressed on, but in vain. The wind arose; the sea roared; and, as with the mighty shock of an earthquake, it split, and cracked with a tremendous and overwhelming sound. The work was soon finished: in a few minutes a tumultuous sea rolled between me and my enemy, and I was left drifting on a scattered piece of ice, that was continually lessening, and thus preparing for me a hideous death.

In this manner many appalling hours passed; several of my dogs died; and I myself was about to sink under the accumulation of distress, when I saw your vessel riding at anchor, and holding forth to me hopes of succour and life. I had no conception that vessels ever came so far north, and was astounded at the sight. I quickly destroyed part of my sledge to construct oars; and by these means was enabled, with infinite fatigue, to move my ice-raft in the direction of your ship. I had determined, if you were going southward, still to trust myself to the mercy of the seas, rather than abandon my purpose. I hoped to induce you to grant me a boat with which I could still pursue my enemy. But your direction was northward.

You took me on board when my vigour was exhausted, and I should soon have sunk under my multiplied hardships into a death, which I still dread,—for my task is unfulfilled.

Oh! when will my guiding spirit, in conducting me to the dæmon, allow me the rest I so much desire; or must I die, and he yet live? If I do, swear to me, Walton, that he shall not escape; that you will seek him, and satisfy my vengeance in his death. Yet, do I dare ask you to undertake my pilgrimage, to endure the hardships that I have undergone? No; I am not so selfish. Yet, when I am dead, if he should appear; if the ministers of vengeance should conduct him to you, swear that he shall not live—swear that he shall not triumph over my accumulated woes, and live to make another such a wretch as I am. He is eloquent and persuasive; and once his words had even power over my heart: but trust him not. His soul is as hellish as his form, full of treachery and fiend-like malice. Hear him not; call on the names[32] of William, Justine, Clerval, Elizabeth, my father, and of the wretched Victor, and thrust your sword into his heart. I will hover near, and direct the steel aright.

***Walton*, in continuation.**

August 26th, 17—.

You have read this strange and terrific story, Margaret; and do you not feel your blood congealed with horror, like that which even now curdles mine? Sometimes, seized with sudden agony, he could not continue his tale; at others, his voice broken, yet piercing, uttered with difficulty the words so replete with agony. His fine and lovely eyes were now lighted up with indignation, now subdued to downcast sorrow, and quenched in infinite wretchedness. Sometimes he commanded his countenance and tones, and related the most horrible incidents with a tranquil voice, suppressing every mark of agitation; then, like a volcano bursting forth, his face would suddenly change to an expression of the wildest rage, as he shrieked out imprecations on his persecutor.

His tale is connected, and told with an appearance of the simplest truth; yet I own to you that the letters of Felix and Safie, which he shewed me, and the apparition of the monster, seen from our ship, brought to me a greater conviction of the truth of his narrative than his asseverations, however earnest and connected. Such a monster has then really existence; I cannot doubt it; yet I am lost in surprise and admiration. Sometimes I endeavoured to gain from Frankenstein the particulars of his creature's formation; but on this point he was impenetrable.

"Are you mad, my friend?" said he, "or whither does your senseless

32. Spirits of the dead.

curiosity lead you? Would you also create for yourself and the world a demoniacal enemy? Or to what do your questions tend? Peace, peace! learn my miseries, and do not seek to increase your own."

Frankenstein discovered that I made notes concerning his history: he asked to see them, and then himself corrected and augmented them in many places; but principally in giving the life and spirit to the conversations he held with his enemy. "Since you have preserved my narration," said he, "I would not that a mutilated one should go down to posterity."

Thus has a week passed away, while I have listened to the strangest tale that ever imagination formed. My thoughts, and every feeling of my soul, have been drunk up by the interest for my guest, which this tale, and his own elevated and gentle manners have created. I wish to soothe him; yet can I counsel one so infinitely miserable, so destitute of every hope of consolation, to live? Oh, no! the only joy that he can now know will be when he composes his shattered feelings to peace and death. Yet he enjoys one comfort, the offspring of solitude and delirium: he believes, that, when in dreams he holds converse with his friends, and derives from that communion consolation for his miseries, or excitements to his vengeance, that they are not the creations of his fancy, but the real beings who visit him from the regions of a remote world. This faith gives a solemnity to his reveries that render them to me almost as imposing and interesting as truth.

Our conversations are not always confined to his own history and misfortunes. On every point of general literature he displays unbounded knowledge, and a quick and piercing apprehension. His eloquence is forcible and touching; nor can I hear him, when he relates a pathetic incident, or endeavours to move the passions of pity or love, without tears. What a glorious creature must he have been in the days of his prosperity, when he is thus noble and godlike in ruin. He seems to feel his own worth, and the greatness of his fall.

"When younger," said he, "I felt as if I were destined for some great enterprise. My feelings are profound; but I possessed a coolness of judgment that fitted me for illustrious achievements. This sentiment of the worth of my nature supported me, when others would have been oppressed; for I deemed it criminal to throw away in useless grief those talents that might be useful to my fellow-creatures. When I reflected on the work I had completed, no less a one than the creation of a sensitive and rational animal, I could not rank myself with the herd of common projectors. But this feeling, which supported me in the commencement of my career, now serves only to plunge me lower in the dust. All my speculations and hopes are as nothing; and, like the archangel who aspired to omnipotence, I am chained in an eternal hell. My imagination was vivid, yet my powers of analysis and application were intense; by the union of these qualities I conceived the idea, and executed the creation of a man. Even now I cannot recollect, without passion, my reveries while the work was incomplete. I trod heaven in my thoughts, now exulting in my powers, now burning with the idea of their effects. From my infancy I was imbued with high hopes and a lofty ambition; but how am I sunk! Oh! my friend, if you had known me as I once was, you would not recognize me in this state of degradation. Despondency rarely visited my heart; a high destiny seemed to bear me on, until I fell, never, never again to rise."

Must I then lose this admirable being? I have longed for a friend; I have sought one who would sympathize with and love me. Behold, on these desert seas I have found such a one; but, I fear, I have gained him only to know his value, and lose him. I would reconcile him to life, but he repulses the idea.

"I thank you, Walton," he said, "for your kind intentions towards so miserable a wretch; but when you speak of new ties, and fresh affections, think you that any can replace those who are gone? Can any man be to me as Clerval was; or any woman another Elizabeth? Even where the affections are not strongly moved by any superior excellence, the companions of our childhood always possess a certain power over our minds, which hardly any later friend can obtain. They know our infantine dispositions, which, however they may be afterwards modified, are never eradicated; and they can judge of our actions with more certain conclusions as to the integrity of our motives. A sister or a brother can never, unless indeed such symptoms have been shewn early, suspect the other of fraud or false dealing, when another friend, however strongly he may be attached, may, in spite of himself, be invaded with suspicion. But I enjoyed friends, dear not only through habit and association, but from their own merits; and, wherever I am, the soothing voice of my Elizabeth, and the conversation of Clerval, will be ever whispered in my ear. They are dead; and but one feeling in such a solitude can persuade me to preserve my life. If I were engaged in any high undertaking or design, fraught with extensive utility to my fellow-creatures, then could I live to fulfil it. But such is not my destiny; I must pursue and destroy the being to whom I gave existence; then my lot on earth will be fulfilled, and I may die."

September 2d.

My beloved Sister,

I write to you, encompassed by peril, and ignorant whether I am ever doomed to see again dear England, and the dearer friends that inhabit it. I am surrounded by mountains of ice, which admit of no escape, and threaten every moment to crush my vessel. The brave fellows, whom I have persuaded to be my companions, look towards me for aid; but I have none to bestow. There is something terribly appalling in our situation, yet my courage and hopes do not desert me. We may survive; and if we do not, I will repeat the lessons of my Seneca, and die with a good heart.

Yet what, Margaret, will be the state of your mind? You will not hear of my destruction, and you will anxiously await my return. Years will pass, and you will have visitings of despair, and yet be tortured by hope. Oh! my beloved sister, the sickening failings of your heart-felt expectations are, in prospect, more terrible to me than my own death. But you have a husband, and lovely children; you may be happy: heaven bless you, and make you so!

My unfortunate guest regards me with the tenderest compassion. He endeavours to fill me with hope; and talks as if life were a possession which he valued. He reminds me how often the same accidents have happened to other navigators, who have attempted this sea, and, in spite of myself, he fills me with cheerful auguries. Even the sailors feel the power of his eloquence: when he speaks, they no longer despair; he rouses their energies, and, while they hear his voice, they believe these vast mountains of ice are mole-hills, which will vanish before the resolutions of man. These feelings are transitory; each day's expectation delayed fills them with fear, and I almost dread a mutiny caused by this despair.

September 5th.

A scene has just passed of such uncommon interest, that although it is highly probable that these papers may never reach you, yet I cannot forbear recording it.

We are still surrounded by mountains of ice, still in imminent danger of being crushed in their conflict. The cold is excessive, and many of my unfortunate comrades have already found a grave amidst this scene of desolation. Frankenstein has daily declined in health: a feverish fire still glimmers in his eyes; but he is exhausted, and, when suddenly roused to any exertion, he speedily sinks again into apparent lifelessness.

I mentioned in my last letter the fears I entertained of a mutiny. This morning, as I sat watching the wan countenance of my friend—his eyes half closed, and his limbs hanging listlessly,—I was roused by half a dozen of the sailors, who desired admission into the cabin. They entered; and their leader addressed me. He told me that he and his companions had been chosen by the other sailors to come in deputation to me, to make me a demand, which, in justice, I could not refuse. We were immured in ice, and should probably never escape; but they feared that if, as was possible, the ice should dissipate, and a free passage be opened, I should be rash enough to continue my voyage, and lead them into fresh dangers, after they might happily have surmounted this. They desired, therefore, that I should engage with a solemn promise, that if the vessel should be freed, I would instantly direct my course southward.

This speech troubled me. I had not despaired; nor had I yet conceived the idea of returning, if set free. Yet could I, in justice, or even in possibility, refuse this demand? I hesitated before I answered; when Frankenstein, who had at first been silent, and, indeed, appeared hardly to have force enough to attend, now roused himself; his eyes sparkled, and his cheeks flushed with momentary vigour. Turning towards the men, he said—

"What do you mean? What do you demand of your captain? Are you then so easily turned from your design? Did you not call this a glorious expedition? and wherefore was it glorious? Not because the way was smooth and placid as a southern sea, but because it was full of dangers and terror; because, at every new incident, your fortitude was to be called forth, and your courage exhibited; because danger and death surrounded, and these dangers you were to brave and overcome. For this was it a glorious, for this was it an honourable undertaking. You were hereafter to be hailed as the benefactors of your species; your name adored, as belonging to brave men who encountered death for honour and the benefit of mankind. And now, behold, with the first imagination of danger, or, if you will, the first mighty and terrific trial of your courage, you shrink away, and are content to be handed down as men who had not strength enough to endure cold and peril; and so, poor souls, they were chilly, and returned to their warm fire-sides. Why, that requires not this preparation; ye need not have come thus far, and dragged your captain to the shame of a defeat, merely to prove yourselves cowards. Oh! be men, or be more than men. Be steady to your purposes, and firm as a rock. This ice is not made of such stuff as your hearts might be; it is mutable, cannot withstand you, if you say that it shall not. Do not return to your families with the stigma of disgrace marked on your brows. Return as heroes who have fought and conquered, and who know not what it is to turn their backs on the foe."

He spoke this with a voice so modulated to the different feelings expressed in his speech, with an eye so full of lofty design and heroism, that can you wonder that these men were moved. They looked at one another, and were unable to reply. I spoke; I told them to retire, and consider of what had been said: that I would not lead them further north, if they strenuously desired the contrary; but that I hoped that, with reflection, their courage would return.

They retired, and I turned towards my friend; but he was sunk in languor, and almost deprived of life.

How all this will terminate, I know not; but I had rather die, than return shamefully,—my purpose unfulfilled. Yet I fear such will be my fate; the men, unsupported by ideas of glory and honour, can never willingly continue to endure their present hardships.

September 7th.

The die is cast; I have consented to return, if we are not destroyed. Thus are my hopes blasted by cowardice and indecision; I come back ignorant and disappointed. It requires more philosophy than I possess, to bear this injustice with patience.

September 12th.

It is past; I am returning to England. I have lost my hopes of utility and glory;—I have lost my friend. But I will endeavour to detail these bitter circumstances to you, my dear sister; and, while I am wafted towards England, and towards you, I will not despond.

September 9th,[33] the ice began to move, and roarings like thunder were heard at a distance, as the islands split and cracked in every direction. We were in the most imminent peril; but, as we could only remain passive, my chief attention was occupied by my unfortunate guest, whose illness increased in such a degree, that he was entirely confined to his bed. The ice cracked behind us, and was driven with force towards the north; a breeze sprung from the west, and on the 11th the passage towards the south became perfectly free. When the sailors saw this, and that their return to their native country was apparently assured, a shout of tumultuous joy broke from them, loud and long-continued. Frankenstein, who was dozing, awoke, and asked the cause of the tumult. "They shout," I said, "because they will soon return to England."

"Do you then really return?"

"Alas! yes; I cannot withstand their demands. I cannot lead them unwillingly to danger, and I must return."

"Do so, if you will; but I will not. You may give up your purpose; but mine is assigned to me by heaven, and I dare not. I am weak; but surely the spirits who assist my vengeance will endow me with sufficient strength." Saying this, he endeavoured to spring from the bed, but the exertion was too great for him; he fell back, and fainted.

It was long before he was restored; and I often thought that life was entirely extinct. At length he opened his eyes, but he breathed with diffi-

33. Incorrectly printed as "19th" in 1818.

culty, and was unable to speak. The surgeon gave him a composing draught, and ordered us to leave him undisturbed. In the mean time he told me, that my friend had certainly not many hours to live.

His sentence was pronounced; and I could only grieve, and be patient. I sat by his bed watching him; his eyes were closed, and I thought he slept; but presently he called to me in a feeble voice, and, bidding me come near, said—"Alas! the strength I relied on is gone; I feel that I shall soon die, and he, my enemy and persecutor, may still be in being. Think not, Walton, that in the last moments of my existence I feel that burning hatred, and ardent desire of revenge, I once expressed, but I feel myself justified in desiring the death of my adversary. During these last days I have been occupied in examining my past conduct; nor do I find it blameable. In a fit of enthusiastic madness I created a rational creature, and was bound towards him, to assure, as far as was in my power, his happiness and well-being. This was my duty; but there was another still paramount to that. My duties towards my fellow-creatures had greater claims to my attention, because they included a greater proportion of happiness or misery. Urged by this view, I refused, and I did right in refusing, to create a companion for the first creature. He shewed unparalleled malignity and selfishness, in evil: he destroyed my friends; he devoted to destruction beings who possessed exquisite sensations, happiness, and wisdom; nor do I know where this thirst for vengeance may end. Miserable himself, that he may render no other wretched, he ought to die. The task of his destruction was mine, but I have failed. When actuated by selfish and vicious motives, I asked you to undertake my unfinished work; and I renew this request now, when I am only induced by reason and virtue.

"Yet I cannot ask you to renounce your country and friends, to fulfil this task; and now, that you are returning to England, you will have little chance of meeting with him. But the consideration of these points, and the well-balancing of what you may esteem your duties, I leave to you; my judgment and ideas are already disturbed by the near approach of death. I dare not ask you to do what I think right, for I may still be misled by passion.

"That he should live to be an instrument of mischief disturbs me; in other respects this hour, when I momentarily expect my release, is the only happy one which I have enjoyed for several years. The forms of the beloved dead flit before me, and I hasten to their arms. Farewell, Walton! Seek happiness in tranquillity, and avoid ambition, even if it be only the apparently innocent one of distinguishing yourself in science and discoveries. Yet why do I say this? I have myself been blasted in these hopes, yet another may succeed."

His voice became fainter as he spoke; and at length, exhausted by his effort, he sunk into silence. About half an hour afterwards he attempted again to speak, but was unable; he pressed my hand feebly, and his eyes closed for ever, while the irradiation of a gentle smile passed away from his lips.

Margaret, what comment can I make on the untimely extinction of this glorious spirit? What can I say, that will enable you to understand the depth of my sorrow? All that I should express would be inadequate and feeble. My tears flow; my mind is overshadowed by a cloud of disappointment. But I journey towards England, and I may there find consolation.

I am interrupted. What do these sounds portend? It is midnight; the breeze blows fairly, and the watch on deck scarcely stir. Again; there is a sound as of a human voice, but hoarser; it comes from the cabin where the remains of Frankenstein still lie. I must arise, and examine. Good night, my sister.

Great God! what a scene has just taken place! I am yet dizzy with the remembrance of it. I hardly know whether I shall have the power to detail it; yet the tale which I have recorded would be incomplete without this final and wonderful catastrophe.

I entered the cabin, where lay the remains of my ill-fated and admirable friend. Over him hung a form which I cannot find words to describe; gigantic in stature, yet uncouth and distorted in its proportions. As he hung over the coffin, his face was concealed by long locks of ragged hair; but one vast hand was extended, in colour and apparent texture like that of a mummy. When he heard the sound of my approach, he ceased to utter exclamations of grief and horror, and sprung towards the window. Never did I behold a vision so horrible as his face, of such loathsome, yet appalling hideousness. I shut my eyes involuntarily, and endeavoured to recollect what were my duties with regard to this destroyer. I called on him to stay.

He paused, looking on me with wonder; and, again turning towards the lifeless form of his creator, he seemed to forget my presence, and every feature and gesture seemed instigated by the wildest rage of some uncontrollable passion.

"That is also my victim!" he exclaimed; "in his murder my crimes are consummated; the miserable series of my being is wound to its close! Oh, Frankenstein! generous and self-devoted being! what does it avail that I now ask thee to pardon me? I, who irretrievably destroyed thee by destroying all thou lovedst. Alas! he is cold; he may not answer me."

His voice seemed suffocated; and my first impulses, which had suggested to me the duty of obeying the dying request of my friend, in destroying his enemy, were now suspended by a mixture of curiosity and compassion.

I approached this tremendous being; I dared not again raise my looks upon his face, there was something so scaring and unearthly in his ugliness. I attempted to speak, but the words died away on my lips. The monster continued to utter wild and incoherent self-reproaches. At length I gathered resolution to address him, in a pause of the tempest of his passion: "Your repentance," I said, "is now superfluous. If you had listened to the voice of conscience, and heeded the stings of remorse, before you had urged your diabolical vengeance to this extremity, Frankenstein would yet have lived."

"And do you dream?" said the dæmon; "do you think that I was then dead to agony and remorse?—He," he continued, pointing to the corpse, "he suffered not more in the consummation of the deed;—oh! not the ten-thousandth portion of the anguish that was mine during the lingering detail of its execution. A frightful selfishness hurried me on, while my heart was poisoned with remorse. Think ye that the groans of Clerval were music to my ears? My heart was fashioned to be susceptible of love and sympathy; and, when wrenched by misery to vice and hatred, it did not endure the violence of the change without torture, such as you cannot even imagine.

"After the murder of Clerval, I returned to Switzerland, heart-broken and overcome. I pitied Frankenstein; my pity amounted to horror: I abhorred myself. But when I discovered that he, the author at once of my existence and of its unspeakable torments, dared to hope for happiness; that while he accumulated wretchedness and despair upon me, he sought his own enjoyment in feelings and passions from the indulgence of which I was for ever barred, then impotent envy and bitter indignation filled me with an insatiable thirst for vengeance. I recollected my threat, and resolved that it should be accomplished. I knew that I was preparing for myself a deadly torture; but I was the slave, not the master of an impulse, which I detested, yet could not disobey. Yet when she died!—nay, then I was not miserable. I had cast off all feeling, subdued all anguish to riot in the excess of my despair. Evil thenceforth became my good.[34] Urged thus far, I had no choice but to adapt my nature to an element which I had willingly chosen. The completion of my demoniacal design became an insatiable passion. And now it is ended; there is my last victim!"

I was at first touched by the expresssions of his misery; yet when I called to mind what Frankenstein had said of his powers of eloquence and persuasion, and when I again cast my eyes on the lifeless form of my friend, indignation was re-kindled within me. "Wretch!" I said, "it is well that you come here to whine over the desolation that you have made. You throw a torch into a pile of buildings, and when they are consumed you

34. Echo of "Evil be thou my Good" from Milton's *Paradise Lost* IV.110.

sit among the ruins, and lament the fall. Hypocritical fiend! if he whom you mourn still lived, still would he be the object, again would he become the prey of your accursed vengeance. It is not pity that you feel; you lament only because the victim of your malignity is withdrawn from your power."

"Oh, it is not thus—not thus," interrupted the being; "yet such must be the impression conveyed to you by what appears to be the purport of my actions. Yet I seek not a fellow-feeling in my misery. No sympathy may I ever find. When I first sought it, it was the love of virtue, the feelings of happiness and affection with which my whole being overflowed, that I wished to be participated. But now, that virtue has become to me a shadow, and that happiness and affection are turned into bitter and loathing despair, in what should I seek for sympathy? I am content to suffer alone, while my sufferings shall endure: when I die, I am well satisfied that abhorrence and opprobrium should load my memory. Once my fancy was soothed with dreams of virtue, of fame, and of enjoyment. Once I falsely hoped to meet with beings, who, pardoning my outward form, would love me for the excellent qualities which I was capable of bringing forth. I was nourished with high thoughts of honour and devotion. But now vice has degraded me beneath the meanest animal. No crime, no mischief, no malignity, no misery, can be found comparable to mine. When I call over the frightful catalogue of my deeds, I cannot believe that I am he whose thoughts were once filled with sublime and transcendant visions of the beauty and the majesty of goodness. But it is even so; the fallen angel becomes a malignant devil. Yet even that enemy of God and man had friends and associates in his desolation; I am quite alone.

"You, who call Frankenstein your friend, seem to have a knowledge of my crimes and his misfortunes. But, in the detail which he gave you of them, he could not sum up the hours and months of misery which I endured, wasting in impotent passions. For whilst I destroyed his hopes, I did not satisfy my own desires. They were for ever ardent and craving; still I desired love and fellowship, and I was still spurned. Was there no injustice in this? Am I to be thought the only criminal, when all human kind sinned against me? Why do you not hate Felix, who drove his friend from his door with contumely? Why do you not execrate the rustic who sought to destroy the saviour of his child? Nay, these are virtuous and immaculate beings! I, the miserable and the abandoned, am an abortion, to be spurned at, and kicked, and trampled on. Even now my blood boils at the recollection of this injustice.

"But it is true that I am a wretch. I have murdered the lovely and the helpless; I have strangled the innocent as they slept, and grasped to death his throat who never injured me or any other living thing. I have devoted my creator, the select specimen of all that is worthy of love and admiration among men, to misery; I have pursued him even to that irremediable ruin. There he lies, white and cold in death. You hate me; but your abhorrence cannot equal that with which I regard myself. I look on the hands which executed the deed; I think on the heart in which the imagination of it was conceived, and long for the moment when they will meet my eyes, when it will haunt my thoughts, no more.

"Fear not that I shall be the instrument of future mischief. My work is nearly complete. Neither your's nor any man's death is needed to consummate the series of my being, and accomplish that which must be done; but it requires my own. Do not think that I shall be slow to perform this sacrifice. I shall quit your vessel on the ice-raft which brought me hither, and shall seek the most northern extremity of the globe; I shall collect my funeral pile, and consume to ashes this miserable frame, that its remains may afford no light to any curious and unhallowed wretch, who would create such another as I have been. I shall die. I shall no longer feel the agonies which now consume me, or be the prey of feelings unsatisfied, yet unquenched. He is dead who called me into being; and when I shall be no more, the very remembrance of us both will speedily vanish. I shall no longer see the sun or stars, or feel the winds play on my cheeks. Light, feeling, and sense, will pass away; and in this condition must I find my happiness. Some years ago, when the images which this world affords first opened upon me, when I felt the cheering warmth of summer, and heard the rustling of the leaves and the chirping of the birds, and these were all to me, I should have wept to die; now it is my only consolation. Polluted by crimes, and torn by the bitterest remorse, where can I find rest but in death?

"Farewell! I leave you, and in you the last of human kind whom these eyes will ever behold. Farewell, Frankenstein! If thou wert yet alive, and yet cherished a desire of revenge against me, it would be better satiated in my life than in my destruction. But it was not so; thou didst seek my extinction, that I might not cause greater wretchedness; and if yet, in some mode unknown to me, thou hast not yet ceased to think and feel, thou desirest not my life for my own misery. Blasted as thou wert, my agony was still superior to thine; for the bitter sting of remorse may not cease to rankle in my wounds until death shall close them for ever.

"But soon," he cried, with sad and solemn enthusiasm, "I shall die, and what I now feel be no longer felt. Soon these burning miseries will be extinct. I shall ascend my funeral pile triumphantly, and exult in the agony of the torturing flames. The light of that conflagration will fade away; my ashes will be swept into the sea by the winds. My spirit will sleep in peace; or if it thinks, it will not surely think thus. Farewell."

He sprung from the cabin-window, as he said this, upon the ice-raft which lay close to the vessel. He was soon borne away by the waves, and lost in darkness and distance.

THE END.

FRANKENSTEIN'S DEPARTURE

The day of my departure at length arrived.

T. Holst, del. • W. Chevalier, sc.

(Engraved title-page from 1831 *Frankenstein*.)

Introduction

to *Frankenstein* (1831)[1]

The Publishers of the Standard Novels, in selecting "Frankenstein" for one of their series, expressed a wish that I should furnish them with some account of the origin of the story. I am the more willing to comply, because I shall thus give a general answer to the question, so very frequently asked me—"How I, then a young girl, came to think of, and to dilate upon, so very hideous an idea?" It is true that I am very averse to bringing myself forward in print; but as my account will only appear as an appendage to a former production, and as it will be confined to such topics as have connection with my authorship alone, I can scarcely accuse myself of a personal intrusion.

It is not singular that, as the daughter of two persons of distinguished literary celebrity, I should very early in life have thought of writing. As a child I scribbled; and my favourite pastime, during the hours given me for recreation, was to "write stories." Still I had a dearer pleasure than this, which was the formation of castles in the air—the indulging in waking dreams—the following up trains of thought, which had for their subject the formation of a succession of imaginary incidents. My dreams were at once more fantastic and agreeable than my writings. In the latter I was a close imitator—rather doing as others had done, than putting down the suggestions of my own mind. What I wrote was intended at least for one other eye—my childhood's companion and friend; but my dreams were all my own; I accounted for them to nobody; they were my refuge when annoyed—my dearest pleasure when free.

I lived principally in the country as a girl, and passed a considerable time in Scotland. I made occasional visits to the more picturesque parts;

1. Reprinted from *Frankenstein: or, The Modern Prometheus,* revised, corrected, and illustrated with a new introduction, by the Author (London: Henry Colburn and Richard Bentley, 1831), pp. v–xii.

but my habitual residence was on the blank and dreary northern shores of the Tay, near Dundee. Blank and dreary on retrospection I call them; they were not so to me then. They were the eyry[2] of freedom, and the pleasant region where unheeded I could commune with the creatures of my fancy. I wrote then—but in a most common-place style. It was beneath the trees of the grounds belonging to our house, or on the bleak sides of the woodless mountains near, that my true compositions, the airy flights of my imagination, were born and fostered. I did not make myself the heroine of my tales. Life appeared to me too common-place an affair as regarded myself. I could not figure to myself that romantic woes or wonderful events would ever be my lot; but I was not confined to my own identity, and I could people the hours with creations far more interesting to me at that age, than my own sensations.

After this my life became busier, and reality stood in place of fiction. My husband, however, was from the first, very anxious that I should prove myself worthy of my parentage, and enrol myself on the page of fame. He was for ever inciting me to obtain literary reputation, which even on my own part I cared for then, though since I have become infinitely indifferent to it. At this time he desired that I should write, not so much with the idea that I could produce any thing worthy of notice, but that he might himself judge how far I possessed the promise of better things hereafter. Still I did nothing. Travelling, and the cares of a family, occupied my time; and study, in the way of reading, or improving my ideas in communication with his far more cultivated mind, was all of literary employment that engaged my attention.

In the summer of 1816, we visited Switzerland, and became the neighbours of Lord Byron. At first we spent our pleasant hours on the lake, or wandering on its shores; and Lord Byron, who was writing the third canto of Childe Harold, was the only one among us who put his thoughts upon paper. These, as he brought them successively to us, clothed in all the light and harmony of poetry, seemed to stamp as divine the glories of heaven and earth, whose influences we partook with him.

But it proved a wet, ungenial summer, and incessant rain often confined us for days to the house. Some volumes of ghost stories, translated from the German into French, fell into our hands. There was the History of the Inconstant Lover, who, when he thought to clasp the bride to whom he had pledged his vows, found himself in the arms of the pale ghost of her whom he had deserted. There was the tale of the sinful founder of his race, whose miserable doom it was to bestow the kiss of death on all the younger sons of his fated house, just when they reached

---

2. Variant spelling of "aerie," the nest of a bird of prey, used here to suggest a desolate retreat or habitation.

the age of promise. His gigantic, shadowy form, clothed like the ghost in Hamlet, in complete armour, but with the beaver up, was seen at midnight, by the moon's fitful beams, to advance slowly along the gloomy avenue. The shape was lost beneath the shadow of the castle walls; but soon a gate swung back, a step was heard, the door of the chamber opened, and he advanced to the couch of the blooming youths, cradled in healthy sleep. Eternal sorrow sat upon his face as he bent down and kissed the forehead of the boys, who from that hour withered like flowers snapt upon the stalk. I have not seen these stories since then; but their incidents are as fresh in my mind as if I had read them yesterday.

"We will each write a ghost story," said Lord Byron; and his proposition was acceded to. There were four of us. The noble author began a tale, a fragment of which he printed at the end of his poem of Mazeppa.[3] Shelley, more apt to embody ideas and sentiments in the radiance of brilliant imagery, and in the music of the most melodious verse that adorns our language, than to invent the machinery of a story, commenced one founded on the experiences of his early life. Poor Polidori had some terrible idea about a skull-headed lady, who was so punished for peeping through a key-hole—what to see I forget—something very shocking and wrong of course; but when she was reduced to a worse condition than the renowned Tom of Coventry, he did not know what to do with her, and was obliged to despatch her to the tomb of the Capulets, the only place for which she was fitted. The illustrious poets also, annoyed by the platitude of prose, speedily relinquished their uncongenial task.

I busied myself *to think of a story,*—a story to rival those which had excited us to this task. One which would speak to the mysterious fears of our nature, and awaken thrilling horror—one to make the reader dread to look round, to curdle the blood, and quicken the beatings of the heart. If I did not accomplish these things, my ghost story would be unworthy of its name. I thought and pondered—vainly. I felt that blank incapability of invention which is the greatest misery of authorship, when dull Nothing replies to our anxious invocations. *Have you thought of a story?* I was asked each morning, and each morning I was forced to reply with a mortifying negative.

Every thing must have a beginning, to speak in Sanchean phrase; and that beginning must be linked to something that went before. The Hindoos give the world an elephant to support it, but they make the elephant stand upon a tortoise. Invention, it must be humbly admitted, does not consist in creating out of void, but out of chaos; the materials must, in the first place, be afforded: it can give form to dark, shapeless sub-

3. Lord Byron, *Mazeppa, a Poem* (London: John Murray, 1819), pp. 59–69.

stances, but cannot bring into being the substance itself. In all matters of discovery and invention, even of those that appertain to the imagination, we are continually reminded of the story of Columbus and his egg. Invention consists in the capacity of seizing on the capabilities of a subject, and in the power of moulding and fashioning ideas suggested to it.

Many and long were the conversations between Lord Byron and Shelley, to which I was a devout but nearly silent listener. During one of these, various philosophical doctrines were discussed, and among others the nature of the principle of life, and whether there was any probability of its ever being discovered and communicated. They talked of the experiments of Dr. Darwin, (I speak not of what the Doctor really did, or said that he did, but, as more to my purpose, of what was then spoken of as having been done by him,) who preserved a piece of vermicelli in a glass case, till by some extraordinary means it began to move with voluntary motion. Not thus, after all, would life be given. Perhaps a corpse would be re-animated; galvanism had given token of such things: perhaps the component parts of a creature might be manufactured, brought together, and endued with vital warmth.

Night waned upon this talk, and even the witching hour had gone by, before we retired to rest. When I placed my head on my pillow, I did not sleep, nor could I be said to think. My imagination, unbidden, possessed and guided me, gifting the successive images that arose in my mind with a vividness far beyond the usual bounds of reverie. I saw—with shut eyes, but acute mental vision,—I saw the pale student of unhallowed arts kneeling beside the thing he had put together. I saw the hideous phantasm of a man stretched out, and then, on the working of some powerful engine, show signs of life, and stir with an uneasy, half vital motion. Frightful must it be; for supremely frightful would be the effect of any human endeavour to mock the stupendous mechanism of the Creator of the world. His success would terrify the artist; he would rush away from his odious handywork, horror-stricken. He would hope that, left to itself, the slight spark of life which he had communicated would fade; that this thing, which had received such imperfect animation, would subside into dead matter; and he might sleep in the belief that the silence of the grave would quench for ever the transient existence of the hideous corpse which he had looked upon as the cradle of life. He sleeps; but he is awakened; he opens his eyes; behold the horrid thing stands at his bedside, opening his curtains, and looking on him with yellow, watery, but speculative eyes.

I opened mine in terror. The idea so possessed my mind, that a thrill of fear ran through me, and I wished to exchange the ghastly image of my fancy for the realities around. I see them still; the very room, the dark *parquet,* the closed shutters, with the moonlight struggling through, and the sense I had that the glassy lake and white high Alps were beyond. I could not so easily get rid of my hideous phantom; still it haunted me. I must try to think of something else. I recurred to my ghost story,—my tiresome unlucky ghost story! O! if I could only contrive one which would frighten my reader as I myself had been frightened that night!

Swift as light and as cheering was the idea that broke in upon me. "I have found it! What terrified me will terrify others; and I need only describe the spectre which had haunted my midnight pillow." On the morrow I announced that I had *thought of a story.* I began that day with the words, *It was on a dreary night of November,* making only a transcript of the grim terrors of my waking dream.

At first I thought but of a few pages—of a short tale; but Shelley urged me to develope the idea at greater length. I certainly did not owe the suggestion of one incident, nor scarcely of one train of feeling, to my husband, and yet but for his incitement, it would never have taken the form in which it was presented to the world. From this declaration I must except the preface. As far as I can recollect, it was entirely written by him.

And now, once again, I bid my hideous progeny go forth and prosper. I have an affection for it, for it was the offspring of happy days, when death and grief were but words, which found no true echo in my heart. Its several pages speak of many a walk, many a drive, and many a conversation, when I was not alone; and my companion was one who, in this world, I shall never see more. But this is for myself; my readers have nothing to do with these associations.

I will add but one word as to the alterations I have made. They are principally those of style. I have changed no portion of the story, nor introduced any new ideas or circumstances.[4] I have mended the language where it was so bald as to interfere with the interest of the narrative; and these changes occur almost exclusively in the beginning of the first volume. Throughout they are entirely confined to such parts as are mere adjuncts to the story, leaving the core and substance of it untouched.

London, October 15. 1831.   M. W. S.

4. Mary Shelley, however, did make a number of alterations—e.g., she changed Elizabeth from a cousin of Frankenstein to a foundling; and she added a chapter to the beginning of the novel. For a full "Collation of the Texts of 1818 and 1831," see Rieger, *Frankenstein: The 1818 Text,* pp. 230–59, 288.

Mathilda

Chapter I[1]

It is only four o'clock; but it is winter and the sun has already set: there are no clouds in the clear, frosty sky to reflect its slant beams, but the air itself is tinged with a slight roseate colour which is again reflected on the snow that covers the ground. I live in a lone cottage on a solitary, wide heath: no voice of life reaches me. I see the desolate plain covered with white, save a few black patches that the noonday sun has made at the top of those sharp pointed hillocks from which the snow, sliding as it fell, lay thinner than on the plain ground: a few birds are pecking at the hard ice that covers the pools—for the frost has been of long continuance.

I am in a strange state of mind. I am alone—quite alone—in the world—the blight of misfortune has passed over me and withered me; I know that I am about to die and I feel happy—joyous.—I feel my pulse; it beats fast: I place my thin hand on my cheek; it burns: there is a slight, quick spirit within me which is now emitting its last sparks. I shall never see the snows of another winter—I do believe that I shall never again feel the vivifying warmth of another summer sun; and it is in this persuasion that I begin to write my tragic history. Perhaps a history such as mine had better die with me, but a feeling that I cannot define leads me on and I am too weak both in body and mind to resist the slightest impulse. While life was strong within me I thought indeed that there was a sacred horror in my tale that rendered it unfit for utterance, and now about to die I

---

1. Reprinted by permission from Mary Wollstonecraft Shelley's *Mathilda*, ed. Elizabeth Nitchie, Extra Series #3 of *Studies in Philology* (Chapel Hill: The University of North Carolina Press, 1959), pp. 1–80, where Nitchie's text is based on Mary Shelley's fair copy MS belonging to Lord Abinger and deposited in the Bodleian Library, Oxford University. The heading to Chapter I in both MS and Nitchie that reads "Florence. Nov. 9th 1819" is here deleted because it dates the MS and is not part of the novella.

pollute its mystic terrors. It is as the wood of the Eumenides none but the dying may enter; and Oedipus is about to die.[2]

What am I writing?—I must collect my thoughts. I do not know that any will peruse these pages except you, my friend, who will receive them at my death. I do not address them to you alone because it will give me pleasure to dwell upon our friendship in a way that would be needless if you alone read what I shall write. I shall relate my tale therefore as if I wrote for strangers. You have often asked me the cause of my solitary life; my tears; and above all of my impenetrable and unkind silence. In life I dared not; in death I unveil the mystery. Others will toss these pages lightly over: to you, Woodville, kind, affectionate friend, they will be dear—the precious memorials of a heart-broken girl who, dying, is still warmed by gratitude towards you: your tears will fall on the words that record my misfortunes; I know they will—and while I have life I thank you for your sympathy.

But enough of this. I will begin my tale: it is my last task, and I hope I have strength sufficient to fulfill it. I record no crimes; my faults may easily be pardoned; for they proceeded not from evil motive but from want of judgement; and I believe few would say that they could, by a different conduct and superior wisdom, have avoided the misfortunes to which I am the victim. My fate has been governed by necessity, a hideous necessity. It required hands stronger than mine; stronger I do believe than any human force to break the thick, adamantine chain that has bound me, once breathing nothing but joy, ever possessed by a warm love and delight in goodness,—to misery only to be ended, and now about to be ended, in death. But I forget myself, my tale is yet untold. I will pause a few moments, wipe my dim eyes, and endeavour to lose the present obscure but heavy feeling of unhappiness in the more acute emotions of the past.

I was born in England. My father was a man of rank: he had lost his father early, and was educated by a weak mother with all the indulgence she thought due to a nobleman of wealth. He was sent to Eton and afterwards to college; and allowed from childhood the free use of large sums of money; thus enjoying from his earliest youth the independance which a boy with these advantages, always acquires at a public school.

Under the influence of these circumstances his passions found a deep soil wherein they might strike their roots and flourish either as flowers or weeds as was their nature. By being always allowed to act for himself his character became strongly and early marked and exhibited a various sur-

---

2. In Sophocles's *Oedipus at Colonus*, the Eumenides or "kindly ones" (actually the Furies) occupied the grove through which Oedipus had to pass. The allusion here also introduces the subject of incest.

face on which a quick sighted observer might see the seeds of virtues and of misfortunes. His careless extravagance, which made him squander immense sums of money to satisfy passing whims, which from their apparent energy he dignified with the name of passions, often displayed itself in unbounded generosity. Yet while he earnestly occupied himself about the wants of others his own desires were gratified to their fullest extent. He gave his money, but none of his own wishes were sacrifised to his gifts; he gave his time, which he did not value, and his affections which he was happy in any manner to have called into action.

I do not say that if his own desires had been put in competition with those of others that he would have displayed undue selfishness, but this trial was never made. He was nurtured in prosperity and attended by all its advantages; every one loved him and wished to gratify him. He was ever employed in promoting the pleasures of his companions—but their pleasures were his; and if he bestowed more attention upon the feelings of others than is usual with schoolboys it was because his social temper could never enjoy itself if every brow was not as free from care as his own.

While at school, emulation and his own natural abilities made him hold a conspicuous rank in the forms among his equals; at college he discarded books; he believed that he had other lessons to learn than those which they could teach him. He was now to enter into life and he was still young enough to consider study as a school-boy shackle, employed merely to keep the unruly out of mischief but as having no real connexion with life—whose wisdom of riding—gaming &c. he considered with far deeper interest—So he quickly entered into all college follies although his heart was too well moulded to be contaminated by them—it might be light but it was never cold. He was a sincere and sympathizing friend—but he had met with none who superior or equal to himself could aid him in unfolding his mind, or make him seek for fresh stores of thought by exhausting the old ones. He felt himself superior in quickness of judgement to those around him: his talents, his rank and wealth made him the chief of his party, and in that station he rested not only contented but glorying, conceiving it to be the only ambition worthy for him to aim at in the world.

By a strange narrowness of ideas he viewed all the world in connexion only as it was or was not related to his little society. He considered queer and out of fashion all opinions that were exploded by his circle of intimates, and he became at the same time dogmatic and yet fearful of not coinciding with the only sentiments he could consider orthodox. To the generality of spectators he appeared careless of censure, and with high disdain to throw aside all dependance on public prejudices; but at the same time that he strode with a triumphant stride over the rest of the world, he cowered, with self-disguised lowliness, to his own party, and although its chief never dared express an opinion or a feeling until he was assured that it would meet with the approbation of his companions.

Yet he had one secret hidden from these dear friends; a secret he had nurtured from his earliest years, and although he loved his fellow collegiates he would not trust it to the delicacy or sympathy of any one among them. He loved. He feared that the intensity of his passion might become the subject of their ridicule; and he could not bear that they should blaspheme it by considering that trivial and transitory which he felt was the life of his life.

There was a gentleman of small fortune who lived near his family mansion who had three lovely daughters. The eldest was far the most beautiful, but her beauty was only an addition to her other qualities—her understanding was clear and strong and her disposition angelically gentle. She and my father had been playmates from infancy: Diana, even in her childhood had been a favourite with his mother; this partiality encreased with the years of this beautiful and lively girl and thus during his school and college vacations they were perpetually together. Novels and all the various methods by which youth in civilized life are led to a knowledge of the existence of passions before they really feel them, had produced a strong effect on him who was so peculiarly susceptible of every impression. At eleven years of age Diana was his favourite playmate but he already talked the language of love. Although she was elder than he by nearly two years the nature of her education made her more childish at least in the knowledge and expression of feeling; she received his warm protestations with innocence, and returned them unknowing of what they meant. She had read no novels and associated only with her younger sisters, what could she know of the difference between love and friendship? And when the development of her understanding disclosed the true nature of this intercourse to her, her affections were already engaged to her friend, and all she feared was lest other attractions and fickleness might make him break his infant vows.

But they became every day more ardent and tender. It was a passion that had grown with his growth; it had become entwined with every faculty and every sentiment and only to be lost with life. None knew of their love except their own two hearts; yet although in all things else and even in this he dreaded the censure of his companions, for thus truly loving one inferior to him in fortune, nothing was ever able for a moment to shake his purpose of uniting himself to her as soon as he could muster courage sufficient to meet those difficulties he was determined to surmount.

Diana was fully worthy of his deepest affection. There were few who could boast of so pure a heart, and so much real humbleness of soul joined to a firm reliance on her own integrity and a belief in that of others. She had from her birth lived a retired life. She had lost her mother when very young, but her father had devoted himself to the care of her education—He had many peculiar ideas which influenced the system he had adopted with regard to her—She was well acquainted with the heroes of Greece and Rome or with those of England who had lived some hundred years ago, while she was nearly ignorant of the passing events of the day: she had read few authors who had written during at least the last fifty years but her reading with this exception was very extensive. Thus although she appeared to be less initiated in the mysteries of life and society than he, her knowledge was of a deeper kind and laid on firmer foundations; and if even her beauty and sweetness had not fascinated him, her understanding would ever have held his in thrall. He looked up to her as his guide, and such was his adoration that he delighted to augment to his own mind the sense of inferiority with which she sometimes impressed him.

When he was nineteen his mother died. He left college on this event and shaking off for a while his old friends he retired to the neighbourhood of his Diana and received all his consolation from her sweet voice and dearer caresses. This short separation from his companions gave him courage to assert his independance. He had a feeling that however they might express ridicule of his intended marriage they would not dare display it when it had taken place; therefore seeking the consent of his guardian which with some difficulty he obtained, and of the father of his mistress which was more easily given, without acquainting any one else of his intention, by the time he had attained his twentieth birthday he had become the husband of Diana.

He loved her with passion and her tenderness had a charm for him that would not permit him to think of aught but her. He invited some of his college friends to see him but their frivolity disgusted him. Diana had torn the veil which had before kept him in his boyhood: he was become a man and he was surprised how he could ever have joined in the cant words and ideas of his fellow collegiates or how for a moment he had feared the censure of such as these. He discarded his old friendships not from fickleness but because they were indeed unworthy of him. Diana filled up all his heart: he felt as if by his union with her he had received a new and better soul. She was his monitress as he learned what were the true ends of life. It was through her beloved lessons that he cast off his old pursuits and gradually formed himself to become one among his fellow men; a distinguished member of society, a Patriot; and an enlightened lover of truth and virtue.—He loved her for her beauty and for her amiable disposition but he seemed to love her more for what he considered her superior wisdom. They studied, they rode together; they were never seperate and seldom admitted a third to their society.

Thus my father, born in affluence, and always prosperous, clombe without the difficulty and various disappointments that all human beings seem destined to encounter, to the very topmost pinacle of happiness. Around him was sunshine, and clouds whose shapes of beauty made the prospect divine concealed from him the barren reality which lay hidden below them. From this dizzy point he was dashed at once as he unawares congratulated himself on his felicity. Fifteen months after their marriage I was born, and my mother died a few days after my birth.

A sister of my father was with him at this period. She was nearly fifteen years older than he, and was the offspring of a former marriage of his father. When the latter died this sister was taken by her maternal relations: they had seldom seen one another, and were quite unlike in disposition. This aunt, to whose care I was afterwards consigned, has often related to me the effect that this catastrophe had on my father's strong and susceptible character. From the moment of my mother's death until his departure she never heard him utter a single word: buried in the deepest melancholy he took no notice of any one; often for hours his eyes streamed tears or a more fearful gloom overpowered him. All outward things seemed to have lost their existence relatively to him and only one circumstance could in any degree recall him from his motionless and mute despair: he would never see me. He seemed insensible to the presence of any one else, but if, as a trial to awaken his sensibility, my aunt brought me into the room he would instantly rush out with every symptom of fury and distraction. At the end of a month he suddenly quitted his house and, unattended by any servant, departed from that part of the country without by word or writing informing any one of his intentions. My aunt was only relieved of her anxiety concerning his fate by a letter from him dated Hamburgh.

How often have I wept over that letter which until I was sixteen was the only relick I had to remind me of my parents. "Pardon me," it said, "for the uneasiness I have unavoidably given you: but while in that unhappy island, where every thing breathes *her* spirit whom I have lost for ever, a spell held me. It is broken: I have quitted England for many years, perhaps for ever. But to convince you that selfish feeling does not entirely engross me I shall remain in this town until you have made by letter every arrangement that you judge necessary. When I leave this place do not expect to hear from me: I must break all ties that at present exist. I shall become a wanderer, a miserable outcast—alone! alone!"—In another part of the letter he mentioned me—"As for that unhappy little being whom I could not see, and hardly dare mention, I leave her under your protection. Take care of her and cherish her: one day I may claim her at your hands; but futurity is dark, make the present happy to her."

My father remained three months at Hamburgh; when he quitted it he changed his name, my aunt could never discover that which he adopted and only by faint hints, could conjecture that he had taken the road of Germany and Hungary to Turkey.

Thus this towering spirit who had excited interest and high expectation in all who knew and could value him became at once, as it were, extinct. He existed from this moment for himself only. His friends remembered him as a brilliant vision which would never again return to them. The memory of what he had been faded away as years passed; and he who before had been as a part of themselves and of their hopes was now no longer counted among the living.

Chapter II

I now come to my own story. During the early part of my life there is little to relate, and I will be brief; but I must be allowed to dwell a little on the years of my childhood that it may be apparent how when one hope failed all life was to be a blank; and how when the only affection I was permitted to cherish was blasted my existence was extinguished with it.

I have said that my aunt was very unlike my father. I believe that without the slightest tinge of a bad heart she had the coldest that ever filled a human breast: it was totally incapable of any affection. She took me under her protection because she considered it her duty; but she had too long lived alone and undisturbed by the noise and prattle of children to allow that I should disturb her quiet. She had never been married; and for the last five years had lived perfectly alone on an estate, that had descended to her through her mother, on the shores of Loch Lomond in Scotland. My father had expressed a wish in his letters that she should reside with me at his family mansion which was situated in a beautiful country near Richmond in Yorkshire. She would not consent to this proposition, but as soon as she had arranged the affairs which her brother's departure had caused to fall to her care, she quitted England and took me with her to her Scotch estate.

The care of me while a baby, and afterwards until I had reached my eighth year devolved on a servant of my mother's, who had accompanied us in our retirement for that purpose. I was placed in a remote part of the house, and only saw my aunt at stated hours. These occurred twice a day; once about noon she came to my nursery, and once after her dinner I was taken to her. She never caressed me, and seemed all the time I stayed in the room to fear that I should annoy her by some childish freak. My good nurse always schooled me with the greatest care before she ventured into the parlour—and the awe my aunt's cold looks and few constrained words inspired was so great that I seldom disgraced her lessons or was betrayed from the exemplary stillness which I was taught to observe during these short visits.

Under my good nurse's care I ran wild about our park and the neighbouring fields. The offspring of the deepest love, I displayed from my earliest years the greatest sensibility of disposition. I cannot say with what passion I loved every thing, even the inanimate objects that surrounded me. I believe that I bore an individual attachment to every tree in our park; every animal that inhabited it knew me and I loved them. Their occasional deaths filled my infant heart with anguish. I cannot number the birds that I have saved during the long and severe winters of that climate; or the hares and rabbits that I have defended from the attacks of our dogs, or have nursed when accidentally wounded.

When I was seven years of age my nurse left me. I now forget the cause of her departure if indeed I ever knew it. She returned to England, and the bitter tears she shed at parting were the last I saw flow for love of me for many years. My grief was terrible: I had no friend but her in the whole world. By degrees I became reconciled to solitude but no one supplied her place in my affections. I lived in a desolate country where

> ———— there were none to praise
> And very few to love.[3]

It is true that I now saw a little more of my aunt, but she was in every way an unsocial being; and to a timid child she was as a plant beneath a thick covering of ice; I should cut my hands in endeavouring to get at it. So I was entirely thrown upon my own resources. The neighbouring minister was engaged to give me lessons in reading, writing, and French, but he was without family and his manners even to me were always perfectly characteristic of the profession in the exercise of whose functions he chiefly shone, that of a schoolmaster. I sometimes strove to form friendships with the most attractive of the girls who inhabited the neighbouring village; but I believe I should never have succeeded [even] had not my aunt interposed her authority to prevent all intercourse between me and the peasantry; for she was fearful lest I should acquire the Scotch accent and dialect; a little of it I had, although great pains was taken that my tongue should not disgrace my English origin.

As I grew older my liberty increased with my desires, and my wanderings extended from our park to the neighbouring country. Our house was situated on the shores of the lake and the lawn came down to the water's

3. Wordsworth. [Mary Shelley's note on William Wordsworth, "She Dwelt Among the Untrodden Ways," published in the 2d ed. of *Lyrical Ballads* (1800).]

edge. I rambled amidst the wild scenery of this lovely country and became a complete mountaineer: I passed hours on the steep brow of a mountain that overhung a waterfall or rowed myself in a little skiff to some one of the islands. I wandered for ever about these lovely solitudes, gathering flower after flower

Ond' era pinta tutta la mia via[4]

singing as I might the wild melodies of the country, or occupied by pleasant day dreams. My greatest pleasure was the enjoyment of a serene sky amidst these verdant woods: yet I loved all the changes of Nature; and rain, and storm, and the beautiful clouds of heaven brought their delights with them. When rocked by the waves of the lake my spirits rose in triumph as a horseman feels with pride the motions of his high fed steed.

But my pleasures arose from the contemplation of nature alone, I had no companion: my warm affections finding no return from any other human heart were forced to run waste on inanimate objects. Sometimes indeed I wept when my aunt received my caresses with repulsive coldness, and when I looked round and found none to love; but I quickly dried my tears. As I grew older books in some degree supplied the place of human intercourse: the library of my aunt was very small; Shakespear, Milton, Pope and Cowper[5] were the strangely assorted poets of her collection; and among the prose authors a translation of Livy and Rollin's ancient history[6] were my chief favourites although as I emerged from childhood I found others highly interesting which I had before neglected as dull.

When I was twelve years old it occurred to my aunt that I ought to learn music; she herself played upon the harp. It was with great hesitation that she persuaded herself to undertake my instruction; yet believing this accomplishment a necessary part of my education, and balancing the evils of this measure or of having some one in the house to instruct me she submitted to the inconvenience. A harp was sent for that my playing might not interfere with hers, and I began: she found me a docile and, when I had conquered the first rudiments, a very apt scholar. I had acquired in my harp a companion in rainy days; a sweet soother of my feelings when any untoward accident ruffled them: I often addressed it as my only friend; I could pour forth to it my hopes and loves, and I fancied

4. Dante. [Mary Shelley's note on Dante's *Purgatorio* XXVIII.42, where Matelda is introduced, gathering flowers "with which all my path was painted" (Mary Shelley changed Dante's "sua via" to "mia via"). This and subsequent translations are from *The Divine Comedy*, trans. Charles S. Singleton, 6 vols., 2d printing (Princeton: Princeton University Press, 1977).]

5. Alexander Pope (1688–1744) and William Cowper (1731–1800).

6. The Roman historian Livy (59 B.C.–A.D. 17) and Charles Rollin (1661–1741), whose *Ancient History* went through numerous eighteenth-century editions.

that its sweet accents answered me. I have now mentioned all my studies.

I was a solitary being, and from my infant years, ever since my dear nurse left me, I had been a dreamer. I brought Rosalind and Miranda and the lady of Comus[7] to life to be my companions, or on my isle acted over their parts imagining myself to be in their situations. Then I wandered from the fancies of others and formed affections and intimacies with the aerial creations of my own brain—but still clinging to reality I gave a name to these conceptions and nursed them in the hope of realization. I clung to the memory of my parents; my mother I should never see, she was dead: but the idea of [my] unhappy, wandering father was the idol of my imagination. I bestowed on him all my affections; there was a miniature of him that I gazed on continually; I copied his last letter and read it again and again. Sometimes it made me weep; and at others I repeated with transport those words,—"One day I may claim her at your hands." I was to be his consoler, his companion in after years. My favourite vision was that when I grew up I would leave my aunt, whose coldness lulled my conscience, and disguised like a boy I would seek my father through the world. My imagination hung upon the scene of recognition; his miniature, which I should continually wear exposed on my breast, would be the means and I imaged the moment to my mind a thousand and a thousand times, perpetually varying the circumstances. Sometimes it would be in a desert; in a populous city; at a ball; we should perhaps meet in a vessel; and his first words constantly were, "My daughter, I love thee!" What extatic moments have I passed in these dreams! How many tears I have shed; how often have I laughed aloud.

This was my life for sixteen years. At fourteen and fifteen I often thought that the time was come when I should commence my pilgrimage, which I had cheated my own mind into believing was my imperious duty: but a reluctance to quit my aunt; a remorse for the grief which, I could not conceal from myself, I should occasion her for ever withheld me. Sometimes when I had planned the next morning for my escape a word of more than usual affection from her lips made me postpone my resolution. I reproached myself bitterly for what I called a culpable weakness; but this weakness returned upon me whenever the critical moment approached, and I never found courage to depart.

7. Characters in Shakespeare's *As You Like It* and *Tempest* and in Milton's *Comus*.

Chapter III

It was on my sixteenth birthday that my aunt received a letter from my father. I cannot describe the tumult of emotions that arose within me as I read it. It was dated from London; he had returned! I could only relieve my transports by tears, tears of unmingled joy. He had returned, and he wrote to know whether my aunt would come to London or whether he should visit her in Scotland. How delicious to me were the words of his letter that concerned me: "I cannot tell you," it said, "how ardently I desire to see my Mathilda. I look on her as the creature who will form the happiness of my future life: she is all that exists on earth that interests me. I can hardly prevent myself from hastening immediately to you but I am necessarily detained a week and I write because if you come here I may see you somewhat sooner." I read these words with devouring eyes; I kissed them, wept over them and exclaimed, "He will love me!"—

My aunt would not undertake so long a journey, and in a fortnight we had another letter from my father, it was dated Edinburgh: he wrote that he should be with us in three days. As he approached, his desire of seeing me, he said, became more and more ardent, and he felt that the moment when he should first clasp me in his arms would be the happiest of his life.

How irksome were these three days to me! All sleep and appetite fled from me; I could only read and re-read his letter, and in the solitude of the woods imagine the moment of our meeting. On the eve of the third day I retired early to my room; I could not sleep but paced all night about my chamber and, as you may in Scotland at midsummer, watched the crimson track of the sun as it almost skirted the northern horizon. At day break I hastened to the woods; the hours past on while I indulged in wild dreams that gave wings to the slothful steps of time, and beguiled my eager impatience. My father was expected at noon but when I wished to return to meet him I found that I had lost my way: it seemed that in every attempt to find it I only became more involved in the intracacies of the woods, and the trees hid all trace by which I might be guided. I grew impatient, I wept, and wrung my hands but still I could not discover my path.

It was past two o'clock when by a sudden turn I found myself close to the lake near a cove where a little skiff was moored—It was not far from our house and I saw my father and aunt walking on the lawn. I jumped into the boat, and well accustomed to such feats, I pushed it from shore, and exerted all my strength to row swiftly across. As I came, dressed in white, covered only by my tartan *rachan*,[8] my hair streaming on my shoulders, and shooting across with greater speed that it could be supposed I could give to my boat, my father has often told me that I looked more like a spirit than a human maid. I approached the shore, my father held the boat, I leapt lightly out, and in a moment was in his arms.

And now I began to live. All around me was changed from a dull uniformity to the brightest scene of joy and delight. The happiness I enjoyed in the company of my father far exceeded my sanguine expectations. We were for ever together; and the subjects of our conversations were inexhaustible. He had passed the sixteen years of absence among nations nearly unknown to Europe; he had wandered through Persia, Arabia and the north of India and had penetrated among the habitations of the natives with a freedom permitted to few Europeans. His relations of their manners, his anecdotes and descriptions of scenery whiled away delicious hours, when we were tired of talking of our own plans of future life.

The voice of affection was so new to me that I hung with delight upon his words when he told me what he had felt concerning me during these long years of apparent forgetfulness. "At first"—said he, "I could not bear to think of my poor little girl; but afterwards as grief wore off and hope again revisited me I could only turn to her, and amidst cities and desarts her little fairy form, such as I imagined it, for ever flitted before me. The northern breeze as it refreshed me was sweeter and more balmy for it seemed to carry some of your spirit along with it. I often thought that I would instantly return and take you along with me to some fertile island where we should live at peace for ever. As I returned my fervent hopes were dashed by so many fears; my impatience became in the highest degree painful. I dared not think that the sun should shine and the moon rise not on your living form but on your grave. But, no, it is not so; I have my Mathilda, my consolation, and my hope."—

My father was very little changed from what he described himself to be

8. Variant spelling of *rauchan*, "a plaid or wrap, the traditional garb of shepherds."

before his misfortunes. It is intercourse with civilized society; it is the disappointment of cherished hopes, the falsehood of friends, or the perpetual clash of mean passions that changes the heart and damps the ardour of youthful feelings; lonely wanderings in a wild country among people of simple or savage manners may inure the body but will not tame the soul, or extinguish the ardour and freshness of feeling incident to youth. The burning sun of India, and the freedom from all restraint had rather encreased the energy of his character: before he bowed under, now he was impatient of any censure except that of his own mind. He had seen so many customs and witnessed so great a variety of moral creeds that he had been obliged to form an independant one for himself which had no relation to the peculiar notions of any one country: his early prejudices of course influenced his judgement in the formation of his principles, and some raw college ideas were strangely mingled with the deepest deductions of his penetrating mind.

The vacuity his heart endured of any deep interest in life during his long absence from his native country had had a singular effect upon his ideas. There was a curious feeling of unreality attached by him to his foreign life in comparison with the years of his youth. All the time he had passed out of England was as a dream, and all the interest of his soul, all his affections belonged to events which had happened and persons who had existed sixteen years before. It was strange when you heard him talk to see how he passed over this lapse of time as a night of visions; while the remembrances of his youth standing seperate as they did from his after life had lost none of their vigour. He talked of my mother as if she had lived but a few weeks before; not that he expressed poignant grief, but his description of her person, and his relation of all anecdotes connected with her was thus fervent and vivid.

In all this there was a strangeness that attracted and enchanted me. He was, as it were, now awakened from his long, visionary sleep, and he felt somewhat like one of the seven sleepers, or like Nourjahad, in that sweet imitation of an eastern tale:[9] Diana was gone; his friends were changed or dead, and now on his awakening I was all that he had to love on earth.

How dear to me were the waters, and mountains, and woods of Loch Lomond now that I had so beloved a companion for my rambles. I visited with my father every delightful spot, either on the islands, or by the side of the tree-sheltered waterfalls; every shady path, or dingle entangled with underwood and fern. My ideas were enlarged by his conversation. I

9. The Seven Sleepers (third-century Christians of Ephesus who slept for two centuries to escape the persecutions of the Emperor Decius) and Nourjahad (a Persian who was convinced that he had slept for decades) are also mentioned in Mary Shelley's "The Mortal Immortal: A Tale." See also the long sleeper in her narrative essay "Roger Dodsworth: The Reanimated Englishman."

felt as if I were recreated and had about me all the freshness and life of a new being: I was, as it were, transported since his arrival from a narrow spot of earth into a universe boundless to the imagination and the understanding. My life had been before as a pleasing country rill, never destined to leave its native fields, but when its task was fulfilled quietly to be absorbed, and leave no trace. Now it seemed to me to be as a various river flowing through a fertile and lovely landscape, ever changing and ever beautiful. Alas! I knew not the desart it was about to reach; the rocks that would tear its waters, and the hideous scene that would be reflected in a more distorted manner in its waves. Life was then brilliant; I began to learn to hope and what brings a more bitter despair to the heart than hope destroyed?

Is it not strange that grief should quickly follow so divine a happiness? I drank of an enchanted cup but gall was at the bottom of its long drawn sweetness. My heart was full of deep affection, but it was calm from its very depth and fulness. I had no idea that misery could arise from love, and this lesson that all at last must learn was taught me in a manner few are obliged to receive it. I lament now, I must ever lament, those few short months of Paradisaical bliss; I disobeyed no command, I ate no apple, and yet I was ruthlessly driven from it. Alas! my companion did, and I was precipitated in his fall. But I wander from my relation—let woe come at its appointed time; I may at this stage of my story still talk of happiness.

Three months passed away in this delightful intercourse, when my aunt fell ill. I passed a whole month in her chamber nursing her, but her disease was mortal and she died, leaving me for some time inconsolable. Death is so dreadful to the living; the chains of habit are so strong even when affection does not link them that the heart must be agonized when they break. But my father was beside me to console me and to drive away bitter memories by bright hopes: methought that it was sweet to grieve that he might dry my tears.

Then again he distracted my thoughts from my sorrow by comparing it with his despair when he lost my mother. Even at that time I shuddered at the picture he drew of his passions: he had the imagination of a poet, and when he described the whirlwind that then tore his feelings he gave his words the impress of life so vividly that I believed while I trembled. I wondered how he could ever again have entered into the offices of life after his wild thoughts seemed to have given him affinity with the unearthly; while he spoke, so tremendous were the ideas which he conveyed that it appeared as if the human heart were far too bounded for their conception. His feelings seemed better fitted for a spirit whose habitation is the earthquake and the volcano than for one confined to a mortal body and human lineaments. But these were merely memories; he was changed since then. He was now all love, all softness: and when I raised my eyes in wonder at him as he spoke the smile on his lips told me that his heart was possessed by the gentlest passions.

Two months after my aunt's death we removed to London where I was led by my father to attend to deeper studies than had before occupied me. My improvement was his delight; he was with me during all my studies and assisted or joined with me in every lesson. We saw a great deal of society, and no day passed that my father did not endeavour to embellish by some new enjoyment. The tender attachment that he bore me, and the love and veneration with which I returned it cast a charm over every moment. The hours were slow for each minute was employed; we lived more in one week than many do in the course of several months, and the variety and novelty of our pleasures gave zest to each.

We perpetually made excursions together. And whether it were to visit beautiful scenery, or to see fine pictures, or sometimes for no object but to seek amusement as it might chance to arise, I was always happy when near my father. It was a subject of regret to me whenever we were joined by a third person, yet if I turned with a disturbed look towards my father, his eyes fixed on me and beaming with tenderness instantly restored joy to my heart. O, hours of intense delight! Short as ye were ye are made as long to me as a whole life when looked back upon through the mist of grief that rose immediately after as if to shut ye from my view. Alas! ye were the last of happiness that I ever enjoyed; a few, a very few weeks and all was destroyed. Like Psyche I lived for awhile in an enchanted palace, amidst odours, and music, and every luxurious delight; when suddenly I was left on a barren rock; a wide ocean of despair rolled around me: above all was black, and my eyes closed while I still inhabited a universal death. Still I would not hurry on; I would pause for ever on the recollections of these happy weeks; I would repeat every word, and how many do I remember, record every enchantment of the faery habitation. But, no, my tale must not pause; it must be as rapid as was my fate,—I can only describe in short although strong expressions my precipitate and irremediable change from happiness to despair.

Chapter IV

Among our most assiduous visitors was a young man of rank, well informed, and agreeable in his person. After we had spent a few weeks in London his attentions towards me became marked and his visits more frequent. I was too much taken up by my own occupations and feelings to attend much to this, and then indeed I hardly noticed more than the bare surface of events as they passed around me; but I now remember that my father was restless and uneasy whenever this person visited us, and when we talked together watched us with the greatest apparent anxiety although he himself maintained a profound silence. At length these obnoxious visits suddenly ceased altogether, but from that moment I must date the change of my father: a change that to remember makes me shudder and then filled me with the deepest grief. There were no degrees which could break my fall from happiness to misery; it was as the stroke of lightning—sudden and entire. Alas! I now met frowns where before I had been welcomed only with smiles: he, my beloved father, shunned me, and either treated me with harshness or a more heart-breaking coldness. We took no more sweet counsel together; and when I tried to win him again to me, his anger, and the terrible emotions that he exhibited drove me to silence and tears.

And this was sudden. The day before we had passed alone together in the country; I remember we had talked of future travels that we should undertake together—there was an eager delight in our tones and gestures that could only spring from deep and mutual love joined to the most unrestrained confidence; and now the next day, the next hour, I saw his brows contracted, his eyes fixed in sullen fierceness on the ground, and his voice so gentle and so dear made me shiver when he addressed me. Often, when my wandering fancy brought by its various images now consolation and now aggravation of grief to my heart, I have compared myself to Proserpine who was gaily and heedlessly gathering flowers on the sweet plain of Enna, when the King of Hell snatched her away to the abodes of death and misery. Alas! I who so lately knew of nought but the joy of life; who had slept only to dream sweet dreams and awoke to incomparable happiness, I now passed my days and nights in tears. I who sought and had found joy in the love-breathing countenance of my father now when I dared fix on him a supplicating look it was ever answered by an angry frown. I dared not speak to him; and when sometimes I had worked up courage to meet him and to ask an explanation, one glance at his face where a chaos of mighty passion seemed for ever struggling made me tremble and shrink to silence. I was dashed down from heaven to earth as a silly sparrow when pounced on by a hawk; my eyes swam and my head was bewildered by the sudden apparition of grief. Day after day passed marked only by my complaints and my tears; often I lifted my soul in vain prayer for a softer descent from joy to woe, or if that were denied me that I might be allowed to die, and fade for ever under the cruel blast that swept over me,

> ———— for what should I do here,
> Like a decaying flower, still withering
> Under his bitter words, whose kindly heat
> Should give my poor heart life?[10]

Sometimes I said to myself, this is an enchantment, and I must strive against it. My father is blinded by some malignant vision which I must remove. And then, like David, I would try music to win the evil spirit from him; and once while singing I lifted my eyes towards him and saw his fixed on me and filled with tears; all his muscles seemed relaxed to softness. I sprung towards him with a cry of joy and would have thrown myself into his arms, but he pushed me roughly from him and left me. And even from this slight incident he contracted fresh gloom and an additional severity of manner.

There are many incidents that I might relate which shewed the diseased yet incomprehensible state of his mind; but I will mention one that occurred while we were in company with several other persons. On this occasion I chanced to say that I thought Myrrha the best of Alfieri's tragedies;[11] as I said this I chanced to cast my eyes on my father and met his: for the first time the expression of those beloved eyes displeased me, and I

10. Fletcher's comedy of the Captain. [Mary Shelley's note on John Fletcher (1579–1625) and his drama *The Captain* (c. 1612) I.iii.237–40.]

11. *Myrrha* by Vittorio Alfieri (1749–1803) was a tragedy about incestuous love between a father and daughter that Mary Shelley apparently had begun translating in 1818: see *Journals*, I: 226 and n. 4; and *The Letters of Percy Bysshe Shelley*, ed. Frederick L. Jones (Oxford: Clarendon Press, 1964), II: 39.

saw with affright that his whole frame shook with some concealed emotion that in spite of his efforts half conquered him: as this tempest faded from his soul he became melancholy and silent. Every day some new scene occurred and displayed in him a mind working as [it] were with an unknown horror that now he could master but which at times threatened to overturn his reason, and to throw the bright seat of his intelligence into a perpetual chaos.

I will not dwell longer than I need on these disastrous circumstances. I might waste days in describing how anxiously I watched every change of fleeting circumstance that promised better days, and with what despair I found that each effort of mine aggravated his seeming madness. To tell all my grief I might as well attempt to count the tears that have fallen from these eyes, or every sign that has torn my heart. I will be brief for there is in all this a horror that will not bear many words, and I sink almost a second time to death while I recall these sad scenes to my memory. Oh, my beloved father! Indeed you made me miserable beyond all words, but how truly did I even then forgive you, and how entirely did you possess my whole heart while I endeavoured, as a rainbow gleams upon a cataract,[12] to soften thy tremendous sorrows.

Thus did this change come about. I seem perhaps to have dashed too suddenly into the description, but thus suddenly did it happen. In one sentence I have passed from the idea of unspeakable happiness to that of unspeakable grief but they were thus closely linked together. We had remained five months in London, three of joy and two of sorrow. My father and I were now seldom alone or if we were he generally kept silence with his eyes fixed on the ground—the dark full orbs in which before I delighted to read all sweet and gentle feeling shadowed from my sight by their lids and the long lashes that fringed them. When we were in company he affected gaiety but I wept to hear his hollow laugh—begun by an empty smile and often ending in a bitter sneer such as never before this fatal period had wrinkled his lips. When others were there he often spoke to me and his eyes perpetually followed my slightest motion. His accents whenever he addressed me were cold and constrained although his voice would tremble when he perceived that my full heart choked the answer to words proffered with a mien yet new to me.

But days of peaceful melancholy were of rare occurrence: they were often broken in upon by gusts of passion that drove me as a weak boat on a stormy sea to seek a cove for shelter; but the winds blew from my native harbour and I was cast far, far out until shattered I perished when the tempest had passed and the sea was apparently calm. I do not know

12. Lord Byron. [Mary Shelley's note: the images of the rainbow and cataract come from Byron's *Childe Harold's Pilgrimage,* Canto IV (1818), stanzas 71–72.]

that I can describe his emotions: sometimes he only betrayed them by a word or gesture, and then retired to his chamber and I crept as near it as I dared and listened with fear to every sound, yet still more dreading a sudden silence—dreading I knew not what, but ever full of fear.

It was after one tremendous day when his eyes had glared on me like lightning—and his voice sharp and broken seemed unable to express the extent of his emotion—that in the evening when I was alone he joined me with a calm countenance, and not noticing my tears which I quickly dried when he approached, told me that in three days that he intended to remove with me to his estate in Yorkshire, and bidding me prepare left me hastily as if afraid of being questioned.

This determination on his part indeed surprised me. This estate was that which he had inhabited in childhood and near which my mother resided while a girl; this was the scene of their youthful loves and where they had lived after their marriage; in happier days my father had often told me that however he might appear weaned from his widow sorrow, and free from bitter recollections elsewhere, yet he would never dare visit the spot where he had enjoyed her society or trust himself to see the rooms that so many years ago they had inhabited together; her favourite walks and the gardens the flowers of which she had delighted to cultivate. And now while he suffered intense misery he determined to plunge into still more intense, and strove for greater emotion than that which already tore him. I was perplexed, and most anxious to know what this portended; ah, what could it portend but ruin!

I saw little of my father during this interval, but he appeared calmer although not less unhappy than before. On the morning of the third day he informed me that he had determined to go to Yorkshire first alone, and that I should follow him in a fortnight unless I heard any thing from him in the mean time that should contradict this command. He departed the same day, and four days afterwards I received a letter from his steward telling me in his name to join him with as little delay as possible. After travelling day and night I arrived with an anxious, yet a hoping heart, for why should he send for me if it were only to avoid me and to treat me with the apparent aversion that he had in London. I met him at the distance of thirty miles from our mansion. His demeanour was sad; for a moment he appeared glad to see me and then he checked himself as if unwilling to betray his feelings. He was silent during our ride, yet his manner was kinder than before and I thought I beheld a softness in his eyes that gave me hope.

When we arrived, after a little rest, he led me over the house and pointed out to me the rooms which my mother had inhabited. Although more than sixteen years had passed since her death nothing had been changed; her work box, her writing desk were still there and in her room a book lay open on the table as she had left it. My father pointed out these circumstances with a serious and unaltered mien, only now and then fixing his deep and liquid eyes upon me; there was something strange and awful in his look that overcame me, and in spite of myself I wept, nor did he attempt to console me, but I saw his lips quiver and the muscles of his countenance seemed convulsed.

We walked together in the gardens and in the evening when I would have retired he asked me to stay and read to him; and first said, "When I was last here your mother read Dante to me; you shall go on where she left off." And then in a moment he said, "No, that must not be; you must not read Dante. Do you choose a book." I took up Spenser and read the descent of Sir Guyon to the halls of Avarice;[13] while he listened his eyes fixed on me in sad profound silence.

I heard the next morning from the steward that upon his arrival he had been in a most terrible state of mind: he had passed the first night in the garden lying on the damp grass; he did not sleep but groaned perpetually. "Alas!" said the old man who gave me this account with tears in his eyes, "it wrings my heart to see my lord in this state: when I heard that he was coming down here with you, my young lady, I thought we should have the happy days over again that we enjoyed during the short life of my lady your mother—But that would be too much happiness for us poor creatures born to tears—and that was why she was taken from us so soon. She was too beautiful and good for us. It was a happy day as we all thought it when my lord married her: I knew her when she was a child and many a good turn has she done for me in my old lady's time—You are like her although there is more of my lord in you—But has he been thus ever since his return? All my joy turned to sorrow when I first beheld him with that melancholy countenance enter these doors as it were the day after my lady's funeral—He seemed to recover himself a little after he had bidden me write to you—but still it is a woful thing to see him so unhappy." These were the feelings of an old, faithful servant: what must be those of an affectionate daughter. Alas! Even then my heart was almost broken.

We spent two months together in this house. My father spent the greater part of his time with me; he accompanied me in my walks, listened to my music, and leant over me as I read or painted. When he conversed with me his manner was cold and constrained; his eyes only seemed to speak, and as he turned their black, full lustre towards me they expressed a living sadness. There was something in those dark deep orbs so liquid, and intense that even in happiness I could never meet their full

13. From Book II, Canto VII of Edmund Spenser's *The Faerie Queene*.

gaze that mine did not overflow. Yet it was with sweet tears; now there was a depth of affliction in their gentle appeal that rent my heart with sympathy; they seemed to desire peace for me; for himself, a heart patient to suffer; a craving for sympathy, yet a perpetual self denial. It was only when he was absent from me that his passion subdued him,—that he clinched his hands—knit his brows—and with haggard looks called for death to his despair, raving wildly, until exhausted he sank down nor was revived until I joined him.

While we were in London there was a harshness and sulleness in his sorrow which had now entirely disappeared. There I shrunk and fled from him, now I only wished to be with him that I might soothe him to peace. When he was silent I tried to divert him, and when sometimes I stole to him during the energy of his passion I wept but did not desire to leave him. Yet he suffered fearful agony; during the day he was more calm, but at night when I could not be with him he seemed to give the reins to his grief: he often passed his nights either on the floor in my mother's room, or in the garden; and when in the morning he saw me view with poignant grief his exhausted frame, and his person languid almost to death with watching, he wept; but during all this time he spoke no word by which I might guess the cause of his unhappiness. If I ventured to enquire he would either leave me or press his finger on his lips, and with a deprecating look that I could not resist, turn away. If I wept he would gaze on me in silence but he was no longer harsh and although he repulsed every caress yet it was with gentleness.

He seemed to cherish a mild grief and softer emotions although sad as a relief from despair—He contrived in many ways to nurse his melancholy as an antidote to wilder passion. He perpetually frequented the walks that had been favourites with him when he and my mother wandered together talking of love and happiness; he collected every relick that remained of her and always sat opposite her picture which hung in the room fixing on it a look of sad despair—and all this was done in a mystic and awful silence. If his passion subdued him he locked himself in his room; and at night when he wandered restlessly about the house, it was when every other creature slept.

It may easily be imagined that I wearied myself with conjecture to guess the cause of his sorrow. The solution that seemed to me the most probable was that during his residence in London he had fallen in love with some unworthy person, and that his passion mastered him although he would not gratify it: he loved me too well to sacrifise me to this inclination, and that he had now visited this house that by reviving the memory of my mother whom he so passionately adored he might weaken the present impression. This was possible; but it was a mere conjecture unfounded on any fact. Could there be guilt in it? He was too upright and noble to *do* aught that his conscience would not approve; I did not yet know of the crime there may be in involuntary feeling and therefore ascribed his tumultuous starts and gloomy looks wholly to the struggles of his mind and not any as they were partly due to the worst fiend of all—Remorse.

But still do I flatter myself that this would have passed away. His paroxisms of passion were terrific but his soul bore him through them triumphant, though almost destroyed by victory; but the day would finally have been won had not I, foolish and presumptuous wretch! hurried him on until there was no recall, no hope. My rashness gave the victory in this dreadful fight to the enemy who triumphed over him as he lay fallen and vanquished. I! I alone was the cause of his defeat and justly did I pay the fearful penalty. I said to myself, let him receive sympathy and these struggles will cease. Let him confide his misery to another heart and half the weight of it will be lightened. I will win him to me; he shall not deny his grief to me and when I know his secret then will I pour a balm into his soul and again I shall enjoy the ravishing delight of beholding his smile, and of again seeing his eyes beam if not with pleasure at least with gentle love and thankfulness. This will I do, I said. Half I accomplished; I gained his secret and we were both lost for ever.

Chapter V

Nearly a year had passed since my father's return, and the seasons had almost finished their round—It was now the end of May; the woods were clothed in their freshest verdure, and the sweet smell of the new mown grass was in the fields. I thought that the balmy air and the lovely face of Nature might aid me in inspiring him with mild sensations, and give him gentle feelings of peace and love preparatory to the confidence I determined to win from him.

I chose therefore the evening of one of these days for my attempt. I invited him to walk with me, and led him to a neighbouring wood of beech trees whose light shade shielded us from the slant and dazzling beams of the descending sun—after walking for some time in silence I seated myself with him on a mossy hillock—It is strange but even now I seem to see the spot—the slim and smooth trunks were many of them wound round by ivy whose shining leaves of the darkest green contrasted with the white bark and the light leaves of the young sprouts of beech that grew from their parent trunks—the short grass was mingled with moss and was partly covered by the dead leaves of the last autumn that driven by the winds had here and there collected in little hillocks—there were a few moss grown stumps about—The leaves were gently moved by the breeze and through their green canopy you could see the bright blue sky—As evening came on the distant trunks were reddened by the sun and the wind died entirely away while a few birds flew past us to their evening rest.

Well it was here we sat together, and when you hear all that passed—all that of terrible tore our souls even in this placid spot, which but for strange passions might have been a paradise to us, you will not wonder that I remember it as I looked on it that its calm might give me calm, and inspire me not only with courage but with persuasive words. I saw all these things and in a vacant manner noted them in my mind while I endeavoured to arrange my thoughts in fitting order for my attempt. My heart beat fast as I worked myself up to speak to him, for I was determined not to be repulsed but I trembled to imagine what effect my words might have on him; at length, with much hesitation I began:

"Your kindness to me, my dearest father, and the affection—the excessive affection—that you had for me when you first returned will I hope excuse me in your eyes that I dare speak to you, although with the tender affection of a daughter, yet also with the freedom of a friend and equal. But pardon me, I entreat you and listen to me: do not turn away from me; do not be impatient; you may easily intimidate me into silence, but my heart is bursting, nor can I willingly consent to endure for one moment longer the agony of uncertitude which for the last four months has been my portion.

"Listen to me, dearest friend, and permit me to gain your confidence. Are the happy days of mutual love which have passed to be to me as a dream never to return? Alas! You have a secret grief that destroys us both: but you must permit me to win this secret from you. Tell me, can I do nothing? You well know that on the whole earth there is no sacrifise that I would not make, no labour that I would not undergo with the mere hope that I might bring you ease. But if no endeavour on my part can contribute to your happiness, let me at least know your sorrow, and surely my earnest love and deep sympathy must soothe your despair.

"I fear that I speak in a constrained manner: my heart is overflowing with the ardent desire I have of bringing calm once more to your thoughts and looks; but I fear to aggravate your grief, or to raise that in you which is death to me, anger and distaste. Do not then continue to fix your eyes on the earth; raise them on me for I can read your soul in them: speak to me, and pardon my presumption. Alas! I am a most unhappy creature!"

I was breathless with emotion, and I paused fixing my earnest eyes on my father, after I had dashed away the intrusive tears that dimmed them. He did not raise his, but after a short silence he replied to me in a low voice: "You are indeed presumptuous, Mathilda, presumptuous and very rash. In the heart of one like me there are secret thoughts working, and secret tortures which you ought not to seek to discover. I cannot tell you how it adds to my grief to know that I am the cause of uneasiness to you; but this will pass away, and I hope that soon we shall be as we were a few months ago. Restrain your impatience or you may mar what you attempt to alleviate. Do not again speak to me in this strain; but wait in submissive patience the event of what is passing around you."

"Oh, yes!" I passionately replied, "I will be very patient; I will not be rash or presumptuous: I will see the agonies, and tears, and despair of my father, my only friend, my hope, my shelter, I will see it all with folded arms and downcast eyes. You do not treat me with candour; it is not true what you say; this will not soon pass away, it will last for ever if you deign not to speak to me; to admit my consolations.

"Dearest, dearest father, pity me and pardon me: I entreat you do not drive me to despair; indeed I must not be repulsed; there is one thing that although it may torture me to know, yet that you must tell me. I demand, and most solemnly I demand if in any way I am the cause of your unhappiness. Do you not see my tears which I in vain strive against— You hear unmoved my voice broken by sobs—Feel how my hand trembles: my whole heart is in the words I speak and you must not endeavour to silence me by mere words barren of meaning: the agony of my doubt hurries me on, and you must reply. I beseech you; by your former love for me now lost, I adjure you to answer that one question. Am I the cause of your grief?"

He raised his eyes from the ground, but still turning them away from me, said: "Besought by that plea I will answer your rash question. Yes, you are the sole, the agonizing cause of all I suffer, of all I must suffer until I die. Now, beware! Be silent! Do not urge me to your destruction. I am struck by the storm, rooted up, laid waste: but you can stand against it; you are young and your passions are at peace. One word I might speak and then you would be implicated in my destruction; yet that word is hovering on my lips. Oh! There is a fearful chasm; but I adjure you to beware!"

"Ah, dearest friend!" I cried, "do not fear! Speak that word; it will bring peace, not death. If there is a chasm our mutual love will give us wings to pass it, and we shall find flowers, and verdure, and delight on the other side." I threw myself at his feet, and took his hand, "Yes, speak, and we shall be happy; there will no longer be doubt, no dreadful uncertainty; trust me, my affection will soothe your sorrow; speak that word and all danger will be past, and we shall love each other as before, and for ever."

He snatched his hand from me, and rose in violent disorder: "What do you mean? You know not what you mean. Why do you bring me out, and torture me, and tempt me, and kill me—Much happier would [it] be for you and for me if in your frantic curiosity you tore my heart from my breast and tried to read its secrets in it as its life's blood was dropping from it. Thus you may console me by reducing me to nothing—but your words I cannot bear; soon they will make me mad, quite mad, and then I shall utter strange words, and you will believe them, and we shall be both lost for ever. I tell you I am on the very verge of insanity; why, cruel girl, do you drive me on: you will repent and I shall die."

When I repeat his words I wonder at my pertinacious folly; I hardly know what feelings resistlessly impelled me. I believe it was that coming out with a determination not to be repulsed I went right forward to my object without well weighing his replies: I was led by passion and drew him with frantic heedlessness into the abyss that he so fearfully avoided— I replied to his terrific words: "You fill me with affright it is true, dearest father, but you only confirm my resolution to put an end to this state of doubt. I will not be put off thus: do you think that I can live thus fearfully from day to day—the sword in my bosom yet kept from its mortal wound by a hair—a word!—I demand that dreadful word; though it be as a flash of lightning to destroy me, speak it.

"Alas! Alas! What am I become? But a few months have elapsed since I believed that I was all the world to you; and that there was no happiness or grief for you on earth unshared by your Mathilda—your child: that happy time is no longer, and what I most dreaded in this world is come upon me. In the despair of my heart I see what you cannot conceal: you no longer love me. I adjure you, my father, has not an unnatural passion seized upon your heart? Am I not the most miserable worm that crawls? Do I not embrace your knees, and you most cruelly repulse me? I know it—I see it—you hate me!"

I was transported by violent emotion, and rising from his feet, at which I had thrown myself, I leant against a tree, wildly raising my eyes to heaven. He began to answer with violence: "Yes, yes, I hate you! You are my bane, my poison, my disgust! Oh! No!" And then his manner changed, and fixing his eyes on me with an expression that convulsed every nerve and member of my frame—"you are none of all these; you are my light, my only one, my life.—My daughter, I love you!" The last words died away in a hoarse whisper, but I heard them and sunk on the ground, covering my face and almost dead with excess of sickness and fear: a cold perspiration covered my forehead and I shivered in every limb—But he continued, clasping his hands with a frantic gesture:

"Now I have dashed from the top of the rock to the bottom! Now I have precipitated myself down the fearful chasm! The danger is over; she is alive! Oh, Mathilda, lift up those dear eyes in the light of which I live. Let me hear the sweet tones of your beloved voice in peace and calm. Monster as I am, you are still, as you ever were, lovely, beautiful beyond expression. What I have become since this last moment I know not; perhaps I am changed in mien as the fallen archangel. I do believe I am for I have surely a new soul within me, and my blood riots through my veins: I am burnt up with fever. But these are precious moments; devil as I am become, yet that is my Mathilda before me whom I love as one was never before loved: and she knows it now; she listens to these words which I thought, fool as I was, would blast her to death. Come, come, the worst is past: no more grief, tears or despair; were not those the words you uttered?—We have leapt the chasm I told you of, and now, mark me, Mathilda, we are to find flowers, and verdure and delight, or is it hell, and fire, and tortures? Oh! Beloved One, I am borne away; I can no longer sustain myself; surely this is death that is coming. Let me lay my head near your heart; let me die in your arms!"—He sunk to the earth fainting, while I, nearly as lifeless, gazed on him in despair.

Yes it was despair I felt; for the first time that phantom seized me; the first and only time for it has never since left me—After the first moments of speechless agony I felt her fangs on my heart: I tore my hair; I raved aloud; at one moment in pity for his sufferings I would have clasped my father in my arms; and then starting back with horror I spurned him with my foot; I felt as if stung by a serpent, as if scourged by a whip of scorpions which drove me—Ah! Whither—Whither?

Well, this could not last. One idea rushed on my mind; never, never may I speak to him again. As this terrible conviction came upon *him* [*me?*] it melted my soul to tenderness and love—I gazed on him as to take my last farewell—he lay insensible—his eyes closed as [and?] his cheeks deathly pale—Above, the leaves of the beech wood cast a flickering shadow on his face, and waved in mournful melody over him—I saw all these things and said, "Aye, this is his grave!" And then I wept aloud, and raised my eyes to heaven to entreat for a respite to my despair and an alleviation for his unnatural suffering—the tears that gushed in a warm and healing stream from my eyes relieved the burthen that oppressed my heart almost to madness. I wept for a long time until I saw him about to revive, when horror and misery again recurred, and the tide of my sensations rolled back to their former channel: with a terror I could not restrain—I sprung up and fled, with winged speed, along the paths of the wood and across the fields until nearly dead I reached our house and just ordering the servants to seek my father at the spot I indicated, I shut myself up in my own room.

Chapter VI

My chamber was in a retired part of the house, and looked upon the garden so that no sound of the other inhabitants could reach it; and here in perfect solitude I wept for several hours. When a servant came to ask me if I would take food I learnt from him that my father had returned, and was apparently well and this relieved me from a load of anxiety, yet I did not cease to weep bitterly. At first, as the memory of former happiness contrasted to my present despair came across me, I gave relief to the oppression of heart that I felt by words, and groans, and heart rending sighs: but nature became wearied, and this more violent grief gave place to a passionate but mute flood of tears: my whole soul seemed to dissolve them. I did not wring my hands, or tear my hair, or utter wild exclamations, but as Boccaccio describes the intense and quiet grief [of] Ghismunda over the heart of Guiscardo,[14] I sat with my hands folded, silently letting fall a perpetual stream from my eyes. Such was the depth of my emotion that I had no feeling of what caused my distress, my thoughts even wandered to many indifferent objects; but still neither moving limb or feature my tears fell until, as if the fountains were exhausted, they gradually subsided, and I awoke to life as from a dream.

When I had ceased to weep, reason and memory returned upon me, and I began to reflect with greater calmness on what had happened, and how it became me to act—A few hours only had passed but a mighty revolution had taken place with regard to me—the natural work of years had been transacted since the morning: my father was as dead to me, and I felt for a moment as if he with white hairs were laid in his coffin and I—youth vanished in approaching age, were weeping at his timely dissolution. But

14. Allusion to the first story of the fourth day of Boccaccio's *Decameron*, which Mary Shelley read in May 1819 (see *Journals*, I: 262–64). Mary Shelley wrote the name Sigismunda, which is here emended to Ghismunda.

it was not so, I was yet young, Oh! far too young, nor was he dead to others; but I, most miserable, must never see or speak to him again. I must fly from him with more earnestness than from my greatest enemy: in solitude or in cities I must never more behold him. That consideration made me breathless with anguish, and impressing itself on my imagination I was unable for a time to follow up any train of ideas. Ever after this, I thought, I would live in the most dreary seclusion. I would retire to the Continent and become a nun; not for religion's sake, for I was not a Catholic, but that I might be for ever shut out from the world. I should there find solitude where I might weep, and the voices of life might never reach me.

But my father; my beloved and most wretched father? Would he die? Would he never overcome the fierce passion that now held pityless dominion over him? Might he not many, many years hence, when age had quenched the burning sensations that he now experienced, might he not then be again a father to me? This reflection unwrinkled my brow, and I could feel (and I wept to feel it) a half melancholy smile draw from my lips their expression of suffering: I dared indulge better hopes for my future life; years must pass but they would speed lightly away winged by hope, or if they passed heavily, still they would pass and I had not lost my father for ever. Let him spend another sixteen years of desolate wandering: let him once more utter his wild compaints to the vast woods and the tremendous cataracts of another clime: let him again undergo fearful danger and soul-quelling hardships: let the hot sun of the south again burn his passion worn cheeks and the cold night rains fall on him and chill his blood.

To this life, miserable father, I devote thee!—Go!—Be thy days passed with savages, and thy nights under the cope of heaven! Be thy limbs worn and thy heart chilled, and all youth be dead within thee! Let thy hairs be as snow; thy walk trembling and thy voice have lost its mellow tones! Let the liquid lustre of thine eyes be quenched; and then return to me, return to thy Mathilda, thy child, who may then be clasped in thy loved arms, while thy heart beats with sinless emotion. Go, Devoted One, and return thus!—This is my curse, a daughter's curse: go, and return pure to thy child, who will never love aught but thee.

These were my thoughts; and with trembling hands I prepared to begin a letter to my unhappy parent. I had now spent many hours in tears and mournful meditation; it was past twelve o'clock; all was at peace in the house, and the gentle air that stole in at my window did not rustle the leaves of the twining plants that shadowed it. I felt the entire tranquillity of the hour when my own breath and involuntary sobs were all the sounds that struck upon the air. On a sudden I heard a gentle step ascending the stairs; I paused breathless, and as it approached glided into an obscure corner of the room; the steps paused at my door, but after a few moments they again receded, descended the stairs and I heard no more.

This slight incident gave rise in me to the most painful reflections; nor do I now dare express the emotions I felt. That he should be restless I understood; that he should wander as an unlaid ghost and find no quiet from the burning hell that consumed his heart. But why approach my chamber? Was not that sacred? I felt almost ready to faint while he had stood there, but I had not betrayed my wakefulness by the slightest motion, although I had heard my own heart beat with violent fear. He had withdrawn. Oh, never, never, may I see him again! Tomorrow night the same roof may not cover us; he or I must depart. The mutual link of our destinies is broken; we must be divided by seas—by land. The stars and the sun must not rise at the same period to us: he must not say, looking at the setting crescent of the moon, "Mathilda now watches its fall."—No, all must be changed. Be it light with him when it is darkness with me! Let him feel the sun of summer while I am chilled by the snows of winter! Let there be the distance of the antipodes between us!

At length the east began to brighten, and the comfortable light of morning streamed into my room. I was weary with watching and for some time I had combated with the heavy sleep that weighed down my eyelids: but now, no longer fearful, I threw myself on my bed. I sought for repose although I did not hope for forgetfulness; I knew I should be pursued by dreams, but did not dread the frightful one that I really had. I thought that I had risen and went to seek my father to inform him of my determination to seperate myself from him. I sought him in the house, in the park, and then in the fields and the woods, but I could not find him. At length I saw him at some distance, seated under a tree, and when he perceived me he waved his hand several times, beckoning me to approach; there was something unearthly in his mien that awed and chilled me, but I drew near. When at short distance from him I saw that he was dead-lily pale, and clothed in flowing garments of white. Suddenly he started up and fled from me; I pursued him: we sped over the fields, and by the skirts of woods, and on the banks of rivers; he flew fast and I followed. We came at last, methought, to the brow of a huge cliff that over hung the sea which, troubled by the winds, dashed against its base, at a distance. I heard the roar of the waters: he held his course right on towards the brink and I became breathless with fear lest he should plunge down the dreadful precipice; I tried to augment my speed, but my knees failed beneath me, yet I had just reached him; just caught a part of his flowing robe, when he leapt down and I awoke with a violent scream. I was trembling and my pillow was wet with my tears; for a few moments my heart beat hard, but the bright beams of the sun and the chirping of the birds quickly restored me to myself, and I rose with a languid spirit, yet wondering what events the day would bring forth. Some time passed before I summoned courage to ring the bell for my servant, and when she came I still dared not utter my father's name. I ordered her to bring my breakfast to my room, and was again left alone—yet still I could make no resolve, but only thought that I might write a note to my father to beg his permission to pay a visit to a relation who lived about thirty miles off, and who had before invited me to her house, but I had refused for then I could not quit my suffering father. When the servant came back she gave me a letter.

"From whom is this letter," I asked trembling.

"Your father left it, madam, with his servant, to be given to you when you should rise."

"My father left it! Where is he? Is he not here?"

"No; he quitted the house before four this morning."

"Good God! He is gone! But tell how this was; speak quick!"

Her relation was short. He had gone in the carriage to the nearest town where he took a post chaise and horses with orders for the London road. He dismissed his servants there, only telling them that he had a sudden call of business and that they were to obey me as their mistress until his return.

Chapter VII

With a beating heart and fearful, I knew not why, I dismissed the servant and locking my door, sat down to read my father's letter. These are the words that it contained.

"My dear Child

"I have betrayed your confidence; I have endeavoured to pollute your mind, and have made your innocent heart acquainted with the looks and language of unlawful and monstrous passion. I must expiate these crimes, and must endeavour in some degree to proportionate my punishment to my guilt. You are I doubt not prepared for what I am about to announce; we must seperate and be divided for ever.

"I deprive you of your parent and only friend. You are cast out shelterless on the world: your hopes are blasted; the peace and security of your pure mind destroyed; memory will bring to you frightful images of guilt, and the anguish of innocent love betrayed. Yet I who draw down all this misery upon you; I who cast you forth and remorselessly have set the seal of distrust and agony on the heart and brow of my own child, who with devilish levity have endeavoured to steal away her loveliness to place in its stead the foul deformity of sin; I, in the overflowing anguish of my heart, supplicate you to forgive me.

"I do not ask your pity; you must and do abhor me: but pardon me, Mathilda, and let not your thoughts follow me in my banishment with unrelenting anger. I must never more behold you; never more hear your voice; but the soft whisperings of your forgiveness will reach me and cool the burning of my disordered brain and heart; I am sure I should feel it even in my grave. And I dare enforce this request by relating how miserably I was betrayed into this net of fiery anguish and all my struggles to release myself: indeed if your soul were less pure and bright I would not attempt to exculpate myself to you; I should fear that if I led you to regard me with less abhorrence you might hate vice less: but in addressing you I feel as if I appealed to an angelic judge. I cannot depart without your forgiveness and I must endeavour to gain it, or I must despair. I conjure you therefore to listen to my words, and if with the good guilt may be in any degree extenuated by sharp agony and remorse that rends the brain as madness, perhaps you may think, though I dare not, that I have some claim to your compassion.

"I entreat you to call to your remembrance our first happy life on the shores of Loch Lomond. I had arrived from a weary wandering of sixteen years, during which, although I had gone through many dangers and misfortunes, my affections had been an entire blank. If I grieved it was for your mother, if I loved it was your image; these sole emotions filled my heart in quietness. The human creatures around me excited in me no sympathy and I thought that the mighty change that the death of your mother had wrought within me had rendered me callous to any future impression. I saw the lovely and I did not love, I imagined therefore that all warmth was extinguished in my heart except that which led me ever to dwell on your then infantine image.

"It is a strange link in my fate that without having seen you I should passionately love you. During my wanderings I never slept without first calling down gentle dreams on your head. If I saw a lovely woman, I thought, does my Mathilda resemble her? All delightful things, sublime scenery, soft breezes, exquisite music seemed to me associated with you and only through you to be pleasant to me. At length I saw you. You appeared as the deity of a lovely region, the ministering Angel of a Paradise to which of all human kind you admitted only me. I dared hardly consider you as my daughter; your beauty, artlessness, and untaught wisdom seemed to belong to a higher order of beings; your voice breathed forth only words of love: if there was aught of earthly in you it was only what you derived from the beauty of the world; you seemed to have gained a grace from the mountain breezes—the waterfalls and the lake; and this was all of earthly except your affections that you had; there was no dross, no bad feeling in the composition. You yet even have not seen enough of the world to know the stupendous difference that exists between the women we meet in daily life and a nymph of the woods such as you were, in whose eyes alone mankind may study for centuries and grow wiser and purer. Those divine lights which shone on me as did those of Beatrice upon Dante, and well might I say with him yet with what different feelings

E quasi mi perdei con gli occhi chini.[15]

15. Canto IV Vers Ult. [Mary Shelley's note, omitted from Nitchie, who also omits the "con" from Dante's *Paradiso* IV.142: "And I almost lost myself with eyes downcast."]

Can you wonder, Mathilda, that I dwelt on your looks, your words, your motions, and drank in unmixed delight?

"But I am afraid that I wander from my purpose. I must be more brief for night draws on apace and all my hours in this house are counted. Well, we removed to London, and still I felt only the peace of sinless passion. You were ever with me, and I desired no more than to gaze on your countenance, and to know that I was all the world to you; I was lapped in a fool's paradise of enjoyment and security. Was my love blamable? If it was I was ignorant of it; I desired only that which I possessed, and if I enjoyed from your looks, and words, and most innocent caresses a rapture usually excluded from the feelings of a parent towards his child, yet no uneasiness, no wish, no casual idea awoke me to a sense of guilt. I loved you as a human father might be supposed to love a daughter borne to him by a heavenly mother; as Anchises[16] might have regarded the child of Venus if the sex had been changed; love mingled with respect and adoration. Perhaps also my passion was lulled to content by the deep and exclusive affection you felt for me.

"But when I saw you become the object of another's love; when I imagined that you might be loved otherwise than as a sacred type and image of loveliness and excellence; or that you might love another with a more ardent affection than that which you bore to me, then the fiend awoke within me; I dismissed your lover; and from that moment I have known no peace. I have sought in vain for sleep and rest; my lids refused to close, and my blood was for ever in a tumult. I awoke to a new life as one who dies in hope might wake in Hell. I will not sully your imagination by recounting my combats, my self-anger, and my despair. Let a veil be drawn over the unimaginable sensations of a guilty father; the secrets of so agonized a heart may not be made vulgar. All was uproar, crime, remorse, and hate, yet still the tenderest love; and what first awoke me to the firm resolve of conquering my passion and of restoring her father to my child was the sight of your bitter and sympathizing sorrows. It was this that led me here: I thought that if I could again awaken in my heart the grief I had felt at the loss of your mother, and the many associations with her memory which had been laid to sleep for seventeen years, that all love for her child would become extinct. In a fit of heroism I determined to go alone; to quit you, the life of my life, and not to see you again until I might guiltlessly. But it would not do: I rated my fortitude too high, or my love too low. I should certainly have died if you had not hastened to me. Would that I had been indeed extinguished!

"And now, Mathilda I must make you my last confession. I have been

16. The father of Aeneas.

miserably mistaken in imagining that I could conquer my love for you; I never can. The sight of this house, these fields and woods which my first love inhabited seems to have encreased it: in my madness I dared say to myself—Diana died to give her birth; her mother's spirit was transferred into her frame, and she ought to be as Diana to me. With every effort to cast it off, this love clings closer, this guilty love more unnatural than hate, that withers your hopes and destroys me for ever.

Better have loved despair, and safer kissed her.[17]

No time or space can tear from my soul that which makes a part of it. Since my arrival here I have not for a moment ceased to feel the hell of passion which has been implanted in me to burn until all be cold, and stiff, and dead. Yet I will not die; alas! how dare I go where I may meet Diana, when I have disobeyed her last request; her last words said in a faint voice when all feeling but love, which survives all things else, was already dead, she then bade me make her child happy: that thought alone gives a double sting to death. I will wander away from you, away from all life—in the solitude I shall seek I alone shall breathe of human kind. I must endure life; and as it is my duty so I shall until the grave, dreaded yet desired, receive me free from pain: for while I feel it will be pain that must make up the whole sum of my sensations. Is not this a fearful curse that I labour under? Do I not look forward to a miserable future? My child, if after this life I am permitted to see you again, if pain can purify the heart, mine will be pure: if remorse may expiate guilt, I shall be guiltless.

———

"I have been at the door of your chamber: every thing is silent. You sleep. Do you indeed sleep, Mathilda? Spirits of Good, behold the tears of my earnest prayer! Bless my child! Protect her from the selfish among her fellow creatures: protect her from the agonies of passion, and the despair of disappointment! Peace, Hope, and Love be thy guardians, oh, thou soul of my soul: thou in whom I breathe!

———

"I dare not read my letter over for I have no time to write another, and yet I fear that some expressions in it might displease me. Since I last saw you I have been constantly employed in writing letters, and have several more to write; for I do not intend that any one shall hear of me after I depart. I need not conjure you to look upon me as one of whom all links that once existed between us are broken. Your own delicacy will not allow you, I am convinced, to attempt to trace me. It is far better for your peace

17. Unidentified.

that you should be ignorant of my destination. You will not follow me, for when I banish myself would you nourish guilt by obtruding yourself upon me? You will not do this, I know you will not. You must forget me and all the evil that I have taught you. Cast off the only gift that I have bestowed upon you, your grief, and rise from under my blighting influence as no flower so sweet ever did rise from beneath so much evil.

"You will never hear from me again: receive these then as the last words of mine that will ever reach you; and although I have forfeited your filial love, yet regard them I conjure you as a father's command. Resolutely shake off the wretchedness that this first misfortune in early life must occasion you. Bear boldly up against the storm: continue wise and mild, but believe it, and indeed it is, your duty to be happy. You are very young; let not this check for more than a moment retard your glorious course; hold on, beloved one. The sun of youth is not set for you; it will restore vigour and life to you; do not resist with obstinate grief its beneficent influence, oh, my child! bless me with the hope that I have not utterly destroyed you.

"Farewell, Mathilda. I go with the belief that I have your pardon. Your gentle nature would not permit you to hate your greatest enemy and though I be he, although I have rent happiness from your grasp; though I have passed over your young love and hopes as the angel of destruction, finding beauty and joy, and leaving blight and despair, yet you will forgive me, and with eyes overflowing with tears I thank you; my beloved one, I accept your pardon with a gratitude that will never die, and that will, indeed it will, outlive guilt and remorse.

"Farewell for ever!"

The moment I finished this letter I ordered the carriage and prepared to follow my father. The words of his letter by which he had dissuaded me from this step were those that determined me. Why did he write them? He must know that if I believed that his intention was merely to absent himself from me that instead of opposing him it would be that which I should myself require—or if he thought that any lurking feeling, yet he could not think that, should lead me to him would he endeavour to overthrow the only hope he could have of ever seeing me again; a lover, there was madness in the thought, yet he was my lover, would not act thus. No, he had determined to die, and he wished to spare me the misery of knowing it. The few ineffectual words he had said concerning his duty were to me a further proof—and the more I studied the letter the more did I perceive a thousand slight expressions that could only indicate a knowledge that life was now over for him. He was about to die! My blood froze at the thought: a sickening feeling of horror came over me that allowed not of tears. As I waited for the carriage I walked up and down with a quick pace; then kneeling and passionately clasping my hands I tried to pray but my voice was choked by convulsive sobs—Oh the sun shone, the air was balmy—he must yet live for if he were dead all would surely be black as night to me!

The motion of the carriage knowing that it carried me towards him and that I might perhaps find him alive somewhat revived my courage: yet I had a dreadful ride. Hope only supported me, the hope that I should not be too late. I did not weep, but I wiped the perspiration from my brow, and tried to still my brain and heart beating almost to madness. Oh! I must not be mad when I see him; or perhaps it were as well that I should be, my distraction might calm his, and recall him to the endurance of life. Yet until I find him I must force reason to keep her seat, and I pressed my forehead hard with my hands—Oh do not leave me; or I shall forget what I am about—instead of driving on as we ought with the speed of lightning they will attend to me, and we shall be too late. Oh! God help me! Let him be alive! It is all dark; in my abject misery I demand no more: no hope, no good: only passion, and guilt, and horror; but alive! Alive! My sensations choked me—No tears fell yet I sobbed, and breathed short and hard; one only thought possessed me, and I could only utter one word, that half screaming was perpetually on my lips: Alive! Alive!—

I had taken the steward with me for he, much better than I, could make the requisite enquiries—the poor old man could not restrain his tears as he saw my deep distress and knew the cause—he sometimes uttered a few broken words of consolation: in moments like these the mistress and servant become in a manner equals and when I saw his old dim eyes wet with sympathizing tears; his gray hair thinly scattered on an age-wrinkled brow I thought oh if my father were as he is—decrepid and hoary—then I should be spared this pain—

When I had arrived at the nearest town I took post horses and followed the road my father had taken. At every inn where we changed horses we heard of him, and I was possessed by alternate hope and fear. At length I found that he had altered his route; at first he had followed the London road; but now he changed it, and upon enquiry I found that the one which he now pursued led *towards the sea*. My dream recurred to my thoughts; I was not usually superstitious but in wretchedness every one is so. The sea was fifty miles off, yet it was towards it that he fled. The idea was terrible to my half-crazed imagination, and almost overturned the little self possession that still remained to me. I journeyed all day; every moment my misery encreased and the fever of my blood became intolerable. The summer sun shone in an unclouded sky; the air was close but all was cool to me except my own scorching skin. Towards evening dark thunder clouds arose above the horizon and I heard its distant roll—after sunset they darkened the whole sky and it began to rain, the lightning lighted up the whole country, and the thunder drowned the noise of our carriage. At the next inn my father had not taken horses; he had left a box there saying he would return, and had walked over the fields to the town of ——— a seacoast town eight miles off.

For a moment I was almost paralized by fear; but my energy returned and I demanded a guide to accompany me in following his steps. The night was tempestuous but my bribe was high and I easily procured a countryman. We passed through many lanes and over fields and wild downs; the rain poured down in torrents, and the loud thunder broke in terrible crashes over our heads. Oh! What a night it was! And I passed on with quick steps among the high, dank grass amid the rain and tempest. My dream was for ever in my thoughts, and with a kind of half insanity that often possesses the mind in despair, I said aloud: "Courage! We are not near the sea; we are yet several miles from the ocean"—Yet it was towards the sea that our direction lay and that heightened the confusion of my ideas. Once, overcome by fatigue, I sunk on the wet earth; about two hundred yards distant, alone in a large meadow stood a magnificent oak; the lightnings shewed its myriad boughs torn by the storm. A strange idea seized me; a person must have felt all the agonies of doubt concerning the life and death of one who is the whole world to them before they can enter into my feelings—for in that state, the mind working unrestrained by the will makes strange and fanciful combinations with outward circumstances and weaves the chances and changes of nature into an immediate connexion with the event they dread. It was with this feeling that I turned to the old steward who stood pale and trembling beside me; "Mark, Gaspar, if the next flash of lightning rend not that oak my father will be alive."

I had scarcely uttered these words than a flash instantly followed by a tremendous peal of thunder descended on it; and when my eyes recovered their sight after the dazzling light, the oak no longer stood in the meadow—The old man uttered a wild exclamation of horror when he saw so sudden an interpretation given to my prophecy. I started up, my strength returned with my terror; I cried, "Oh, God! Is this thy decree? Yet perhaps I shall not be too late."

Although still several miles distant we continued to approach the sea. We came at last to the road that led to the town of ——— and at an inn there we heard that my father had passed by somewhat before sunset; he had observed the approaching storm and had hired a horse for the next town which was situated a mile from the sea that he might arrive there before it should commence: this town was five miles off. We hired a chaise here, and with four horses drove with speed through the storm. My garments were wet and clung around me, and my hair hung in straight locks on my neck when not blown aside by the wind. I shivered, yet my pulse was high with fever. Great God! What agony I endured. I shed no tears but my eyes wild and inflamed were starting from my head; I could hardly support the weight that pressed upon my brain. We arrived at the town of ——— in a little more than half an hour. When my father had arrived the storm had already begun, but he had refused to stop and leaving his horse there he walked on—*towards the sea.* Alas! it was double cruelty in him to have chosen the sea for his fatal resolve; it was adding madness to my despair.

The poor old servant who was with me endeavoured to persuade me to remain here and to let him go alone—I shook my head silently and sadly; sick almost to death I leant upon his arm, and as there was no road for a chaise dragged my weary steps across the desolate downs to meet my fate, now too certain for the agony of doubt. Almost fainting I slowly approached the fatal waters; when we had quitted the town we heard their roaring. I whispered to myself in a muttering voice—"The sound is the same as that which I heard in my dream. It is the knell of my father which I hear."

The rain had ceased; there was no more thunder and lightning; the wind had paused. My heart no longer beat wildly; I did not feel any fever: but I was chilled; my knees sunk under me—I almost slept as I walked with excess of weariness; every limb trembled. I was silent: all was silent except the roaring of the sea which became louder and more dreadful. Yet we advanced slowly: sometimes I thought that we should never arrive; that the sound of waves would still allure us, and that we should walk on for ever and ever: field succeeding field, never would our weary journey cease, nor night nor day; but still we should hear the dashing of the sea, and to all this there would be no end. Wild beyond the imagination of the happy are the thoughts bred by misery and despair.

At length we reached the overhanging beach; a cottage stood beside the path; we knocked at the door and it was opened: the bed within instantly caught my eye; something stiff and straight lay on it, covered by a sheet; the cottagers looked aghast. The first words that they uttered confirmed what I before knew. I did not feel shocked or overcome: I believe that I asked one or two questions and listened to the answers. I hardly know, but in a few moments I sank lifeless to the ground; and so would that then all had been at an end!

Chapter VIII

I was carried to the next town: fever succeeded to convulsions and faintings, and for some weeks my unhappy spirit hovered on the very verge of death. But life was yet strong within me; I recovered: nor did it a little aid my returning health that my recollections were at first vague, and that I was too weak to feel any violent emotion. I often said to myself, my father is dead. He loved me with a guilty passion, and stung by remorse and despair he killed himself. Why is it that I feel no horror? Are these circumstances not dreadful? Is it not enough that I shall never more meet the eyes of my beloved father; never more hear his voice; no caress, no look? All cold, and stiff, and dead! Alas! I am quite callous: the night I was out in was fearful and the cold rain that fell about my heart has acted like the waters of the cavern of Antiparos and has changed it to stone. I do not weep or sigh; but I must reason with myself, and force myself to feel sorrow and despair. This is not resignation that I feel, for I am dead to all regret.

I communed in this manner with myself, but I was silent to all around me. I hardly replied to the slightest question, and was uneasy when I saw a human creature near me. I was surrounded by my female relations, but they were all of them nearly strangers to me: I did not listen to their consolations; and so little did they work their designed effect that they seemed to me to be spoken in an unknown tongue. I found if sorrow was dead within me, so was love and desire of sympathy. Yet sorrow only slept to revive more fierce, but love never woke again—its ghost, ever hovering over my father's grave, alone survived—since his death all the world was to me a blank except where woe had stampt its burning words telling me to smile no more—the living were not fit companions for me, and I was ever meditating by what means I might shake them all off, and never be heard of again.

My convalescence rapidly advanced, yet this was the thought that haunted me, and I was for ever forming plans how I might hereafter contrive to escape the tortures that were prepared for me when I should mix in society, and to find that solitude which alone could suit one whom an untold grief seperated from her fellow creatures. Who can be more solitary even in a crowd than one whose history and the never ending feelings and remembrances arising from it is known to no living soul. There was too deep a horror in my tale for confidence; I was on earth the sole depository of my own secret. I might tell it to the winds and to the desart heaths but I must never among my fellow creatures, either by word or look give allowance to the smallest conjecture of the dread reality: I must shrink before the eye of man lest he should read my father's guilt in my glazed eyes: I must be silent lest my faltering voice should betray unimagined horrors. Over the deep grave of my secret I must heap an impenetrable heap of false smiles and words: cunning frauds, treacherous laughter, and a mixture of all light deceits would form a mist to blind others and be as the poisonous simoon to me. I, the offspring of love, the child of the woods, the nursling of Nature's bright self was to submit to this? I dared not.

How must I escape? I was rich and young, and had a guardian appointed for me; and all about me would act as if I were one of their great society, while I must keep the secret that I really was cut off from them for ever. If I fled I should be pursued; in life there was no escape for me: why then I must die. I shuddered; I dared not die even though the cold grave held all I loved; although I might say with Job

> Where is now my hope? For my hope who shall see it?
> They shall go down together to the bars of the pit,
> when our rest together is in the dust—[18]

Yes my hope was corruption and dust and all to which death brings us.— Or after life—No, no, I will not persuade myself to die, I may not, dare not. And then I wept; yes, warm tears once more struggled into my eyes soothing yet bitter; and after I had wept much and called with unavailing anguish, with outstretched arms, for my cruel father; after my weak frame was exhausted by all variety of plaint I sank once more into reverie, and once more reflected on how I might find that which I most desired; dear to me if aught were dear, a death-like solitude.

I dared not die, but I might feign death, and thus escape from my comforters: they will believe me united to my father, and so indeed I shall be. For alone, when no voice can disturb my dream, and no cold

18. Job 17:15–16.

eye meet mine to check its fire, then I may commune with his spirit; on a lone heath, at noon or at midnight, still I should be near him. His last injunction to me was that I should be happy; perhaps he did not mean the shadowy happiness that I promised myself, yet it was that alone which I could taste. He did not conceive that never again I could make one of the smiling hunters that go coursing after bubbles that break to nothing when caught, and then after a new one with brighter colours; my hope also had proved a bubble, but it had been so lovely, so adorned that I saw none that could attract me after it; besides I was wearied with the pursuit, nearly dead with weariness.

I would feign to die; my contented heirs would seize upon my wealth, and I should purchase freedom. But then my plan must be laid with art; I would not be left destitute, I must secure some money. Alas! to what loathsome shifts must I be driven? Yet a whole life of falsehood was otherwise my portion: and when remorse at being the contriver of any cheat made me shrink from my design I was irresistibly led back and confirmed in it by the visit of some aunt or cousin, who would tell me that death was the end of all men. And then say that my father had surely lost his wits ever since my mother's death; that he was mad and that I was fortunate, for in one of his fits he might have killed me instead of destroying his own crazed being. And all this, to be sure, was delicately put; not in broad words for my feelings might be hurt but

> Whispered so and so
> In dark hint soft and low[19]

with downcast eyes, and sympathizing smiles or whimpers; and I listened with quiet countenance while every nerve trembled; I that dared not utter aye or no to all this blasphemy. Oh, this was a delicious life quite void of guile! I with my dove's look and fox's heart: for indeed I felt only the degradation of falsehood, and not any sacred sentiment of conscious innocence that might redeem it. I who had before clothed myself in the bright garb of sincerity must now borrow one of divers colours: it might sit awkwardly at first, but use would enable me to place it in elegant folds, to lie with grace. Aye, I might die my soul with falsehood until I had quite hid its native colour. Oh, beloved father! Accept the pure heart of your unhappy daughter; permit me to join you unspotted as I was or you will not recognize my altered semblance. As grief might change Constance[20]

---

19. Coleridge's Fire, Famine and Slaughter. [Mary Shelley's note: she has adapted Famine's lines to Slaughter ("Whisper it, sister! so and so! / In a dark hint, soft and slow"), ll. 17–18 of S. T. Coleridge's 1798 poem "Fire, Famine, and Slaughter: A War Eclogue."]

20. Allusion to Constance's speeches on grief in Shakespeare's *King John*: see, e.g., III.i.67–74 and III.iv.93–105.

so would deceit change me until in heaven you would say, "This is not my child"—My father, to be happy both now and when again we meet I must fly from all this life which is mockery to one like me. In solitude only shall I be myself; in solitude I shall be thine.

Alas! I even now look back with disgust at my artifices and contrivances by which, after many painful struggles, I effected my retreat. I might enter into a long detail of the means I used, first to secure myself a slight maintenance for the remainder of my life, and afterwards to ensure the conviction of my death: I might, but I will not. I even now blush at the falsehoods I uttered; my heart sickens: I will leave this complication of what I hope I may in a manner call innocent deceit to be imagined by the reader. The remembrance haunts me like a crime—I know that if I were to endeavour to relate it my tale would at length remain unfinished. I was led to London, and had to endure for some weeks cold looks, cold words and colder consolations: but I escaped; they tried to bind me with fetters that they thought silken, yet which weighed on me like iron, although I broke them more easily than a girth formed of a single straw and fled to freedom.

The few weeks that I spent in London were the most miserable of my life: a great city is a frightful habitation to one sorrowing. The sunset and the gentle moon, the blessed motion of the leaves and the murmuring of waters are all sweet physicians to a distempered mind. The soul is expanded and drinks in quiet, a lulling medecine—to me it was as the sight of the lovely water snakes to the bewitched mariner—in loving and blessing Nature I unawares, called down a blessing on my own soul.[21] But in a city all is closed shut like a prison, a wiry prison from which you can peep at the sky only. I cannot describe to you what were the frantic nature of my sensations while I resided there; I was often on the verge of madness. Nay, when I look back on many of my wild thoughts, thoughts with which actions sometimes endeavoured to keep pace; when I tossed my hands high calling down the cope of heaven to fall on me and bury me; when I tore my hair and throwing it to the winds cried, "Ye are free, go seek my father!" And then, like the unfortunate Constance, catching at them again and tying them up, that nought might find him if I might not. How, on my knees I have fancied myself close to my father's grave and struck the ground in anger that it should cover him from me. Oft when I have listened with gasping attention for the sound of the ocean mingled with my father's groans; and then wept until my strength was gone and I was calm and faint, when I have recollected all this I have asked myself if this were not madness. While in London these and many

21. Allusion to the blessing of the water snakes in Coleridge's "Rime of the Ancient Mariner," ll. 272–87.

other dreadful thoughts too harrowing for words were my portion: I lost all this suffering when I was free; when I saw the wild heath around me, and the evening star in the west, then I could weep, gently weep, and be at peace.

Do not mistake me; I never was really mad. I was always conscious of my state when my wild thoughts seemed to drive me to insanity, and never betrayed them to aught but silence and solitude. The people around me saw nothing of all this. They only saw a poor girl broken in spirit, who spoke in a low and gentle voice, and from underneath whose downcast lids tears would sometimes steal which she strove to hide. One who loved to be alone, and shrunk from observation; who never smiled; oh, no! I never smiled—and that was all.

Well, I escaped. I left my guardian's house and I was never heard of again; it was believed from the letters that I left and other circumstances that I planned that I had destroyed myself. I was sought after therefore with less care than would otherwise have been the case; and soon all trace and memory of me was lost. I left London in a small vessel bound for a port in the north of England. And now having succeeded in my attempt, and being quite alone peace returned to me. The sea was calm and the vessel moved gently onwards, I sat upon deck under the open canopy of heaven and methought I was an altered creature. Not the wild, raving and most miserable Mathilda but a youthful Hermitess dedicated to seclusion and whose bosom she must strive to keep free from all tumult and unholy despair—The fanciful nun-like dress that I had adopted; the knowledge that my very existence was a secret known only to myself; the solitude to which I was for ever hereafter destined nursed gentle thoughts in my wounded heart. The breeze that played in my hair revived me, and I watched with quiet eyes the sunbeams that glittered on the waves, and the birds that coursed each other over the waters just brushing them with their plumes. I slept too undisturbed by dreams; and awoke refreshed to again enjoy my tranquil freedom.

In four days we arrived at the harbour to which we were bound. I would not remain on the sea coast, but proceeded immediately inland. I had already planned the situation where I would live. It should be a solitary house on a wide plain near no other habitation: where I could behold the whole horizon, and wander far without molestation from the sight of my fellow creatures. I was not misanthropic, but I felt that the gentle current of my feelings depended upon my being alone. I fixed myself on a wide solitude. On a dreary heath bestrewn with stones, among which short grass grew; and here and there a few rushes beside a little pool. Not far from my cottage was a small cluster of pines the only trees to be seen for many miles: I had a path cut through the furze from my door to this little wood, from whose topmost branches the birds saluted the rising sun and awoke me to my daily meditation. My view was bounded only by the horizon except on one side where a distant wood made a black spot on the heath, that every where else stretched out its faint hues as far as the eye could reach, wide and very desolate. Here I could mark the net work of the clouds as they wove themselves into thick masses: I could watch the slow rise of the heavy thunder clouds and could see the rack as it was driven across the heavens, or under the pine trees I could enjoy the stillness of the azure sky.

My life was very peaceful. I had one female servant who spent the greater part of the day at a village two miles off. My amusements were simple and very innocent; I fed the birds who built on the pines or among the ivy that covered the wall of my little garden, and they soon knew me: the bolder ones pecked the crumbs from my hands and perched on my fingers to sing their thankfulness. When I had lived here some time other animals visited me and a fox came every day for a portion of food appropriated for him and would suffer me to pat his head. I had besides many books and a harp with which when despairing I could soothe my spirits, and raise myself to sympathy and love.

Love! What had I to love? Oh many things: there was the moonshine, and the bright stars; the breezes and the refreshing rains; there was the whole earth and the sky that covers it: all lovely forms that visited my imagination, all memories of heroism and virtue. Yet this was very unlike my early life although as then I was confined to Nature and books. Then I bounded across the fields; my spirit often seemed to ride upon the winds, and to mingle in joyful sympathy with the ambient air. Then if I wandered slowly I cheered myself with a sweet song or sweeter day dreams. I felt a holy rapture spring from all I saw. I drank in joy with life; my steps were light; my eyes, clear from the love that animated them, sought the heavens, and with my long hair loosened to the winds I gave my body and my mind to sympathy and delight. But now my walk was slow—My eyes were seldom raised and often filled with tears; no song; no smiles; no careless motion that might bespeak a mind intent on what surrounded it—I was gathered up into myself—a selfish solitary creature ever pondering on my regrets and faded hopes.

Mine was an idle, useless life; it was so; but say not to the lily laid prostrate by the storm, "Arise, and bloom as before." My heart was bleeding from its death's wound; I could live no otherwise—Often amid apparent calm I was visited by despair and melancholy; gloom that nought could dissipate or overcome; a hatred of life; a carelessness of beauty; all these would by fits hold me nearly annihilated by their powers. Never for one moment when most placid did I cease to pray for death. I could be found in no state of mind which I would not willingly have exchanged for nothingness. And morning and evening my tearful eyes raised to heaven, my hands clasped tight in the energy of prayer, I have repeated with the poet—

> Before I see another day
> Oh, let this body die away![22]

Let me not be reproached then with inutility; I believed that by suicide I should violate a divine law of nature, and I thought that I sufficiently fulfilled my part in submitting to the hard task of enduring the crawling hours and minutes—in bearing the load of time that weighed miserably upon me and that in abstaining from what I in my calm moments considered a crime, I deserved the reward of virtue. There were periods, dreadful ones, during which I despaired—and doubted the existence of all duty and the reality of crime—but I shudder, and turn from the rememberance.

22. William Wordsworth, "The Complaint of a Forsaken Indian Woman," ll. 1–2, published in *Lyrical Ballads* (1798).

Chapter IX

Thus I passed two years. Day after day so many hundreds wore on; they brought no outward changes with them, but some few slowly operated on my mind as I glided on towards death. I began to study more; to sympathize more in the thoughts of others as expressed in books; to read history, and to lose my individuality among the crowd that had existed before me. Thus perhaps as the sensation of immediate suffering wore off, I became more human. Solitude also lost to me some of its charms: I began again to wish for sympathy; not that I was ever tempted to seek the crowd, but I wished for one friend to love me. You will say perhaps that I gradually became fitted to return to society. I do not think so. For the sympathy that I desired must be so pure, so divested of influence from outward circumstances that in the world I could not fail of being balked by the gross materials that perpetually mingle even with its best feelings. Believe me, I was then less fitted for any communion with my fellow creatures than before. When I left them they had tormented me but it was in the same way as pain and sickness may torment; something extraneous to the mind that galled it, and that I wished to cast aside. But now I should have desired sympathy; I should wish to knit my soul to some one of theirs, and should have prepared for myself plentiful draughts of disappointment and suffering; for I was tender as the sensitive plant, all nerve. I did not desire sympathy and aid in ambition or wisdom, but sweet and mutual affection; smiles to cheer me and gentle words of comfort. I wished for one heart in which I could pour unrestrained my plaints, and by the heavenly nature of the soil blessed fruit might spring from such bad seed. Yet how could I find this? The love that is the soul of friendship is a soft spirit seldom found except when two amiable creatures are knit from early youth, or when bound by mutual suffering and pursuits; it comes to some of the elect unsought and unaware; it descends as gentle dew on chosen spots which however barren they were before become under its benign influence fertile in all sweet plants; but when desired it flies; it scoffs at the prayers of its votaries; it will bestow, but not be sought.

I knew all this and did not go to seek sympathy; but there on my solitary heath, under my lowly roof where all around was desart, it came to me as a sunbeam in winter to adorn while it helps to dissolve the drifted snow.—Alas the sun shone on blighted fruit; I did not revive under its radiance for I was too utterly undone to feel its kindly power. My father had been and his memory was the life of my life. I might feel gratitude to another but I never more could love or hope as I had done; it was all suffering; even my pleasures were endured, not enjoyed. I was as a solitary spot among mountains shut in on all sides by steep black precipices; where no ray of heat could penetrate; and from which there was no outlet to sunnier fields. And thus it was that although the spirit of friendship soothed me for a while it could not restore me. It came as some gentle visitation; it went and I hardly felt the loss. The spirit of existence was dead within me; be not surprised therefore that when it came I welcomed not more gladly, or when it departed I lamented not more bitterly the best gift of heaven—a friend.

The name of my friend was Woodville. I will briefly relate his history that you may judge how cold my heart must have been not to be warmed by his eloquent words and tender sympathy; and how he also being most unhappy we were well fitted to be a mutual consolation to each other, if I had not been hardened to stone by the Medusa head of Misery. The misfortunes of Woodville were not of the heart's core like mine; his was a natural grief, not to destroy but to purify the heart and from which he might, when its shadow had passed from over him, shine forth brighter and happier than before.

Woodville was the son of a poor clergyman and had received a classical education. He was one of those very few whom fortune favours from their birth; on whom she bestows all gifts of intellect and person with a profusion that knew no bounds, and whom under her peculiar protection, no imperfection however slight, or disappointment however transitory has leave to touch. She seemed to have formed his mind of that excellence which no dross can tarnish, and his understanding was such that no error could pervert. His genius was transcendant, and when it rose as a bright star in the east all eyes were turned towards it in admiration. He was a Poet. That name has so often been degraded that it will not convey the idea of all that he was. He was like a poet of old whom the muses had crowned in his cradle, and on whose lips bees had fed. As he walked among other men he seemed encompassed with a heavenly halo that divided him from and lifted him above them. It was his surpassing beauty, the dazzling fire of his eyes, and his words whose rich accents wrapt the listener in mute and extatic wonder, that made him transcend all others so that before him they appeared only formed to minister to his superior excellence.

He was glorious from his youth. Every one loved him; no shadow of envy or hate cast even from the meanest mind ever fell upon him. He was, as one the peculiar delight of the gods, railed and fenced in by his own divinity, so that nought but love and admiration could approach him. His heart was simple like a child, unstained by arrogance or vanity. He mingled in society unknowing of his superiority over his companions, not because he undervalued himself but because he did not perceive the inferiority of others. He seemed incapable of conceiving of the full extent of the power that selfishness and vice possesses in the world: when I knew him, although he had suffered disappointment in his dearest hopes, he had not experienced any that arose from the meanness and self-love of men: his station was too high to allow of his suffering through their hardheartedness; and too low for him to have experienced ingratitude and encroaching selfishness: it is one of the blessings of a moderate fortune, that by preventing the possessor from conferring pecuniary favours it prevents him also from diving into the arcana of human weakness or malice— To bestow on your fellow men is a godlike attribute—So indeed it is and as such not one fit for mortality;—the giver like Adam and Prometheus, must pay the penalty of rising above his nature by being the martyr to his own excellence. Woodville was free from all these evils; and if slight examples did come across him he did not notice them but passed on in his course as an angel with winged feet might glide along the earth unimpeded by all those little obstacles over which we of earthly origin stumble. He was a believer in the divinity of genius and always opposed a stern disbelief to the objections of those petty cavillers and minor critics who wish to reduce all men to their own miserable level—"I will make a scientific simile" he would say, "in the manner, if you will, of Dr. Darwin—I consider the alledged errors of a man of genius as the aberrations of the fixed stars. It is our distance from them and our imperfect means of communication that makes them appear to move; in truth they always remain stationary, a glorious centre, giving us a fine lesson of modesty if we would thus receive it."[23]—

I have said that he was a poet: when he was three and twenty years of age he first published a poem, and it was hailed by the whole nation with enthusiasm and delight. His good star perpetually shone upon him; a

23. Compare Mary Shelley's similar phrasing in the introductory paragraph to her essay "Giovanni Villani," printed below.

reputation had never before been made so rapidly: it was universal. The multitude extolled the same poems that formed the wonder of the sage in his closet: there was not one dissentient voice.

It was at this time, in the height of his glory, that he became acquainted with Elinor. She was a young heiress of exquisite beauty who lived under the care of her guardian: from the moment they were seen together they appeared formed for each other. Elinor had not the genius of Woodville but she was generous and noble, and exalted by her youth and the love that she every where excited above the knowledge of aught but virtue and excellence. She was lovely; her manners were frank and simple; her deep blue eyes swam in a lustre which could only be given by sensibility joined to wisdom.

They were formed for one another and they soon loved. Woodville for the first time felt the delight of love; and Elinor was enraptured in possessing the heart of one so beautiful and glorious among his fellow men. Could any thing but unmixed joy flow from such a union?

Woodville was a Poet—he was sought for by every society and all eyes were turned on him alone when he appeared; but he was the son of a poor clergyman and Elinor was a rich heiress. Her guardian was not displeased with their mutual affection: the merit of Woodville was too eminent to admit of cavil on account of his inferior wealth; but the dying will of her father did not allow her to marry before she was of age and her fortune depended upon her obeying this injunction. She had just entered her twentieth year, and she and her lover were obliged to submit to this delay. But they were ever together and their happiness seemed that of Paradise: they studied together: formed plans of future occupations, and drinking in love and joy from each other's eyes and words they hardly repined at the delay to their entire union. Woodville for ever rose in glory; and Elinor become more lovely and wise under the lessons of her accomplished lover.

In two months Elinor would be twenty one: every thing was prepared for their union. How shall I relate the catastrophe to so much joy; but the earth would not be the earth it is, covered with blight and sorrow, if one such pair as these angelic creatures had been suffered to exist for one another: search through the world and you will not find the perfect happiness which their marriage would have caused them to enjoy; there must have been a revolution in the order of things as established among us miserable earth-dwellers to have admitted of such consummate joy. The chain of necessity ever bringing misery must have been broken and the malignant fate that presides over it would not permit this breach of her eternal laws. But why should I repine at this? Misery was my element, and nothing but what was miserable could approach me; if Woodville had been happy I should never have known him. And can I who for many years was fed by tears, and nourished under the dew of grief, can I pause to relate a tale of woe and death?

Woodville was obliged to make a journey into the country and was detained from day to day in irksome absence from his lovely bride. He received a letter from her to say that she was slightly ill, but telling him to hasten to her, that from his eyes she would receive health and that his company would be her surest medecine. He was detained three days longer and then he hastened to her. His heart, he knew not why, prognosticated misfortune; he had not heard from her again; he feared she might be worse and this fear made him impatient and restless for the moment of beholding her once more stand before him arrayed in health and beauty; for a sinister voice seemed always to whisper to him, "You will never more behold her as she was."

When he arrived at her habitation all was silent in it: he made his way through several rooms; in one he saw a servant weeping bitterly: he was faint with fear and could hardly ask, "Is she dead?" and just listened to the dreadful answer, "Not yet." These astounding words came on him as of less fearful import than those which he had expected; and to learn that she was still in being, and that he might still hope was an alleviation to him. He remembered the words of her letter and he indulged the wild idea that his kisses breathing warm love and life would infuse new spirit into her, and that with him near her she could not die; that his presence was the talisman of her life.

He hastened to her sick room; she lay, her cheeks burning with fever, yet her eyes were closed and she was seemingly senseless. He wrapt her in his arms; he imprinted breathless kisses on her burning lips; he called to her in a voice of subdued anguish by the tenderest names; "Return Elinor; I am with you; your life, your love. Return; dearest one, you promised me this boon, that I should bring you health. Let your sweet spirit revive; you cannot die near me: What is death? To see you no more? To part with what is a part of myself; without whom I have no memory and no futurity? Elinor die! This is frenzy and the most miserable despair: you cannot die while I am near."

And again he kissed her eyes and lips, and hung over her inanimate form in agony, gazing on her countenance still lovely although changed, watching every slight convulsion, and varying colour which denoted life still lingering although about to depart. Once for a moment she revived and recognized his voice; a smile, a last lovely smile, played upon her lips. He watched beside her for twelve hours and then she died.

Chapter X

It was six months after this miserable conclusion to his long nursed hopes that I first saw him. He had retired to a part of the country where he was not known that he might peacefully indulge his grief. All the world, by the death of his beloved Elinor, was changed to him, and he could no longer remain in any spot where he had seen her or where her image mingled with the most rapturous hopes had brightened all around with a light of joy which would now be transformed to a darkness blacker than midnight since she, the sun of his life, was set for ever.

He lived for some time never looking on the light of heaven but shrouding his eyes in a perpetual darkness far from all that could remind him of what he had been; but as time softened his grief, like a true child of Nature he sought in the enjoyment of her beauties for a consolation in his unhappiness. He came to a part of the country where he was entirely unknown and where in the deepest solitude he could converse only with his own heart. He found a relief to his impatient grief in the breezes of heaven and in the sound of waters and woods. He became fond of riding; this exercise distracted his mind and elevated his spirits; on a swift horse he could for a moment gain respite from the image that else for ever followed him; Elinor on her death bed, her sweet features changed, and the soft spirit that animated her gradually waning into extinction. For many months Woodville had in vain endeavoured to cast off this terrible remembrance; it still hung on him until memory was too great a burthen for his loaded soul, but when on horseback the spell that seemingly held him to this idea was snapt; then if he thought of his lost bride he pictured her radiant in beauty; he could hear her voice, and fancy her "a sylvan Huntress by his side,"[24] while his eyes brightened as

24. Unidentified.

he thought he gazed on her cherished form. I had several times seen him ride across the heath and felt angry that my solitude should be disturbed. It was so long [since] I had spoken to any but peasants that I felt a disagreeable sensation at being gazed on by one of superior rank. I feared also that it might be some one who had seen me before: I might be recognized, my impostures discovered and I dragged back to a life of worse torture than that I had before endured. These were dreadful fears and they even haunted my dreams.

I was one day seated on the verge of the clump of pines when Woodville rode past. As soon as I perceived him I suddenly rose to escape from his observation by entering among the trees. My rising startled his horse; he reared and plunged and the rider was at length thrown. The horse then galloped swiftly across the heath and the stranger remained on the ground stunned by his fall. He was not materially hurt, a little fresh water soon recovered him. I was struck by his exceeding beauty, and as he spoke to thank me the sweet but melancholy cadence of his voice brought tears into my eyes.

A short conversation passed between us, but the next day he again stopped at my cottage and by degrees an intimacy grew between us. It was strange to him to see a female in extreme youth. I was not yet twenty, evidently belonging to the first classes of society and possessing every accomplishment an excellent education could bestow, living alone on a desolate heath—One on whose forehead the impress of grief was strongly marked, and whose words and motions betrayed that her thoughts did not follow them but were intent on far other ideas; bitter and overwhelming miseries. I was dressed also in a whimsical nun-like habit which denoted that I did not retire to solitude from necessity, but that I might indulge in a luxury of grief, and fanciful seclusion.

He soon took great interest in me, and sometimes forgot his own grief to sit beside me and endeavour to cheer me. He could not fail to interest even one who had shut herself from the whole world, whose hope was death, and who lived only with the departed. His personal beauty; his conversation which glowed with imagination and sensibility; the poetry that seemed to hang upon his lips and to make the very air mute to listen to him were charms that no one could resist. He was younger, less worn, more passionless than my father and in no degree reminded me of him: he suffered under immediate grief yet its gentle influence instead of calling feelings otherwise dormant into action, seemed only to veil that which otherwise would have been too dazzling for me. When we were together I spoke little, yet my selfish mind was sometimes borne away by the rapid course of his ideas; I would lift my eyes with momentary brilliancy until memories that never died and seldom slept would recur, and a tear would dim them.

Woodville for ever tried to lead me to the contemplation of what is beautiful and happy in the world. His own mind was constitutionally bent to a firmer[25] belief in good than in evil and this feeling which must even exhilarate the hopeless ever shone forth in his words. He would talk of the wonderful powers of man, of their present state and of their hopes: of what they had been and what they were, and when reason could no longer guide him, his imagination as if inspired shed light on the obscurity that veils the past and the future. He loved to dwell on what might have been the state of the earth before man lived on it, and how he first arose and gradually became the strange, complicated, but as he said, the glorious creature he now is. Covering the earth with their creations and forming by the power of their minds another world more lovely than the visible frame of things, even all the world that we find in their writings. A beautiful creation, he would say, which may claim this superiority to its model, that good and evil is more easily seperated: the good rewarded in the way they themselves desire; the evil punished as all things evil ought to be punished, not by pain which is revolting to all philanthropy to consider but by quiet obscurity, which simply deprives them of their harmful qualities; why kill the serpent when you have extracted his fangs?

The poetry of his language and ideas which my words ill convey held me enchained to his discourses. It was a melancholy pleasure to me to listen to his inspired words; to catch for a moment the light of his eyes; to feel a transient sympathy and then to awaken from the delusion, again to know that all this was nothing,—a dream—a shadow for which[26] there was no reality for me; my father had for ever deserted me, leaving me only memories which set an eternal barrier between me and my fellow creatures. I was indeed fellow to none. He—Woodville, mourned the loss of his bride: others wept the various forms of misery as they visited them: but infamy and guilt was mingled with my portion; unlawful and detestable passion had poured its poison into my ears and changed all my blood, so that it was no longer the kindly stream that supports life but a cold fountain of bitterness corrupted in its very source. It must be the excess of madness that could make me imagine that I could ever be aught but one alone; struck off from humanity; bearing no affinity to man or woman; a wretch on whom Nature had set her ban.

Sometimes Woodville talked to me of himself. He related his history

25. Printed incorrectly as "former" in Nitchie, p. 61.
26. Changed from "that" in Nitchie and in manuscript.

brief in happiness and woe and dwelt with passion on his and Elinor's mutual love. "She was," he said, "the brightest vision that ever came upon the earth: there was something in her frank countenance, in her voice, and in every motion of her graceful form that overpowered me, as if it were a celestial creature that deigned to mingle with me in intercourse more sweet than man had ever before enjoyed. Sorrow fled before her; and her smile seemed to possess an influence like light to irradiate all mental darkness. It was not like a human loveliness that these gentle smiles went and came; but as a sunbeam on a lake, now light and now obscure, flitting before as you strove to catch them, and fold them for ever to your heart. I saw this smile fade for ever. Alas! I could never have believed that it was indeed Elinor that died if once when I spoke she had not lifted her almost benighted eyes, and for one moment like nought beside on earth, more lovely than a sunbeam, slighter, quicker than the waving plumage of a bird, dazzling as lightning and like it giving day to night, yet mild and faint, that smile came; it went, and then there was an end of all joy to me."

Thus his own sorrows, or the shapes copied from nature that dwelt in his mind with beauty greater than their own, occupied our talk while I railed in my own griefs with cautious secresy. If for a moment he shewed curiosity, my eyes fell, my voice died away and my evident suffering made him quickly endeavour to banish the ideas he had awakened; yet he for ever mingled consolation in his talk, and tried to soften my despair by demonstrations of deep sympathy and compassion. "We are both un-happy—" he would say to me; "I have told you my melancholy tale and we have wept together the loss of that lovely spirit that has so cruelly deserted me; but you hide your griefs: I do not ask you to disclose them, but tell me if I may not console you. It seems to me a wild adventure to find in this desart one like you quite solitary: you are young and lovely; your manners are refined and attractive; yet there is in your settled melancholy, and something, I know not what, in your expressive eyes that seems to seperate you from your kind: you shudder; pardon me, I entreat you but I cannot help expressing this once at least the lively interest I feel in your destiny.

"You never smile: your voice is low, and you utter your words as if you were afraid of the slight sound they would produce: the expression of awful and intense sorrow never for a moment fades from your countenance. I have lost for ever the loveliest companion that any man could ever have possessed, one who rather appears to have been a superior spirit who by some strange accident wandered among us earthly creatures, than as belonging to our kind. Yet I smile, and sometimes I speak almost forgetful of the change I have endured. But your sad mien never alters; your pulses beat and you breathe, yet you seem already to belong to another world; and sometimes, pray pardon my wild thoughts, when you touch my hand I am surprised to find your hand warm when all the fire of life seems extinct within you.

"When I look upon you, the tears you shed, the soft deprecating look with which you withstand enquiry; the deep sympathy your voice expresses when I speak of my lesser sorrows add to my interest for you. You stand here shelterless. You have cast yourself from among us and you wither on this wild plain forlorn and helpless: some dreadful calamity must have befallen you. Do not turn from me; I do not ask you to reveal it: I only entreat you to listen to me and to become familiar with the voice of consolation and kindness. If pity, and admiration, and gentle affection can wean you from despair let me attempt the task. I cannot see your look of deep grief without endeavouring to restore you to happier feelings. Unbend your brow; relax the stern melancholy of your regard; permit a friend, a sincere, affectionate friend, I will be one, to convey some relief, some momentary pause to your sufferings.

"Do not think that I would intrude upon your confidence: I only ask your patience. Do not for ever look sorrow and never speak it; utter one word of bitter complaint and I will reprove it with gentle exhortation and pour on you the balm of compassion. You must not shut me from all communion with you: do not tell me why you grieve but only say the words, 'I am unhappy,' and you will feel relieved as if for some time excluded from all intercourse by some magic spell you should suddenly enter again the pale of human sympathy. I entreat you to believe in my most sincere professions and to treat me as an old and tried friend: promise me never to forget me, never causelessly to banish me; but try to love me as one who would devote all his energies to make you happy. Give me the name of friend; I will fulfill its duties; and if for a moment complaint and sorrow would shape themselves into words, let me be near to speak peace to your vext soul."

I repeat his persuasions in faint terms and cannot give you at the same time the tone and gesture that animated them. Like a refreshing shower on an arid soil they revived me, and although I still kept their cause secret he led me to pour forth my bitter complaints and to clothe my woe in words of gall and fire. With all the energy of desperate grief I told him how I had fallen at once from bliss to misery; how that for me there was no joy, no hope; that death however bitter would be the welcome seal to all my pangs; death the skeleton was to be beautiful as love. I know not why but I found it sweet to utter these words to human ears; and though I derided all consolation yet I was pleased to see it offered me with gentleness and kindness. I listened quietly, and when he paused would again pour out my misery in expressions that shewed how far too deep my wounds were for any cure.

But now also I began to reap the fruits of my perfect solitude. I had become unfit for any intercourse, even with Woodville the most gentle and sympathizing creature that existed. I had become captious and unreasonable: my temper was utterly spoilt. I called him my friend but I viewed all he did with jealous eyes. If he did not visit me at the appointed hour I was angry, very angry, and told him that if indeed he did feel interest in me it was cold, and could not be fitted for me, a poor worn creature, whose deep unhappiness demanded much more than his worldly heart could give. When for a moment I imagined that his manner was cold I would fretfully say to him—"I was at peace before you came; why have you disturbed me? You have given me new wants and now you trifle with me as if my heart were as whole as yours, as if I were not in truth a shorn lamb thrust out on the bleak hill side, tortured by every blast. I wished for no friend, no sympathy. I avoided you, you know I did, but you forced yourself upon me and gave me those wants which you see with triumph give you power over me. Oh the brave power of the bitter north wind which freezes the tears it has caused to shed! But I will not bear this; go: the sun will rise and set as before you came, and I shall sit among the pines or wander on the heath weeping and complaining without wishing for you to listen. You are cruel, very cruel, to treat me who bleed at every pore in this rough manner."

And then, when in answer to my peevish words, I saw his countenance bent with living pity on me. When I saw him

> Gli occhi drizzo ver me con quel sembiante
> Che madre fa sopra figlioul deliro[27]

I wept and said, "Oh, pardon me! You are good and kind but I am not fit for life. Why am I obliged to live? To drag hour after hour, to see the trees wave their branches restlessly, to feel the air, and to suffer in all I feel keenest agony. My frame is strong, but my soul sinks beneath this endurance of living anguish. Death is the goal that I would attain, but, alas! I do not even see the end of the course. Do you, my compassionate friend, tell me how to die peacefully and innocently and I will bless you: all that I, poor wretch, can desire is a painless death."

But Woodville's words had magic in them, when beginning with the sweetest pity, he would raise me by degrees out of myself and my sorrows until I wondered at my own selfishness: but he left me and despair returned; the work of consolation was ever to begin anew. I often desired

27. Paradiso. C 1. [Mary Shelley's incomplete note on Dante, *Paradiso* I.101–102: "she turned her eyes on me with the look that a mother casts on her delirious child."]

his entire absence; for I found that I was grown out of the ways of life and that by long seclusion, although I could support my accustomed grief, and drink the bitter daily draught with some degree of patience, yet I had become unfit for the slightest novelty of feeling. Expectation, and hopes, and affection were all too much for me. I knew this, but at other times I was unreasonable and laid the blame upon him, who was most blameless, and peevishly thought that if his gentle soul were more gentle, if his intense sympathy were more intense, he could drive the fiend from my soul and make me more human. I am, I thought, a tragedy; a character that he comes to see act: now and then he gives me my cue that I may make a speech more to his purpose: perhaps he is already planning a poem in which I am to figure. I am a farce and play to him, but to me this is all dreary reality: he takes all the profit and I bear all the burthen.

Chapter XI

It is a strange circumstance but it often occurs that blessings by their use turn to curses; and that I who in solitude had desired sympathy as the only relief I could enjoy should now find it an additional torture to me. During my father's life time I had always been of an affectionate and forbearing disposition, but since those days of joy alas! I was much changed. I had become arrogant, peevish, and above all suspicious. Although the real interest of my narration is now ended and I ought quickly to wind up its melancholy catastrophe, yet I will relate one instance of my sad suspicion and despair and how Woodville with the goodness and almost the power of an angel, softened my rugged feelings and led me back to gentleness.

He had promised to spend some hours with me one afternoon but a violent and continual rain prevented him. I was alone the whole evening. I had passed two whole years alone unrepining, but now I was miserable. He could not really care for me, I thought, for if he did the storm would rather have made him come even if I had not expected him, than, as it did, prevent a promised visit. He would well know that this drear sky and gloomy rain would load my spirit almost to madness: if the weather had been fine I should not have regretted his absence as heavily as I necessarily must, shut up in this miserable cottage with no companions but my own wretched thoughts. If he were truly my friend he would have calculated all this; and let me now calculate this boasted friendship, and discover its real worth. He got over his grief for Elinor, and the country became dull to him, so he was glad to find even me for amusement; and when he does not know what else to do he passes his lazy hours here, and calls this friendship—It is true that his presence is a consolation to me, and that his words are sweet, and, when he will, he can pour forth thoughts that win me from despair. His words are sweet,—and so, truly, is the honey of the bee, but the bee has a sting, and unkindness is a worse smart than that received from an insect's venom. I will put him to the proof. He says all hope is dead to him, and I know that it is dead to me, so we are both equally fitted for death. Let me try if he will die with me; and as I fear to die alone, if he will accompany to cheer me, and thus he can shew himself my friend in the only manner my misery will permit.

It was madness I believe, but I so worked myself up to this idea that I could think of nothing else. If he dies with me it is well, and there will be an end of two miserable beings; and if he will not, then will I scoff at his friendship and drink the poison before him to shame his cowardice. I planned the whole scene with an earnest heart and franticly set my soul on this project. I procured Laudanum and placing it in two glasses on the table, filled my room with flowers and decorated the last scene of my tragedy with the nicest care. As the hour for his coming approached, my heart softened and I wept; not that I gave up my plan, but even when resolved the mind must undergo several revolutions of feeling before it can drink its death.

Now all was ready and Woodville came. I received him at the door of my cottage and leading him solemnly into the room, I said: "My friend, I wish to die. I am quite weary of enduring the misery which hourly I do endure, and I will throw it off. What slave will not, if he may, escape from his chains? Look, I weep; for more than two years I have never enjoyed one moment free from anguish. I have often desired to die; but I am a very coward. It is hard for one so young who was once so happy as I was voluntarily to divest themselves of all sensation and to go alone to the dreary grave; I dare not. I must die, yet my fear chills me; I pause and shudder and then for months I endure my excess of wretchedness. But now the time is come when I may quit life. I have a friend who will not refuse to accompany me in this dark journey; such is my request: earnestly do I entreat and implore you to die with me. Then we shall find Elinor and what I have lost. Look, I am prepared; there is the death draught, let us drink it together and willingly and joyfully quit this hated round of daily life.

"You turn from me; yet before you deny me reflect, Woodville, how sweet it were to cast off the load of tears and misery under which we now labour: and surely we shall find light after we have passed the dark valley. That drink will plunge us in a sweet slumber, and when we awaken what joy will be ours to find all our sorrows and fears past. *A little patience, and all will be over*; aye, a very little patience; for, look, there is the key of our prison; we hold it in our own hands, and are we more debased than slaves to cast it away and give ourselves up to voluntary bondage? Even now if we had courage we might be free. Behold, my cheek is flushed with pleasure at the imagination of death; all that we love are dead. Come, give me your hand, one look of joyous sympathy and we will go together and seek them; a lulling journey; where our arrival will bring bliss and our waking be that of angels. Do you delay? Are you a coward, Woodville? Oh fie! Cast off this blank look of human melancholy. Oh! that I had words to express the luxury of death that I might win you. I tell you we are no longer miserable mortals; we are about to become gods; spirits free and happy as gods. What fool on a bleak shore, seeing a flowery isle on the other side with his lost love beckoning to him from it would pause because the wave is dark and turbid?

> What if some little payne the passage have
> That makes frayle flesh to fear the bitter wave?
> Is not short payne well borne that brings long ease,
> And lays the soul to sleep in quiet grave?[28]

"Do you mark my words; I have learned the language of despair: I have it all by heart, for I am Despair; and a strange being am I, joyous, triumphant Despair. But those words are false, for the wave may be dark but it is not bitter. We lie down, and close our eyes with a gentle good night, and when we wake, we are free. Come then, no more delay, thou tardy one! Behold the pleasant potion! Look, I am a spirit of good, and not a human maid that invites thee, and with winning accents (oh, that they would win thee!) says, Come and drink."

As I spoke I fixed my eyes upon his countenance, and his exquisite beauty, the heavenly compassion that beamed from his eyes, his gentle yet earnest look of deprecation and wonder even before he spoke wrought a change in my high-strained feelings taking from me all the sternness of despair and filling me only with the softest grief. I saw his eyes humid also as he took both my hands in his; and sitting down near me, he said:

"This is a sad deed to which you would lead me, dearest friend, and your woe must indeed be deep that could fill you with these unhappy thoughts. You long for death and yet you fear it and wish me to be your companion. But I have less courage than you and even thus accompanied I dare not die. Listen to me, and then reflect if you ought to win me to your project, even if with the overbearing eloquence of despair you could make black death so inviting that the fair heaven should appear darkness. Listen I entreat you to the words of one who has himself nurtured desperate thoughts, and longed with impatient desire for death, but who has at length trampled the phantom under foot, and crushed his sting.

28. Spencer's Faery Queen Book 1-Canto. [Mary Shelley's incomplete note on Spenser's *Faerie Queene* I.9.xl, where the Red Cross Knight is being tempted by Despair before being saved by Una.]

Come, as you have played Despair with me I will play the part of Una with you and bring you hurtless from his dark cavern. Listen to me, and let yourself be softened by words in which no selfish passion lingers.

"We know not what all this wide world means; its strange mixture of good and evil. But we have been placed here and bid live and hope. I know not what we are to hope; but there is some good beyond us that we must seek; and that is our earthly task. If misfortune come against us we must fight with her; we must cast her aside, and still go on to find out that which it is our nature to desire. Whether this prospect of future good be the preparation for another existence I know not; or whether that it is merely that we, as workmen in God's vineyard, must lend a hand to smooth the way for our posterity. If it indeed be that; if the efforts of the virtuous now, are to make the future inhabitants of this fair world more happy; if the labours of those who cast aside selfishness, and try to know the truth of things, are to free the men of ages, now far distant but which will one day come, from the burthen under which those who now live groan, and like you weep bitterly; if they free them but from one of what are now the necessary evils of life, truly I will not fail but will with my whole soul aid the work. From my youth I have said, I will be virtuous; I will dedicate my life for the good of others; I will do my best to extirpate evil and if the spirit who protects ill should so influence circumstances that I should suffer through my endeavour, yet while there is hope, and hope there ever must be, of success, cheerfully do I gird myself to my task.

"I have powers; my countrymen think well of them. Do you think I sow my seed in the barren air, and have no end in what I do? Believe me, I will never desert life until this last hope is torn from my bosom, that in some way my labours may form a link in the chain of gold with which we ought all to strive to drag Happiness from where she sits enthroned above the clouds, now far beyond our reach, to inhabit the earth with us. Let us suppose that Socrates, or Shakespear, or Rousseau had been seized with despair and died in youth when they were as young as I am; do you think that we and all the world should not have lost incalculable improvement in our good feelings and our happiness through their destruction? I am not like one of these; they influenced millions: but if I can influence but a hundred, but ten, but one solitary individual, so as in any way to lead him from ill to good, that will be a joy to repay me for all my sufferings, though they were a million times multiplied; and that hope will support me to bear them.

"And those who do not work for posterity; or working, as may be my case, will not be known by it; yet they, believe me, have also their duties. You grieve because you are unhappy; it is happiness you seek but you despair of obtaining it. But if you can bestow happiness on another; if you can give one other person only one hour of joy ought you not to live to do it? And every one has it in their power to do that. The inhabitants of this world suffer so much pain. In crowded cities, among cultivated plains, or on the desert mountains, pain is thickly sown, and if we can tear up but one of these noxious weeds, or more, if in its stead we can sow one seed of corn, or plant one fair flower, let that be motive sufficient against suicide. Let us not desert our task while there is the slightest hope that we may in a future day do this.

"Indeed I dare not die. I have a mother whose support and hope I am. I have a friend who loves me as his life, and in whose breast I should infix a mortal sting if I ungratefully left him. So I will not die. Nor shall you, my friend; cheer up; cease to weep, I entreat you. Are you not young, and fair, and good? Why should you despair? Or if you must for yourself, why for others? If you can never be happy, can you never bestow happiness? Oh! believe me, if you beheld on lips pale with grief one smile of joy and gratitude, and knew that you were parent of that smile, and that without you it had never been, you would feel so pure and warm a happiness that you would wish to live for ever again and again to enjoy the same pleasure.

"Come, I see that you have already cast aside the sad thoughts you before franticly indulged. Look in that mirror; when I came your brow was contracted, your eyes deep sunk in your head, your lips quivering; your hands trembled violently when I took them; but now all is tranquil and soft. You are grieved and there is grief in the expression of your countenance but it is gentle and sweet. You allow me to throw away this cursed drink; you smile. Oh! Congratulate me, hope is triumphant, and I have done some good."

These words are shadowy as I repeat them but they were indeed words of fire and produced a warm hope in me (I, miserable wretch, to hope!) that tingled like pleasure in my veins. He did not leave me for many hours; not until he had improved the spark that he had kindled, and with an angelic hand fostered the return of something that seemed like joy. He left me but I still was calm, and after I had saluted the starry sky and dewy earth with eyes of love and a contented good night, I slept sweetly, visited by dreams, the first of pleasure I had had for many long months.

But this was only a momentary relief and my old habits of feeling returned; for I was doomed while in life to grieve, and to the natural sorrow of my father's death and its most terrific cause, imagination added a ten-fold weight of woe. I believed myself to be polluted by the unnatural love I had inspired, and that I was a creature cursed and set apart by nature. I thought that like another Cain, I had a mark set on my forehead to shew mankind that there was a barrier between me and them.

Woodville had told me that there was in my countenance an expression as if I belonged to another world; so he had seen that sign: and there it lay a gloomy mark to tell the world that there was that within my soul that no silence could render sufficiently obscure. Why when fate drove me to become this outcast from human feeling; this monster with whom none might mingle in converse and love; why had she not from that fatal and most accursed moment, shrouded me in thick mists and placed real darkness between me and my fellows so that I might never more be seen; and as I passed, like a murky cloud loaded with blight, they might only perceive me by the cold chill I should cast upon them; telling them, how truly, that something unholy was near? Then I should have lived upon this dreary heath unvisited, and blasting none by my unhallowed gaze. Alas! I verily believe that if the near prospect of death did not dull and soften my bitter feelings, if for a few months longer I had continued to live as I then lived, strong in body, but my soul corrupted to its core by a deadly cancer, if day after day I had dwelt on these dreadful sentiments I should have become mad, and should have fancied myself a living pestilence: so horrible to my own solitary thoughts did this form, this voice, and all this wretched self appear; for had it not been the source of guilt that wants a name?

This was superstition. I did not feel thus franticly when first I knew that the holy name of father was become a curse to me: but my lonely life inspired me with wild thoughts; and then when I saw Woodville and day after day he tried to win my confidence and I never dared give words to my dark tale, I was impressed more strongly with the withering fear that I was in truth a marked creature, a pariah, only fit for death.

Chapter XII

As I was perpetually haunted by these ideas, you may imagine that the influence of Woodville's words was very temporary; and that although I did not again accuse him of unkindness, yet I soon became as unhappy as before. Soon after this incident we parted. He heard that his mother was ill, and he hastened to her. He came to take leave of me, and we walked together on the heath for the last time. He promised that he would come and see me again; and bade me take cheer, and to encourage what happy thoughts I could, until time and fortitude should overcome my misery, and I could again mingle in society.

"Above all other admonition on my part," he said, "cherish and follow this one: do not despair. That is the most dangerous gulph on which you perpetually totter; but you must reassure your steps, and take hope to guide you. Hope, and your wounds will be already half healed: but if you obstinately despair, there never more will be comfort for you. Believe me, my dearest friend, that there is a joy that the sun and earth and all its beauties can bestow that you will one day feel. The refreshing bliss of Love will again visit your heart, and undo the spell that binds you to woe, until you wonder how your eyes could be closed in the long night that burthens you. I dare not hope that I have inspired you with sufficient interest that the thought of me, and the affection that I shall ever bear you, will soften your melancholy and decrease the bitterness of your tears. But if my friendship can make you look on life with less disgust, beware how you injure it with suspicion. Love is a delicate sprite and easily hurt by rough jealousy. Guard, I entreat you, a firm persuasion of my sincerity in the inmost recesses of your heart out of the reach of the casual winds that may disturb its surface. Your temper is made unequal by suffering, and the tenor of your mind is, I fear, sometimes shaken by unworthy causes; but let your confidence in my sympathy and love be deeper far, and incapable of being reached by these agitations that come and go, and if they touch not your affections leave you uninjured."

These were some of Woodville's last lessons. I wept as I listened to him; and after we had taken an affectionate farewell, I followed him far with my eyes until they saw the last of my earthly comforter. I had insisted on accompanying him across the heath towards the town where he dwelt: the sun was yet high when he left me, and I turned my steps towards my cottage. It was at the latter end of the month of September when the nights have become chill. But the weather was serene, and as I walked on I fell into no unpleasing reveries. I thought of Woodville with gratitude and kindness and did not, I know not why, regret his departure with any bitterness. It seemed that after one great shock all other change was trivial to me; and I walked on wondering when the time would come when we should all four, my dearest father restored to me, meet in some sweet Paradise. I pictured to myself a lovely river such as that on whose banks Dante describes Mathilda gathering flowers, which ever flows

> —————— bruna, bruna,
> Sotto l'ombra perpetua, che mai
> Raggiar non lascia sole ivi, nè Luna.[29]

And then I repeated to myself all that lovely passage that relates the entrance of Dante into the terrestrial Paradise; and thought it would be sweet when I wandered on those lovely banks to see the car of light descend with my long lost parent to be restored to me. As I waited there in expectation of that moment, I thought how, of the lovely flowers that grew there, I would wind myself a chaplet and crown myself for joy: I would sing *sul margine d'un rio*,[30] my father's favourite song, and my voice gliding through the windless air would announce to him, in whatever bower he sat expecting the moment of our union, that his daughter was come. Then the mark of misery would have faded from my brow, and I should raise my eyes fearlessly to meet his, which ever beamed with the soft lustre of innocent love. When I reflected on the magic look of those deep eyes I wept, but gently, lest my sobs should disturb the fairy scene.

I was so entirely wrapt in this reverie that I wandered on, taking no heed of my steps until I actually stooped down to gather a flower for my wreath on that bleak plain where no flower grew, when I awoke from my day dream and found myself I knew not where.

The sun had set and the roseate hue which the clouds had caught from

29. Dante, *Purgatorio* XXVIII.31–33: "quite dark under the perpetual shade, which never lets sun or moon beam enter there."

30. "On the edge of a brook." Nitchie (p. 88, n. 77) notes that an "air with this title was published about 1800 in London by Robert Birchall."

him in his descent had nearly died away. A wind swept across the plain, I looked around me and saw no object that told me where I was; I had lost myself, and in vain attempted to find my path. I wandered on, and the coming darkness made every trace indistinct by which I might be guided. At length all was veiled in the deep obscurity of blackest night; I became weary and knowing that my servant was to sleep that night at the neighbouring village, so that my absence would alarm no one; and that I was safe in this wild spot from every intruder, I resolved to spend the night where I was. Indeed I was too weary to walk further: the air was chill but I was careless of bodily inconvenience, and I thought that I was well inured to the weather during my two years of solitude, when no change of seasons prevented my perpetual wanderings.

I lay upon the grass surrounded by a darkness which not the slightest beam of light penetrated—There was no sound for the deep night had laid to sleep the insects, the only creatures that lived on the lone spot where no tree or shrub could afford shelter to aught else—There was a wondrous silence in the air that calmed my senses yet which enlivened my soul; my mind hurried from image to image and seemed to grasp an eternity. All in my heart was shadowy yet calm, until my ideas became confused and at length died away in sleep.

When I awoke it rained: I was already quite wet, and my limbs were stiff and my head giddy with the chill of night. It was a drizzling, penetrating shower; as my dank hair clung to my neck and partly covered my face, I had hardly strength to part with my fingers, the long straight locks that fell before my eyes. The darkness was much dissipated and in the east where the clouds were least dense the moon was visible behind the thin grey cloud—

> The moon is behind, and at the full
> And yet she looks both small and dull.[31]

Its presence gave me a hope that by its means I might find my home. But I was languid and many hours passed before I could reach the cottage, dragging as I did my slow steps, and often resting on the wet earth unable to proceed.

I particularly mark this night, for it was that which has hurried on the last scene of my tragedy, which else might have dwindled on through long years of listless sorrow. I was very ill when I arrived and quite incapable of taking off my wet clothes that clung about me. In the morning, on her return, my servant found me almost lifeless, while possessed by a high fever I was lying on the floor of my room.

31. S. T. Coleridge, *Christabel* (1816), ll. 18–19.

I was very ill for a long time, and when I recovered from the immediate danger of fever, every symptom of a rapid consumption declared itself. I was for some time ignorant of this and thought that my excessive weakness was the consequence of the fever. But my strength became less and less; as winter came on I had a cough; and my sunken cheek, before pale, burned with a hectic fever. One by one these symptoms struck me; and I became convinced that the moment I had so much desired was about to arrive and that I was dying. I was sitting by my fire, the physician who had attended me ever since my fever had just left me, and I looked over his prescription in which digitalis was the prominent medecine. "Yes," I said, "I see how this is, and it is strange that I should have deceived myself so long; I am about to die an innocent death, and it will be sweeter even than that which the opium promised."

I rose and walked slowly to the window; the wide heath was covered by snow which sparkled under the beams of the sun that shone brightly through the pure, frosty air: a few birds were pecking some crumbs under my window. I smiled with quiet joy; and in my thoughts, which through long habit would for ever connect themselves into one train, as if I shaped them into words, I thus addressed the scene before me:

"I salute thee, beautiful Sun, and thou, white Earth, fair and cold! Perhaps I shall never see thee again covered with green, and the sweet flowers of the coming spring will blossom on my grave. I am about to leave thee; soon this living spirit which is ever busy among strange shapes and ideas, which belong not to thee, soon it will have flown to other regions and this emaciated body will rest insensate on thy bosom

> Rolled round in earth's diurnal course
> With rocks, and stones, and trees.[32]

"For it will be the same with thee, who art called our Universal Mother, when I am gone. I have loved thee; and in my days both of happiness and sorrow I have peopled your solitudes with wild fancies of my own creation. The woods, and lakes, and mountains which I have loved, have for me a thousand associations; and thou, oh, Sun! hast smiled upon, and borne your part in many imaginations that sprung to life in my soul alone, and which will die with me. Your solitudes, sweet land, your trees and waters will still exist, moved by your winds, or still beneath the eye of noon, though what I have felt about ye, and all my dreams which have often strangely deformed thee, will die with me. You will exist to reflect other images in other minds, and ever will remain the same, although

---

32. William Wordsworth, "A slumber did my spirit seal," published in 2d ed. of *Lyrical Ballads* (1800), ll. 7–8.

your reflected semblance vary in a thousand ways, changeable as the hearts of those who view thee. One of these fragile mirrors, that ever doted on thine image, is about to be broken, crumbled to dust. But ever teeming Nature will create another and another, and thou wilt lose nought by my destruction.[33]

"Thou wilt ever be the same. Receive then the grateful farewell of a fleeting shadow who is about to disappear, who joyfully leaves thee, yet with a last look of affectionate thankfulness. Farewell! Sky, and fields and woods; the lovely flowers that grow on thee; thy mountains and thy rivers; to the balmy air and the strong wind of the north, to all, a last farewell. I shall shed no more tears for my task is almost fulfilled, and I am about to be rewarded for long and most burthensome suffering. Bless thy child even in death, as I bless thee; and let me sleep at peace in my quiet grave."

I feel death to be near at hand and I am calm. I no longer despair, but look on all around me with placid affection. I find it sweet to watch the progressive decay of my strength, and to repeat to myself, another day and yet another, but again I shall not see the red leaves of autumn; before that time I shall be with my father. I am glad Woodville is not with me for perhaps he would grieve, and I desire to see smiles alone during the last scene of my life; when I last wrote to him I told him of my ill health but not of its mortal tendency, lest he should conceive it to be his duty to come to me for I fear lest the tears of friendship should destroy the blessed calm of my mind. I take pleasure in arranging all the little details which will occur when I shall no longer be. In truth I am in love with death; no maiden ever took more pleasure in the contemplation of her bridal attire than I in fancying my limbs already enwrapt in their shroud: is it not my marriage dress? Alone it will unite me to my father when in an eternal mental union we shall never part.

I will not dwell on the last changes that I feel in the final decay of nature. It is rapid but without pain: I feel a strange pleasure in it. For long years these are the first days of peace that have visited me. I no longer exhaust my miserable heart by bitter tears and frantic complaints; I no longer reproach the sun, the earth, the air, for pain and wretchedness. I wait in quiet expectation for the closing hours of a life which has been to me most sweet and bitter. I do not die not having enjoyed life; for sixteen years I was happy: during the first months of my father's re-

---

33. Omitted in *Mathilda* at this point but present in "The Fields of Fancy" (Mary Shelley's rough draft for her novella) is this footnote: "Dante in his *Purgatorio* describes a grifon as remaining unchanged but his reflection in the eyes of Beatrice as perpetually varying (Purg. Cant. 31) So nature is ever the same but seen differently by almost every spectator and even by the same at various times. All minds, as mirrors, receive her forms—yet in each mirror the shapes apparently reflected vary & are perpetually changing—" (quoted from Nitchie, *Mathilda*, p. 89, n. 84).

turn I had enjoyed ages of pleasure: now indeed I am grown old in grief; my steps are feeble like those of age; I have become peevish and unfit for life; so having passed little more than twenty years upon the earth I am more fit for my narrow grave than many are when they reach the natural term of their lives.

Again and again I have passed over in my remembrance the different scenes of my short life: if the world is a stage and I merely an actor on it my part has been strange, and, alas! tragical. Almost from infancy I was deprived of all the testimonies of affection which children generally receive; I was thrown entirely upon my own resources, and I enjoyed what I may almost call unnatural pleasures, for they were dreams and not realities. The earth was to me a magic lantern and I [a] gazer, and a listener but no actor; but then came the transporting and soul-reviving era of my existence: my father returned and I could pour my warm affections on a human heart; there was a new sun and a new earth created to me; the waters of existence sparkled: joy! joy! but, alas! what grief! My bliss was more rapid than the progress of a sunbeam on a mountain, which discloses its glades and woods, and then leaves it dark and blank; to my happiness followed madness and agony, closed by despair.

This was the drama of my life which I have now depicted upon paper. During three months I have been employed in this task. The memory of sorrow has brought tears; the memory of happiness a warm glow the lively shadow of that joy. Now my tears are dried; the glow has faded from my cheeks, and with a few words of farewell to you, Woodville, I close my work; the last that I shall perform.

Farewell, my only living friend; you are the sole tie that binds me to existence, and now I break it. It gives me no pain to leave you; nor can our seperation give you much. You never regarded me as one of this world, but rather as a being, who for some penance was sent from the Kingdom of Shadows; and she passed a few days weeping on the earth and longing to return to her native soil. You will weep but they will be tears of gentleness. I would, if I thought that it would lessen your regret, tell you to smile and congratulate me on my departure from the misery you beheld me endure. I would say: Woodville, rejoice with your friend, I triumph now and am most happy. But I check these expressions; these may not be the consolations of the living; they weep for their own misery, and not for that of the being they have lost. No; shed a few natural tears due to my memory: and if you ever visit my grave, pluck from thence a flower, and lay it to your heart; for your heart is the only tomb in which my memory will be interred.

My death is rapidly approaching and you are not near to watch the flitting and vanishing of my spirit. Do not regret this; for death is too terrible an object for the living. It is one of those adversities which hurt insead of purifying the heart; for it is so intense a misery that it hardens and dulls the feelings. Dreadful as the time was when I pursued my father towards the ocean, and found there only his lifeless corpse; yet for my own sake I should prefer that to the watching one by one his senses fade; his pulse weaken—and sleeplessly as it were devour his life in gazing. To see life in his limbs and to know that soon life would no longer be there; to see the warm breath issue from his lips and to know they would soon be chill—I will not continue to trace this frightful picture; you suffered this torture once; I never did. And the remembrance fills your heart sometimes with bitter despair when otherwise your feelings would have melted into soft sorrow.

So day by day I become weaker, and life flickers in my wasting form, as a lamp about to lose its vivifying oil. I now behold the glad sun of May. It was May, four years ago, that I first saw my beloved father; it was in May, three years ago that my folly destroyed the only being I was doomed to love. May is returned, and I die. Three days ago, the anniversary of our meeting; and, alas! of our eternal seperation, after a day of killing emotion, I caused myself to be led once more to behold the face of nature. I caused myself to be carried to some meadows some miles distant from my cottage; the grass was being mowed, and there was the scent of hay in the fields; all the earth looked fresh and its inhabitants happy. Evening approached and I beheld the sun set. Three years ago and on that day and hour it shone through the branches and leaves of the beech wood and its beams flickered upon the countenance of him whom I then beheld for the last time. I now saw that divine orb, gilding all the clouds with unwonted splendour, sink behind the horizon; it disappeared from a world where he whom I would seek exists not; it approached a world where he exists not. Why do I weep so bitterly? Why does my heart heave with vain endeavour to cast aside the bitter anguish that covers it "as the waters cover the sea."[34] I go from this world where he is no longer and soon I shall meet him in another.

Farewell, Woodville, the turf will soon be green on my grave; and the violets will bloom on it. *There* is my hope and my expectation; your's are in this world; may they be fulfilled.

34. Isaiah 11:7.

MARY WOLLSTONECRAFT SHELLEY
Miniature by Reginald Easton
(Courtesy of Bodleian Library, Oxford.)

MARY WOLLSTONECRAFT SHELLEY
Painting by Richard Rothwell
(Courtesy of National Portrait Gallery, London.)

PERCY BYSSHE SHELLEY
Painting by Amelia Curran

(Courtesy of National Portrait Gallery, London.)

MARY WOLLSTONECRAFT GODWIN
Painting by John Opie
(Courtesy of National Portrait Gallery, London.)

WILLIAM GODWIN
Painting by James Northcote
(Courtesy of National Portrait Gallery, London.)

Tales and Stories

Recollections of Italy[1]

After three weeks of incessant rain, at Midsummer, the sun shone on the town of Henley upon Thames.[2] At first the roads were deep with mud, the grass wet, and the trees dripping; but after two unclouded days, on the second afternoon, pastoral weather commenced; that is to say, weather when it is possible to sit under a tree or lie upon the grass, and feel neither cold nor wet. Such days are too rare not to be seized upon with avidity. We English often feel like a sick man escaping into the open air after a three months' confinement within the four walls of his chamber; and if "an ounce of sweet be worth a pound of sour," we are infinitely more fortunate than the children of the south, who bask a long summer life in his rays, and rarely feel the bliss of sitting by a brook's side under the rich foliage of some well-watered tree, after having been shut up week after week in our carpeted rooms, beneath our white ceilings.

The sun shone on the town of Henley upon Thames. The inhabitants, meeting one another, exclaimed: "What enchanting weather! It has not rained these two days; and, as the moon does not change till Monday, we shall perhaps enjoy a whole week of sunshine!" Thus they congratulated themselves, and thus also I thought as, with the Eclogues of Virgil in my

1. Reprinted from *Tales and Stories*, pp. 24–31, where text is based on *London Magazine* 9 (January 1824): 21–26.
2. In this narrative essay, Mary Shelley fused together a number of elements from her own and her husband's previous writings and experiences: the introductory description of the Thames is taken in part from her "Eighteenth-Century Tale: A Fragment" (see *Tales and Stories*, p. 345); the six-line quotation that is footnoted as "Spenser's Ruins of Rome" is to be found in her journal entry for 5 March 1819 (see *Journals*, I: 251); Edmund Malville presents the author's own recollections of Italy; Malville's excursion from Pisa to Vico Pisano on 15 September 18— reproduces the Shelley's trip to the same place with Edward and Jane Williams on 15 September 1821 (see *Journals*, I: 380); Malville's "'best, and now lost friend'" was actually Percy B. Shelley; and this friend's eloquent description of the scenery on the return to Pisa reproduces with but slight variation Percy Shelley's MS prose fragment, which was later published by Richard Garnett, ed., *Relics of Shelley* (London: Edward Moxon & Co., 1862), pp. 89–90.

pocket, I walked out to enjoy one of the best gifts of heaven, a rainless, windless, cloudless day. The country around Henley is well calculated to attune to gentlest modulations the rapturous emotions to which the balmy, ambient air, gave birth in my heart. The Thames glides through grassy slopes, and its banks are sometimes shaded by beechwood, and sometimes open to the full glare of the sun. Near the spot towards which I wandered several beautiful islands are formed in the river, covered with willows, poplars, and elms. The trees of these islands unite their branches with those of the firm land, and form a green archway which numerous birds delight to frequent. I entered a park belonging to a noble mansion; the grass was fresh and green; it had been mown a short time before; and, springing up again, was softer than the velvet on which the Princess Badroulboudour walked to Aladdin's palace. I sat down under a majestic oak by the river's side; I drew out my book and began to read the Eclogue of Silenus.

A sigh breathed near me caught my attention. How could an emotion of pain exist in a human breast at such a time. But when I looked up I perceived that it was a sigh of rapture, not of sorrow. It arose from a feeling that, finding no words by which it might express itself, clothed its burning spirit in a sigh. I well knew the person who stood beside me; it was Edmund Malville, a man young in soul, though he had passed through more than half the way allotted for man's journey. His countenance was pale; when in a quiescent state it appeared heavy; but let him smile, and Paradise seemed to open on his lips; let him talk, and his dark blue eyes brightened, the mellow tones of his voice trembled with the weight of feeling with which they were laden; and his slight, insignificant person seemed to take the aspect of an ethereal substance (if I may use the expression), and to have too little of clay about it to impede his speedy ascent to heaven. The curls of his dark hair rested upon his clear brow, yet unthinned.

Such was the appearance of Edmund Malville, a man whom I reverenced and loved beyond expression. He sat down beside me, and we entered into conversation on the weather, the river, Parry's voyage, and the Greek revolution. But our discourse dwindled into silence; the sun declined; the motion of the fleckered shadow of the oak tree, as it rose and fell, stirred by a gentle breeze; the passage of swallows, who dipt their wings into the stream as they flew over it; the spirit of love and life that seemed to pervade the atmosphere, and to cause the tall grass to tremble beneath its presence; all these objects formed the links of a chain that bound up our thoughts in silence.

Idea after idea passed through my brain; and at length I exclaimed, why or wherefore I do not remember,—"Well, at least this clear stream is better than the muddy Arno."

Malville smiled. I was sorry that I had spoken; for he loved Italy, its soil, and all that it contained, with a strange enthusiasm. But, having delivered my opinion, I was bound to support it, and I continued: "Well, my dear friend, I have also seen the Arno, so I have some right to judge. I certainly was never more disappointed with any place than with Italy— that is to say, taken all in all. The shabby villas; the yellow Arno; the bad taste of the gardens, with their cropped trees and deformed statues; the suffocating scirocco; the dusty roads; their ferries over their broad, uninteresting rivers, or their bridges crossing stones over which water never flows; that dirty Brenta (the New River Cut is an Oronooko to it); and Venice, with its uncleaned canals and narrow lanes, where Scylla and Charybdis meet you at every turn; and you must endure the fish and roasted pumpkins at the stalls, or the smell—"

"Stop, blasphemer!" cried Malville, half angry, half laughing, "I give up the Brenta; but Venice, the Queen of the sea, the city of gondolas and romance—"

"Romance, Malville, on those ditches?—"

"Yes, indeed, romance!—genuine and soul-elevating romance! Do you not bear in mind the first view of the majestic city from Fusina, crowning the sea with Cybele's diadem? How well do I remember my passage over, as with breathless eagerness I went on the self-same track which the gondolas of the fearless Desdemona, the loving Moor, the gentle Belvidera, and brave Pierre, had traced before me; they still seemed to inhabit the palaces that thronged on each side, and I figured them to myself gliding near, as each dark, mysterious gondola passed by me. How deeply implanted in my memory is every circumstance of my little voyage home from the opera each night along what you call ditches; when sitting in one of those luxurious barks, matched only by that which bore Cleopatra to her Antony, all combined to raise and nourish romantic feeling. The dark canal, shaded by the black houses; the melancholy splash of the oar; the call, or rather chaunt made by the boat-men, 'Ca Stali!' (the words themselves delightfully unintelligible) to challenge any other bark as we turned a corner; the passing of another gondola, black as night and silent as death—Is not this romantic? Then we emerged into the wide expanse before the Place of St. Mark; the cupolas of the church of Santa Maria de la Salute were silvered by the moonbeams; the dark tower rose in silent majesty; the waves rippled; and the dusty line of Lido afar off was the pledge of calm and safety. The Paladian palaces that rose from the Canale Grande; the simple beauty of the Rialto's single arch—"

"Horrible place! I shall never forget crossing it—"

"Ay, that is the way with you of this world. But who among those who love romance ever thinks of going on the Rialto when they have once heard that the fish-market is held there? No place, trust an adept, equals Venice in giving 'a local habitation and a name,'[3] to the restless imaginations of those who pant to quit the 'painted scene of this new world—'[4] for the old world, peopled by sages who have lived in material shape, and heroes whose existence is engendered in the mind of man alone. I have often repeated this to myself as I passed the long hours of the silent night watching the far lights of the distant gondolas, and listening to the chaunt of the boatmen as they glided under my window. How quiet is Venice! no horses; none of the hideous sounds and noises of a town. I grant that in lanes—but why talk of what belongs to every town; dirty alleys, troublesome market-women, and the mark of a maritime city, the luckless smell of fish? Why select defects, and cast from your account the peculiar excellencies of this wonderful city? The buildings rising from the waves; the silence of the watery pavement; the mysterious beauty of the black gondolas; and, not to be omitted, the dark eyes and finely-shaped brows of the women peeping from beneath their fazioles.

"You were three months in Italy?"

"Six, if you please, Malville."

"Well, six, twelve, twenty, are not sufficient to learn to appreciate Italy. We go with false notions of God knows what—of orange groves and fields of asphodel; we expect what we do not find, and are therefore disappointed with the reality; and yet to my mind the reality is not inferior to any scene of enchantment that the imagination ever conjured."

"Or rather say, my friend, that the imagination can paint objects of little worth in gaudy colours, and then become enamoured of its own work."

"Shall I tell you," continued Malville, with a smile, "how you passed your time in Italy? You traversed the country in your travelling chariot, cursing the postillions and the bad inns. You arrived at a town and went to the best hotel, at which you found many of your countrymen, mere acquaintances in England, but hailed as bosom friends in that strange land. You walked about the streets of a morning expecting to find gorgeous temples and Cyclopean ruins in every street in Florence; you came to some broken pillar, wondered what it could be, and laughed at the idea of this being one of the relics which your wise countrymen came so far to see; you lounged into a coffee-house and read Galignani; and

3. Shakespeare, *A Midsummer-Night's Dream* V.i.17.
4. Percy B. Shelley, *The Cenci* V.i.78.

then perhaps wandered with equal apathy into the gallery, where, if you were not transported to the seventh heaven, I can undertake your defence no further."

"My defence, Malville?"

"You dined; you went to a conversazione, where you were neither understood nor could understand; you went to the opera to hear probably the fifty-second repetition of a piece to which nobody listened; or you found yourself in Paradise at the drawing-room of the English ambassador, and fancied yourself in Grosvenor-square.

"I am a lover of nature. Towns, and the details of mixed society, are modes of life alien to my nature. I live to myself and to my affections, and nothing to that tedious routine which makes up the daily round of most men's lives. I went to Italy young, and visited with ardent curiosity and delight all of great and glorious which that country contains. I have already mentioned the charms which Venice has for me; and all Lombardy, whose aspect indeed is very different from that of the south of Italy, is beautiful in its kind. Among the lakes of the north we meet with alpine scenery mixed with the more luxuriant vegetation of the south. The Euganean hills in gentler beauty remind one of the hills of our own country, yet painted with warmer colours. Read Ugo Foscolo's description of them in the first part of his 'Ultime lettere di Jacopo Ortis,' and you will acknowledge the romantic and even sublime sentiments which they are capable of inspiring. But Naples is the real enchantress of Italy; the scenery there is so exquisitely lovely, the remains of antiquity so perfect, wondrous, and beautiful; the climate so genial, that a festive appearance seems for ever to invest it, mingled strangely with the feeling of insecurity with which one is inspired by the sight of Vesuvius, and the marks which are every where manifest of the violent changes that have taken place in that of which in other countries we feel most certain, good Mother Earth herself. With us this same dame is a domestic wife, keeping house, and providing with earnest care and yet penurious means for her family, expecting no pleasure, and finding no amusement. At Naples my fair lady tricks herself out in rich attire, she is kept in the best humour through the perpetual attentions of her constant cavaliere servente, the sun—and she smiles so sweetly on us that we forgive her if at times she plays the coquette with us and leaves us in the lurch. Rome is still the queen of the world,—

> All that Athens ever brought forth wise,
> All that Afric ever brought forth strange,
> All that which Asia ever had of prize,

Was here to see;—O, marvellous great change!
Rome living was the world's sole ornament,
And dead is now the world's sole monument.[5]

If this be true, our forefathers have, in faith! a rare mausoleum for their decay, and Artemisia built a far less costly repository for her lord than widowed Time has bestowed on his dead companion, the Past; when I die may I sleep there and mingle with the glorious dust of Rome! May its radiant atmosphere enshroud these lifeless limbs, and my fading clay give birth to flowers that may inhale that brightest air.

"So I have made my voyage in that fair land, and now bring you to Tuscany. After all I have said of the delights of the south of Italy I would choose Tuscany for a residence. Its inhabitants are courteous and civilized. I confess that there is a charm for me in the manners of the common people and servants. Perhaps this is partly to be accounted for from the contrast which they form with those of my native country; and all that is unusual, by divesting common life of its familiar garb, gives an air of gala to everyday concerns. These good people are courteous, and there is much *piquance* in the shades of distinction which they make between respect and servility, ease of address and impertinence. Yet this is little seen and appreciated among their English visitors. I have seen a countrywoman of some rank much shocked at being cordially embraced in a parting scene from her cook-maid; and an Englishman think himself insulted because when, on ordering his coachman to wait a few minutes for orders, the man quietly sat down: yet neither of these actions were instigated by the slightest spirit of insolence. I know not why, but there was always something heartfelt and delightful to me in the salutation that passes each evening between master and servant. On bringing the lights the servant always says, 'Felicissima sera, Signoria;' and is answered by a similar benediction. These are nothings, you will say; but such nothings have conduced more to my pleasure than other events usually accounted of more moment.

"The country of Tuscany is cultivated and fertile, although it does not bear the same stamp of excessive luxury as in the south. To continue my half-forgotten simile, the earth is here like a young affectionate wife, who loves her home, yet dresses that home in smiles. In spring, nature arises in beauty from her prison, and rains sunbeams and life upon the land. Summer comes up in its green array, giving labour and reward to the peasants. Their plenteous harvests, their Virgilian threshing floors, and looks of busy happiness, are delightful to me. The balmy air of night, Hesperus in his glowing palace of sunlight, the flower-starred earth, the

5. Spenser's *Ruins of Rome*. [Mary Shelley's note referring to sonnet 29 of Edmund Spenser's *Ruins of Rome*.]

glittering waters, the ripening grapes, the chestnut copses, the cuckoo, and the nightingale,—such is the assemblage which is to me what balls and parties are to others. And if a storm come, rushing like an armed band over the country, filling the torrents, bending the proud heads of the trees, causing the clouds' deafening music to resound, and the lightning to fill the air with splendour; I am still enchanted by the spectacle which diversifies what I have heard named the monotonous blue skies of Italy.

"In Tuscany the streams are fresh and full, the plains decorated with waving corn, shadowed by trees and trellised vines, and the mountains arise in woody majesty behind to give dignity to the scene. What is a land without mountains? Heaven disdains a plain; but when the beauteous earth raises her proud head to seek its high communion, then it descends to meet her, it adorns her in clouds, and invests her in radiant hues.

"On the 15th of September, 18—, I remember being one of a party of pleasure from the baths of Pisa to Vico Pisano, a little town formerly a frontier fortress between the Pisan and Florentine territories. The air inspired joy, and the pleasure I felt I saw reflected in the countenance of my beloved companions. Our course lay beneath hills hardly high enough for the name of mountains, but picturesquely shaped and covered with various wood. The cicale chirped, and the air was impregnated with the perfume of flowers. We passed the Rupe de Noce, and proceeding still at the foot of hills arrived at Vico Pisano, which is built at the extreme point of the range. The houses are old and surmounted with ancient towers; and at one end of the town there is a range of old wall, weed-grown; but never did eye behold hues more rich and strange than those with which time and the seasons have painted this relic. The lines of the cornice swept downwards, and made a shadow that served even to diversify more the colours we beheld. We returned along the same road; and not far from Vico Pisano ascended a gentle hill, at the top of which was a church dedicated to Madonna, with a grassy platform of earth before it. Here we spread and ate our rustic fare, and were waited upon by the peasant girls of the cottage attached to the church, one of whom was of extreme beauty, a beauty heightened by the grace of her motions and the simplicity of her manner. After our pic-nic we reposed under the shade of the church, on the brow of the hill. We gazed on the scene with rapture. 'Look,' cried my best, and now lost friend, 'behold the mountains that sweep into the plain like waves that meet in a chasm; the olive woods are as green as a sea, and are waving in the wind; the shadows of the clouds are spotting the bosoms of the hills; a heron comes sailing over us; a butterfly flits near; at intervals the pines give forth their sweet and prolonged response to the wind, the myrtle bushes are in bud, and the soil beneath us is carpeted with odoriferous flowers.'—My full heart could only sigh, he alone was eloquent enough to clothe his thoughts in language."

Malville's eyes glistened as he spoke, he sighed deeply; then turning away, he walked towards the avenue that led from the grounds on which we were. I followed him, but we neither of us spoke; and when at length he renewed the conversation, he did not mention Italy; he seemed to wish to turn the current of his thoughts, and by degrees he reassumed his composure.

When I took leave of him I said, smiling, "You have celebrated an Italian party of pleasure; may I propose an English one to you? Will you join some friends next Thursday in an excursion down the Thames? Perhaps the sight of its beautiful banks, and the stream itself, will inspire you with some of the delight you have felt in happier climes."

Malville consented. But dare I tell the issue of my invitation? Thursday came, and the sky was covered with clouds; it looked like rain. However, we courageously embarked, and within an hour a gentle mizzling commenced. We made an awning of sails, and wrapt ourselves up in boat-cloaks and shawls. "It is not much," cried one, with a sigh. "I do not think it will last," remarked another, in a despairing voice. A silence ensued. "Can you contrive to shelter me at this corner?" said one; "my shoulder is getting wet." In about five minutes another observed, that the water was trickling in his neck. Yet we went on. The rain ceased for a few minutes, and we tethered our boat in a small cove under dripping trees; we ate our collation, and raised our spirits with wine, so that we were able to endure with tolerable fortitude the heavy rain that accompanied us as we slowly proceeded homewards up the river.

The Bride
of Modern Italy[1]

My heart is fixt:
This is the sixt.
Elia[2]

On a serene winter morning two young ladies, Clorinda and Teresa,
walked up and down the garden of the convent of St. S——, at Rome.
If my reader has never seen a convent, or if he has only seen the better
kind, let him dismiss from his mind all he may have heard or imagined
of such abodes, or he can never transport himself into the garden of
St. S——. He must figure it to himself as bounded by a long, low, straggling, white-washed, weather-stained building, with grated windows, the
lower ones glassless. It is a kitchen garden, but the refuse of the summer
stock alone remained, except a few cabbages, which perfumed the air
with their rank exhalations. The walks were neglected, yet not overgrown,
but strewed with broken earthen-ware, ashes, cabbage-stalks, orange-peel,
bones, and all that marks the vicinity of a much frequented, but dis-
orderly mansion. The beds were intersected by these paths, and the whole
was surrounded by a high wall. This common scene was, however, unlike
what it would have been in this country. You saw the decayed and
straggling boughs of the passion-flower against the walls of the convent;
here and there a geranium, its luxuriant foliage starred by scarlet flowers,
grew unharmed by frost among the cabbages; the lemon plants had been
removed to shelter, but orange trees were nailed against the wall, the

1. Reprinted from *Tales and Stories*, pp. 32–42, where text is based on *London Magazine* 9 (April 1824): 357–63.
2. This epigraph from Charles Lamb epitomizes this gentle satire on the fickleness
of Clorinda, whom Mary Shelley modeled to some degree on Emilia Viviani, a young
Italian woman whom the Shelleys met in Pisa. Emilia, living in a convent while await-
ing the arrangement of her marriage, enthralled Percy B. Shelley, whose "Italian Pla-
tonics" were the subject of his poem *Epipsychidion* (1821).

golden fruit peeping out from amidst the dark leaves; the wall itself was variegated by a thousand rich hues; and thick and pointed aloes grew beneath it. Under the highest wall, opposite the back door of the convent, a corner of ground was enclosed; this was the burial place of the nuns; and in the path that led from the door to this enclosure Clorinda and Teresa walked up and down.

"He will never come!" exclaimed Clorinda.

"I fear the dinner bell will ring and interrupt us, if he does come," observed Teresa.

"Some cruel obstacle doubtless prevents him," continued Clorinda, sighing—"and I have prayed to St. Giacomo, and vowed to give him the best flowers and a candle a foot long next Easter."

Teresa smiled: "I remember," she said, "that at Christmas you fulfilled such a vow to San Francesco,—was not that for the sake of Cieco Magni? for you change your saint as your lover changes name;—tell me, sweet Clorinda, how many saints have been benefited by your piety?"

Clorinda looked angry, and then sorrowful; the large drops gathered in her dark eyes: "You are unkind to taunt me thus, Teresina;—when did I love truly until now? believe me, never; and if heaven bestows Giacomo upon me—oh! that is his bell!—naughty Teresa, you will cause me to meet him with tears in my eyes."

Away they ran to the parlour of the convent, and were joined there by an old woman purblind and nearly deaf, who was to be present at the visit of Giacomo de' Tolomei, the brother of Teresa. He kissed the hands of the young ladies, and then they commenced a conversation, which, by the lowness of their tones, and an occasional intermixture of French, was quite incomprehensible to their Argus, who was busily employed in knitting a large green worsted shawl.

"Well?"—said Clorinda, in a tone of inquiry.

"Well, dear Clorinda, I have executed our design, though I hope little from it. I have written a proposal of marriage; if you approve of it, I will send it to your parents. Here it is."

"What is that paper?" cried the Argus.

Teresa bawled in her ear: "Only the history of the late miracle performed at Asisa" (Italians, male or female, are not great patronizers of truth), "look at it, dear Eusta." (Eusta could not read.) "I will read it to you by and bye." Eusta went on with her knitting.

The two girls looking over one another, read the proposal of marriage, which Giacomo de' Tolomei made to the parents of Clorinda Saviani. The paper was divided into two columns, one headed: "The Proposal,"—the other "Observations to be made thereon"—and this latter column was left blank. The proposal itself was divided into several heads and numbered. It premised that a noble family of Sienna wishing to ally themselves to the family of the Saviani of Rome, in the persons of their eldest son and Clorinda, they presented the following considerations to the heads of that house first, that the young man was well-made, good-looking, healthy, studiously inclined, and of irreproachable morals. The circumstances of his fortune were then detailed, and the claims of dowry: it concluded by saying, that if the parents of Clorinda approved of the terms proposed, the young people might be introduced to each other, and if mutually pleased at their interview, the nuptials might be celebrated in the course of a few months. When Clorinda had finished reading, the tears that had gathered in her eyes fell drop after drop upon the paper.—"Wherefore do you weep?" asked Giacomo, "why do you distress me thus?"

"This proposal will never be accepted. You have asked twelve thousand crowns in dowry; my parents will not give more than six."

"And yet," replied Giacomo, "I have named a sum to which I am convinced my father will never agree; he will require twenty thousand at least; even if your parents accede I shall have to win his consent; but if prayers and tears can move him, I will not be chary of either."

The bell rang for dinner, old Eusta arose, and Giacomo retired. Dinner!—what dainty feast of convent-like confectionaries does the reader picture?—Let him see, in truth, a long, brick-paved floor, with long deal tables, and benches ditto; the tables covered with not white cloths; cellars of black salt; bottles of sour wine, and small loaves of bitter bread. Then came the minestra, consisting (for it was fast day) of what we call macaroni, water, oil, and cheese; then a few vegetables swimming in oil; a concluding dish of eggs fried with garlic, and the repast of one of the most highborn and loveliest girls in Rome was finished. Clorinda Saviani was indeed handsome, and all her fine features expressed the *bisogna d'amare*[3] which ruled her heart. She was just eighteen, and had been five years in this convent, waiting until her father should find a husband of noble birth, who would be content with a slender dowry. During this time she had formed several attachments for various youths, who, under different pretexts, had visited the convent. She had written letters, prayed and wept, and then yielding to insurmountable difficulties she had changed her idol, though she had never ceased to love. The fastidious English must not be disgusted with this picture. It is, perhaps, only a coarse representation of what takes place at every ball-room with us. And if it went beyond;—the nature of the Catholic religion, which crushes the innate conscience by giving a false one in its room; the system of artifice and heartlessness that subsists in a convent; the widely spread maxim in Italy, that dishonour attaches itself to the discovered not the concealed

3. "Need for love."

fault—all this forms the excuse why with a tender heart and much native talent, there was neither constancy in Clorinda's love, nor dignity in her conduct.

After their repast the friends retired to Clorinda's cell; a small, though high room, floored with brick, miserably furnished, and neither clean nor orderly. A prie-dieu was beside the little bed with a crucifix over it, together with two or three prints (like our penny children's prints) of saints, among which St. Giacomo appeared with the freshest and cleanest face; beside these was a glass (resembling a bird's drinking vessel) containing holy water, rather the worse for long standing; in a closet, with the door a-jar, among tattered books and female apparel, hung a glass-case enclosing a waxen Gesu Bambino, and some flowers, gathered for this holy dedication and drooping for want of light, were placed beneath him; some mignionette, basil, and heliotrope, weeds o'ergrown, flowered in a wooden trough at the window; a broken looking glass; a leaden ink stand—such was Clorinda's boudoir.

"I despair," she exclaimed—"I see no end to my evils—and but one road open——flight——"—"Which would ruin my brother."—"How?—he is of another state."—"And your honour?"—"Honour in this dungeon!—O, let me breathe the fresh air of heaven; let me no longer see this prison room; these high walls and all the circumstances of my convent life, and I care not for the rest." "But how? You may get people into the convent—but to get out yourself is a different affair." "I have many plans:—if this proposal of your brother fail, as it will, I will disclose them to him."

A lay sister now came in to ask the young ladies if they would take coffee with the Superior. They found her alone; a little, squat, snuff-taking old woman; she was in high ill-humour: "Body of Bacchus!" she began, "you introduce strange laws in St. S——!—This coffee is detestable—Your brother, Teresina, is here every day—I detest coffee without rum—Clorinda sees him, and it begins to be talked of—when he comes to-morrow, you only must receive him, and request him to discontinue his visits."

Clorinda's tears mingled with her coffee—"The old witch!" she said, when they had retired, "she is fishing for a present."—"And must have one; what shall Giacomo bring her?"—"Let him send some rum. Did you not see the faces she made over her coffee? yet she is too niggardly to buy it herself." A note was hastily dispatched to Giacomo by Teresa, to inform him of the necessary oblation. He came the next day well provided; for the waiter of a neighbouring inn accompanied him bearing six bottles of what bore the name of *Romme*. Teresa was called and dispatched to solicit the presence of the Superior. She came; Giacomo took off his hat:

"Signora," said he, "it is winter time, and I bring you a wintry gift.—Will you favour me by accepting this rum?"—"Signor, you are too courteous."—"The courtesy is yours, Signora, in honouring me by receiving my present. I hope that you will find it good."—He uncorked a bottle; Teresa ran for a glass; Giacomo filled it, and the Superior emptied it. Clorinda at the same moment tripped into the room. She started with a natural air, and after saluting Giacomo was going away, but he detained her, and they all sat down together, until the Superior was called away to give out bread for supper, and the three young people remained together.

The girls turned to Giacomo with inquiring looks: his were sorrowful. "My proposal has not been received. Your parents replied that they have proposed you to some one, and cannot break off the treaty."—"And thus I am to be sacrificed!" cried Clorinda, casting up her beautiful eyes.—"Will you consent?" said Giacomo reproachfully.—"What means have I? I have talked of flight" (Giacomo's countenance fell); "and that, although difficult, is not impossible."—"How?"—"Why, my cell adjoins that of the Superior. She is fond of sweet things; on the next holiday I will make some cakes for her, filled with sugar and a little opium. I can then steal away the keys, make an impression on wax (I have a large piece ready), and you can easily get them counterfeited."—"You would engage my brother in a dangerous enterprize," said Teresa.—"My dear, dear Clorinda, my sweet friend," said Giacomo, "you are ignorant of the world's ways. I would sacrifice my life for you; but you would thus lose your honour, I should be imprisoned, and you would be sent to some dreary convent among the mountains, till forced to marry some boor who would render you miserable for life."—"What is to be done then?" asked Clorinda, discontentedly.—"It requires thought. Something must, something shall, be done; do you be faithful to me, and refuse your parents' offer, and I do not despair. In the mean time I will set out for Sienna to-morrow and see my father."

Giacomo had formed an intimacy with a young English artist residing at Rome, and he left the cares of his love in the hands of this gentleman, while he by short days' journeys, and with a heavy heart, proceeded towards Sienna. The following day brought a letter of five pages, in a nearly illegible hand, to be delivered to Clorinda. Our Englishman had been a year in Rome, but he had never yet been within a convent. As he passed the prison-like building of St. S——, and measured with his eye the lofty walls of its garden, he had peopled it with nuns of all ages, states, and dispositions;—the solemn and demure, the ambitious, the bigoted, and those who, repenting of their vows, wetted their pallet with their midnight tears, and then, prostrate on the damp marble before the crucifix, prayed God to pardon them for being human. And then he thought of the novices fearful as brides, but not so hopeful; and of the boarders who dreamt of the world outside, as we of Paradise beyond the grave. He pictured echoing corridors, painted windows, the impenetrable grate, the religious cloister, and the garden, that most immaculate of asylums, with grassy walks, majestic trees, and veiled forms flitting under their shade. Well, thought he, I am now in for it; and if I do not lose my heart, I shall at least gain some excellent hints for my picture of the Profession of Eloisa.

He crossed the outer hall, rang at the bell, and the old tottering portress came towards the door. He asked for "the Signora Teresa de' Tolomei." He was shown into the parlour—a vaulted room, the floor bricked, the furniture mean, without fire or chimney, though the cold east wind covered the ground with hoar frost. In a few minutes the two friends tripped into the room, followed by Eusta, who, instead of her knitting, carried a fire-pot filled with wood ashes, over which she held her withered hands and her blue nose, frost bitten. The girls were somewhat startled on seeing the stranger, who advanced, and announcing himself as Signor Marcott Alleyn, a friend of the brother of Teresa, delivered a little packet, together with a note which bade his sister confide implicitly in the Englishman.

The conversation became animated. No bashfulness intruded to prevent Clorinda from discoursing eloquently of her passion, especially when she observed the deep interest which her account excited. Alleyn was a man of infinitely pleasing manners; he had a soft tone of voice and eyes full of expression. Italian ladies are not accustomed to the English system of gallantry; since in that country either downright love is made, or the most distant coldness preserved between the sexes. Alleyn's compassion was excited in various ways. He heard that Clorinda had been imprisoned in that convent for five years; he saw the desolate garden, he felt the bitter cold, which was unalleviated by any thing except fire-pots; he had a glance at the blank corridors and squalid cells, and he saw in the victim an elegance of manners and a delicate sensitiveness that ill accorded with such dreary privations. Several visits ensued, and Alleyn became a favourite in the convent. He was only seventeen; his spirits were high; he diverted the friends, brought presents of rum and confectionary to the nuns, kissed some of the least ugly, made covert game of the Superior, and established himself with greater freedom in this seclusion in a week than Giacomo had done in a year. At first he sympathised with Clorinda, now he did more—he amused her. If she wept for the absence of Giacomo, he made her laugh at some story told *apropos,* which diverted her. If she complained of the petty tyranny of the nuns, he laid some plot of droll revenge, which she executed. He introduced a system of English jokes and hoaxes, at which the poor Italians were perfectly aghast, and to which no experience prevented their becoming victims; so utterly unable were they to comprehend the meaning of such machinations; and then, when their loud voices pealed through the arched passages in wonder and anger, they were appeased by soft words and well-timed gifts.

But this sunshine could not last for ever. Clorinda was at first more happy and gay than she had ever been. She in vain endeavoured to lament the absence of her lover. Alleyn prevented every emotion except gaiety from finding a place in her heart. She looked forward with delight for the hour of his visit, and the merriment that he excited left its traces on the rest of the day. Her step was light; and the cold of her cheerless cell was unfelt, since it had been adorned with caricatures of the Superior and nuns; their tyranny was either laid asleep or revenged, and Giacomo was, alas! forgotten. Her love-breathing letters lost their fire, and the writing them became an irksome task; her sighs were changed into smiles—but suddenly these again vanished, and Clorinda became more pensive and sad than ever. She avoided Teresa, and passed most of her time in lonely walks up and down the straight paths of the garden. She was fretful if Alleyn did not come; when he was announced, she would blush, sit silent in his presence, and, if any of his sallies provoked her laughter, it was quickly quenched by her tears. Her devotions even lost their accustomed warmth; Alleyn had no tutelar saint; no Marcott had ever been honoured with canonization, nor had any of the bones found in the catacombs been baptized with the transalpine name. "Marry, this is miching Mallecho; it means mischief,"[4]—the brief mischief of inconstancy, new love, and all the evils attendant on such a change. Alleyn did not suspect this turn in the tide, till, left tête-à-tête one morning, some slight attentions on his part painted her cheeks with blushes; the confession was not far behind, he heard with mingled surprise and delight, and one kiss sealed their infidelity to the absent Giacomo just as Teresa and Eusta entered.

Alleyn was only seventeen. At that age men look on women as living Edens which they dare not imagine they can ever enjoy; they love, and dream not of being loved; they seek, and their wildest fancies do not picture themselves as sought: so it was small wonder that the heart of Alleyn beat with exultation, that his step was light and his eyes sparkling as he left the convent on that day. His visits were now more frequent; Teresa was confined to her room by illness, and the lovers (though that sacred name is prophaned by such an application) were left together unwatched. Clorinda's thoughts turned wholly upon escape, and Alleyn heedlessly fostered such thoughts, until one day she said: "If I quit the convent this night, will you be under the walls to receive me?"—"My sweet Clorinda,

4. Shakespeare, *Hamlet* III.ii.147–48.

are you serious?"—"Alas! no, I cannot. But in a few nights I trust that I shall be able to execute my project. Look, here is wax with an impression of the keys of the convent; you must get others made from it. The sisters shall sleep well that night, and before morning we will be far on our journey towards your happy country. Fear not; my disguise is ready—all will go well."

"The devil it will!" thought Alleyn, as he quitted St. S——, and carefully placing the waxen impression he had received against a sunny wall, he paced up the Corso,—"and the devil take me if ever I go within those walls again! I have sown a pretty crop, but I am not mad enough to reap it; and, as the fates will have it, here is Tolomei returned to tax me with my false proceedings. I wish all convents and women——."

Tolomei now accosted him. They walked together towards the Coliseum, talking of indifferent things. They climbed to the highest part of the ruin, and then, seated amid leafy shrubs and fragrant violets and wall flowers, looking over the desert lanes and violated Forum of Rome, Giacomo asked—"What news of Clorinda?" Alleyn wished himself hanged, and, with a look that almost indicated that his wish was about to be fulfilled, replied briefly to his friend's questions, and then began a string himself, that he might escape his keen, lover-like looks—more painful than his words. Giacomo's hopes were nearly dead. His father was inexorable; and he had learnt, besides, that the person selected by her parents as a husband for Clorinda had arrived in Rome, and this accomplished his misery. He shed abundance of tears as he related this, and ended by declaring that if he still found Clorinda faithful and affectionate, the contrariety of his destiny would urge him to some desperate measure. They separated at length, having appointed to go together to St. S—— on the following day.

Alleyn broke this appointment. He sent an excuse to Giacomo, who accordingly went alone. In the evening he received a note from Clorinda. She lamented his absence; declared her utter aversion for Giacomo; bewailed her hard fate, and having acquainted him that she was to spend the following day with her parents, entreated him to call on the succeeding one. Alleyn passed the intermediate time at Tivoli, that he might avoid his injured friend, and at the appointed hour went to the convent. Teresa and Clorinda were together; they both looked disturbed and angry; when Alleyn appeared, Teresa arose, and casting a disdainful look on the conscious pair, left the parlour. Clorinda burst into tears. "Oh, my beloved friend," she cried, "I have gone through heart-breaking scenes since I last saw you. This cruel Teresa is continually upbraiding me, and Giacomo's silent looks of grief are a still greater reproach. Yet I am innocent. This heart has escaped from my control; its overwhelming sensations defy all the efforts of my reason, and I passionately love without hope, almost without a return—nor is this all." She then related, that during her visit of the day before, she had been introduced to the person on whom her parents had resolved to bestow her. "At first," she continued, "I was ignorant of the design on foot, and saw him with indifference. Presently my mother took me aside; she began with a torrent of reproaches; told me that all my artifices were discovered, and then showed me a letter of mine to Giacomo which had been intercepted by that artful monster the Superior, and concluded by telling me that I must agree instantly to marry the personage to whom I had been introduced. 'Not that you shall be forced,' she said; 'beware therefore of spreading that report; but your conduct necessitates the strongest measures. If you refuse this match, which is in every way suitable to you, you must prepare to be sent to a convent of Carthusian Nuns at Benevento, where if you do not take the veil, you will be strictly guarded, and your plots, letters, and lovers, will be of no avail.' Without permitting me to reply, this cruel mother led me back to the drawing room; this personage, whose name is Romani, came near me, and presently took an opportunity of asking whether I agreed to the arrangement of my parents. What could I say? I gave an ungracious assent, and they consider the matter settled. His estate is near Spoleto, and he is gone to prepare for my reception. The writings are drawing up; the time will soon arrive when I shall change my cage and be miserable for life. You alone, Alleyn, you, generous and brave Englishman, can aid me; take me hence; bear me away to freedom and love, and let me not be sacrificed to this unknown bridegroom, whose person I hardly know, and the idea of whom fills my heart with despair." Alleyn replied as he best might, with expressions of real sorrow, but of small consolation, and the inexorable dinner-bell rang and separated them just as he concluded his reply.

The same evening Alleyn received a note from her. "My horror of this marriage," she wrote, "increases in proportion as the period of its accomplishment approaches. I hear to-day that my parents have already given my *corrèdo*[5] to Romani, which he is to expend in jewels and dresses for me, and thus my fate is nearly sealed. I shall be banished from Rome and my friends; I shall live with a stranger—I must be miserable. Giacomo is better than this. But as an union with him is impossible, and you refuse to aid me, and to liberate one whom you say you love, listen to a plan I have formed; some years ago I was addressed by one, who at that time gained my heart, and whom I still regard with tenderness. The smallness of my dowry caused his father to break off the treaty; this father is now dead. Go to this gentleman—find out whether he still loves me. Married

5. Used here to mean "dowry."

to him, I should be united to one whose merits I know—I should live at Rome, and there would be some alleviation to my cruel fate. At least come to-morrow to the convent, and endeavour to console your miserable friend."

Alleyn, as may easily be supposed, did not pay the required visit to the quondam lover of Clorinda. Perhaps she expected this; for the same night she wrote to him herself. Her letter was long and eloquent. Its expressions seemed to proceed from the over-flowings of a passionate and loving heart. She referred to Alleyn as a common friend, and urged expedition in every measure that was to be pursued. This letter was intercepted and carried to her parents. On the following day Alleyn received a despairing note, entreating him not to attempt to come to the convent. "Alas!" she wrote, "how truly miserable I am! What a fate! I suffer, and am the cause of a thousand griefs to others. Oh heaven! I were better dead; then I should cease to lament, or at least to occasion wretchedness to others. Now I am hated by others, and even by myself—Oh, my incomparable friend! Angel of my heart! Can I be the cause of misery even to you? See Giacomo, my beloved friend; tell him how deeply I pity him, but counsel him in my name to desist from all further pursuit. He must permit me to obey my parents, and they will never consent. My sole aim now is to escape from this prison."

Another and another letter came; and she most earnestly begged him not to come to the convent. Thus nearly a month passed, when one morning early Alleyn was surprised by a visit from the Superior of the convent of St. S——. The old lady seemed very full of matter. She drank the rosoglio presented to her, took snuff, and opened her budget. She talked of the trouble she had ever had with poor Clorinda; inveighed against Giacomo; during her long discourse she praised her own sagacity, the tender affection of Clorinda's parents, and related how she had always opposed the entrance of young men into the convent and their free communication with Clorinda, except his own; but that his politeness and known integrity had in this particular caused her to relax her discipline; and she concluded by inviting him to visit the convent whenever it should be agreeable to him. She then took her leave.

Alleyn was much disturbed. He wished not to go to St. S——; he knew that he ought not to see Clorinda again. He resolved not to go out at all, and sat thinking of her beauty, love, and unaffected manners, until he resolved to walk that he might get rid of such thoughts. He hurried down the Corso, and before he was aware found himself before the door of the convent of St. S——. He paused, again he moved, and entered the outer hall—his hand was on the bell, when the door opened and Giacomo came out. Seeing Alleyn, he threw himself into his arms, shedding a torrent of tears. This exordium startled our Englishman; the conclusion was soon told: Clorinda had married Romani the day before, and on the same evening had quitted Rome for Spoleto.

This news sobered Alleyn at once; he shuddered almost to think of the folly he had been about to commit, feeling as one who is stayed by a friendly hand when about to place his foot beyond the brink of a high precipice. They turned from the convent door. "And yet," said Alleyn as he walked on, "are you secure of the truth of your account? The Superior called on me yesterday and invited me to visit St. S——. Why should she do this if Clorinda were gone? I have half a mind to go and fathom this mystery."

"Ay, go by all means," replied Giacomo bitterly, "you will be welcome; fill your pockets with sugar plums; dose the old lady with rosoglio, and kiss the gentle nuns, the youngest of whom bears the weight of sixty years under the fillet on her brow. They miss your good cheer, and who knows, Clorinda gone, what other nets they may weave to secure so valuable a prize. True, you are an Englishman and a heretic; words which, interpreted into pure Tuscan, mean an untired prodigal, and one, pardon me, whose conscience will no more stickle at violating yon sanctuary than at eating flesh on Fridays. Go by all means, and make the best of your good fortune among these Houris."

"Rather say, take post horses for Spoleto, friend Giacomo. And yet neither—it is all vanity and vexation of spirit. I will go paint my Profession of Eloisa."

Roger Dodsworth
The Reanimated Englishman[1]

It may be remembered, that on the fourth of July last,[2] a paragraph appeared in the papers importing that Dr. Hotham, of Northumberland, returning from Italy, over Mount St. Gothard, a score or two of years ago, had dug out from under an avalanche, in the neighbourhood of the mountain, a human being whose animation had been suspended by the action of the frost. Upon the application of the usual remedies, the patient was resuscitated, and discovered himself to be Mr. Dodsworth, the son of the antiquary Dodsworth, who perished in the reign of Charles I. He was thirty-seven years of age at the time of his inhumation, which had taken place as he was returning from Italy, in 1654. It was added that as soon as he was sufficiently recovered he would return to England, under the protection of his preserver. We have since heard no more of him, and various plans for public benefit, which have started in philanthropic minds on reading the statement, have already returned to their pristine nothingness. The antiquarian society had eaten their way to several votes for medals, and had already begun, in idea, to consider what prices it could afford to offer for Mr. Dodsworth's old clothes, and to conjecture what treasures in the way of pamphlet, old song, or autographic letter his pockets might contain. Poems from all quarters, of all kinds, elegiac, congratulatory, burlesque and allegoric, were half written. Mr. Godwin had suspended for the sake of such authentic information the history of

1. Reprinted from *Tales and Stories*, pp. 43–50, where text is based on untitled narrative essay published by Cyrus Redding, *Yesterday and To-day* (London: T. Cautley Newby, Publisher, 1863), II: 150–65.
2. That is, 1826. Between 4 and 9 July of that year, no less than six British newspapers translated and published the report from the 28 June 1826 issue of the *Journal du Commerce de Lyon* that announced the discovery and reanimation of Roger Dodsworth. For more on this hoax and Mary Shelley's delightfully witty essay, see Charles E. Robinson, "Mary Shelley and the Roger Dodsworth Hoax," *Keats-Shelley Journal* 24 (1975): 20–28.

the Commonwealth he had just begun. It is hard not only that the world should be baulked of these destined gifts from the talents of the country, but also that it should be promised and then deprived of a new subject of romantic wonder and scientific interest. A novel idea is worth much in the commonplace routine of life, but a new fact, an astonishment, a miracle, a palpable wandering from the course of things into apparent impossibilities, is a circumstance to which the imagination must cling with delight, and we say again that it is hard, very hard, that Mr. Dodsworth refuses to appear, and that the believers in his resuscitation are forced to undergo the sarcasms and triumphant arguments of those sceptics who always keep on the safe side of the hedge.

Now we do not believe that any contradiction or impossibility is attached to the adventures of this youthful antique. Animation (I believe physiologists agree) can as easily be suspended for an hundred or two years, as for as many seconds. A body hermetically sealed up by the frost, is of necessity preserved in its pristine entireness. That which is totally secluded from the action of external agency, can neither have any thing added to nor taken away from it: no decay can take place, for something can never become nothing; under the influence of that state of being which we call death, change but not annihilation removes from our sight the corporeal atoma; the earth receives sustenance from them, the air is fed by them, each element takes its own, thus seizing forcible repayment of what it had lent. But the elements that hovered round Mr. Dodsworth's icy shroud had no power to overcome the obstacle it presented. No zephyr could gather a hair from his head, nor could the influence of dewy night or genial morn penetrate his more than adamantine panoply. The story of the Seven Sleepers rests on a miraculous interposition—they slept. Mr. Dodsworth did not sleep; his breast never heaved, his pulses were stopped; death had his finger pressed on his lips which no breath might pass. He has removed it now, the grim shadow is vanquished, and stands wondering. His victim has cast from him the frosty spell, and arises as perfect a man as he had lain down an hundred and fifty years before. We have eagerly desired to be furnished with some particulars of his first conversations, and the mode in which he has learnt to adapt himself to his new scene of life. But since facts are denied to us, let us be permitted to indulge in conjecture. What his first words were may be guessed from the expressions used by people exposed to shorter accidents of the like nature. But as his powers return, the plot thickens. His dress had already excited Doctor Hotham's astonishment—the peaked beard—the love locks—the frill, which, until it was thawed, stood stiff under the mingled influence of starch and frost; his dress fashioned like that of one of Vandyke's portraits, or (a more familiar similitude) Mr. Sapio's costume in Winter's

Opera of the Oracle, his pointed shoes—all spoke of other times. The curiosity of his preserver was keenly awake, that of Mr. Dodsworth was about to be roused. But to be enabled to conjecture with any degree of likelihood the tenor of his first inquiries, we must endeavour to make out what part he played in his former life. He lived at the most interesting period of English History—he was lost to the world when Oliver Cromwell had arrived at the summit of his ambition, and in the eyes of all Europe the commonwealth of England appeared so established as to endure for ever. Charles I. was dead; Charles II. was an outcast, a beggar, bankrupt even in hope. Mr. Dodsworth's father, the antiquary, received a salary from the republican general, Lord Fairfax, who was himself a great lover of antiquities, and died the very year that his son went to his long, but not unending sleep, a curious coincidence this, for it would seem that our frost-preserved friend was returning to England on his father's death, to claim probably his inheritance—how short lived are human views! Where now is Mr. Dodsworth's patrimony? Where his co-heirs, executors, and fellow legatees? His protracted absence has, we should suppose, given the present possessors to his estate—the world's chronology is an hundred and seventy years older since he seceded from the busy scene, hands after hands have tilled his acres, and then become clods beneath them; we may be permitted to doubt whether one single particle of their surface is individually the same as those which were to have been his—the youthful soil would of itself reject the antique clay of its claimant.

Mr. Dodsworth, if we may judge from the circumstance of his being abroad, was no zealous commonwealth's man, yet his having chosen Italy as the country in which to make his tour and his projected return to England on his father's death, renders it probable that he was no violent loyalist. One of those men he seems to be (or to have been) who did not follow Cato's advice as recorded in the Pharsalia; a party, if to be of no party admits of such a term, which Dante recommends us utterly to despise, and which not unseldom falls between the two stools, a seat on either of which is so carefully avoided. Still Mr. Dodsworth could hardly fail to feel anxious for the latest news from his native country at so critical a period; his absence might have put his own property in jeopardy; we may imagine therefore that after his limbs had felt the cheerful return of circulation, and after he had refreshed himself with such of earth's products as from all analogy he never could have hoped to live to eat, after he had been told from what peril he had been rescued, and said a prayer thereon which even appeared enormously long to Dr. Hotham—we may imagine, we say, that his first question would be: "If any news had arrived lately from England?"

"I had letters yesterday," Dr. Hotham may well be supposed to reply.

"Indeed," cries Mr. Dodsworth, "and pray, sir, has any change for better or worse occurred in that poor distracted country?"

Dr. Hotham suspects a Radical, and coldly replies: "Why, sir, it would be difficult to say in what its distraction consists. People talk of starving manufacturers, bankruptcies, and the fall of the Joint Stock Companies—excrescences these, excrescences which will attach themselves to a state of full health. England, in fact, was never in a more prosperous condition."

Mr. Dodsworth now more than suspects the Republican, and, with what we have supposed to be his accustomed caution, sinks for awhile his loyalty, and in a moderate tone asks: "Do our governors look with careless eyes upon the symptoms of over-health?"

"Our governors," answers his preserver, "if you mean our ministry, are only too alive to temporary embarrassment." (We beg Doctor Hotham's pardon if we wrong him in making him a high Tory; such a quality appertains to our pure anticipated cognition of a Doctor, and such is the only cognizance that we have of this gentleman.) "It were to be wished that they showed themselves more firm—the king, God bless him!"

"Sir!" exclaims Mr. Dodsworth.

Doctor Hotham continues, not aware of the excessive astonishment exhibited by his patient: "The king, God bless him, spares immense sums from his privy purse for the relief of his subjects, and his example has been imitated by all the aristocracy and wealth of England."

"The King!" ejaculates Mr. Dodsworth.

"Yes, sir," emphatically rejoins his preserver; "the king, and I am happy to say that the prejudices that so unhappily and unwarrantably possessed the English people with regard to his Majesty are now, with a few" (with added severity) "and I may say contemptible exceptions, exchanged for dutiful love and such reverence as his talents, virtues, and paternal care deserve."

"Dear sir, you delight me," replies Mr. Dodsworth, while his loyalty late a tiny bud suddenly expands into full flower; "yet I hardly understand; the change is so sudden; and the man—Charles Stuart, King Charles, I may now call him, his murder is I trust execrated as it deserves?"

Dr. Hotham put his hand on the pulse of his patient—he feared an access of delirium from such a wandering from the subject. The pulse was calm, and Mr. Dodsworth continued: "That unfortunate martyr looking down from heaven is, I trust, appeased by the reverence paid to his name and the prayers dedicated to his memory. No sentiment, I think I may venture to assert, is so general in England as the compassion and love in which the memory of that hapless monarch is held?"

"And his son, who now reigns?—"

"Surely, sir, you forget; no son; that of course is impossible. No descendant of his fills the English throne, now worthily occupied by the house of Hanover. The despicable race of the Stuarts, long outcast and wandering, is now extinct, and the last days of the last Pretender to the crown of that family justified in the eyes of the world the sentence which ejected it from the kingdom for ever."

Such must have been Mr. Dodsworth's first lesson in politics. Soon, to the wonder of the preserver and preserved, the real state of the case must have been revealed; for a time, the strange and tremendous circumstance of his long trance may have threatened the wits of Mr. Dodsworth with a total overthrow. He had, as he crossed Mount Saint Gothard, mourned a father—now every human being he had ever seen is "lapped in lead,"[3] is dust, each voice he had ever heard is mute. The very sound of the English tongue is changed, as his experience in conversation with Dr. Hotham assures him. Empires, religions, races of men, have probably sprung up or faded; his own patrimony (the thought is idle, yet, without it, how can he live?) is sunk into the thirsty gulph that gapes ever greedy to swallow the past; his learning, his acquirements, are probably obsolete; with a bitter smile he thinks to himself, I must take to my father's profession, and turn antiquary. The familiar objects, thoughts, and habits of my boyhood, are now antiquities. He wonders where the hundred and sixty folio volumes of MS. that his father had compiled, and which, as a lad, he had regarded with religious reverence, now are—where—ah, where? His favourite play-mate, the friend of his later years, his destined and lovely bride; tears long frozen are uncongealed, and flow down his young old cheeks.

But we do not wish to be pathetic; surely since the days of the patriarchs, no fair lady had her death mourned by her lover so many years after it had taken place. Necessity, tyrant of the world, in some degree reconciles Mr. Dodsworth to his fate. At first he is persuaded that the later generation of man is much deteriorated from his contemporaries; they are neither so tall, so handsome, nor so intelligent. Then by degrees he begins to doubt his first impression. The ideas that had taken possession of his brain before his accident, and which had been frozen up for so many years, begin to thaw and dissolve away, making room for others. He dresses himself in the modern style, and does not object much to anything except the neck-cloth and hardboarded hat. He admires the texture of his shoes and stockings, and looks with admiration on a small Genevese watch, which he often consults, as if he were not yet assured that time had made progress in its accustomed manner, and as if he should find on its dial plate occular demonstration that he had exchanged

3. Shakespeare, *The Passionate Pilgrim*, 1. 396.

his thirty-seventh year for his two hundredth and upwards, and had left A.D. 1654 far behind to find himself suddenly a beholder of the ways of men in this enlightened nineteenth century. His curiosity is insatiable; when he reads, his eyes cannot purvey fast enough to his mind, and every now and then he lights upon some inexplicable passage, some discovery and knowledge familiar to us, but undreamed of in his days, that throws him into wonder and interminable reverie. Indeed, he may be supposed to pass much of his time in that state, now and then interrupting himself with a royalist song against old Noll[4] and the Roundheads, breaking off suddenly, and looking round fearfully to see who were his auditors, and on beholding the modern appearance of his friend the Doctor, sighing to think that it is no longer of import to any, whether he sing a cavalier catch or a puritanic psalm.

It were an endless task to develope all the philosophic ideas to which Mr. Dodsworth's resuscitation naturally gives birth. We should like much to converse with this gentleman, and still more to observe the progress of his mind, and the change of his ideas in his very novel situation. If he be a sprightly youth, fond of the shows of the world, careless of the higher human pursuits, he may proceed summarily to cast into the shade all trace of his former life, and endeavour to merge himself at once into the stream of humanity now flowing. It would be curious enough to observe the mistakes he would make, and the medley of manners which would thus be produced. He may think to enter into active life, become whig or tory as his inclinations lead, and get a seat in the, even to him, once called chapel of St. Stephens. He may content himself with turning contemplative philosopher, and find sufficient food for his mind in tracing the march of the human intellect, the changes which have been wrought in the dispositions, desires, and powers of mankind. Will he be an advocate for perfectibility or deterioration? He must admire our manufactures, the progress of science, the diffusion of knowledge, and the fresh spirit of enterprise characteristic of our countrymen. Will he find any individuals to be compared to the glorious spirits of his day? Moderate in his views as we have supposed him to be, he will probably fall at once into the temporising tone of mind now so much in vogue. He will be pleased to find a calm in politics; he will greatly admire the ministry who have succeeded in conciliating almost all parties—to find peace where he left feud. The same character which he bore a couple of hundred years ago, will influence him now; he will still be the moderate, peaceful, unenthusiastic Mr. Dodsworth that he was in 1647.

For notwithstanding education and circumstances may suffice to direct

4. Nickname given to Oliver Cromwell by the Cavaliers; the song was probably "Old Noll's Jig."

and form the rough material of the mind, it cannot create, nor give intellect, noble aspiration, and energetic constancy where dulness, wavering of purpose, and grovelling desires, are stamped by nature. Entertaining this belief we have (to forget Mr. Dodsworth for awhile) often made conjectures how such and such heroes of antiquity would act, if they were reborn in these times: and then awakened fancy has gone on to imagine that some of them are reborn; that according to the theory explained by Virgil in his sixth Æneid, every thousand years the dead return to life, and their souls endued with the same sensibilities and capacities as before, are turned naked of knowledge into this world, again to dress their skeleton powers in such habiliments as situation, education, and experience will furnish. Pythagoras, we are told, remembered many transmigrations of this sort, as having occurred to himself, though for a philosopher he made very little use of his anterior memories. It would prove an instructive school for kings and statesmen, and in fact for all human beings, called on as they are, to play their part on the stage of the world, could they remember what they had been. Thus we might obtain a glimpse of heaven and of hell, as, the secret of our former identity confined to our own bosoms, we winced or exulted in the blame or praise bestowed on our former selves. While the love of glory and posthumous reputation is as natural to man as his attachment to life itself, he must be, under such a state of things, tremblingly alive to the historic records of his honour or shame. The mild spirit of Fox would have been soothed by the recollection that he had played a worthy part as Marcus Antoninus—the former experiences of Alcibiades or even of the emasculated Steeny of James I. might have caused Sheridan to have refused to tread over again the same path of dazzling but fleeting brilliancy. The soul of our modern Corinna would have been purified and exalted by a consciousness that once it had given life to the form of Sappho. If at the present moment the witch, memory, were in a freak, to cause all the present generation to recollect that some ten centuries back they had been somebody else, would not several of our free thinking martyrs wonder to find that they had suffered as Christians under Domitian, while the judge as he passed sentence would suddenly become aware, that formerly he had condemned the saints of the early church to the torture, for not renouncing the religion he now upheld—nothing but benevolent actions and real goodness would come pure out of the ordeal. While it would be whimsical to perceive how some great men in parish affairs would strut under the consciousness that their hands had once held a sceptre, an honest artizan or pilfering domestic would find that he was little altered by being transformed into an idle noble or director of a joint stock company; in every way we may suppose that the humble would be exalted, and the noble and the proud would feel their stars and honours dwindle into baubles and child's play when they called to mind the lowly stations they had once occupied. If philosophical novels were in fashion, we conceive an excellent one might be written on the development of the same mind in various stations, in different periods of the world's history.

But to return to Mr. Dodsworth, and indeed with a few more words to bid him farewell. We entreat him no longer to bury himself in obscurity; or, if he modestly decline publicity, we beg him to make himself known personally to us. We have a thousand inquiries to make, doubts to clear up, facts to ascertain. If any fear that old habits and strangeness of appearance will make him ridiculous to those accustomed to associate with modern exquisites, we beg to assure him that we are not given to ridicule mere outward shows, and that worth and intrinsic excellence will always claim our respect.

This we say, if Mr. Dodsworth is alive. Perhaps he is again no more. Perhaps he opened his eyes only to shut them again more obstinately; perhaps his ancient clay could not thrive on the harvests of these latter days. After a little wonder; a little shuddering to find himself the dead alive—finding no affinity between himself and the present state of things— he has bidden once more an eternal farewell to the sun. Followed to his grave by his preserver and the wondering villagers, he may sleep the true death-sleep in the same valley where he so long reposed. Doctor Hotham may have erected a simple tablet over his twice-buried remains, inscribed—

To the Memory of R. Dodsworth,
An Englishman,
Born April 1, 1617; Died July 16, 1826; Aged 209.

An inscription which, if it were preserved during any terrible convulsion that caused the world to begin its life again, would occasion many learned disquisitions and ingenious theories concerning a race which authentic records showed to have secured the privilege of attaining so vast an age.

FRANCIS THE FIRST & HIS SISTER
Painted by Richard Parkes Bonington · Engraved by Charles Heath
(Plate from *The Keepsake for MDCCCXXX*.)

The False Rhyme[1]

Come, tell me where the maid is found
Whose heart can love without deceit,
And I will range the world around
To sigh one moment at her feet.

Thomas Moore[2]

On a fine July day, the fair Margaret, Queen of Navarre,[3] then on a visit to her royal brother, had arranged a rural feast for the morning following, which Francis declined attending. He was melancholy; and the cause was said to be some lover's quarrel with a favourite dame. The morrow came, and dark rain and murky clouds destroyed at once the schemes of the courtly throng. Margaret was angry, and she grew weary: her only hope for amusement was in Francis, and he had shut himself up—an excellent reason why she should the more desire to see him. She entered his apartment: he was standing at the casement, against which the noisy shower beat, writing with a diamond on the glass. Two beautiful dogs were his sole companions. As Queen Margaret entered, he hastily let down the silken curtain before the window, and looked a little confused.

"What treason is this, my liege," said the queen, "which crimsons your cheek? I must see the same."

"It is treason," replied the king, "and therefore, sweet sister, thou mayest not see it."

This the more excited Margaret's curiosity, and a playful contest ensued: Francis at last yielded: he threw himself on a huge high-backed settee; and as the lady drew back the curtain with an arch smile, he grew grave and sentimental, as he reflected on the cause which had inspired his libel against all womankind.

"What have we here?" cried Margaret: "nay, this is lèse majesté—

1. Reprinted from *Tales and Stories*, pp. 117–20, where text is based on *The Keepsake for MDCCCXXX*, ed. Frederic Mansel Reynolds (London: Hurst, Chance, and Co. [1829]), pp. 265–68.
2. From Thomas Moore's four-stanza lyric, "Come, tell me where the maid is found."
3. Marguerite d'Angoulême (1492–1549): sister of Francis I (1494–1547), King of France; wife of Henri d'Albret, King of Navarre; author and patroness of letters.

> 'Souvent femme varie,
> Bien fou qui s'y fie!'[4]

Very little change would greatly amend your couplet:—would it not run better thus—

> 'Souvent homme varie,
> Bien folle qui s'y fie'?

I could tell you twenty stories of man's inconstancy."

"I will be content with one true tale of woman's fidelity," said Francis, drily; "but do not provoke me. I would fain be at peace with the soft Mutabilities, for thy dear sake."

"I defy your grace," replied Margaret, rashly, "to instance the false-hood of one noble and well reputed dame."

"Not even Emilie de Lagny?" asked the king.

This was a sore subject for the queen. Emilie had been brought up in her own household, the most beautiful and the most virtuous of her maids of honour. She had long loved the Sire de Lagny, and their nuptials were celebrated with rejoicings but little ominous of the result. De Lagny was accused but a year after of traitorously yielding to the emperor a fortress under his command, and he was condemned to perpetual imprisonment. For some time Emilie seemed inconsolable, often visiting the miserable dungeon of her husband, and suffering on her return, from witnessing his wretchedness, such paroxysms of grief as threatened her life. Suddenly, in the midst of her sorrow, she disappeared; and inquiry only divulged the disgraceful fact, that she had escaped from France, bearing her jewels with her, and accompanied by her page, Robinet Leroux. It was whis-pered that, during their journey, the lady and the stripling often occupied one chamber; and Margaret, enraged at these discoveries, commanded that no further quest should be made for her lost favourite.

Taunted now by her brother, she defended Emilie, declaring that she believed her to be guiltless, even going so far as to boast that within a month she would bring proof of her innocence.

"Robinet was a pretty boy," said Francis, laughing.

"Let us make a bet," cried Margaret: "if I lose, I will bear this vile rhyme of thine as a motto to my shame to my grave; if I win——"

"I will break my window, and grant thee whatever boon thou askest."

The result of this bet was long sung by troubadour and minstrel. The queen employed a hundred emissaries—published rewards for any intel-ligence of Emilie—all in vain. The month was expiring, and Margaret

---

4. "Often a woman is inconstant, / A great fool is the man who trusts in her!" The sexes are reversed when Margaret emends the couplet.

would have given many bright jewels to redeem her word. On the eve of the fatal day, the jailor of the prison in which the Sire de Lagny was confined sought an audience of the queen; he brought her a message from the knight to say, that if the Lady Margaret would ask his pardon as her boon, and obtain from her royal brother that he might be brought before him, her bet was won. Fair Margaret was very joyful, and readily made the desired promise. Francis was unwilling to see his false servant, but he was in high good humour, for a cavalier had that morning brought intelligence of a victory over the Imperialists. The messenger himself was lauded in the despatches as the most fearless and bravest knight in France. The king loaded him with presents, only regretting that a vow prevented the soldier from raising his visor or declaring his name.

That same evening as the setting sun shone on the lattice on which the ungallant rhyme was traced, Francis reposed on the same settee, and the beautiful Queen of Navarre, with triumph in her bright eyes, sat beside him. Attended by guards, the prisoner was brought in: his frame was attenuated by privation, and he walked with tottering steps. He knelt at the feet of Francis, and uncovered his head; a quantity of rich golden hair then escaping, fell over the sunken cheeks and pallid brow of the suppliant. "We have treason here!" cried the king: "sir jailor, where is your prisoner?"

"Sire, blame him not," said the soft faltering voice of Emilie; "wiser men than he have been deceived by woman. My dear lord was guiltless of the crime for which he suffered. There was but one mode to save him:—I assumed his chains—he escaped with poor Robinet Leroux in my attire— he joined your army: the young and gallant cavalier who delivered the despatches to your grace, whom you overwhelmed with honours and reward, is my own Enguerrard de Lagny. I waited but for his arrival with testimonials of his innocence, to declare myself to my lady, the queen. Has she not won her bet? And the boon she asks——"

"Is de Lagny's pardon," said Margaret, as she also knelt to the king: "spare your faithful vassal, sire, and reward this lady's truth."

Francis first broke the false-speaking window, then he raised the ladies from their supplicatory posture.

In the tournament given to celebrate this "Triumph of Ladies," the Sire de Lagny bore off every prize; and surely there was more loveliness in Emilie's faded cheek—more grace in her emaciated form, type as they were of truest affection—than in the prouder bearing and fresher complexion of the most brilliant beauty in attendance on the courtly festival.

Transformation[1]

Forthwith this frame of mine was wrench'd
With a woful agony,
Which forced me to begin my tale,
And then it set me free.
Since then, at an uncertain hour,
That agony returns;
And till my ghastly tale is told
This heart within me burns.
Coleridge's Ancient Mariner.

I have heard it said, that, when any strange, supernatural, and necromantic adventure has occurred to a human being, that being, however desirous he may be to conceal the same, feels at certain periods torn up as it were by an intellectual earthquake, and is forced to bare the inner depths of his spirit to another. I am a witness of the truth of this. I have dearly sworn to myself never to reveal to human ears the horrors to which I once, in excess of fiendly pride, delivered myself over. The holy man who heard my confession, and reconciled me to the church, is dead. None knows that once——

Why should it not be thus? Why tell a tale of impious tempting of Providence, and soul-subduing humiliation? Why? answer me, ye who are wise in the secrets of human nature! I only know that so it is; and in spite of strong resolve—of a pride that too much masters me—of shame, and even of fear, so to render myself odious to my species—I must speak.

Genoa! my birth-place—proud city! looking upon the blue waves of the Mediterranean sea—dost thou remember me in my boyhood, when thy cliffs and promontories, thy bright sky and gay vineyards, were my world? Happy time! when to the young heart the narrow-bounded universe, which leaves, by its very limitation, free scope to the imagination, enchains our physical energies, and, sole period in our lives, innocence and enjoyment are united. Yet, who can look back to childhood, and not remember its sorrows and its harrowing fears? I was born with the most imperious, haughty, tameless spirit, with which ever mortal was gifted. I quailed before my father only; and he, generous and noble, but capricious and tyrannical, at once fostered and checked the wild impetuosity of my

---

1. Reprinted from *Tales and Stories*, pp. 121–35, where text is based on *The Keepsake for MDCCCXXXI*, ed. Frederic Mansel Reynolds (London: Hurst, Chance, and Co. [1830]), pp. 18–39.

character, making obedience necessary, but inspiring no respect for the motives which guided his commands. To be a man, free, independent; or, in better words, insolent and domineering, was the hope and prayer of my rebel heart.

My father had one friend, a wealthy Genoese noble, who in a political tumult was suddenly sentenced to banishment, and his property confiscated. The Marchese Torella went into exile alone. Like my father, he was a widower: he had one child, the almost infant Juliet, who was left under my father's guardianship. I should certainly have been an unkind master to the lovely girl, but that I was forced by my position to become her protector. A variety of childish incidents all tended to one point,—to make Juliet see in me a rock of refuge; I in her, one, who must perish through the soft sensibility of her nature too rudely visited, but for my guardian care. We grew up together. The opening rose in May was not more sweet than this dear girl. An irradiation of beauty was spread over her face. Her form, her step, her voice—my heart weeps even now, to think of all of relying, gentle, loving, and pure, that was enshrined in that celestial tenement. When I was eleven and Juliet eight years of age, a cousin of mine, much older than either—he seemed to us a man—took great notice of my playmate; he called her his bride, and asked her to marry him. She refused, and he insisted, drawing her unwillingly towards him. With the countenance and emotions of a maniac I threw myself on him—I strove to draw his sword—I clung to his neck with the ferocious resolve to strangle him: he was obliged to call for assistance to disengage himself from me. On that night I led Juliet to the chapel of our house: I made her touch the sacred relics—I harrowed her child's heart, and profaned her child's lips with an oath, that she would be mine, and mine only.

Well, those days passed away. Torella returned in a few years, and became wealthier and more prosperous than ever. When I was seventeen, my father died; he had been magnificent to prodigality; Torella rejoiced that my minority would afford an opportunity for repairing my fortunes. Juliet and I had been affianced beside my father's deathbed—Torella was to be a second parent to me.

I desired to see the world, and I was indulged. I went to Florence, to Rome, to Naples; thence I passed to Toulon, and at length reached what had long been the bourne of my wishes, Paris. There was wild work in Paris then. The poor king, Charles the Sixth, now sane, now mad, now a monarch, now an abject slave, was the very mockery of humanity. The queen, the dauphin, the Duke of Burgundy, alternately friends and foes—now meeting in prodigal feasts, now shedding blood in rivalry—were blind to the miserable state of their country, and the dangers that impended over it, and gave themselves wholly up to dissolute enjoyment or savage strife. My character still followed me. I was arrogant and self-willed; I loved display, and above all, I threw all control far from me. Who could control me in Paris? My young friends were eager to foster passions which furnished them with pleasures. I was deemed handsome—I was master of every knightly accomplishment. I was disconnected with any political party. I grew a favourite with all: my presumption and arrogance were pardoned in one so young: I became a spoiled child. Who could control me? not the letters and advice of Torella—only strong necessity visiting me in the abhorred shape of an empty purse. But there were means to refill this void. Acre after acre, estate after estate, I sold. My dress, my jewels, my horses and their caparisons, were almost un-rivalled in gorgeous Paris, while the lands of my inheritance passed into possession of others.

The Duke of Orleans was waylaid and murdered by the Duke of Burgundy. Fear and terror possessed all Paris. The dauphin and the queen shut themselves up; every pleasure was suspended. I grew weary of this state of things, and my heart yearned for my boyhood's haunts. I was nearly a beggar, yet still I would go there, claim my bride, and rebuild my fortunes. A few happy ventures as a merchant would make me rich again. Nevertheless, I would not return in humble guise. My last act was to dispose of my remaining estate near Albaro for half its worth, for ready money. Then I despatched all kinds of artificers, arras, furniture of regal splendour, to fit up the last relic of my inheritance, my palace in Genoa. I lingered a little longer yet, ashamed at the part of the prodigal returned, which I feared I should play. I sent my horses. One matchless Spanish jennet I despatched to my promised bride; its caparisons flamed with jewels and cloth of gold. In every part I caused to be entwined the initials of Juliet and her Guido. My present found favour in hers and in her father's eyes.

Still to return a proclaimed spendthrift, the mark of impertinent wonder, perhaps of scorn, and to encounter singly the reproaches or taunts of my fellow-citizens, was no alluring prospect. As a shield between me and censure, I invited some few of the most reckless of my comrades to accompany me: thus I went armed against the world, hiding a rankling feeling, half fear and half penitence, by bravado and an insolent display of satisfied vanity.

I arrived in Genoa. I trod the pavement of my ancestral palace. My proud step was no interpreter of my heart, for I deeply felt that, though surrounded by every luxury, I was a beggar. The first step I took in claiming Juliet must widely declare me such. I read contempt or pity in the looks of all. I fancied, so apt is conscience to imagine what it deserves, that rich and poor, young and old, all regarded me with derision. Torella came not near me. No wonder that my second father should expect a son's deference from me in waiting first on him. But, galled and stung by a sense of my follies and demerit, I strove to throw the blame on others. We kept nightly orgies in Palazzo Carega. To sleepless, riotous nights, followed listless, supine mornings. At the Ave Maria we showed our dainty persons in the streets, scoffing at the sober citizens, casting insolent glances on the shrinking women. Juliet was not among them—no, no; if she had been there, shame would have driven me away, if love had not brought me to her feet.

I grew tired of this. Suddenly I paid the Marchese a visit. He was at his villa, one among the many which deck the suburb of San Pietro d'Arena. It was the month of May—a month of May in that garden of the world— the blossoms of the fruit trees were fading among thick, green foliage; the vines were shooting forth; the ground strewed with the fallen olive blooms; the fire-fly was in the myrtle hedge; heaven and earth wore a mantle of surpassing beauty. Torella welcomed me kindly, though seriously; and even his shade of displeasure soon wore away. Some resemblance to my father—some look and tone of youthful ingenuousness, lurking still in spite of my misdeeds, softened the good old man's heart. He sent for his daughter—he presented me to her as her betrothed. The chamber became hallowed by a holy light as she entered. Hers was that cherub look, those large, soft eyes, full dimpled cheeks, and mouth of infantine sweetness, that expresses the rare union of happiness and love. Admiration first possessed me; she is mine! was the second proud emotion, and my lips curled with haughty triumph. I had not been the *enfant gâté*[2] of the beauties of France not to have learnt the art of pleasing the soft heart of woman. If towards men I was overbearing, the deference I paid to them was the more in contrast. I commenced my courtship by the display of a thousand gallantries to Juliet, who, vowed to me from infancy, had never admitted the devotion of others; and who, though accustomed to expressions of admiration, was uninitiated in the language of lovers.

For a few days all went well. Torella never alluded to my extravagance; he treated me as a favourite son. But the time came, as we discussed the preliminaries to my union with his daughter, when this fair face of things should be overcast. A contract had been drawn up in my father's lifetime. I had rendered this, in fact, void, by having squandered the whole of the wealth which was to have been shared by Juliet and myself. Torella, in consequence, chose to consider this bond as cancelled, and proposed another, in which, though the wealth he bestowed was immeasurably

2. Literally "spoiled child," but here "pampered darling."

increased, there were so many restrictions as to the mode of spending it, that I, who saw independence only in free career being given to my own imperious will, taunted him as taking advantage of my situation, and refused utterly to subscribe to his conditions. The old man mildly strove to recall me to reason. Roused pride became the tyrant of my thought: I listened with indignaton—I repelled him with disdain.

"Juliet, thou art mine! Did we not interchange vows in our innocent childhood? are we not one in the sight of God? and shall thy cold-hearted, cold-blooded father divide us? Be generous, my love, be just; take not away a gift, last treasure of thy Guido—retract not thy vows—let us defy the world, and setting at nought the calculations of age, find in our mutual affection a refuge from every ill."

Fiend I must have been, with such sophistry to endeavour to poison that sanctuary of holy thought and tender love. Juliet shrank from me affrighted. Her father was the best and kindest of men, and she strove to show me how, in obeying him, every good would follow. He would receive my tardy submission with warm affection; and generous pardon would follow my repentance. Profitless words for a young and gentle daughter to use to a man accustomed to make his will, law; and to feel in his own heart a despot so terrible and stern, that he could yield obedience to nought save his own imperious desires! My resentment grew with resistance; my wild companions were ready to add fuel to the flame. We laid a plan to carry off Juliet. At first it appeared to be crowned with success. Midway, on our return, we were overtaken by the agonized father and his attendants. A conflict ensued. Before the city guard came to decide the victory in favour of our antagonists, two of Torella's servitors were dangerously wounded.

This portion of my history weighs most heavily with me. Changed man as I am, I abhor myself in the recollection. May none who hear this tale ever have felt as I. A horse driven to fury by a rider armed with barbed spurs, was not more a slave than I, to the violent tyranny of my temper. A fiend possessed my soul, irritating it to madness. I felt the voice of conscience within me; but if I yielded to it for a brief interval, it was only to be a moment after torn, as by a whirlwind, away—borne along on the stream of desperate rage—the plaything of the storms engendered by pride. I was imprisoned, and, at the instance of Torella, set free. Again I returned to carry off both him and his child to France; which hapless country, then preyed on by freebooters and gangs of lawless soldiery, offered a grateful refuge to a criminal like me. Our plots were discovered. I was sentenced to banishment; and, as my debts were already enormous, my remaining property was put in the hands of commissioners for their payment. Torella again offered his mediation, requiring only my promise not to renew my abortive attempts on himself and his daughter. I spurned his offers, and fancied that I triumphed when I was thrust out from Genoa, a solitary and penniless exile. My companions were gone: they had been dismissed the city some weeks before, and were already in France. I was alone—friendless; with nor sword at my side, nor ducat in my purse.

I wandered along the sea-shore, a whirlwind of passion possessing and tearing my soul. It was as if a live coal had been set burning in my breast. At first I meditated on what *I should do*. I would join a band of free-booters. Revenge!—the word seemed balm to me:—I hugged it—caressed it—till, like a serpent, it stung me. Then again I would abjure and despise Genoa, that little corner of the world. I would return to Paris, where so many of my friends swarmed; where my services would be eagerly accepted; where I would carve out fortune with my sword, and might, through success, make my paltry birth-place, and the false Torella, rue the day when they drove me, a new Coriolanus, from her walls. I would return to Paris—thus, on foot—a beggar—and present myself in my poverty to those I had formerly entertained sumptuously? There was gall in the mere thought of it.

The reality of things began to dawn upon my mind, bringing despair in its train. For several months I had been a prisoner: the evils of my dungeon had whipped my soul to madness, but they had subdued my corporeal frame. I was weak and wan. Torella had used a thousand artifices to administer to my comfort; I had detected and scorned them all—and I reaped the harvest of my obduracy. What was to be done?—Should I crouch before my foe, and sue for forgiveness?—Die rather ten thousand deaths!—Never should they obtain that victory! Hate—I swore eternal hate! Hate from whom?—to whom?—From a wandering outcast—to a mighty noble. I and my feelings were nothing to them: already had they forgotten one so unworthy. And Juliet!—her angel-face and sylph-like form gleamed among the clouds of my despair with vain beauty; for I had lost her—the glory and flower of the world! Another will call her his!—that smile of paradise will bless another!

Even now my heart fails within me when I recur to this rout of grim-visaged ideas. Now subdued almost to tears, now raving in my agony, still I wandered along the rocky shore, which grew at each step wilder and more desolate. Hanging rocks and hoar precipices overlooked the tideless ocean; black caverns yawned; and for ever, among the seaworn recesses, murmured and dashed the unfruitful waters. Now my way was almost barred by an abrupt promontory, now rendered nearly impracticable by fragments fallen from the cliff. Evening was at hand, when, seaward, arose, as if on the waving of a wizard's wand, a murky web of clouds, blotting the late azure sky, and darkening and disturbing the till now placid deep. The clouds had strange fantastic shapes; and they changed, and mingled, and seemed to be driven about by a mighty spell. The waves raised their white crests; the thunder first muttered, then roared from across the waste of waters, which took a deep purple dye, flecked with foam. The spot where I stood, looked, on one side, to the wide-spread ocean; on the other, it was barred by a rugged promontory. Round this cape suddenly came, driven by the wind, a vessel. In vain the mariners tried to force a path for her to the open sea—the gale drove her on the rocks. It will perish!—all on board will perish!—Would I were among them! And to my young heart the idea of death came for the first time blended with that of joy. It was an awful sight to behold that vessel struggling with her fate. Hardly could I discern the sailors, but I heard them. It was soon all over!—A rock, just covered by the tossing waves, and so unperceived, lay in wait for its prey. A crash of thunder broke over my head at the moment that, with a frightful shock, the skiff dashed upon her unseen enemy. In a brief space of time she went to pieces. There I stood in safety; and there were my fellow-creatures, battling, how hopelessly, with annihilation. Methought I saw them struggling—too truly did I hear their shrieks, conquering the barking surges in their shrill agony. The dark breakers threw hither and thither the fragments of the wreck: soon it disappeared. I had been fascinated to gaze till the end: at last I sank on my knees—I covered my face with my hands: I again looked up; something was floating on the billows towards the shore. It neared and neared. Was that a human form?—It grew more distinct; and at last a mighty wave, lifting the whole freight, lodged it upon a rock. A human being bestriding a sea-chest!—A human being!—Yet was it one? Surely never such had existed before—a misshapen dwarf, with squinting eyes, distorted features, and body deformed, till it became a horror to behold. My blood, lately warming towards a fellow-being so snatched from a watery tomb, froze in my heart. The dwarf got off his chest; he tossed his straight, straggling hair from his odious visage:

"By St. Beelzebub!" he exclaimed, "I have been well bested." He looked round and saw me. "Oh, by the fiend! here is another ally of the mighty one. To what saint did you offer prayers, friend—if not to mine? Yet I remember you not on board."

I shrank from the monster and his blasphemy. Again he questioned me, and I muttered some inaudible reply. He continued:—

"Your voice is drowned by this dissonant roar. What a noise the big ocean makes! Schoolboys bursting from their prison are not louder than these waves set free to play. They disturb me. I will no more of their ill-timed brawling.—Silence, hoary One!—Winds, avaunt!—to your homes!—Clouds, fly to the antipodes, and leave our heaven clear!"

As he spoke, he stretched out his two long lank arms, that looked like spider's claws, and seemed to embrace with them the expanse before him. Was it a miracle? The clouds became broken, and fled; the azure sky first peeped out, and then was spread a calm field of blue above us; the stormy gale was exchanged to the softly breathing west; the sea grew calm; the waves dwindled to riplets.

"I like obedience even in these stupid elements," said the dwarf. "How much more in the tameless mind of man! It was a well got up storm, you must allow—and all of my own making."

It was tempting Providence to interchange talk with this magician. But *Power*, in all its shapes, is venerable to man. Awe, curiosity, a clinging fascination, drew me towards him.

"Come, don't be frightened, friend," said the wretch: "I am good-humoured when pleased; and something does please me in your well-proportioned body and handsome face, though you look a little woe-begone. You have suffered a land—I, a sea wreck. Perhaps I can allay the tempest of your fortunes as I did my own. Shall we be friends?"—And he held out his hand; I could not touch it. "Well, then, companions—that will do as well. And now, while I rest after the buffeting I underwent just now, tell me why, young and gallant as you seem, you wander thus alone and downcast on this wild sea-shore."

The voice of the wretch was screeching and horrid, and his contortions as he spoke were frightful to behold. Yet he did gain a kind of influence over me, which I could not master, and I told him my tale. When it was ended, he laughed long and loud: the rocks echoed back the sound: hell seemed yelling around me.

"Oh, thou cousin of Lucifer!" said he; "so thou too hast fallen through thy pride; and, though bright as the son of Morning, thou art ready to give up thy good looks, thy bride, and thy well-being, rather than submit thee to the tyranny of good. I honour thy choice, by my soul!—So thou hast fled, and yield the day; and mean to starve on these rocks, and to let the birds peck out thy dead eyes, while thy enemy and thy betrothed rejoice in thy ruin. Thy pride is strangely akin to humility, methinks."

As he spoke, a thousand fanged thoughts stung me to the heart.

"What would you that I should do?" I cried.

"I!—Oh, nothing, but lie down and say your prayers before you die. But, were I you, I know the deed that should be done."

I drew near him. His supernatural powers made him an oracle in my

eyes; yet a strange unearthly thrill quivered through my frame as I said—
"Speak!—teach me—what act do you advise?"

"Revenge thyself, man!—humble thy enemies!—set thy foot on the old
man's neck, and possess thyself of his daughter!"

"To the east and west I turn," cried I, "and see no means! Had I gold,
much could I achieve; but, poor and single, I am powerless."

The dwarf had been seated on his chest as he listened to my story.
Now he got off; he touched a spring; it flew open!—What a mine of
wealth—of blazing jewels, beaming gold, and pale silver—was displayed
therein. A mad desire to possess this treasure was born within me.

"Doubtless," I said, "one so powerful as you could do all things."

"Nay," said the monster, humbly, "I am less omnipotent than I seem.
Some things I possess which you may covet; but I would give them all for
a small share, or even for a loan of what is yours."

"My possessions are at your service," I replied, bitterly—"my poverty,
my exile, my disgrace—I make a free gift of them all."

"Good! I thank you. Add one other thing to your gift, and my treasure
is yours."

"As nothing is my sole inheritance, what besides nothing would you
have?"

"Your comely face and well-made limbs."

I shivered. Would this all-powerful monster murder me? I had no
dagger. I forgot to pray—but I grew pale.

"I ask for a loan, not a gift," said the frightful thing: "lend me your
body for three days—you shall have mine to cage your soul the while, and,
in payment, my chest. What say you to the bargain?—Three short days."

We are told that it is dangerous to hold unlawful talk; and well do I
prove the same. Tamely written down, it may seem incredible that I
should lend any ear to this proposition; but, in spite of his unnatural
ugliness, there was something fascinating in a being whose voice could
govern earth, air, and sea. I felt a keen desire to comply; for with that
chest I could command the world. My only hesitation resulted from a fear
that he would not be true to his bargain. Then, I thought, I shall soon die
here on these lonely sands, and the limbs he covets will be mine no
more:—it is worth the chance. And, besides, I knew that, by all the rules
of art-magic, there were formula and oaths which none of its practisers
dared break. I hesitated to reply; and he went on, now displaying his
wealth, now speaking of the petty price he demanded, till it seemed
madness to refuse. Thus is it: place our bark in the current of the stream,
and down, over fall and cataract it is hurried; give up our conduct to the
wild torrent of passion, and we are away, we know not whither.

He swore many an oath, and I adjured him by many a sacred name; till

I saw this wonder of power, this ruler of the elements, shiver like an autumn leaf before my words; and as if the spirit spake unwillingly and per force within him, at last, he, with broken voice, revealed the spell whereby he might be obliged, did he wish to play me false, to render up the unlawful spoil. Our warm life-blood must mingle to make and to mar the charm.

Enough of this unholy theme. I was persuaded—the thing was done. The morrow dawned upon me as I lay upon the shingles, and I knew not my own shadow as it fell from me. I felt myself changed to a shape of horror, and cursed my easy faith and blind credulity. The chest was there—there the gold and precious stones for which I had sold the frame of flesh which nature had given me. The sight a little stilled my emotions: three days would soon be gone.

They did pass. The dwarf had supplied me with a plenteous store of food. At first I could hardly walk, so strange and out of joint were all my limbs; and my voice—it was that of the fiend. But I kept silent, and turned my face to the sun, that I might not see my shadow, and counted the hours, and ruminated on my future conduct. To bring Torella to my feet—to possess my Juliet in spite of him—all this my wealth could easily achieve. During dark night I slept, and dreamt of the accomplishment of my desires. Two suns had set—the third dawned. I was agitated, fearful. Oh expectation, what a frightful thing art thou, when kindled more by fear than hope! How dost thou twist thyself round the heart, torturing its pulsations! How dost thou dart unknown pangs all through our feeble mechanism, now seeming to shiver us like broken glass, to nothingness— now giving us a fresh strength, which can *do* nothing, and so torments us by a sensation, such as the strong man must feel who cannot break his fetters, though they bend in his grasp. Slowly paced the bright, bright orb up the eastern sky; long it lingered in the zenith, and still more slowly wandered down the west: it touched the horizon's verge—it was lost! Its glories were on the summits of the cliff—they grew dun and gray. The evening star shone bright. He will soon be here.

He came not!—By the living heavens, he came not!—and night dragged out its weary length, and, in its decaying age, "day began to grizzle its dark hair;"[3] and the sun rose again on the most miserable wretch that ever upbraided its light. Three days thus I passed. The jewels and the gold—oh, how I abhorred them!

Well, well—I will not blacken these pages with demoniac ravings. All too terrible were the thoughts, the raging tumult of ideas that filled my soul. At the end of that time I slept; I had not before since the third

3. Lord Byron, *Werner* III.iv.152–53.

sunset; and I dreamt that I was at Juliet's feet, and she smiled, and then she shrieked—for she saw my transformation—and again she smiled, for still her beautiful lover knelt before her. But it was not I—it was he, the fiend, arrayed in my limbs, speaking with my voice, winning her with my looks of love. I strove to warn her, but my tongue refused its office; I strove to tear him from her, but I was rooted to the ground—I awoke with the agony. There were the solitary hoar precipices—there the plashing sea, the quiet strand, and the blue sky over all. What did it mean? was my dream but a mirror of the truth? was he wooing and winning my betrothed? I would on the instant back to Genoa—but I was banished. I laughed—the dwarf's yell burst from my lips—*I* banished! O, no! they had not exiled the foul limbs I wore; I might with these enter, without fear of incurring the threatened penalty of death, my own, my native city.

I began to walk towards Genoa. I was somewhat accustomed to my distorted limbs; none were ever so ill adapted for a straight-forward movement; it was with infinite difficulty that I proceeded. Then, too, I desired to avoid all the hamlets strewed here and there on the sea-beach, for I was unwilling to make a display of my hideousness. I was not quite sure that, if seen, the mere boys would not stone me to death as I passed, for a monster: some ungentle salutations I did receive from the few peasants or fishermen I chanced to meet. But it was dark night before I approached Genoa. The weather was so balmy and sweet that it struck me that the Marchese and his daughter would very probably have quitted the city for their country retreat. It was from Villa Torella that I had attempted to carry off Juliet; I had spent many an hour reconnoitring the spot, and knew each inch of ground in its vicinity. It was beautifully situated, embosomed in trees, on the margin of a stream. As I drew near, it became evident that my conjecture was right; nay, moreover, that the hours were being then devoted to feasting and merriment. For the house was lighted up; strains of soft and gay music were wafted towards me by the breeze. My heart sank within me. Such was the generous kindness of Torella's heart that I felt sure that he would not have indulged in public manifestations of rejoicing just after my unfortunate banishment, but for a cause I dared not dwell upon.

The country people were all alive and flocking about; it became necessary that I should study to conceal myself; and yet I longed to address some one, or to hear others discourse, or in any way to gain intelligence of what was really going on. At length, entering the walks that were in immediate vicinity to the mansion, I found one dark enough to veil my excessive frightfulness; and yet others as well as I were loitering in its shade. I soon gathered all I wanted to know—all that first made my very heart die with horror, and then boil with indignation. To-morrow Juliet was to be given to the penitent, reformed, beloved Guido—to-morrow my bride was to pledge her vows to a fiend from hell! And I did this!—my accursed pride—my demoniac violence and wicked self-idolatry had caused this act. For if I had acted as the wretch who had stolen my form had acted—if, with a mien at once yielding and dignified, I had presented my-self to Torella, saying, I have done wrong, forgive me; I am unworthy of your angel-child, but permit me to claim her hereafter, when my al-tered conduct shall manifest that I abjure my vices, and endeavour to become in some sort worthy of her. I go to serve against the infidels; and when my zeal for religion and my true penitence for the past shall appear to you to cancel my crimes, permit me again to call myself your son. Thus had he spoken; and the penitent was welcomed even as the prodigal son of scripture: the fatted calf was killed for him; and he, still pursuing the same path, displayed such open-hearted regret for his follies, so humble a concession of all his rights, and so ardent a resolve to reacquire them by a life of contrition and virtue, that he quickly conquered the kind, old man; and full pardon, and the gift of his lovely child, followed in swift succession.

O! had an angel from Paradise whispered to me to act thus! But now, what would be the innocent Juliet's fate? Would God permit the foul union—or, some prodigy destroying it, link the dishonoured name of Carega with the worst of crimes? To-morrow at dawn they were to be married: there was but one way to prevent this—to meet mine enemy, and to enforce the ratification of our agreement. I felt that this could only be done by a mortal struggle. I had no sword—if indeed my distorted arms could wield a soldier's weapon—but I had a dagger, and in that lay my every hope. There was no time for pondering or balancing nicely the question: I might die in the attempt; but besides the burning jealousy and despair of my own heart, honour, mere humanity, demanded that I should fall rather than not destroy the machinations of the fiend.

The guests departed—the lights began to disappear; it was evident that the inhabitants of the villa were seeking repose. I hid myself among the trees—the garden grew desert—the gates were closed—I wandered round and came under a window—ah! well did I know the same!—a soft twi-light glimmered in the room—the curtains were half withdrawn. It was the temple of innocence and beauty. Its magnificence was tempered, as it were, by the slight disarrangements occasioned by its being dwelt in, and all the objects scattered around displayed the taste of her who hallowed it by her presence. I saw her enter with a quick light step—I saw her ap-proach the window—she drew back the curtain yet further, and looked out into the night. Its breezy freshness played among her ringlets, and wafted them from the transparent marble of her brow. She clasped her hands, she raised her eyes to Heaven. I heard her voice. Guido! she softly murmured, Mine own Guido! and then, as if overcome by the fulness of her own heart, she sank on her knees:—her upraised eyes—her negligent but graceful attitude—the beaming thankfulness that lighted up her face— oh, these are tame words! Heart of mine, thou imagest ever, though thou canst not pourtray, the celestial beauty of that child of light and love.

I heard a step—a quick firm step along the shady avenue. Soon I saw a cavalier, richly dressed, young and, methought, graceful to look on, advance.—I hid myself yet closer.—The youth approached; he paused beneath the window. She arose, and again looking out she saw him, and said—I cannot, no, at this distant time I cannot record her terms of soft silver tenderness; to me they were spoken, but they were replied to by him.

"I will not go," he cried: "here where you have been, where your memory glides like some Heaven-visiting ghost, I will pass the long hours till we meet, never, my Juliet, again, day or night, to part. But do thou, my love, retire; the cold morn and fitful breeze will make thy cheek pale, and fill with languor thy love-lighted eyes. Ah, sweetest! could I press one kiss upon them, I could, methinks, repose."

And then he approached still nearer, and methought he was about to clamber into her chamber. I had hesitated, not to terrify her; now I was no longer master of myself. I rushed forward—I threw myself on him—I tore him away—I cried, "O loathsome and foul-shaped wretch!"

I need not repeat epithets, all tending, as it appeared, to rail at a person I at present feel some partiality for. A shriek rose from Juliet's lips. I neither heard nor saw—I *felt* only mine enemy, whose throat I grasped, and my dagger's hilt; he struggled, but could not escape: at length hoarsely he breathed these words: "Do!—strike home! destroy this body— you will still live: may your life be long and merry!"

The descending dagger was arrested at the word, and he, feeling my hold relax, extricated himself and drew his sword, while the uproar in the house, and flying of torches from one room to the other, showed that soon we should be separated—and I—oh! far better die: so that he did not survive, I cared not. In the midst of my frenzy there was much calculation:—fall I might, and so that he did not survive, I cared not for the death-blow I might deal against myself. While still, therefore, he thought I paused, and while I saw the villanous resolve to take advantage of my hesitation, in the sudden thrust he made at me, I threw myself on his sword, and at the same moment plunged my dagger, with a true desperate aim, in his side. We fell together, rolling over each other, and the tide of blood that flowed from the gaping wound of each mingled on the grass. More I know not—I fainted.

JULIET

Painted by Miss Sharpe · Engraved by J. C. Edwards

(Plate from *The Keepsake for MDCCCXXXI.*)

Again I returned to life: weak almost to death, I found myself stretched upon a bed—Juliet was kneeling beside it. Strange! my first broken request was for a mirror. I was so wan and ghastly, that my poor girl hesitated, as she told me afterwards; but, by the mass! I thought myself a right proper youth when I saw the dear reflection of my own well-known features. I confess it is a weakness, but I avow it, I do entertain a considerable affection for the countenance and limbs I behold, whenever I look at a glass; and have more mirrors in my house, and consult them oftener than any beauty in Venice. Before you too much condemn me, permit me to say that no one better knows than I the value of his own body; no one, probably, except myself, ever having had it stolen from him.

Incoherently I at first talked of the dwarf and his crimes, and reproached Juliet for her too easy admission of his love. She thought me raving, as well she might, and yet it was some time before I could prevail on myself to admit that the Guido whose penitence had won her back for me was myself; and while I cursed bitterly the monstrous dwarf, and blest the well-directed blow that had deprived him of life, I suddenly checked myself when I heard her say—Amen! knowing that him whom she reviled was my very self. A little reflection taught me silence—a little practice enabled me to speak of that frightful night without any very excessive blunder. The wound I had given myself was no mockery of one—it was long before I recovered—and as the benevolent and generous Torella sat beside me, talking such wisdom as might win friends to repentance, and mine own dear Juliet hovered near me, administering to my wants, and cheering me by her smiles, the work of my bodily cure and mental reform went on together. I have never, indeed, wholly recovered my strength— my cheek is paler since—my person a little bent. Juliet sometimes ventures to allude bitterly to the malice that caused this change, but I kiss her on the moment, and tell her all is for the best. I am a fonder and more faithful husband—and true is this—but for that wound, never had I called her mine.

I did not revisit the sea-shore, nor seek for the fiend's treasure; yet, while I ponder on the past, I often think, and my confessor was not backward in favouring the idea, that it might be a good rather than an evil spirit, sent by my guardian angel, to show me the folly and misery of pride. So well at least did I learn this lesson, roughly taught as I was, that I am known now by all my friends and fellow-citizens by the name of Guido il Cortese.

The Dream[1]

Chi dice mal d'amore
Dice una falsità!
Italian Song[2]

The time of the occurrence of the little legend about to be narrated, was that of the commencement of the reign of Henry IV.[3] of France, whose accession and conversion, while they brought peace to the kingdom whose throne he ascended, were inadequate to heal the deep wounds mutually inflicted by the inimical parties. Private feuds, and the memory of mortal injuries, existed between those now apparently united; and often did the hands that had clasped each other in seeming friendly greeting, involuntarily, as the grasp was released, clasp the dagger's hilt, as fitter spokesman to their passions than the words of courtesy that had just fallen from their lips. Many of the fiercer Catholics retreated to their distant provinces; and while they concealed in solitude their rankling discontent, not less keenly did they long for the day when they might show it openly.

In a large and fortified chateau built on a rugged steep overlooking the Loire, not far from the town of Nantes, dwelt the last of her race and the heiress of their fortunes, the young and beautiful Countess de Villeneuve. She had spent the preceding year in complete solitude in her secluded abode; and the mourning she wore for a father and two brothers, the victims of the civil wars, was a graceful and good reason why she did not appear at court, and mingle with its festivities. But the orphan countess inherited a high name and broad lands; and it was soon signified to her that the king, her guardian, desired that she should bestow them, together with her hand, upon some noble whose birth and accomplishments should entitle him to the gift. Constance, in reply, expressed her intention of

---

1. Reprinted from *Tales and Stories*, pp. 153–65, where text is based on *The Keepsake for MDCCCXXXII*, ed. Frederic Mansel Reynolds (London: Longman, Rees, Orme, Brown, and Green [1831]), pp. 22–38.

2. "Whoever speaks badly about love / Utters a falsehood!"

3. Henry IV (1553–1610), King of France who was raised a Protestant, who acceded to the throne in 1589, and who converted to Catholicism in 1593.

CONSTANCE
Painted by Miss Louisa Sharpe · Engraved by Charles Heath
(Plate from *The Keepsake for MDCCCXXXII*.)

taking vows, and retiring to a convent. The king earnestly and resolutely forbade this act, believing such an idea to be the result of sensibility overwrought by sorrow, and relying on the hope that, after a time, the genial spirit of youth would break through this cloud.

A year passed, and still the countess persisted; and at last Henry, unwilling to exercise compulsion—desirous, too, of judging for himself of the motives that led one so beautiful, young, and gifted with fortune's favours, to desire to bury herself in a cloister—announced his intention, now that the period of her mourning was expired, of visiting her chateau; and if he brought not with him, the monarch said, inducement sufficient to change her design, he would yield his consent to its fulfillment.

Many a sad hour had Constance passed—many a day of tears, and many a night of restless misery. She had closed her gates against every visitant; and, like the Lady Olivia in "Twelfth Night," vowed herself to loneliness and weeping. Mistress of herself, she easily silenced the entreaties and remonstrances of underlings, and nursed her grief as it had been the thing she loved. Yet it was too keen, too bitter, too burning, to be a favoured guest. In fact, Constance, young, ardent, and vivacious, battled with it, struggled, and longed to cast it off; but all that was joyful in itself, or fair in outward show, only served to renew it; and she could best support the burthen of her sorrow with patience, when, yielding to it, it oppressed but did not torture her.

Constance had left the castle to wander in the neighbouring grounds. Lofty and extensive as were the apartments of her abode, she felt pent up within their walls, beneath their fretted roofs. The clear sky, the spreading uplands, the antique wood, associated to her with every dear recollection of her past life, enticed her to spend hours and days beneath their leafy coverts. The motion and change eternally working, as the wind stirred among the boughs, or the journeying sun rained its beams through them, soothed and called her out of that dull sorrow which clutched her heart with so unrelenting a pang beneath her castle roof.

There was one spot on the verge of the well-wooded park, one nook of ground, whence she could discern the country extended beyond, yet which was in itself thick set with tall umbrageous trees—a spot which she had forsworn, yet whither unconsciously her steps for ever tended, and where now again, for the twentieth time that day, she had unaware found herself. She sat upon a grassy mound, and looked wistfully on the flowers she had herself planted to adorn the verdurous recess—to her the temple of memory and love. She held the letter from the king which was the parent to her of so much despair. Dejection sat upon her features, and her gentle heart asked fate why, so young, unprotected, and forsaken, she should have to struggle with this new form of wretchedness.

"I but ask," she thought, "to live in my father's halls—in the spot familiar to my infancy—to water with my frequent tears the graves of those I loved; and here in these woods, where such a mad dream of happiness was mine, to celebrate for ever the obsequies of Hope!"

A rustling among the boughs now met her ear—her heart beat quick—all again was still. "Foolish girl!" she half muttered: "dupe of thine own passionate fancy: because here we met; because seated here I have expected, and sounds like these have announced, his dear approach; so now every coney as it stirs, and every bird as it awakens silence, speaks of him. O Gaspar!—mine once—never again will this beloved spot be made glad by thee—never more!"

Again the bushes were stirred, and footsteps were heard in the brake. She rose; her heart beat high: it must be that silly Manon, with her impertinent entreaties for her to return. But the steps were firmer and slower than would be those of her waiting-woman; and now emerging from the shade, she too plainly discerned the intruder. Her first impulse was to fly:—but once again to see him—to hear his voice:—once again before she placed eternal vows between them, to stand together, and find the wide chasm filled which absence had made, could not injure the dead, and would soften the fatal sorrow that made her cheek so pale.

And now he was before her the same beloved one with whom she had exchanged vows of constancy. He, like her, seemed sad, nor could she resist the imploring glance that entreated her for one moment to remain.

"I come, lady," said the young knight, "without a hope to bend your inflexible will. I come but once again to see you, and to bid you farewell before I depart for the Holy Land. I come to beseech you not to immure yourself in the dark cloister to avoid one as hateful as myself:—one you will never see more. Whether I die or live in Palestine, France and I are parted for ever!"

"Palestine!" said Constance; "that were fearful, were it true; but King Henry will never so lose his favourite cavalier. The throne you helped to build, you still will guard. Nay, as I ever had power over thought of thine, go not to Palestine."

"One word of yours could detain me—one smile—Constance——" and the youthful lover knelt before her; but her harsher purpose was recalled by the image once so dear and familiar, now so strange and so forbidden.

"Linger no longer here!" she cried. "No smile, no word of mine will ever again be yours. Why are you here—here, where the spirits of the dead wander, and, claiming these shades as their own, curse the false girl who permits their murderer to disturb their sacred repose?"

"When love was young and you were kind," replied the knight, "you taught me to thread the intricacies of these woods—you welcomed me to this dear spot, where once you vowed to be my own—even beneath these ancient trees."

"A wicked sin it was," said Constance, "to unbar my father's doors to the son of his enemy, and dearly is it punished!"

The young knight gained courage as she spoke; yet he dared not move, lest she, who, every instant, appeared ready to take flight, should be startled from her momentary tranquillity; but he slowly replied:—"Those were happy days, Constance, full of terror and deep joy, when evening brought me to your feet; and while hate and vengeance were as its atmosphere to yonder frowning castle, this leafy, star-lit bower was the shrine of love."

"*Happy?*—miserable days!" echoed Constance; "when I imagined good could arise from failing in my duty, and that disobedience would be rewarded of God. Speak not of love, Gaspar!—a sea of blood divides us for ever! Approach me not! The dead and the beloved stand even now between us: their pale shadows warn me of my fault, and menace me for listening to their murderer."

"That am not I!" exclaimed the youth. "Behold, Constance, we are each the last of our race. Death has dealt cruelly with us, and we are alone. It was not so when first we loved—when parent, kinsman, brother, nay, my own mother breathed curses on the house of Villeneuve; and in spite of all I bless'd it. I saw thee, my lovely one, and bless'd it. The God of peace planted love in our hearts, and with mystery and secrecy we met during many a summer night in the moon-lit dells; and when daylight was abroad, in this sweet recess we fled to avoid its scrutiny, and here, even here, where now I kneel in supplication, we both knelt and made our vows.—Shall they be broken?"

Constance wept as her lover recalled the images of happy hours. "Never," she exclaimed, "O never! Thou knowest, or wilt soon know, Gaspar, the faith and resolves of one who dare not be yours. Was it for us to talk of love and happiness, when war, and hate, and blood were raging around? The fleeting flowers our young hands strewed were trampled by the deadly encounter of mortal foes. By your father's hand mine died; and little boots it to know whether, as my brother swore, and you deny, your hand did or did not deal the blow that destroyed him. You fought among those by whom he died. Say no more—no other word: it is impiety towards the unreposing dead to hear you. Go, Gaspar; forget me. Under the chivalrous and gallant Henry your career may be glorious; and many a fair girl will listen, as once I did, to your vows, and be made happy by them. Farewell! May the Virgin bless you! In my cell and cloister-home I will not forget the best Christian lesson—to pray for our enemies. Gaspar, farewell!"

She glided hastily from the bower: with swift steps she threaded the glade and sought the castle. Once within the seclusion of her own apartment she gave way to the burst of grief that tore her gentle bosom like a tempest; for hers was that worst sorrow which taints past joys, making remorse wait upon the memory of bliss, and linking love and fancied guilt in such fearful society as that of the tyrant when he bound a living body to a corpse. Suddenly a thought darted into her mind. At first she rejected it as puerile and superstitious; but it would not be driven away. She called hastily for her attendant. "Manon," she said, "didst thou ever sleep on St. Catherine's couch?"

Manon crossed herself. "Heaven forefend! None ever did, since I was born, but two: one fell into the Loire and was drowned; the other only looked upon the narrow bed, and returned to her own home without a word. It is an awful place; and if the votary have not led a pious and good life, woe betide the hour when she rests her head on the holy stone!"

Constance crossed herself also. "As for our lives, it is only through our Lord and the blessed saints that we can any of us hope for righteousness. I will sleep on that couch to-morrow night!"

"Dear, my lady! and the king arrives to-morrow."

"The more need that I resolve. It cannot be that misery so intense should dwell in any heart, and no cure be found. I had hoped to be the bringer of peace to our houses; and is the good work to be for me a crown of thorns? Heaven shall direct me. I will rest to-morrow night on St. Catherine's bed: and if, as I have heard, the saint deigns to direct her votaries in dreams, I will be guided by her; and believing that I act according to the dictates of Heaven, I shall feel resigned even to the worst."

The king was on his way to Nantes from Paris, and he slept on this night at a castle but a few miles distant. Before dawn a young cavalier was introduced into his chamber. The knight had a serious, nay, a sad aspect; and all beautiful as he was in feature and limb, looked way-worn and haggard. He stood silent in Henry's presence, who, alert and gay, turned his lively blue eyes upon his guest, saying gently, "So thou foundest her obdurate, Gaspar?"

"I found her resolved on our mutual misery. Alas! my liege, it is not, credit me, the least of my grief, that Constance sacrifices her own happiness when she destroys mine."

"And thou believest that she will say nay to the gaillard chevalier whom we ourselves present to her?"

"Oh! my liege, think not that thought! it cannot be. My heart deeply, most deeply, thanks you for your generous condescension. But she whom her lover's voice in solitude—whose entreaties, when memory and seclusion aided the spell—could not persuade, will resist even your majesty's commands. She is bent upon entering a cloister; and I, so please you, will now take my leave:—I am henceforth a soldier of the cross, and will die in Palestine."

"Gaspar," said the monarch, "I know woman better than thou. It is not by submission nor tearful plaints she is to be won. The death of her relatives naturally sits heavy at the young countess' heart; and nourishing in solitude her regret and her repentance, she fancies that Heaven itself forbids your union. Let the voice of the world reach her—the voice of earthly power and earthly kindness—the one commanding, the other pleading, and both finding response in her own heart—and by my fay and the Holy Cross, she will be yours. Let our plan still hold. And now to horse: the morning wears, and the sun is risen."

The king arrived at the bishop's palace, and proceeded forthwith to mass in the cathedral. A sumptuous dinner succeeded, and it was afternoon before the monarch proceeded through the town beside the Loire to where, a little above Nantes, the Chateau Villeneuve was situated. The young countess received him at the gate. Henry looked in vain for the cheek blanched by misery, the aspect of downcast despair which he had been taught to expect. Her cheek was flushed, her manner animated, her voice scarce tremulous. "She loves him not," thought Henry, "or already her heart has consented."

A collation was prepared for the monarch; and after some little hesitation, arising even from the cheerfulness of her mien, he mentioned the name of Gaspar. Constance blushed instead of turning pale, and replied very quickly, "To-morrow, good my liege; I ask for a respite but until to-morrow;—all will then be decided;—to-morrow I am vowed to God—or—"

She looked confused, and the king, at once surprised and pleased, said, "Then you hate not young De Vaudemont;—you forgive him for the inimical blood that warms his veins."

"We are taught that we should forgive, that we should love our enemies," the countess replied with some trepidation.

"Now by Saint Denis that is a right welcome answer for the nonce," said the king, laughing. "What ho! my faithful serving-man, Dan Apollo in disguise! come forward, and thank your lady for her love."

In such disguise as had concealed him from all, the cavalier had hung behind, and viewed with infinite surprise the demeanour and calm countenance of the lady. He could not hear her words: but was this even she whom he had seen trembling and weeping the evening before?—this she whose very heart was torn by conflicting passion?—who saw the pale ghosts of parent and kinsman stand between her and the lover whom more than her life she adored? It was a riddle hard to solve. The king's call was in unison with his impatience, and he sprang forward. He was at her feet; while she, still passion-driven, overwrought by the very calmness she had assumed, uttered one cry as she recognised him, and sank senseless on the floor.

All this was very unintelligible. Even when her attendants had brought her to life, another fit succeeded, and then passionate floods of tears; while the monarch, waiting in the hall, eyeing the half-eaten collation, and humming some romance in commemoration of woman's waywardness, knew not how to reply to Vaudemont's look of bitter disappointment and anxiety. At length the countess' chief attendant came with an apology: "her lady was ill, very ill. The next day she would throw herself at the king's feet, at once to solicit his excuse, and to disclose her purpose."

"To-morrow—again to-morrow!—Does to-morrow bear some charm, maiden?" said the king. "Can you read us the riddle, pretty one? What strange tale belongs to to-morrow, that all rests on its advent?"

Manon coloured, looked down, and hesitated. But Henry was no tyro in the art of enticing ladies' attendants to disclose their ladies' counsel. Manon was besides frightened by the countess' scheme, on which she was still obstinately bent, so she was the more readily induced to betray it. To sleep in St. Catherine's bed, to rest on a narrow ledge overhanging the deep rapid Loire, and if, as was most probable, the luckless dreamer escaped from falling into it, to take the disturbed visions that such uneasy slumber might produce for the dictate of Heaven, was a madness of which even Henry himself could scarcely deem any woman capable. But could Constance, her whose beauty was so highly intellectual, and whom he had heard perpetually praised for her strength of mind and talents, could *she* be so strangely infatuated! And can passion play such freaks with us?—like death, levelling even the aristocracy of the soul, and bringing noble and peasant, the wise and foolish, under one thraldom? It was strange—yet she must have her way. That she hesitated in her decision was much; and it was to be hoped that St. Catherine would play no ill-natured part. Should it be otherwise, a purpose to be swayed by a dream might be influenced by other waking thoughts. To the more material kind of danger some safeguard should be brought.

There is no feeling more awful than that which invades a weak human heart bent upon gratifying its ungovernable impulses in contradiction to the dictates of conscience. Forbidden pleasures are said to be the most agreeable:—it may be so to rude natures, to those who love to struggle, combat, and contend; who find happiness in a fray, and joy in the conflict of passion. But softer and sweeter was the gentle spirit of Constance; and love and duty contending crushed and tortured her poor heart. To commit her conduct to the inspirations of religion, or, if it was so to be named, of superstition, was a blessed relief. The very perils that threatened her undertaking gave a zest to it;—to dare for his sake was happiness;—the very difficulty of the way that led to the completion of her wishes, at once gratified her love and distracted her thoughts from her despair. Or if it was decreed that she must sacrifice all, the risk of danger and of death were of trifling import in comparison with the anguish which would then be her portion for ever.

The night threatened to be stormy—the raging wind shook the casements—and the trees waved their huge shadowy arms, as giants might in fantastic dance and mortal broil. Constance and Manon, unattended, quitted the chateau by a postern, and began to descend the hill side. The moon had not yet risen; and though the way was familiar to both, Manon tottered and trembled; while the countess, drawing her silken cloak round her, walked with a firm step down the steep. They came to the river's side, where a small boat was moored, and one man was in waiting. Constance stepped lightly in, and then aided her fearful companion. In a few moments they were in the middle of the stream. The warm, tempestuous, animating, equinoctial wind swept over them. For the first time since her mourning, a thrill of pleasure swelled the bosom of Constance. She hailed the emotion with double joy. It cannot be, she thought, that Heaven will forbid me to love one so brave, so generous, and so good as the noble Gaspar. Another I can never love; I shall die if divided from him: and this heart, these limbs, so alive with glowing sensation, are they already predestined to an early grave? Oh, no! life speaks aloud within them. I shall live to love. Do not all things love?—the winds as they whisper to the rushing waters? the waters as they kiss the flowery banks, and speed to mingle with the sea? Heaven and earth are sustained by, live through, love; and shall Constance alone, whose heart has ever been a deep, gushing, overflowing well of true affection, be compelled to set a stone upon the fount to lock it up for ever?

These thoughts bid fair for pleasant dreams; and perhaps the countess, an adept in the blind god's lore, therefore indulged them the more readily. But as thus she was engrossed by soft emotions, Manon caught her arm:—"Lady, look," she cried; "it comes—yet the oars have no sound. Now the Virgin shield us! Would we were at home!"

A dark boat glided by them. Four rowers, habited in black cloaks, pulled at oars which, as Manon said, gave no sound; another sat at the helm: like the rest, his person was veiled in a dark mantle, but he wore no cap; and though his face was turned from them, Constance recognised her lover. "Gaspar," she cried aloud, "dost thou live?"—but the figure in the boat neither turned its head nor replied, and quickly it was lost in the shadowy waters.

How changed now was the fair countess' reverie! Already Heaven had begun its spell, and unearthly forms were around, as she strained her eyes through the gloom. Now she saw and now she lost view of the bark that occasioned her terror; and now it seemed that another was there, which held the spirits of the dead; and her father waved to her from shore, and her brothers frowned on her.

Meanwhile they neared the landing. Her bark was moored in a little cove, and Constance stood upon the bank. Now she trembled, and half yielded to Manon's entreaty to return; till the unwise *suivante*[4] mentioned the king's and De Vaudemont's name, and spoke of the answer to be given to-morrow. What answer, if she turned back from her intent?

She now hurried forward up the broken ground of the bank, and then along its edge, till they came to a hill which abruptly hung over the tide. A small chapel stood near. With trembling fingers the countess drew forth the key and unlocked its door. They entered. It was dark—save that a little lamp, flickering in the wind, showed an uncertain light from before the figure of Saint Catherine. The two women knelt; they prayed; and then rising, with a cheerful accent the countess bade her attendant good night. She unlocked a little low iron door. It opened on a narrow cavern. The roar of waters was heard beyond. "Thou mayest not follow, my poor Manon," said Constance,—"nor dost thou much desire:—this adventure is for me alone."

It was hardly fair to leave the trembling servant in the chapel alone, who had neither hope nor fear, nor love nor grief, to beguile her; but, in those days, esquires and waiting-women often played the part of subalterns in the army, gaining knocks and no fame. Besides, Manon was safe in holy ground. The countess meanwhile pursued her way groping in the dark through the narrow tortuous passage. At length what seemed light to her long-darkened sense gleamed on her. She reached an open cavern in the overhanging hill's side, looking over the rushing tide beneath. She looked out upon the night. The waters of the Loire were speeding, as since that day have they ever sped—changeful, yet the same; the heavens were thickly veiled with clouds, and the wind in the trees was as mournful and ill-omened as if it rushed round a murderer's tomb. Constance shuddered a little, and looked upon her bed—a narrow ledge of earth and a moss-grown stone bordering on the very verge of the precipice. She doffed her mantle—such was one of the conditions of the spell;—she bowed her head, and loosened the tresses of her dark hair—

4. "Waiting-maid."

she bared her feet—and thus, fully prepared for suffering to the utmost the chill influence of the cold night, she stretched herself on the narrow couch that scarce afforded room for her repose, and whence, if she moved in sleep, she must be precipitated into the cold waters below.

At first it seemed to her as if she never should sleep again. No great wonder that exposure to the blast and her perilous position should forbid her eyelids to close. At length she fell into a reverie so soft and soothing that she wished even to watch—and then by degrees her senses became confused—and now she was on St. Catherine's bed—the Loire rushing beneath, and the wild wind sweeping by—and now—O whither?—and what dreams did the saint send, to drive her to despair, or to bid her be blest for ever?

Beneath the rugged hill, upon the dark tide, another watched, who feared a thousand things, and scarce dared hope. He had meant to precede the lady on her way, but when he found that he had outstaid his time, with muffled oars and breathless haste he had shot by the bark that contained his Constance, nor even turned at her voice, fearful to incur her blame, and her commands to return. He had seen her emerge from the passage, and shuddered as she leant over the cliff. He saw her step forth, clad as she was in white, and could mark her as she lay on the ledge beetling above. What a vigil did the lovers keep!—she given up to visionary thoughts, he knowing—and the consciousness thrilled his bosom with strange emotion—that love, and love for him, had led her to that perilous couch; and that while dangers surrounded her in every shape, she was alive only to the small still voice that whispered to her heart the dream which was to decide their destinies. She slept perhaps—but he waked and watched; and night wore away, as, now praying, now entranced by alternating hope and fear, he sat in his boat, his eyes fixed on the white garb of the slumberer above.

Morning—was it morning that struggled in the clouds? Would morning ever come to waken her? And had she slept? and what dreams of weal or woe had peopled her sleep? Gaspar grew impatient. He commanded his boatmen still to wait, and he sprang forward, intent on clambering the precipice. In vain they urged the danger, nay, the impossibility of the attempt; he clung to the rugged face of the hill, and found footing where it would seem no footing was. The acclivity, indeed, was not high; the dangers of St. Catherine's bed arising from the likelihood that any one who slept on so narrow a couch would be precipitated into the waters beneath. Up the steep ascent Gaspar continued to toil, and at last reached the roots of a tree that grew near the summit. Aided by its branches, he made good his stand at the very extremity of the ledge, near the pillow on which lay the uncovered head of his beloved. Her hands were folded on her bosom; her dark hair fell round her throat and pillowed her cheek; her face was serene: sleep was there in all its innocence and in all its helplessness; every wilder emotion was hushed, and her bosom heaved in regular breathing. He could see her heart beat as it lifted her fair hands crossed above. No statue hewn of marble in monumental effigy was ever half so fair; and within that surpassing form dwelt a soul true, tender, self-devoted, and affectionate as ever warmed a human breast.

With what deep passion did Gaspar gaze, gathering hope from the placidity of her angel countenance! A smile wreathed her lips; and he too involuntarily smiled, as he hailed the happy omen; when suddenly her cheek was flushed, her bosom heaved, a tear stole from her dark lashes, and then a whole shower fell, as starting up she cried, "No!—he shall not die!—I will unloose his chains!—I will save him!" Gaspar's hand was there. He caught her light form ready to fall from the perilous couch. She opened her eyes and beheld her lover, who had watched over her dream of fate, and who had saved her.

Manon also had slept well, dreaming or not, and was startled in the morning to find that she waked surrounded by a crowd. The little desolate chapel was hung with tapestry—the altar adorned with golden chalices—the priest was chanting mass to a goodly array of kneeling knights. Manon saw that King Henry was there; and she looked for another whom she found not, when the iron door of the cavern passage opened, and Gaspar de Vaudemont entered from it, leading the fair form of Constance; who, in her white robes and dark dishevelled hair, with a face in which smiles and blushes contended with deeper emotion, approached the altar, and kneeling with her lover, pronounced the vows that united them for ever.

It was long before the happy Gaspar could win from his lady the secret of her dream. In spite of the happiness she now enjoyed, she had suffered too much not to look back even with terror to those days when she thought love a crime, and every event connected with them wore an awful aspect. Many a vision, she said, she had that fearful night. She had seen the spirits of her father and brothers in Paradise; she had beheld Gaspar victoriously combating among the infidels; she had beheld him in King Henry's court, favoured and beloved, and she herself—now pining in a cloister, now a bride—now grateful to Heaven for the full measure of bliss presented to her, now weeping away her sad days—till suddenly she thought herself in Paynim land; and the saint herself, Saint Catherine, guiding her unseen through the city of the infidels. She entered a palace and beheld the miscreants rejoicing in victory; and then descending to the dungeons beneath, they groped their way through damp vaults, and low mildewed passages, to one cell, darker and more frightful than the rest. On the floor lay one with soiled and tattered garments, with unkempt locks and wild matted beard. His cheek was worn and thin; his eyes had lost their fire; his form was a mere skeleton; the chains hung loosely on the fleshless bones.

"And was it my appearance in that attractive state and winning costume that softened the hard heart of Constance?" asked Gaspar, smiling at this painting of what would never be.

"Even so," replied Constance; "for my heart whispered me that this was my doing: and who could recall the life that waned in your pulses—who restore, save the destroyer? My heart never warmed to my living happy knight as then it did to his wasted image, as it lay, in the visions of night, at my feet. A veil fell from my eyes; a darkness was dispelled from before me. Methought I then knew for the first time what life and what death was. I was bid believe that to make the living happy was not to injure the dead; and I felt how wicked and how vain was that false philosophy which placed virtue and good in hatred and unkindness. You should not die: I would loosen your chains and save you, and bid you live for love. I sprung forward, and the death I deprecated for you would, in my presumption, have been mine—then, when first I felt the real value of life—but that your arm was there to save me, your dear voice to bid me be blest for evermore."

The Mortal Immortal
A Tale[1]

July 16, 1833.—This is a memorable anniversary for me; on it I complete my three hundred and twenty-third year!

The Wandering Jew?—certainly not. More than eighteen centuries have passed over his head. In comparison with him, I am a very young Immortal.

Am I, then, immortal? This is a question which I have asked myself, by day and night, for now three hundred and three years, and yet cannot answer it. I detected a gray hair amidst my brown locks this very day—that surely signifies decay. Yet it may have remained concealed there for three hundred years—for some persons have become entirely white-headed before twenty years of age.

I will tell my story, and my reader shall judge for me. I will tell my story, and so contrive to pass some few hours of a long eternity, become so wearisome to me. For ever! Can it be? to live for ever! I have heard of enchantments, in which the victims were plunged into a deep sleep, to wake, after a hundred years, as fresh as ever: I have heard of the Seven Sleepers—thus to be immortal would not be so burthensome: but, oh! the weight of never-ending time—the tedious passage of the still-succeeding hours! How happy was the fabled Nourjahad!——But to my task.

All the world has heard of Cornelius Agrippa. His memory is as immortal as his arts have made me. All the world has also heard of his scholar, who, unawares, raised the foul fiend during his master's absence, and was destroyed by him. The report, true or false, of this accident, was attended with many inconveniences to the renowned philosopher. All his scholars at once deserted him—his servants disappeared. He had no one

1. Reprinted from *Tales and Stories*, pp. 219-30, where text is based on *The Keepsake for MDCCCXXXIV*, ed. Frederic Mansel Reynolds (London: Longman, Rees, Orme, Brown, Green, and Longman [1833]), pp. 71-87.

near him to put coals on his ever-burning fires while he slept, or to attend to the changeful colours of his medicines while he studied. Experiment after experiment failed, because one pair of hands was insufficient to complete them: the dark spirits laughed at him for not being able to retain a single mortal in his service.

I was then very young—very poor—and very much in love. I had been for about a year the pupil of Cornelius, though I was absent when this accident took place. On my return, my friends implored me not to return to the alchymist's abode. I trembled as I listened to the dire tale they told; I required no second warning; and when Cornelius came and offered me a purse of gold if I would remain under his roof, I felt as if Satan himself tempted me. My teeth chattered—my hair stood on end:—I ran off as fast as my trembling knees would permit.

My failing steps were directed whither for two years they had every evening been attracted,—a gently bubbling spring of pure living waters, beside which lingered a dark-haired girl, whose beaming eyes were fixed on the path I was accustomed each night to tread. I cannot remember the hour when I did not love Bertha; we had been neighbours and playmates from infancy—her parents, like mine, were of humble life, yet respectable—our attachment had been a source of pleasure to them. In an evil hour, a malignant fever carried off both her father and mother, and Bertha became an orphan. She would have found a home beneath my paternal roof, but, unfortunately, the old lady of the near castle, rich, childless, and solitary, declared her intention to adopt her. Henceforth Bertha was clad in silk—inhabited a marble palace—and was looked on as being highly favoured by fortune. But in her new situation among her new associates, Bertha remained true to the friend of her humbler days; she often visited the cottage of my father, and when forbidden to go thither, she would stray towards the neighbouring wood, and meet me beside its shady fountain.

She often declared that she owed no duty to her new protectress equal in sanctity to that which bound us. Yet still I was too poor to marry, and she grew weary of being tormented on my account. She had a haughty but an impatient spirit, and grew angry at the obstacles that prevented our union. We met now after an absence, and she had been sorely beset while I was away; she complained bitterly, and almost reproached me for being poor. I replied hastily,—

"I am honest, if I am poor!—were I not, I might soon become rich!"

This exclamation produced a thousand questions. I feared to shock her by owning the truth, but she drew it from me; and then, casting a look of disdain on me, she said—

"You pretend to love, and you fear to face the Devil for my sake!"

I protested that I had only dreaded to offend her;—while she dwelt on the magnitude of the reward that I should receive. Thus encouraged—shamed by her—led on by love and hope, laughing at my late fears, with quick steps and a light heart, I returned to accept the offers of the alchymist, and was instantly installed in my office.

A year passed away. I became possessed of no insignificant sum of money. Custom had banished my fears. In spite of the most painful vigilance, I had never detected the trace of a cloven foot; nor was the studious silence of our abode ever disturbed by demoniac howls. I still continued my stolen interviews with Bertha, and Hope dawned on me—Hope—but not perfect joy; for Bertha fancied that love and security were enemies, and her pleasure was to divide them in my bosom. Though true of heart, she was somewhat of a coquette in manner; and I was jealous as a Turk. She slighted me in a thousand ways, yet would never acknowledge herself to be in the wrong. She would drive me mad with anger, and then force me to beg her pardon. Sometimes she fancied that I was not sufficiently submissive, and then she had some story of a rival, favoured by her protectress. She was surrounded by silk-clad youths—the rich and gay——What chance had the sad-robed scholar of Cornelius compared with these?

On one occasion, the philosopher made such large demands upon my time, that I was unable to meet her as I was wont. He was engaged in some mighty work, and I was forced to remain, day and night, feeding his furnaces and watching his chemical preparations. Bertha waited for me in vain at the fountain. Her haughty spirit fired at this neglect; and when at last I stole out during the few short minutes allotted to me for slumber, and hoped to be consoled by her, she received me with disdain, dismissed me in scorn, and vowed that any man should possess her hand rather than he who could not be in two places at once for her sake. She would be revenged!—And truly she was. In my dingy retreat I heard that she had been hunting, attended by Albert Hoffer. Albert Hoffer was favoured by her protectress, and the three passed in cavalcade before my smoky window. Methought that they mentioned my name—it was followed by a laugh of derision, as her dark eyes glanced contemptuously towards my abode.

Jealousy, with all its venom, and all its misery, entered my breast. Now I shed a torrent of tears, to think that I should never call her mine; and, anon, I imprecated a thousand curses on her inconstancy. Yet, still I must stir the fires of the alchymist, still attend on the changes of his unintelligible medicines.

Cornelius had watched for three days and nights, nor closed his eyes. The progress of his alembics was slower than he expected: in spite of his anxiety, sleep weighed upon his eyelids. Again and again he threw off drowsiness with more than human energy; again and again it stole away his senses. He eyed his crucibles wistfully. "Not ready yet," he murmured; "will another night pass before the work is accomplished? Winzy, you are vigilant—you are faithful—you have slept, my boy—you slept last night. Look at that glass vessel. The liquid it contains is of a soft rose-colour: the moment it begins to change its hue, awaken me—till then I may close my eyes. First, it will turn white, and then emit golden flashes; but wait not till then; when the rose-colour fades, rouse me." I scarcely heard the last words, muttered, as they were, in sleep. Even then he did not quite yield to nature. "Winzy, my boy," he again said, "do not touch the vessel—do not put it to your lips; it is a philter—a philter to cure love; you would not cease to love your Bertha—beware to drink!"

And he slept. His venerable head sunk on his breast, and I scarce heard his regular breathing. For a few minutes I watched the vessel—the rosy hue of the liquid remained unchanged. Then my thoughts wandered—they visited the fountain, and dwelt on a thousand charming scenes never to be renewed—never! Serpents and adders were in my heart as the word "Never!" half formed itself on my lips. False girl!—false and cruel! Never more would she smile on me as that evening she smiled on Albert. Worthless, detested woman! I would not remain unrevenged—she should see Albert expire at her feet—she should die beneath my vengeance. She had smiled in disdain and triumph—she knew my wretchedness and her power. Yet what power had she?—the power of exciting my hate—my utter scorn—my—oh, all but indifference! Could I attain that—could I regard her with careless eyes, transferring my rejected love to one fairer and more true, that were indeed a victory!

A bright flash darted before my eyes. I had forgotten the medicine of the adept; I gazed on it with wonder: flashes of admirable beauty, more bright than those which the diamond emits when the sun's rays are on it, glanced from the surface of the liquid; an odour the most fragrant and grateful stole over my sense; the vessel seemed one globe of living radiance, lovely to the eye, and most inviting to the taste. The first thought, instinctively inspired by the grosser sense, was, I will—I must drink. I raised the vessel to my lips. "It will cure me of love—of torture!" Already I had quaffed half of the most delicious liquor ever tasted by the palate of man, when the philosopher stirred. I started—I dropped the glass—the fluid flamed and glanced along the floor, while I felt Cornelius's gripe at my throat, as he shrieked aloud, "Wretch! you have destroyed the labour of my life!"

The philosopher was totally unaware that I had drunk any portion of his drug. His idea was, and I gave a tacit assent to it, that I had raised the

BERTHA

Painted by Henry P. Briggs · Engraved by Frederick Bacon

(Plate from *The Keepsake for MDCCCXXXIV.*)

vessel from curiosity, and that, frighted at its brightness, and the flashes of intense light it gave forth, I had let it fall. I never undeceived him. The fire of the medicine was quenched—the fragrance died away—he grew calm, as a philosopher should under the heaviest trials, and dismissed me to rest.

I will not attempt to describe the sleep of glory and bliss which bathed my soul in paradise during the remaining hours of that memorable night. Words would be faint and shallow types of my enjoyment, or of the gladness that possessed my bosom when I woke. I trod air—my thoughts were in heaven. Earth appeared heaven, and my inheritance upon it was to be one trance of delight. "This it is to be cured of love," I thought; "I will see Bertha this day, and she will find her lover cold and regardless; too happy to be disdainful, yet how utterly indifferent to her!"

The hours danced away. The philosopher, secure that he had once succeeded, and believing that he might again, began to concoct the same medicine once more. He was shut up with his books and drugs, and I had a holiday. I dressed myself with care; I looked in an old but polished shield, which served me for a mirror; methought my good looks had wonderfully improved. I hurried beyond the precincts of the town, joy in my soul, the beauty of heaven and earth around me. I turned my steps towards the castle—I could look on its lofty turrets with lightness of heart, for I was cured of love. My Bertha saw me afar off, as I came up the avenue. I know not what sudden impulse animated her bosom, but at the sight, she sprung with a light fawn-like bound down the marble steps, and was hastening towards me. But I had been perceived by another person. The old high-born hag, who called herself her protectress, and was her tyrant, had seen me, also; she hobbled, panting, up the terrace; a page, as ugly as herself, held up her train, and fanned her as she hurried along, and stopped my fair girl with a "How, now, my bold mistress? whither so fast? Back to your cage—hawks are abroad!"

Bertha clasped her hands—her eyes were still bent on my approaching figure. I saw the contest. How I abhorred the old crone who checked the kind impulses of my Bertha's softening heart. Hitherto, respect for her rank had caused me to avoid the lady of the castle; now I disdained such trivial considerations. I was cured of love, and lifted above all human fears; I hastened forwards, and soon reached the terrace. How lovely Bertha looked! her eyes flashing fire, her cheeks glowing with impatience and anger, she was a thousand times more graceful and charming than ever—I no longer loved—Oh! no, I adored—worshipped—idolized her!

She had that morning been persecuted, with more than usual vehemence, to consent to an immediate marriage with my rival. She was reproached with the encouragement that she had shown him—she was threatened with being turned out of doors with disgrace and shame. Her proud spirit rose in arms at the threat; but when she remembered the scorn that she had heaped upon me, and how, perhaps, she had thus lost one whom she now regarded as her only friend, she wept with remorse and rage. At that moment I appeared. "O, Winzy!" she exclaimed, "take me to your mother's cot; swiftly let me leave the detested luxuries and wretchedness of this noble dwelling—take me to poverty and happiness."

I clasped her in my arms with transport. The old lady was speechless with fury, and broke forth into invective only when we were far on our road to my natal cottage. My mother received the fair fugitive, escaped from a gilt cage to nature and liberty, with tenderness and joy; my father, who loved her, welcomed her heartily; it was a day of rejoicing, which did not need the addition of the celestial potion of the alchymist to steep me in delight.

Soon after this eventful day, I became the husband of Bertha. I ceased to be the scholar of Cornelius, but I continued his friend. I always felt grateful to him for having, unawares, procured me that delicious draught of a divine elixir, which, instead of curing me of love (sad cure! solitary and joyless remedy for evils which seem blessings to the memory), had inspired me with courage and resolution, thus winning for me an inestimable treasure in my Bertha.

I often called to mind that period of trance-like inebriation with wonder. The drink of Cornelius had not fulfilled the task for which he affirmed that it had been prepared, but its effects were more potent and blissful than words can express. They had faded by degrees, yet they lingered long—and painted life in hues of splendour. Bertha often wondered at my lightness of heart and unaccustomed gaiety; for, before, I had been rather serious, or even sad, in my disposition. She loved me the better for my cheerful temper, and our days were winged by joy.

Five years afterwards I was suddenly summoned to the bedside of the dying Cornelius. He had sent for me in haste, conjuring my instant presence. I found him stretched on his pallet, enfeebled even to death; all of life that yet remained animated his piercing eyes, and they were fixed on a glass vessel, full of a roseate liquid.

"Behold," he said, in a broken and inward voice, "the vanity of human wishes! a second time my hopes are about to be crowned, a second time they are destroyed. Look at that liquor—you remember five years ago I had prepared the same, with the same success;—then, as now, my thirsting lips expected to taste the immortal elixir—you dashed it from me! and at present it is too late."

He spoke with difficulty, and fell back on his pillow. I could not help saying,—

"How, revered master, can a cure for love restore you to life?"

A faint smile gleamed across his face as I listened earnestly to his scarcely intelligible answer.

"A cure for love and for all things—the Elixir of Immortality. Ah! if now I might drink, I should live for ever!"

As he spoke, a golden flash gleamed from the fluid; a well-remembered fragrance stole over the air; he raised himself, all weak as he was—strength seemed miraculously to re-enter his frame—he stretched forth his hand—a loud explosion startled me—a ray of fire shot up from the elixir, and the glass vessel which contained it was shivered to atoms! I turned my eyes towards the philosopher; he had fallen back—his eyes were glassy—his features rigid—he was dead!

But I lived, and was to live for ever! So said the unfortunate alchymist, and for a few days I believed his words. I remembered the glorious drunkenness that had followed my stolen draught. I reflected on the change I had felt in my frame—in my soul. The bounding elasticity of the one—the buoyant lightness of the other. I surveyed myself in a mirror, and could perceive no change in my features during the space of the five years which had elapsed. I remembered the radiant hues and grateful scent of that delicious beverage—worthy the gift it was capable of bestowing——I was, then, IMMORTAL!

A few days after I laughed at my credulity. The old proverb, that "a prophet is least regarded in his own country," was true with respect to me and my defunct master. I loved him as a man—I respected him as a sage— but I derided the notion that he could command the powers of darkness, and laughed at the superstitious fears with which he was regarded by the vulgar. He was a wise philosopher, but had no acquaintance with any spirits but those clad in flesh and blood. His science was simply human; and human science, I soon persuaded myself, could never conquer nature's laws so far as to imprison the soul for ever within its carnal habitation. Cornelius had brewed a soul-refreshing drink—more inebriating than wine—sweeter and more fragrant than any fruit: it possessed probably strong medicinal powers, imparting gladness to the heart and vigor to the limbs; but its effects would wear out; already were they diminished in my frame. I was a lucky fellow to have quaffed health and joyous spirits, and perhaps long life, at my master's hands; but my good fortune ended there: longevity was far different from immortality.

I continued to entertain this belief for many years. Sometimes a thought stole across me—Was the alchymist indeed deceived? But my habitual credence was, that I should meet the fate of all the children of Adam at my appointed time—a little late, but still at a natural age. Yet it was certain that I retained a wonderfully youthful look. I was laughed at for my vanity in consulting the mirror so often, but I consulted it in vain—my brow was untrenched—my cheeks—my eyes—my whole person continued as untarnished as in my twentieth year.

I was troubled. I looked at the faded beauty of Bertha—I seemed more like her son. By degrees our neighbours began to make similar observations, and I found at last that I went by the name of the Scholar bewitched. Bertha herself grew uneasy. She became jealous and peevish, and at length she began to question me. We had no children; we were all in all to each other; and though, as she grew older, her vivacious spirit became a little allied to ill-temper, and her beauty sadly diminished, I cherished her in my heart as the mistress I had idolized, the wife I had sought and won with such perfect love.

At last our situation became intolerable: Bertha was fifty—I twenty years of age. I had, in very shame, in some measure adopted the habits of a more advanced age; I no longer mingled in the dance among the young and gay, but my heart bounded along with them while I restrained my feet; and a sorry figure I cut among the Nestors of our village. But before the time I mention, things were altered—we were universally shunned; we were—at least, I was—reported to have kept up an iniquitous acquaintance with some of my former master's supposed friends. Poor Bertha was pitied, but deserted. I was regarded with horror and detestation.

What was to be done? we sat by our winter fire—poverty had made itself felt, for none would buy the produce of my farm; and often I had been forced to journey twenty miles, to some place where I was not known, to dispose of our property. It is true we had saved something for an evil day—that day was come.

We sat by our lone fireside—the old-hearted youth and his antiquated wife. Again Bertha insisted on knowing the truth; she recapitulated all she had ever heard said about me, and added her own observations. She conjured me to cast off the spell; she described how much more comely gray hairs were than my chestnut locks; she descanted on the reverence and respect due to age—how preferable to the slight regard paid to mere children: could I imagine that the despicable gifts of youth and good looks outweighed disgrace, hatred, and scorn? Nay, in the end I should be burnt as a dealer in the black art, while she, to whom I had not deigned to communicate any portion of my good fortune, might be stoned as my accomplice. At length she insinuated that I must share my secret with her, and bestow on her like benefits to those I myself enjoyed, or she would denounce me—and then she burst into tears.

Thus beset, methought it was the best way to tell the truth. I revealed it as tenderly as I could, and spoke only of a *very long life*, not of immortality—which representation, indeed, coincided best with my own ideas. When I ended, I rose and said,

"And now, my Bertha, will you denounce the lover of your youth?— You will not, I know. But it is too hard, my poor wife, that you should suffer from my ill-luck and the accursed arts of Cornelius. I will leave you—you have wealth enough, and friends will return in my absence. I will go; young as I seem, and strong as I am, I can work and gain my bread among strangers, unsuspected and unknown. I loved you in youth; God is my witness that I would not desert you in age, but that your safety and happiness require it."

I took my cap and moved towards the door; in a moment Bertha's arms were round my neck, and her lips were pressed to mine. "No, my husband, my Winzy," she said, "you shall not go alone—take me with you; we will remove from this place, and, as you say, among strangers we shall be unsuspected and safe. I am not so very old as quite to shame you, my Winzy; and I dare say the charm will soon wear off, and, with the blessing of God, you will become more elderly-looking, as is fitting; you shall not leave me."

I returned the good soul's embrace heartily. "I will not, my Bertha; but for your sake I had not thought of such a thing. I will be your true, faithful husband while you are spared to me, and do my duty by you to the last."

The next day we prepared secretly for our emigration. We were obliged to make great pecuniary sacrifices—it could not be helped. We realised a sum sufficient, at least, to maintain us while Bertha lived; and, without saying adieu to any one, quitted our native country to take refuge in a remote part of western France.

It was a cruel thing to transport poor Bertha from her native village, and the friends of her youth, to a new country, new language, new customs. The strange secret of my destiny rendered this removal immaterial to me; but I compassionated her deeply, and was glad to perceive that she found compensation for her misfortunes in a variety of little ridiculous circumstances. Away from all tell-tale chroniclers, she sought to decrease the apparent disparity of our ages by a thousand feminine arts—rouge, youthful dress, and assumed juvenility of manner. I could not be angry— Did not I myself wear a mask? Why quarrel with hers, because it was less successful? I grieved deeply when I remembered that this was my Bertha, whom I had loved so fondly, and won with such transport—the dark-eyed, dark-haired girl, with smiles of enchanting archness and a step like a fawn—this mincing, simpering, jealous old woman. I should have revered her gray locks and withered cheeks; but thus!——It was my work, I knew; but I did not the less deplore this type of human weakness.

Her jealousy never slept. Her chief occupation was to discover that, in spite of outward appearances, I was myself growing old. I verily believe that the poor soul loved me truly in her heart, but never had woman so tormenting a mode of displaying fondness. She would discern wrinkles in my face and decrepitude in my walk, while I bounded along in youthful vigour, the youngest looking of twenty youths. I never dared address another woman: on one occasion, fancying that the belle of the village regarded me with favouring eyes, she bought me a gray wig. Her constant discourse among her acquaintances was, that though I looked so young, there was ruin at work within my frame; and she affirmed that the worst symptom about me was my apparent health. My youth was a disease, she said, and I ought at all times to prepare, if not for a sudden and awful death, at least to awake some morning white-headed, and bowed down with all the marks of advanced years. I let her talk—I often joined in her conjectures. Her warnings chimed in with my never-ceasing speculations concerning my state, and I took an earnest, though painful, interest in listening to all that her quick wit and excited imagination could say on the subject.

Why dwell on these minute circumstances? We lived on for many long years. Bertha became bed-rid and paralytic: I nursed her as a mother might a child. She grew peevish, and still harped upon one string—of how long I should survive her. It has ever been a source of consolation to me, that I performed my duty scrupulously towards her. She had been mine in youth, she was mine in age, and at last, when I heaped the sod over her corpse, I wept to feel that I had lost all that really bound me to humanity.

Since then how many have been my cares and woes, how few and empty my enjoyments! I pause here in my history—I will pursue it no further. A sailor without rudder or compass, tossed on a stormy sea—a traveller lost on a wide-spread heath, without landmark or star to guide him—such have I been: more lost, more hopeless than either. A nearing ship, a gleam from some far cot, may save them; but I have no beacon except the hope of death.

Death! mysterious, ill-visaged friend of weak humanity! Why alone of all mortals have you cast me from your sheltering fold? O, for the peace of the grave! the deep silence of the iron-bound tomb! that thought would cease to work in my brain, and my heart beat no more with emotions varied only by new forms of sadness!

Am I immortal? I return to my first question. In the first place, is it not more probable that the beverage of the alchymist was fraught rather with longevity than eternal life? Such is my hope. And then be it remembered, that I only drank *half* of the potion prepared by him. Was not the whole necessary to complete the charm? To have drained half the Elixir of Immortality is but to be half immortal—my For-ever is thus truncated and null.

But again, who shall number the years of the half of eternity? I often try to imagine by what rule the infinite may be divided. Sometimes I fancy age advancing upon me. One gray hair I have found. Fool! do I lament? Yes, the fear of age and death often creeps coldly into my heart; and the more I live, the more I dread death, even while I abhor life. Such an enigma is man—born to perish—when he wars, as I do, against the established laws of his nature.

But for this anomaly of feeling surely I might die: the medicine of the alchymist would not be proof against fire—sword—and the strangling waters. I have gazed upon the blue depths of many a placid lake, and the tumultuous rushing of many a mighty river, and have said, peace inhabits those waters; yet I have turned my steps away, to live yet another day. I have asked myself, whether suicide would be a crime in one to whom thus only the portals of the other world could be opened. I have done all, except presenting myself as a soldier or duellist, an object of destruction to my—no, *not* my fellow-mortals, and therefore I have shrunk away. They are not my fellows. The inextinguishable power of life in my frame, and their ephemeral existence, place us wide as the poles asunder. I could not raise a hand against the meanest or the most powerful among them.

Thus I have lived on for many a year—alone, and weary of myself—desirous of death, yet never dying—a mortal immortal. Neither ambition nor avarice can enter my mind, and the ardent love that gnaws at my heart, never to be returned—never to find an equal on which to expend itself—lives there only to torment me.

This very day I conceived a design by which I may end all—without self-slaughter, without making another man a Cain—an expedition, which mortal frame can never survive, even endued with the youth and strength that inhabits mine. Thus I shall put my immortality to the test, and rest for ever—or return, the wonder and benefactor of the human species.

Before I go, a miserable vanity has caused me to pen these pages. I would not die, and leave no name behind. Three centuries have passed since I quaffed the fatal beverage: another year shall not elapse before, encountering gigantic dangers—warring with the powers of frost in their home—beset by famine, toil, and tempest—I yield this body, too tenacious a cage for a soul which thirsts for freedom, to the destructive elements of air and water—or, if I survive, my name shall be recorded as one of the most famous among the sons of men; and, my task achieved, I shall adopt more resolute means, and, by scattering and annihilating the atoms that compose my frame, set at liberty the life imprisoned within, and so cruelly prevented from soaring from this dim earth to a sphere more congenial to its immortal essence.

Essays and Reviews

from Giovanni Villani[1]

Among the many accusations that have been made against modern writers by the exclusive lovers of ancient literature, none has been more frequently repeated than the want of art manifested in the conception of their works, and of unity in the execution. They compare the Greek temples to Gothic churches, and bidding us remark the sublime simplicity of the one, and the overcharged ornament of the other, they tell us, that such is the perfection of antiquity compared with the monstrous distortions of modern times. These arguments and views, followed up in all their details, have given rise to volumes concerning the Classic and the Romantic, a difference much dwelt on by German writers, and treated at length by Madame de Staël in her "L'Allemagne."[2] All readers, who happen at the same time to be thinkers, must have formed their own opinion of this question; but assuredly the most reasonable is that which would lead us to admire the beauties of all, referring those beauties to the standard of excellence that must decide on all merit in the highest resort, without reference to narrow systems and arbitrary rules. Methinks it is both presumptuous and sacrilegious to pretend to give the law to genius. We are too far removed from the point of perfection to judge with accuracy of what ought to be, and it is sufficient if we understand and feel what is. The fixed stars appear to aberrate; but it is we that move, not they. The regular planets make various excursions into the heavens, and we are told that some among them never return to the point whence they departed, and by no chance ever retrace the same path in the pathless sky. Let us, applying the rules which appertain to the sublimest objects in

1. Reprinted from "Giovanni Villani," *The Liberal*, No. 4 (1823), pp. 281–97—only pp. 281–86 reprinted here.

2. Mary Shelley had read *De l'Allemagne (On Germany)* in 1815—for this and other works by Madame de Staël (1766–1817) that she read, see "Reading List," *Journals*, I: 89 and n.; and II: 678.

nature, to the sublimest work of God, a Man of Genius,—let us, I say, conclude, that though one of this species appear to err, the failure is in our understandings, not in his course; and though lines and rules, "centric and eccentric scribbled o'er,"[3] have been marked out for the wise to pursue, that these in fact have generally been the leading-strings and go-carts of mediocrity, and have never been constituted the guides of those superior minds which are themselves the law, and whose innate impulses are the fiats, of intellectual creation.

But zeal for the cause of genius has carried me further than I intended. Let us again recur to the charges brought against modern writers, and instead of cavilling at their demerits, let me be pardoned if I endeavour to discover that which is beautiful even in their defects, and to point out the benefits we may reap in the study of the human mind from this capital one—the want of unity and system.

It is a frequent fault among modern authors, and peculiarly among those of the present day, to introduce themselves, their failings and opinions, into the midst of works dedicated to objects sufficiently removed, as one might think, from any danger of such an incursion. This has sometimes the effect of a play-house anecdote I once heard, of a man missing his way behind the scenes, in passing from one part of the house to the other, and suddenly appearing in his hat and unpicturesque costume, stalking amidst the waves of a frightful storm, much to the annoyance of the highly-wrought feelings of the spectators of the impending catastrophe of a disastrous melodrame. Thus the Poet, in propriâ personâ, will elbow his way between the despairing fair one and her agitated lover; he will cause a murderer's arm to be uplifted till it ought to ache, and his own hobby will sometimes displace the more majestic quadruped that just before occupied the scene.

These are the glaring defects of the intrusion of self in a work of art. But well-managed, there are few subjects, especially in poetry, that excite stronger interest or elicit more beautiful lines. To sit down for the purpose of talking of oneself, will sometimes freeze the warmth of inspiration; but, when elevated and carried away by the subject in hand, some similitude or contrast may awaken a chord which else had slept, and the whole mind will pour itself into the sound; and he must be a critic such as Sterne describes, his stop-watch in his hand, who would arrest the lengthened echo of the deepest music of the soul. Let each man lay his hand on his heart and say, if Milton's reference to his own blindness and personal circumstances does not throw an interest over Paradise Lost,

3. Milton, *Paradise Lost* VIII.83.

which they would not lose to render the work as much no man's or any man's production as the Æneid—supposing *Ille ego* to be an interpolation, which I fondly trust it is not.[4]

This habit of self-analysation and display has also caused many men of genius to undertake works where the individual feeling of the author embues the whole subject with a peculiar hue. I have frequently remarked, that these books are often the peculiar favourites among men of imagination and sensibility. Such persons turn to the human heart as the undiscovered country. They visit and revisit their own; endeavour to understand its workings, to fathom its depths, and to leave no lurking thought or disguised feeling in the hiding places where so many thoughts and feelings, for fear of shocking the tender consciences of those inexpert in the task of self-examination, delight to seclude themselves. As a help to the science of self-knowledge, and also as a continuance of it, they wish to study the minds of others, and particularly of those of the greatest merit. The sight of land was not more welcome to Columbus, than are these traces of individual feeling, chequering their more formal works of art, to the voyagers in the noblest of terræ incognitæ, the soul of man. Sometimes, despairing to attain to a knowledge of the secrets of the best and wisest, they are pleased to trace human feeling wherever it is artlessly and truly pourtrayed. No book perhaps has been oftener the vade-mecum of men of wit and sensibility than Burton's Anatomy of Melancholy; the zest with which it is read being heightened by the proof the author gave in his death of his entire initiation into the arcana of his science. The essential attributes of such a book must be truth; for else the fiction is more tame than any other; and thus Sterne may become this friend to the reading man, but his imitators never can; for affectation is easily detected and deservedly despised. Montaigne is another great favourite; his pages are referred to as his conversation would be, if indeed his conversation was half so instructive, half so amusing, or contained half so vivid a picture of his internal spirit as his essays. Rousseau's Confessions, written in a more liberal and even prodigal spirit of intellectual candour, is to be ranked as an inestimable acquisition to this class of production. Boswell's Life of Johnson has the merit of carrying light into the recesses not of his own, but another's peculiar mind. Spence's Anecdotes is a book of the same nature, but less perfect in its kind. Half the beauty of Lady Mary Montagu's Letters consists in the *I* that adorns them; and this *I*,

4. See Laurence Sterne (1713–68), *The Life and Opinions of Tristram Shandy, Gentleman* (1760–67), vol. III, chap. xii; Milton's introductory lines to Book III of *Paradise Lost*; and Virgil's personal four-line introduction (beginning "I am he") to the *Aeneid* that mentions his other poetry but that is most often judged an interpolation.

this sensitive, imaginative, native, suffering, enthusiastic pronoun, spreads an inexpressible charm over Mary Wollstonecraft's Letters from Norway.[5]

An historian is perhaps to be held least excusable, if he intrude personally on his readers. Yet they might well follow the example of Gibbon, who, while he left the pages of his Decline and Fall unstained by any thing that is not applicable to the times of which he treated, has yet, through the medium of his Life and Letters, given a double interest to his history and opinions. Yet an author of Memoirs, or a History of his own Times, must necessarily appear sometimes upon the scene. Mr. Hyde gives greater interest to Lord Clarendon's History of the Rebellion, though I have often regretted that a quiet *I* had not been inserted in its room.[6]

And now drawing the lines of this reasoning together, it may be conjectured why I like, and how I would excuse, the dear, rambling, old fashioned pages of Giovanni Villani, the author of the Croniche Fiorentine; the writer who makes the persons of Dante's Spirits familiar to us; who guides us through the unfinished streets and growing edifices of Firenze la bella, and who in short transports us back to the superstitions, party spirit, companionship, and wars of the thirteenth and fourteenth centuries.[7] Dante's commentators had made me familiar with the name of Villani, and I became desirous of obtaining what appeared to be the key of the mysterious allusions of the Divina Comedia. There is something venerable and endearing in the very appearance of this folio of the sixteenth century. The Italian is old and delightfully ill-spelt: I say delightfully, for it is spelt for Italian ears, and the mistakes let one into the secret of the pronunciation of Dante and Petrarch better than the regular orthography of the present day. The abbreviations are many, and the stops in every instance misplaced; the ink is black, the words thickly set, so that the most seems to have been made of every page. It requires

5. I cannot help here alluding to the papers of "Elia," which have lately appeared in a periodical publication. When collected together, they must rank among the most beautiful and highly valued specimens of the kind of writing spoken of in the text. [Mary Shelley's note, referring to Charles Lamb's essays published in *London Magazine* in 1820–23. The other authors and works praised here are *The Anatomy of Melancholy* (1621) by Robert Burton (1577–1640); *Essais* (1580) by Michel de Montaigne (1533–92); *Confessions* (1783) by Jean-Jacques Rousseau (1712–78); *Life of Samuel Johnson* (1791) by James Boswell (1740–95); *Anecdotes, Observations, and Characters, of Books and Men* (posthumously, 1820) by Rev. Joseph Spence (1699–1768); *Letters . . . Written, during her Travels in Europe, Asia and Africa* (1763) by Lady Mary Wortley Montagu (1689–1762); and *Letters Written during a Short Residence in Sweden, Norway, and Denmark* (1796) by Mary Shelley's mother, Mary Wollstonecraft (1759–97).]

6. Mary Shelley's Reading Lists include *The Decline and Fall of the Roman Empire* (1776–88) by Edward Gibbon (1737–94) and *The History of the Rebellion and Civil Wars in England* (1702–1704) by Edward Hyde, 1st Earl of Clarendon (1609–74).

7. Giovanni Villani (c. 1275–1348) was a Florentine whose twelve-book *Cronica* or *Storia Fiorentina* was begun about 1308. Mary Shelley read Villani at various times in 1820 and 1821 (see *Journals*).

a little habit to read it with the same fluency as another book, but when this difficulty is vanquished, it acquires additional charms from the very labour that has been bestowed.

I know that in describing the outward appearance of my friend, I perform a thankless office, since few will sympathise in an affection which arises from a number of associations in which they cannot participate. But in developing the spirit that animates him, I undertake a more grateful task, although, by stripping him of his original garb and dressing him in a foreign habiliment, I divest him of one of his greatest beauties. Though in some respects rather old fashioned, his Italian is still received as a model of style; and those Italians who wish to purify their language from Gallicisms, and restore to it some of its pristine strength and simplicity, recur with delight to his pages. All this is lost in the English; but even thus I trust that his facts will interest, his simplicity charm, and his real talent be appreciated.[8]

8. This essay continues for another thirteen paragraphs, five of which are passages translated from Villani's chronicle.

On Ghosts[1]

> *I look for ghosts—but none will force*
> *Their way to me; 'tis falsely said*
> *That there was ever intercourse*
> *Between the living and the dead.*
>
> Wordsworth[2]

What a different earth do we inhabit from that on which our forefathers dwelt! The antediluvian world, strode over by mammoths, preyed upon by the megatherion, and peopled by the offspring of the Sons of God, is a better type of the earth of Homer, Herodotus, and Plato, than the hedged-in cornfields and measured hills of the present day. The globe was then encircled by a wall which paled in the bodies of men, whilst their feathered thoughts soared over the boundary; it had a brink, and in the deep profound which it overhung, men's imaginations, eagle-winged, dived and flew, and brought home strange tales to their believing auditors. Deep caverns harboured giants; cloudlike birds cast their shadows upon the plains; while far out at sea lay islands of bliss, the fair paradise of Atlantis or El Dorado sparkling with untold jewels. Where are they now? The Fortunate Isles have lost the glory that spread a halo round them; for who deems himself nearer to the golden age, because he touches at the Canaries on his voyage to India? Our only riddle is the rise of the Niger; the interior of New Holland, our only terra incognita; and our sole mare incognitum, the north-west passage. But these are tame wonders, lions in leash; we do not invest Mungo Park, or the Captain of the Hecla, with divine attributes; no one fancies that the waters of the unknown river bubble up from hell's fountains, no strange and weird power is supposed to guide the ice-berg, nor do we fable that a stray pick-pocket from Botany Bay has found the gardens of the Hesperides within the circuit of the Blue Mountains. What have we left to dream about? The clouds are no longer the charioted servants of the sun, nor does he any more bathe his glowing brow in the bath of Thetis; the

---

1. Reprinted from *London Magazine* 9 (March 1824): 253–56.
2. Epigraph from William Wordsworth, "The Affliction of Margaret" (ll. 57–60), published in *Poems in Two Volumes* (1807).

rainbow has ceased to be the messenger of the Gods, and thunder is no longer their awful voice, warning man of that which is to come. We have the sun which has been weighed and measured, but not understood; we have the assemblage of the planets, the congregation of the stars, and the yet unshackled ministration of the winds:—such is the list of our ignorance.

Nor is the empire of the imagination less bounded in its own proper creations, than in those which were bestowed on it by the poor blind eyes of our ancestors. What has become of enchantresses with their palaces of crystal and dungeons of palpable darkness? What of fairies and their wands? What of witches and their familiars? and, last, what of ghosts, with beckoning hands and fleeting shapes, which quelled the soldier's brave heart, and made the murderer disclose to the astonished noon the veiled work of midnight? These which were realities to our forefathers, in our wiser age—

> —— Characterless are grated
> To dusty nothing.[3]

Yet is it true that we do not believe in ghosts? There used to be several traditionary tales repeated, with their authorities, enough to stagger us when we consigned them to that place where that is which "is as though it had never been." But these are gone out of fashion. Brutus's dream has become a deception of his over-heated brain, Lord Lyttleton's vision is called a cheat; and one by one these inhabitants of deserted houses, moonlight glades, misty mountain tops, and midnight church-yards, have been ejected from their immemorial seats, and small thrill is felt when the dead majesty of Denmark blanches the cheek and unsettles the reason of his philosophic son.

But do none of us believe in ghosts? If this question be read at noonday, when—

> Every little corner, nook, and hole,
> Is penetrated with the insolent light—[4]

at such a time derision is seated on the features of my reader. But let it be twelve at night in a lone house; take up, I beseech you, the story of the Bleeding Nun; or of the Statue, to which the bridegroom gave the wedding ring, and she came in the dead of night to claim him, tall, white, and cold; or of the Grandsire, who with shadowy form and breathless lips stood over the couch and kissed the foreheads of his sleeping grand-

---

3. Shakespeare, *Troilus and Cressida* III.ii.195–96.
4. Percy B. Shelley, *The Cenci* II.i.179–80.

children, and thus doomed them to their fated death; and let all these
details be assisted by solitude, flapping curtains, rushing wind, a long and
dusky passage, an half open door—O, then truly, another answer may be
given, and many will request leave to sleep upon it, before they decide
whether there be such a thing as a ghost in the world, or out of the world,
if that phraseology be more spiritual. What is the meaning of this feeling?

For my own part, I never saw a ghost except once in a dream. I feared
it in my sleep; I awoke trembling, and lights and the speech of others
could hardly dissipate my fear. Some years ago I lost a friend, and a few
months afterwards visited the house where I had last seen him. It was
deserted, and though in the midst of a city, its vast halls and spacious
apartments occasioned the same sense of loneliness as if it had been situated on an uninhabited heath. I walked through the vacant chambers
by twilight, and none save I awakened the echoes of their pavement. The
far mountains (visible from the upper windows) had lost their tinge of
sunset; the tranquil atmosphere grew leaden coloured as the golden stars
appeared in the firmament; no wind ruffled the shrunk-up river which
crawled lazily through the deepest channel of its wide and empty bed;
the chimes of the Ave Maria had ceased, and the bell hung moveless in
the open belfry: beauty invested a reposing world, and awe was inspired
by beauty only. I walked through the rooms filled with sensations of the
most poignant grief. He had been there; his living frame had been caged
by those walls, his breath had mingled with that atmosphere, his step had
been on those stones, I thought:—the earth is a tomb, the gaudy sky a
vault, we but walking corpses. The wind rising in the east rushed through
the open casements, making them shake;—methought, I heard, I felt—I
know not what—but I trembled. To have seen him but for a moment, I
would have knelt until the stones had been worn by the impress, so I told
myself, and so I knew a moment after, but then I trembled, awe-struck
and fearful. Wherefore? There is something beyond us of which we are
ignorant. The sun drawing up the vaporous air makes a void, and the
wind rushes in to fill it,—thus beyond our soul's ken there is an empty
space; and our hopes and fears, in gentle gales or terrific whirlwinds,
occupy the vacuum; and if it does no more, it bestows on the feeling
heart a belief that influences do exist to watch and guard us, though they
be impalpable to the coarser faculties.

I have heard that when Coleridge was asked if he believed in ghosts,—
he replied that he had seen too many to put any trust in their reality;
and the person of the most lively imagination that I ever knew echoed
this reply. But these were not real ghosts (pardon, unbelievers, my mode
of speech) that they saw; they were shadows, phantoms unreal; that while

they appalled the senses, yet carried no other feeling to the mind of others than delusion, and were viewed as we might view an optical deception which we see to be true with our eyes, and know to be false with our understandings. I speak of other shapes. The returning bride, who claims the fidelity of her betrothed; the murdered man who shakes to remorse the murderer's heart; ghosts that lift the curtains at the foot of your bed as the clock chimes one; who rise all pale and ghastly from the church-yard and haunt their ancient abodes; who, spoken to, reply; and whose cold unearthly touch makes the hair stand stark upon the head; the true old-fashioned, foretelling, flitting, gliding ghost,—who has seen such a one?

I have known two persons who at broad daylight have owned that they believed in ghosts, for that they had seen one. One of these was an Englishman, and the other an Italian. The former[5] had lost a friend he dearly loved, who for awhile appeared to him nightly, gently stroking his cheek and spreading a serene calm over his mind. He did not fear the appearance, although he was somewhat awe-stricken as each night it glided into his chamber, and,

Ponsi del letto in su la sponda manca.[6]

This visitation continued for several weeks, when by some accident he altered his residence, and then he saw it no more. Such a tale may easily be explained away;—but several years had passed, and he, a man of strong and virile intellect, said that "he had seen a ghost."

The Italian[7] was a noble, a soldier, and by no means addicted to super-stition: he had served in Napoleon's armies from early youth, and had been to Russia, had fought and bled, and been rewarded, and he unhesi-tatingly, and with deep relief, recounted his story.

This Chevalier, a young, and (somewhat a miraculous incident) a gal-lant Italian, was engaged in a duel with a brother officer, and wounded him in the arm. The subject of the duel was frivolous; and distressed therefore at its consequences he attended on his youthful adversary dur-ing his consequent illness, so that when the latter recovered they became firm and dear friends. They were quartered together at Milan, where the youth fell desperately in love with the wife of a musician, who disdained

---

5. This Englishman was the Shelleys' friend Thomas Jefferson Hogg, who told his personal ghost story on the evening of 22 December 1814 (see *Journals*, I: 54–55).

6. "It put itself on the left side of the bed"—source unidentified.

7. This Italian Chevalier was Angelo Mengaldo, whom Mary Shelley met in Venice, where on the evening of 20 October 1818 she heard him relate this and several other ghost stories (see *Journals*, I: 231–32).

his passion, so that it preyed on his spirits and his health; he absented himself from all amusements, avoided all his brother officers, and his only consolation was to pour his love-sick plaints into the ear of the Chevalier, who strove in vain to inspire him either with indifference towards the fair disdainer, or to inculcate lessons of fortitude and heroism. As a last resource he urged him to ask leave of absence; and to seek, either in change of scene, or the amusement of hunting, some diversion to his passion. One evening the youth came to the Chevalier, and said, "Well, I have asked leave of absence, and am to have it early to-morrow morning, so lend me your fowling-piece and cartridges, for I shall go to hunt for a fortnight." The Chevalier gave him what he asked; among the shot there were a few bullets. "I will take these also," said the youth, "to secure myself against the attack of any wolf, for I mean to bury myself in the woods."

Although he had obtained that for which he came, the youth still lingered. He talked of the cruelty of his lady, lamented that she would not even permit him a hopeless attendance, but that she inexorably banished him from her sight, "so that," said he, "I have no hope but in oblivion." At length he rose to depart. He took the Chevalier's hand and said, "You will see her to-morrow, you will speak to her, and hear her speak; tell her, I entreat you, that our conversation to-night has been concerning her, and that her name was the last that I spoke." "Yes, yes," cried the Chevalier, "I will say any thing you please; but you must not talk of her any more, you must forget her." The youth embraced his friend with warmth, but the latter saw nothing more in it than the effects of his affection, combined with his melancholy at absenting himself from his mistress, whose name, joined to a tender farewell, was the last sound that he uttered.

When the Chevalier was on guard that night, he heard the report of a gun. He was at first troubled and agitated by it, but afterwards thought no more of it, and when relieved from guard went to bed, although he passed a restless, sleepless night. Early in the morning some one knocked at his door. It was a soldier, who said that he had got the young officer's leave of absence, and had taken it to his house; a servant had admitted him, and he had gone up stairs, but the room door of the officer was locked, and no one answered to his knocking, but something oozed through from under the door that looked like blood. The Chevalier, agitated and frightened at this account, hurried to his friend's house, burst open the door, and found him stretched on the ground—he had blown out his brains, and the body lay a headless trunk, cold, and stiff.

The shock and grief which the Chevalier experienced in consequence of this catastrophe produced a fever which lasted for some days. When he got well, he obtained leave of absence, and went into the country to try to divert his mind. One evening at moonlight, he was returning home from a walk, and passed through a lane with a hedge on both sides, so high that he could not see over them. The night was balmy; the bushes gleamed with fireflies, brighter than the stars which the moon had veiled with her silver light. Suddenly he heard a rustling near him, and the figure of his friend issued from the hedge and stood before him, mutilated as he had seen him after his death. This figure he saw several times, always in the same place. It was impalpable to the touch, motionless, except in its advance, and made no sign when it was addressed. Once the Chevalier took a friend with him to the spot. The same rustling was heard, the same shadow stept forth, his companion fled in horror, but the Chevalier staid, vainly endeavouring to discover what called his friend from his quiet tomb, and if any act of his might give repose to the restless shade.

Such are my two stories, and I record them the more willingly, since they occurred to men, and to individuals distinguished the one for courage and the other for sagacity. I will conclude my "modern instances," with a story told by M. G. Lewis, not probably so authentic as these, but perhaps more amusing. I relate it as nearly as possible in his own words.[8]

"A gentleman journeying towards the house of a friend, who lived on the skirts of an extensive forest, in the east of Germany, lost his way. He wandered for some time among the trees, when he saw a light at a distance. On approaching it he was surprised to observe that it proceeded from the interior of a ruined monastery. Before he knocked at the gate he thought it proper to look through the window. He saw a number of cats assembled round a small grave, four of whom were at that moment letting down a coffin with a crown upon it. The gentleman startled at this unusual sight, and, imagining that he had arrived at the retreats of fiends or witches, mounted his horse and rode away with the utmost precipitation. He arrived at his friend's house at a late hour, who sate up waiting for him. On his arrival his friend questioned him as to the cause of the traces of agitation visible in his face. He began to recount his adventures after much hesitation, knowing that it was scarcely possible

8. Mary Shelley did not actually hear these words spoken by Matthew Gregory ("Monk") Lewis (1775–1818), the Gothic novelist whom she met in Geneva in the summer of 1816. Instead, Percy B. Shelley went up to Diodati to visit with Byron and Lewis on the evening of 18 August 1816 and then recorded a total of five supernatural stories, the last being the source for Mary Shelley's retelling of the "king of the cats" (see *Journals*, I: 129). Lewis was famous for such stories, including that of the "Bleeding Nun" (from his 1796 novel *The Monk*), to which Mary Shelley also alludes in this essay "On Ghosts."

that his friend should give faith to his relation. No sooner had he mentioned the coffin with the crown upon it, than his friend's cat, who seemed to have been lying asleep before the fire, leaped up, crying out, 'Then I am king of the cats;' and then scrambled up the chimney, and was never seen more."

Σζ.

The English in Italy[1]

When peace came, after many long years of war, when our island prison was opened to us, and our watery exit from it was declared practicable, it was the paramount wish of every English heart, ever addicted to vagabondizing, to hasten to the continent, and to imitate our forefathers in their almost forgotten custom, of spending the greater part of their lives and fortunes in their carriages on the post-roads of the continent. With the brief and luckless exception of the peace of Amiens, the continent had not been open for the space of more than one-and-twenty years; a new generation had sprung up, and the whole of this, who had money and time at command, poured, in one vast stream, across the Pas de Calais into France: in their numbers, and their eagerness to proceed forward, they might be compared to the Norwegian rats, who always go right on, and when they come to an opposing stream, still pursue their route, till a bridge is formed of the bodies of the drowned, over which the living pass in safety. The simile holds good in more ways than one: the first emigrants, it is true, were not wholly killed, but the miseries they endured, of dirty packets and wretched inns, were the substratum from which has arisen the elegant steam-packet, and the improved state of the continental hotels. But in those early days of migration, in the summer of 1814,[2] every inconvenience was hailed as a new chapter in the romance

1. Reprinted from Article IV of *Westminster Review* 6 (October 1826): 325–41, this review essay dealt with three works: Constantine Henry Phipps, 1st Marquis of Normanby, *The English in Italy*, 3 vols. (London: Saunders and Otley, 1825); Charlotte Anne Eaton, *Continental Adventures: A Novel*, 3 vols. (London: Hurst, Robinson, 1826); and Anna Brownell Jameson, *Diary of an Ennuyée* (London: H. Colburn, 1826). Normanby's work contains the following stories: "L'Amoroso"; "Il Politico"; "I Zingari" (a series of shorter sketches); "Sbarbuto"; and "Il Critico."

2. That is, when Mary Godwin and Percy B. Shelley eloped, accompanied by Claire Clairmont, to France. See Mary Shelley's *History of a Six Weeks' Tour through a Part of France, Switzerland, Germany, and Holland* (London: T. Hookham, Jun., and C. and J. Ollier, 1817).

of our travels; the worst annoyance of all, the Custom-house, was amusing as a novelty; we saw with extasy the strange costume of the French women, read with delight our own descriptions in the passport, looked with curiosity on every *plât*,[3] fancying that the fried-leaves of artichokes were frogs; we saw shepherds in opera-hats, and post-boys in jack-boots; and (*pour comble de merveille*[4]) heard little boys and girls talk French: it was acting a novel, being an incarnate romance. But these days are now vanished: frequent landings at Calais have deprived it of its captivating novelty. Many of our children, under the guidance of foreign nursery-maids, lisp French as well as any little wood-shod urchin among the natives. We have learned to curse the *douane*,[5] and denounce passports as tyrannical and insufferable impediments to our free progress.

When France palled on our travelled appetites, which always crave for something new, Italy came into vogue. As preparatives for our pilgrimage to that country, whose charm is undying, we devoured the fabulous descriptions of Eustace, and well-poised sentences of Forsyth, and a traveller from Italy inspired us almost with devotional respect. We do not think that we are guilty of any exaggeration when we affirm, that even now that the English are almost cloyed with foreign travel, a journey to Italy is still regarded with enthusiastic transport, and when visited, that country is quitted with greater regret than any other, and the peculiarity of its situation accounts for this. We all wish to burst our watery bound, and to wander in search of a more genial climate than that enjoyed (according to the vulgarism, *he enjoys a very bad state of health*) by our native land. Neither France, Germany, nor Switzerland, content the swallow English. La belle France is now acknowledged to be the most unpicturesque, dull, miserable-looking country in the world. The name of Germany is sufficient in itself to inspire a kind of metaphysical gloom, enlightened only by meteoric flashes from the Hartz or the Elbe. Passing the Jura, surrounded by the mighty Alps, we ramble delightedly over Switzerland, till the snow and ice, ushered in by the chilling Biz, cause us to escape from the approach of a winter more severe than our own. We fly to Italy; we eat the lotus; we cannot tear ourselves away. It is the land of romance, and therefore pleases the young; of classic lore, and thus possesses charms for the learned. Its petty states and tiny courts, with all the numerous titles enjoyed by their frequenters, gild it for the worldly. The man of peace and domesticity finds in its fertile soil, and the happiness of its peasantry, an ameliorated likeness of beloved but starving England. The society is facile; the towns illustrious by the reliques they contain of the

3. "Dish" or "meal."
4. "As a crowning wonder."
5. "Customs."

arts of ancient times, or the middle ages; while its rural districts attach us, through the prosperity they exhibit, their plenteous harvests, the picturesque arrangement of their farms, the active life every where apparent, the novelty of their modes of culture, the grace which a sunny sky sheds over labours which in this country are toilsome and unproductive.

This preference accorded to Italy by the greater part of the emigrant English has given rise to a new race or sect among our countrymen, who have lately been dubbed Anglo-Italians. The Anglo-Italian has many peculiar marks which distinguish him from the mere traveller, or true John Bull. First, he understands Italian, and thus rescues himself from a thousand ludicrous mishaps which occur to those who fancy that a little Anglo-French will suffice to convey intelligence of their wants and wishes to the natives of Italy; the record of his travels is no longer confined, according to lord Normanby's vivid description, to how he had been "starved here, upset there, and robbed every where" [*English in Italy,* vol. ii. p. 229].[6] Your Anglo-Italian ceases to visit the churches and palaces, guide-book in hand; anxious, not to see, but to say that he has seen. Without attempting to adopt the customs of the natives, he attaches himself to some of the most refined among them, and appreciates their native talent and simple manners; he has lost the critical mania in a real taste for the beautiful, acquired by a frequent sight of the best models of ancient and modern art.

Upon the whole, the Anglo-Italians may be pronounced a well-informed, clever, and active race; they pity greatly those of their un-Italianized countrymen, who are endowed with Spurzheim's bump,[7] denominated stayathomeativeness; and in compassion of their narrow experience have erected a literature calculated to disseminate among them a portion of that taste and knowledge acquired in the Peninsula. Lord Byron may be considered the father of the Anglo-Italian literature, and Beppo as being the first product of that school; lord Normanby brings up the rear. The plan of his work, entitled, "The English in Italy," is excellent. It is difficult, after a long residence in a foreign country, to collect one's variety of experience into one focus. The detached anecdotes and observations on manners, made at various periods and places, are grouped in the mind, while it is impossible to select any form of journal, letter, or narrative, which will combine the mass in an intelligible form, and cause the reader to seize, as the author did, the conclusions to be drawn from such multifarious materials. Besides, though mere travellers are culpably neg-

---

6. Mary Shelley's brackets.

7. Johann Gaspar Spurzheim (1776–1832) was a practitioner of phrenology, by which character traits (such as Mary Shelley's clever "stayathomeativeness") were deduced from bumps on the skulls.

ligent on this score, the resident Anglo-Italian is withheld by honour, from the exposition of facts and names. Lord Normanby has hit upon a medium both novel and entertaining. He has given a series of tales, in which the English and Italians alike figure; the contrast between the two nations adds to the interest of these sketches, while the colouring of fiction is thrown over truths, which it would be difficult to convey in any other manner. It is impossible to read "The English in Italy" without being struck at every page with the verity of the delineations of character and manners, and without admiring the skill with which the noble author has seized and expressed the slight shadowings, and evanescent lights, peculiar to the complicated form of Italian society, which must have escaped a ruder pen. We frequently, it is true, dissent from his lordship's opinions and conclusions, but we always assent to the truth of his facts.

The first (and it is the best) of his longer stories is entitled L'Amoroso. It is the tale of a high-bred English girl, who, enchanted with the beauty of Naples, the softness of its climate, the vivacious and easy tone of society, and the ardour of her Italian lover, sacrifices her first *half* love (first loves are, for the most part, we fear, half loves), and gives her hand to a Neapolitan count. The gradual development of her Italian husband's feelings, her awakening to the truth of her situation, and the growth of her despair, is admirably managed; yet in all this there is something besides the comparative merits of English and Italian domestic customs. We can none of us attempt, with impunity, to engraft ourselves on foreign stocks: the habits of our childhood cling to us, and we seek in vain for sympathy from those who have travelled life quite on a different road from that which we have followed. We are far from advocating the Italian conjugal system, which puts the axe to domestic happiness, and deeply embitters the childhood of the offspring of the divided parents; nevertheless, we must observe, that the misery suffered by the English girl in Italy would on other accounts, but in no minor degree, become the lot of an Italian married to an Englishman. Let us imagine the daughter of a Neapolitan noble, dragged from her beautiful country and sunny clime, deprived of her box at the opera, her ride on the Corso, her cortège of devoted servants, her circle of complaisant friends, her *dolce far niente*;[8] to the toils and dulness of an English home—to the cares of housekeeping—a charge not imposed on Italian females—her snug, but monotonous, fire-side, her sentry-box of a house; to our cloudy sky; to the labour of giving dinners and entertaining evening parties; to those numerous etiquettes easy to the natives, unattainable by foreigners; to the *sotto voce*[9] tone (if the metaphor be admissible) which characterizes our social inter-

8. "Sweet idleness."
9. "In a whisper."

course, to the necessity of for ever wearing that thick and ample veil of propriety which we throw over every act and word: introduce the ardent, simple-hearted, undisguising Italian to this world, so opposite to her own, and she would experience the same heart-sickening disappointment that visited the heart of the heroine of the Amoroso. To us, and particularly to our females, these laws of constraint are the music, the accompaniment by which they regulate their steps until they cannot walk without it; and the veil before spoken of is as necessary to their sense of decency as their very habiliments. It is natural, therefore, that the English girl of the tale should be transfixed with grief at the request from her husband to conform with Italian customs; and it is also inevitable that the first step she takes in compliance with this request must sin against Italian etiquette, and, though liberty is offered her, that she should find that even the excess of freedom does not permit her the exact liberty she wants.

The "Politico" contains a rapid but masterly sketch of the Piedmontese revolution. The author, it is true, judging only from the apparent effects, blames this sudden burst of impatience on the part of Italians any longer to bear their galling chains. He says, that they had better have waited a few years, as if the capacity of waiting did not engender a callousness to the evils of tyranny, incompatible with a generous love of liberty. The revolution ended unfortunately, it is true; but, most certainly, if the attempt had not been made, the Italians would have lost their characteristic of being slaves "ognor frementi,"[10] and have sunk into as degraded an existence as that of the Fanariotes of Constantinople. From the smothered fire of this crushed revolt a brighter flame will hereafter rise: it was a glimmer, a flash, a reflection, sent back from the blaze just then kindled by the Spaniards: both are quenched now, but not for ever.

If the Italians could have viewed the Spanish struggle, and still submitted uncontending to the Austrian, they could never more have lifted their heads as a nation, nor possessed any claim to our commiseration. One of the chief causes, indeed, of the failure of the revolt of 1820–21 was political despair. This despair originated in the disarmed state of the natives, and the terror engendered by the Austrian bayonets. In every Italian state, except Tuscany, this fear was joined to a never-dying hatred of their oppressive rulers; which made them on the alert to seize every opportunity to rebel against their tyrants. While the flame of revolt spread from the Alps to Brundusium, Tuscany alone was tranquil. They

10. "Always trembling with restlessness." In her revisions to the original Chapter I of *Frankenstein*, Mary Shelley made Elizabeth's father into "one of those Italians nursed in the memory of the antique glory of Italy,—one among the *schiavi ognor frementi*, who exerted himself to obtain the liberty of his country" (*Frankenstein* [1831], p. 22). The phrase is also used in Mary Shelley's letter of 30 December 1830 to Frances Wright (*Letters*, II:124).

talked of liberty, but their enthusiasm began and ended in talk. The grand duke appreciated so well the quiescence of his loving subjects, that when the Austrian minister presented him with a list of sixty-seven Carbonari worthy of incarceration, Ferdinand refused to look at it. He did not believe, he said, that these men were Carbonari, but he was sure if he imprisoned them they would become so. Who, indeed, were to form the patriotic band? Not the peasants: the idea of political liberty never entered their heads. They work hard, and their genial climate lightens their labour of all the misery which renders the peasant's life so irksome in this country; yet still, from the utter want of money and traffic, their hardest labour only enables them to labour on. In the cities neither the rich nor the poor are willing to risk their wealth or their safety. There is another class of persons, the men of letters and students at the universities. The first are peacefully inclined, the second unprincipled: they are ready for riot, but they are little fitted for any commotion which has for its aim a noble and enlightened purpose. Yet we do not think the emancipation of Italy far off. In one circumstance, Italy is far better situated than Spain—in case of a revolution. Religion is here no enemy of political liberty. Napoleon gave a blow to Italian superstition, from which it will never recover. By destroying the wealth of the priests, he has destroyed their influence. The higher classes are liberal in their opinions, and the little bigotry that subsists among the lower orders is wholly untinged by the spirit of persecution. The great and immoveable foundation-stone, the boundary mark of Italian liberty, which still subsists, though no superstructure is thereto added, is their natural talent. In spite of college restrictions, in spite of almost universal ignorance, their native genius flourishes; their untaught courtesy, their love for the fine arts, the poetry with which their sunny sky endows them, prevent their being brutified; and thus Italy possesses in her own bosom the germs of regeneration, which, in spite of their late overthrow, will in the end give birth to their emancipation.

But to return to "The English in Italy." The "Sbarbuto" approaches nearest to a failure of any of the sketches; the hero is a kind of ideal of lord Byron. The "dear Corsair expression," now going out of fashion, is introduced, and the mixed character of bandit and dandy is carried to its height. Truth of description and liveliness of narrative, two chief characteristics of this author, render even this strange anomaly interesting. The conclusion of the tale is singularly abrupt, but it may be observed that all lord Normanby's catastrophes are faulty; that of "Matilda" has been justly censured. The author wished to pourtray the evils resulting from certain modes of action, and yet the tragic conclusion of the tale is entirely independent of the chain of unhappy events which were to appear of necessity to arise from the heroine's departure from the moral laws of her country. The conclusion of the "Sbarbuto" is still worse, and our imagination received a most disagreeable baulk, when, on turning the last page of this tale, we found that was indeed the last.

The sketches called the "Zingari," which detail a variety of adventures which have befallen the gipsy English in Italy, are perhaps the best part of the book. There is nothing outré,[11] nothing of caricature in any of these portraits. We recognize many well-known faces, and at each successive narration remember a *pendant*[12] that has come within our own experience. Utter ignorance of the Italian language is the source of many of the ludicrous situations in which the English get involved. French does not, as has been said, carry the traveller through Italy; those who depend on it, will find their support fail them at the first Italian town they enter. Besides, the Italians speak French with peculiar awkwardness; they are unable to accentuate its unutterable consonants and slip-shod vowels. When an Italian has welcomed a foreigner with gravity, and even with sulkiness, answering their introduction with a few mispronounced French phrases, if replied to in their own language, their ease of manner returns, and they become as graceful and facile in conversation as before they were repulsive.[13] The tales of the "Zingari" may serve as so many lessons to all future travellers as to what they may seek and what they may shun in Italy. We may learn the perils of Vetturino[14] travelling from "The Economist," assured that the details are by no means caricatured; and we may reap still more serious profit from the sketches entitled, "Change of Air," and "Boyhood Abroad." And yet, as is frequently the case, further experience overthrows the minor one, and the discomforts and dangers which are the lot of an invalid traveller in Italy will change to comforts and safety, if he becomes a resident there. If, indeed, the invalid

11. "Exaggerated."

12. "Counterpart."

13. Innumerable are the anecdotes that might be related of the ridiculous mistakes of the un-Italianized English in Italy. A gentleman at Rome said to us one day, "These Italians have no idea of morality or virtue; the fine arts are the only things they think worth praising. I was speaking to signora D—— of a young lady whom I described as, Di gran genio, bella, amabile, e poi virtuosissima, on which the signora asked with vivacity, Davvero si conosce forse nella musica?" We were near the same gentleman at a conversazione, he was looking over some pieces of music, when an Italian lady, apropos of his occupation, asked, "È virtuoso lei?"—"Lo spero," replied the astonished Englishman, and then turned to us to remark on the oddity of catechising a gentleman concerning his virtue; forgetful that even with us virtù is not virtue. Foreigners may murder English, but an Englishman's assassination of French and Italian is even more entire and remorseless. We heard one of our countrymen in Paris, in felicitous Anglo-French, ask the driver of a fiacre, "Pouvez-vous aller à rue Saint Honoré dans vingt cinq minuits?" [Mary Shelley's note.]

14. According to this sketch in Lord Normanby's *The English in Italy* (II: 101), this Vetturino or coachman was "one of those keen and plush-clad tribe of Florentines" who with mules arranged for the very slow transport of carriages.

travel, like lord Normanby's hero, from one town to another, from one bad inn and cold lodging to another a match for the last, he may certainly return from such pursuit of health worse than he went. But let him fix on some city for a constant residence: Pisa[15] we recommend as most equable in climate; let him get his English comforts about him, as he may with ease and cheapness from the free port of Leghorn, not twelve miles distant, and he will then find the advantage of a southern residence. The streets of Pisa are quiet, and the whole town wears a sober, scholastic aspect. The north side of the Lung Arno, looking towards the south, is warm at mid-winter, and always presents a delightful promenade. The rides round the town are beautiful; you have your choice of the pine forest of the Cascina, or the road along the plain that skirts the neighbouring hills, which, covered with olives, chesnuts, and last, toward their summit, with pines, are, though not high, remarkably picturesque. The whole road from Vico Pisano to Lucca, some twenty or thirty miles, presenting successive pictures of fertility in the plain, and of the view of ravine or precipice in the mountains, is within four miles of one or other of the gates of Pisa. The neighbourhood to the sea is an advantage not to be omitted. Let an invalid do this, and he will speedily acquire the health and spirits, the promise of which drew him from his home.[16]

We are surprised that lord Normanby has not introduced more of the country life of Italy, which bears a peculiar stamp, and which is pregnant with interest and beauty. Generally speaking, our countrymen see only the surface of the country, and are unaware of the minutiæ of the peasants' life, and their mode of agriculture. They are connoisseurs in paintings, and frequenters of drawing-rooms; but the inferior classes of their fellow beings possess no interest for them: and yet it is in the country of Italy that you see most of the true Italian character, and most enjoy the exhaustless delights of that sunny clime. The very aspect of the country to a cursory observer will prove this assertion. The use of oxen in their agricultural labours is seemingly a small, and yet, in truth, a great improvement to the picturesque of the rural scene. The oxen of Italy surpass, in beauty of form, in the sleekness of their dove-coloured skin, and the soft expression of their large eyes, all other animals of their species. In every part of Italy we encounter, during our walks, in lanes bordered by elms and sallows, to which the vines are trained and fes-

15. Where the Shelleys lived in 1820–22.
16. We were about to add that in the Professor Vaccà he would find an able substitute for any English medical aid; but alas! this estimable man is now dead, and we can do no more than consecrate this note to his memory. His talents were of the highest order, and as a practical surgeon he stood in the first rank of his profession. His private virtues secured for him universal esteem; he was gentle, yet full of enthusiasm; a select specimen of Italian virtue and genius. [Mary Shelley's note on Andrea Vaccà Berlinghieri, the physician who treated the Shelleys in Pisa.]

tooned, frequent wains drawn by these animals, yoked by the neck; and the dark-eyed driver, with his sun-burnt limbs, in no manner detracts from the beauty of the picture. It is curious in Italy to observe the great advantage the peasants possess as to personal appearance, over the town's-people. The inhabitants of the cities, whether rich or poor, are for the most part low in stature, sallow-complexioned, bent shouldered; but if while you are induced, by the appearance of the citizens, to lament the degeneracy of Italian beauty, you wander in the country, or enter the market-place, to which, on certain days, the country people resort, you are immediately convinced that you now behold the models of the Italian painters. You are struck by groups resembling those fine fellows repre-sented in the paintings of the Adoration of the Shepherds. Their very occupation adds to their pictorial appearance. They are employed among the vines, or following the oxen-drawn plough, whose rough mechanism is such as Virgil describes; frequently in summer they work merely in a shirt, and the white colour of the linen contrasts well with limbs whose veins seem to flow with dark wine. The women, less hard-worked than the French *paysannes*,[17] perform the lighter labours of the farm, and, notwithstanding the shade of their large straw-hats, soon acquire a deep but healthy hue; in an evening they are seen returning from fetching water at the spring, bearing their pitchers of an antique shape on their heads, stepping freely under the burthen. Of course we do not pretend to say that all, or even that the greater part of them, are handsome; but they have, for the most part, pleasing expressions of countenance, and the beauty you do encounter is of a high character; their brows are finely moulded, their eyes soft and large; the cheeks sink gently towards the chin, and their lips remind you of those chiselled by Greek sculptors. Such we have seen in the evening emerging from the trellised *pergole,* or vine-walks, singing in perfect tune, and with clear, though loud voices, the simple but beautiful melodies peculiar to the Italian peasantry.

It is true that, in thus eulogizing the country of Italy, our remarks must be understood as being principally confined to Tuscany. In Lom-bardy the abundance of pasture-land is inimical to the happiness of the peasantry: nor are we sufficiently acquainted with the rural districts of the Roman and Neapolitan states, to speak with precision concerning their inhabitants. In Tuscany the farms are usually small, and held at long leases; the rent is often paid in kind, and the landlord receives as his share one half of the produce. The expenses are also shared between the landholder and the cultivator, the former providing the heavy stock, cattle, ploughs, out-houses, wine-presses, &c.; the peasantry the lighter

17. "Peasant women."

utensils, and repairs of hedges, sluices, &c. The smallness of the farms renders the farmer almost always the labourer; a hired workman is rare among them; and the cottager, we should almost call him, with a farm of twelve acres, whose family is sufficiently large to cultivate the land, and whose share of corn and wine suffices to maintain that family without extra purchase, considers himself rich; for, then, the superfluous money he obtains by the sale of vegetables, fruit, and the better kind of wine, clothes his family, and keeps his farm and house in repair. Their lives would be deemed, and justly deemed, hard in England, for our unbenign climate would render painful the continual out-door work, which is light to them.

The Tuscan name for their small farms is *podere,* and in appearance they resemble what we imagine to have been the first attempts at agriculture, every thing being cultivated in patches. A podere generally contains six or eight acres; they are hedged in; in the neighbourhood of Leghorn the hedges are of myrtle, which, like all evergreens, are fragrant even when out of bloom; and when in flower, their spicy odour gives a taste of Indian climes. Little hay is raised, for the Indian corn is much used in its stead; so after the spring-labour of pruning the vines, the wheat is the first harvest. The wheat-fields are planted with rows of trees, to which the vines cling; and the shade, far from being detrimental, is considered a shelter for the crops. When the wheat is gathered in, and threshed on the threshing-floor, constructed in the open air, with all the care Virgil advises, the land is again sown with Indian corn. This is a beautiful harvest. The men cut it down, and the women and children sit round the threshing-floor, taking the grain from the pod, loosening it from the stalk, and spreading it in the sun, till its paler orange hue deepens to a fiery glow. The vintage follows—an universal feast. The men pluck the fruit from the trees, which is received and deposited in the vats by the women and children. The plucking of the olives brings up the rear of their *raccolte*.[18] But it is not the mere sowing, and the harvests that demand labour; the long droughts force them to construct sluices through every part of the podere, and the water-wheel is for ever at work to irrigate the land; nature the while is busy and noisy. During the day the loud cicale, with ceaseless chirp, fill the air with sound, and in the evening the fire-flies come out from the myrtle hedges, and form a thousand changing and flashing constellations on the green corn-fields, which is their favourite resort. Meanwhile the *contadini*[19] cheer themselves with songs, either singly, in harmony, or in response. One of the favourite games among the Tuscan peasants (we have forgotten the name of it),

18. "Harvests."
19. "Peasants."

especially during the time of the vintage, is singularly poetic. A man on one tree, will challenge another perched afar off, calling out the name of a flower; the challenged responds with an extempore couplet, sometimes founded on the metaphoric meaning attached, of the flower's name, sometimes given at random, and then returns the challenge by naming another flower, which is replied to in the same manner. We have unluckily preserved but two of these impromptus, and they are both on the same flower:—

> Fior di cent' erbe!
> Non bimbi voglion bene a loro mamma,
> Quanto io alla speranza mia.
> Fior di cent' erbe!
> Se un sospiro avesse la parola,
> Quanto bell' ambasciator sarebbe.[20]

It is this exhaustless fertility that makes Italy a paradise, and affords never-ending variety of object to the residents. With us nature is parsimonious, if not frugal; her very magnificence is that of a well-regulated mansion, where, though great show is made, there is no waste. In Italy she superabounds, overflows, and, like a prodigal, casts immense treasures to the winds. This abundance is not displayed alone in inanimate nature; but among the Italians themselves there exist rich stores of talent, useless it is true, in the general sense of the term, which are displayed to the delight of their countrymen and astonishment of travellers. We cannot give a better idea of what we mean than by instancing their improvisatori, who pour out, as a cataract does water, poetic imagery and language; but except that the genial moisture somewhat fertilizes the near bordering banks, it reaches the ocean of oblivion, leaving no trace behind. Sgricci[21] may be given as an example. He is well read, and profoundly versed in the works of the Greek metaphysicians and historians, as well as their poets. The mode of his improvisation is wonderful, and different from the usual style of these exhibitions. When he comes on the stage, his personal appearance, animated countenance, and regular features, lost in his daily costume, strike you with admiration. It is the custom for those who choose, to leave at the door of the theatre a slip of paper, on which is written a subject for a tragic drama. We were present at three of these performances. The subject of the first was "Ifegenia in Tauride;"

20. "Flower from a hundred seeds! / Children do not love their mother, / As much as I love my hope." "Flower from a hundred seeds! / If a sigh would have a voice, / What a wonderful messenger would it be."

21. Mary Shelley met the famous improvisatore Tommaso Sgricci in 1820 and, as noted in this essay, attended three of his performances: see entries for 21 December 1820 and for 12 and 22 January 1821 in *Journals*, I: 343, 348–50, and nn.

the plan of the tragedy was closely copied from Euripides; but the words and poetry were his own, and we were continually startled by images of dazzling beauty, and a flow of language which never degenerated into mere words, but, on the contrary, was instinct with energy and pathos.

Inez de Castro was a tragedy he gave at Lucca, the subject being imposed on him by the arch-duchess, who was in the theatre. When towards the end, he caused the audience to understand that the prince, Don Pedro, husband of Inez, drawing a curtain, suddenly displays to his father the bodies of his murdered wife and children, the same thrill was felt, nay, far greater than if the real mock bodies (the implied bull must be excused) had been brought forward. His words were so living, that you saw them, not decked out with stage trickery, but in the true livery of death, livid, stiff, and cold. The last tragedy we heard was the Death of Hector.[22] In it you were transported within the walls of Troy, and heard mad Cassandra denouncing its fall. Speaking afterwards to the poet, he said that he did not remember much about any other part; but he had a vivid recollection that when he poured forth the ravings of the prophetess, he no longer saw the theatre; Troy was around him; Troy burning; Priam stabbed at his altar, and the women dragged lamenting away in chains. From all this magical creation of talent, what resulted? The poet himself forgets all his former imaginations, and is hurried on to create fresh imagery, while the effects of his former inspirations are borne away with the breath that uttered them, never again to be recalled—

Nec revocare situs, aut jungere carmina curat.[23]

For the rest, he acquires the enthusiastic praises of some few of the more refined of his countrymen—for Sgricci's poetry is of too classic and elevated a nature to please the multitude—and the animated recollection of those few English who understand sufficient Italian to appreciate his genius.

Italy is an exhaustless theme to those who, having been long residents there, are familiar with its novel and beauteous aspect. But our limits warn us not to pursue our digression, and oblige us to turn our attention

22. The same subject was subsequently given him at Turin, and a short-hand writer took it down, and it was published. The plot resembled the one we heard, otherwise it struck us as inferior in poetry, and was certainly a very different production. The plot is not the least admirable part of these impromptu dramas. When a novel subject is given, it is of course arranged during the heat of inspiration and delivery; it never lags; the interest is continually increasing, and the scenes grow naturally from each other. They are shorter than our five-act plays, being, on the Greek plan, interspersed with choruses. [Mary Shelley's note.]

23. Virgil, *Aeneid* III.451: "Nor does [the Sibyl] care to recover [the leaves'] places or to unite the verses."

to those other works whose titles head our article. We shall not dilate much upon them; for the scope of our present writing is to treat of Italy, and as these volumes do not bear the same perfect Italian stamp as those of lord Normanby, they may be passed more cursorily over.

"Continental Adventures" are the production of the very clever authoress of "Rome in the Nineteenth Century."[24] This latter publication is an inestimable guide to all who visit the Eternal City, and even to those at home, more than any other work on the same subject, gives a faithful account of the wonders of that metropolis of the world. "Continental Adventures" is on another and a worse plan. It mixes real scenes with fictitious ones, not in the style of the "English in Italy," where the manners of the natives form the ground-work of the tales, but in the mode of a common novel—a novel of the day: a lady and her lover, the baulks to love, the rival, and the denouement, all English: and the "Continental Adventures" are merely, that while the hero and heroine are *progressing* towards the fulfilment of their hopes, they ramble about Switzerland, and the lady, in particular, endures so many perils, that we really think that no female in real life could have undergone them without becoming prematurely grey. She commences by breaking her collar-bone and two of her fingers; is twice in imminent danger of perishing in snow-drifts; narrowly escapes tumbling down a precipice; is nearly shot by a robber in one of the Alpine Ravines; and last, is carried away by Italian banditti, at whose hands death was the least evil she expected, and from whom she saves herself by the administration of a piece of opium, which she had fortunately put into her *pocket* the day before. The story of the novel is commonplace enough, and the gordian knot, tied just at the end, then to be cut, is confused, and even displeasing. The discovery of relationship in a forbidden degree between lovers is always disagreeable; and the mode by which these lovers are found to be related, disfiguring the sacred associations always blended with a mother's name, is even revolting. The authoress is evidently nearly related to Scotland, though we believe she is not Scotch. She has a taste for humour, and her comedy is generally very entertaining, though she too often falls into a comedian's worst fault, of wire-drawing a comic scene, till it becomes tedious; and once or twice she is guilty of giving them for their foundation subjects hardly admissible on the score of propriety. The book is, however, written with great spirit, and is very entertaining. Some of the scenes of real life are sketched with fidelity and true humour. The Côche-d'Eau on the Rhone is one of these, and the Reverend Saunders M'Muckleman is throughout a genuine

24. Charlotte Anne Eaton's popular *Rome in the Nineteenth Century* had gone through four editions since 1820.

comic character. Her descriptions of scenery are, however, the best part of the book; they are varied and faithful. We select one, as a specimen of the style in which they are executed:—

The glaciers of the Aar, which we visited from the Grimsel, present a scene which I am convinced the world cannot equal; which none who have beheld it can ever forget, and none who have not seen it can ever conceive. I will not mock you with a futile attempt at description. You cannot picture the scene; but you can form some idea of the awe-struck astonishment which filled our minds, when, after surmounting all the difficulties of the way, we found ourselves standing amidst a world of ice, extending around, beneath, above us; far beyond where the straining sight, in every direction, vainly sought to follow the interminable frozen leagues of glaciers, propped up in towering pyramids or shapeless heaps, or opening into yawning gulphs and unfathomable fissures. The tremendous barren rocks and mountains of the impenetrable Alps, amidst which the terrific Finsteraarhorn reared his granitic pyramid of fourteen thousand feet, appeared alone amidst this world of desolation. Eternal and boundless wastes of ice, naked and inaccessible mountains of rock, which had stood unchanged and untrodden from creation, were the only objects which met our view. Hitherto, with all we had seen of desolation and horror, there was some contrast, some relief. The glaciers of Chamouni are bordered by glowing harvests; the glaciers of Grindelwald are bounded by its romantic vale; the glaciers of the Schiedeck shine forth amidst its majestic woods. Even among the savage rocks and torrents of the Grimsel, though animated life is seen no more, the drooping birch and feathery larch protrude their storm-beaten branches from the crevices of the precipices; and the lonely pine-tree is seen on high, where no hand can ever reach it. But here there is no trace of vegetation, no blade of grass, no bush, no tree; no spreading weed or creeping lichen invades the cold still desolation of the icy desert. It is the death of nature. We seemed placed in a creation in which there is no principle of life; translated to another orb, where existence is extinct, and where death, unresisted, holds his terrific reign. The only sound which meets the ear is that of the loud detonation of the ice, as it burst open into new abysses, with the crash of thunder, and reverberates from the wild rocks like the voice of the mountain storms.—Vol. ii. p. 134.

These volumes contain the best description and guide to Switzerland that we have ever seen, but Italy makes only a small portion of them. We have some animated scenes on the romantic lake of Como, and visit, with the personages of the novel, the galleries and palaces of Florence; but a guide-book and a romance form an incongruous mixture, and we certainly wish that they should be separated in future.

"The Diary of an Ennuyée," is a very well written and interesting imposture. Well written and interesting it is true, but still an imposture, and that not of a kind which is admissible. The very laws of *cavaliere serventei*sm[25] in Italy are not more delicate, subtle, and yet strict, than those of fiction, and they are transgressed in the volume before us. A fiction must contain no glaring improbability, and yet it must never divest itself of a certain idealism, which forms its chief beauty. Once in Italy we saw a drama, which was any thing but dramatic, and we were reminded of it by the pages of the book before us. The hero was an English Milord who had a diseased arm; no medical attendant was able to afford him any relief; one doctor, one alone could cure this otherwise mortal disorder; but this doctor refused to exert his skill until his friend *Jenkisson,* who was imprisoned in the Tower under suspicion of treasonable practices, should be liberated by the sick Milord, who was also a secretary of state; but Milord was too patriotic to sacrifice public good to his private advantage. Miledi, in the mean time, ran from her husband to the doctor, adjuring the one and supplicating the other, while Milord, with his bound-up arm, groaning when on the stage, and shrieking while behind it, formed a most distressing foreground to the picture. You actually felt for the poor man; and a greater verity of scenic illusion (such as it was) was produced by that bandaged arm, and the moaning and crippled action of the patient than Kean or Pasta usually effect in their portentous identifications with ideal woe. That our readers may not be left in a painful suspense, we proceed to inform them, that when Milord was at his last gasp, and the doctor stood unmoved in the midst of his kneeling and supplicating relatives, Jenkisson himself, whose innocence had been discovered, appeared; a general reconciliation took place; and the doctor was proceeding to work a cure, when the curtain fell.

We do not wish to cast an air of ridicule over the volume before us, which we read, really believing in it as we read, with great interest; but having discovered that the sensitive, heart-broken, dying, dead diarist is a fictitious personage, we are angry at the trick of art that excited our real sympathy; and we were led to a conviction that the circumstances that demand our deepest interest as a reality, are, when feigned, not of an high order of idealism, and consequently the fraud being discovered, the fictitious part of the book falls below the usual rate of novel interest.

But to leave this criticism, or hypercriticism, let us advert to the real merits of the work. It is written with great spirit and great enthusiasm: the descriptions are vivid, the anecdotes entertaining, and the whole style displays intelligence and feeling. The few traits recorded of Italian manners are felicitously seized, and the English party is well sketched, from the quiet, retiring, suffering, ideal authoress, to the blundering and viva-

25. The social code that allows a married Italian woman to be attended by a lover.

cious L——, who may stand as a specimen of a whole tribe of English rovers in Italy. We turn over the pages to find an extract, which our limits will not permit us to make long. We hesitated between the account of the eruption of Vesuvius, the description of the improvisatore Sestini, the Capanna and Gesu Bambino, always exhibited in the convents during Christmas, the Diarist's Adventure with the Governor of Lerici—between these and the following one, which we have fixed upon as one of the most interesting anecdotes in the book:—

Last night we had a numerous party, and Signor P—— and his daughter came to sing. *She* is a private singer of great talent, and came attended by her lover, or her *fiancé,* who, according to the Italian custom, attends his mistress every where during the few weeks which precede their marriage. He is a young artist, a favourite pupil of Camuccini, and of very quiet, unobstrusive manners. La P. has the misfortune to be plain; her features are irregular, her complexion of a sickly paleness, and though her eyes are large and dark, they appeared totally devoid of lustre and expression. Her plainness, the bad taste of her dress, her awkward figure, and her timid and embarrassed deportment, all furnished matter of amusement and observation to some young people (English of course), whose propensities for *quizzing* exceeded their good breeding and good nature. Though La P. does not understand a word of either French or English, I thought she could not mistake the significant looks and whispers of which she was the object, and I was in pain for her and for her modest lover. I drew my chair to the piano, and tried to divert her attention, by keeping her in conversation, but could get no farther than a few questions, which were answered in monosyllables. At length she sang, and sang divinely; I found the pale automaton had a soul as well as a voice. After giving us with faultless execution, as well as great expression, some of Rossini's finest songs, she sang the beautiful and difficult cavatina in Otello *"Assisa al piè d' un salice,"*[26] with the most enchanting style and pathos, and then stood as unmoved as a statue, while the company applauded loud and long. A moment afterwards, as she stooped to take up a music-book, her lover, who had edged himself by degrees from the door to the piano, bent his head too, and murmured, in a low voice, but with the most passionate accent, "O, brava, brava, cara!" She replied only by a look, but it was such a look! I never saw a human countenance so entirely, so instantaneously changed in character: the vacant eyes kindled and beamed with tenderness; the pale cheek glowed, and a bright smile playing round her mouth, just parted her lips sufficiently to discover a set of teeth like pearls. I could have called her at that moment beautiful; but the change was as transient as sudden; it passed like a gleam of light over her face, and vanished; and by the time the book was placed on the

26. "Seated at the foot of a willow-tree," from *Otello* (first performance, 1816), by Gioachino Antonio Rossini (1792–1868).

desk, she looked as plain, as stupid, and statue-like as ever. I was the only person who witnessed this little bye-scene, and it gave me pleasant thoughts and interest for the rest of the evening.—p. 207.

We hope to heaven all this is true, and not false as the Ennuyée herself. One thing alone at all atones for her deception. We longed, while reading her work, to thank the fair authoress for reviving many a half-forgotten Italian scene, and for shedding a beautiful light over many a favourite spot; we regretted that our gratitude was due to the dead; but since the writer lives, we no longer have this painful debt heavy at our hearts, and we pay it with the praise she entirely merits.

We shall hail with pleasure any new production from the pen of any one of the writers of these works; and we were not a little gratified at the announcement of lord Normanby's "Historiettes." We hope that in these he has a little abated an offensive display of superiority of rank. It is unworthy of the enlightened heir of a peerage thus to prize himself above nine-tenths of his readers on account of his adventitious advantages, and very absurd to shew it. We remember, in former times, that this nobleman had a warm love for talent, though its possessor was unendowed either with rank or fashion; we hope the generous feeling is not dead. His lordship has too much real talent not to feel and appreciate the nobility of nature as well as that of birth, and some indication of such a feeling would give a grace to his productions, in which, at present, they are deficient.

from Modern Italy[1]

Happy is the man who, leaving the Alps behind him, has the plains of Lombardy on his right hand and on his left, the Apennines in view, and Florence as the city towards which he directs his steps. His way is through a country where corn grows under groves of fruit trees, whose tops are woven into green arcades by thickly-clustering garlands of vines; the dark masses of foliage and verdure which every where appear, melt insensibly, as he advances, into a succession of shady bowers that invite him to their depths; the scenery is monotonous, and yet ever various from the richness of its sylvan beauty, possessing all the softness of forest glades without their gloom. Towards Bologna, the landscape roughens into hills, which grow into Apennines, but Arcadia still breathes from slopes and lawns of tender green, which take their rise in the low stream-watered vallies, and extend up the steep ascent till met midway by the lofty chesnut groves which pale them in. To these gentler features succeeds the passage of the Apennines, which here, at least, are not as the author of "Italy as it Is," describes them, "the children of the Alps—smiling and gentle and happy as children should be,"[2] but, as we remember them, their summits form themselves into a wild, dreary region, sown with sterile mountain-tops, and torn to pieces by wind and storm: the only glimpse of peace is derived from the view on either side of the sea, which sometimes shews itself on the horizon, a misty line, half silver, half æther. This barren wilderness again softens into gracefully-swelling hills turned towards Florence. The fair olive tree and the dark cypress mingle their foliage with

1. Reprinted from Article IX of *Westminster Review* 11 (July 1829), 127–40, a review of Henry Digby Beste's *Italy as it Is; or Narrative of an English Family's Residence for Three Years in That Country* (London: Henry Colburn, 1828); and Louis Simond's *A Tour in Italy and Sicily* (London: Longman, Rees, Orme, Brown, and Green, 1828)— only pp. 127–33 reprinted here.
2. *Italy as it Is*, pp. 126–27.

the luxuriant chesnut boughs, and the frequent marble villa flashes a white gleam from amid its surrounding laurel bowers. The sky is more beautiful than earth, and each symbolize peace and serene enjoyment.

Both the country and the climate increase in beauty as you approach Rome. The Queen of the world, humble in her glory, sits in a lowly plain; she is hid in the misty expanse of the Campagna, till within a few miles, when the long boundary line is broken, and the dome of St. Peter's emerges in single majesty from behind. One by one, like stars in the twilight sky, the smaller cupolas shine out, and a vast extent of dome, tower, and verdurous wall, discloses itself to the traveller's thirsty gaze.

Here we pause. The high-wrought expectations which the name of Rome, the picturesque and desolate Campagna, and the first glorious lifting of the curtain at the Porta del Popolo, had fully realized, are often visited with disappointment during a residence in the city. The confused mixture of monuments of all ages disturbs the imagination. The vile hut of an artificer, the abode of dirt, smoke, and noise, rising in the hollow of a temple checks our enthusiasm.—In one place we remember being struck by the ridiculous juxta-position of a variety of structures—a stunted gothic tower, leaving its mother church, cheated our imperfect, distance-deluded optics, by assuming the appearance of a night-cap placed upon four Grecian columns elevated in its front. No line of demarcation is drawn between such dissimilar objects, and yet there is no affinity between them. Modern Rome is the lineal descendant of the ancient city, yet it is impossible to trace the slightest likeness of one to the other; and they form a contrast rendered more striking by their being forcibly brought into comparison. Paganism and Christianity were not more hostile in the days of Julian the Apostate,[3] than is now the spirit breathed from the works of art, children of various eras, that strew the area, which the walls of Rome inclosed. At each step the genial temper of ancient philosophy stands corrected by the austere self-denying precepts of Catholicism. To render this intelligible, let us only compare the structure of their tombs. The sarcophagi of the ancients are adorned by images of living grace, and the sculptured resemblance of all that is jocund; sorrow is cheated of her tears, and melancholy death becomes a plaything. Let us view a modern monument. Here the dread misshapen shape is depicted in a grim, yet ridiculous form; he figures like the lean horse of an hardworking country apothecary, who in his master's service has bared his ribs, and displays his fleshless bones in token of a steady but sad attachment, while his victim waits eternal centuries upon his knees, with uplifted eyes and clasped hands, for the coming of the grand audit day; and

3. Flavius Claudius Julianus (331–63), Roman emperor (361–63) who publicly announced his conversion to paganism from Christianity—hence "Apostate."

did the stone image sympathise with the believer it is meant to represent, the marble features would be deep trenched with lines of terror for its result.

Go to Rome,[4] but seek not to find even a dim shadow of the city of the consuls, nor even the silent burial place of her bygone heroes. We do not discover the crowded forum, the well-filled amphitheatre, nor baths, the resort of the voluptuous;—neither do we find the ruins of all these in their untainted simplicity; traces of the altered faith gather around; gloomy records of martyrdom, and interminable portraitures of saintly miracles, stand side by side with the relics of Roman glory and Roman power. Each are interesting, both may be good, but they accord ill. Again, the manners of the Romans of our days, their worldliness and covetousness, disturb the solemn emotions we desire to indulge among these time-eaten ruins. The love of money, the characteristic trait of the modern Italians, becomes a perfect thirst of gain, as you advance southwards. A Roman accosts you with solemn reverence—to view his respectful aspect and to listen to his tender adulations, you might fancy yourself an apostle travelling in disguise; but the salvation aimed at by such pious attention is purely temporal, and to be arrived at through your purse; egged on by hope of approaching with his fingers the idolized coin, he thrusts himself between you and your enthusiasm, and standing under the shadow of the capitol, will call a quattrino (farthing) his dear friend. As you love the memory of the past, and would cherish exalted association with the relics of the eternal city, shun daylight in Rome, avoid the garish sun which displays the ill-assorted marriage of ancient with modern; wander forth beneath the moon's illusory rays; then the undergrowth of the puny sons of the latter years, fades in the shade of night, the great and glorious monuments of past ages stand forth "in single blessedness,"[5] and succeed to one another, till Rome grows out of Rome, and the mirror of her past existence stands unstained by any base reflection in simple majesty before you. She becomes the sepulchre of antiquity, and, as a sepulchre, ought to be lonely. Thus, in truth, we have sometimes wished her to become wholly depopulate; we have desired that the profound solitude which reigns without her precincts, should also exist within. To render Rome really a Roman scene (an expression which Simond supposes to be the origin of the word romantic), every inhabitant should be dismissed; let the modern usurpers of the sacred soil build elsewhere, on less consecrated ground, homes for their degenerate race, and let the crumbling of her ruins and the flowing of her fountains be the only

4. Echo of Percy B. Shelley, *Adonais* (1821), stanzas 48–49.
5. Shakespeare, *A Midsummer-Night's Dream* I.i.78.

sounds to salute the ear of the classic pilgrim, who visits this venerable conservatory of old Time's rarest treasures.

But we are not permitted thus to foster our enthusiasm: pursued by Locandieri, ciceroni,[6] and dread tales of bandits, who ever retreat as we advance, we quit degraded Rome. From her extent of palace and temple and garden, we make what the Italians call a *salto mortale*,[7] and fall from the extreme heights of civilization upon the Pontine Marshes, a remnant of the reign of old Chaos, when earth and water lay in hideous and unfruitful torpor together. This dismal swamp serves as a curtain to veil the shrine and select abode of beauty. After the pass of Fondi, the sea retreats from the land, and spreads itself into a placid expanse of limpid blue, while the earth swells into a thousand lovely forms; sharp promontories shoot into the waves, and the crescent shores, painted bright by the gleaming fruit of the orange trees (called by the imaginative Italians *conche d'oro*, golden shells) lie in radiant beauty at the foot of the purple hills, paling in the Mediterranean, while the islands which rise from their clear-ocean bath, complete the seclusion and beauty of the scene. On the extreme verge of sea and land, separating the two elements—Naples stands glittering like a gem—*Vede Napoli, e poi mori!*[8] is a well-known saying—which every spectator echoes; for who that has been at Naples does not feel that all other places appear sad and gloomy as a cloister, after a residence in this "piece of Heaven fallen upon earth."

We have been led into this enlargement upon Italian scenery by the absence of any thing like description in the volume entitled "Italy as it Is"—Mr. Best is already known as the author of an account of a residence of four years in France,[9] whose chief interest consists in the development of the character, and a detail of the death of his eldest son. There is good sense and useful knowledge in the work, and we easily pardon the absence of the graces of a higher species of composition in the history of the minutiæ of a family's abode in a country town in France. But something more is required of a traveller in Italy. Besides, Mr. Best is a Roman Catholic, and the desire of defending his faith warps his views and diminishes the justice or utility of his observations. In consonance with his opinion of the superior merits of the faith of our fathers, he chooses to imagine that since the twelfth century, civilization has enjoyed a complete sabbath, making no sort of advance during the latter ages. Discontented with the changes, which he will not consider improvements, which

6. Innkeepers and guides.
7. "Somersault."
8. "See Naples, and then die!"
9. *Four Years in France; or, Narrative of an English Family's Residence There during That Period; Preceded by Some Account of the Conversion of the Author to the Catholic Faith* (London: Henry Colburn, 1826).

have had place since, he retrogrades with his intellect back to that æra, and employs himself by picking up in his way all the exploded errors dropped by Time in his progress, as useless lumber out of his baggage cart; these he sets up as idols, extols them, and has written a book in honour of their memory, so pathetically worded, that we begin to repine at the law of nature which has placed our birth in the nineteenth century. Nor can we agree in the judgments he passes on the works of art, though they often amused us from their whimsicality. We are told that the Coliseum is too ruinous—that the Egyptian Museum in the Vatican puts him in mind of the five wigs in the barber Figaro's shop window—that the Apollo Belvidere[10] looks like a broken-backed young gentleman shooting at a target for the amusement of young ladies. Works of art belong to the imagination, certain forms of which they realize; those who do not possess this portion of mind are incapable of perceiving the excellence of the objects created only to be understood by it—their criticisms stand for nothing, and an artist has a natural right to demur at submitting his works to their tribunal.

It may be prejudice, but as before in Eustace,[11] so now in the present volume, we are disgusted by the Catholics setting the corruption, profligacy and imbecility of Papal Rome, in comparison with her ancient glories. He glories over the consecration of the Pantheon as "a trophy of the greatest victory that ever was achieved; a victory in comparison with which all those obtained by brute force, or military art, are less than nothing in the estimate of right reason, justice, and benevolence—A victory of truth over error, of virtuous principle over deplorable perversion, over vacillating morality."—[p. 301.][12]—Does the reader wish to understand these assertions? Let him turn from the pages of Livy, to those of the history of the Popes, and he will find its just comment and elucidation. It is in this spirit that the convert travels through Italy, exulting in the overthrow of the magnificent, the intellectual, soul-stirring times of the Scipios and Catos,[13] and the superstructure of tiaras, red-stockinged cardinals—of pardons, priestcraft and simony.

As the next best thing to the power of the Pope, Mr. Best reveres that which Austria has established to degrade to the lowest possible depth the degenerate Italians. He sets out by endeavouring to refute all the stories told of the barbaric stupidity of the Austrian government; but this

---

10. Usually spelled Apollo Belvedere, a famous statue in the Vatican Museum.

11. Rev. John Chetwode Eustace, whose *A Tour Through Italy* (1813) was written with explicit endorsements of the Catholic faith.

12. Mary Shelley's brackets.

13. Scipio Africanus Major (?236–183 B.C.) and Scipio Africanus Minor (185–129 B.C.), Roman generals; Cato the Elder (234–149 B.C.) and Cato the Younger (95–46 B.C.), Roman statesmen.

admiration yields to the annoyances inflicted on him by the Austrian custom-house officers. Some of the most amusing passages of the book are allotted to a recital of teazing delays occasioned by the absence of these officials from their post of duty, and of the wanderings of the whole unhappy party in different directions through an unknown city in search of them—they, when found, shut the door like Pope's "good John,"[14] in their faces, bidding them wait—not exactly ten years, but till ten tomorrow, which is pretty much the same to the author's six innocent children, standing in the market-place, wanting their night-caps. At last, one of the *Liberators* is prevailed upon to attend; he begins the long progress of inquisitorial research, and just as the business seems drawing to a peaceable close, some forbidden trifle peeps through the respectable common-places of ordinary wearing apparel, and the turn-out of the whole box is insisted upon. Scenes like this make a rebel of the passive non-resistant—and he seditiously contradicts his previous account of the perfection of Austrian sway, by an assertion that "none can travel in that empire with tolerable comfort, but pedlars, and men to whom combs and tooth-brushes are luxuries unknown."[15]

Mr. Best's work will not be revered by men of taste, nor consulted for its philosophy and enlarged views—but it is, after all, both an amusing and useful production. It is amusing from the anecdotes and native repartees scattered through the narration, which taken from the lips of the Italians themselves are characteristic and worthy of Goldoni.[16] It is useful, for he details the minutiæ of his domestic life—his bargains, his contracts—he gives an exact list of prices, and accurate information as to a foreigner's best mode of living in the country—a family going to reside there will derive considerable benefit from consulting him and following his directions.

It has seldom been our lot to read a work more unpretending, more manly in its style, extensive in its information, amusing from its variety, and just in its conclusions than the "Tour in Italy and Sicily, by L. Simond." If all travellers wrote and described as he does, their productions would attain the highest places in the literary scale. He entered Italy by the Simplon, and condenses his progress southward into one magnificent panorama, where nothing is omitted, and nothing overdone. If we were at all inclined to quarrel with him, it would be with his opinions concerning works of art;—he does not sufficiently admire—and this arises from not having sufficiently studied—the productions of the great masters.—

14. "Shut, shut the door, good John! (fatigued, I said)," Alexander Pope, *Epistle to Dr. Arbuthnot*, l. 1—"good John" being Pope's gardener John Serle.
15. *Italy as it Is*, p. 81.
16. Carlo Goldoni (1707–93), dramatist, often considered father of Italian realistic comedy.

The knowledge of beauty is not a simple perception gained by the eyes; it requires refinement and education merely to perceive the intention of an artist, to pass judgment; we must not only, as it were, turn over the leaves hastily, reading merely the heads of the chapters, and table of contents, we must scan each page, peruse each line. A good picture requires at least as much time for its perusal as the volume of a novel.

In giving an account of the manners and usages of the country, Mr. Simond has not put down each vague assertion of the people he met, or the crude result of his own hasty observations; he has conversed with sensible men, seen with penetrating eyes, and the reader may depend on the truth and justness of his deductions. As an interesting specimen of his narrations we present one extract; and, as long sojourners in the country he describes, can vouch for every part of the detail.[17]

17. This essay continues for another twenty paragraphs, eleven of which are extracts from Simond's *Tour in Italy and Sicily*.

Loves of the Poets[1]

The Loves of the Poets! that we may understand why the conjunction of ideas represented by these words, presents the most resplendent image of beauty, grace, and happiness, that the human mind can well conceive, let us analyze them, and learn what Love, and what a Poet is.

There is much in the world afforded by nature and contrived by man, to yield satisfaction and enjoyment to our senses and our physical wants. In this northern clime the rich engross much of these. Carriages, horses, palaces with all their appendages, costly dress, and luxurious tables. The poor, (*i.e.* the unopulent, not the absolutely poor, those shut out from nature's table, the starving and miserable), have a counterbalance in a keener sense of the delights of leisure—they bring appetite instead of fastidious taste to season their plain viands; repose after labour, instead of downy beds, and silken hangings. With the omission of the necessitous and sick, our physical nature is replete with agreeable sensations; and yet how many ministered to, even to superfluity, are unhappy.

The mind requires more contribution than even our corporeal frame; ennui is the offspring of plenty and comfort; and while we contrive to shut out the evil elements, listlessness and weariness pervade the soul and pall every enjoyment. If the poor suffer less from this annoyance, it is not because they receive more pleasure; but because care, anxiety, or labour, occupy them; the rich also invent employments; books, operas, concerts, hunting, shooting, balls, picture-dealing, building, planting, travelling, fanciful changes of dress, and gambling. Yet these suffice not, nor professions, trades, nor ambition, to afford pleasure, though they waste the time; even the pursuits of wisdom, and the discoveries of sci-

1. Reprinted from Article X of *Westminster Review* 11 (October 1829): 472–77, a review of Anna Brownell Jameson's *The Loves of the Poets,* 2 vols. (London: Henry Colburn, 1829).

ence, engrossing as they are, and often delightful, are inefficient to take the sting from life, changing its burthen to gladness: this miracle is left for the affections; and the best form of affection, from the excess of its sympathy, is Love.

Who can feel satiety or sorrow when he loves?—"Love," Plato says, "showers benignity upon the world; before his presence, all harsh passions flee and perish. He is the author of all soft affections, the destroyer of all ungentle thoughts, possessed by the fortunate, and desired by the unhappy, therefore unhappy, because they possess him not; he is the father of grace and delicacy, and gentleness and delight and persuasion, and desire; the cherisher of all that is good, the abolisher of all that is evil, our most excellent pilot, defence, saviour and guardian, in labour and in fear, in desire and in reason; the ornament and governor of all things human and divine; the best, the loveliest."[2]

"Love," Shelley writes, "is that powerful attraction towards all we conceive, or fear, or hope beyond ourselves, when we find within our own thoughts the chasm of an insufficient void, and seek to awaken in all things that are, a community with what we experience within ourselves. The meeting with an understanding capable of clearly estimating our own, an imagination which should enter into, and seize upon the subtle and delicate peculiarities we have delighted to cherish and unfold in secret, with a frame whose nerves, like the chords of two exquisite lyres strung to the accompaniment of one delightful voice, vibrate with the vibrations of our own; this is the unattainable point to which Love tends; and to attain which, it urges forth the powers of man to arrest the faintest shadow of that, without the possession of which there is no rest or respite to the heart over which it rules."[3]

If so imperious, intense and pervading, be the spirit of Love, most powerful in the best and most delicate natures, how earnestly must women, whose being is formed for tenderness and sympathy, desire to know among whom in the harder, harsher sex this feeling exists in its greatest purity and force. And is not a poet an incarnation of the very essence of Love?

What is a Poet? Is he not that which wakens melody in the silent chords of the human heart? A light which arrays in splendor things and thoughts

2. Plato's Symposium. [Mary Shelley's note; she quotes from Agathon's speech in Percy B. Shelley's translation of the *Symposium*.]

3. Essay on Love by Shelley, published in the Keepsake for 1829. [Mary Shelley's note. Either Mary Shelley or the *Westminster Review* elided numerous sentences from "On Love" as printed in *The Keepsake for MDCCCXXIX*, ed. Frederic Mansel Reynolds (London: Hurst, Chance, and Co., [1828]), pp. 47–49. Rather than "an inefficient void" in the first sentence quoted by Mary Shelley, the *Keepsake* had printed "an insufficient void," which is here restored.]

which else were dim in the shadow of their own insignificance. His soul is like one of the pools in the Ilex woods of the Maremma,[4] it reflects the surrounding universe, but it beautifies, groupes, and mellows their tints, making a little world within itself, the copy of the outer one; but more entire, more faultless. But above all, a poet's soul is Love; the desire of sympathy is the breath that inspires his lay, while he lavishes on the sentiment and its object, his whole treasure-house of resplendent imagery, burning emotion, and ardent enthusiasm. He is the mirror of nature, reflecting her back ten thousand times more lovely; what then must not his power be, when he adds beauty to the most perfect thing in nature—even Love.

Lady Morgan who writes many things, not because they are true, but because they come into her head, has devoted some pages of the "Book of the Boudoir" to the villifying a poet's love. Another scrap in the same volume may serve as a comment. The few lines she has written on "Sentiment" sufficiently show why she depreciates the breathing sentiment of love, which is a poet's treasure and his gift.[5]

Let us instead of refuting an opinion which this lady may already have discarded as false, turn to the pages of the book before us, which propose to give us the history of the Loves of the Poets, of modern poets that is, for with many declarations of ignorance, yet with no little presumption, the fair authoress sweeps out of her list the loves of the classic authors; she shall have her way, however, and with her we will confine ourselves to the poets of modern Europe.

This work is the production of the authoress of the "Diary of an Ennuyée,"[6] a book we have heard described as the offspring of a singular union of a light head and a heavy heart—whose defect is to have made reality and fiction, who are brother and sister, and who may not therefore too closely unite, marry, and produce an offspring which is neither true nor false. Yet notwithstanding this defect, which disturbs and confuses the reader throughout, it is an interesting, clever, and graceful work.

The book dwells somewhat on the Troubadours, and then commences with the early Italian poets. So much has been said concerning Petrarch and Laura, that we find the account here given concise. She seems to have neglected his letters, which are abundant in testimonies of the truth, ardour, and reality of his attachment, and to have confined herself to his poems only, and to repeat what is already known, without research, to

4. In southwest Tuscany.

5. See Lady Morgan, "Poets' Loves" and "Sentiment," *The Book of the Boudoir* (London: Henry Colburn, 1829), II: 21–24 and 184. Such comments as "Poets seldom make good lovers, except on paper" and "Sentiment is at best an invention of vanity to mask the infirmities of mind and body" angered Mary Shelley. Mary Shelley and Lady Morgan became friends in 1835.

6. Which Mary Shelley reviewed in "The English in Italy," reprinted above.

every one. Dante and Beatrice are a pair more veiled in obscurity. Dante, like our own gentle affectionate Milton, has been stigmatized with the accusation of moroseness. Few know, that while bad institutions and bad men awoke stern resistance and severe animosity in the fervent souls of both, their hearts were the abode of Love, the realm over which sweet womanhood reigned and ruled. Dante's "Vita Nuova" is a beautiful and fanciful history of his love; and who that reads the vivid description of his trembling before the beauteous girl he almost worshipped, would figure the harsh proud Dante, so often pourtrayed to us? The loves of Ariosto, but little known, are on that account interesting; while the melancholy, impassioned, mysterious sentiment of Tasso, borrowing its grace from suffering, fascinates the imagination. In these pages this sad romance is unravelled much to our satisfaction. An extract on this subject will serve as a specimen of the work, and excite the curiosity of the reader to peruse the whole of these little volumes, replete as they are with the beautiful and unknown.

Leonora then was not unworthy of her illustrious conquest, either in person, heart, or mind. To be summoned daily into the presence of a princess thus beautiful and amiable, to read aloud his verses to her, to hear his own praises from her lips, to bask in her approving smiles, to associate with her in retirement, to behold her in all the graceful simplicity of her familiar life, was a dangerous situation for Tasso, and surely not less so for Leonora herself. That she was aware of his admiration, and perfectly understood his sentiments, and that a mysterious intelligence existed between them, consistent with the utmost reverence on his part, and the most perfect delicacy and dignity on hers, is apparent from the meaning and tendency of innumerable passages scattered through his minor poems, too significant in their application to be mistaken. Though that application be not avowed, and even disguised, the very disguise, when once detected, points to the object. Leonora knew, as well as her lover, that a princess "was no love-mate for a bard." She knew far better than her lover—until *he* too had been taught by wretched experience—the haughty and implacable temper of her brother Alphonso, who was never known to brook an injury or forgive an offender. She must have remembered too well the twelve years imprisonment and the narrow escape from death, of her unfortunate mother, for a less cause. She was of a timid reserved nature, increased by the extreme delicacy of her constitution. Her hand had been frequently sought by princes and nobles, whom she had uniformly rejected, at the risk of displeasing her brother; and the eyes of a jealous court were upon her. Tasso, on the other hand, was imprudent, hot-headed, fearless, and ardently attached. For both their sakes it was necessary for Leonora to be guarded and reserved, unless she would have made herself the fable of all Italy.—Vol. i. p. 296.

The reader must be referred to the volume itself for the proofs brought of these premises.

Perhaps the most interesting portion of these volumes, is that dedicated to the commemoration of conjugal poetry—the poets being for the most part women. The soft sweetness of Clotilde de Surville, the impassioned grace of Vittoria Colonna,[7] bear the palm. Complaint here is superseded by tender regret; solicitation by acknowledged sympathy; jealousy and suspense by gratitude and joy. The authoress is not pleased that while women mourn till death the loss of their companion, men usually change the elegiac strain composed for their first love, for epithalamiums on a marriage with a second. It is probably one among the many superstitions which rather injure than exalt the characters of women, which makes us, in spite of ourselves, set so high a price on their constancy even to the dead. Human beings in every stage of life need companions; women protectors; and except that, for the highminded and delicate, there are few worthy companions and protectors, and that if once a woman find one man on whom she may bestow without sorrow her tenderness, it is very unlikely that, losing him, she find a second, we know no cause in reason and morality, and hardly in good taste, which should condemn the lovely, bereaved, and ardent heart to perpetual widowhood.

A woman's love is tenderness, and may wed itself to the lost and dead. A man's is passion, and must expend itself on the living. A woman's domesticity is of her own making, and her home may be replete with elegance though she be alone. An unmarried man has no home. A solitary woman is the world's victim, and there is heroism in her consecration. A man whose fate is not allied to a female, from whatever cause, is divested of every poetical attribute—there is something rugged, harsh, and unnatural in the very idea. After all, the worthiness of the beloved object must always stand as an excuse for inconstancy; or, with a poet, the fervency and truth of his passion: since, through the force of his imagination, he may dress in jewels richer than those that adorned the doll at Loretto, a black-visaged Madonna;[8] nor be aware that the beauty of the object resides in his eyes instead of in her mind or form.

The latter part of these volumes forms a very amusing and sentimental scandalous chronicle. We pity Pope, who, in default of better, lavished his verses and his poetical attentions on so uninteresting a personage as

7. Clotilde de Surville (the purported fifteenth-century author of *Poésies de Clotilde,* first published in 1803) and Vittoria Colonna (1490–1547) were both famous for their love poetry.

8. A statue that, together with the shrine of the Holy House of Virgin, had supposedly been transported by angels from Nazareth to Loreto, Italy, at the end of the thirteenth century. The statue, taken to Paris in 1798 and returned by Napoleon in 1801, was destroyed by fire in 1921.

Martha Blount. Our authoress says, "me thinks, had I been a poet, or Pope, I would rather have been led about in triumph by the spirited, accomplished lady Mary, than chained to the footstool of two paltry girls" [vol. ii. p. 284]. Yet as no satisfactory account is given for the cause of the quarrel between Pope and that lady, we may believe, judging from the hardness and peremptoriness of her character, her love of ridicule, and her talent for sarcasm, that she first awoke the sting of the "Wasp of Twickenham;"[9] and he, with all the bitterness of one whose person was but too open to vulgar derision, could not bear to have his genuine tenderness scoffed at; while the spiteful, jealous, bitter disposition, usually characteristic of deformed persons, gave poison to the wound she had provoked.

If we smile somewhat at the loves of the "Wasp" and the Sappho[10] of the satires, whom Horace Walpole so amusingly describes [vol. ii. p. 307], what shall we say to the French philosophers by nature—poets by courtesy—Du Châtelet and Voltaire.[11] Had either of them had one spark of real poetry in their composition, it had led to different results than those ridiculous, disgusting, violent and laughable scenes commemorated in these volumes [vol. ii. p. 322]. The same observations may apply to Swift. Lovers in verse are not, therefore, poets. Swift's victims were beautiful accomplished women. He was clever, and could forge even rhythm and rhyme in his head, but the spirit of poetry disdained to take up its abode in his coarse-grained, ill-fashioned, hard-natured soul. Of these modern moderns the greatest portion of interest has been thrown over the rustic loves of Burns,—thus redeeming a poet's name,—shewing that the high born and bred, and clever lady Mary Montagu, Voltaire and his *femme terrible*,[12] and Swift, were lovers, but not poets, and therefore neither gentle, imaginative, nor interesting; while the lowly-born Burns, being instinct with Apollo's fire, sheds a glory over the humble objects of his attachment, which a princess might envy [vol. ii. p. 195].[13] Monti and his wife[14] are also an interesting pair [vol. ii. p. 209], and we are charmed by the sweetness displayed in the loves of Klopstock and Meta [vol. ii. p.

9. The nickname of Alexander Pope, whose lifelong friend was Martha Blount (1690–1763). The brackets in this and subsequent paragraphs are Mary Shelley's.

10. Lady Mary Wortley Montagu.

11. Gabrielle-Emilie Le Tonnelier de Breteuil, Marquise du Châtelet (1706–49) and François Marie Arouet de Voltaire (1694–1778) were lovers. The names in the original review are incorrectly preceded by "Messrs.", which has here been deleted. Also, "322" at the end of the next sentence corrects the printing error of "222".

12. A phrase Voltaire once used to describe Madame du Châtelet.

13. Mary Shelley refers to the "Bonnie Jean" in the poetry of Robert Burns (1759–96).

14. Vincenzo Monti (1754–1828), Italian Neoclassical poet, and his wife Teresa Pichler; Mary Shelley later wrote the life of Monti for Lardner's Cabinet Cyclopædia.

154],[15] though there is a Germanism about it, which, giving effeminacy to the man, dims the picture by a mist of what appears to us almost like affectation.

The authoress sums up her work by a glance at the poets of the day, and their loves—a chapter as well left out, for she, fearing to tread on forbidden ground, tells us, in fact, nothing. Unable to throw the ideality of distance over the near and distinct—and afraid, justly so—for the practice of shewing up our friends is the vice and shame of our literature,— of dragging into undesired publicity the modest and retiring,—she does not even bestow the interest of reality upon her undefined sketches. Besides, there are certain names she dreads to mention. May we not say, in the somewhat hacknied phrase of Tacitus: Sed perfulgebant, eo ipso quod *nomines* eorum non visebantur?[16]

15. The German poet Friedrich Gottlieb Klopstock (1724–1803) and his wife Margareta (Meta) Moller, herself a writer. They were married in 1754, and she died in 1758.
16. Tacitus, *Annals*, III. 76. Mary Shelley deletes the names "Cassius atque Brutus" from the original and substitutes for "effigies" her *"nomines"*: "But they shone brighter than all by the very fact that their *names* were unseen."

from A Review
of William Godwin's
Cloudesley[1]

In his able preface to this work, Mr Godwin sets the writer of fiction in a very high place. He compares him with the historian and the dramatist, and gives him the preference. He says—and his late occupation of the History of the Commonwealth[2] has informed him of the truth of the assertion—that "individual history and biography are mere guesses in the dark." "The writer collects his information of what the great men on the theatre of the world are reported to have said and done, and then endeavours with his best sagacity to find out the explanation; to hit on that thread, woven through the whole contexture of the piece, which, being discovered, we are told

> No prodigies remain,
> Comets are regular, and Wharton plain.[3]

But man is a more complex machine than is dreamed of in our philosophy, and it is probable that the skill of no moral anatomist has yet been consummate enough fully to solve the obscurities of any one of the great worthies of ancient or modern times." While the writer of fiction, Mr Godwin goes on to say, "when he introduces his ideal personage to the public, enters upon the task with a preconception of the qualities that belong to this being, the principle of his actions and its concomitants. He has thus two advantages: in the first place, his express office is to draw just conclusions from assigned premises, a task of no extraordinary diffi-

---

1. Reprinted from *Blackwood's Edinburgh Magazine* 27 (May 1830): 711–16, a review of William Godwin's *Cloudesley: A Tale,* 3 vols. (London: Henry Colburn and Richard Bentley, 1830)—only pp. 711–13 reprinted here.

2. William Godwin, *History of the Commonwealth of England: From its Commencement, to the Restoration of Charles the Second* (1824–28).

3. Godwin quotes from Alexander Pope, "Epistle to Sir Richard Temple, Lord Viscount Cobham," ll. 208–209.

culty; and, secondly, while he endeavours to aid those conclusions by consulting the oracle in his bosom, the suggestions of his own heart, instructed as he is besides by a converse with the world, and a careful survey of the encounters that present themselves to his observation, he is much less liable to be cribbed and cabined in by those unlooked-for phenomena, which in the history of an individual seem to have a malicious pleasure in thrusting themselves forward to subvert the best digested theories. In this sense, then, it is infallibly true that fictitious history, when it is the work of a competent hand, is more to be depended upon, and comprises more of the science of man, than whatever can be exhibited by the historian." The writer of fiction, Mr Godwin asserts, has besides many advantages over the dramatist; "he has leisure to ripen his materials; to draw out his results one by one, even as they grow up and unfold themselves in the 'seven ages' of man. He is not confined, like the dramatist, to put down the words that his characters shall utter. He accompanies the language made use of by them with his comments, and explains the inmost thoughts that pass in the bosom of the upright man and the perverse."

Such, indeed, have been the characteristics of Mr Godwin's novels. While other writers represent manners rather than passions, or passions at once vague and incomplete, he conceives, in its entireness, the living picture of an event with all its adjuncts; he sets it down in its vivid reality: no part is dim, no part is tame. We have the clear and distinct representation of his conception, and are made to feel that his portraiture is endowed with the very essence and spirit of our nature. Mr Bulwer has, in his delightful novel of "Pelham," described his idea of a work of fiction.[4] Story, he renders the subordinate. The almost common events of life are his groundwork; or where he mingles the romantic, it is made rather an episode than an intrinsic part of his machinery. Mr Bulwer does not take the materials of the world around, first separating, and then, by aid of the inventive faculty, moulding them into a new form, whose exact appearance depends on a preconceived notion of what must be, to fulfil his idea; but he gives us rather himself, his experience, his opinions, his emotions. The high-wrought and noble tone of his mind spreads a sacred and even mysterious grandeur over his pages. His wit enlivens them, his acute observations and peculiar and beautiful power of poetically linking the apparently dissimilar by their real similitudes, are the value and charm of his works.

But though Mr Bulwer's exceeding talent exalts this species of com-

---

4. Edward George Earle Lytton Bulwer (1803–73), later Bulwer-Lytton, explained his ideas on fiction in his Preface to the 2d ed. of *Pelham; or, The Adventures of a Gentleman* (1828).

position, it is not in itself of so high a grade as the other, which in fact almost infringes on the ideality of the drama by a sort of unity, wanting, in what we may call in comparison with this the "narrative," the "didactic novel." The temple which presents to our eyes the proportions and harmonious accords of architecture, is a finer production than a rambling palace, though the apartments of the latter may be more glittering, lustrous, and delightful. There seems in our human nature a necessity of self-restraint, before we can reach the highest kind of excellence. If simplicity is the best,—if those,

> Who, in love and truth,
> Where no misgiving is, rely
> Upon the genial sense of youth,
> Glad hearts without reproach or blot,
> Who do thy work and know it not,—[5]

and if the works which are the type of this artless celestial nature hold the first rank, yet both characters and productions of this kind are too rare and too individual to form a class:[6] an example they cannot be, for their characteristic is, that they are genuine and untaught. Putting, therefore, these out of the question, I repeat, that a certain degree of obedience to rule and law is necessary for the completion and elevation of our nature and its productions. Of all writers, Shakspeare, whom the ignorant have deemed irregular, is the closest follower of these laws, for he has always a scope and an aim, which, beyond every other writer, he fulfils. The merely copying from our own hearts will no more form a first-rate work of art, than will the most exquisite representation of mountains, water, wood, and glorious clouds, form a good painting, if none of the rules of grouping or colouring are followed. Sir Walter Scott has not attained this master art; his wonderful genius developes itself in individual characters and scenes, unsurpassed, except by Shakspeare, for energy and truth; but his wholes want keeping—often even due connexion.

Of all modern writers, Mr Godwin has arrived most sedulously, and most successfully, at the highest species of perfection his department of art affords. He sketches in his own mind, with a comprehensive and bold imagination, the plan of his work; he digs at the foundations, and learns all the due bearings of his position; he examines his materials, and sees

5. William Wordsworth, "Ode to Duty," ll. 10–14, published in *Poems in Two Volumes* (1807).
6. The beautiful tale of Rosamond Gray, by Charles Lamb, occurs to us as the most perfect specimen of the species of writing to which we allude. [Mary Shelley's note on Lamb's *A Tale of Rosamund Gray and Old Blind Margaret* (1798).]

exactly to what purpose each is best fitted; he makes an incident; he un-
erringly divines the results, both of the event and passion, which this
incident will bring forth. By dint of the mastery of thought, he transfuses
himself into the very souls of his personages; he dives into their secret
hearts, and lays bare, even to their anatomy, their workings; not a pulsation escapes him,—while yet all is blended into one whole, which forms
the pervading impulse of the individual he brings before us. Who, remembering Falkland, but feels as if he had stood by that noble ruin, and
watched its downfall! Who but writhes under the self-dejection of Mandeville, and feels the while his own heart whisper fearful oracles of the
tameless and sad incongruities of our souls! Who but exulted madly with
St Leon, when he obtained his specious gifts![7] We pass with their creator
into the very form and frame of his creatures: our hearts swell responsive
to every emotion he delineates. When we heard of another tale by the
same author, we wondered what new magic circle was traced, within
which we were to stand side by side with the enchanter, seeing the spirits
that rise to his call, enthralled by the spell he casts over us.

Cloudesley is before us, a fresh example of what we have been saying.
This tale contains a train of events, each naturally flowing one from the
other, and each growing in importance and dignity as they proceed. We
have no extraneous ornaments; no discursive flights. Comparing this book
with others, we felt as if we had quitted gardens and parks, and tamer
landscapes, for a scene on nature's grandest scale; that we wandered
among giants' rocks, "the naked bones of the world waiting to be
clothed."[8] We use this quotation, because it suggested itself to our minds
as we read these volumes, but we must guard our meaning from the idea
of there being any turgidness in Cloudesley. Grace and dignity, joined to
power, are its characteristics. The first volume is the least interesting. The
author digs at the foundation, and then places the first stones; then we
begin to feel the just proportions and promising beauty of the plan, till
the tantalizing work of preparation finally yields to the full manifestation
of the conception of the artist. If we may be permitted another metaphor,
and this last is the most just, we will say that this work reminds us of the
solemn strain of some cathedral organ. First, a few appropriate chords are
fitfully and variously struck; a prelude succeeds to awaken our attention,
and then rises the full peal, which swells upon the ear, till the air appears
overcharged and overflowing with majestic harmonies. As far as an image

7. Characters from Godwin's *Things As They Are; or, The Adventures of Caleb
Williams* (1794), *Mandeville* (1817), and *St. Leon* (1799).
   8. Unidentified.

can go, this exactly pourtrays our sensations on reading Cloudesley. The composer rapts us from ourselves, filling our bosoms with new and extraordinary emotions, while we sit soul-enchained by the wonders of his art.[9]

9. The review continues for another thirteen paragraphs, six of which are extracts from *Cloudesley*.

Preface

to *The Poetical Works of*
Percy Bysshe Shelley (1839)[1]

Obstacles have long existed to my presenting the public with a perfect edition of Shelley's Poems. These being at last happily removed, I hasten to fulfil an important duty,—that of giving the productions of a sublime genius to the world, with all the correctness possible, and of, at the same time, detailing the history of those productions, as they sprung, living and warm, from his heart and brain. I abstain from any remark on the occurrences of his private life; except, inasmuch as the passions which they engendered, inspired his poetry. This is not the time to relate the truth; and I should reject any colouring of the truth. No account of these events has ever been given at all approaching reality in their details, either as regards himself or others; nor shall I further allude to them than to remark, that the errors of action, committed by a man as noble and generous as Shelley, may, as far as he only is concerned, be fearlessly avowed, by those who loved him, in the firm conviction, that were they judged impartially, his character would stand in fairer and brighter light than that of any contemporary. Whatever faults he had, ought to find extenuation among his fellows, since they proved him to be human; without them, the exalted nature of his soul would have raised him into something divine.

The qualities that struck any one newly introduced to Shelley, were, first, a gentle and cordial goodness that animated his intercourse with warm affection, and helpful sympathy. The other, the eagerness and ardour with which he was attached to the cause of human happiness and improvement. To defecate life of its misery and its evil, was the ruling passion of his soul: he dedicated to it every power of his mind, every pulsation of his heart. He looked on political freedom as the direct agent to effect the happiness of mankind; and thus any new-sprung hope of liberty

1. Reprinted from *The Poetical Works of Percy Bysshe Shelley*, ed. Mrs. Shelley, 4 vols. (London: Edward Moxon, 1839), I: vii–xvi.

inspired a joy and an exultation more intense and wild than he could have felt for any personal advantage. Those who have never experienced the workings of passion on general and unselfish subjects, cannot understand this; and it must be difficult of comprehension to the younger generation rising around, since they cannot remember the scorn and hatred with which the partizans of reform were regarded some few years ago, nor the persecutions to which they were exposed. He had been from youth the victim of the state of feeling inspired by the reaction of the French Revolution; and believing firmly in the justice and excellence of his views, it cannot be wondered that a nature as sensitive, as impetuous, and as generous as his, should put its whole force into the attempt to alleviate for others the evils of those systems from which he had himself suffered. Many advantages attended his birth; he spurned them all when balanced with what he considered his duties. He was generous to imprudence, devoted to heroism.

These characteristics breathe throughout his poetry. The struggle for human weal; the resolution firm to martyrdom; the impetuous pursuit; the glad triumph in good; the determination not to despair. Such were the features that marked those of his works which he regarded with most complacency, as sustained by a lofty subject and useful aim.

In addition to these, his poems may be divided into two classes,—the purely imaginative, and those which sprung from the emotions of his heart. Among the former may be classed "The Witch of Atlas," "Adonais," and his latest composition, left imperfect, "The Triumph of Life." In the first of these particularly, he gave the reins to his fancy, and luxuriated in every idea as it rose; in all, there is that sense of mystery which formed an essential portion of his perception of life—a clinging to the subtler inner spirit, rather than to the outward form—a curious and metaphysical anatomy of human passion and perception.

The second class is, of course, the more popular, as appealing at once to emotions common to us all; some of these rest on the passion of love; others on grief and despondency; others on the sentiments inspired by natural objects. Shelley's conception of love was exalted, absorbing, allied to all that is purest and noblest in our nature, and warmed by earnest passion; such it appears when he gave it a voice in verse. Yet he was usually averse to expressing these feelings, except when highly idealised; and many of his more beautiful effusions he had cast aside, unfinished, and they were never seen by me till after I had lost him. Others, as for instance, "Rosalind and Helen," and "Lines written among the Euganean Hills," I found among his papers by chance; and with some difficulty urged him to complete them. There are others, such as the "Ode to the Sky Lark," and "The Cloud," which, in the opinion of many critics, bear a purer poetical stamp than any other of his productions. They were written as his mind prompted, listening to the carolling of the bird, aloft in the azure sky of Italy; or marking the cloud as it sped across the heavens, while he floated in his boat on the Thames.

No poet was ever warmed by a more genuine and unforced inspiration. His extreme sensibility gave the intensity of passion to his intellectual pursuits; and rendered his mind keenly alive to every perception of outward objects, as well as to his internal sensations. Such a gift is, among the sad vicissitudes of human life, the disappointments we meet, and the galling sense of our own mistakes and errors, fraught with pain; to escape from such, he delivered up his soul to poetry, and felt happy when he sheltered himself from the influence of human sympathies, in the wildest regions of fancy. His imagination has been termed too brilliant, his thoughts too subtle. He loved to idealise reality; and this is a taste shared by few. We are willing to have our passing whims exalted into passions, for this gratifies our vanity; but few of us understand or sympathise with the endeavour to ally the love of abstract beauty, and adoration of abstract good, the τὸ ἀγαθὸν καὶ τὸ καλὸν[2] of the Socratic philosophers, with our sympathies with our kind. In this Shelley resembled Plato; both taking more delight in the abstract and the ideal, than in the special and tangible. This did not result from imitation; for it was not till Shelley resided in Italy that he made Plato his study; he then translated his Symposium and his Ion; and the English language boasts of no more brilliant composition, than Plato's Praise of Love, translated by Shelley. To return to his own poetry. The luxury of imagination, which sought nothing beyond itself, as a child burthens itself with spring flowers, thinking of no use beyond the enjoyment of gathering them, often showed itself in his verses: they will be only appreciated by minds who have resemblance to his own; and the mystic subtlety of many of his thoughts will meet the same fate. The metaphysical strain that characterises much of what he has written, was, indeed, the portion of his works to which, apart from those whose scope was to awaken mankind to aspirations for what he considered the true and good, he was himself particularly attached. There is much, however, that speaks to the many. When he would consent to dismiss these huntings after the obscure, which, entwined with his nature as they were, he did with difficulty, no poet ever expressed in sweeter, more heart-reaching, or more passionate verse, the gentler or more forcible emotions of the soul.

A wise friend once wrote to Shelley, "You are still very young, and in certain essential respects you do not yet sufficiently perceive that you are so." It is seldom that the young know what youth is till they have got be-

2. "The good and the beautiful."

yond its period; and time was not given him to attain this knowledge. It must be remembered that there is the stamp of such inexperience on all he wrote; he had not completed his nine and twentieth year when he died. The calm of middle life did not add the seal of the virtues which adorn maturity to those generated by the vehement spirit of youth. Through life also he was a martyr to ill health, and constant pain wound up his nerves to a pitch of susceptibility that rendered his views of life different from those of a man in the enjoyment of healthy sensations. Perfectly gentle and forbearing in manner, he suffered a good deal of internal irritability, or rather excitement, and his fortitude to bear was almost always on the stretch; and thus, during a short life, had gone through more experience of sensation, than many whose existence is protracted. "If I die to-morrow," he said, on the eve of his unanticipated death, "I have lived to be older than my father." The weight of thought and feeling burdened him heavily; you read his sufferings in his attenuated frame, while you perceived the mastery he held over them in his animated countenance and brilliant eyes.

He died, and the world shewed no outward sign; but his influence over mankind, though slow in growth, is fast augmenting, and in the ameliorations that have taken place in the political state of his country, we may trace in part the operation of his arduous struggles. His spirit gathers peace in its new state from the sense that, though late, his exertions were not made in vain, and in the progress of the liberty he so fondly loved.

He died, and his place among those who knew him intimately, has never been filled up. He walked beside them like a spirit of good to comfort and benefit—to enlighten the darkness of life with irradiations of genius, to cheer it with his sympathy and love. Any one, once attached to Shelley, must feel all other affections, however true and fond, as wasted on barren soil in comparison. It is our best consolation to know that such a pure-minded and exalted being was once among us, and now exists where we hope one day to join him;—although the intolerant, in their blindness, poured down anathemas, the Spirit of Good, who can judge the heart, never rejected him.

In the notes appended to the poems, I have endeavoured to narrate the origin and history of each. The loss of nearly all letters and papers which refer to his early life, renders the execution more imperfect than it would otherwise have been. I have, however, the liveliest recollection of all that was done and said during the period of my knowing him. Every impression is as clear as if stamped yesterday, and I have no apprehension of any mistake in my statements, as far as they go. In other respects, I am, indeed, incompetent; but I feel the importance of the task, and regard it as my most sacred duty. I endeavour to fulfil it in a manner he would himself approve; and hope in this publication to lay the first stone of a monument due to Shelley's genius, his sufferings, and his virtues:

> S'al seguir son tarda,
> Forse avverrà che 'l bel nome gentile
> Consacrerò con questa stanca penna.[3]

3. Petrarch (1304–74), Sonnet CCXCVII: "if I am late to follow, / Perhaps it will be seen that her [his] dear name / I shall make sacred with this weary pen." Translation by Anna Maria Armi, *Petrarch: Sonnets and Songs* (New York: Grosset & Dunlap, 1968), p. 419.

Preface to

Rambles in Germany and Italy,
in 1840, 1842, and 1843 [1]

I have found it a pleasant thing while travelling to have in the carriage the works of those who have passed through the same country. Sometimes they inform, sometimes they excite curiosity. If alone, they serve as society; if with others, they suggest matter for conversation.

These Volumes were thus originated. Visiting spots often described, pursuing a route such as form for the most part the common range of the tourist—I could tell nothing new, except as each individual's experience possesses novelty. While I passed in haste from city to city; as I travelled through mountain-passes or over vast extents of country, I put down the daily occurrences—a guide, a pioneer, or simply a fellow-traveller, for those who came after me.

When I reached Italy, however, and came south, I found that I could say little of Florence and Rome, as far as regarded the cities themselves, that had not been said so often and so well before, that I was satisfied to select from my letters such portions merely as touched upon subjects that I had not found mentioned elsewhere. It was otherwise as regarded the people, especially in a political point of view; and in treating of them my scope grew more serious.

I believe that no one can mingle much with the Italians without becoming attached to them. Their faults injure each other; their good qualities make them agreeable to strangers. Their courtesy, their simplicity of manner, their evident desire to serve, their rare and exceeding intelligence, give to the better specimens among the higher classes, and to many among the lower, a charm all their own. In addition, therefore, to being a mere gossiping companion to a traveller, I would fain say something

1. Reprinted from Mrs. Shelley, *Rambles in Germany and Italy, in 1840, 1842, and 1843*, 2 vols. (London: Edward Moxon, 1844), I: vii–xvi.

that may incite others to regard them favourably; something explanatory of their real character.[2] But to speak of the state of Italy and the Italians—

> Non è poleggio da picciola barca
> Quel, che fendendo va l'ardita prora,
> Nè da nocchier, ch'a se medesmo parca.[3]

When I began to put together what I knew, I found it too scant of circumstance and experience to form a whole. I could only sketch facts, guess at causes, hope for results. I have said little, therefore; but what I have said, I believe that I may safely declare, may be depended upon.

Time was, when travels in Italy were filled with contemptuous censures of the effeminacy of the Italians—diatribes against the vice and cowardice of the nobles—sneers at the courtly verses of the poets, who were content to celebrate a marriage or a birth among the great:—their learned men fared better, for there were always writers in Italy whose names adorned European letters—yet still contempt was the general tone; and of late years travellers (with the exception of Lady Morgan, whose book[4] is dear to the Italians), parrot the same, not because these things still exist, but because they know no better.

Italy is, indeed, much changed. Their historians no longer limit themselves to disputing dates, but burn with enthusiasm for liberty; their poets, Manzoni and Niccolini[5] at their head, direct their efforts to elevating and invigorating the public mind. The country itself wears a new aspect; it is struggling with its fetters,—not only with the material ones that weigh on it so heavily, and which they endure with a keen sense of shame, but

2. Assassination is of frequent occurrence in Italy: these are perpetrated chiefly from jealousy. There are crimes frequent with us and the French of which they are never guilty. Brutal murders committed for "filthy lucre" do not occur among them. We never hear of hospitality violated, or love used as a cloak that the murderers may possess themselves of some trifle more or less of property. Their acts of violence are, indeed, assassinations, committed in the heat of the moment—never cold-blooded. Even the history of their banditti was full of redeeming traits, as long as they only acted for themselves and were not employed by government. There is plenty of cheating in Italy—not more, perhaps, than elsewhere, only the system is more artfully arranged; but there is no domestic robbery. I lived four years in Tuscany. I was told that the servant who managed my expenditure cheated me dreadfully, and had reason to know that during that time she saved nearly a hundred crowns: but I never at any time, when stationary or travelling, was robbed of the smallest coin or the most trifling article of property. On the contrary, instances of scrupulous honesty are familiar to all travellers in Italy, as practised among the poorest peasantry. [Mary Shelley's note.]

3. Dante, *Paradiso* XXIII.67–69, with Mary Shelley's choice of "poleggio" rather than the preferred "pareggio": "It is no voyage for a little bark, this which my daring prow cleaves as it goes, nor for a pilot who would spare himself."

4. *Italy* (1821) by Lady Sydney Morgan (1783–1859).

5. Allesandro Francesco Tommaso Antonio Manzoni (1785–1873) and Giovanni Battista Niccolini (1782–1861).

with those that have entered into and bind the soul—superstition, luxury, servility, indolence, violence, vice.

Since the date of these letters Italy has been much disturbed,—but the risings and their unfortunate consequences to individuals, are regarded by us with contempt, or excite only a desire of putting an end to them as detrimental to the sufferers, without being of any utility to the cause of civilisation and moral improvement. Yet it ought not to be forgotten, that the oppression suffered in that portion of the country which has been recently convulsed, is such as to justify Dr. Johnson's proposition, that "if the abuse be enormous, Nature will rise up, and claiming her original rights, overturn a corrupt political system."[6]

Englishmen, in particular, ought to sympathise in their struggles: for the aspiration for free institutions all over the world has its source in England. Our example first taught the French nobility to seek to raise themselves from courtiers into legislators. The American war of independence, it is true, quickened this impulse, by showing the way to a successful resistance to the undue exercise of authority; but the seed was all sown by us. The swarms of English that overrun Italy keep the feeling alive. An Italian gentleman naturally envies an Englishman, hereditary or elective legislator. He envies him his pride of country, in which he himself can in no way indulge. He knows, at best, that his sovereign is a weak tool in the hands of a foreign potentate; and that all that is aimed at by the governments that rule him, is to benefit Austria—not Italy. But this forms but a small portion of his wrongs. He sees that we enjoy the privilege of doing and saying whatever we please, so that we infringe no law. If he write a book, it is submitted to the censor, and if it be marked by any boldness of opinion, it is suppressed. If he attempt any plan for the improvement of his countrymen, he is checked; if a tardy permission be given him to proceed, it is clogged with such conditions as nullify the effect. If he limit his endeavours to self-improvement, he is suspected—surrounded by spies; while his friends share in the odium that attaches to him. The result of such persecution is to irritate or discourage. He either sinks into the Circean Stye, in which so many drag out a degraded existence, or he is irresistibly impelled to resist. No way to mitigate the ills he groans under, or to serve his countrymen, is open, except secret societies. The mischievous effects of such to those who are implicated in them, are unspeakably great. They fear a spy in the man who shares their oath; their acts are dark, and treachery hovers close. The result is inevitable; their own moral sense is tampered with, and becomes vitiated; or, if they escape this evil, and preserve the ingenuousness of a free and noble nature, they are victims.

6. James Boswell, *Life of Samuel Johnson,* 6 July 1763.

While thus every passion, bad and good, ferments—a touch is given, and up springs armed revolt. This must be put down or the peace of Europe will be disturbed. Peace is a lovely thing. It is horrible to image the desolation of war; the cottage burnt, the labour of the husbandman destroyed—outrage and death there, where security of late spread smiles and joy:—and the fertility and beauty of Italy exaggerate still more the hideousness of the contrast. Cannot it be that peaceful mediation and a strong universal sense of justice may interpose, instead of the cannon and bayonet?

There is another view to be taken. We have lately been accustomed to look on Italy as a discontented province of Austria, forgetful that her supremacy dates only from the downfall of Napoleon. From the invasion of Charles VIII.[7] till 1815, Italy has been a battle-field, where the Spaniard, the French, and the German, have fought for mastery; and we are blind indeed, if we do not see that such will occur again, at least among the two last. Supposing a war to arise between them, one of the first acts of aggression on the part of France would be to try to drive the Germans from Italy. Even if peace continue, it is felt that the papal power is tottering to its fall—it is only supported, because the French will not allow Austria to extend her dominions, and the Austrian is eager to prevent any change that may afford pretence for the French to interfere. Did the present pope[8] act with any degree of prudence, his power thus propped might last some time longer; but as it is, who can say, how soon, for the sake of peace in the rest of Italy, it may not be necessary to curtail his territories.

The French feel this and begin to dream of dominion across the Alps—the occupation of Ancona was a feeler put out—it gained no positive object except to check Austria—for the rest its best effect was to reiterate the lesson they have often taught, that no faith should be given to their promises of liberation.

The Italians consider that the hour will arrive sooner or later when the stranger will again dispute for dominion over them; when the peace of their wealthy towns and smiling villages will be disturbed by nations meeting in hostility on their soil. The efforts of their patriots consequently tend to make preparation, that such an hour may find them, from the Alps to Brundusium, united. They feel the necessity also of numbering military leaders among themselves. The most enlightened Italians instead of relying on the mystery of oaths, the terror of assassination, the perpetual conspiracy of secret associations, are anxious that their young men should exercise themselves in some school of warfare—they wish that the new generation may be emancipated by their courage, their

7. Charles VIII the Adventurous (1470–98), King of France (1483–98).
8. Pope Gregory XVI (1831–46), born Bartolommeo Capellari (1765–1846).

knowledge, their virtues; which should oppose an insurmountable barrier to foreign invasion and awe their rulers into concession.

Niccolini, in his latest work, Arnaldo da Brescia,[9] has put these sentiments in the mouth of his hero. That poem, replete with passionate eloquence and striking incident, presents a lively picture of the actual state of Italy. The insolence of the German, the arrogance of the popes, the degraded state of the people, and the aspirations of the patriots, each find a voice. It is impossible not to hope well for a country, whose poets, whose men of reflection and talent, without one exception, all use the gifts of genius or knowledge, to teach the noblest lessons of devotion to their country; and whose youth receive the same with devoted enthusiasm.

When we visit Italy, we become what the Italians were censured for being,—enjoyers of the beauties of nature, the elegance of art, the delights of climate, the recollections of the past, and the pleasures of society, without a thought beyond. Such to a great degree was I while there, and my book does not pretend to be a political history or dissertation. I give fragments—not a whole. Such as they are, I shall be repaid for the labour and anxiety of putting them together, if they induce some among my countrymen to regard with greater attention, and to sympathise in the struggles of a country, the most illustrious and the most unfortunate in the world.

9. A tragedy published in 1843.

Letters

Letters

To Percy Bysshe Shelley[1]

[5 Church Terrace, Pancras   25 October 1814][2]
For what a minute did I see you yesterday—is this the way my beloved that we are to live till the sixth[3] in the morning I look for you and when I awake I turn to look on you—dearest Shelley you are solitary and uncomfortable why cannot I be with you to cheer you and to press you to my heart oh my love you have no friends why then should you be torn from the only one who has affection for you—But I shall see you tonight and that is the hope that I shall live on through the day—be happy dear Shelley and think of me—why do I say this dearest & only one   I know how tenderly you love me and how you repine at this absence from me—when shall we be free from fear of treachery?—

I send you the letter I told you of from Harriet and a letter we received yesterday from fanny[4] the history of this interview I will tell you when I

1. This and the following letters are reprinted, with rewritten and condensed notes, from *Letters*, I: 1, 4-5, 71, 205-8, 244-50, 299, 377-81; II: 115, 117-18; III: 1-3, 17-18. See *Letters* for fuller annotations and for explanation of the editorial principles. The brackets in these letters serve the following functions: square brackets [   ] enclose editorial additions, corrections, conjectures, and comments; empty square brackets designate unknown words that are missing due to holes, tears, or deterioration in the manuscripts; curly brackets {   } enclose words, letters, or punctuation omitted by Mary Shelley; empty curly brackets designate unknown words omitted by Mary Shelley; angle brackets ⟨   ⟩ enclose words that Mary Shelley wrote and then deleted.
2. Mary Godwin and Shelley had eloped on 28 July 1814 for their six weeks' tour on the continent, returned to London on 13 September, and resided there under financial strain until May 1815. On 27 September 1814 they took lodgings at 5 Church Terrace, but Shelley from 23 October until 9 November lived elsewhere in order to avoid arrest for debt.
3. That is, 6 November, when Mary Godwin expected to be reunited permanently with Shelley.
4. Letters from Harriet Westbrook Shelley (1795–1816), Shelley's first wife; and from Fanny Imlay (1794–1816), Mary Godwin's half sister.

come—but perhaps as it is so rainy a day Fanny will not be allowed to come at all—

My love my own one be happy—

I was so dreadfully tired yesterday that I was obliged to take a coach home forgive this extravagance but I am so very weak at present[5] & I had been so agitated through the day that I was not able to stand a morning rest however will set me quite right again and I shall be quite well when I meet you this evening—will you be at the door of the coffee house at five oclock as it is disagreeable to go into those places and I shall be there exactly at that time & we will go into St. Pauls where we can sit down

I send you Diogenes as you have no books—Hookham[6] was so ill tempered as not to send the books I asked for

To Percy Bysshe Shelley

[5 Church Terrace, Pancras   3 November 1814]

Dearest Love—I am so out of spirits   I feel so lonely but we shall meet tomorrow so I will try to be happy—Grays inn Gardens is I fear a dangerous place yet can you think of any other.

I received your letter tonight   I wanted one for I had {not} received one for almost two day but do not think I mean any thing by this my love—I know you took a long long walk yesterday so you could not write but I who am at home who do not walk out I could write to you all day love—

Another circumstance has made me feel more solitary that letter I received today[7]—dear Shelley you will say I was deceived   I know I am not—I know her unexampled frankness and sweetness of character but what must that character be who resists opinions preach——

Oh dear what am I writing   I am indeed disappointed—I did think Isabel perfectly unprejudiced—she adores the shade of my mother—but then a married man it is impossible to knock into some peoples heads that Harriet is selfish & unfeeling and that my father might be happy if he chose—by that cant concerning selling his daughter I should half suspect that there has been some communication between ⟨my⟩ the Skinner St.[8] folks and them

5. She was pregnant at this time.

6. Thomas Hookham, Jr. (1787–1867), publisher, bookseller, and Shelley's friend. Shelley had begun reading Diogenes Laertius (c. 200–50) in September: see *Journals*, I:29.

7. From David Booth (1766–1846), lexicographer. In 1812 and 1813, for reasons of health, Mary Godwin had been sent to live with the family of William Thomas Baxter in Dundee, Scotland. There she formed a deep friendship for Isabella Baxter, who in 1814 married Booth, widower of Isabella's sister Margaret and some twenty years her senior. Booth, disapproving of the elopement and probably concerned about his own questionable matrimonial status, refused to allow the continuation of the friendship.

8. The Godwins' residence.

Higho love such is the world

How you reason & philosophize about love—do you know if I had been asked I could not have given one reason in its favour—yet I have as great an opinion as you concerning its exaltedness and love very tenderly to prove my theory—adieu for the present it has struck eight & in an hour or two I will wish you goodnight.

Well so now I am to write a goodnight with the old story of I wish I could say it to you—yes my love it has indeed become an old story but I hope the last chapter is come—I shall meet you tomorrow love & if you do but get money love which indeed you must we will defy our enemies & our friends (for aught I see they are all as bad as one another) and we will not part again—Is not that a delightful word it shall cheer my dreams

No answer from Hooper[9]—I wish he would write oh how I long {to} be at our dear home where nothing can trouble us neither friends or ene-mies—dont be angry at this you know my love they are all a bad set—But Nantgwilt do you not wish to be settled there at a home you know love—with your own Mary nothing to disturb you studying walking & other such like amusements—oh its much better {I} believe not to be able to see the the light of the sun for mountains than for houses

You dont say a word in your letter—you naughty love to ease one of my anxietie not a word of Lambert of Harriet of M[rs] Stuart[10] of money or anythink [*anything*]—but all the reasonings you used to persuade M[r] Peacock[11] love was a good thing   Now you know I did not want con-verting—but my love do not be displeased at my chattering in this way for you know the expectation of a letter from you when absent always makes my heart jump so do you think it says nothing when one actually arrives.

Your own Mary who loves you so tenderly

To [*Sir Walter Scott*][12]

Bagni di Lucca[13]   14 June—1818

Sir

Having received from the publisher of Frankenstein the notice taken of that work in Blackwood's magasine, and intelligence at the same time that it was to your kindness that I owed this favourable notice I hasten to re-

9. Shelley had lived in Mr. Hooper's house in Nantgwillt, Wales, in 1812 and had written to inquire about letting the house again.

10. John Lambert, a creditor who threatened William Godwin with arrest; Harriet Westbrook Shelley; and Mrs. Stewart, one of Shelley's creditors.

11. Thomas Love Peacock (1785–1866), author and friend of Shelley.

12. Sir Walter Scott (1771–1832) favorably reviewed *Frankenstein* in *Blackwood's Edinburgh Magazine* 2 (March 1818): 613–20.

13. The Shelleys departed England in March 1818, arrived in Milan on 4 April, and lived at Bagni di Lucca in the summer.

turn my acknowledgements and thanks, and at the same time to express the pleasure I receive from approbation of so high a value as yours.

Mr Shelley soon after its publication took the liberty of sending you a copy but as both he and I thought in a manner which would prevent you from supposing that he was the author we were surprised therefore to see him mentioned in the notice as the probable author,—I am anxious to prevent your continuing in the mistake of supposing Mr Shelley guilty of a juvenile attempt of mine; to which—from its being written at an early age, I abstained from putting my name—and from respect to those persons from whom I bear it. I have therefore kept it concealed except from a few friends.

I beg you will pardon the intrusion of this explanation—

Your obliged &c &c

Mary Wollst^{ft} Shelley.

To Isabella Hoppner[14]

Pisa.[15]   August 10th 1821

My dear Mrs Hoppner—

After a silence of nearly two years I address you again, and most bitterly do I regret the occasion on which I now write. Pardon me that I do not write in french; you understand English well, and I am too much impressed to shackle myself in a foreign language; even in my own, my thoughts far outrun my pen, so that I can hardly form the letters. I write ⟨in⟩ to defend ⟨of⟩ him to whom I have the happiness to be united, whom I love and esteem beyond all creatures, from the foulest calumnies; and to you I write this, who were so kind, to Mr Hoppner; to both of whom I indulged the pleasing ⟨hope⟩ idea that I have every reason to feel gratitude. This is indeed a painful task.

⟨M^r⟩ Shelley is at present on a visit to Lord Byron at Ravenna and I received a letter[16] from him today containing accounts that make⟨s⟩ my hand tremble so much that I can hardly hold the pen. It tells me that Elise wrote to you relating the most hideous stories against him, and that you have believed them. Before I speak of these falsehoods permit {me} to say a few words concerning this miserable girl. You well know that she

---

14. Wife of Richard Belgrave Hoppner (1786–1872), English Consul General at Venice.

15. Where the Shelleys had moved in 1820.

16. Shelley's letter of 7 August 1821 (*Letters of P. B. Shelley,* II: 316–19) had reported that the Hoppners believed the scandalous gossip spread by Elise, the Shelleys' Swiss nursemaid, who became pregnant by Paolo Foggi, the Shelleys' servant. Dismissed by the Shelleys, Elise and Paolo maintained that Claire Clairmont was Shelley's mistress and that Elena Adelaide Shelley (the "Neapolitan charge") was Shelley and Claire's child. For more information on this complicated matter, see *Letters,* I: 149n.; and *Journals,* I: 249n.–50n.

formed an attachment with Paolo when we proceeded to Rome, & at Naples their marriage was talked of—We all tried to dissuade her; we knew Paolo to be a rascal and we thought so well of her that we believed him to be unworthy of her. An accident led me to the knowledge that without marrying they had formed a connexion; she was ill we sent for a docter who said there was danger of a miscarriage—I w^d not turn the girl on the world without in some degree binding her to this man—we had them married at Sir W. A'Courts—she left us; turned catholic at Rome, married him & then went to Florence. After the disastrous death of my child we came to Tuscany—we have seen little of them; but we have had knowledge that Paolo has formed a scheme of extorting money from Shelley by false accusations—he has written him threatning letters saying that he w^d be the ruin of him &c—we placed these in the hands of a celebrated lawyer here who has done what he can to silence him. Elise has never interfered in this and indeed the other day I received a letter from her entreating with great professions of love that I w^d send her money—I took no notice of this; but although I knew her to be in Evil hands I w^d not believe that she was wicked enough to join in his plans without proof.

And now I come to her accusations—and I must indeed summon all my courage while I transcribe them; for tears will force their way, and how can it be otherwise? You knew Shelley, you saw his face, & could you believe them? Believe them only on the testimony of a girl whom you despised? I had hopes that such a thing was impossible, and that although ⟨stange⟩ strangers might believe the calumnies that this man propogated, that none who had ever seen my husband could for a moment credit them.

She says Claire was Shelley's ⟨miss⟩ mistress, that—Upon my word, ⟨I vow by all that I hold⟩ I solemnly assure you that I cannot write the words, I send you a part of Shelleys letter that you may see what I am now about to refute—but I had rather die that [than] copy any thing so vilely so wickedly false, so beyond all imagination fiendish.

I am perfectly convinced, in my own mind that Shelley never had an improper connexion with Claire—At the time specified in ⟨Claires⟩ Elise's letter, the winter after we quited ⟨Nap⟩ Este, I suppose while she was was with us, and that was at Naples, we lived in lodgings where I had momentary entrance into every room and such a thing could not have passed unknown to me. The malice of the girl is beyond all thought—I now do remember that Claire did keep her bed there for two days—but I attended on her—I saw the physician—her illness was one that she had been accustomed to for years—and the same remedies were employed as I had before ministered to her in England.

Claire had no child—the rest must be false—but that you should believe it—⟨I th⟩ That my beloved Shelley should stand thus slandered in your minds—⟨He⟩ He, the gentlest & most humane of creatures, is more painful to me, oh far more painful than any words can express.

It is all a lie—Claire ⟨if anything⟩ is timid; she always shewed respect even for me—poor dear girl! she has ⟨many⟩ some faults—you know them as well as I—but her heart is good—and if ever we quarelled, which was seldom, it was I, and not she, that was harsh, and our instantaneous reconciliations were sincere & affectionate.

Need I say that the union between my husband and ⟨hims⟩ myself has ever been undisturbed—Love caused our first imprudences, love which improved by esteem, a perfect trust one in the other, a confidence and affection, which visited as we have been by severe calamities (have we not lossed two children?) has encreased daily and knows no bounds.

I will add that Claire has been seperated from us for about a year—She lives with a respectable German family at Florence—The reasons of this were obvious—her connexion with us made her manifest as the Miss Clairmont, the Mother of Allegra[17]—besides we live much alone—she enters much into society there—and solely occupied with the idea of the welfare of her child, she wished to ⟨be⟩ appear such that she may not be thought in aftertimes to be unworthy of fulfilling the maternal duties—you ought to have paused before you tried to convince the father of her child of such unheard of atrocities on her part—If his generosity & knowledge of the world had not made him reject the slander with the ridicule it deserved ⟨of⟩ what irretrievable mischief you would have occasioned her.

Those who know me ⟨we⟩ well believe my simple word—it is not long ago that my father said in a letter to me, that he had never known me utter a falsehood—but you, easy as you have been to credit evil, who may be more deaf to truth—to you I swear—by all that I hold sacred upon heaven & earth by a vow which I should die to write if I affirmed a falsehood—I swear by the life of my child, by my blessed & beloved child, that I know these accusations to be false—

Shelley is as incapable of cruelty as the softest woman—To those who know him his humanity is almost as a proverb.—He has been unfortunate as a father. the laws of his country & death has cut him off from his dearest hopes—⟨But⟩ His enemies have done him incredible mischief—but that you should believe such a tale coming from such a hand, is beyond all belief, a blow quite unexpected, and the very idea of it beyond words shockings—

But I have said enough to convince you   And are you not convinced? Are not my words the words of truth? Repair—I conjure you the evil you have done by retracting you confidence in one so vile as Elise, and by

17. Allegra, the daughter of Claire Clairmont and Lord Byron.

writing to me that you now reject as false every circumstance of her infamous tale.

You were kind to us, and I shall never forget it; now I require justice; You must believe me, and do me, I solemnly entreat you, the justice to confess that you do so.

Mary W. Shelley

I send this letter to Shelley at Ravenna, that he may see it. For although I ought, the subject is too odious to me to copy it. I wish also that Lord Byron should see it[18]—He gave no credit to the tale, but it is as well that he should see how entirely fabulous it is.   ⟨, and I⟩

To Maria Gisborne[19]

Pisa   August 15th 1822

I said in a letter to Peacock, my dear Mrs Gisborne, that I would send you some account of the last miserable months of my disastrous life. From day to day I have put this off, but I will now endeavour to fulfill my design. The scene of my existence is closed & though there be no pleasure in retracing the scenes that have preceded the event which has crushed my hopes yet there seems to be a necessity in doing so, and I obey the impulse that urges me. I wrote to you either at the end of May or the beginning of June. I described to you the place we were living in:[20]—Our desolate house, the beauty yet strangeness of the scenery and the delight Shelley took in all this—he never was in better health or spirits than during this time. I was not well in body or mind. My nerves were wound up to the utmost irritation, and the sense of misfortune hung over my spirits. No words can tell you how I hated our house & the country about it. Shelley reproached me for this—his health was good & the place was quite after his own heart—What could I answer—that the people were wild & hateful, that though the country was beautiful yet I liked a more countryfied place, that there was great difficulty in living—that all our Tuscans would leave us, & that the very jargon of these Genovese was disgusting—This was all I had to say but no words could describe my feelings—the beauty of the woods made me weep & shudder—so vehement was my feeling of dislike that I used to rejoice when the winds & waves permitted me to go out in the boat so that I was not obliged to take my usual walk among tree shaded paths, allies of vine festooned trees—all that before I doated on—& that now weighed on me. My only moments of peace were on board

18. Because this letter was given to Byron and found among his papers after his death, it may not have ever reached Mrs. Hoppner.

19. Maria Gisborne (1770–1836) and her husband John, the Shelleys' friends in Italy, had returned to London in 1821.

20. Casa Magni, at San Terenzo, near Lerici, on the Gulf of Spezia.

that unhappy boat, when lying down with my head on his knee I shut my eyes & felt the wind & our swift motion alone. My ill health might account for much of this—bathing in the sea somewhat relieved me—but on the 8th of June (I think it was) I was threatened with a miscarriage, & after a week of great ill health on sunday the 16th this took place at eight in the morning. I was so ill that for seven hours I lay nearly lifeless—kept from fainting by brandy, vinegar eau de Cologne &c—at length ice was brought to our solitude—it came before the doctor so Claire & Jane[21] were afraid of using it but Shelley overuled them & by an unsparing application of it I was restored. They all thought & so did I at one time that I was about to die—I hardly wish that I had, my own Shelley could never have lived without me, the sense of eternal misfortune would have pressed to heavily upon him, & what would have become of my poor babe? My convalescence was slow and during it a strange occurence happened to retard it. But first I must describe our house to you. The floor on which we lived was thus

1 is a terrace that went the whole length of our house & was precipitous to the sea. 2 the large dining hall— 3, a private staircase. 4 my bedroom 5 M^{rs} [*Williams's*] bedroom, 6 Shelleys & 7 the entrance from the great staircase. Now to return. As I said Shelley was at first in perfect health but having over fatigued himself one day, & then the fright my illness gave him caused a return of nervous sensations & visions as bad as in his worst times. I think it was the saturday after my illness while yet unable to walk I was confined to my bed—in the middle of the night I was awoke by hearing him scream & come rushing into my room; I was sure that he was asleep & tried to waken him by calling on him, but he continued to scream which inspired me with such a panic that I jumped out of bed & ran across the hall to M^{rs} W's room where I fell through weakness, though I was so frightened that I got up again immediately—she let me in & Williams went to S. who had been wakened by my getting out of bed—he said that he had not been asleep & that it was a vision that he saw that had frightened him—But as he declared that he had not screamed it was certainly a dream & no waking vision—What had frightened him was this—He dreamt that lying as he did in bed Edward & Jane came into him, they were in the most horrible condition, their bodies lacerated—their bones starting through their skin, the faces pale yet stained with blood, they could hardly walk, but Edward was the weakest & Jane was supporting him—Edward said—Get up, Shelley, the sea is flooding the house & it is all

21. Claire Clairmont and Jane Williams (1798–1884), common-law wife of Edward Ellerker Williams (1793–1822). The Williamses joined the Pisan Circle in January 1821; Edward Williams died at sea with Shelley on 8 July 1822.

coming down." S. got up, he thought, & went to the his window that looked on the terrace & the sea & thought he saw the sea rushing in. Suddenly his vision changed & he saw the figure of himself strangling me, that had made him rush into my room, yet fearful of frightening me he dared not approch the bed, when my jumping out awoke him, or as he phrased it caused his vision to vanish. All this was frightful enough, & talking it over the next morning he told me that he had had many visions lately—he had seen the figure of himself which met him as he walked on the terrace & said to him—"How long do you mean to be content"—No very terrific words & certainly not prophetic of what has occurred. But Shelley had often seen these figures when ill; but the strangest thing is that Mrs W. saw him. Now Jane though a woman of sensibility, has not much imagination & is not in the slightest degree nervous—neither in dreams or otherwise. She was standing one day, the day before I was taken ill, at a window that looked on the Terrace with Trelawny[22]—it was day— she saw as she thought Shelley pass by the window, as he often was then, without a coat or jacket—he passed again—now as he passed both times the same way—and as from the side towards which he went each time there was no way to get back except past the window again (except over a wall twenty feet from the ground) she was struck at seeing him pass twice thus & looked out & seeing him no more she cried—"Good God can Shelley have leapt from the wall? Where can he be gone?" Shelley, said Trelawny—"No Shelley has past—What do you mean?" Trelawny says that she trembled exceedingly when she heard this & it proved indeed that Shelley had never been on the terrace & was far off at the time she saw him. Well we thought {no} more of these things & I slowly got better. Having heard from Hunt[23] that he had sailed from Genoa, on Monday July 1st S., Edward & Captain Roberts (the Gent. who built our boat)[24] departed in our boat for Leghorn to receive him—I was then just better, had begun to crawl from my bedroom to the terrace; but bad spirits succeded to ill health, and this departure of Shelley's seemed to add insuferably to my misery. I could not endure that he should go—I called him back two or three times, & told him that if I did not see him soon I would go to Pisa with the child—I cried bitterly when he went away. They went & Jane, Claire & I remained alone with the children—I could not walk out, & though I gradually gathered strength it was slowly & my ill spirits encreased; in my letters to him I entreated him to return—"the feeling

22. Edward John Trelawny (1792–1881), a friend of the Williamses who joined them in Pisa on 14 January 1822. Trelawny gained fame from his associations with Shelley and Byron.

23. Leigh Hunt, who had finally arrived in Pisa to join Shelley and Byron and to establish their journal *The Liberal.*

24. Captain Daniel Roberts, Trelawny's friend, a boatbuilder who built Byron's *Bolivar* and Shelley's *Don Juan.*

that some misfortune would happen," I said, "haunted me": I feared for
the child, for the idea of danger connected with him never struck me—
When Jane & Claire took their evening walk I used to patrole the terrace,
oppressed with wretchedness, yet gazing on the most beautiful scene in
the world. This Gulph of Spezia is subdivided into many small bays of
which ours was far the most beautiful—the two horns of the bay (so to
express myself) were wood covered promontories crowned with castles—at
the foot of these on the furthest was Lerici on the nearest San^t Arenzo—
Lerici being above a mile by land from us & San Arenzo about a hundred
or two yards—trees covered the hills that enclosed this bay & then beautiful groups were picturesquely contrasted with the rocks the castle on [*and*]
the town—the sea lay far extended in front while to the west we saw the
promontory & islands which formed one of the extreme boundarys of the
Gulph—to see the sun set upon this scene, the stars shine & the moon rise
was a sight of wondrous beauty, but to me it added only to my wretchedness—I repeated to myself all that another would have said to console me,
& told myself the tale of love peace & competence which I enjoyed—but I
answered myself by tears—did not my William die? & did I hold my Percy
by a firmer tenure?[25]—Yet I thought when he, when my Shelley returns I
shall be happy—he will comfort me, if my boy be ill he will restore him
& encourage me. I had a letter or two from Shelley mentioning the difficulties he had in establishing the Hunts, & that he was unable to fix the
time of his return. Thus a week past. On Monday 8th Jane had a letter
from Edward, dated saturday, he said that he waited at Leghorn for S.
who was at Pisa   That S's return was certain, "but" he continued, "if he
should not come by monday I will come in a felucca, & you may expect
me teusday evening at furthest." This was monday, the fatal monday, but
with us it was stormy all day & we did not at all suppose that they could
put to sea. At twelve at night we had a thunderstorm; Teusday it rained
all day & was calm—the sky wept on their graves—on Wednesday—the
wind was fair from Leghorn & in the evening several felucca's arrived
thence—one brought word that they had sailed monday, but we did not
believe them—thursday was another day of fair wind & when twelve at
night came & we did not see the tall sails of the little boat double the
promontory before us we began to fear not the truth, but some illness—
some disagreable news for their detention. Jane got so uneasy that she
determined to proceed the next day to Leghorn in a boat to see what was
the matter—friday came & with it a heavy sea & bad wind—Jane however
resolved to be rowed to Leghorn (since no boat could sail) and busied
herself in preparations—I wished her to wait for letters, since friday was

25. The Shelleys' son William had died in Rome in 1819; their son Percy Florence
outlived Mary Shelley.

letter day—she would not—but the sea detained her, the swell rose so that no boat would venture out—At 12 at noon our letters came—there was one from Hunt to Shelley, it said—"pray write to tell us how you got home, for they say that you had bad weather after you sailed monday & we are anxious"—the paper fell from me—I trembled all over—Jane read it—"Then it is all over!" she said. "No, my dear Jane," I cried, "it is not all over, but this suspense is dreadful—come with me, we will go to Leghorn, we will post to be swift & learn our fate." We crossed to Lerici, despair in our hearts; they raised our spirits there by telling us that no accident had been heard of & that it must have been known &c—but still our fear was great—& without resting we posted to Pisa It must have been fearful to see us—two poor, wild, aghast creatures—driving (like Matilda)[26] towards the <u>sea</u> to learn if we were to be for ever doomed to misery. I knew that Hunt was at Pisa at Lord Byron's house but I thought that L. B. was at Leghorn. I settled that we should drive to Casa Lanfranchi that I should get out & ask the fearful question of Hunt, "do you know any thing of Shelley?" On entering Pisa the idea of seeing Hunt for the first time for four years under such circumstances, & asking him such a question was so terrific to me that it was with difficulty that I prevented myself from going into convulsions—my struggles were dreadful—they knocked at the door & some one called out "Chi è?" it was the Guiccioli's maid L.B. was in Pisa—Hunt was in bed, so I was to see LB. instead of him—This was a great relief to me; I staggered up stairs—the Guiccioli[27] came to meet me smiling while I could hardly say—"Where is he—Sapete alcuna cosa di Shelley"[28]—They knew nothing—he had left Pisa on sunday—on Monday he had sailed—there had been bad weather monday afternoon—more they knew not. Both LB & the lady have told me since—that on that terrific evening I looked more like a ghost than a woman—light seemed to emanate from my features, my face was very white I looked like marble—Alas. I had risen almost from a bed of sickness for this journey—I had travelled all day—it was now 12 at night—& we, refusing to rest, proceeded to Leghorn—not in despair—no, for then we must have died; but with sufficient hope to keep up the agitation of the spirits which was all my life. It was past two in the morning when we arrived—They took us to the wrong inn—neither Trelawny or Capⁿ Roberts were there nor did we exactly know where they were so we were obliged to wait until daylight. We threw ourselves drest on our beds & slept a little but at 6 o'clock we went to one or two inns to ask for one or the other of these

26. That is, Mary Shelley's heroine Mathilda who pursued her father *"towards the sea"* (see above, pp. 212, 214).

27. Countess Teresa Gamba Guiccioli (c. 1800–73), Lord Byron's "last attachment," who loved and lived with Byron.

28. "Do you know anything about Shelley?"

gentlemen. We found Roberts at the Globe. He came down to us with a face which seemed to tell us that the worst was true, and here we learned all that had occurred during the week they had been absent from us, & under what circumstances they had departed on their return.——— Shelley had past most of the time a[t] Pisa—arranging the affairs of the Hunts—& skrewing LB's mind to the sticking place[29] about the journal. He had found this a difficult task at first but at length he had succeeded to his heart's content with both points. Mrs Mason[30] said that she saw him in better health and spirits than she had ever known him, when he took leave of her sunday July 7th His face burnt by the sun, & his heart light that he had succeeded in rendering the Hunts' tolerably comfortable. Edward had remained at Leghorn. On Monday July 8th during the morning they were employed in buying many things—eatables &c for our solitude. There had been a thunderstorm early but about noon the weather was fine & the wind right fair for Lerici—They were impatient to be gone. Roberts said, "Stay until tomorrow to see if the weather is settled; & S. might have staid but Edward was in so great an anxiety to reach home—saying they would get there in seven hours with that wind—that they sailed! S. being in one of those extravagant fits of good spirits in which you have sometimes seen him. Roberts went out to the end of the mole & watched them out of sight—they sailed at one & went off at the rate of about 7 knots—About three—Roberts, who was still on the mole—saw wind coming from the Gulph—or rather what the Italians call a temporale anxious to know how the boat w^d weather the storm, he got leave to go up the tower & with the glass discovered them about ten miles out at sea, off Via Reggio, they were taking in their topsails—"The haze of the storm," he said, "hid them from me & I saw them no more—when the storm cleared I looked again fancying that I should see them on their return to us—but there was no boat on the sea."—This then was all we knew, yet we did not despair—they might have been driven over to Corsica & not knowing the coast & Gone god knows where. Reports favoured this belief.—it was even said that they had been seen in the Gulph—We resolved to return with all possible speed—We sent a courier to go from tower to tower along the coast to know if any thing had been seen or found, & at 9 AM. we quitted Leghorn—stopped but one moment at Pisa & proceeded towards Lerici. When at 2 miles from Via Reggio we rode down to that town to know if they knew any thing—here our calamity first began to break on us—a little boat & a water cask had been found five miles off—they had manufactured a <u>piccolissima lancia</u> of thin planks

29. See Shakespeare, *Macbeth* I.vii.60.
30. Mrs. Mason, whose real name was Margaret King Moore, Lady Mount Cashell (1773–1835) and who had been Mary Wollstonecraft's pupil some thirty years before, lived with George William Tighe as Mr. and Mrs. Mason.

stitched by a shoemaker just to let them run on shore without wetting themselves as our boat drew 4 feet water.—the description of that found tallied with this—but then this boat was very cumbersome & in bad weather they might have been easily led to throw it overboard—the cask frightened me most—but the same reason might in some sort be given for that. I must tell you that Jane & I were not now alone—Trelawny accompanied us back to our home. We journied on & reached the Magra about ½ past ten P.M.   I cannot describe to you what I felt in the first moment when, fording this river, I felt the water splash about our wheels—I was suffocated—I gasped for breath—I thought I should have gone into convulsions, & I struggled violently that Jane might not perceive it—looking down the river I saw the two great lights burning at the foce[31]—A voice from within me seemed to cry aloud that is his grave. After passing the river I gradually recovered. Arriving at Lerici we {were} obliged to cross our little bay in a boat—San Arenzo was illuminated for a festa—what a scene—the roaring sea—the scirocco wind—the lights of the town towards which we rowed—& our own desolate hearts—that coloured all with a shroud—we landed; nothing had been heard of them. This was saturday July 13. & thus we waited until Thursday July 25th[32] thrown about by hope & fear. We sent messengers along the coast towards Genoa & to Via Reggio—nothing had been found more than the lancetta; reports were brought us—we hoped—& yet to tell you all the agony we endured during those 12 days would be to make you conceive a universe of pain—each moment intolerable & giving place to one still worse. The people of the country too added to one's discomfort—they are like wild savages—on festa's the men & women & children in different bands—the sexes always separate—pass the whole night in dancing on the sands close to our door running into the sea then back again & screaming all the time one perpetuel air—the most detestable in the world—then the scirocco perpetually blew & the sea for ever moaned their dirge. On thursday 25th Trelawny left us to go to Leghorn to see what was doing or what could be done. On friday I was very ill but as evening came on I said to Jane—"If any thing had been found on the coast Trelawny would have returned to let us know. He has not returned so I hope." About 7 o'clock P.M. he did return—all was over—all was quiet now, they had been found washed on shore—Well all this was to be endured.

Well what more have I to say? The next day we returned to Pisa   And here we are still—days pass away—one after another—& we live thus. We are all together—we shall quit Italy together. Jane must proceed to London—if letters do not alter my views I shall remain in Paris.—Thus we

---

31. "Mouth of the river."
32. An error for Thursday, 18 July. The error is repeated later in the paragraph.

live—Seeing the Hunts now & then. Poor Hunt has suffered terribly as you may guess. Lord Byron is very kind to me & comes with the Guiccioli to see me often.

Today—this day—the sun shining in the sky—they are gone to the desolate sea coast to perform the last offices to their earthly remains.[33] Hunt, LB. & Trelawny. The quarantine laws would not permit us to remove them sooner—& now only on condition that we burn them to ashes. That I do not dislike—His rest shall be at Rome beside my child—where one day I also shall join them—Adonais is not Keats's it is his own elegy—he bids you there go to Rome.[34]—I have seen the spot where he now lies—the sticks that mark the spot where the sands cover him—he shall not be there it is too nea[r] Via Reggio—They are now about this fearful office—& I live!

One more circumstance I will mention. As I said he took leave of M[rs] Mason in high spirits on sunday—"Never," said she, "did I see him look happier than the last glance I had of his countenance." On Monday he was lost—on monday night she dreamt—that she was somewhere—she knew not where & he came looking very pale & fearfully melancholy—she said to him—"You look ill, you are tired, sit down & eat." "No," he replied, "I shall never eat more; I have not a <u>soldo</u> left in the world."—"Nonsense," said she, "this is no inn—you need not pay—"—"Perhaps, he answered, "it is the worse for that." Then she awoke & going to sleep again she dreamt that my Percy was dead & she awoke crying bitterly ⟨—so bitterly th⟩ & felt so miserable—that she said to herself—"why if the little boy should die I should not feel it in this manner." She [was] so struck with these dreams that she mentioned them to her servant the next day—saying she hoped all was well with us.

Well here is my story—the last story I shall have to tell—all that might have been bright in my life is now despoiled—I shall live to improve myself, to take care of my child, & render myself worthy to join him. soon my weary pilgrimage will begin—I rest now—but soon I must leave Italy—& then—there is an end of all despair. Adieu I hope you are well & happy. I have an idea that while he was at Pisa that he received a letter from you that I have never seen—so not knowing where to direct I shall send this letter to Peacock—I shall send it open—he may be glad to read it—

Your's ever truly Mary WS.—Pisa

I shall probably write to you soon again.

33. Edward Williams's body was disinterred and cremated on 15 August; Shelley's, the next day.

34. See stanzas 47–48 of *Adonais*, Shelley's elegy on John Keats. Shelley's remains were not buried beside his son William's, for the child's grave was not located.

I have left out a material circumstance—A Fishing boat saw them go down—It was about 4 in the afternoon—they saw the boy at mast head, when baffling winds struck the sails, they had looked away a moment & looking again the boat was gone—This is their story but there is little down [*doubt*] that these men might have saved them, at least Edward who could swim. They c^d not they said get near her—but 3 quarters of an hour after passed over the spot where they had seen her—they protested no wreck of her was visible, but Roberts going on board their boat found several spars belonging to her.—perhaps they let them perish to obtain these. Trelawny thinks he can get her up, since another fisherman things [*thinks*] that he has found the spot where she lies, having drifted near shore. T. does this to know perhaps the cause of her wreck—but I care little about it

To Lord Byron

[Albaro]   Saturday.   [?14 December 1822][35]
Your Lordships MS. was very difficult to decypher, so pardon blunders & omissions

I like your Canto extremely; it has only touches of your highest style of poetry, but it is very amusing & delightful. It is a comfort to get anything to gild the dark clouds now my sun is set.—Sometimes when very melancholy I repeat your lyric in "The Deformed", & that for a while enlivens me:—But—

But I will not scrawl nonsense to you

Adieu   Yours   MaryS.

To Leigh Hunt

[14 Speldhurst Street   Brunswick Square]
September 9th   (Sep. 11th) [1823]
My dear Hunt

Bessy promised me to relieve you from any inquietude you might suffer from not hearing from me, so I indulged myself with not writing to you until I was quietly settled in lodgings of my own. Want of time is not my excuse, I had plenty—but until I saw all quiet around me I had not the spirit to write a line—I thought of you all—how much! and often longed to write, yet would not till I called myself free. To turn Southward; to imagine you all, to put myself in the midst of you would have destroyed all my philosophy. But now I do so. I am in little neat lodgeings—my boy

35. Mary Shelley, living near Byron in the environs of Genoa, often copied his manuscripts. This letter, conjecturally placed at its earliest possible date, refers to later cantos of Byron's *Don Juan* (1819–24) and to his dramatic fragment *The Deformed Transformed* (1824).

in bed, I quiet—and I will now talk to you; tell you what I have seen and heard, and with as little repining as I can try, by making the best of what I have, the certainty of your friendship & kindness, to rest half content tho' I am not in the "Paradise of Exiles."[36]—Well—first I will tell you journal wise the history of my 16 days in London. I arrived monday the 25th of August—My father & William[37] came for me to the Wharf. I had an excellent passage of 11½ hours—a glassy sea & a contrary wind—the smoke of our fire was wafted right aft & streamed out behind us—but wind was of little consequence—the tide was with us—& though the Engine gave a "short uneasy motion"[38] to the vessel, the water was so smooth that no one on board was sick & Persino[39] played about the deck in high glee. I had a very kind reception in the Strand[40] and all was done that could be done to make me comfortable—I exerted myself to keep up my spirits— the house though rather dismal, is infinitely better than the Skinner St. one—I resolved not to think of certain things, to take all as a matter of course and thus contrived to keep myself out of the gulph of melancholy, on the edge of which I was & am continually peeping.—

But lo & behold! I found myself famous—Frankenstein had prodigious success as a drama & was about to be repeated for the 23rd night at the English opera house.[41] The play bill amused me extremely, for in the list of dramatis personæ came, ———— by Mr T. Cooke: this nameless mode of naming the un{n}ameable is rather good. On Friday Aug. 29th Jane My father William & I went to the theatre to see it. Wallack looked very well as F [*Frankenstein*]—he is at the beginning full of hope & expectation— at the end of the 1st Act. the stage represents a room with a staircase leading to F workshop—he goes to it and you see his light at a small window, through which a frightened servant peeps, who runs off in terror when F. exclaims "It lives!"—Presently F himself rushes in horror & trepi- dation from the room and while still expressing his agony & terror ———— throws down the door of the labratory, leaps the staircase & presents his unearthly & monstrous person on the stage. The story is not well man- aged—but Cooke played ————'s part extremely well—his seeking as it were for support—his trying to grasp at the sounds he heard—all indeed he does was well imagined & executed. I was much amused, & it appeared to excite a breathelss eagerness in the audience—it was a third piece   a

36. That is, Italy, where Leigh Hunt and his family remained. The quotation is from Shelley, "Julian and Maddalo," l. 57.
37. William Godwin and William Godwin, Jr.
38. S. T. Coleridge, "The Rime of the Ancient Mariner" (1798).
39. Her son, Percy Florence.
40. At the Godwins'.
41. *Presumption, or the Fate of Frankenstein*, by Richard Brinsley Peake (1792– 1847), opened on 28 July, with Thomas Potter Cooke (1786–1864) as Frankenstein's unnamed creature and James William Walleck (?1791–1864) as Victor Frankenstein.

scanty pit filled at half price—& all stayed till it was over. They continue to play it even now.

On Saturday Aug. 30ᵗʰ I went with Jane to the Gisbornes. I know not why, but seeing them seemed more than anything else to remind me of Italy. Evening came on drearily, the rain splashed on the pavement, nor star, nor moon deigned to appear—I looked upward to seek an image of Italy but the blotted sky told me only of my change. I tried to collect my thoughts, and then again dared not think—for I am a ruin where owls & bats live only and I lost my last singing bird when I left Albaro. It was my birthday and it pleased me to tell the people so—to recollect & feel that time flies & what is to arrive is nearer, & my home not so far off as it was a year ago. This same evening on my return to the Strand I saw Lamb who was very entertaining & amiable though a little deaf. One of the first questions he asked me was whether they made puns in Italy—I said—{"}Yes, now Hunt is there"—He said that Burney made a pun in Otaheite,[42] the first that was ever made in that country: At first the natives could not make out what he meant, but all at once they discovered the pun & danced round him in transports of joy. L. [*Lamb*] said one thing which I am sure will give you pleasure. He corrected for Hazlitt a new collection of Elegant Extracts, in which the Living Poets are included.[43] He said he was much pleased with many of your things, with a little of Montgomery & a little of Crabbe—Scott he found tiresome—Byron had many fine things but was tiresome but yours appeared to him the freshest & best of all. These Extracts have never been published—they have been offered to Mʳ Hunter & seeing the book at his house I had the curiosity to look at what the extracts were that pleased L. There was the Canto of the Fatal Passion from Rimini several things from Foliage & from the Amyntas.[44] L. mentioned also your conversation with Coleridge & was much pleased with it. He was very gracious to me, and invited me to see him when Miss L. should be well.

On the strength of the drama my father had published for my benefit a new edition of F.[45] & this seemed all I had to look to, for he despaired utterly of my doing anything with S.T.S. [*Sir Timothy Shelley*]—I wrote

42. Tahiti. Charles Lamb here refers to his friend Captain James Burney (1750–1821), rear admiral and man of letters.

43. William Hazlitt (1778–1830), *Select British Poets, or New Elegant Extracts from Chaucer to the Present Time* (1824), which apparently was withdrawn when it was finally published in June 1824 because the selections from contemporary poets had been reprinted without permission. The poets named here include James Montgomery (1771–1854), George Crabbe (1754–1832), Sir Walter Scott, Lord Byron.

44. At the house of the publisher Rowland Hunter, whom Leigh Hunt's widowed mother-in-law had married, Mary Shelley read extracts from Hunt's *The Story of Rimini, A Poem* (1816), *Foliage; or Poems Original and Translated* (1818), and *Amyntas, A Tale of the Woods* (1820).

45. The two-volume reprinting of *Frankenstein*, published by G. and W. B. Whittaker in 1823.

to him however to tell him I had arrived & on the following Wednesday had a note from Whitton[46] where he invited me, if I wished for an explanation of S.T.S.'s intentions concerning my boy to call on him. I went with my father. W. [*Whitton*] was very polite though long winded—his great wish seemed to be to prevent my applying again to STS, whom he represented as old, infirm & irritable—however he advanced me £100 for my immediate expences, told me that he c^d not speak positively until he had seen STS. but that he doubted not but that I should receive the same annually for my child, & with a little time & patience, I should get an allowance for myself. This, you see relieved me from a load of anxieties— I hesitated no longer to quit the Strand and having secured neat cheap lodgings—removed hither last night. Such, dear Hunt is the outline of your poor Exile's history. After two days of rain the weather has been <u>uncommonly fine</u> cioè without rain, & cloudless I believe, though I trust to other eyes for that fact, since the whitewashed sky is any thing but blue to any but the perceptions of the Natives themselves. It is so cold however that the fire I am now sitting by is not the first that has been lighted, for my father had one two days ago. The wind is East and piercing—but I comfort myself with the hope that softer gales are now fanning your <u>not</u> throbbing temples, that the climate of Florence will prove kindly to you, & that your health & spirits will return to you.—Why am I not there? This is quite a foreign country to me; the names of the places sound strangely— the voices of the people are new & grating—the Vulgar English they speak particularly displeasing—but for my father, I should be with you next spring—but his heart & soul are set on my stay, and in this world it always seems one's duty to sacrifice one's own desires, & that claim ever appears the strongest which claims such a sacrifice.

On Tuesday (Sep. 2nd) I dined with Mr Hunter and Bessy[47] & she afterwards drank tea with me at the Strand—She is certainly much improved in countenance. Her mouth which used always to express violence & anger now seems habitually to wear a good tempered smile—Mrs Godwin herself observed the change—this is certainly to Bessy's credit since she is far from happy as you may guess. It would be useless for me to repeat Bessy's news since doubtless she has told you all herself & you already know that the Novello's have from motives of economy, retired to the country.[48]—One thing at Mr Hunter's amused me very much—Your piping Fau[n] & kneeling Venus are on the piano, but, from a feeling {of} delicacy, they are turned with their backs [   ] company. I think of going down to

46. William Whitton, Shelley's father's solicitor.
47. Elizabeth Kent (?1790–1861), Hunt's sister-in-law and author of *Flora Domestica* (1823).
48. The famous composer Vincent Novello (1781–1861) had moved with his large family to Shacklewell Green.

Richmond on Friday & take a last peep at green fields & [   ] leaves
before I return to my winter cage. You must know that Jane is a great
favourite w[ith] Mrs H. [*Hunter*]—Poor thing she is much persecuted by
Edward's Mother in Law[49] Who to save her own credit spreads false reports about her as much as she can. She even called on Mrs Godwin to
warn her that I ought not to know her—at the same time that she tells
other people that she can never forgive <u>her</u>, for knowing <u>me</u>. England is
no place for Jane—how I wish we could leave it together next spring.
Hogg & Peacock[50] are both out of town.

I have now renewed my acquaintance with the friend of my girlish
days[51]—she has been ill a long time, even disturbed in her reason, and the
remains of this still hang over her. She is delighted to see me, although
she is just now on the point of going to Scotland for a few weeks. The
great affection she displays for me endears her to me & the memory of
early days—Else all is so changed for me that I should hardly feel pleasure
in cultivating her society. We never do what we wish when we wish it,
and when we desire a thing earnestly, & it does arrive, that or we are
changed so that we slide from the summit of our wishes & find ourselves
where we were. Two years ago I looked forward with eagerness to your
arrival, & pictured to myself all that I should enjoy with you & dear
Marianne to make a part of our pleasures—You came, 12 dreary months
past, I just began to regain your affection & to delight in your society & I
am here, to pine for it again. This is life!—And what more have I {   }
to you with its painful bitterness—sour sweets & sweet sours?—What will
happen when I see you again?

Your brother[52] has been out of town all this time. I heard that he was
to return yesterday & expect him to call on me today. Of course I did not
talk to Henry of all that I have to say to his father. Henry is <u>not</u> handsome. He is stiff in his manners though polite to me. They seem to be
going on well and he says that the literary Examiner is succeeding. The
truth how ever is, dear Hunt, that there is nothing in it Except the
<u>Indicator</u> which is worth reading—but you will see them and judge. They
have offered that I should contribute to fill up the few pages that follow
the Criticism on books (which is written by a Mr Gordon, I think is his
name) & when I can I will—but I have not that talent which enlivens a
half page.—Do you know that your friend R^d Mr Collyer (who so shamefully attacked dearest S.) has been accused of the <u>Bishop's crime</u>[53] & has

---

49. That is, Mary Ann Williams, the stepmother of Edward Williams.
50. Thomas Jefferson Hogg and Thomas Love Peacock.
51. Isabella Baxter Booth.
52. John Hunt (1775–1848) and his son Henry had begun publishing in July 1823
the weekly *Literary Examiner* which contained and continued Leigh Hunt's *Indicator*.

absconded.—This will become quite a clerical amusement, it unnaturalness befits their habitual hypocrisy & cant—When a man belies his conscience to the world—he will soon bely it to himself and what comes next, may easily be as bad as poor Joslin. Adieu dear friend I will finish the rest when I have seen your brother.

(Sep. 11th) I saw your brother yesterday. Being the first time that I saw him you may guess that I looked curiously at him. In features he is very like Henry, but softened from his immoveability of feature by time and suffering. He does not look so old as he is, & LB. w^d envy his unchanged looks, but I do not think him at all like your picture. He was all politeness & even kindness to me—I soon found that I had two feelings to remove in his mind[54]—one your not having managed well with the D in M Stores—the other poor dear M⟨a⟩r.'s [*Marianne's*] extravagance—I believe that I succeeded in both these points at least he said that I did. He spoke with great affection of you & when he went away said, that he was reserved & had the character perhaps of being more so than he was but that he did not wish to be so with you or with me—In fact though obstinacy is written on his brow, & reserve in all his solemn address yet he encouraged me so far that I look forward with less apprehension to the final result of my next conversation with him. I feel that I must not be reserved, nor shall I be so—I told him as it was that he ought to write oftenor, spoke of regular remittances—& urged him to send an immediate one; he said that he would write by the same post as that by which this letter will go, and that I trust will contain a permission for you to draw. I expect to see him soon again. Direct to me 14 Speldhurst St.—Brunswick Square. I will write again speedily—& wait anxiously to hear from you—Keep well—be all well, dear, dearest friends, be as happy as you can, &, while it be of value to you, & even after, depend upon the unremitting affection of your Exiled

Mary WS.

To [*John Murray III*][55]

Park Cottage—Paddington   8 Sep^{br} 1830

My Dear Sir

I presume, since I have not heard from you, that you have received no communication from Mr Murray in reply to my letter. My idea has been that he intended to delay any until his return. I find however that he is

53. Rev. William Bengo Collyer (1782–1854) had been accused of homosexual activity.
54. Leigh Hunt and his brother John were in the midst of financial disagreements, primarily concerning Leigh Hunt's proprietary rights to their newspaper, the *Examiner*.
55. During the temporary absence of the publisher John Murray II (1778–1843), his son John Murray III (1808–92) managed the firm.

not expected back for a month. Meanwhile if Mr Murray's silence proceeds from his deciding on declining my offers, I should be very glad not any longer to be kept in a suspense, which is very inconvenient to me.

May I request you at your earliest convenience, to make my desire known to Mr Murray. If he desires to postpone any arrangement until his return—yet ⟨means⟩ if he considers it most probable that then one will be made, of course I shall be most happy to wait. For I own I shall have great pleasure in contributing to the Family Library—I suggested several subjects in my last letter—I almost forget now whether some I am going ⟨now⟩ to mention were included. One subject I have thought of, is an History of the Earth—in its earlier state—that is an account both of the anti diluvian remains—of the changes on the surface of the Earth, and of the relics of States and Kingdoms before the period of regular history. Mr Murray will judge how far there is any danger of intrenching upon <u>orthodoxy</u> on this subject—He is aware that I have a great distaste to obtruding any opinions, even if I have any, differing from general belief, of which I am not aware—and also how far such a history would be amusing. To me these speculations have always been the source of great interest, but this may not be the public taste.

I have thought also of the Lives of Celebrated women—or a history of Woman—her position in society & her influence upon it—historically considered. and a History of Chivalry.

My friend. Mr Marshall, mentioned some time ago the idea of writing for the Quarterly[56]—and liberal as that publication has become, and clever and distinguished as it has always been, I should be very much pleased to contribute—I wrote once a Review for the Westminster—it appeared in one of the earlier numbers I forget which—it was upon "The English in Italy"[57] and as I received a good many Compliments about it— I suppose in some degree it may be received as a specimin—if the Editor wished to have one on the subject.

I am so aware of Mr Murray's gentlemanly feeling & I must say kindness towards me, that I am sure if you will inform how desirous I am of some kind of answer upon all these points, that he will no longer delay to furnish me with one.

I am Dear Sir
Y^s Ob^ly &cc
MaryW Shelley

56. The *Quarterly Review,* published by John Murray.
57. Reprinted above.

To General Lafayette

London 33 Somerset St Portman Sq.

11 Nov. 1830

My dear General

It is with great diffidence that so humble an individual as myself addresses herself to the Hero of three Revolutions. Yet I cannot refuse myself the pleasure of congratulating that Hero on his final triumph.[58] How has France redeemed herself in the eyes of the world—washing off the stains of her last attempt in the sublime achievements of this July. How does every heart in Europe respond to the mighty voice, which spoke in your Metropolis, bidding the world be free. For that word is said—one by one the nations take up the echo and mine will not be the last. May England imitate your France in its moderation and heroism. There is great hope that any change operated among us, will originate with the Government. Our king[59] is desirous of popularity; careless of opinions, leaning through family connexions to the liberal party—He will willingly accede to any measures for the good of the people. But our position is critical and dreadful—for what course of measures can annihilate the debt? and so reduce the taxation, which corrodes the very vitals of the suffering population of this country.

Pardon a woman, my dear and most respected General, for intruding these observations. I was the wife of a man who—held dear the opinions you espouse, to which you <u>were</u> the martyr and <u>are</u> the ornament; and to sympathize with successes which would have been matter of such delight to him, appears to me a sacred duty—and while I deeply feel my incapacity to understand or treat such high subjects, I rejoice that the Cause to which Shelley's life was devoted, is crowned with triumph.

Your amiable family and yourself must have almost forgotten a stranger who came among you under disastrous circumstances,[60] for so short a time, and so long ago—I trust that one day it will be my fate to visit you again; meanwhile I feel satisfaction in remembering—that sick & unlike myself as I was when in Paris—yet then I became acquainted with its most illustrious citizen and that I can boast of having conversed with La Fayette

Most respectfully Y[rs] MaryShelley

58. Lafayette (1757–1834) was a key figure in the July 1830 revolution in France.

59. George IV died on 26 June 1830 and was succeeded by his brother William (1765–1837).

60. A reference to the smallpox that attacked her during her 1828 visit to Paris.

To Everina Wollstonecraft[61]

Lake of Como[62]   20 July [1840]

My dear Aunt—Yours is the only letter that I have yet received from England—it was therefore doubly welcome. I hope all will continue well with you—You do not mention Charles Robinson—By this time I hope you or his family have heard from him.[63]

We had a very long journey here. Our party consisted of Percy, I, Julian (a brother of Charles) Robinson & another young Cantab.[64] To please Julian we took a circuitous route—& thus made an interesting though long journey. On the 25. June we left Paris for Metz (look for our route in a map) by the diligence. The country for the most part was eccessively fertile rich in vines & corn lands, & the year promises abundance. The Moselle runs under the walls of Metz & the town is pleasant & clean enough, but not picturesque. Another diligence took us in 14 hours to Trêves—a distance of 55 miles—this was <u>German</u> travelling. The driver was up & down from his seat every 10 minutes—& we delayed two hours at the Custom House on the Prussian frontier to have our luggage examined—Not that much was done—but it served as an excuse for loitering. Here too we began to experience the inconvenience of not understanding German.—It was our wish to go down the Moselle from Treves to Coblentz in a boat—there was no steamer—the passage boat plies only twice a week & had left that morning—so we & two other young men Cantabs, engaged a boat to ourselves. We ⟨did⟩ made the voyage in 3 days—it ought not to have occupied more than 2—but we were very lazy about it. One of our new companions knew a little German, which was a great convenience. The scenery on the banks of the river was monotonous but pleasing—hills of picturesque shapes—the bases clothed with vines—the summits with trees form the banks of the river—ruined towers & castles crowned the heights—& numberless villages studded the ravines. Here the Moselle wine is grown. The villages however & their inhabitants are dirty & poor—though the vineyards belong to the peasants, the wine merchants reap the profits. After winding down the many meanderings of this river on 1st July we reached Coblentz—& the next day embarked on the Rhine in the steam boat for Mayence. You know how Ld Byron celebrates this

---

61. Everina Wollstonecraft (1765–1843), Mary Wollstonecraft's youngest sister.

62. Mary Shelley and Percy Florence left England in mid-June 1840 for a tour of the Continent. On 22 June they arrived at Paris, where they were met by Percy's friends who were to travel with them: Julian Robinson (1818–99) and George Hibbert Deffell (1819–95). On 15 July they arrived at Cadenabbia, on Lake Como, where they remained at the Albergo Grande until 8 September (see *Rambles in Germany and Italy*, I: 62–104).

63. A friend of Mary Shelley and Percy Florence, Charles Robinson went to Australia with a recommendation from Everina to Elizabeth Berry (see *Letters*, II: 321).

64. That is, George Hibbert Deffell; a *Cantabrigian* attended Cambridge University.

river—& it is described in a portion of the two volumes of Shelley's works[65]—No description can equal the reality. The promontories & mountain peaks,—the castles that crown them the villages beneath—the fertility of the vallies, the various aspect of the many folded hills present an exhaustless series of landscapes—which as the sun declines grow in beauty. We went from Mayence to Frankfort by the railroad—which is comfortable & well conducted. Here we engaged a Voiturier[66] to take us to Shauffhausen in 7 days. I cannot in this letter describe the scenery in any detail—We passed through Darmstadt, Heidelburg, Carlsruhe, Baden & Freiburg. The towns are spacious airy & clean. The people courteous. The country pretty uniform; a fertile plain to the right—to the left a range of low but pleasing hills varied as usual by many a shattered tower & ruined Castle: at Heidelburg & Baden we turned in among the hills—& these places are surrounded by verdurous & woody uplands. After leaving Freiburg, the scenery became altered as we entered the Mountainous district of the Black forest. At the commencement we traversed a pass called the Valley of Hell—from the close meeting of the dark precipices between which the road winds—The country continues mountainous & varies by patches of the dark old forest, interspersed by tracts of cultivated land. At Shauffhausen we saw the falls of the Rhine—which is wondrously beautiful, & one view from a jutting platform when you look up to sky & rock through the spray & mist of the cataract is quite sublime. Our route now lay thro' Switzerland, by Zurich—the lake of Wallenstadt, Loire, Splungen across the Splungen to Chiavenna—We wound among enormous mountains—the lower Alps—through the valley of the Rhine which is now a mountain stream. The Mountains are precipitous, dark & rugged. One pass on the way from Loire to Splungen is sublime—A Mountain many hundred feet high is cleft to its base—in the depth the Rhine flows—on each side rises a bare precipice—It was considered impassable till very talely [*lately*]. Your Cyclopedia will I am sure give an account of the Via Mala—A shelf has been made by force of blasting the rock with gun powder to form the road—in parts it is protected by a parapet—in others it runs within the rock—it crosses from one side of the ravine to the other by bridges of a single arch—As you look down you see far below the torrent of the Rhine—far above the almost meeting precipices leave only a strip of sky open to the view. The passage of the Mountain of the Splungen is also very grand & the descent on the Italian side scarcely less magnificent & more beautiful than the Swiss passes. The weather had been

65. See Byron, *Childe Harold's Pilgrimage*, Canto III; and Shelley, *Essays, Letters from Abroad, Translations and Fragments*, II: 33–34.

66. "Public carrier."

cool during the whole of our journey. On the top of the Splungen it snowed—but the sun came out as we reached Chiavenna

On the 13th we reached the shores of Como—& embarked in the steam boat. The shores of the lake are [*p. 1, cross-written*] formed of huge mountains—dark—rugged—the summits jagged—divided by deep chasms formed by fierce torrents—Half way down the lake divides in two & here the scenery of that portion called Como—(the other branch is called the lake of Lecco) becomes more mild & lovely—the bases of the vast mountains subside into hills planted with olives & vines—studded with villages & villas. Here we have settled ourselves for a few weeks. One portion of the plan of our journey was that Percy & his Friend Deffell should study for the degree they are to take at Xmas. Accordingly our lives are secluded & quiet. The mornings are devoted to study The afternoons to boating &c—I often suffer from the terror I have of any accident happening to Percy on the water otherwise I am comfortable & happy. In the middle of September we recross the Alps—and we shall not go further than Milan southwards—all our space time & money being expended [*p. 6, cross-written*] during our long journey.

There is something strange & dreamlike in returning to Italy after so many many years—the language the mode of life the people—the houses the vegetation are as familiar to me as if I had left them only yesterday—yet since I saw them Youth has fled—my baby boy become a man—& still I have struggled on poor & alone. The weather is now hot—but there is almost always a breeze from the lake—The Evenings are delicious—The scene as I see it now from my window—the wide lake & dark high Mountains beyond all that can be imagined of grand—Nor is it less delightful to wander inland up the mountain paths among the vineyards—or under the overarching boughs of the chesnuts—catching glimpses of the lake hearing the dash of the waterfalls—while the monotonous [*p. 3, cross-written*] but pleasing song of the boat man is wafted across the lake.

I am delighted you see something of Mrs Hogg[67]—She is very clever, agreable & kind—Her daughter is very pretty. Will you shew Mrs Hogg this letter. Percy is quite well—He was much delighted with the more rugged & sublime part of our journey—The Via Mala & the Splungen especially—& the scenery of the lake is to his taste. He sighs a little for the society of some young persons of the other sex—but we are very solitary here—& his shyness prevents his making acquaintances as easily as other young men might.

Adieu my dear Aunt—I hope to find you on my return well—& prosper-

67. Jane Williams and Thomas Jefferson Hogg had formed a common-law marriage.

ous. The account you give of the life of Hamilton Rowan is charming
I long to see the book[68] [*p. 4, cross-written*] Among my fathers papers I
found one or two letters from him to my Mother

Remember me to your kind friends & believe me

Aff[y] Y[s]

MWShelley

To Edward Moxon[69]

Dolgelley.   N. W. [North Wales]

14 July [1841]

Dear M[r] Moxon

I know not what to say to your refusal of compensati{o}n for all the
expence which the Liberals have put you to. Since the evil sprung from
them solely—I think you ought to let them repair it—not by a formal sub-
scription—but by allowing them to take the fine &c on themselves. Thanks
for Talfourd's speech[70]—it is very eloquent—& so conclusive that I wonder that the Jury was not persuaded by it; they ought to have been—But I
suppose there was some bigotted fool among them who made them go
wrong. I like <u>some</u> things he says about Shelley very much—& he makes
out an admirable case for you—You must receive some comfort from the
kind & just representation he makes of your character & position.

I shall certainly add a postscript with regard to the trial. I will send
you in a day or two. I must mention that by an unaccountable oversight
a poem of Shelley, printed in the Posthumous Poems is omitted in my
editions it the one beginning

Rough wind that moanest loud

I think the title is a dirge—It can now be added. As to filling up the vacant space of Queen Mab—it is difficult. I object to Leigh Hunt's account—because it looks like patchwork taking a thing already printed &
published. I should like what was inserted to be original. What I should
like would be if M[r] Hogg would write an Essay on Shelley's life & writ-

68. The *Autobiography* (1840) of Archibald Hamilton Rowan (1751–1834), an Irish
patriot who knew Mary Wollstonecraft in Paris in 1794.

69. The publisher Edward Moxon had been prosecuted for blasphemous libel because
he had published the complete text of Shelley's *Queen Mab* in the one-volume edition
of Shelley's *Poetical Works*. The trial was instigated by liberal and radical booksellers
and publishers who sought to protect themselves from discriminatory treatment under
the law of libel by bringing charges against the highly respected Moxon.

70. The author and lawyer Thomas Noon Talfourd (1795–1854), *Speech for the De-
fendant in the Prosecution of the Queen versus Moxon, for the Publication of Shelley's
Works. Delivered at the Court of Queen's Bench, June 23, 1841*, and *Revised* (1841).

ings—original—though it might embody the substance of his Articles in the New Monthly.[71] This would cost something. Perhaps you would see him & learn what it would cost & then I would write to him & arrange it on my own account. Let me know what you think of this—

Let me have 25 copies of Talfourd's speech—send one to [*p. 1, cross-written*] Miss Clairmont—3 Golden Sq—one to Mrs Hogg 12 Maida Vale Edgware Road—one directed to Mrs Boinville to the care of J. Flather Esq Lincoln's Inn 24 Old Square—written outside from Mrs Shelley, to be forwarded.

I am dear Sir
Y^s truly
MWShelley

71. "Percy Bysshe Shelley at Oxford," *New Monthly Magazine* (January 1832 through May 1833), collected and published as Hogg's *Life of Percy Bysshe Shelley* (1858).

Selected Bibliography

PRIMARY WORKS

Mounseer Nongtongpaw; or, the Discoveries of John Bull in a Trip to Paris. London: Proprietors of the Juvenile Library [M. J. Godwin & Co.], 1808. [4th ed., 1812.]

History of a Six Weeks' Tour through a Part of France, Switzerland, Germany, and Holland: With Letters Descriptive of a Sail round the Lake of Geneva, and of the Glaciers of Chamouni. [With Percy Bysshe Shelley.] London: T. Hookham, Jun.; and C. and J. Ollier, 1817.

Frankenstein; or, The Modern Prometheus. 3 vols. London: Lackington, Hughes, Harding, Mavor, & Jones, 1818.

Valperga: or, The Life and Adventures of Castruccio, Prince of Lucca. 3 vols. London: G. and W. B. Whittaker, 1823.

The Last Man. 3 vols. London: Henry Colburn, 1826.

The Fortunes of Perkin Warbeck, A Romance. 3 vols. London: Henry Colburn and Richard Bentley, 1830.

Frankenstein: or, The Modern Prometheus. A revised one-volume edition. London: Henry Colburn and Richard Bentley, 1831.

"Proserpine: A Mythological Drama, in Two Acts." In *The Winter's Wreath for MDCCCXXXII.* London: Whittaker, Treacher, and Arnot [1831], pp. 1–20.

Lodore. 3 vols. London: Richard Bentley, 1835.

Lives of the Most Eminent Literary and Scientific Men of Italy, Spain and Portugal. [With James Montgomery and Sir David Brewster.] 3 vols. (Vols. 86–88 of The Cabinet Cyclopædia, edited by the Rev. Dionysius Lardner.) London: Longman, Rees, Orme, Brown, Green, & Longman; and John Taylor, 1835, 1837.

Falkner: A Novel. 3 vols. London: Saunders and Otley, 1837.

Lives of the Most Eminent Literary and Scientific Men of France. 2 vols. (Vols. 102 and 103 of The Cabinet Cyclopædia, edited by the Rev. Dionysius

Lardner.) London: Longman, Orme, Brown, Green, & Longmans; and John Taylor, 1838, 1839.

Rambles in Germany and Italy, in 1840, 1842, and 1843. 2 vols. London: Edward Moxon, 1844.

The Choice: A Poem on Shelley's Death. Edited by H. Buxton Forman. London: Privately printed, 1876.

Proserpine & Midas: Two Unpublished Mythological Dramas by Mary Shelley. Edited by A[ndre]. Koszul. London: Humphrey Milford, 1922.

Mathilda. Edited by Elizabeth Nitchie. Extra Series #3 of *Studies in Philology.* Chapel Hill: The University of North Carolina Press, 1959.

Mary Shelley: Collected Tales and Stories, with Original Engravings. Edited by Charles E. Robinson. Baltimore: The Johns Hopkins University Press, 1976.

EDITED WORKS

Posthumous Poems of Percy Bysshe Shelley. [Edited by Mary W. Shelley.] London: John and Henry L. Hunt, 1824.

The Poetical Works of Percy Bysshe Shelley. Edited by Mrs. Shelley. 4 vols. London: Edward Moxon, 1839.

The Poetical Works of Percy Bysshe Shelley. Edited by Mrs. Shelley. One-volume edition with Postscript added to the Preface. London: Edward Moxon, 1840 [1839].

Essays, Letters from Abroad, Translations and Fragments, By Percy Bysshe Shelley. Edited by Mrs. Shelley. 2 vols. London: Edward Moxon, 1840 [1839].

SECONDARY AND OTHER WORKS

Bennett, Betty T., and William T. Little. "Seven Letters from Prosper Mérimée to Mary Shelley." *Comparative Literature* 31 (1979): 134–53.

Cameron, Kenneth Neill. *Shelley: The Golden Years.* Cambridge: Harvard University Press, 1974.

The Complete Works of Percy Bysshe Shelley. Edited by Roger Ingpen and Walter E. Peck. (Julian Edition.) 10 vols. London: Ernest Benn, 1926–30.

"Current Bibliography." *Keats-Shelley Journal* I (1952) to the present. [An extraordinarily good annual and indexed bibliography.]

The Diary of Dr. John William Polidori, 1816. Edited by William Michael Rossetti. London: Elkin Mathews, 1911.

Dowden, Edward. *The Life of Percy Bysshe Shelley.* London: Kegan Paul, Trench & Co., 1886.

Dunbar, Clement. *A Bibliography of Shelley Studies: 1823–1950.* New York: Garland Publishing, Inc., 1976.

The Endurance of Frankenstein: Essays on Mary Shelley's Novel. Edited by

George Levine and U. C. Knoepflmacher. Berkeley: University of California Press, 1979.

Frankenstein; or, The Modern Prometheus: The 1818 Text. Edited by James Rieger. Chicago: The University of Chicago Press, 1982. [1st published, 1974.]

Gilbert, Sandra, and Susan Gubar. *The Madwoman in the Attic.* New Haven: Yale University Press, 1979.

Holmes, Richard. *Shelley: The Pursuit.* London: Weidenfeld and Nicolson, 1974.

Ingpen, Roger. *Shelley in England: New Facts and Letters from the Shelley-Whitton Papers.* 2 vols. Boston: Houghton Mifflin Company, 1917.

The Journals of Claire Clairmont. Edited by Marion Kingston Stocking with the assistance of David Mackenzie Stocking. Cambridge: Harvard University Press, 1968.

The Journals of Mary Shelley 1814–1844. Edited by Paula R. Feldman and Diana Scott-Kilvert. 2 vols. Oxford: Clarendon Press, 1987.

Ketterer, David. *Frankenstein's Creation: The Book, The Monster, and Human Reality.* (English Literary Studies No. 16.) Victoria, British Columbia: University of Victoria Press, 1979.

The Letters of Mary Wollstonecraft Shelley. Edited by Betty T. Bennett. 3 vols. Baltimore: The Johns Hopkins University Press, 1980, 1983, 1988.

The Letters of Percy Bysshe Shelley. Edited by Frederick L. Jones. 2 vols. Oxford: Clarendon Press, 1964.

Lyles, W. H. *Mary Shelley: An Annotated Bibliography.* New York: Garland Publishing, Inc., 1975.

Marchand, Leslie A. *Byron: A Biography.* 3 vols. New York: Alfred A. Knopf, 1957.

Maria Gisborne & Edward E. Williams, Shelley's Friends: Their Journals and Letters. Edited by Frederick L. Jones. Norman, Oklahoma: University of Oklahoma Press, 1951.

Marshall, Mrs. Julian. *The Life & Letters of Mary Wollstonecraft Shelley.* 2 vols. London: Richard Bentley & Son, 1889.

Massey, Irving. *Posthumous Poems of Shelley: Mary Shelley's Fair Copy Book.* Montreal: McGill-Queen's University Press, 1969.

Mellor, Anne K. *Mary Shelley: Her Life, her Fiction, her Monsters.* New York and London: Methuen, 1988.

Murray, E. B. "Shelley's Contribution to Mary's *Frankenstein.*" *Keats-Shelley Memorial Bulletin* 29 (1978): 50–68.

Nitchie, Elizabeth. *Mary Shelley: "Author of Frankenstein."* New Brunswick: Rutgers University Press, 1953.

Norman, Sylva. *Flight of the Skylark: The Development of Shelley's Reputation.* London: Max Reinhardt, 1954.

Palacio, Jean de. *Mary Shelley dans son œuvre: Contributions aux etudes shelleyennes.* Paris: Editions Klincksieck, 1969.

Paul, C. Kegan. *William Godwin: His Friends and Contemporaries.* 2 vols. London: Henry S. King & Co., 1876.

The Romance of Mary W. Shelley, John Howard Payne and Washington Irving. Boston: The Bibliophile Society, 1907.

Shelley and his Circle 1773–1822. 8 vols. to date: I–IV edited by Kenneth Neill Cameron; V–VI edited by Donald H. Reiman; VII–VIII edited by Donald H. Reiman and Doucet Devin Fischer. Cambridge: Harvard University Press, 1961–86.

Shelley and Mary. Edited by Lady Jane Shelley. 4 vols. London: Privately published, 1882.

Small, Christopher. *Ariel Like a Harpy: Shelley, Mary and Frankenstein.* London: Victor Gollancz Ltd., 1972.

Spark, Muriel. *Child of Light: A Reassessment of Mary Shelley.* Hadleigh, Essex: Tower Bridge Publications Limited, 1951. Revised and republished as *Mary Shelley.* New York: E. P. Dutton, 1987.

St. Clair, William. *The Godwins and the Shelleys: The Biography of a Family.* London: Faber and Faber, 1989.

Sunstein, Emily W. *Mary Shelley: Romance and Reality.* Boston: Little, Brown and Company, 1989.

Veeder, William. *Mary Shelley & Frankenstein: The Fate of Androgyny.* Chicago: The University of Chicago Press, 1986.

Walling, William A. *Mary Shelley.* New York: Twayne Publishers, Inc., 1972.

White, Newman Ivey. *Shelley.* 2 vols. London: Secker & Warburg, 1947.